Maureen Taylor. 2013

Rain Around The Moon

Rain Around The Moon

Maureen Taylor

ISBN 978-0-9570858-0-0

Printed in the UK by
CPI Group (UK) Ltd, Croydon, CR0 4YY

First published in 2011 by

Jomo Publishing
26 Bedgebury Close, Maidstone, Kent ME14 5QZ

For Alan Denton Read (Uncle)
Known for only a short time,
Always remembered

Acknowledgements

My husband, for his endless patience, and without whom this book would not have been written.

Jan Fautley, for her editing skills and encouragement.

Roger Wickham, for his unstinting efforts to make this book a success.

The 'paws on' experience of 'TIZZIE' the Yorkshire terrier.

Chapter One

The End

The little car crunching the shingle on the drive, pulled up at the house on Acacia Avenue in the leafy suburbs of London. Two little tear-stained and sad faces peered from behind the front door, as their mother jumped out and ran to cuddle her two small daughters. They were too young to understand how this day had begun, but they somehow knew that their young lives would never be the same again. Their mother had left them early in the morning, in the care of a trusted neighbour. She had kissed them tenderly, and had promised to return as quickly as she could. She had carefully explained to them at great length that she had to go and say goodbye to their beloved Kat, who had been there with them for all of their tiny lives. She had told them that Kat was needed by God to become a new star in heaven, and that if they were to look to the right hand side of the moon, they would see where she lived, and she would always be watching them, even if they could not see her. She would be there, especially at night if they were frightened by the dark.

It was thus that Katy Louise Brown arrived home after the funeral of her godmother. There had been but a few mourners, and across the coffin lay a single red rose, which during one of their many conversations over the years had been requested by the old lady. She had always been there, so much a part of their lives. She was there when Katy had first focused her eyes on the outside world. Her loving arms had held her when she cried. Her smiling eyes had cried when she took her first steps, and when her mother had said, 'You spoil her so much I can't do anything with her when you aren't there,' but there had been an undying love in the heart of Katy's mother too. Such was the charisma of this old lady, now gone to her final rest. She would live on in their hearts forever, and in the indelible memory of how she looked, and how she dressed. How she held her head proudly as she moved, and the enormous dark eyes that seemed to shine with an indefinable radiance when she observed the circle of her life that contained everything precious that she had ever known.

As Katy sat, now holding her two children tightly in her arms, she could see Kat, in her long black skirt, her shiny patent shoes with gold buckles, and a pure white shirt always tucked neatly into the top of her skirt. Around her neck always, the large gold locket on its long gold chain. The locket always seemed to catch the light, and was a source of fascination to both Katy and, more recently, her daughters, who loved to touch it, which in turn brought a strange faraway look to the old lady's eyes. Katy had asked her many times, where she had come from? Did she have any family? Why did she never talk about her life? The answers to these questions were always negative, and had left the old lady with a look of fear and sadness in her eyes, so that the subject was dropped, and the questions remained unanswered. Now the light of their lives, the joy of their living, the binding love that they all felt for her had been taken away, and they would never know any more about her than that she had given her life to them, completely and unconditionally. How would they live without her?

Katy Louise gently released her children, and sat them down at the kitchen table. She had prepared a special tea for them, just as Kat would have done. The little cakes covered with Smarties, and jam sandwiches with the crusts cut off, their own little cups with a picture of Pooh Bear on, filled to the top with lovely cold milk. Their tummies full, and their eyes very close to sleep, she ushered them upstairs to be bathed and put into their twin beds, close to one another for comfort. The first normal part of the day thus completed, Katy gently kissed them, and returned to the kitchen to start her husband's meal. The end of the saddest day of her life was now coming to a close.

Tomorrow she would look at the parcel that had been given to her by the solicitor, who was the executor of her godmother's will. Tonight she would lay in her husband's arms and suffer the grief of a loss so total that her life would forever be the poorer by its existence.

Chapter Two

The Box

Katy Louise had risen early, finding it difficult to sleep with so many thoughts and memories invading the silent darkness, with only the rhythmic sound of the clock ticking, and the gentle breathing of her husband as he lay quietly beside her, his head close to hers on the pillow. She had peeped in at her daughters, who she found asleep holding hands across the gap between the identical beds. Slowly she crept downstairs and into the kitchen. The familiarity of this room had a calming influence upon her as she reached for the kettle. Since she was quite young she had shared this moment with her godmother. Early mornings together, her godmother would sit, often with the cat on her lap, knitting needles clicking as she made her a cardigan or jumper, and a cup of steaming tea would stand side by side with Katy's favourite bright red mug full of hot chocolate.

Now Katy sat alone with her own cup of tea. She wanted so much to open the box which stood against the wall. A piece of sticky tape hung untidily from its side, as if it had been torn from the box, and re-stuck. Had something been removed or added to the box, Katy mused idly as she sat there. She knew that before she could satisfy her curiosity she would have to see her husband off to work, and get her children ready for their day at school. So, another two hours passed, while the everyday routine took place.

Home once again, and with the gentle hum of her newly acquired washing machine bringing a sort of reality to the situation, Katy sat at the kitchen table, bent and picked up the box, placed it on the table, and with trembling hands pulled it toward her. She pulled on the tape, which it appeared had been removed before, and, resisting at first, taking a strip of the cardboard from the side of the box as it finally released, Katy lifted the lid. The box, full of tissue paper, gave up its first treasure. Carefully wrapped. with two twisted ends to resemble a sweet paper, Katy lifted it gently and undid the ends to find the locket. The same locket that Katy had loved so much, but had never held in her hand, for the locket had never left Kat's neck. Now as she turned it over in her hand she saw a sort of crest engraved on the back. It was well worn, and so difficult to identify a specific design, but it was so beautiful, it brought sudden tears to Katy's eyes. She could do no more than hold it tight, and feel its warmth against her palm. Her fingers exploring its rim came in contact with the catch. Pressing it, the lid flew open to reveal two old photographs, both suffering badly from what appeared to be water damage. One was of a handsome man in some sort of uniform, and the other a slim beautiful woman, surrounded by a cloud of filmy material and with a glittering tiara on her head. Oh Kat! Why if you knew who these people were, did you not explain to me as I matured; how will I ever find out now? I loved you so much, and yet you could not bring yourself to confide in me.

Katy was now feeling dejected and sad, in spite of owning the most beautiful piece of jewellery she had ever seen. She placed it around her neck, and felt the strangest feeling of belonging to something more precious than she had ever dreamed of. Under another sheet of tissue, in the top corner of the box, was an envelope, unsealed, and from it issued the most beautiful smell. Inside was a handkerchief with a tiny K. embroidered in the corner. As Katy drew it carefully from the envelope and opened it, she found a tiny lock of pale blond hair tied with a pink ribbon. The lock of hair was like silk, and not a lot different in colour to her shoulder length fair hair. Did Kat cut a piece of her hair when she was a baby and keep it, but why? Did she wish that she had had a family of her own, or had she in time begun to think of Katy as her own, as she had cared for her for so long. There were no clues here, except the beautiful baby smell and an address in Milan, Italy, hastily scribbled on the corner of the envelope. Katy had no answer to this, as she slowly replaced it in the handkerchief and closed the envelope.

There were now two things remaining in the box, one of which was also in a box whose dimensions were approximate to that of a shoe box. The other was a small velvet pouch in which Katy could feel a solid object, round, with a hole at its centre. Closing her eyes, she passed her hands across the surface of the tissue paper until they came to rest. It was the turn of the box to give up its secret. The box itself had been covered by what looked like old fashioned wallpaper, cream in colour, with a dark red design of raised velvet, in tight swirls of roses. The lid lifted off easily, and inside, again, tissue paper, but this time it was red tissue paper, and unlike that which had filled the large box it was badly creased and torn in places. Katy removed it slowly and, gently straightening it as she went, folded it and lay it in a neat pile next to the box on the table. As each piece was removed, slowly coming into view was indeed a pair of shoes, but no ordinary shoes were these, they were a pair of ballet shoes. Small exquisite ballet shoes in pink satin with long ribbons that looked as if they had been tied around a very small foot many times. The block toes hard as Katy touched them, had scuff marks around the area of the toes that would have come into contact with the floor on which they had been used. Katy, without a second thought, kicked off her shoe and pushed her foot into the ballet shoe. A remarkable fit she thought, as with a small giggle she said to herself, 'Cinderella you will go to the ball.' Another mystery. How was she going to live with the contents of this box? She had no one to ask.

She had never really known her own mother. Kat had been her godmother, but she never really knew why, and now all this had come to her from Kat, and again she knew not why. Tears filled her eyes, and now she felt drained of energy. One more to go; perhaps this would be the answer she was looking for. She could not stop until the final gift was unwrapped. The black velvet pouch with a silk string gave up the strangest thing of all. Inside was an earring of large proportions. It was sitting in Katy's hand and felt heavy. It was obviously made of solid gold. It was fashioned in the style of a wedding ring, but much larger, and wound around its entire circumference was a fine chain of gold. There was a gold hook at the top of the ring to one side of a gap, the whole thing being about one and a half inches in diameter. Only one earring; had there been two, and who did it belong to? She had never seen Kat wear earrings, and this one looked much too heavy for a female ear. Did it therefore belong to a man, and if it did, who did it belong to? Kat had never mentioned a man in her life at any time, as far as Katy remembered.

The last item from the box, and still no clues. Why would her godmother leave such things to her; were they the only treasured things she had owned in her entire life. Not very much for all those years, thought Katy, and yet she had a feeling so strong inside her heart that Kat had a reason for leaving them to her, other than the reason of her being her god-daughter.

She had wanted to tell Katy something that she found very difficult, maybe something that she had never told another soul. Katy knew that somehow, somewhere, she would find the answers, and she would never rest until she did. How she would start she had no idea, but start she would, and soon, but today was over.

It was time to fetch her children from school, and give them her undivided attention for the rest of the day, and then she would sit with her husband and relate her findings to him, perhaps to get some advice on her search for the truth. She would close the box on it all for today. She lifted the box from its place on the floor and, as she did so, something slid from one end to the other. She tipped it back the other way, and the same thing happened. Opening the box again, she removed all the remaining tissue paper, and beneath it she found a book. Heart pounding, she lifted it from its hiding place. It was an old hard cover exercise book, thick with many pages, with a leather spine like an old-fashioned accounts book. She opened it at a random page, and saw handwriting, neat and precise. She flicked the pages, and from cover to cover it was filled with the most beautifully handwritten script, and it was Kat's handwriting. Tears streaming down her face now, and with little time to do anything, she closed the book, put it back in the box, and silently whispered, 'Tomorrow'.

Chapter Three

The Beginning

Maria Valencia, face flushed, eyes shining, ran from the stage of the theatre. Her arms full of flowers, bouquets with ribbons, and single red roses by the score. 'Encore! Encore!' came with the thunderous applause from an entranced audience. At sixteen, the youngest ballerina ever to perform as the prima ballerina in *The Sleeping Beauty*, and she had executed it to perfection. As the shouts grew louder, she returned to the stage to take her bow once again. Her mother, standing in the wings, wept unashamedly as her daughter took her final bow to even more rapturous applause and more flowers.

Maria had danced from a tiny child around the cramped kitchen of her mother's house in the downtrodden area of Milan, where the poorest of the poor made their dwelling places as comfortable as possible. Maria had loved to dance; with bare feet she would pirouette in the little skirt that her mother had made from an old curtain. Never had a dream been weaved so carefully. Her mother had taken in washing and ironing, had scrubbed floors, and mended sheets for a few coins which she would hide in a blue jar on the shelf with a few treasured pieces of china which one by one she would sell to raise funds.

Maria, now three years old, was so eager to learn that the quest for funds became urgent. Her mother was finding it hard to feed them, much less try to pay for ballet lessons. However, fate took a hand one day when taking Maria with her to a large house where she was doing some housework. A young girl came skipping down to the servants' quarters where Maria was patiently waiting for her mother to finish her work. Maria smiled shyly at the pretty young girl, and noticed that she carried a small canvas bag with a long cord handle. Following in her wake was an old lady dressed in black, who took the canvas bag, and hung it on a hook in a little alcove along with coats, hats, and other items of outdoor clothing. As she removed the girl's coat, Maria noticed that she had on a tunic in black, edged with red piping, and on her feet a pair of bright red socks. When Maria's mother's work was finished, and she returned to the servants' quarters, she learned that the young girl was the only daughter of a rich merchant who owned the house. She was lonely and had no friends. She had brothers who were unkind to her, and her mother had suggested that ballet school might be the answer. Ballet had however proved to be difficult for her; she found the movements hard, and the learning of them even harder.

Maria's mother boldly suggested that Maria might help her, as she had a natural aptitude for dance, and would love the company. So it was sealed. Maria would join Cordelia, and her ballet lessons would be paid for. She would have all the necessary clothing and shoes, and she would accompany Cordelia, and help her, if not to find her niche in the world of dance, at least to develop a healthy attitude to life.

Cordelia took to Maria with a hungry need for friendship, and Maria responded. She was so happy to be able to go to ballet classes, and even more so to go with a friend who could share all her happy times, and also be there when things did not always go to plan. Cordelia was no match for Maria in the ballet class, although she had been attending for some time. Now four years old, she was not fleet of foot in any direction, but at ballet she was ungainly and very uncertain of her balance. Maria, on the other hand, light as thistledown, with the grace of a much older pupil, had taken the eye of the tutor, so much so that she had been taken from the back row of the class, and placed at the front, so as to be under much closer scrutiny.

The move did not please Cordelia, and she showed her disapproval on the journey home, becoming morose and sulky. Maria, not allowing herself to become upset by Cordelia's actions, stayed very close to her and tried to help her as much as she could with her steps. For such a young child, Maria had a kindly disposition, and her radiance captured the heart of Cordelia who gradually leaned more heavily on the younger child in all sorts of aspects. All this never seemed to weigh Maria down; she was unselfish and happy in her own little life, and wanted all around her to be happy too.

Life for the two little girls went on, each accepting the other's capabilities, and in spite of their differences they formed a very special friendship. Cordelia's mother, however, found herself beginning to dislike Maria, solely because of her genius, and genius it was. In one so young she was leaping ahead at an alarming speed. Learning to her was a pure joy, and she never wanted her lessons to end, although her feet were sore and very often had to be attended to by the nurse who was on duty for the older ballerinas. She never gave up, and along with her schoolwork which she now also had to cope with, she fell into bed at night exhausted, but so happy.

The first blow came when Cordelia's mother decided that she would withdraw Cordelia from the school, and therefore would not be able to fund Maria's ballet education any more. Her fees had been paid to the end of term, but after that she would have to find other funding. Both Maria and her mother were devastated by the decision, and knew that now the fees would be much higher as Maria would be moving to another grade, having passed her first grade examination with a distinction. Cordelia pleaded with her mother to help her friend, but to no avail. She hugged Maria, and in floods of tears, and promises always to remain friends, they parted.

Maria's mother had a while to think about Maria's future, and how she could help her to fulfil her dreams. She sold her precious china that she had collected over the years, but this would only scratch the surface of the cost of the ballet tuition that Maria would need to achieve her destiny. She would also soon need new ballet shoes, and a new tunic. The latter her mother could make, as she had a leaning toward design and sewing, and she had been given an old sewing machine to make some curtains for their room in the house to which they had recently moved. The ballet shoes however were a different thing all together, they had to be properly fitted so as not to cause damage to young feet, which if all went to plan would be encased in them for many years to come.

Maria, although overcome with sadness, not only at the loss of her chance to attend the next term at the ballet school, but the loss of her friendship with Cordelia, never lost hope, and never gave up for one moment. In fact she worked harder than ever before on her dancing. Her ankles now were becoming stronger, and she could hold her pirouettes and her changes for much longer without feeling the strain. She was also now studying her theory, which would become more important in her next grade if by some chance she were able to continue.

The months went by with amazing speed; the end of term approached, and still she danced. Now nearly seven years old, she knew how important ballet was in her life. She lived, breathed, and dreamed it. Surely it could not end here with all her hopes and hard work dashed to the ground. She hated to see her mother so desperate to acquire the fees that she would need, just to see her through one more term. She knew how hard it was for her mother, and she never complained when she was not there to cook her dinner after school, or to take her out on Saturday, as she had when Maria was small. Her mother, she knew, worked every hour that she could, doing anything that came to hand in order to earn a few coins to go into the blue pot.

The term ended, and there was just nowhere near the amount needed for Maria to stay at ballet school. As her mother met her on the last day, she looked so sad that Maria ran to her, and put her arms around her. They walked together from the school arm in arm, two people both deep in thought, and hurt by the sadness of life, but sure in their love of each other. Maria's dream had ended before it had barely begun, and all her mother's striving and toiling had not been enough.

A few months had passed since Maria's exit from the ballet school. Her mother still worked hard in the hope that in some way she could still help her daughter realise her ambition to become a ballerina, but Maria's was downcast and had lost all her enthusiasm, not only for her beloved ballet, but for everything, almost for life itself. She sat, after coming home from school, and stared out of the window at the other children playing in the streets below. When she was working hard on her ballet, she would sometimes wish that she could be playing outside with the children too, but now she had no interest. Her mother despaired of her.

One day she decided to go to Cordelia's house, and ask her mother if she would allow Cordelia to come and visit Maria to see if that would cheer her up. Cordelia's mother agreed to let her see her daughter, but at the big house and not at Maria's. Cordelia was excited by the thought of seeing Maria, and now that she had found her ideal hobby of horse riding, she felt that she could meet Maria, and have something to talk about other than ballet, which seemed to be all that Maria was interested in.

The friends met the next afternoon after Cordelia had had her private tuition, and Maria had come home from school. They hugged, and went and sat in the kitchen, where cook made them some cucumber sandwiches, followed by jelly and ice cream. Cordelia chatted away about 'Arturo', her new horse, which her father had bought for her birthday. Maria listened politely, and was pleased to see Cordelia so happy. They went to see the horse, who was indeed beautiful, and who nuzzled Maria, and made her laugh when he snatched a carrot from her hand narrowly missing taking her finger too.

At this point, Cordelia's two older brothers came running out of the stables whooping and hollering, so as to cause Arturo to canter off in the opposite direction, leaving a disappointed Maria, who liked the comfort of touching this lovely animal, and having him respond so warmly to her touch. She suddenly felt a softening of her pain, realising in her own young way, that all of life was there for the taking, and the trust of this creature proved that it wasn't all to do with what you wanted in life, but what you could give in comfort and love to another being. Maria went home with her mother feeling a mite happier, with a resolve to do well in her lessons, and to see what fate had in store for her, also with the promise that she could go and see Cordelia and Arturo any time she wished.

One stormy Saturday afternoon when Maria and her mother were sitting at the fireside, content in each other's company. A knock came at the front door. Peeping from behind the lace curtains, Maria saw the familiar black cloak of her old ballet teacher. Her mother answered the door, and brought the elegant lady into the lounge. Maria immediately jumped to her feet and dropped a low curtsey at the ballet teacher's feet.

'Stand up, child,' the teacher commanded, and turning to Maria's mother introduced herself as Madame Lapello. 'I have been asked to enquire as to why Maria left ballet school so suddenly at the end of last term,' she said.

'I am afraid that I could not raise enough money to pay for her lessons, or the equipment that she needs to carry on dancing,' replied her mother with honesty.

'Maria,' said the ballet teacher, 'would you wish to carry on with your ballet lessons, given the chance?'

'Oh yes, madame,' cried Maria, her heart now leaping about in her rib cage, 'but it is just not possible. My mother has worked too hard for me to be able to continue, and I cannot allow her to do it any more.'

'My child, you have been noticed by the Maitre de ballet, and I have been asked to bring you back to school, to continue your ballet studies. Your fees and all your expenses will be paid, and you will have private tutoring for your normal school studies, so that the maximum amount of time can be spent on your dancing.' The ballet teacher continued. 'If you complete your ballet training, and reach the highest grade, you will be offered a place at the Academy of Ballet, and the rest will be up to you, and finally,' she said, 'we believe that you have an incredible talent for one so young, but the road will be hard and long, and if you reach the end of it and still feel the hurt and heartbreak has been worthwhile, then you, Maria, will be a ballerina.'

Chapter Four

Rise To Fame – Maria's Story

The road was long, and the work harder than she had ever imagined. The ballet teacher who used to smile at her and applaud her childish attempts to perform the difficult steps, now wore a hard expression, and exclaimed, 'Again Maria, turn the ankles in, and hold that line.' Her back ached, and her legs felt heavy, but determined, she never faltered or complained. She responded to her tutor, and corrected every error that she made, no matter how long it took her. When she left the ballet school, she turned her mind to her school lessons. Her mother was adamant that she studied subjects which allowed her to find a career outside of the theatre, if her dancing failed her. She put everything she had left in her to do this successfully, but her heart was in her dancing, and that was where she was sure her future lay.

Now turning twelve, she was fast passing her theory examinations, and heading toward the time when she would have to go to the Academy of Ballet, sit the final paper on her theory, and dance the final dances that would seal her fate. This would dictate whether she would enter the academy, to follow the path that could lead her to her dream of becoming a professional ballerina, and performing on stage, maybe even reach the pinnacle of dancing at the most famous theatre of all in Milan. With each day she grew stronger. Her ankles were now able to hold her pirouettes, and her changes were performed to perfection. With her head held high, and her hands held in position beautifully, she looked exquisite as she executed each section of her dance, flowing from one to the other with immaculate fluency. Her point work was such that the Maitre de Ballet, watching from the edge of the practice area, one day was heard to comment,

'From one so young, this is unbelievable.' The days, weeks, and months passed, and for Maria it was the hardest, but happiest time she had spent in all her young life.

Eventually the time came when she had to go to the Academy to sit her final examinations for entry into the Academy of Ballet. As she was younger than most dancers to take the entry examination, her mother was allowed to accompany her. As they passed through the enormous oak doors into the reception area, Maria was asked to pass her application papers across the desk, and sign the form that would take her through to the innermost room where all the applicants completed each section of the entrance papers. At this point she had to leave her mother, who reluctantly walked to a row of chairs placed against the wall, on which sat anyone who was a parent or guardian of the applicant. Maria would not see her mother again until she had completed the rigorous tasks.

The examination consisted of three sections of theory, based on the whole of her learning, from her beginnings in the ballet school to the present day, when all the knowledge of ballet culminated in the answers to the questions. Also finally, each applicant had to perform three dances, the first two choreographed by tutors of the academy, and the last dance, which was the one that caused most worry to Maria, was a free dance in which the applicant had to do their own choreography. It was over at last, and Maria joined her mother. It would be about two months before they knew the results, and the waiting would be almost impossible to bear. Maria and her mother left the building hand in hand, and walked across the road into the park, where they had the biggest ice cream that the vendor could push into a cornet, and sat on the park bench, quietly watching the ducks, as if this was about the most normal day they had ever spent. Both were exhausted, and both did not know whether to laugh or cry, so they hugged one another, and just sat like two statues frozen in time as if waiting to be brought back to reality.

Maria's entry into the academy came finally one September morning. Saying goodbye to her mother was one of the hardest things she had ever had to do. All of her dancing years were spent with her mother by her side, and now she would be on her own, having to get used to the company of other ballerinas all with their own hopes and dreams, some with attitudes which worried Maria, as she had always been a happy, friendly child, and had grown into a pleasant natured teenager without aggression. She realised that she would now have to stand up for herself. She had a rare beauty, with her pale skin, and titian hair, and she made a perfect picture as she appeared at the barre in her new leotard, and ankle warmers. Her soft-toed practice shoes in practical black standing out against her pure white ballet tights.

Each day would begin thus, with a warm up at the barre for balance, so as to attain a perfect position for every movement. The hours of practice were long, with a few breaks for rest and refreshment. Dance routines would be gradually built up and rehearsed every day, until the steps became a part of the dancer's body, which produced arcs and lines in perfect symmetry. No sharp angles, no rapid moves which gave way to ugly angles. Everything had to flow like water. Maria once again shone above all the others. It was as if a grace far beyond her years came from within this young body, and lifted her to heights that her tutors found astounding. She loved it, and nothing, not the jibes from some of the other dancers, or the speed with which she was gaining knowledge, worried her. She accepted everything as if she knew how it would all be. She danced at a local theatre in minor roles, and in the chorus, which delighted her, and of course her mother, who was able to come and watch her daughter, and marvel at her prowess. Life was a miracle for Maria as she headed toward her fifteenth birthday, and fame she felt was hers just for the taking.

Maria would go on studying at the Academy de Ballet; her time there would reach its climax when her tutors set her the ultimate challenge of making her way through the minefield of dance in the corps de ballet, until every aspect of it was covered, until she had, along with all the ballerinas who were also struggling to be recognised in the world of ballet, danced as supporting ballerinas to the lead dancers, and prima ballerinas on the circuit. The most famous theatre in Milan was the pinnacle of their ambitions, and to appear there in any capacity was totally daunting, as well as being the goal to which they all aspired.

During this time, as spaces were few and far between for stage work, Maria would go to visit Cordelia at her house. She was welcomed now by Cordelia's mother, who recognised that their friendship had surpassed the earlier differences, and that her daughter had grown both in beauty and confidence, so that she could compete with Maria in many ways. She was now an excellent horse woman, and had taken to giving Maria riding lessons. Arturo, the black stallion, had been passed over to the boys to ride, and Cordelia now had a silver grey mare called Stardust, an altogether more gentle horse, but with a touch of speed that fired Cordelia to ride her strongly, and give her her head when the going was good. She was a good jumper, and Cordelia loved to feel the power of her as she sailed over the obstacles around the countryside surrounding the big house where she lived.

Maria, however, still found herself being drawn to Arturo, and whenever the boys were not around, she would ask Cordelia if she would let her practise her trotting and cantering around the paddock on him. Arturo seemed to sense Maria's presence and would poke his head out of the stable door, or come ambling across the paddock whenever she was near. She would breathe into his nostril, and he would give a low whinny, as if to say, 'You're here, come ride me,' and ride him she did, gently, because her riding prowess was not yet good enough to do any more, but as with her ballet, she would keep on trying, content to just sit on his back and let him take her wherever he wanted to.

Cordelia would sometimes canter off on her own little tracks, and leave Maria to practise. Now and then, Maria would turn Arturo around and head him out of the paddock, and gently hack him around the area, but never straying far. Arturo, for his part, carried his precious cargo very carefully, never pulling at the reins, and always bringing her safely back to the paddock, standing still as she dismounted and gave him his favourite carrot which she had childishly but lovingly peeled before coming to see him. Maria loved these days spent with Cordelia, and their friendship blossomed as they spent time together at the big house, telling each other about their lives. Cordelia was studying beauty and design, and was considering going to Switzerland to finishing school, sometime next year. Cordelia would reach her sixteenth birthday a few months before Maria.

Maria had been offered a small part, not in the Corps de ballet, but as one of the main dancers in the ballet 'Copelia'. She was overcome, and entered into the part with a great deal of enthusiasm. As the night of her performance drew near, she became nervous and excited. Her mother would be there, and also Cordelia and her mother. She had to dance better than she had ever done before, so as to prove to herself, as well as to her audience, that at last she had become a ballerina.

Dance well she did, not only for her own private audience, but for some more important people who she did not know were present at the performance. A casting agent had been impressed, and had been accompanied by the Maitre de ballet. They agreed that they would like

Maria to dance for them in private. Another free dance like the one she had danced at her entrance examination to the academy. They wanted to see just how far her talent would stretch, and how she would cope with the stress that went hand in hand with the training of a prima ballerina.

The year passed so quickly that Maria's feet hardly touched the ground. She danced whereever and whenever the chance came about. She shone like a star in the heavens. She laughed, and she cried, each with equal passion, at the highs and lows of her life in the theatre. The dream at last fulfilled, and with the pure talent that was hers alone, she danced on to the stage in her theatre of dreams, and straight into the hearts of her audience.

Chapter Five

All That Glitters, For Love of Maria

The public loved her. The theatre was fully booked for her performances. The press hounded her and her mother for stories of her life, which up to now had only been a single sheet. Her love of dance, her unstinting love and passion for the dream that at such a young age she had brought to fruition. Her mother now was extremely possessive of her, and went with her to every performance, waiting in the wings or backstage somewhere, so as to escort her away from the hurly burly of life in the theatre. She would take her home where peace and quiet gave her some time to reflect, and become Maria again, the child that she had raised to show respect, and work hard, to repay her mother's devotion and selfless denial in order that she could reach the pinnacle of success. This she had done, and much, much more.

So much was the pride that her mother had for her only daughter, she could hardly bear her out of her sight. The only friend she had was Cordelia, and there, her mother knew she would be out of danger, and cared for. Maria had no reason to dislike the arrangement, as she and Cordelia enjoyed one another's company with relish, and it also gave her the chance to ride Arturo on a regular basis, which for her and the horse was pure joy.

Every night at the stage door, there was a crowd of theatre-goers waiting to see the ballerinas leave the theatre. Bursts of applause could be heard from a distance, as the dancers left for home, or a rendezvous that had been planned prior to the performance. Maria's mother always made sure that Maria was ushered quickly from the theatre, so as not to be disturbed by a meeting with any casual fly-by-night who may be hanging around.

Maria, on several occasions, received bouquets from well-wishers, and twice had received, via the main entrance and delivered by a young page boy, one dozen red roses, tied with a ribbon, and with a little message of devotion attached. This was not unusual for a prima ballerina and the star of the show to receive, and so not that much notice was taken. Maria of course was thrilled, and removed the message, tucking it in the inside pocket of her jacket.

Now seventeen, Maria had romantic notions as to who the donor of the roses might be, and on one quiet night, at a time when her mother had an appointment with one of the dressmakers, Maria had a visitor. A soft knock sounded on her dressing room door, and she moved slowly to open it. A tiny young girl, who she recognised as one of her dressers from back stage, stood there timidly. Maria bade her come in, and asked what she could do for her. The girl replied that a young man had been coming to the stage door quite often to leave flowers for Maria, and had caught her on her way in to the theatre, and asked if there was any possibility that he could just say hello to Maria. He would not be a nuisance, and would not ask to stay if she wasn't there. 'How did Maria feel?' asked the young dresser. Maria felt a fluttering inside and a secret excitement that maybe she could do something grown up without her mother knowing anything about it. She told the girl, 'yes!' but only if she was sure that her mother would be occupied in other places during the meeting. The scene was set, the girl went away, and Maria leaned against the now closed door, wondering what she had just agreed to.

Many days went by, and Maria saw nothing of the young girl, and heard nothing more of the donor of the roses, but the roses kept coming, sometimes directly to the stage door, which was noted with interest by the stage door keeper, and sometimes via the main entrance, but always left outside her door.

Her mother began to take an interest, and took it upon herself to find out from whence they were coming. Maria now became concerned because she knew that her mother would step in, and if she found it not to be in Maria's best interest, she would put a stop to it, and Maria would never know the identity of her secret admirer. Maria also knew that her dancing must never be put into second place to anything, and so she tried to forget all the messages that were hidden in the roses. She danced her way from success to success, never faltering, taking each role in her stride, and dancing it to magic perfection.

It was Saturday morning, and Maria had been rehearsing. Tired and hot from vigorous exercise, she sank on to the settee in her dressing room and closed her eyes. She had to dance a matinee today, as well as an evening performance. Pads over her eyes, as the glare from the footlights often made them ache, she relaxed and let her mind drift. A knock at the door startled her. She jumped up to answer it, to find the small girl standing there, and behind her a tall man in dark trousers with a pure white ruffled shirt, who doffed his hat in recognition of Maria.

'Miss,' the girl whispered, 'your mother is doing some fittings for the chorus, and will be some time. I will go and watch, and hurry back to tell you when she is finished.'

Maria noticed that in the young man's other hand was the largest bouquet of red roses she had ever seen. 'May I come in for just one moment?' he asked.

'Yes, sir,' answered Maria in a barely audible whisper.

The young man stood in front of Maria, hat in hand, lowering the bouquet of roses on to the table which already held cards full of good wishes, and small tokens of good luck. Slowly he lifted her tiny hand to his lips and kissed it.

'I am Alexi Sergio, my lady, and am greatly honoured to meet you at last. I have watched from a distance each night as you performed, and find myself enthralled to be allowed to visit and speak to you. The newspapers tell that you are of a very young age, and therefore I find myself in great dilemma, as I would dearly love to invite you to join me for a quiet repast, somewhere near to the theatre, so that I could assure your guardians that you would be returned safely. Do you think that this would be at all possible?'

Maria, having not moved an inch since the young man entered the room, now turned toward him and exclaimed. 'Sir, I, Maria Valencia, would be extremely honoured to join you for a repast as you request, but I am under the total care of my mother, who is very strict about any movement I make outside of the theatre. I do not believe that she would agree to any such meeting at any time. I am truly sorry.'

At that moment, the young girl rapped at the door, and told Maria that her mother was hastening down the corridor.

'Please go, sir! I would not like my mother to turn you out in anger. I so hope that one day I will see you again, and be able to speak more freely to you. I am truly flattered by your presence here today, and so glad that I now know who sent me all the roses. I thank you from the bottom of my heart, and wish you god speed on your way.'

Alexi Sergio the third took his leave of Maria, vowing that they would meet again, and that she would become much more to him than the beautiful ballerina who had danced her way into his very soul. Maria's mother, entering the room and turning to close the door, caught a glimpse of the red roses. She turned to Maria, whose face was flushed, and her eyes bright.

'More roses,' she uttered. 'Who delivered these, Maria? I need to talk to them.' She lifted them from the table, and searched for a card, but there was no card there.

'One of the dressers; I do not know her name,' Maria answered, carefully hiding the message that she had quickly rescued before her mother saw it.

Her mother watched her daughter suspiciously and noted her colour, and nervous movements. She would make it her business now to find the giver of all these roses, and nip this in the bud before things got out of control. She could not risk her daughter's future as a ballerina under any circumstances. She would fight and, if necessary, lose her love for a short while until she came to her senses.

Maria knew her mother well enough to know that talking to her would do no good at all; even asking if she could see Alexi under her supervision would be met with a definite refusal. With this in mind, Maria started to hatch a plan.

Her good friend Cordelia would help her she was sure. She would ask to go and see her the following weekend, and her mother would be pleased to have some free time, and not have to be worrying as to the whereabouts of Maria. Of course, Cordelia's mother would have to be involved as well, so the plan was quite a dangerous one, and to involve two innocent people was worrying for Maria, but she so much needed to see this beautiful man who had pulled at her young heartstrings.

As for Alexi Sergio, who never had had any trouble attracting young ladies, he was now suffering from a feeling he had never experienced before. A longing just to see her was with him all the time. A desperate need to talk to her, to know everything that there was to know about her, to see her face light up with a smile, to hold her hand in his if only for a second. The only contact he had with her was through the theatre, and that was fraught with the danger of being caught by her mother, obviously a dragon of a woman, who cared only for her daughter's career, and not for her happiness. He had to get a message to her somehow. The young dresser seemed to be the only chance he had to communicate, and so he waited, day after day outside the theatre until he finally saw her. He had written a long note, and begged that Maria answer it, and give the said answer to the young girl, so that she might pass it back to him the next time she saw him.

Neither of them knew of each other's plans, and so it all took a long time to come to any kind of conclusion. Come it did in the end. Alexi's note reached Maria, and Maria's answer reached Alexi, and finally with the help of Cordelia and, under great pressure, the silence of Cordelia's mother, the arrangement was made. Sergio would make his way to the big house, and be lent one of the horses from the stables. Maria, of course, would ride Arturo, and they would meet in the apple orchard on the perimeter of the surrounding land on a mellow summer afternoon just before Maria's eighteenth birthday.

Thus the tryst between them began. They sat together and spoke of their lives, and learned of each other's commitment to family and, in Maria's case, career. Life would be at the best difficult, and at worst impossible. Alexi was of noble birth, and as such would be expected to marry someone of the same social standing. Maria, although now famous and rich for a young girl, was born in poverty, and as such would not be entertained as a possible wife for Alexi. With all the support that they had from Cordelia's family and household, Maria and Alexi were able to meet and be together without Maria's mother becoming the least bit suspicious.

Maria's dancing was impeccable always, and her leading roles became almost continuous. Although she never let it show, her love for Alexi was beginning to weigh heavily, and his need for her became almost impossible for her to refuse. She knew he would never ask her to marry him, because of his nobility, but she loved him so much, and she knew he loved her too. The roles she danced, in a strange way, led her to believe that whatever the end may be, love makes you follow its path even if it leads you to destruction.

So follow she did, and after the last night of her dancing the role of Aurora in the Sleeping Beauty, for the second time in her career, she took her first few steps along the dangerous path of first love. As the curtain fell for the last time, separating Maria from her audience, Alexi was waiting outside the theatre in a carriage. Maria slipped away while her mother was revelling in her success, and taking all the praise. He pulled her aboard the carriage and they sped away, she knew not where; neither did she care, for she was with him and that was all that mattered.

They drove for what seemed like an eternity, but they were in each other's arms, and nothing else mattered. Finally, the carriage wheels were still. Alexi jumped out, took her hand, and led her to the old inn. The landlord appeared to know Alexi, and smiled at Maria. They were ushered inside, and a maid bade them follow her up a mellow wooded staircase to a minstrel gallery where the beautiful sounds of pipes and strings played softly. On they went down a narrow corridor, and stopped at a large oak door. As the maid turned the key, and ushered them in, Maria saw a roaring fire in a fireplace that stretched across the entire side of the room. There stood a table with silver dishes, all with covers on, being kept warm by tiny lights underneath on a silver tray. There were two chairs, and two placements for a meal. On the opposite side of the room there were two armchairs, and a bed of enormous proportions with the whitest of linen covers.

Alexi looked at Maria to see that she had tears in her eyes, but she smiled, and he knew she was his. They sat at the table to eat, but Maria had little appetite. Her heart was thudding in her chest, and her head was telling her that this was foolish to say the least, but she had made her decision, and now there was no going back. The wine they drank calmed her panic, and later as Alexi gently undressed her, she felt little else than the all-consuming love that enveloped her body. The pain that she felt was short and sharp, and once over was washed away by an uncontrollable wave of feeling that took over her body and mind, until she floated above herself and watched with amazement as Alexi, riding the same wave, brought her down with him to lay exhausted and complete within the realms of the reality of their love.

Morning broke with birdsong filtering its way through the open window, and pale streaks of sunlight reflecting the pattern of the lace curtains across the bed where two innocents lay curled in each other's arms, oblivious of the sound or movement coming from the early morning activities of a working inn.

Alexi was first to awake and turn to see the vision of loveliness that lay by his side, and the fullness of her lips that had brought him such temptations. The texture of her hair that now lay fanned out upon the pillow, bade him bury his face in its glory. The body which he had seen dance before him, now laid in perfect repose by his side, crying out to be caressed, and loved until once again it surrendered to his touch. Maria woke to feel the warmth of Alexi, as he gently moved against her. She turned to him, and with the utmost grace and agility moved beneath him, and gave herself completely to his passion, which now raged within him as he took her. The gentleness of the last evening was forgotten, both of them consummating their love with a fierceness which neither frightened nor surprised them, and without thought of where they were or what was to become of them, until the last ounce of joy was wasted. Their bodies satisfied, and their love compounded, they clung together, close to tears, and realised that they now had to escape from the fantasy, and somehow grasp the reality of what they had done.

Cordelia's mother, now showing signs of worry as Alexi had not, as promised, returned Maria safely, the time now closing in on midday without sight or sound of them. The boys were becoming tiresome, and casting doubt as to the whereabouts of Maria. Cordelia, out riding Stardust, seeing a cloud of dust in the distance, was hoping against hope that it was the coach bringing Maria back just in time to return her to the theatre, before rehearsals for the evening performance.

With a rattle of the horse's hooves, and the squeal of the brake against the wooden wheel, the coach came to a standstill. Maria, white-faced, jumped from the open door, bade a hasty goodbye to the other occupant, and raced up the steps to meet Cordelia's mother standing on the veranda, with a look that was enough to send the dogs, boys, and Cordelia scuttling in all directions, leaving Maria to face the onslaught of her words.

'You, young lady, will not use my good will in this way,' shouted Cordelia's mother. 'I will not be held responsible for such stupidity. Did you not think that your mother may enquire about your rapid disappearance, which incidentally she did? I covered for you, but will not do so in future. You have betrayed my trust, Maria, and now you had better make ready to leave for the theatre. Think hard about what you have done and what you intend to do in the future. I do not wish you to confide in me, neither do I wish to hear any more about this young man who is equally responsible for whatever has befallen you.'

Maria, head now bowed and silent, retired to the bedroom she shared with Cordelia to find her friend waiting with open arms to befriend her. She flew to her, sobbing out the story that left Cordelia breathless and unbelieving. What had her dear friend done, and, what would be the consequences, she wondered. Maria, with head throbbing, managed to get herself ready to go to the theatre. She had to control every ounce of feeling that she had in order not to think of Alexi, and the last thing he had said to her as the coach neared its homeward destination. 'I love you Maria with all that is in me, but I will never be able to marry you.' Maria accepted his words, but in her heart she thought that maybe she could change his mind.

She hurried to rehearsals, shedding her outer garments as she arrived, and straightening her leotard, which she had quickly put on before she left Cordelia. Shoes in hand she took a deep breath, entered the rehearsal room, and prepared to dance. Cordelia had witnessed the beautiful body of her friend shaking as she changed out of the clothes she had travelled in. She also saw blood stains on some of her underwear, and was disturbed by the sight of it.

Maria had taken risks that both she and Cordelia said they would never take outside of marriage, and Cordelia had been in on the scheme and so felt guilty at letting Maria go away with the young man who Cordelia thought was beautiful, and would never have believed that he could act so irresponsibly. Why did this have to happen, just as everything was going well, when life was sheer enjoyment, when Maria was a wonderful ballerina with such a future ahead of her, and Cordelia was feeling great and totally in charge of her life, looking forward with hope and happiness.

Flowers arrived for Maria as usual, but this time they were white lilies, and on the card the words read 'For Ever'. Maria held them to her, and placed a kiss on the card, as she tucked it into her bodice. She danced the dying swan that night, which she normally found very difficult, but tonight she danced as if she was possessed by its very meaning. Drained and full of emotion, she left the stage to be met by her mother who realised the distress that her daughter was feeling. She held out her arms, and Maria let herself be held and comforted by the mother who had always been her strength and light. They left the theatre together, and walked with arms around one another as they had done when Maria was a child with all her hopes and aspirations still only a dream.

A few weeks passed by, and always the flowers arrived at the stage door, but now no note was on them. Maria knew from whence they came but could not understand why Alexi had not tried to see her, and was not putting a note in the flowers.

Alexi was distraught at not being able to see Maria, but he knew that she would be feeling hurt, as he was. Why did he have to bow to the tradition of the nobility? Why couldn't he marry Maria, and lead a normal life with her, but he knew this would never be possible. He would not be able to live in the land of his birth. Maria would never be accepted, and any children that they may have had would never be able to claim their birthright. He would have to let her go, and he would have to proceed to find himself a wife of the correct lineage and upbringing. He had hurt her beyond belief, he knew this, and felt guilt like no other he had ever known.

He would have to see her one last time and try to convey how much he loved her, and how much he would suffer the loss of their love. He would leave her with something to remind her of their togetherness, and the love they felt in such a short time. He waited at the stage door night after night, but always she was with her mother. He thought how pale she looked and wanted to run from the crowd, and tell her that everything would be all right, and that nothing would come between them and their love for each other. He always stayed far enough away so that she could not see him, not yet, not until he had his mind set upon what he would say.

The time came one evening when he had stood there from the end of the matinee, to the beginning of the evening performance, for which he had managed to get a ticket that would allow him to watch her without any chance of her knowing he was there. He sat in anguish as she danced to the music of Tchaikovsky, in the role of Juliet. His sight blurred by tears, his heart so heavy that the stage became nothing but a dungeon into where his beloved had been placed beyond his touch. The end of the performance came suddenly, and brought him out of his reverie of doom. His fingers reached into the pocket of his jacket, and surrounded the parting gift that he was going to give her that night.

He had met the young dresser earlier, and had agreed to pay her a substantial amount of money to keep Maria's mother occupied for one hour after the performance. All went according to plan and Maria wrapped her cloak around her tightly, and followed Alexi to the waiting cab. He took her to the edge of Cordelia's home where the paddocks and the surrounding land gave them a small piece of solitude, and the comfort of knowing that their togetherness would not be interrupted. Cordelia's mother had agreed, with misgivings, to allow this to happen, knowing the reason that Alexi had for needing the meeting.

As the cab stopped, and Maria helped by Alexi got out, the moon clouded over, and rain clouds gathered. They sat in the shelter of a lean-to that the Cordelia's brothers had built as a hideaway. Alexi took her hand, turned it palm upward, and placed a tiny parcel in it. Maria closed her hand over it, and leaned to kiss Alexi. He held her at a distance, and said gently , 'This has to be goodbye, my darling. I can't let you go on thinking that we would one day be together as husband and wife. This will never happen. I am so sorry. I will love you to beyond the grave, but it will be a love within my heart that I will never be able to share with you. You will find happiness with someone else. You are young and beautiful, and life will be good to you.'

She unclenched her fist, and looked at what he had given her. There, shining in the moonlight, as just for a moment the shadow of the rain had moved to reveal its radiance, was a locket of pure gold, oval in shape with a deckled edge, giving the impression that it was studded with gems. Maria was stunned. How beautiful, how perfect. She felt for the clasp, and pushed until the locket flew open to reveal a picture of her as she was when she appeared for the first time he saw her dance in the *Sleeping Beauty*, swathed in white voile and with the princess's tiara on her head. Alexi, looking every inch a nobleman, had on tight breeches and a long military-style jacket with shiny brass buttons. Maria had never seen him dressed like this, and asked where the picture had been taken. Alexi explained that he had for a short time been trained as an officer in the Italian armed forces, and had had the picture taken for his mother to soften the blow of losing her son to the military.

This was to be Maria's only memento of the hours that they had spent in each other's arms, losing her virginity to him willingly, and with a joy that only a deep undying love can allow.

Now as they sat silently side by side, one barely touching the other, each afraid to break the silence of the moment, knowing that the next words that were spoken would be their last. The hurt on both sides was so deep that it took its toll on them, and rendered them both to immortal beings lost in time and space, with an unending torture of just being there. Finally, drenched in their sorrow, and drowned in their belief of the reasons for their not being able to spend their lives together were so wrong, they stood up and held each other in silence for a short while.

The sound of the second carriage brought them from the realms of despair. As the carriage came to a halt, Cordelia's mother alighted, gently took hold of Maria's arm, and led her away from Alexi, who now headed toward the carriage that had brought them there. Cordelia had been sitting waiting, and from behind the curtained window had witnessed the separation. Now as Maria rested in her arms sobbing quietly, she comforted her friend, and at the same time thought of poor Alexi. Who would comfort him in his sorrow? Deep down inside she wished it could be her.

Chapter Six

A Life For a Life, Maria Immortal

Her dancing now her only love, once again Maria worked until every ounce of strength and self indulgence were drained from her heart and soul. She took on every lesson with such violent activity that her tutors began to worry that she may be taking some sort of stimulant. She seemed to draw in the crowds even more, each performance equalling, and even bettering the last. Her mother was now seeing her daughter as a different being. She had an ethereal appearance, very pale, but the paleness seeming to add to her beauty, as she floated across the floor on her points. The result of all this made her mother more than a little uneasy. Something had happened; she was not sure what it was, but she believed that it had something to do with the mystery deliverer of the flowers. The small dresser, who always seemed to be where Maria was, had she was sure also been involved in some way. Cordelia, and her mother, who both held back in any conversation that Maria's mother tried to guide toward the situation that turned Maria from a happy child, and a beautiful ballerina into a lonely dancer who danced only to salve the unhappiness inside her. Maria became angry when her mother questioned her, and pulled away when she tried to comfort her.

Days turned into weeks, and the despair in her heart never left her. Maria, feeling a strange lack of energy and motivation, danced as if there was a memory indelibly etched in her head, as to the character she was dancing. Her mother, watching her daughter more closely than ever before, now felt a panic rising inside her, and was trying to push to the back of her mind the suspicions that were manifesting themselves. Maria was moody, and treated her mother with disdain when she approached her on the subject of her appearance. Maria knew that the weight gain and the sickness that sent her running to the toilet in the early hours of the morning could only mean one thing. She knew she was carrying Alexi's child. She tried to keep her mother's thoughts away from the subject until she could reach Alexi, knowing that he would come back to her if he knew that she was with child. Maria's mother, however, had already set up a meeting with Cordelia's mother without Maria's knowledge, and had also cornered the young dresser, and had worn her down until she had spilled the beans and told the whole story.

Horrified and angry beyond belief, she faced Cordelia's mother, who unlike the young dresser, held on to Maria's story, and hedged her way through all the questions until she left without the evidence she needed. Convinced in her own mind as to her daughter's condition, she was aware that this would be the end of a career that she had worked so terribly hard to bring to the point where it now was. Frustrated and burning with resentment and anger, she waited for the end of Maria's performance, which lacked its normal fire, and left the audience giving just an enthusiastic round of applause, instead of its usual rapturous shouts of encore!

She had a cab ready as Maria left the stage door. With little sympathy, and a heavy hand, she unceremoniously pushed her daughter inside. She sat in silence until they reached the home that she had worked her fingers to the bone to keep as a base for Maria to be herself, and be loved for no other reason than that she was her daughter, all be it a very famous one, and one who could have repaid her mother handsomely for all her trouble.

Now it was gone; now there would be no reward, only a bastard baby, fathered by some fly-by-night son of a nobleman who she knew would not care a jot for what he had done. Well, she would no longer be the doting mother, giving up everything she had possessed for this. She would give no more. As far as she was concerned, her daughter was no longer a part of her. She could make her own decisions, which she obviously thought she was capable of doing, and that was that; she would tell her as much as soon as they were in the privacy of her home.

Maria left her mother's house in a state of disbelief and desperation. She had nowhere to go, except back to the theatre in the hope that they would let her stay in her dressing room, and sleep in the small truckle bed that she used to rest on between performances. The old doorman, taking pity on her, gave her the key, and told her that he would come in at dawn and unlock the doors for her. He, in his pity, left his flask filled with hot coffee, and some bread and cheese that was to be his supper. He asked her no questions; the sight of her shivering and crying was enough to tell him that something very bad had befallen her. He had always liked this beautiful, bright, and happy child, and, at this moment, a very vulnerable one, who needed help. He would do anything he could to help her, but for tonight she needed to rest. Unbeknown to anyone, he stayed at the theatre within reach of her to see that she suffered no more harm than had already put her into his care.

Chapter Seven

Maria Lost to the World

The morning following Maria's last ever dance, was for her a succession of misty moments, of people standing over her, talking in whispers, walking away again in clouds of grey. Her head was reeling, and her heart pounding. She was constantly feeling a dreadful sickness washing over her. The old stage door keeper she recognised above anyone else, because he was constantly by her side, trying to comfort her as he plied her with warm drinks, which only served to make her feel more sick. Finally, when a doctor was brought to her bedside, and a decision was made to move her to somewhere away from the environment of the theatre, she seemed to regain a little calmness, and allowed him to lift her head and administer some medication.

They moved her to a small hospital, a few blocks from the theatre. It was cool and quiet, and she was laid in a soft and clean smelling bed. A nurse with an enormous hat, pale blue with large stiff wings at each side, stood over her with a kindness in her smile that made Maria shut her eyes and drift into sleep. They bathed and dried her, and put her into a white cotton gown. She looked just like the child she once was, at peace now and not alone in the nightmare of the previous night, when she had run through the streets stumbling and crying at the terrifying trauma that had bestowed itself upon her.

The hours of the day passed without recognition. People came and went. The old stage door keeper was there at intervals, sitting by her side, worried and tired, not knowing what to do to help this beautiful child in her hour of great need. He would have to try and see her mother. He wondered why she was not here to care for her beloved daughter. Had something awful happened to her, and was this why Maria was so distressed? She had not uttered one word since she had thrown herself through the stage door and begged for his help. How could he help her when he had not a clue as to her situation, and what had made her so ill throughout the long night when he had stayed by her side. In moments when her delirium left her, and she became lucid, she would whisper a few random words, none of them meaning very much, but he wrote them down and studied them when she drifted back into sleep. 'Baby… gone… Arturo… Mama… Gone… Alex… Gone… Cordelia. Shoes... gone... locket... gone... help.'

Two days drifted by. Maria started to take in some fluids, and the fever abated slightly. The sickness remained, but now not racking her body as it had done on the first night. The hospital decided that it was time to make some enquiries, and to try to get Maria to remember what happened on that fateful night when a young talented ballerina fell into the depths of dull despair, and nearly died as a consequence. It was mainly down to the diligence of the old stage door keeper, who kept her warm, and comforted, during the hours of the cold night as she lay in a shivering heap in the cramped conditions of her dressing room at the theatre. It was therefore him who was asked if he could find the answers to some of the questions. He sat with her whenever they allowed him to be away from the theatre. He also made enquiries there. He knew that there was some sort of connection with Maria and a young dresser. He needed to find her to see if she knew anything about Maria's family, and most of all where her mother could be found.

Maria started to take small portions of food, but still she had not the strength to stand un-supported. It was almost a week before she was able to sit up and be aware of how she now felt, which was not as she wished it would be. She had no visitors, only Aldo the stage door keeper with whom, in spite of herself, she had formed a kind of friendship. She talked quietly, not of her circumstances, but of her days when as a young child she had danced around the kitchen in her mother's house, and how they had sat in the park, eaten ice creams, and fed the ducks. She also talked of a horse called Arturo, who belonged to a friend, and who she was allowed to ride sometimes. She never asked if she could go home, nor did she ask for her mother.

This was a worry to both the stage door keeper and the hospital, as they were aware that her mother had been at every one of her performances, and that she had been the one to usher her away from the theatre at the end of each show. Therefore it appeared that her mother had to be the priority in their search for the reason why Maria was here fighting for survival.

The theatre now was in total chaos. They had lost their prima ballerina to some mystery illness. No one seemed to have any relevant information. The girl's mother who had always seemed so reliable, and in control of Maria, was now not available for comment, neither could she be seen anywhere in the vicinity of the theatre. The stage door keeper looked as if he had spent a week sleeping rough, and at this time could not offer them any explanation, as nothing that Maria said to him could lead him to any conclusions.

The hospital had asked him if he could help them to find her a safe place to go and be cared for until arrangements could be made for something more permanent. They also felt that, as he had shown such genuine concern for her, he should be made aware of the results of their examinations. The next statement they made left him shaken and desperately unhappy.

'The girl is pregnant. Have you any idea who the father may be?' the sister asked gently, as she could see that the old man was in shock. He had no idea what had happened in Maria's life. Once she left the theatre, he had no more to do with her than with any of the other ballerinas; it was just her joyous zest for life that enthralled him, and he would have given anything to have a daughter like her.

Now he was angry and determined to find out all he could. He knew that she was friendly with the young dresser who attended to all the leading dancers in the theatre. Maybe she could help, and maybe between them they could find her mother and tell her of her daughter's predicament.

Going back to the room where Maria was, he went to the chair where she sat looking out of the window. There was a sadness in her that made him crumple, and he gently put his arms around her. She turned to him and buried her head into his arms and wept.

In silence, she listened as he told her he knew about the baby, but still she would not confide in him, except to say, 'I loved him, and he will love our baby.' He touched the locket that she wore around her neck. He had noticed it when she came back to the theatre, but had not seen it since, until today. He asked the sister who had looked after her where it had been, and she told him that it had been in the hospital safe, as it was considered to be of great value. Now Maria held it in her hand, as if it were a life line. His visiting time now over, it was time to return to the theatre for the evening performance.

As he approached the stage door, he noticed none of the usual crowds waiting for a glimpse of the magical ballerina who had captured their hearts over the last couple of years. There was a sort of dullness around, and last minute bookings were being taken for the evening performance. It seemed that ticket sales were down as well. He was about to walk through the stage door when the young dresser appeared. She was talking in low whispers to one of the other ballerinas. Noticing him walking toward her, she hastily moved away from the other girl and began to walk up the spiral staircase that led to the wardrobe area. The stage door now firmly closed, the doorman headed in her direction, and asked her if she could spare him a moment of her time.

The answer came briefly and sharply: 'No! sorry, I'm very busy', and with this she scuttled up the stairs and quickly disappeared behind a mass of costumes. This was a territory that no unauthorized person was allowed to enter. He now had no alternative but to turn around and return to his job at the stage door, but his curiosity was aroused. He knew in his heart that she was hiding something, and he would find out what it was, however long it took, and however hard it was to make her tell him.

Maria, meanwhile, was beginning to come to terms with her condition. The hospital had been wonderful to her, but she knew that she was getting stronger, and there would be a limit to the time she could stay in this safe environment. The money she had earned from her dancing, had gone mostly to pay for all the things she needed, and the rest had been left in her mother's care. How would she get hold of it now, when her mother had totally disowned her.

She would need help in many areas of her life, none more important than the welfare of her baby, now growing noticeably in her once flat stomach. She had to find Alexi; she knew if she did, all her problems would be gone, and he would marry her when he knew she was carrying his child. She would somehow get in touch with Cordelia, and once again ask her for help. She wondered if Cordelia's mother would allow her daughter to be involved with the now pregnant Maria, and would she in turn refuse to have Maria in her house, if so she would never again be able to see her beloved Arturo, let alone ride him.

The stage door keeper now made it the quest of his life to corner the elusive young dresser and, by hook or by crook, get the information he needed to start the ball rolling in the direction of finding Maria's mother, and the father of her child. Who could possibly walk out on someone as beautiful in body, mind, and spirit as Maria? When he found him, he would have a lot to answer for.

So, as each performance came to a close, and the costumes were returned to the wardrobe mistresses, he waited every afternoon, and evening, until the day when the young dresser, unaware of his presence, made the mistake of talking to the understudy ballerina. He heard her mention Maria and a clandestine meeting that she had arranged for her with a wealthy young man who had plied her with gifts and flowers.

The stage door keeper, now incensed, jumped from his hiding place and stood in front of her, refusing to move until she told him everything she knew. She was obviously frightened and was not easily going to give up her information. He had heard her mention about being paid to get Maria's mother out of the way, and so he had a chance to either up the bribe, or threaten to tell all to the theatre management and put her job in jeopardy. The dresser, now clearly irritated, was somewhat scared of the usually polite and helpful stage door keeper, who was now beginning to show an anger that no one at the theatre had ever seen.

'You will come with me now and answer my questions, or I will report your refusal to co-operate to the management.' The old man ushered her to the room just behind the booking office, where interviews for all aspects of the theatre were conducted. Access to the manager's office was easy from here. 'Please sit down,' he said, calmer now that he had her utmost attention. 'I am going to be straight with you because I believe that you are in some way involved with Maria, and therefore may be responsible for her being held in a hospital, in a state of collapse, and with little or no will to live at present. Thanks to the care of the sisters at the hospital, she has improved physically, but unfortunately that will be of little good if her mental state does not improve accordingly. I am going to ask you now to tell me everything you know. If you need permission for my request from the hospital, there will not be a problem, I assure you. They are as worried as I am.'

He proceeded to open the notebook that he had started at the hospital. He raised his eyes in expectation, but was disappointed.

'I don't know nothing,' the young girl whimpered, 'had all kind of visitors she did. Always hiding things in her pockets she was. I only passed her messages to the people she asked me to.'

'OK,' sighed the stage door keeper. 'Then please give me descriptions of the things they bought her. Tell me what they said. You must have heard, just as I heard you whispering to the other ballerina. You need to consider your options, because either you talk to me, and it goes no further, or I call the management and you talk to them. I think if the truth comes out, you will find yourself out of the theatre, and probably out of any future job that you may wish to hold in this field. I believe you are a good costume mistress, and a well-liked member of the theatre staff. Think very hard about what I have just said, and also imagine the plight of Maria, laying broken-hearted and ill in a hospital bed, without even her mother to comfort her.'

At this the girl raised her head, and with a questioning glance said, 'Her mother? Her mother is always there. Why is she not there when she is ill?'

'If I knew that, dear,' answered the stage door keeper, 'I may be able to put some of the pieces together.' He was noticing a change in the girl's attitude, and suddenly had an idea. 'Would you consider coming with me to the hospital and talking to Maria? I would leave the room while you did so. If you could rethink your reasoning, and be assured that I would do everything I could to protect you, you may just be able to bring Maria back to the world she so loved. Would you not think that was a worthy thing to do?'

The girl, now aware of the stage door keeper's desperation, knew she could find not just one of Maria's acquaintances, but all of them, including the mystery donor of the hundreds of roses sent to Maria in just a few weeks. Could she take the risk? Could she trust this old man that she only knew as the person who ran the comings and goings at the stage door? Why? she wondered, had he not remembered the man with all the roses. She herself would never forget that handsome face of the man who dressed with such flair, and who was never far from the stage door each day. With some reluctance she agreed to go and see Maria. She would have to risk the chance of the old man telling someone that he had heard her say she received money to arrange meetings and cover up disappearances of the prima ballerina from the theatre. Also the liaison she had with the mother and daughter at the big house to help Maria in her escapades. Aside from all of these reasons for her to visit Maria, she felt a fondness for her, and knew her as an extremely happy and generous person, who was after all only human, and under her mother's thumb to a great extent.

She would visit, and she would try to help Maria, and along with the stage door keeper they could maybe find answers to all the questions. The stage door keeper was elated with her decision, but decided to keep the knowledge of her pregnancy to himself for the time being. Having this young girl around her could possibly spark Maria into talking, as long as he could instil upon her not to divulge any of the information to any outsider; to just keep it between themselves until Maria was well enough to deal with it in her own way.

Maria woke to the sound of a soft footfall near to her bed. She had been dreaming that she was dancing, and the wicked fairy had visited her and told her that she would sleep for a hundred years, and that all the bad people that surrounded her would no longer be there when she awoke. Maria was frightened and crying out for her mother. She felt a cool hand gently stroke her brow as she woke, and she whispered, 'Mother', but she stared at the face that bent over her, and found a young pale-faced girl whom she hardly recognised.

'It is me, miss. I'm Zarah. I am the dresser from the theatre; do you remember me? I helped you to meet your friend, the one who sent you flowers. Also I know your other friend, the one who let you ride her horse; you used to tell me about them all. I have come to see if I can help you get better. Aldo, you know the old stage door keeper who has been sitting with you, asked me if I could come too, as he thought you would like to have some female company. I would be glad to sit and talk to you; it is my morning off, and I have nothing important to do.'

Maria, suddenly realising that she had been having a bad dream, smiled shyly at the young Zarah. They both looked at one another for what seemed to be an eternity, and then Maria held out her hand, and took hold of Zarah's hand so gently, it felt as if no strength could be found to grip in friendship the hand that was offered. 'I have nothing to talk about, except the loneliness I feel, the rejection and the loss of the love of those I held most dear, and that has all gone. I would love to just lie and listen to you. Won't you tell me of the theatre, of all its dancers, and of the work that you are all doing. My life as a dancer is over, at least I know that much. I will never stand on a stage again. There is just one thing I would ask you to do if you could.'

'Anything, miss, I will do anything you ask,' Zarah said, secretly hoping to get a little information for Aldo to go to work on.

Maria looked at her sadly and said, 'Could you find my belongings in the theatre, and bring me my ballet shoes? They are the only things that really belong to me and I need to keep them close to me always to remind me of the life I so carelessly threw away.'

Zarah left the hospital at noon, with little to show for her being there, except an inexplicable feeling that Maria would someday need her, and she would be there in whatever capacity she could to help her. She would go and see her often. Not now as a favour to the stage door keeper, but in her own right as a friend, and as one who felt there was a far greater problem with Maria than she or the stage door keeper could at present envisage.

The days went by, and Maria grew stronger. She was able to walk in the beautiful grounds that surrounded the hospital. She would always sit in her favourite spot, near to the duck pond where the calmness of the water gave her peace, where the only noise was from the ducks as they paddled their way to and fro across the shiny surface, sometimes accompanied by a brilliant flash of a dragonfly as it dipped and hovered near to her.

It was on one such day as this that Maria's thoughts turned to Cordelia, her long lost friend. How she would like to see her, but she knew she couldn't. She could not tell her that she was carrying Alexi's child, and very soon now it would become evident to all who looked at her. She would confide in Zarah, whom she had become very fond of, and with whom she had sometimes been able to laugh when she had regaled her with some of the exploits of the theatre dancers.

At last, Zarah had a clue to work on. Maria had told her of her pregnancy, and Zarah had been a kind and sympathetic friend, but one who could not offer any help as to the future when Maria would have to leave the hospital, and fend for not only herself but for the forthcoming birth of her child. Aldo and Zarah sat with their heads together one evening during the show, both now in full knowledge of the immediate situation. How could they find Cordelia?

In a moment of deep thought, Zarah remembered Maria talking about the big house on the hill where she had first had the chance to go to ballet lessons. The house belonged to Cordelia and her mother, and of course it was there that Maria was supposed to be when she headed off with the handsome stranger who plied her with gifts and roses by the dozen. All she had to do was find out who the ballet teacher was at that time, and she would have the address of Cordelia, and probably the address of Maria's mother. Had they finally made a giant step toward securing some sort of future for Maria? They would start their search tomorrow, but for now they would do it without Maria's awareness, so as to not raise her hopes.

They would go on as normal, keep up their visits, and aim at getting her to open up her heart to them. They were after all, at this moment, the only two people that she had in the world.

The breakthrough came without warning one morning when Zarah was called to the practice hall, to help with the newest ballerinas that had joined the corps de ballet. They all needed leotards and headbands, each one matching the next, so as to give them the feeling of dancing as one when the time came to put into operation all that they had been taught over the last few years in the academy school, and before that at their particular dancing school. Teachers from different schools were allowed if they wished to watch their protégées perform on occasions like these. It helped them to assess their own tuition, and relate to a much larger area of their particular form of art. There were four teachers present at this session, and Zara decided to take a risk and step outside her role of wardrobe assistant.

She approached the little cluster of teachers with much trepidation, and stood quietly in front of them trying to give an enquiring look into their midst. One of them turned and, to Zarah's absolute amazement, addressed her by name and enquired as to her well being. She then said that she remembered Zarah when she was looking after Maria, and she had heard that a terrible illness had befallen her, and that she had decided not to dance again.

She asked if Zarah was aware of all that had happened, and did she know where Maria was, as she would like to see her once again. She had been such a perfect pupil, and she could not imagine anything coming between Maria and her dancing. Zarah stood as if she had been welded to the spot, her eyes wide and full of tears. She explained that she could not talk here, but could the teacher meet her when she had finished as it was so important both to her and to Maria that she could not bear it if the meeting did not take place.

It was well into the afternoon when Zarah was called to the stage manager's office. She went with many a doubt, as she knew that the result of this meeting could in some way affect her life at the theatre. Nevertheless she went. She had taken this so far now that it was impossible to back out, and she did not want to anyway. Maria and her plight had gripped her so hard that she felt closer to her than she had done to anyone in her life before.

She knocked quietly on the door, and entered, to find only the teacher standing there. No stage manager, no one else, just the teacher. The strained expression on her face softened as the teacher beckoned her to sit at the desk opposite to her. A silver tray sat between them, with two cups and saucers, and a plate of chocolate biscuits. The teacher passed the plate across to Zarah, and poured her a cup of tea.

'I have a feeling that we will both need this before the meeting has ended,' she said with a slight smile that denied the feeling of misgiving that she felt inside. 'Now, do you feel that you can tell me what happened to Maria? If I can help, I will, if not then this conversation will not be heard of outside of these four walls.'

Zarah knew that this was the only chance she would ever have of helping Maria, and so she poured out the story word for word from the beginning to the end, taking her own share of the blame, and not flinching as she admitted to the part she played in the terrible outcome of it all. The teacher sat in silence, her eyes never leaving the face of the young woman, so tied up in the torment of it all that her face, as young and as pretty as it was, screwed up in an effort to ward off the tears that threatened to overcome her at any moment. She reached the end of the story, and sighed as she said, 'What are we to do? She needs her mother; she needs the lover who is responsible for her condition, and most of all she needs a friend whom she can trust above all others, not only to talk to, but who has the power and the means to find and talk to these people who appear to have deserted her when she needs them most. I do not know where to start, neither do I have the authority to call them to book. I will always befriend her, but most of all I would like to see her through this trauma, and at least give her a chance to find happiness with her expected child. I also have a friend here in the theatre who has been a lifeline to her from the beginning of all this. He too will be unconditionally involved in any search that is needed to reach someone in whom she can find some solace, at least until the birth of her baby.'

The teacher, head in hands now, wiping the tears from her eyes, looked up at Zarah and said, 'I wish to see Maria; will you take me to her? I do not want her to know that I am going, and yes, Zarah, I will help, but I need to talk to Maria first as it has to be her wish too that we contact these people. I have to have her permission to go to my records of her dancing career, and see what their pages bring to light, but my child if all else fails I personally will see that she is cared for, at least until after the birth of her child, so let your worries be at least shared by a third person and, between us, who knows what we might achieve.'

Zarah left the office, and flew down the corridor straight into the arms of Aldo the doorkeeper; she dragged him into his tiny cubby hole of an office, and words just tumbled out one after the other until he had to shake her, and make her stop. He was elated, and she was exhausted, but between them they started to laugh and cry together, in joy and relief, until passing traffic through the corridors of the theatre made them stop and remember where they were, and what jobs they were supposed to be doing.

Chapter Eight

Maria's Final Steps

The process of finding Maria's nearest and dearest was slow. Her mother had moved from the house where she and Maria shared the early days of untiring work that would allow Maria to enter the world of dance, and then the fame and fortune of attaining their dreams. Neighbours had seen her scowling, ignoring all of their comments and enquiries as she hurried back and forth to the house, removing much of its content, suitcases, and bags of clothing, some of which appeared to be theatre apparel. She never looked back at the house. Each time she made haste down the road, and disappeared from sight. No one had any idea where she had gone, but they had witnessed the arrival of a new tenant and assumed that Maria's mother had no wish to stay in the area.

The next enquiry held a little more hope when the ballet mistress visited the house where she knew Cordelia had lived during the time that Maria had taken her ballet lessons, and had remembered the close friendship that the girls had enjoyed. Cordelia's mother, after receiving the letter that the ballet mistress had sent, invited her to call at the house. She was curious to know of the whereabouts of Maria too. She had grown quite fond of the child, and was happy that Maria had helped Cordelia grow in confidence, enough now to have gained a place at a university in Switzerland to complete her studies.

The interview went better than the ballet mistress could ever have hoped for. Before she left, it was arranged that Maria could stay at the house, and be looked after until Cordelia returned at Christmas. By this time she would have her baby, and hopefully, if the father of the child was not forthcoming, she would find herself able somehow to support both of them.

It was armed with this wonderful news that the ballet mistress hurried back to the theatre to tell Aldo and Zarah. She would let them go and tell Maria, and in the meantime she would try and find some clothes, both for Maria and the baby. She would then arrange transport for her so that she could leave the hospital with as little fuss as possible, and without the knowledge of the theatre press who had been seen lurking around the area for some while. Maria needed time now to regain her strength, and come to terms with the possible struggles she would encounter in her future life.

A week later, with a tiny suitcase that the ballet mistress had so neatly packed with sensible clothes for Maria, and three tiny outfits for the baby, including nappies and some essential toiletries for them both, and on top a pair of ballet shoes, Maria left the hospital. Aldo walked with her, and they boarded a carriage at the iron gates. A little further down the road, and out of sight of any onlookers, Aldo climbed from the carriage and bade Maria a fond farewell. Maria cried, and hugged him, and promised to keep in touch as soon as she could. She sent much love to Zarah, and eternal thanks to the ballet mistress, then she was on her own and heading for the big house, where in her childhood she had spent so many happy hours and had later experienced the torment of a lost love. Cordelia's mother had always supported her, and she knew she would help her now, so it was with no doubts and with much courage that she faced the future.

Looking down at her thickening figure, and feeling the gentle movement of the life within her for the first time in many weeks, she managed a tiny smile, and as she reached to touch the locket that hung from its gold chain around her neck, she wondered if eventually she would have all the things that she craved. She would never give up the hope that the father of her child would come back to her; she would live with that hope for the rest of her life.

She had taken her last steps on the stage, but now her life held far greater challenges than the life she had led as a ballerina. She had always been strong and able to cope with everything that had been asked of her. Now she would ask seemingly impossible things of herself, and she would carry them through. Her child would have everything she could offer it. She would work as her mother had to, and see it had every possible chance to do the things that it wanted most to do. At the thought of her mother, her smile faded and she hoped that one day she would forgive her, and come and meet her grandchild. All these thoughts poured in and out of her mind as the carriage pulled up outside the big house, and as Maria gazed toward the stables she saw him, the massive frame of Arturo as he cantered toward the fence as if to welcome her home.

She jumped from the coach as Cordelia's mother hastened towards her, arms outstretched. Clutching the small suitcase to her chest, as if all of her life was encased in it, she went with Cordelia's mother into the house. Nothing much had changed, except for all of the playthings and clothes that had been Cordelia's. Now they were missing, and so was Cordelia. The house had a strange quietness about it, but Maria was content to spend as much time as she was allowed to be there, and with the thought that she would be able to see Arturo every day, and feel him nuzzle her, was just wonderful. She had loved the horse from the first moment she had seen it, and the horse seemed to sense it and responded with gusto by nudging her, often catching her off guard and sending her sprawling to the ground. At the sound of her laughter, his head would go down and nudge her up again. She would have to be more careful now so as not to hurt the baby.

Cordelia, according to her mother, came home some weekends, but more often stayed with friends. She had become quite a party goer, and was popular amongst the students. Her mother had told her that Maria was staying, and that it would be nice if she could spend a little time with her old friend. She had not informed her of her pregnancy, as she thought that should come from Maria herself.

Days passed quite pleasantly for Maria. She was rested, and had engaged the services of a midwife for the forthcoming birth of her child. She was, in spite of all that she had been through, in good health, and all was going well with the baby. She wandered out in the surrounding countryside, walking through the meadows, and across fields that glowed red with the swaying poppies that were growing there. It was an idyllic place to be. She would have loved to ride Arturo, but it was of general consensus that it would be foolish to risk it as she was now getting heavy with child. Arturo, however, was not to be left out, and followed her on her walks, content in her company, sometimes leading the way through small gullies and over tiny rushing streams with Maria holding his rein and talking to him as if he understood all she said. She told him of her love for Alexi, and her sorrow that he had decided that she was not good enough to become his wife. She told him that she would one day explain all this to her daughter, because she knew that it was a daughter she would have. Alexi was so beautiful, he just would have had to have given her a beautiful daughter. 'Not that boys weren't beautiful as well,' she commented to Arturo, so as not to upset his male ego. He just whinnied, and walked on.

One evening, Maria, feeling restless, and with Cordelia's mother sitting in the library with her head firmly planted in a book, she decided to walk across to the paddock to see Arturo. The evening was lovely, bathed in mellow sunlight. Her step was light, and she felt as if good things were going to happen. As she turned to head toward the stables, she noticed the door ajar, and as she approached it she saw him. 'Alexi,' she whispered, closing her eyes as if to wipe away the vision, but upon opening them, she saw him again. He had his back to her, and she took a breath and started to call his name, but the words died on her lips, and her hand flew to her mouth in disbelief. He was there, and so was Cordelia, locked in his arms. Out of sight, Maria crept a bit closer and heard the words spoken by Alexi: 'Marry me...' That was all Maria waited to hear, and then she turned on her heels and ran toward the house.

She silently entered the back door, so as not to disturb Cordelia's mother, and climbed the stairs to her bedroom. She picked up her small bag, pushed as much as she could carry into it, lastly cramming in her ballet shoes, and headed once more for the back door. She skirted the stable block, out of sight of its occupants, and headed to where Arturo was standing. With no time to gather riding tackle, and in blind panic, she climbed onto his back, leaning forward with her bag tightly held between her and the horse's body, and dug her heels into his side, heading him out of the gate.

They flew like two fugitives, away from the house, him with flaring nostrils, and her blinded by tears. They headed they knew not where. The horse, exhilarated now, not knowing what precious cargo he was carrying, headed for the wooded hills, a place where he had frequently been ridden during the hunting season. For him it was no problem, but for her it was life threatening. She was feeling faint now from exhaustion and the memory of the words that kept hammering through her head like bullets. She clung to his mane, but it was all in vain. The horse slipped as it jumped a small stream, and Maria could not hold on any longer. Her body flew through the air and slumped to the ground at the bottom of a bramble bush.

Cordelia's mother, growing tired of reading, wandered from the library and called to Maria, as she so often did. They both enjoyed one another's company. Not receiving any reply, she decided to walk across to the stables. Invariably, that was where Maria could be found. Lost in thought, the sounds that emitted from the stables startled her; two voices talking in hushed tones, and the occasional giggle. Walking toward the door, she stopped, and the blood in her veins went cold. The voice of her daughter was fully recognisable, but the voice of the man, although slightly familiar, filled her with horror when she heard the conversation that was going on between them. She opened the door, and the sight that greeted her shocked her beyond belief. Her daughter, scantily dressed, and Alexi, with his clothing disturbed, were laying on an old horse blanket. Both jumped up at the exclamation that issued from Cordelia's mother's lips.

'It's all right, Mummy,' she said in a sweet voice. 'Alexi and I are going to be married, and I am pregnant. Isn't that just wonderful?'

Cordelia's mother was frozen to the spot, and mortified, and at that moment, in spite of the shock she had just received, all she could think of was Maria... Maria... where was she? Had she witnessed the same scene as she had? Where had she gone? Oh my god! Where is Arturo? 'You!' she addressed herself to Alexi, 'leave my house immediately,' and to her daughter, she turned and said, 'just get out of my sight now!'

Then the panic began to manifest itself; she ran to the paddock, and then to the stables where Arturo's stall was. The riding tackle and saddle were all on their hooks; they had not been disturbed. She ran back to the house, and up the stairs to Maria's room. The bed was undisturbed, but her precious suitcase and all its belongings had gone. Now she knew what Maria had heard and seen. Darkness was falling now; she must find Maria. She flew down the stairs, grabbing a coat and a torch, screaming to the members of staff still in the house. 'Search everywhere, go wherever you think, but find Maria and bring her home.'

In her wildness, the full implications of the situation had not entered her mind, but as she hastened across the garden, and out into the fields, she began to realize the full horror of it all. Cordelia was pregnant by the same man that had fathered Maria's child. How much did Maria know? How was she going to handle the shame of Cordelia's condition? How could she let Cordelia marry this man while Maria was under her roof in the final stages of her pregnancy, and was Alexi aware that Maria was pregnant, and, if he was, would he marry her, and not Cordelia, who definitely did not know of Maria's condition, as she had not yet seen her, or had she? What had Maria heard to make her take flight? It could only be that she had overheard more or less the same as she had. She must find her, and find out before anyone else did. Where was Arturo? The only person whom he would have gone with was Maria. How could she ride him bareback in her condition? She couldn't. Oh my God! Had she had an accident, was she hurt? All these thoughts sent Cordelia's mother's mind into turmoil, and she kept on running with no sense of direction. 'Please somebody find her,' she screamed into the chill night air.

The search party, now spreading out, were leaving the estate and heading toward the wild land beyond its boundaries. The local woodman lived in the tiny cottage deep in the wooded countryside, and was eating supper when his wife heard an unusual sound. The woods were usually quiet at night, and only the soft sounds of the local wild life could be heard. She moved to the window, but could see nothing, and so went to the front door and opened it. The sound was now quite clear. It was the whinny of a horse. It was strange for anyone to be out riding at this time. She also thought she heard voices, including the shrill one of a woman. Shouting to her husband that she was going to have a look around, she took her shawl and closed the door. She moved toward the sound, and she could hear a scratching sound upon the ground in the direction of the coppice.

She shouted 'Who is that?' to which there was no answer, just another whinny. She thought that there was a horse in trouble, maybe it had slipped its harness, taken off and got lost. She saw him then and recognised him as Arturo. He was raised on hind legs, and was covered in sweat, and then she saw the body, still and crumpled at his feet. Running now toward the scene, she saw Maria; she saw the blood in a small pool around her head. At the same time she heard shouts, and saw a torch frantically being waved as the search party and Cordelia's mother reached her side.

'Go and get my husband,' screamed Martha, 'and tell him to bring the cart as quickly as possible; we need to get her to safety. She is still breathing, but we need to act fast as she is very cold, and her pulse is faint,' she cried to the search party, as she took her shawl and placed it over Maria.

The tiny procession began to form into sections. The woodman guiding the old cart across the rough ground, next to him his wife cradling the damaged head of Maria in her hands, issuing tiny curses. Arturo, now frothing at the mouth, galloping forward, and then coming back to the party as if to assess the situation.

Cordelia's mother, silent now, and in a state of shock, white-faced and with hands clenched, eyes wild with fright and anguish, and finally the stragglers that had joined the search, not quite knowing what to do but follow on.

Cordelia's mother turned to them and shouted, 'Go back to your homes, and do not breathe one word of what you have just witnessed. If you do, have no doubt you will suffer at my hands, and your future employment in my service will be terminated.'

The servants and stable hands stopped and stood in a small circle, not uttering a word but aware that the sound of the voice of the mistress was like a sentence being pronounced against them. They did not understand, but they would obey without question or discussion. They stood silently and watched the figures in front of them disappear into the mist. Cordelia's mother, now in utter silence, followed the cart as it made its way into the wood.

Eventually, the cart came to rest outside the small cottage that belonged to the woodman and his wife. No one spoke, but everyone seemed to follow the lead of the woodman as he opened the door and turned to his wife to whisper a command. Between them they lifted the unconscious body of Maria, and gently guided her through the door. Following in their wake was Cordelia's mother. Arturo gave a whinny, and turned to stand by the cart. There he would remain until his precious Maria was returned to him. They laid Maria on the bed, and Martha, the woodman's wife, took over. She was gentle but efficient as she bathed the head that was now caked in blood; she took the pulse, and raised her head to the onlookers. The doubt in her eyes was enough to tell them that all was far from well. To get to a doctor at this time of night would take hours. There was no means of communication from the cottage; someone would have to go on foot, and the only one was the woodman, and if he rode Arturo, he would maybe make it in an hour or so to the town, but Arturo was not saddled and in no mood to be ridden by a stranger. The woodman had no desire to sit on the back of this massive creature anyway.

It was decided he would walk and hopefully meet someone who would take over on the way, so that he could return to this pitiful scene, and be of help here. There was no response from Maria, and as Martha lifted her eyelids she could see that she was in a state of deep unconsciousness. She could only make her comfortable, and wait. As she tidied her mud-sodden clothes in an effort not to move her any more than necessary, she saw the blood issuing now from beneath her skirt. The bed was also soaked in water. With no movement from Maria, she had not realised that the baby was about to be born; dead or alive it was on its way, and now her concentration must be focused on this.

The infant was delivered with little trouble, causing no pain to Maria. The cord was cut, but no sound issued from its tiny body. 'It's a girl,' announced the woodman's wife, 'but it appears no life is present.' She placed the baby to one side, as Maria now seemed to be bleeding quite profusely.

Cordelia's mother just looked on in utter disbelief. Wickedly, she thought this could be the answer to this impossible situation. If the baby did not live, nobody need know of its existence, and Cordelia could marry Alexi. Horrified by her thoughts, she cried, 'let me help.' She picked up the baby to clean her, and wrap her in a towel to keep her warm. As she did so, she felt a small movement, and then heard the tiny strangled cry of a baby born too soon, with no food, no comfort, and nowhere to be. 'It's alive,' she whispered to Martha, but Martha's back was toward her, and she thought that she had not heard.

About to repeat the revelation, Martha turned and with a great sigh said, 'I am afraid that Maria is not.' They both turned to see the beautiful pale face of a once famous ballerina devoid of expression, lying blood soaked and damaged beyond belief.

In an unkempt bed, in a tiny cottage in the middle of a wood where few people ventured, Maria's child was born. For Maria, the hurt was over, but for her child, life was just beginning, with little hope, and with little knowledge of those around her as to her future.

Chapter Nine

Katherine Anne

A baby born in horror and turmoil, Katherine Anne given life in spite of the death of her mother from a tragic accident caused by trying to escape her own life, now left alone, wrapped in an old towel, and without the warmth and nourishment of her mother's breast. A cry so small that it could not be heard above the noises in the adjoining room of two women faced with the trauma of death in such terrifying circumstances. Cordelia's mother was now in a frenzy, not helping the woodman's wife who was desperately trying to wash the now stiffening body of a young girl, no longer beautiful in death, and not at peace as she might have been had the death been from any other cause.

She wandered to the door to see Arturo standing so still beside the wagon that had borne the beautiful lady with the soft hands that had so often caressed his mane. She saw Maria's tiny suitcase, carelessly thrown into the cart, and now she approached and gently removed it under the close inspection of Arturo. Once back inside the cottage, she opened the case and found the tiny clothes for a baby inside, also a dress and shoes belonging to Maria, and underneath them the ballet shoes.

She felt the tears sting her eyes, and her heart felt so heavy with guilt at the thoughts that she had nurtured, and anger at the behaviour of Alexi and her own daughter. What could she do! Cordelia was pregnant and gaily planning her wedding to Alexi, not aware of Maria's condition, or the fact that Maria had still been in love with Alexi. Now she would have to know that her old friend had died in a horrendous accident involving Arturo, but, her mother thought, did she have to know there was a baby? Maria could not be hurt anymore, so could she find a mother for the child without anyone knowing that it had survived the accident. So far only Martha the woodman's wife knew. She would have to confide in her, and do it quickly before the woodman returned with a doctor.

She returned to the cottage, finding Maria clean now with her hair cascading over her shoulders, and covered by a clean white sheet, and Martha nursing the scrap of humanity that was clinging to life in her arms. She had made a makeshift bottle, with a teat fashioned from a finger of an old leather glove, which she had sterilised in boiling water, and had filled with sugared water. Miraculously, the baby responded and sucked with a gentle motion, ensuring slow penetration of the liquid into her system. Cordelia's mother watched, enthralled, as a plot began to form in her mind. She smiled at Martha, as she looked up and said, 'I have always longed for a child, and now this one has no one to care for her. Life is so unfair!'

Cordelia's mother could not believe what was happening. She took her courage in both hands, and decided to put her plan to Martha, who, as she continued, began to see a future so perfect that she would be prepared to go to any lengths to bring it to fruition.

'Take the baby, and keep her out of sight for a few months,' she suggested. 'Very few people pass by this way, so it would be possible. The child would be yours, and as far as anyone would know, the baby could have been aborted and the foetus destroyed with the blood that had poured in profusion from Maria's body.'

The doctor would have to accept that as the cleaning of Maria was now complete, and all that was there was a frail body. All the clothing had been thrown on the bonfire that was burning dead cuttings from the surrounding trees. The woodman would be told after the doctor had gone. The baby in the meantime, now peacefully sleeping, was placed in the loft in a soft straw bed, and as a gesture of love and a wish for forgiveness, Cordelia's mother placed Maria's locket over the baby's head.

'Whatever becomes of this child, the locket must go with her; it will be her inheritance, very small, but I feel it will serve her with some happiness in the future. Also, I will pay you for the cost of her raising, education, and anything that she may need to make her life possible, but it is you Martha who will give her love, and this you will offer until the day she leaves you to venture into her own world, or until the day you die, whichever comes first. The little case that belonged to her mother, and which she held so close to her heart, must go with her. Inside are a few tiny clothes, and a pair of ballet shoes.'

Finally that night, Martha sat with a glow around her, cherishing her new role as a mother. Cordelia's mother could now allow her daughter to enter into a marriage that would bring her financial security and the love of a handsome man. A tiny child, without even a name for a few months, would know the love of a woman who would be every bit as precious to her as any mother to her child.

It was a sad group of people, clad in black, who followed the cart that bore the body of Maria to her final resting place in the small church graveyard in the local village. The rough coffin, covered in a black lace cloth, had atop of it a single white rose. Cordelia and Alexi, hand in hand, quietly speaking to each other. Cordelia's mother, hands clasped in front of her carrying a tiny posy of wild flowers, and Martha and her husband. Three people who showed the most signs of distress also stood there, the ballet mistress with Zarah, and Aldo who had been advised of her death by Cordelia's mother. Clinging to each other in disbelief and anger that life should end this way for Maria, who was so loved by all who encountered her talent and beauty, and those who grew close to her as she took her final steps. Last of all, and given the final honour of being tethered to the cart and gently pulling it across the countryside that had seen her die, was Arturo, who stayed long after the procession had departed as if to leave her would break his big heart.

Katherine Anne was now a bonny baby, happily gurgling and propped on her mother's hip as she wandered around the cottage and surrounding woodland. Martha had blossomed, and her husband was happy for her to occupy her time, especially when he could head for the village and share a beer with the locals. No mention of the child that had died with her mother was ever made by anyone. Gradually, Martha ventured farther with Katherine Anne, and the time had come, she thought, to have her christened. She would talk to her husband, and decide whether to keep the name that she had given her as soon as she became her responsibility.

Katherine had been the name of Martha's elder sister, who, like Martha, had lived in England for the greater part of her young life, and had also met with a tragic accident at a very young age. Anne was the name of Martha's mother who had, against her will, been persuaded by her husband to move to Italy where he had been offered a position as manager of a winery. Martha's father was a good man but one who could not resist the wine, or the attraction of a pretty face, both of which brought him down, cost him his marriage, and caused the death of his eldest daughter. Katherine, running from what she had seen her father doing to one of her young friends in one of the holding bays where the great vats were, and not looking ahead of her, ran into one of the threshing machines that stripped the vines. Her death was instant. Life from that moment was unbearable for Martha, and her mother. One night, her father went to a quiet corner in the vineyard and committed suicide, swallowing oxalic acid which resulted in a writhing agonising death, leaving his face twisted and burned for his wife to discover the following morning.

Martha, only ten years old, cared for her mother as best she could, but soon it was impossible, as her mother lost her mind and was taken to an institute for the mentally deranged. Martha moved into care and was looked after by an Italian family with whom she grew to find much happiness. Every now and then she would yearn to go back to where she spent the early days of her life, living in a cottage in Southern England, where her garden was full of grape vines and pretty flowers. She had brought with her to Italy many books. She was never one for playing games like her sister; she preferred to sit in the hammock on a bright summer day and read a book. When Katherine Anne was big enough, she would teach her English and show her pictures of England, and, who knows, one day she may be able to take her there.

Martha began to think of the life she had finally made for herself. She had been taught to sew, and as she grew up she was put to work as a seamstress in a local boutique where hand-made lingerie was made for discerning Italian ladies of noble status. A young man with a mop of curly black hair, and a pair of the bluest eyes, passed the window each day where she sat and worked. On his cart he would ride, with his logs piled high in neatly stacked bundles. He would slow his horse and wave to her. He won her heart, and she finally married him, a woodman, with not many prospects, and as it turned out not very much at all. She went to live with him in his cottage, which was cold and sparsely furnished. He would leave her for many hours on her own, not only while he worked, but when he would go she knew not where, and return smelling strongly of alcohol, and demand her favours. She would have dearly loved a child, but nothing happened despite his intense love making.

Her husband agreed to have the baby christened. Anything that would keep his wife happy was all right by him. So arrangements were made, forms were signed, and a beautiful gown was made by Martha from some old lace that she had saved from the lingerie that she had fashioned before she was married. She walked to the church and passed her baby to the priest who duly christened her Katherine Anne, and ensured that promises were made to keep the child in the ways of the church. Martha now took her baby back, looked at her and wept unashamedly as her tiny face wrinkled, about to cry, until she saw her mother and gave her the most wonderful smile.

Now the world would know that the child she had nurtured from birth was hers; only a few people knew that she hadn't borne her, and none of them would decry her. She could raise her, and watch her grow in strength and beauty. The latter being a foregone conclusion, for the child had her natural mother's pale skin, beautiful eyes, and the beginnings of the stunning titian locks that were her mother's crowning glory. Martha made for her a bedroom fit for a princess, using some of the money that Cordelia's mother had left her. She bought some pretty white furniture, and made curtains that were covered in tiny pink and white flowers, and had frilled edges that were gathered into a pink bow so that the window was framed by them, and from underneath, a froth of white tulle to protect her from any prying eyes passing the cottage, whilst keeping the room cool in the heat of summer.

Her room was next to the room where Martha had her sewing machine, and all her collection of precious items she had brought with her as a tiny child from England. Next to that was a room that Martha had turned into a tiny bathroom, with a bath that stood in the middle which had to be emptied by hand into a sink that carried the water down an outside drain pipe.

The days and months passed in idyllic happiness for Martha, and Katherine thrived on the simple regime. Martha found a new mother in the village who agreed to express enough milk for the baby, as well as feeding her own little boy. They became great friends, and gleaned knowledge and understanding of the life of a mother from each other. Vittorio, the woodman, in spite of himself, also grew fond of the infant, and made her playthings. Roughly hewn from the old wood of fallen trees, he also made a pram for her, a simple box shape with four large metal wheels from an old wagon that he found in his shed. He could not fashion a hood, so Martha used an umbrella that she had never opened, and with some of the material she had left from the nursery curtains, covered it. She then took a large pillow from the bed to make a comfortable mattress, and made a small pillow and quilt from the last piece of the curtain material. Her friend in the village gave her a pink blanket that she had been given before her own baby's birth; pink just didn't look right on a boy's pram. With the umbrella clamped to the top of the pram, all was ready for the first trip. So proudly she wheeled Katherine Anne into the village. People smiled, openly and without question. As far as they were all concerned, the woodman's wife was now a mother and to all intents and purposes a very good one.

Katherine was such a good baby, she slept through the night nearly always, which Martha was so pleased about, as Vittorio often came home the worse for drink. Sometimes, Martha suffered his drunken attentions to the point of exhaustion that caused her to come and sit by Katherine in the small hours, and cry, hurting physically and mentally while he snored his way to the morning, when he would shout for his cup of tea, breakfast, and his clean clothes for the day. Her days were filled with joy. Each smile that Katherine gave her, was etched in her brain, and Katherine smiled a lot. Now she was aware of all that went on around her, Martha would prop her up in the pram after she had fed her, and sit her by the back door so that she could watch the chickens clucking around Martha's skirts as she fed them. She watched as tiny rabbits popped out of the trees and fed hungrily on the vegetable greenery that was scattered around the yard.

Martha now took her to market. It was a long walk, but both Martha and Katherine enjoyed it. There was always a skip in Martha's step, and Katherine would just sit and gurgle, and sometimes, just for fun, she would throw one of her wooden toys from the pram and wait for Martha to scold her, but Martha never did, she just gave a waggle of a finger that sent Katherine into gales of giggles. She responded to the people who stopped to look at her. She raised a tiny hand, if they put their hand near to her, and took hold of a finger, which endeared them to her completely. Her hair was now growing, and it laid in masses of titian curls on her tiny forehead. Her eyelashes for a baby were long, and had little golden flecks in them, which mirrored those that in certain lights appeared in her eyes. She will break someone's heart one day, commented one of the villagers who stopped to pass the time of day with Martha. 'I hope not,' she said silently, remembering the night that she came to her and gave her a reason to live.

Martha would only spend a small amount of the money that Cordelia's mother sent her regularly. She wanted to be sure that as she grew, she would be able to set her on the right path to lead as normal a life as possible. She saved some money every month, and she tucked it in a box at the bottom of the case that Maria had with her the night she died. The locket was lodged there too, and when Katherine was old enough, she would tell her of its where-abouts, and explain all she could to her about it. She was dreading doing that, because there would always be the possibility that she would resent her not being her natural mother. She would not think about that, hopefully for a long time yet, and she would live the rest of her life for Katherine.

It seemed such a short time, and here it was, Katherine's first birthday. A year had passed since that terrible night when they had lost the fight to save Maria, and she had gained the love and the joy of her life, Katherine Anne Carrera; she had been given Martha's married name at her christening. Martha had no proof, although she had her suspicions as to the identity of her father. She had to keep that a secret, and never reveal it to anyone. If she did, the money would no longer be coming from Cordelia's mother, and who knows how long she would be prepared to support her anyway. Cordelia would soon be married and have a family of her own. Her mother could, if pushed, deny all knowledge of the happenings that night. On her birthday, Katherine would have a new pretty dress and her first pair of tiny shoes. She was beginning to perform a few tottering steps, much to the amazement of the woodman and his wife to whom the raising of a child had been a complete mystery just a short while ago. Shoes maybe would play a small part in her trying to keep upright. She would have a birthday cake, lovingly baked by her mother, and it would be iced in pink with one pink candle, which her friend and her own one-year-old would join in and try to blow out. Katherine Anne sat there on her birthday at the head of the table, and acted like the perfect hostess. She smiled, and laughed, slapped her spoon in her small dish of jelly, and sent it in a myriad of strawberry fragments across the table. This was to cause an uproar among her guests, and she laid her head on the table, followed by her little boy friend, both of whom spent the rest of the day in competition and hysterical laughter much to the amusement of the onlookers. When bedtime finally came, and in her mother's arms, she listened with no understanding to the little poem that Martha used to say to her in English. She looked into Martha's eyes, and sleepily she mouthed the word Mama.

> Darling child to me you came,
> With not a home and not a name,
> And now you smile and love me too,
> And I will give my life for you.

Martha stayed with her, and watched her drift into the land of dreams. A tiny smile played around her rosebud mouth. Her heart was so full of love for her, she felt it would burst, and almost in panic she thought of the day she might lose her. She would give her gladly in love to someone who would care for her, and make her happy, but she would die for her if anyone should hurt her. Finally she left her to sleep, and in the morning a new beginning she would face as her darling child would begin to grow and face the future. It would be many years yet before she would have to plan her departure, and she would live every day until then in happiness. She would teach her to read, and she would learn to speak English as well as Italian. She would be clever, and beautiful, and no harm would befall her with her mother there to guide and protect her.

Ten years passed with amazing speed. Katherine grew beyond all her mother's expectations. She was tall for her age, and in good proportion. She loved to run, which she did every morning in front of her mother as they made their way to pick up Martha's special friend, and her young son who was just a day older than Katherine. Then together they would race toward the school house. Katherine loved school, and according to her teachers showed promise in all manner of subjects. She loved to draw and to paint, but also loved reading and arithmetic. Above all this, she had a special talent, and that was to sing; she never stopped singing the songs that Martha had taught her, but, much to the annoyance of the other children, she sang them in English. Martha promised that she would try and translate them into Italian, so that she could sing them at a concert that the school was going to put on at the end of the term.

It was the learning of one of these songs that caused her one day to wander a little further from the cottage than she was normally allowed to do. Concentrating on fitting the Italian words to the tune that she had learned in English, which she found a little tiresome, she would step in time to the tune, stop at the end of the sentence, and then repeat it over again until she had it right, counting a step to a note. Not noticing where she was going, she found herself on the edge of the trees that formed the boundary of the woodman's land. She stopped, felt a little frightened, turned to try and see the cottage, but instead saw a horseman approaching. The horse it seemed was a little frightened too, as he raised his front legs, as if to quickly stop, turned and then headed straight for her at a gentle trot. The rider dismounted, and holding the reins walked beside it until they reached the little girl. The horse dropped its head, and stood quietly in front of her, giving a gentle whinny. Katherine, delighted, reached and touched its nose;

she had never been this close to a horse. She had only seen the woodman with his dirty tired old horses dragging the old cart full of logs. The gentleman asked if she was all right, and where she was from; to be out here in this part of the woods on her own was unusual.

'I live in the woodman's cottage, but I am lost, sir,' she said in her best Italian. The gentleman looked at her curiously... the hair... the eyes... the forthright attitude. The likeness was amazing. No! it was his imagination. However he walked with her and the horse until the cottage came into view. Martha was at the gate, wringing her hands at the disappearance of her daughter as she caught sight of her coming toward her.

'Katherine,' she cried with an anger that the child had never seen. 'Come here now.'

Katherine ran to her, arms outstretched. 'I'm sorry, Mama, I got lost.'

Martha had also seen the horse and rider, one of whom she recognised with little trouble. The other made her tremble inside as she had an idea who it may be, but would not accept her feelings, and prayed the episode would be forgotten by both parties.

This was not to be. Alexi arrived back at the house, unsaddled Arturo, who to say the least was skittish, and made his way to the study where Cordelia's mother was sitting at her desk.

'I have just seen a child in the woods who said she lived in the woodman's cottage. Do you know who she is?' he said, somewhat irritably.

'She is the woodman's daughter,' said Cordelia's mother in a calm voice that belied the feeling she felt inside.

No comment had ever been made by anyone in relation to the child that had now been fully accepted by them all as Martha's daughter. Katherine, on the other hand, never mentioned the incident again, although she would always remember the beautiful horse that helped her on the day that she was lost and frightened. Martha knew that one day she would have to tell Katherine Anne, but she was secretly glad that it would not have to be today. She would carry on preparing her for the concert in which she would star. She would sit in the audience and be proud of the beautiful little girl, who had repaid her tenfold for all the care and love she had given unconditionally to her for the first ten years of her life.

Alexi could not forget her! Cordelia, now heavily pregnant with their third child, was being her usual tempestuous self. Living in the house with her mother was not easy in spite of the size of it, and their own apartments being entirely self-contained. He was not a happy man. The richness of his title was not enhanced by financial status. Therefore, Cordelia's mother held the purse strings, and the wellbeing of her daughter came first. It had to be shown that the marriage was perfect, and that Cordelia was the perfect wife and mother, when in fact she had no hand in the raising of their children, or the running of the household. Alexi now had regrets about his past that he found almost impossible to live with, but to live with it he had to. He would run the risk of complete banishment from his family, and the loss of any inheritance that may be due to him in time, if he were to denounce his marriage to Cordelia. His children showed him no love, or respect. All their benefits came from their grandmother, who doted on them, and spoiled them, thus making them ill-mannered and obnoxious.

Martha sat with Katherine for hours on end, and helped her with her reading, and with the rehearsals for the concert, which was getting ever closer. Martha had been asked by the head mistress for her permission to allow Katherine to perform with the higher class for the concert. Her voice was sweet, and clear as a bell, and there was no one who could render a particular song in the way that Katherine could. Martha of course consulted Katherine, who duly whooped for joy, hugged her mother, and said, 'But I am so afraid.'

'You will be just fine, and the older girls will look after you, they all like you,' said her mother with pride.

So mother and child would sit in the warmth of late summer in the garden, and they would talk and laugh. Katherine was learning all the time, and when her studying got a little too tiring, Martha would tell her stories of her childhood in England. Katherine was enthralled and often asked if her mother thought that one day they might visit England. She promised to work hard at her studies, and when she was old enough she would work and earn lots of money so that they could both go to England. Martha smiled wistfully, and said 'maybe'. Katherine in the meantime set herself a target. She would one day go to England, and she would take her mother. She would study her singing, and she would be the best singer in the world, so that people would pay to hear her sing, and she would be rich. Martha made her dress for the part she would play in the concert. It had to be quite plain, the teachers said, not too grown-up, but it could be down to the ground, and it was to be in a dark green to contrast with the rest of the choir when Katherine sang her solo. Martha spent a little more of the savings she had collected than she meant to, but this was important for Katherine to have something really special to remember.

The great day arrived. Martha brushed her hair till it shone like spun gold on the little proud head that walked to school, sedately now. The days of running with her friends of a couple of years ago were over. Now she was a girl, not a child, and she would act like one, practising with her head held high, and arms to her sides, gracefully swinging them, although her satchel sometimes got in the way. It was so heavy with all the books for her homework that her graceful movements were slightly restricted. She was twelve years old this year, and would soon be moving to a higher grade. She faced this with all the confidence that Martha had instilled in her. It was tonight that she had at this moment to focus on.

All the dresses were behind the stage, and there was a buzz of excitement everywhere. Parents and friends were gathering, to be ushered into the assembly hall, to sit and wait, each one, for their children to perform. Martha found a spot about midway down the hall, and to one side, where she thought she would have a good overall view. She sat, never taking her eyes from the stage, and waiting patiently for Katherine's moment.

The choirs from all the classes sang with vigour, and were applauded with gusto by a larger than expected audience. Martha did not notice the man who entered the hall at the last moment before the concert began. Alexi stood in the shadow of a pillar that stood at the side of the hall, matched exactly by one on the opposite side. Had he stood at that one, chances are Martha would have seen him, but he went unnoticed, and with an almost ghostly look on his face, he watched as if he had been transported back in time.

A child in the spotlight, with a slight beautiful frame, and titian hair that glinted like a halo around her head, stood in front of an audience and gave a performance close to perfection. It could not possibly be, but he had to find out without causing a commotion, and without giving a reason for wanting to know who she was. The woodman's daughter, was she, he would find out somehow.

In the throng of people leaving the school, he was able to slip away, and make his way to where the teachers were standing in happy conversation as to how well it had all gone. 'May I offer,' the gentleman said, 'congratulations on an excellent concert. A great deal of talent was evident in the last performance. May I ask what age group they were in? I would like to compare it to my own daughter's ability.'

'These are the thirteen to fourteen-year-olds, in their last year with us here,' one of the teachers said with some pride.

'Thank you,' he said, somewhat taken aback. He walked away with a dull ache in his stomach. So it can't be then. He worked out how old she would have to be, if she had been... He could not bring himself to say the word... He went home to his wife and children, with a feeling that he had just lost his only hope in life.

Martha in the meantime had picked up her daughter and danced her all the way back to the cottage. Too excited to sleep, mother and child went upstairs and sat in Martha's sewing room, where remnants of the material from her beautiful dress were still scattered around.

'Mama, I know I will be famous one day, and you and I will go to England. Please tell me about it again.'

Martha did so, thinking she would never go because of her husband, but there was no reason why her daughter shouldn't. There were many years to go yet, and all of them would be special, just as her daughter was. How lucky she had been to be blessed with a child so beautiful.

'Please god, may she stay that way always. And may I always be a part of her life.'

Alexi was a haunted man, he had an overwhelming feeling that the child was Maria's, and if she was, who was the father? It could not be his if the age he had been given at the school was correct. Then he thought about Maria, and realized just how much he had loved her. What a fool he was to give her up for something as flimsy as the heritage that it was thought his family had. There may be nothing. They could all have been living a lie. He had nothing from his family when he married Cordelia. She in fact had more social standing than him. Her mother came from high aristocracy in her own right. Her husband was an Italian count, so the breeding was immaculate. Cordelia was a perfect choice for a wife, and the choice was mainly made by her mother, and was highly approved of by Alexi's family. So he was trapped in a situation from which he could never escape. The only thing he could have done was to go away with Maria and renounce his heritage, if she had been pregnant and he had known about it.

'Oh my god, I would have gone,' he shouted out loud, in the hope that she would hear him. He knew that he would have to go to the graveside and just be near her for a while; he had to say the words out loud, and he could do it nowhere but there. He had not been near the churchyard in thirteen years. Perhaps there would be no sign of her burial place left, but he knew where it was; he remembered every step he took that day, and he remembered resenting Cordelia hanging on to his arm. He wanted to be there on his own. So with that set firmly in his mind, he carefully worked out how he could go, and not be seen by Cordelia, her mother, or in fact anyone who knew of him. He wanted the moment to be as the moment was when he first made love to the beautiful Maria, barely more than a child, but so full of love and warmth. His heart felt as if it was bleeding at the very thought of her.

Katherine sat one evening in Martha's room. Martha was clearing up after her husband had eaten his supper, and gone off on one of his evening jaunts to the village. Katherine always felt happy and contented in this room. She wanted to be away from the woodman, as the way he treated Martha, and the way he looked at her, made her feel uncomfortable. She knew Martha cried a lot. Sometimes she pretended to be asleep as Martha crept into her bedroom, and sat in the little rattan chair by the window, and softly cried so as not to waken and upset her.

Tonight Katherine felt restless. The excitement of the concert had left her tired, but without the desire to sleep. She pulled out the little case that Martha had given her when she was ten years old, and told her that she would explain where it came from when she was a bit older. Often when she was on her own upstairs, she would carefully lift out the pair of ballet shoes that were carefully wrapped in tissue paper. She had tried them on, and smiled because her little feet did not quite fill them, but they would one day, and when they did, she would try to stand on her toes as she had seen in the pictures that Martha had shown her in one of the books. She tried them on, and felt that it would not be too long before they fitted her. She turned over the baby clothes that had been carefully washed and folded and laid in the case.

Then Katherine lifted the pouch that had in it a gold locket. She always held it in her hand and wondered at its beauty, and when she clicked it open she saw the beautiful lady swathed in white. She looked at it closely, and then at the gentleman in the opposite window. Slowly she gazed at it, put it down, and then picked it up again, and looked closer at his face, which in the picture was quite small. She stared at it for a long time, and then felt a fluttering inside her. The face without a doubt was the face of the gentleman who stopped, walked, and talked with her, when she got lost in the woods. She was sitting staring at it as Martha came into the room.

'What is it my darling?'

'Mama, the man in this picture is the man in the woods. Did you see him closely when he brought me back to the cottage?'

Martha's worst moment had arrived, and now she knew she had to tell her darling daughter, who had only been lent to her, about her life and the reason for her being here.

'Come here, Katherine, and sit with me. I have to tell you a story which I had hoped not to tell you for a while yet. You are still so young to understand the things that happen in the story. It will not be like the stories that you have read with me up to now. It will be a grown-up story. Do you think you can be brave enough to listen to it all?'

'Yes of course, Mama, as long as you are near I will be as brave as I had to be to sing in the concert with the older girls,' said Katherine.

This brought tears to Martha's eyes. She was not sure where to start, and how much to tell this innocent child. With Katherine held tight sitting on her lap and with her arms around her, she started at the beginning. She decided that this was the only thing to do. She had to give Katherine the right to decide whether she had done the correct thing by waiting this long to tell her that she was not her mother.

'Thirteen years ago, my precious child, there was a terrible accident. A lady unknown to me at the time fell from her horse a short way from the cottage. I could hear the horse crying out, and thought it was hurt, so I went alone to find out what had happened. What I found was so horrible that I can't bring myself to describe it to you. The young lady had fallen from the horse and was very badly injured. Help was at hand from some of the locals, and she was brought here to the cottage where another lady and myself administered to her. We spent hours trying to help her while Vittorio went for a doctor. We lost the fight for her, and she died, but there was a baby born that night, and we believed that it was dead too, and so paid not too much attention until we saw a movement and heard a tiny cry. We realized that the baby inside the mother's body had survived the accident. I wrapped her in a towel, made her a makeshift bottle, and fed her. Rightly or wrongly, the other lady and I decided that I would keep her and raise her as my own. The reason for this I can't tell you yet, but I will one day when you are old enough. The lady in the picture was your mother, Katherine, and she did not know that you had been born, as the accident had caused you to be born earlier than you should have been. She was a famous ballerina, and had performed in a theatre in Milan. The ballet shoes were hers. I do not know about the man in the picture. He could be your father, but I have no way of finding out because I kept you illegally. As far as everyone who has met you knows, you are my daughter. I hope you do not hate me for what I have done, but I truly believe I saved your life that night, and that is the only excuse I have, and the fact that I love you more than life itself.' Martha stopped, and looked at the child to find tears streaming down her face.

'I only want you for my Mama, and I too love you more than life itself. Thank you for my lovely life, and I want to be with you always. I do not care who my father is. If he had loved my mother, he wouldn't have allowed her to ride a horse with a baby inside her, would he?'

'I can't say, my darling, what was right or wrong. It is now a long while ago, and I have told you all that I can at this time, except to say that your mother is buried in the little churchyard behind our village. If you wish to go and visit her grave, I will take you there.'

It was with some thought that Katherine decided that she should at least visit even though she had no feelings for the mother she never knew. The ballet shoes and the locket, however, now took on a different dimension in the course of things, and in her mind as she held them, a moment of sadness and a strange feeling of belonging took hold of her. Katherine Anne had in a couple of days grown to gain knowledge of a life so far removed from the sweet joys of a child to the reality which encountered sadness, loss, and the enduring love of a complete stranger who had played the part of the mother that she loved beyond anything in the world for the past twelve years and, who, in spite of all that she had just learned, she would love until her dying day.

Carrying a small bunch of flowers that she had picked from the garden, she headed off with Martha to see her secret mother's grave. Martha had told her about the reason for keeping it a secret, and Katherine had no wish to call anyone her mother, except for Martha. The woman lying in the ground was a stranger from the past, and had no part in her life. She had decided however that she would wear the locket round her neck from now on to remind her of how her life had begun, and how lucky she was to have been given a mother who cared and loved her instead of a woman who cared only for herself, and a wicked man who had obviously not loved her mother at all, and who she hoped she would never come into contact with... not ever...

The graveyard was quiet and empty as the two of them entered, and followed the path toward the now flattened mound of earth with the tiny wooden cross at its head which simply read 'Maria'. Martha stood and watched as her daughter knelt and placed the flowers by the cross, and gently touched it with one finger. Katherine looked up at Martha and said quietly , 'Can we go now, please?' and holding tightly to her hand walked quickly toward the gate.

Alexi had tethered Arturo a few yards from the gate and, continuing on foot, had seen the cameo, as one stood, and one knelt at the grave of the woman he had loved with an all-consuming love. Now he knew. This child was his, and if there had been any doubt, apart from her colouring and natural grace, the locket, hit by a sudden shaft of sunlight as they left the graveside, gave him the final evidence that he needed. He stood there transfixed, but, before he could hide, the two were at the gate, and all three stopped as if frozen in time. Katherine hesitated, but only for a second, and then pulled at Martha's sleeve and said, 'Come Mama, it's time we were home to get Papa's tea. Alexi could do nothing but stare; no words would come. No expression could give a clue to his turmoil. He wanted to run, and yet he wanted to stay and talk to her. Arturo on the other hand restlessly pulled at the reigns that held him fast to the railings. He gave a whinny in vain. Martha and Katherine were running down the lane hand in hand to the safety of the cottage.

Alexi now moved with heavy foot toward the grave at which his daughter had knelt just a few seconds ago. He too knelt and lifted the flowers to his lips, gently kissing them. 'Maria,' he whispered, his body now racked with sobs as he realised what he had done and how it had cost him not only the only woman he had truly loved, but the sweetest, most beautiful daughter any man could have fathered.

Martha left Katherine at the bottom of the stairs, and headed for the kitchen. She knew that she had to let her be alone with her thoughts for a while; her own heart was worried by the happenings of the afternoon, and she too was now sure that the man was Katherine's father. Although the likeness was vague, Katherine was definitely her mother's daughter, but this man could cause her untold problems, and if he was her father, all their futures were in question. She could do nothing. She could not protect her enough without smothering her, and she could not do that to a free spirit like Katherine, who had such a zest for life. The next few years until she came of age could be the most difficult of both hers and Katherine's.

Katherine sat on her bed, head reeling. She undid the locket yet again. He was the man in the picture, of that she was sure, but could he possibly be her father, and if he was, why was he not with her mother? There were so many questions. Her mother was just a picture, but this man was real. Martha was her mother too, and she could reach out and touch her, talk to her, hug her, and know she would care for her forever. It was with this thought that she decided that she would have nothing to do with this man. She didn't want a father, she had Vittorio, although he was not, if she was honest, someone she would have chosen to be a father.

In fact he frightened her. She hated the way he treated Martha, and often made her cry. She never liked being alone with him in the cottage. He would creep up behind her and make her jump, and then hold her too tight in an effort to say sorry. She stayed sitting on the bed until much later when Martha came upstairs. Mother! Mother! she kept repeating to herself, not realising Martha was within earshot. She came to her and held her close. 'I always will be, until you say you don't need me any more,' she whispered, and they sat in silent closeness until the sound of the door slamming forced them apart. Katherine lay on her bed unable to sleep, as throughout the night the woodman both verbally and physically abused her darling mother.

Life continued in a sort of formality for a while. There was no sign of the man, or the horse. Katherine continued her studies. She knew she had to do her best, so that one day she could keep her promise to her mother and take her to England, if only for a while to get her away from her ugly husband. She had almost reached her thirteenth year, and tried to keep away from Vittorio. He seemed to act more badly to her mother when she was there, saying horrible things to her, and snatching his food, and then throwing the dishes noisily in the sink, often breaking them and blaming Martha. When Katherine came home from school, he would put his arm around her, and place a wet mouth upon her cheek, which made her want to retch, but she kept calm for Martha's sake.

Once or twice he came up the stairs and stood in the doorway of Martha's work room when Katherine was doing her homework. He would say not a word, but just stare at her in a way that sent shivers of fear down her back. She knew that Martha had enough worries, and so never mentioned her fear to her. Her school work was beginning to suffer, and her teachers noticed a difference in her that they could not quite understand. They had seen the man with the horse sometimes ride by, and wondered if he had something to do with her vagueness. They had discussions and decided to monitor her closely, and if necessary have a word with her mother who they considered to be a perfect parent.

Alexi lived a life of total mortification. He could not talk to anyone. He paid respectful attention to Cordelia's mother in relation to the children and his responsibilities to them. To Cordelia herself, he remained cool, but was in all purposes a perfect husband. She in her turn was happy not to have his physical advances. It gave her freedom to think of the good times she could have when meeting her social companions, which she did often. With a nanny and her mother to care for and nurture the children, she had few worries. Money was easily come by from her mother, who, recognizing the situation for what it was, constantly gave her daughter the wherewithal to purchase fine clothes, and give the impression that all was well in her marriage, and life.

Alexi, like a tortured soul, moved around as if borne on a mist to a place far beyond this life. He visited Maria's grave often, and sat silently watching the gate and the path that led to this haven where he found a restless peace. He prayed that one of these days his daughter may come also to visit her long lost and unknown mother, but she never did. He so wished he could just talk to her to explain how he had loved Maria, to tell her the reason why he did not marry her, and to tell her of the unforgiving grief he felt for leaving her an illegitimate child when she would have been the most beautiful thing in his life, and how he knew that her mother would have cared and loved her. He would also be sure that she knew how grateful he was to Martha whom he knew had saved her life, and given her all that she could and who had selflessly loved her beyond all else.

One day as he sat there wishing he could just lie down beside her, and never leave, he had to make a decision, and he decided that he would go and visit the woodman's cottage, whether or not Katherine was there. He could perhaps talk to Martha and learn a little about this child who was fast becoming a young lady. Older than his eldest daughter, she was so different, slight of build, where his daughter was the image of her mother, a rather large and pouting child with an angry attitude to things she considered below her status. It was mostly to just look at Katherine. She was so much like Maria. Would she one day take the heart of a young man, and hold it until it rendered him with only the power to love her? He had loved her mother like that, but had not had the courage to take his love and give it to her unconditionally. Regret was the only feeling he would now live with until he died. If he could do just one thing for Katherine, with the blessing of Martha, it would in no way make up for all the wrongs, but it would leave a tiny part of his heart undamaged.

So it was, on a cold winter afternoon, that Alexi set off on foot towards the woodman's cottage. He had gone to the stables to saddle up Arturo, but one of the stable lads had taken him out to hack him across country, which the horse loved to do. Alexi shrugged off the cold, and set out with head bent against the wind. It was some time later, as he neared the edge of the trees where he had first set eyes on Katherine, that he heard the screams. He stopped and listened. The screams, now growing in intensity, were coming from the cottage. He began to run, forgetting why he had come. He flew through the garden gate and ran for the door; another scream issued forth, this time from the garden. Unthinking, he automatically picked up a pitch fork that was standing beside the kitchen door, hit the stairs two at a time, to see Martha going in to Katherine's bedroom, an axe held precariously in her hand, and screaming.

In an instant he saw his daughter lying helpless, clothing ripped, under the woodman. He saw Martha move toward them, and with a strength that no woman should possess, he saw her grab her husband's hair, with one arm, and pull him from Katherine, who in half flight fell from the bed. 'Run,' screamed Martha, to her. Alexi moved, and Katherine flew past him, and down the stairs. He followed her, and as he reached the bottom of the stairs, he heard an almighty crash, a blood curdling curse, and, looking up, he saw Martha hurl the axe at Vittorio's head. Blood started to flow, but being too strong for Martha he pushed her aside. She fell with a sickening thud to the floor, and Vittorio made for Alexi.

'Who the hell are you then? You can have some of the same.' He made to leap the last half a dozen stairs as Alexi held out the pitch fork to defend himself. Vittorio missed his footing, and plunged at full stretch to be impaled upon its spikes. Landing on the floor underneath the body of Vittorio, Alexi, writhing with blood pouring all over his suit, face, and neck, released himself, and climbed the stairs to Martha. She had been knocked out cold by her husband, but suffered little damage. She reeled as Alexi picked her up.

'Where is he?' she cried. 'I am going to kill him.'

'He is downstairs,' answered Alexi.

Martha, now seeing the blood, said, 'Have you done it already?'

'I don't know,' said Alexi.

They headed for the stairs together to see Vittorio, mouth wide open as if he was about to scream, but no utterance would come from his mouth ever again, only blood came running from the corner of his lips, dark and thick.

Martha felt his pulse, and then shouted at Alexi, 'Where's Katherine? We must find her. He will not hurt her or me any more.' And with that and all her strength, she kicked her husband's face until it was unrecognisable. Alexi threw a sheet over the body, went to the door, and shouted for Katherine. There was no answer.

'Katherine knows this land and its buildings well. She will be frightened, but she will be safe for now,' she said with quiet satisfaction. Martha, thinking quickly, began to collect some bread and milk, and a warm coat to cover the ripped clothing that Katherine had fled in. 'Can I trust you? I know you are her father, and you must know too now,' she cried to Alexi. 'I must go and find her, and make her stay where she is until I can think what to do about Vittorio. I am not going to tell her yet what has happened.'

'Go,' said Alexi, 'I will stay here and try to clean up some of the mess. When you return we will decide what to do together.' Martha looked at him and saw determination in his face. This man would, like her, go to any lengths to protect his daughter.

Katherine was crouched in the big shed behind a pile of logs, shivering and crying. As Martha pushed open the door, she lay down and covered her face with her hands so as not to see the creature that she thought was coming for her. 'Katherine,' Martha called quietly, 'where are you, darling'? Katherine stayed still until she saw Martha move toward the pot bellied stove that stood in the centre of the floor. 'Katherine, are you here? Can you hear me? Answer if you can.'

'I'm here, Mama,' she cried in a strangled voice. In a second, Martha had her in her arms, and cradled her, rocking her back and forth, and cooing to her as she had done so long ago when she was a tiny baby. 'Where is he?' she cried in fear. 'He will come for us. I know he will.'

'He will not, my darling, he has gone, and I don't think he will be coming back.'

'I'm so sorry, Mama, it was all my fault. He was hammering on the door, and I let him in, and now he has hurt you. I can see you're bleeding.'

'It is nothing, my angel, and it is not your fault.'

Katherine, sobbing now, said, 'It is my fault. I let him touch me, and I was frightened.'

'Darling, I can't talk to you right now, I have to go and clear up your room. We had a fight, and a mess was made of your bed and floor. I want you to stay here until I come for you. It may take a while, and this I must tell you, my dearest child, the man in the picture is your father, and he is going to help me. Don't be afraid. Vittorio is long gone, and he will be far, far away by now. You will have to be brave because things will have to happen that you may not understand, but I will always love you, and I think your father will too. His name is Alexi. Martha lit the coals in the fire, and gently put the thick coat around Katherine's shoulders, made a little seat from old sacks for her to sit on, gave her the bread and milk. She held her for a second and then left her.

What she would do now she knew not, but she would face whatever befell her. Please god she would not be taken from Katherine. With all this in mind, she headed back to the scene of the terrible crime that had been committed, partly by her, and partly by a man whom she really did not know, and who now would be intrinsically linked to her forever.

Alexi had in fact set about cleaning up with a vengeance. He had wrapped the body in some old sacking, tying it tightly at the neck and feet, and with the arms tucked in at the side of the body, had bound the lot together with a linen line that he had ripped from its hooks on garden walls. Upstairs, he had taken up all the rugs that had adorned the floors, and had scrubbed the bare boards until there was not a sign of the blood that had spurted from the head of the victim. The bed linen had been removed and placed in a pile on the rugs.

Downstairs, where the blood was in great pools, he had thrown wood shavings all over the floor to soak up the worst of it, and was waiting for it to dry before he started to scrub that floor as he had done upstairs. The axe handle had been removed, and rammed in between the bindings, and the handle of the pitchfork was also dealt with. The heads of both implements would be dealt with later, and were sitting outside clean and shiny from being dipped in some oil that he had found at the back of the house, which was used for just that purpose to clean the woodman's implements.

As Martha entered the house, he was just about finished, and she was astounded by his alacrity. His face was set in a determined line, and he said to her, 'We will take him now, and bury him in the woods where no one will find him. I know a place where digging will be easy. We will burn every remaining particle of his belongings. No one will question a fire, as the woodman continually had one burning for all the waste that he collected. You will tell anyone who asks that he has left without trace and left you in poverty. That will be accepted as he was well known and not well liked in the local villages.

Katherine was still cold in spite of the warm coat, because she had little on underneath it. She had eaten the bread, and drunk the milk. She moved cautiously to the door and opened it a crack, still convinced that Vittorio would appear at any moment; she was ready for flight if he did. The night was bright with stars, and the view to the cottage was no longer obscured by trees, as they had been felled recently. Katherine watched as she saw two figures carrying a third between them, and with slow but positive steps head toward the thick woods beyond the cottage boundaries. Now she knew that she would never see Vittorio again. They were carrying his body away wrapped in cloth, and dragging behind them spades and forks. Her mother and her father had murdered Martha's husband. They were taking him to bury him. It was her fault, and now her beloved mother would go to prison, and probably her newly found father. If they were caught, that would be exactly what would happen. She would not stay and make things worse for them; she would go now while they were in the woods. She crept from the shed, now quite calm in her decision. She could not bear to see her mother suffer such terrible things. If she wasn't there, her mother would not feel responsible for her, and perhaps she could run too. But for her stupidity, this whole thing would not have happened.

The back door was left ajar; she saw blood-stained clothes, and linen in a pile in the yard. She felt sick, ran inside and upstairs to find only bare boards in her beautiful bedroom, and a wooden bed with no linen on it. She grabbed as many clothes as she could, and she carefully put all of them on, one on top of the other, three skirts, three blouses, two cardigans, and two pairs of thick socks, along with the coat that Martha had brought for her. She reached beneath the bed and pulled out her little case that held the small amount of money that her mother had secretly saved for her, and her treasures, the baby clothes, the locket, and the ballet shoes. She found a scrap of paper, and with one of her colouring pencils she wrote a note to her mother.

I love you with all of my heart, and I will one day bring you to England. This is where I will head for, and I will write to you as soon as I can to let you know where I am. I am so sorry for all the trouble that I have caused you. Thank my father for helping you, but I have no thoughts of ever seeing him again. Please forgive me. I love you, Katherine

The darkness, now complete, hid the silent figures of Alexi and Martha as they carried the body of Martha's husband to the spot that Alexi had suggested as being the least likely place for anyone to be, except for Vittorio himself, which in its own bizarre way seemed apt. They laid him down reverently, and started to dig. At first the ground held a lot of resistance, but as they proceeded the roots of bushes and trees became less of a problem, and the earth beneath them became softer.

'I know it is a hard and long process, but we have to bury him as deep as possible, so that passing animals do not detect a scent,' said Alexi.

Martha just looked at him, nodded, and continued to dig. She was a strong woman, and the anger and hurt that she felt spurred her on. An hour or so passed, and they began to see some results of their labours. The grave now was almost three feet deep, but had to be lengthened to allow the body to lie as straight and as flat as possible. The pile of earth from the dig was becoming too high, and so they had to change direction so as to make anther pile, which made their bodies ache more, and more.

Three hours later, their task was complete. They had made an even base to the grave, and shaped the sides so that the body was held secure. They threw some rotted leaves, and vegetation over it, and then slowly but surely raked the earth mound into the hole. When it was filled to the top and soundly pounded flat by their spades, and feet, they pulled all the bottom branches of the surrounding trees over it. There were no loose branches or twigs left, and so it was that they started to make their way silently back to the cottage.

Martha carefully stoked the fire that had been burning bracken the day before, and she took every piece of blood-stained clothing, including that which Alexi was still wearing, tore it into shreds, so that it would burn easier, and piece by piece placed it into the heart of the fire. Alexi found some old clothes of Vittorio's in the kitchen, and quickly changed into them. He threw an old leather jacket over the top. It was Martha's, but it was unlikely anyone would see him. He would be able to discard them on returning to the house, and change into riding apparel that he had left at the stables.

The two of them checked the downstairs, and tidied up so that the evidence of a fight was no longer visible. Martha washed herself in the kitchen, and put on her working skirt, thick and long, and a dark blouse, covered by a heavy cardigan. She now felt cold and shivery as the shock of what had happened manifested itself. She then climbed the stairs, checking side to side that no blood stains remained, went into their bedroom, which was as it was, not touched by what had transpired; her work room too was unmarked as no one had been in there. She then went to Katherine's room to make her bed and put a new rug down so that she could return to the house when all the horror of the evening was gone from sight. Tears stung her eyes as she saw bare boards and a bed devoid of its lovely covers that she had made. Never mind, she could soon have it spic and span again; she would take a small amount of money from the box and replace it all. As she turned, her eye caught the note. She glanced under the bed to see the little suitcase was missing, and with trembling fingers she opened and read the contents of Katherine's letter. A silent scream issued from her lips and, sobbing, she ran to Alexi who was attending to the fire.

'She's gone,' she cried. 'We must go and find her. Will you help me, Alexi?'

Alexi silently took the letter, put his head in his hands and wept. He had just found a daughter, and now she was gone from him, and from choice had decided that she did not want to know him.

'I will help you, Martha, but we need to sit and think of where she would be likely to go. We both know that she will never make it to England, and so that narrows the search to where she may head in Italy.'

They decided that to start now, with nothing in their hands and with no knowledge of the direction she would take on leaving the cottage, would be foolish, and so they sat at the kitchen table and thought it through. The only place that she could make for would be Milan. She now knew that Milan was the place where her mother had lived, and danced, and also from there, although it was almost impossible, she could get a train that would finally get her to England. She was a clever girl, and had plenty of courage and spirit.

Alexi then said, 'Wait here, Martha, and I will return. I need to somehow go back to the house, change my clothes, and wait until morning, when I will explain that I have to go away on business for a few days. No one will question this, as I do it often, and they do not care anyway; life without me there is always easier and more fun for all of them. I will get a carriage and we will head for Milan, and search the areas where Maria would have been. Pack a few things, and pack some food; she will be hungry. If, with the greatest luck in the world, we happen upon her on the way, we will feed her and bring her back. She will follow familiar roads if she is walking.

She will not have enough money to take any form of transport. All this may be in vain but we have to try. Do you agree with my plan?'

'I have to, Alexi, for I truly know not what to do,' answered Martha, now in desperation at the thought of the love of her life being out there somewhere at nearly thirteen years of age with little money, few warm clothes, and frightened beyond the powers of Martha's imagination. She sat on the stairs, huddled in a blanket, and waited for Alexi.

Katherine had counted the money that Martha had carefully saved for her; it was not a lot, but she would use it to get to Milan. Once there, perhaps she could earn a few lira, by cleaning. She had helped Martha many times to sweep and polish and tidy up after Vittorio's rages, which had left dishes scattered across the table and floor. The thought of him made her shudder uncontrollably. She had carefully put the ballet shoes in the bottom of the case, taken the small piece of paper that had the address of a house in Milan, and tucked it inside the ballet shoes, on top of which she placed the baby clothes and some underwear. Feeling cold, she grabbed a woollen hood that Martha had made for her 'to keep your ears warm' she had said with a laugh. Finally, she lifted the locket, and for a moment held it to her heart, before finally placing it securely around her neck, tucked down inside all the layers of clothing, until she could feel it cold against her bare skin.

Slowly and sadly, she made her way back downstairs, leaving everything as it was, left by the back door, and made her way, staying very close to the trees, toward the road that she had so happily tripped along just a few days ago to school. It was still dark, and the moon only gave a hazy light, being hidden by the clouds of a rain-leaden sky. She would stay away from the main road as much as she could, because, even at this hour, an odd cart or carriage could pass by. It would be the end of her plan if she was found so soon and taken back. She would not be able to bear witness to the things that she had seen, and could not face the terrible unhappiness of her mother.

She would walk out of the village, past the post office, and then past the old inn where the inn sign swaying made a sad moaning sound, she thought as she glanced at it. Martha had brought her this way on one summer's evening, and she remembered hearing the whistle of a distant train as it passed through the countryside. She figured if she could find the railway track, and follow it, she would come to a station, and there, if she was lucky, no one would recognise her, and they would let her buy a ticket that would take her on the first part of her journey to Milan. This was not going to be easy; the road was not familiar, and the night so dark. Occasionally she heard a sound, but it was nothing like a train whistle. She walked for what seemed like hours, and was tiring from the weight of all the clothing she had had to put on because she had nothing to carry them in.

When she had gone into the cottage, she had found the remnants of the meal that Martha had quickly put together for her, and she had wrapped them in a large handkerchief and tied them to an old stick from the garden. She had remembered Martha reading her the story of Dick Whittington, and he had carried small amounts of food thus. The path she walked crossed a small river that was gushing over stones beneath the bridge. Carefully she made her way down the bank, and she filled the small cup that had once held the milk that Martha had brought to the shed for her. She drank thirstily and sat and nibbled at a piece of bread. She could not afford to eat it all, as she knew not when she would be able to find more. She rested a while, and then decided to move on. She had to get as far away from the village as she could, before it got light to reduce the risk of being seen, or approached for whatever reason. She just needed to find a train. At this moment in time she didn't even care which way it was going, at least she would be warm.

On she walked, not stopping again, and her feet were now getting very sore, but on she went. Dawn slowly spread its light across her path, and the pale winter sun provided a very small amount of warmth, which gave her just a tiny bit more energy. She hastened her step. The road took her between two fields which had been ploughed for a while, and the furrows looked hard and unrelenting, so instead of leaving the road which seemed to wind more than a straight line across the fields would have, she followed it with unfaltering steps. She saw in the distance what appeared to be a raised platform, and standing on it a woman in peasant dress holding a lead attached to the necks of two goats, who seemed oblivious to their surroundings and stood quietly by her side. In her basket she carried what looked like long sticks of bread. Katherine, too tired to run and hide, carried on walking toward her.

Then she saw the rail track. Quite narrow it was, but none the less a train track. She looked to the left and to the right, but there was no sign of a station. She climbed the steps toward the woman.

'Catching the next one, are you?' she said in a matter-of-fact voice.

'Yes,' said Katherine, 'but I have lost my way, and I don't know where I am.'

'Where do you want to be?' said the woman.

'Milan,' replied Katherine with her fingers crossed tightly behind her back.

The woman laughed. 'You'll not get there from here, but you can get a little closer, not much mind you.'

'Where do I pay?' said Katherine.

'Stay with me, dear, and you won't have to. My husband drives this one, and I hop on and off as I want to.'

Katherine could not believe her luck; she was on her way, and this small bit was not going to cost her anything. She could have a rest, get warm, and trust in this woman to point her in the right direction when they arrived whereever this train was going to take them.

The dirty black smoke that billowed its way up into the sky heralded the arrival of the train. The whistle blew a long hard note as it rounded the bend toward the makeshift station, which was by now occupied by more than a few locals who knew the driver or his wife, and regularly hitched a ride to a local market town where they would buy or sell all manner of things, from home grown vegetables, eggs, fruit, and hand-made garments, to animals like goats, sheep, and lots of laying hens. Katherine stayed near to the wife of the driver, hoping that somehow she would be able to point her on the right track to Milan. Katherine hoped that once there she would find it possible to hide, and find some work so that she could buy food. None of her fellow passengers seemed to take much notice of her. Dressed in well-worn clothes, and with them being in many layers, she looked very much like any one of the peasants that stood there around her. The only difference being that she had no goods to barter, only a small suitcase, which raised a couple of eyebrows. She tucked it under her large warm coat, and hugged it to her body as if it were her only lifeline, and indeed it was, it held the whole of her life under its lid, and without it she had nothing and no one.

The train wheels screeched on the rusty tracks as it slowed to allow the rabble on the platform to scramble aboard. Katherine jumped with the rest of them, and fell unceremoniously into a carriage that smelled of old vegetation and smoke. She found a seat, and the wife of the driver fell in beside her, her large frame pinning Katherine's shoulder to the window.

Once all were aboard, the train started to pick up a slow speed again. Wheels developing a rhythm as it headed once more into wooded countryside, occasionally broken by rippling streams and small lakes. In the distance, tall pines stood like soldiers against the horizon. The sky, now a vivid blue, reflected in the water and made the pines look as if they had a twin upside down in the lake. Katherine thought how beautiful it all looked, and wished she was here with Martha, nestling into her side, safe and loved. She never stopped thinking of Martha, and was hurting inside for her, and the way she had had to leave her. She stopped instantly, because she knew that she could only think of her future, and eventually being able to see Martha again when she finally found her way to England. This was her dream, and she would hold it until it finally came true. She had no doubt in her mind that it would.

'Where do you want to go in Milan?' asked her travelling companion, who had allowed her to travel free thus far, 'and may I ask why you want to go? Milan is not a good place for someone as young as you. You will be in trouble if you are not very careful,' she warned. 'If you like, I will get my husband to give you a couple of addresses where you might be safe for a short while. Do you have any one there that you know? Why are you travelling with so little luggage, and why were you walking from the same direction as you could have caught a train from? I do not understand.'

She looked into Katherine's eyes to see fear and desperation there, and for a moment felt pity for the young woman. Katherine did not answer her; she held her head low and pulled her coat around her. The woman, looking into her face, then said in a soft but firm voice. 'Perhaps I could help you more if you told me your problems; you obviously have some, and you may find it very difficult to find somewhere in Milan to stay. Let me help you. I have many friends and relatives there.'

With this, Katherine crumpled and began to tell the wife about her beautiful mother who had died from a riding accident the night that she was born, and about the father that she had never known until after the burial of her mother, and whom she hated. She told her also about the wonderful woman who had raised her, and loved her more than any mother could have, and who she had had to leave because of something terrible that had happened because of her. She told her how her real father was rich, and would find her somehow, and how she was frightened, and did not want to be taken back. He already had a wife and children, and complained of his unhappiness with them, and his life in the big house outside the village.

84

The wife listened intently to all of this, torn between sadness for the girl, and fascination as to the circumstances of her departure from an obviously happy life spent with her adoptive parent. Katherine would not be drawn on the reason for her fleeing; she would only insist that she could never go back. The journey was long, and Katherine was so tired, she finally succumbed to sleep. Uncomfortable as it was, she leaned her head, which by now was throbbing, against the cold glass of the window, and fell into an uneasy sleep. The wife watched her and began to realise that the young woman that she had been helping was a lot younger than she had originally thought. A mere child, she thought, with a rich father who would probably pay anything to get her back. She would talk to her husband when they reached their destination.

Katherine awoke to find herself alone in the compartment; the last of her travelling companions was hitching her skirt, picking up a large crate of eggs, and easing herself through the open door. It was then that Katherine heard the voice of the wife, and one of a man talking in animated conversation. Two parts of the conversation she heard, the sound of their voices over ridden by noises from the hubbub going on. She heard the words 'rich father', and the words 'inform the authorities'. She froze and stayed completely still, her mind racing in panic. Could she escape here and run? Then she heard the man say, 'I will do it at Milan. There could be some reward,' and then to his wife he said, 'Stay calm and put her on the Milan train. I will ride on it with the new driver, and we will see that she is caught as she leaves the station.'

Katherine, heart pounding, now stayed exactly as she was, head against the window. She planned an escape; she knew not where or how she would do it, but do it she had to. If she could manage to get through the next part of the journey without paying, she would still have enough money to find a hideaway until they all gave up looking for her. The wife then appeared in the doorway. 'Come on then, dear. My husband has agreed to get you a seat on the train for Milan. I have told him your story, and him being a good honest man is very sorry to hear of your plight and will help you. He has a relation in the city, and he thinks he will allow you to work in his shop, and earn your keep for a while. How does that sound?' the wife said with a smile.

Feeling sick, half with anger, and half with anticipation of outwitting these two people, she just kept her head down and, nodding vigorously, quietly said, 'Thank you for your kindness. I will never forget it.'

The wife and husband, one each side of her, then walked her across the station forecourt toward the big main line train that was already pumping steam from its engine. They took her to the first class section of the train, and opened a carriage door for her to enter. Clutching her tiny suitcase close to her body under her coat, she climbed up the high step with some difficulty. Unaided, she managed to deposit herself on the seat farthest from them, facing the way that the train would travel, and nearest the window. They closed the door with a sort of satisfied look on their faces, as Katherine, now trembling, started to think of a way that she could escape, as near as she could to Milan so that she could make her way there under her own steam. As she waited, a young couple with a child entered the carriage, and an elderly gentleman whom she noted carried a black cane with an ornate silver top, and wore a sombre black suit. She mused that maybe he would rescue her, but ignoring all of them he calmly sat, removed his gloves, placed them with his cane in the luggage rack, and opened his newspaper. With each precious minute, Katherine tried to figure out a plan of escape. Could she jump from the train somewhere when it slowed or stopped at a station, but she figured the driver may have alerted station staff along the route as to her description and situation. Could she hide somewhere on the train, and not get off at Milan? She had but a couple of hours to decide her fate.

The train stood in the platform for what, to Katherine, seemed like an awfully long time. She risked a glance out of the window. The wife and husband had disappeared. Katherine knew that the wife would be going about her business in, what appeared to be, this small market town. She could see in the distance, brightly coloured market stalls, bedecked with flags and banners. The wife no longer held any fear for her. All the plans had been left to the husband to carry out. He, she knew, was somewhere on the train. She suspected he would probably be riding in the driver's cab and, without any doubt, she knew he would be giving the driver the story that his wife had left him with. Could she hide amongst the crowd heading out of the station? No of course she couldn't. She had not realised it at the time, being so shaken by the overheard conversation, but the offer of being allowed to ride into Milan on this train had not been backed up by giving her a ticket, so she would be stopped at the barrier, and not allowed to pass. The husband would then be able to call the authorities and give them all the information that they needed to take her away. In her turmoil, she decided to walk along the corridor of the train, just to clear her mind and give her some air from the outside windows. She picked up her little case and excused herself to the young couple, the old gentleman, and another couple of people who had joined the train before it departed the station. They looked at her with little interest and settled down again into their own thoughts and conversations.

Glancing into the carriages, she swayed along with the movement of the huge train that was belching smoke backwards past the windows, creeping in where ever it could find a slight opening. All the time she moved along, she was frantically thinking of what she could do. The train must slow down at some point; she would open a door and jump, but she would have to be at the back of the train for this, so that no one would see her as the train journeyed on. She had moved forward towards the front of the train. She now had to turn around and start the journey back. She would have to pass the carriage she had been sitting in, and so she had to work out which one it was as she approached. She did not realise how far she had gone, and began to think that she had already passed it when she recognised one of the late arrivals. She stopped, looked around to be sure that no one was watching, dropped to her knees, and crawled past that one, and another, just to be sure. Carefully she raised herself in between the next two carriages, straightened her coat and re-arranged her tiny suitcase, still tightly crushed to her body. Now it was just a case of making her way to the very back of the train, and waiting. She had no idea how long the journey was to Milan, but she hoped she could wait long enough to see the outskirts of the city. If she could, she would easily be able to make it on foot, and her oppressors would be outwitted, with little or no chance of finding her. She would then show someone the address that was on the small piece of paper that she had found in the suitcase, and hope it would take her to someone who would help her.

The final door in the final compartment was locked, and so that was as far as she could go. The carriage luckily was empty, and although she was frightened, sitting there on her own, she prayed that no one would find her there. She would then be able to choose her moment, and take a leap from the now speeding train. The afternoon light was fading, and dusk was spreading across the passing countryside. Katherine's eyes were glued to the window for just a glimpse of city lights. She had never been out of her local environment, and could only guess what it would be like. Martha too had only lived locally, and so they had talked together about visiting a big city one day, and imagining together how it would be. Oh how she wished she had Martha with her now. She would know what to do. She sat until her eyes could no longer focus, and then she fell asleep. Curled in the corner of the carriage, sleep enveloped her, and she knew nothing.

She woke to the screaming of wheels as they braked on the rails; she jumped up, picked up her suitcase, and made for the door. The train had slowed. Now she could do it. She then heard the booming voice of the station announcer. 'Milan... This is Milan...' It was too late, she had been asleep as the train had approached Milan, and now she was trapped. Whichever way she went, she would be caught. Could she quickly change her clothes? She had four sets of clothes, all of them she was wearing. Could she attach herself to a crowd of people, and chance getting through? No! She could not risk it. She sat back down in the now freezing cold carriage, and wept. She slid down in the seat so that no one could see her, and there she stayed. The train would have to move at sometime, and maybe she could stay on until it made its way out of Milan again, back where it came from.

After a while, much sooner than Katherine had expected, the train did move. It was dark so Katherine could see nothing. The train seemed to go backwards for a while, and then it started to go forward again. Panic struck at her heart. It was taking her back into Milan. This time there would be no escape, because the authorities would now have been notified, and would be looking for her. She just sat there and thought of Martha. At least she would be able to see her again. She would do whatever it took to see Martha all right. She would go with Alexi, if that was what he wanted. She would hate it, and she would have to see Martha hurt which was almost more than she could bear. The train kept on moving, not now at the tremendous speed that had brought it to Milan, but with a more gentle motion it rumbled on and on, and then it slowed down almost to a stop. Without a second thought, Katherine made a decision. She gathered her thoughts, clutched her little suitcase, wrenched open the great heavy door, and jumped into oblivion.

Her lithe young body hit the ground with a thud, and the corner of her little suitcase dug into her ribs, causing her to scream in pain. She slowly moved her limbs, and found there was no lasting damage. The clothes that she had piled, one on top of the other on her small body helped to soften the impact of the fall. She sat up, and in the pitch darkness she watched as the rear lights of the train disappeared into the distance. She felt around her, and felt soft damp grass; there seemed to be nothing hurting her, no stones, no bushes, in fact nothing but grass. Her first emotion was one of relief, then joy. She was free, and now she had a chance to escape. The realisation that she had to move away from the track immediately, wiped out her previous feelings of elation.

She could not wait until it was light for fear that the authorities, once they knew she was missing would organise a search, and it would initially be along the railway. First she would change her clothes, so that her description, if anyone saw her and suspected anything, would be changed from that of the husband. She removed her coat, and the hat that she had been wearing when she first walked onto the train. She swapped the top layer of clothing with the set underneath, and turned her coat inside out. She always loved the lining of the coat that Martha had made for her. It was made of a warm material, and was green with a gold thread running through in the design of leaves. This she thought would be good against the green of the land, maybe she would be able to hide amongst bushes and trees. Just a few minutes after her leap from the moving train, she stood up, and started to move away from the track. The night was unforgiving in its blackness. She touched her locket which was intact around her neck, and tucked tightly under the last piece of clothing close to her skin. She felt the locks on her little suitcase, and ensured that they were tightly shut. The next few hours would lead her, she knew not where, but hopefully they would put enough space between her and all those who searched for her.

Dawn slowly reached the land, spreading its pale yellow light around her. She was desperately tired, and her body and legs were aching, her eyes were sore from trying to see in the darkness where she was walking. Now the dawn light, although comforting, gave her no help at all. She could see distant hills, and beyond that a suspicion of mountains that seemed to paint a pale purple outline on the horizon. There were fields of long grass, dotted here and there with long stemmed flowers waving in the gentle breeze. She noted that the weather here had a warmer feel to it, and now the layers of clothes she wore were becoming heavy and hindering her progress. She could not afford to discard any of them in case she left clues to anyone who may be still looking for her.

Carefully now, she moved on. She was hungry, really hungry. Inside her coat pocket she had secreted a couple of pieces of bread that one of the ladies had given her on the first part of the journey to Milan. She withdrew a piece and took a bite. It was so hard that her teeth could not penetrate its mass, so she broke it into small pieces and sucked it until it became soft enough to swallow. That done, she was now so thirsty she could hardly swallow. She had no idea of time, but the lightness of the sky told her that morning had broken.

Now she had to be careful. She needed to find some shelter, to hide away from everyone that moved. She would look for trees. There was no road in sight, nothing to give her an idea as to the direction she was walking in. She needed desperately to rest a while, she needed a drink so badly that her tongue was beginning to stick to the roof of her mouth, and her mouth was sticking to her teeth. She felt sick with hunger and fatigue. There was no relief, and on she walked, getting slower all the while without realising it. Finally she found a little copse of trees, and collapsed. She put her head on the little case, and fell into a restless sleep. Later, as she slowly opened her eyes, and felt her face, it was damp, and she felt cool; she sat up to find it raining quite heavily. She crawled from under the tree, turned her face to the sky, opened her mouth, and allowed the rain to pour into her parched mouth. She raised herself, and knew she had to move on to find some food and drink. Wherever she was she knew that this was the first priority, for without either she would not be able to carry on.

She had kept to the edge of the trees which had developed into a more dense area, bordering on woodland. This sort of terrain she was used to. She remembered with a shudder the woodman's cottage where she was raised, and the surrounding woodland. She moved through the trees stealthily, spurred on by the change in the environment. She left the trees, and moved across some well maintained land, and then she saw what appeared to be trees with fruit upon them, massive clumps of oranges, close enough to reach out and touch. She could see no house, nor any movement.

Just one, she thought, and her mouth tingled with the thought of biting into the flesh of an orange, and drinking its juice. The temptation was too much; there was no wire protecting the trees, and so she inched her way to the nearest tree and pulled at the fruit. The first one she held in her hand, and then closed her eyes, bit into its skin and removed it to reveal the bright orange flesh. Holding it high, she squeezed it until the juice issued forth, and ran into her mouth, down her chin, and dripped on to her coat. She ate with relish until the whole fruit was gone. She then quickly picked a few more, stuffing them in her pockets, and down her clothes, until no more space was available.

She left as she had arrived, quietly with no interference, with the knowledge that she could live for a day or more if necessary on oranges. On she went for the rest of the day, never seeing a soul. Now she was tired, so tired that her legs felt like lead. Night fell and still she walked. Now again, with no light to guide her, she walked. She suddenly felt a change in the weather. There was quite a strong breeze, and she felt a sudden chill. The ground became soft and her feet seemed to be sinking slightly into the land. She knelt and felt around her, but nothing seemed to be obvious. She was now failing in strength, and feeling quite ill. The oranges had kept her going, but she had been without solid food now for almost four days. She was dragging herself along. The wind was getting stronger, and a smell was reaching her, one that she couldn't place. It was tangy but fresh with a slight saltiness.

On she walked, and now the land was rising under her feet. Feeling that she was climbing, but knowing that she could not keep it up, she would have to stop and rest. As this thought left her brain, her right foot slipped, and she could not save herself. Clinging to her little case she plummeted downward, and she hit the water. Her feet would not go down, she could feel nothing under them, and then her face was hit by a wave of water caused by her body flailing about. She reached out, but there was nothing. Her head went under the water, and with the heavy clothing, she had not got the strength to pull herself up. Suddenly she hit something hard, grabbed at it to try to steady herself. It turned her body around, and she felt herself being held up by what appeared to be a long piece of flat wood. Now her head was held above water, but her feet were floating. She pulled on the wood, and it remained steady, but now things were beginning to blur. She could see a pinpoint of bright light, and reached out for it, but she could hear Martha saying, 'I am here, my darling, come back.' The light got brighter, and she wanted to go to it. The last thing she heard was Martha saying, 'I love you, Katherine.' Then all went black.

Chapter Ten

The Fisherman's Cottage

It had been a long day out in the boat. The fisherman headed for the shore, the darkness of the night only broken by a few lights, and by the light in the bow of his little boat. It flickered on the water, as the swell moved the boat from side to side. He would off-load his catch and fill the crates that stood against the quay side. At dawn he would go to the local market and hopefully sell most of it, after he had picked a couple of choice specimens for his own dinner which he would cook when he arrived back at his cottage that night. As he approached the jetty, he saw what he thought to be a bundle of cloth hanging from one of the supports that held up the steps to the platform. On closer inspection his heart leaped as he saw it was a body limply balanced across the bottom step. Forgetting the job that he was about to do, he jumped from the boat and grabbed at the clothing, pulling the body clear of the water and lifting it enough to roll it over to the safety of the jetty floor. It was quite heavy, and there was no movement.

Once safe from the water, he had to leave it for a second to pull in his boat and secure it. This done he returned to the body. He turned it on to its back, so that he could see what was happening. Then he watched in horror, as he lifted the clothing away from its face, to see that it was just a young girl with a wound on her forehead. He felt for a pulse, and amazingly there was one, albeit very faint. She was unconscious, but how long she had been there he could not guess. He had to work quickly.

He picked her up and carried her as swiftly as he could to the cottage in which he lived close to the sea where he made his living. Once inside the door, he pulled each piece of sodden clothing from her body. He knew that she had not been close to drowning, because her breathing, although shallow, was not laboured. Her face was white and drawn, and she was freezing cold. She was just a child, so what in heaven was she doing wandering about in this isolated spot. Finally, having removed all her clothing, he rolled her in the largest towel he could find, rubbing her body as hard as he could without hurting her, and then laying her on a bundle of sheep skins that he used as covers on his bed. Keeping a couple to cover her, he lit a fire in the old stack set in the middle of the big room that was the total space of his accommodation.

What more could he do? He had no communication with the outside world; he didn't need it when all he did was fish all day, sleep for a few hours each night, and repeat it the next day and the day after that. He knew that she needed food and drink, but could not administer either until she woke. He had decided that it was sheer exhaustion that had made her pass out, and he didn't think she had been in the water for very long. Her skin was still taut, and it would have been swollen and discoloured if she had been there for any length of time. He decided that she had been walking in the dark and fallen. He would not at this time question her reasons for being there; he would let her recover, feed her, and take it from there. He thought this was the best thing he could do.

He lit the oil lamp that hung from the ceiling, and looked at her once more to see that she was sleeping. She was breathing much easier than she had been when he fished her out of the water. He had now to go and attend to his catch; he could not afford for the fish to be wasted. It was his living. It was not easy, but it suited him, and brought him enough for the simple life that he lived. 'Here, dog,' he called to the young terrier that shared his boat by day, and his bed by night, 'Stay here, lad, and keep this young lady company while I see to the catch.'

So it was, as Katherine slowly opened her eyes, she felt the warm body of the tiny dog at her side, and the gentle lick of his tongue on a shoulder that peeped from under the skins that covered her. She looked around, and had not got the strength to raise herself, but she felt warm. She saw a fire, and the light from the lamp turned the large room that was hung with fishing nets and baskets into a magical place. She reached out to stroke the ears of the little dog, whose tail was now wagging furiously, and shut her eyes to drift into a world of comfort and contentment, and just for now forgetting all that had brought her to this place.

The fisherman returned from his chores and closed the door quietly so as not to disturb her. Dog seemed to have coped with the situation admirably, so he picked up four fish, placed them on the table and proceeded to gut and clean them. Then he rolled them in some damp paper, placed them in a shallow pan and put them on the top of the stove. The room began to fill with a delicious smell. The dog began to show considerable interest, and decided that his charge could be left long enough for him to eat the supper that he had earned helping his master get through his day. The fisherman decided that he would keep some of the cooked fish on the side, and would make some thick fish soup, chop some potatoes, and boil them, add a carrot, and when this child finally returned to the land of the living, he would gently feed her the soup, thus warming her inside as the skins had warmed her on the outside. In the meantime, he would grab a few hours sleep, and decide in the morning whether or not he could leave her alone in the cottage with the dog while he took the boat out for another day's work. Dog lay down with Katherine, and the fisherman took to his huge bed against the far wall of the room. He took off his boots and fell asleep, feeling quite tired after all that had happened that night.

Katherine did not wake at all; in fact the fisherman was quite worried the following morning, when he realised that she had not stirred or changed position since he had put her there the night before. He started to gather the things that he needed for the day, moving quietly around so as to allow her to wake in her own time, hopefully before he had to leave her with dog. Dog was also getting restless. He thought he had found a playmate. His master never played with his ears; he just called, and dog went obediently to answer his call. Perhaps if he was to nuzzle her a little, she would respond, and so he nosed his way beneath her covers, found her hand and, nudging it gently, received a response. The child stirred, reached out, and touched the small body that was hiding under her covers.

The child's eyes slowly opened. She gazed around, fixing her gaze on the fire, and the lamp still reflecting the shadows of the room in the dawn's pale light. The green and orange nets that hung in pretty drapes around the room were the last thing she saw before her eyes came to rest on the man with a face half-covered by hair, and topped by a white hat with a large peak. Her eyes, hardly leaving him, took in the large thick knitted cream coloured jumper, and the black heavy trousers, down to the enormous wellington boots with thick white socks carefully folded over the top. She went to jump up, but realized that she had no clothes on. Panic in her heart sent her hands to grab the skins that covered her, and pull them up around her neck. No words would come, so she just sat there and stared. Dog, impatient now, began to nudge her again. She stroked his head, feeling the comfort of contact. She risked another look at the man.

'Are you hungry?' he asked in a soft husky voice.

'Yes,' she replied quietly but honestly. She was actually feeling sick with lack of food, but apart from that she felt no pain, and no discomfort. She could remember nothing, but running from the train, frightened of being captured. The man just quietly got on with heating up the liquid food that he had so carefully prepared the night before. He poured it into a large silver coloured mug, and passed it to her.

'Be careful, it will be very hot,' he warned.

She sipped it cautiously, and the feeling of it sliding down into her tummy was something beyond description. As she drank, she didn't utter a word. It was as though, if she stopped, it would all go away, and in truth she wanted none of it to go away. When the entire contents of the mug had gone, the man refilled it, and this time she drank with enjoyment rather than relish. Finally, when she lay back and looked at him with eyes full of tears, and questions, he told her how he had found her last night, and how she was, and why he had removed all her clothes, and left her with the dog for company. She clutched at her neck, and looked at him accusingly.

'My locket,' she cried. He raised his hand to the shelf above her head, reached for the locket, and dangled it in front of her eyes, she reached out gently, and took it from him, and said in a whisper, 'Thank you.' Then, half sitting up resting on one elbow, frantically looked around, and said, 'My case.'

'I have no case,' said the man. 'There was no case when I fished you out of the water.'

Then she began to sob, 'my case, my case.'

Dog began to fret, and went to the door and barked, wagged his tail, and looked at his master in expectation. 'Come on then, let's see if we can find it. Stay there and keep warm,' he said to the child. 'We will be back,' and back they came. Dog victorious with the case handle held securely in his teeth, dragging it across the ground bounding through the door to drop it at her feet. 'You were lucky, you must have dropped the case as you fell; it was stuck in the bank, along with one of your shoes. You only had one on when I reeled you in,' he said with a cheeky smile.

She smiled too now. If she felt any fear when she first saw him, she had none now; she knew she was safe if only for a while.

'My name is Joseph,' he said. I am but a poor fisherman, and I have to go now and sell my catch for last night. I will leave dog with you, so don't be afraid. You will be safe here until I return, and I will bring some food, and then we will talk.'

'Mine is Katherine,' she replied, 'and as I have no clothes, I will not be able to move any further than this. Thank you for saving my life, and yes we will talk when you get back, and thank you for lending me dog; he is wonderful. Has he not got a name? Every dog should have a name, shouldn't it?' she ventured.

'You give him a name,' laughed the fisherman, with a twinkle in his bright blue eyes. She heard him whistling a merry tune as he plodded from the cottage. After he had gone, and dog had settled between her and the fire, Katherine opened her case. To her great joy and surprise, everything was as she had packed it when she left all that time ago. It seemed like a lifetime now since then, and so much had happened. Frightening things, adventurous things, things that she knew she could not face again. She would have to change her appearance, somehow change her clothes. What had happened to them she wondered as she lay there, quite lazily for her. She was used to being up and about when she was at home with Martha. Dear Martha, what would become of her? One day she knew she would see her again, she had promised, and she would keep her promise, both to herself and Martha.

The day seemed long with nothing to do. Dog kept coming over for a bit of fussing. 'What are we going to call you, dog? Every dog should have a proper name,' and then she remembered Martha telling her that when she was a child in England she had a little dog, and she called him Pip. Pip was short for Pipsqueak she told her, and a pipsqueak was a little thing that made a lot of noise, but never did very much. Well she was sure that dog did a lot when he was out with Joseph, otherwise he would not have taken him every day on his fishing trips because he would have been a nuisance. Pip, she thought, was a nice name, and she tried it on dog who at first just ignored her and snoozed by the fire, but after a few tries, and by changing the tone of her voice. 'Pip', brought him to her side.

Joseph had been a long time gone as he had heard at the market that the fish were running well, and he went in order to get a little more money for his catch. He had needed to buy extra food, and get Katherine something that she could wear. Her own clothes were in a pretty sorry state, and he was not used to clothes other than his old sweaters and trousers that he washed in a bucket of water pulled from the well, after he had used it to wash himself. He had made a makeshift line out of sight at the rear of the cottage between the tree and the sea wall, and had hung her clothes there. Being so close to the sea, the winds were always quite strong, and washing dried easily.

The cottage was small, and was built hugging an enormous rock to its rear. The roof was steep, and roughly tiled from its pointed top to the width of the walls below. One side was against a part of the sea wall. High tides never reached the cottage, but the sea wall protruded so that it formed a barrier around the small piece of land, that had become a tiny garden, with wild flowers in profusion clinging to its side. The door was smartly painted black and white, and had a large round knocker, also painted black. The house had no number, as it was the only one there, and it was just known as 'The Fisherman's Cottage'.

Joseph returned with his purchases, and opened the door to a sight that pleased him. Katherine was sitting up, with the skins all pulled around her, laughing and playing with dog. He entered, carrying his fish bag with the usual bounty of a few fish, but also tonight he had brought from the market some cheese and a long freshly baked loaf, two apples, and some milk. He was also carrying a paper bag. He handed it to her without looking at her.

'Had to ask the woman on the stall to pack it for you; told her my niece was stopping for a while, and I needed another change of clothes for her. Don't know what's in there, but she said it would do nicely. Told her you were fourteen. Didn't know how old you were. Hope it will help until you can see to your own clothes; they are pretty bad, I'm afraid.'

'Thank you so much,' said Katherine. 'I am thirteen, but I look older, don't you think?' she said.

'I don't have much to do with young ladies. My brother has two children, but I don't ever see them; they live a long way away,' answered Joseph.

Moving away to the stove, he banked up the fire and set about getting some supper. The hour was late, but he thought she must be hungry, and time would not hold much significance for her, as she had lost so much during her traumatic experience.

Katherine watched him, fascinated by his deftness of hand as he gutted the fish, and prepared it for them.

'I've called him Pip,' Katherine said to break the silence. She held the bag, not quite knowing what to do, as she could not dress in front of him.

'Pip,' he said. 'What sort of name is that for a working dog?' Looking at her and seeing the sadness in her eyes, he said, 'but it is a nice name, and dog seems to like it. Do you like it PIP?' he said to the dog, at which

Pip gave a little bark, and rubbed himself against his leg. 'Pip it is then, although I don't know its meaning.'

Katherine then told him the story that Martha had told her, and he grinned, and said that he thought dog was indeed a pipsqueak. Then, moving from the table, he said, 'I have to go to the garden and pull some carrots from the earth. Perhaps madam would like to dress for dinner before I return.' Smiling at Katherine's obvious shyness he quietly went out and shut the door.

Katherine quickly opened the bag, and found a pretty white cotton shift, some underwear, a pair of baggy trousers in faded blue, and a pair of rubber shoes in white. Also there was a thick woollen jacket rather like the one that Joseph had worn to go out in the boat. Not knowing how long he would be, she hastily donned the underwear, and the shift, which was quite long, so she felt that she did not need to wear the trousers, but tomorrow she would venture into the garden, and then she would put them on. Barefooted, she was sitting by the fire with Pip when he returned.

'Well now, that is better,' he said. 'You can borrow Pip's hair brush, if you wish; I'm sure he wouldn't mind. I always bath him and brush his coat. I washed your hair when I brought you in. You weren't aware, but I had to do it to untangle it, and attend to the wound that was on your forehead.'

Katherine gently touched her forehead, and could feel a grazed patch, but it didn't hurt, just a bit sore. 'Thank you again. I know I would have died but for you, and for me hearing Martha call me back.'

Joseph, now with dinner in the pot, pulled the other chair to the fire, and sat opposite her, saying, 'You can stay here until you are better, and able to travel, and then you must go on and fulfil your plans. I know nothing about looking after anybody, only Pip. I will feed you, and see that you are well, but you will have to do all the other things that need to be done yourself. Are you happy about that?'

She looked at him and said, 'Yes, of course, I will be on my way very soon. I do not wish to be a worry to you; you have been too kind, and I will never forget what you have done. I have a little money so I will pay you for the clothes, and give you some money for the food that you have bought because of me.'

'I don't want any money from you,' he replied. 'While you are here, perhaps you could tidy up my cottage for me. That would be payment enough.'

They sat in comfortable silence and ate the meal that Joseph had carefully placed on clean plates, with a fork to eat it. He usually used the same knife to eat with as he used for gutting his fish, but didn't think that would be proper for Katherine to see. After they had finished, Katherine said, 'I feel I must tell you why I ended up where I did. I don't want to bore you with my story because it is a long and not a very pleasant one. I don't know where I am, because I was running away, and I jumped from a train that was heading for Milan. I was being looked for by the authorities. I have done no wrong; the people who I thought were helping me, were just after money. I have none, but my father has lots, and I foolishly told one of them this.'

'Stop,' said Joseph, 'you don't have to tell me anything that you don't want to.' He could see how very close to tears she was, and he knew that sooner or later she would feel like talking. He didn't know whether he could help her, but he knew how much he wanted to. 'I don't know where you could possibly have jumped from a train heading for Milan, but I will tell you that you must have walked for many miles. You have made it to the coastline close to Lake Como. This is a tiny fishing village with hardly any inhabitants, only other fishermen like me, and we are a tight-knit community who care for each other come what may, so you will be safe here. I live here because of my grandfather; he too was a fisherman, and as a child I lived here with him because I loved him and wanted to be with him. My mother was alone and had my younger brother to care for, so I spent my life with my grandfather until he died at sea a couple of years ago. He built this cottage himself, and promised me it would be mine when he died. I would not live anywhere else. I love it so, and I am happy to fish like he did, in the same boat as he did, and I still wear his wellingtons. They gave them to me when I brought back his body. He had a heart attack while we were pulling in the nets. I tried so hard, but I could not save him. This earring that I wear was his. You will see that most fishermen wear one earring. This you may think is strange for a man to wear such jewellery, but there is a good reason for it. We wear it so that if we die at sea, and our bodies are not claimed by any relative, the earring can then be exchanged for enough money to bury us. I could not bring myself to sell it to get money to bury my grandfather, so I paid for his burial, and kept his earring which I will wear until the day I die, and then, who knows?'

Katherine sat wide-eyed as the fisherman told her his story. She had known him but a few hours, and yet she knew it would be the saddest moment when she would have to leave him to continue her plan to one day go to England, and maybe forget this land of her birth that really had brought her so much trouble, except for the joy that Martha had given her. But she belonged in England too, so her quest would be a lifelong determination to fulfil.

Joseph stood up and looked around the room. He began to haul some nets from the rafters, and with deft fingers, he tied them at the top, and climbed over the makeshift bed that he had fashioned for Katherine. He hooked the top of the nets that he had gathered tightly, and brought the fullness of them down around her bed, fixing them to the wooden floor with metal pegs, until he had made her a perfect tent. It was a private little domain, where she could sleep comfortably, and be safe. She could also make a space for her little case, and not have to hide it any more like she used to. Joseph knew it was hers and respected that. She could also dress and undress here, and keep her few clothes tidy. Tomorrow she would look at the clothes that she had so cleverly worn, layer upon layer, until she fell in the water and ruined them. Well maybe Joseph didn't realise just how good she was with needle and thread, and if she could get them clean and dry, and fold them neatly, placing them under her mattress, she maybe could salvage the best of them, and use some of the better pieces to replace those that were beyond repair. She could end up with a couple of good outfits, and then Joseph would be really impressed.

Tomorrow dawned, with pale sunlight catching the dust that hung around the cottage. Joseph left for market with her still sleeping in her tiny corner. Pip jumped at Joseph's heels, hoping to go with him. It had been nice looking after Katherine, but he missed his master's company on the boat. Joseph gently put him down, and said that he would return after market and take him on the boat, if Katherine was happy to stay on her own here at the cottage.

As the cottage door shut, Katherine awoke to hear the latch go down firmly, and to find Pip sitting forlornly at the door, missing his master already. 'Pip, you must go with Joseph now I am well enough to stay here without you.' The dog, seeming to understand what she said, bounded over to her, and licked her outstretched hand. Katherine now began to see the cottage, not any more as a refuge, but as a rather beautiful place. The picture that hung over Joseph's bed was of his grandfather. This she knew because the likeness was unbelievable. The face, the hair, the size of the man, and the smile that even from a picture seemed to light up the room. She found a large piece of gauze on the floor next to the fire. She picked it up, climbed on the large bed, and gently removed the dust from the picture.

Then she gradually moved around the room, and dusted all the surfaces, lifting pots, pans, and other objects to dust beneath them. She sang quietly as she performed the chores. This done, she carefully removed a pan from over the fire, that was full of boiling water. She filled a bowl that stood on the table, and with her own little bar of soap and a flannel that she had thoughtfully put on the top of her case, when she left Martha, she washed herself. Oh, it felt so good. She could not remember the last time she had felt the pleasure of hot water next to her skin. She knew that Joseph had cleaned her up, and dried her, when he had rescued her two days ago now, but to do it one's self, and linger with the hot flannel pressed to her skin was just wonderful.

This accomplished, she dried herself on the towel that she was wrapped in when she first awoke, and then she put on her new clothes that Joseph had bought for her, this time with the trousers as well. They fitted her very well, and as she looked at her reflection in the window, she thought how different she looked from the little girl that ran to school with the little boy down the road, and the one who sang a solo in the school choir. She picked up Pip's brush, and, apologising to him, she brushed her hair and swept it up on top of her head; then she tied it with a belt that had been threaded through the waist of the shift, and which she had left off to let the shift hang loose over the trousers. She let the rest of her hair hang down in a pony tail. The final result was quite pleasing, she thought. How could she feel so good now, when only a week ago she was feeling like the whole world had deserted her, and that her life was hanging in the balance.

Whatever happened now, she felt that she would be able to deal with it, and that, in all fairness, was mostly down to Joseph who had not only saved her life, but had given her the will to live again. In the time that she was going to stay with him, she would in some way repay him for his total undemanding kindness. Although she was only thirteen years old, she felt she had already lived a lifetime. The water that she had used to wash with, she now took into the garden and poured onto the parched roots of a rose tree trying to survive in the harsh coastal conditions.

Joseph returned from market to find her, head bent in the garden, picking out weeds from amongst the riot of flowers which miraculously grew without any attention from him. He stood for a moment and watched her, marvelling at the change in her in two short days. She looked almost beautiful with the sun shining on her golden red hair, which had been a matted clump held together with blood and water when he picked her up.

She looked up and smiled at him, gave Pip a shove, and said, 'please take Pip with you, he needs you, and you him. I will be just fine here.'

Joseph nodded and moved inside the cottage to see the evening dishes washed and stacked tidily, and noticed how the surfaces gleamed in the morning sunlight. Was this child real, or was he dreaming? No she was real, and he felt that he didn't want to let her go until he was sure that she would achieve all her dreams. Was that possible with the life that he lived? Anything was possible when it was that important he thought, and this was as important as anything he had ever done in his life. He would give everything he had to see her reach her goal. He so wanted to know all about her and what had prompted her at such a young age to run away. One day maybe she would tell him, before he had to let her go. He would make sure that she was strong and sure of herself, and if anyone tried to hurt her, he would kill them. He was shocked at feeling so strongly about the welfare of a child. Perhaps it was because he had never had any children of his own, but he felt protective of her as if she were a baby.

She was still in the garden when he left with Pip. She waved and smiled as if she had been there all her life. What a special place this was, she thought, as she wandered toward the sea wall and, upon reaching it, saw a band of pale yellow sand that stretched for miles. Washing it clean with every movement, was the bluest sea that she could ever have imagined.

She turned back, and then she saw all her tattered clothes, hanging on a line at the back of the cottage. When she looked at them, she realised how lucky she had been to survive. They were muddy and torn, and her lovely coat that Martha had made was all odd shapes where the water had ravaged it, and the lining had shrunk, making all the seams of the coat look as if they had been gathered up. The wind had dried them completely, so that they could not be stretched into anything like the shape they once were. The underwear and nightdress could be salvaged, as they were pure cotton, and a good wash in hot water would revive them and hopefully get the muddy brown stains out. She removed them all from the line and took them inside the cottage. She would take them one at a time, and work on them until they were wearable. Those that weren't, she would tear into squares and use them to clean with.

First she took the nightdress. She had been sleeping with nothing on, and was plenty warm enough beneath the mountain of sheep skin that

Joseph had laid on her bed, but she thought that now the nets had given her a little corner of her own, it would be lovely to slip into the pretty night gown that Martha had spent hours on embroidering the top with tiny flowers. Gently she lifted it from the filthy pile, and placing hot water from the already boiling pot on the fire into the large white sink, lowered in the stained garment. She had found a rough square of very strong smelling soap on the side of the sink which she had seen Joseph scrubbing his hands with after gutting and handling the fish. The smell, though strong, did have quite a breezy scent, she decided, and so she set to work. Laying each piece that was stained, bit by bit, on the wooden side table, she rubbed and scrubbed until she thought would she make a hole in it. Finally, pleased with the result, she plunged it back into the water and, pulling and pushing it up and down, then wringing it out tightly as hard as her little hands could cope with, she left it on the side and headed for the next white piece of clothing she could find.

Continuing thus, until all the white and pale pieces were dealt with this way, she happily realised that not one of them would have to be cut into squares for cleaning. A couple of dresses perhaps could be handled in the same way, but these were a bit more difficult, as Joseph, in an effort to pull them from her sodden body, had had to cut them down the back. He never ceased to wonder why she had worn layer upon layer of clothes, which of course had weighed her down in the water. She would wash them as they were, and then face the task of trying to repair them later when they had dried. The knitted jumper and cardigan that somehow she had managed to wear as well were, she was afraid, going to be casualties. They had stretched in the water, and they smelled horrible. Martha had made them for her, and so it hurt terribly to have to decide to throw them away, but she thought Martha would not mind in the least if she knew she was alive, and now feeling so well.

Once the washing part was done, she threw the dirty water outside on the parched ground, filled the bucket from the well water, and rinsed all the clothes in fresh cold water. She then took them and hung them on the makeshift line that Joseph had put up. Once all this was done, she turned her hands to the chores inside the cottage. She loved this little place. Although it was only one room, it had corners, and alcoves, with a steep sloping roof and, at night when the oil lamp was alight, it threw shadows that lengthened as they reached the floor. She carefully made her bed, folding each sheep skin neatly and placing them as to form cushions, so that if she had some books she would be able to sit in there with her back against the wall and read. Perhaps Joseph would be able to buy a book for her at the market. Martha had made her read a lot in Italian and in English.

Joseph spoke only Italian, and she wondered if he could read, if not, perhaps while she was here she could teach him a little. It would make her feel good, to repay some of his kindness. If she carried on getting better each day, she would not be staying very long. For some strange reason that saddened her, and she decided not to think about it until it happened. She proceeded then to make Joseph's bed. The bedding on it was rough and scratchy, and she thought he deserved better for all the hard work he did. However, she plumped his pillows, took off his covers and shook them vigorously outside, and returned them tidily tucked in at the corners, another of Martha's teachings. She owed her so much, and maybe one day she would be able to repay her.

When she got to England, she would write to her, and let her know that she was all right, and then set about earning enough to bring her back to her country that she had spoken of so lovingly to Katherine. She refilled the pot that hung over the fire with water in, so that it boiled, and then stayed hot for Joseph when he returned. With all that done, she pulled from her case her tiny little set of needles and cotton, that had been one of the things she always kept in her purse, and found a piece of cotton thread that would reasonably match one of the dresses that sat on the pile of now dry clothes. She set about neatening the slit that Joseph had made, using a large pair of scissors that she had found in the drawer along with the knives and forks. They weren't very sharp, but they did the job, and she started to sew a new seam down the back of the dress. This would of course make the dress slightly smaller, but she always thought it was a bit too large. 'You'll grow into it,' Martha had said. After the seam was completed, she had to neaten the edges, as the material had frayed. Martha had shown her how to do this too, and although it took a lot of thread, and time and patience, the result was excellent. She couldn't wait to show Joseph, because he said he felt bad about having to cut them in the first place. The other dress she would do tomorrow as the light was beginning to fade, and such tiny stitches hurt her eyes. She would put it on the pile under her mattress to press it. Perhaps it wouldn't be long now before Joseph and Pip returned.

This was the first day that she had been on her own since the fateful night when, disorientated by the dark, and exhaustion, she had fallen into the water. She started to remember some of the things that had happened, like the oranges she ate with nothing else that had given her pains in the stomach. Like the feeling that someone was always behind her looking for her, and ready to grab her, and take her back from where she had run away, and the last and most terrifying thing when she was trying to fight against the water dragging her down until she lost all her strength.

Now as evening drew nigh, and the little cottage became darker, she wished that Joseph would come home. She couldn't light the lamp, she didn't know how, and Joseph had to pull it down from the roof by a long chain in order to light it. She put a couple of logs in the stove, and a myriad of sparks flew from the old ones as they collapsed under the weight of the new ones. She sat on the chair near to the stove, placed her head on her arms that she rested on the wooden arms of the chair, and as Joseph and Pip came through the door together they found her dozing. Pip scampered to her side and tried clumsily to jump on her lap. She woke with a start, and then gently chastised the little dog, only to end up hugging him with the sheer joy of him being there.

Joseph pulled down the lamp and lit it, and suddenly the whole room became aglow. Joseph gazed around in amazement when he saw how clean and tidy everything was, and the little pile of clothes all clean laying on her bed, and her in her shift curled up in the chair asleep. It was a picture he would remember for the rest of his life. He had never seen anything as perfect as this. He wished so much that he had been an artist and been able to capture this scene, and pin it to his wall so that it was the first thing he saw whenever he entered this place that before was just his grandfather's cottage, and a place to live. In a few days this child had turned it into something magical. They enjoyed their supper. Pip curled up by the stove after he had cleaned the plates of all the leftovers, not to mention his share which was always comparable with his master's.

Katherine and Joseph just sat in companionable silence, neither of them wanting to talk about the situation, although both feeling that they should. Perhaps it was just too soon. Katherine had recovered so quickly it had surprised Joseph, and pleased Katherine because she could now allow herself to be happy in the knowledge that she was on her way to keeping her promise to Martha. This was what she told herself, if only half heartedly, because she loved being here, and she wanted to stay a while, by the beach, and in this little cottage, and secretly, she admitted, with Joseph, and of course Pip. Coming out of her thoughts, she showed Joseph her clothing, and the sewing that she had done. Joseph was impressed, as she thought he would be, and said she should get a job as a needlewoman; she was really excellent, especially doing all the tiny stitches on the dress. Smiling, he said, 'You could make me a shirt. I could take you to the market, and maybe buy some material, and you could have some to make a dress for yourself.'

Excited now, she explained that she had already thought of how much she would love to go to the market. She had a little money, because she had managed to get on and off the train without paying, and she had loved the clothes that Joseph had managed to get her. Excitement now took over, and she rambled on about a book to read, and some paper and a pencil to do some drawing, and also some material with which to make a whole dress instead of having to repair one. She looked apologetically at Joseph, thinking he might feel guilty for cutting the only other dress she had. Joseph sat there and watched her, fascinated by the flush on her cheeks and the sparkle in her eyes, and he just smiled, and said, 'You will have to be up very early in the morning if you wish to go with me. I sell my fish at about six o'clock in the morning. I will not wait, but if you are ready I will take you.

Early the following morning, peeping out from inside her tent, Katherine saw that Joseph was still in his bed, in fact he was gently snoring which quite amused her. Pip was awake, but Katherine putting her finger to her lips to make a please be quiet sign. She quickly dressed herself, brushed her hair, put out the plate, with the bread and the cheese that Joseph ate every morning, and put the jug of cold water, and the mug, that it appeared he also used every morning. She helped herself to a little milk to add to a bowl of oats, and she quietly ate, and sat patiently for what seemed to be an eternity. Finally, Joseph woke, looked across, and let out a whoop of laughter.

'Determined child, aren't you?' he said. 'A few minutes, and we will be on our way. You can talk to the lady that made up your parcel of clothes, and thank her.'

'That I will,' answered Katherine, and then her face clouded.

'What's wrong?' said Joseph.

'I'm frightened someone from the train will be there and recognise me,' she cried.

'No one will know you,' he said, 'except that you are my niece, and are staying with me for a while. Your mother is having another baby, and your father is working away, so I am given the job of caring for you until you can be returned to your family.'

Katherine, happy with the explanation, was ready to go. The hustle and bustle of the market was a revelation to Katherine; all the faces looked happy, and were animated in conversation, each stall holder to the next. Vegetables, meat, and fish of course, but Joseph didn't have a stall, he just sold his fish from the crates that they had been placed in a few hours ago, to which salt had now been added. The fish sold amazingly quickly. Joseph explained that one of the big hotels on the lake took a large part of his catch. He had a good reputation for the fresh fish that he supplied. In about an hour he was free, and he took Katherine to the stall where, to Katherine's astonishment, there was everything that she needed. Beautiful materials, cottons, and ribbons, and she noticed that the next stall had drawing paper, pencils, and, to her utmost joy, a few books. She found the lady on the material stall very friendly and helpful. She asked her how much material she would need to make a dress, to which the lady picked out the chosen bale, and pulled the material from it until it billowed out in all its pale pink glory. Katherine was mesmerised as the lady measured the correct length, and added a reel of cotton in a matching pink. She folded it neatly, and passed it to Katherine, who held out a handful of money. The lady then took a note and a few coins, smiled and said, 'Thank you.'

Katherine, now feeling confidence that belied her years, passed to the next stall and picked up two sheets of paper, a pencil, and five crayons, paid for them, and turned to Joseph, happy and ready to go home. The material lady said as they departed, 'Please come and show me your dress when it is finished,' and the other lady said, 'I would like to see your drawings.'

Katherine walked home with Joseph, helping him pull the cart that now had empty crates on. They chatted easily about their days to come. How they would both spend them, what they would like to do, neither mentioning that the length of her stay had to be discussed. Joseph said that he would take her out in the fishing boat, but that he would have to make her a proper seat, and make her a float, so that if she did happen to fall in she would stay afloat until he could rescue her. After her experience in the water, she was afraid of going, even if she was with Joseph whom she trusted implicitly. She had lots to do at home, so she wouldn't mind if that didn't happen for a while. She would love to see the boat though, and maybe just go on board to see what it was like.

Thus Joseph and Pip set off again for another day's fishing, and Katherine settled down at the cottage, trying to decide which of the wares she had bought at the market, she would set about using first. At this moment she just felt suddenly very tired, so she undid the ties on the opening of her little tent, crept inside, laid on her bed, and fell into a contented slumber.

As the days passed, Katherine almost forgot the reason why she was here. She kept a clean cottage for Joseph; she mended all the clothes that had been salvaged from the water, with the exception of her coat, and a woolly cardigan which now served as dusters and cleaning cloths. She started on the making of the dress; cutting the skirt was easy. Martha had told her to cut a piece of material twice the width of her waist, and to the length that she needed, adding a bit for the bottom hem. The scissors that Joseph used were really not sharp enough for delicate material, so it was a little difficult to do it neatly. The bodice was not at all easy, in fact she had not a notion how to cut the correct shape. She wondered if she could go to the market with Joseph, and ask the lady on the material stall if she could help her. Once she knew, she would be able to carry on herself. This in mind, she started to stitch the skirt and, running a thread through the material at the waist edge, she could pull it in until it fitted perfectly. This done, she was happy, so she folded it neatly with the bodice material, and packed it away until she could ask Joseph to take her to the market.

Joseph had planned to take her on his boat, and felt quite excited at the prospect. His life had been a lonely one. He had never had the company before, and never had the chance to show anyone his boat, his pride and joy, his grandfather's, and now his. He would spend hours in his little makeshift boathouse situated to the rear of his cottage at the other end of the sea wall. He had his own reel-way, which began at the water's edge, and ended well above normal sea level. The shelter itself was in fact a protruding escarpment of the rock face which offered shelter and room a plenty for his little boat, and room for him to raise the boat on wooden blocks to work on it. He had fashioned himself a winch so that he could fasten it to the boat and pull it easily into the boathouse.

He had days when things were not quite as demanding as others, and on one such day he took Katherine to the boathouse. She laughed as she slipped and slithered up the shingle bank in her little rubber shoes that had been bought for just this purpose, and sighed with relief when she finally reached the top, grabbing Joseph's hand for the last few steps on to the solid rock flooring, where for the first time she saw the tiny vessel that had saved her life on that fateful night, and brought her to the sanctuary of Joseph's cottage. The small blue boat, which now sat perfectly secured in its dry haven, stood facing the sea ready to go to work, with its crates neatly packed one on top of the other. On the front, under a lamp which hung from a metal stand, there was a painting of an eye. Joseph explained that the eye would always see him through a storm. Katherine laughed at his explanation, but thought that it really was quite a good idea.

In the main body of the boat, Joseph had built a small seat with straight sides, and with its base secured to one of the wooden rails that ran along the side of the boat. 'It will serve to keep you still,' said Joseph. 'Sit in and I will reel you down to the sea.'

Katherine, feeling very nervous, sat rigidly in the seat, clinging to the sides as Joseph carefully let the winch ease the boat down to the water's edge. Joseph followed on foot and jumped easily aboard, took up the large oars and pushed them off from the safety of land, to the unknown quantity of the sea. He rowed them out until the sea wall was a mere speck in the distance, threw out a couple of nets, and turned to Katherine, who was quite pale-faced and clearly not enjoying this venture. Pip, on the other hand, who had jumped aboard at the last minute to answer his master's call, sat in the bow, head proudly held high, and eyes riveted on the horizon for any sight of ripples, which amazingly he knew was where his master would be heading, and he would give a bark of satisfaction. Today, Katherine was just a passenger on his boat, and would be treated as such, no pulling of ears, or stroking of tummies, as much as he loved it, today he was working and had to concentrate, or his master would be cross.

On returning to dry land, Katherine felt quite sick, and Joseph noticed her nervousness. He decided that perhaps fishing was not for her, but he felt for her own safety he would have to teach her how to swim. This he would do at some later date; he thought about how long he would have to put this into action before she left. He pushed the thought to the back of his mind. Summer was approaching and it would do her good to live in the sunshine, on a beach for a while. She would be all the stronger for that, and he would be happier if he knew that she was strong in confidence, as well as in body. He had plans in this direction, and would let her go happily if he could even put some of them into place. He would still take her to market when she wanted to go, as long as it fell in with his time schedules. His life had changed since Katherine came into it. One small scrap, so close to death when he had found her, was now a thriving young lady with ideas beyond her age. He would maybe need some help and advice on how to cope with her general wellbeing, always having to remember that in spite of her intelligence and an inner knowledge which sometimes astounded him, she was still a child, and as such needed to have some childish fun, and just be happy. Being a single man with little or no knowledge of children let alone female ones, maybe he would have to get some help and advice from another woman. He would talk to Lena at the market. Maybe she would let Katherine meet her children. All be it they were younger they could still be company for her.

With this thought out he felt satisfied, and took Katherine back to the cottage to spend the rest of the day quietly, while he went on to market as usual. She was tired, he could see, and the trip out in the boat had not been a complete success. He had not been out long because of her, and so his catch was small. He so much wanted her to enjoy herself, and forget the horrors of the past. She had loved the boat house, and the boat; he knew that because of her look. He had learned that much about her in the short time he had known her. She had a light around her, a radiance that shone from her very being, when something pleased her.

Katherine, back at the cottage, although pleased to be off the boat, was sorry because she felt as if she had let Joseph down, but she really was afraid of the water now. She had had no experience of it in her life before, never seen it, never been on it, and certainly never been in it, drowning, fighting for life and breath. She never wanted ever to feel that way again. Restless, she took a piece of her paper that she had purchased at the market, and her crayons, walked to the end of the stone wall, and a way down the beach.

The sea was far away, and so she felt at ease. She sat cross-legged as a child would, and drew the scene in front of her. She just caught the end of the rock that was Joseph's boat house, and the edge of the wall with the sand and sea taking up most of the picture. When it was finished, she sat and looked at it critically. It wasn't what she had wanted it to be. The colours were too bright, the lines too harsh, and the rock was small and out of proportion with the rest of the picture. She didn't want to show the lady at the market, and even more, she didn't want to show it to Joseph, but she knew he would want to see it.

She walked back to the cottage, and left it on the table where she knew he would see it, and then went back out on to the beach, walked along it, lost in thought, casually picking up a shell or two on her way. As she slowly made her way to where the beach narrowed and had a few rocks on its soft sand, she thought how much she would like to live in a place like this. Tiny rock pools appeared here and there, and an odd crab scuttled from its hiding place, to run to another. She watched fascinated. How could creatures this small survive in a world so big, she wondered sadly, thinking that one day one of these would end up in Joseph's net, and its sublime life on the beach would be over.

Joseph returned later to see the picture sitting a bit crumpled on the table. He smiled, looked around to see Katherine, but she was not there. He called but there was no answer. He looked from the door, and spotted in the distance the white shift. It was sitting on a rock at the far end of the beach, with Katherine inside it. He wandered out, but on his way he picked up the second piece of paper and a pencil, made for the spot from where she had made her drawing, and started to sketch. Lost in what he was doing, he failed to hear her quietly walking up behind him. He turned to see tears running down her face. 'I'm so sorry, I didn't mean to take your paper. I will replace it tomorrow,' he said, taking her hand.

'No, it's not that,' whispered Katherine. 'It is so beautiful, your picture. I hated mine and didn't want you to see it.'

Joseph replied, 'Your picture has its own beauty, and I would like to keep it. I will give you mine if you will let me keep yours.'

'I will keep it forever,' said Katherine, turning away so that he would not see the further tears that she could not stop.

They walked back to the cottage, both clasping one another's drawings, in the knowledge that they both would be treasured items in their separate lives. Joseph watched her after supper, and could see she was in deep thought, not worrying thoughts, but she was thinking carefully. He knew this much, but about what he knew not.

'Joseph, I will have to think about going soon. I am well now, and I can't let you go on looking after me. I am beginning to love this place, and I'm afraid that I will not want to go at all,' said Katherine suddenly.

'I was thinking the same,' answered Joseph, 'but I thought you would maybe like to spend the summer here. The weather is so lovely, and you could meet some friends to make your time here happier.'

'My time here could not be any happier however many friends I had,' said Katherine.

'Stay anyway,' pleaded Joseph, 'just until the end of summer.'

'Yes I will, provided you will not let me disturb your way of life, and only if I can help in some way to repay you for all your kindness.'

Joseph would take her tomorrow to speak to Lena at the market, to see if she could keep her occupied while he worked. Maybe she could let her help on the stall, and earn a few coins to buy herself the things that young girls like to buy; then when he was able he would take her a little further afield to see how the people around here lived.

The people mainly belonged to fishing families, some were local fishermen who owned their own boats and worked the waters just outside the harbour. Others worked on large vessels for captains, who in turn worked for the owners, some of whom had large fleets and sailed much wider areas across the seas to earn much better rewards for a fishing trip. The women spent their days, as most women did, cooking and cleaning, looking after their children, but also most of them were quite clever and turned their hands to craft work, and growing fruit and vegetables on their sparse areas of land around their cottages. It was commonplace for them to rent a space at the market, and every day they would take their wares, and display them on makeshift stalls. It was colourful, with banners being attached to each stall, some with the names of the owner. They would buy and sell to and from each other, but sometimes visitors would come to the market on hearsay that good bargains could be bought there.

Lena came every day. She worked hard, as her husband spent many weeks away from home, working for the fleet owners, and at the end of his time away he would come home with not so much money to account for the hours that he had been away fishing. Lena never asked questions; she was just happy that he did come home, and the children loved him, and he always brought them something back when he returned. Lena in the meantime had to care for, feed, and clothe the children, which she did very well.

Joseph brought Katherine back to the market, and she brought her unfinished dress to ask Lena if she could show her how to make the bodice for it. Sitting at the back of the stall, cutting and stitching as Lena showed her in between her dealing with customers, she felt important and loved being there. Lena also let her do a couple of easy sales, and asked her if she would do some stitching for her as she was impressed with the neatness shown on the dress seams. Katherine was delighted, and asked Joseph if he would bring her every time he came. She would be ready when he was, and she would be sure that she cleaned and tidied the cottage just as she did now. It was agreed, and Katherine, good as her word, did everything as she promised, and more. She began to bring home tiny bunches of flowers from the end-of-day displays, and also she was given ripe fruit, and unsold vegetables, and occasionally a meat pie that had been left over. She loved it, and Lena soon became quite close to her.

Joseph saw this, and hoped she would confide in Lena some of her hopes and fears, for he felt that to confide in him may be very difficult for a young girl to a man not much more than ten years older than her. He really didn't think he made much of a father figure, but he did his best to make her life happy for the time she would be his responsibility. The dress was finally completed, and buttons were placed down the front, each one with a buttonhole, some stitched by Lena, but the majority by Katherine, with Lena showing her how to do buttonhole stitch.

The time had come for the fashion show. Lena and her three children had come to the tiny cottage, and they sat on the floor with Joseph holding council in his high-backed rocking chair that no one else sat in, not even Pip. Katherine walked shyly from behind her curtain of nets, and did a curtsey. She had a smile on her face to light up the room. A round of applause broke out from the audience, and Pip barked his approval.

'You look like a princess,' said Joseph. 'I shall have to take you somewhere special to wear that.'

'I shall find you a pair of shoes,' said Lena, pride showing in her voice. She liked the child very much. She found her polite, and very anxious to learn, always enjoyed laughing when something funny happened, and showed no bitterness for all that had seemingly happened to her. Joseph had told Lena the truth about how he had come to find her, and that for all intents and purposes she was his niece. He trusted her, and she him, and she told him that she would give him all the support he needed.

Katherine's summer was idyllic. She spent most of her days at the market, and was becoming quite an astute saleswoman. Lena and her children spent their Sundays at the beach with her, and most times Joseph was there as well. Between them they made a tasty picnic which they all devoured with relish. The children taught Katherine to swim, for which Joseph was eternally grateful, as he was sure that she would have taken many a ducking if he had had a hand in it. Katherine for her part did not in all honesty find it enjoyable. She hated her face under water, but she knew Joseph was very pleased with her progress, and was proud on the day she threw away the float he had made for her, and swam from the end of the jetty to him sitting in his boat mending his nets. He reached over the side, pulled her aboard and gave her a hug.

In the late evenings, she, Joseph, and Pip, would sit beside the fire. Although it was summer, the evenings were chilly, because of the cottage's close proximity to the sea. Anyway a fire was cosy with its red glow, and they all felt tired after their busy days. Katherine was usually first to say goodnight and take herself off to the bedroom that was a feather mattress, a pile of sheep skins, and miles of green and orange netting. She sank into its softness, and thought that nothing anywhere in the world could feel like this. She always picked up her book, but the words jumped up and down before her eyes more times than not, so she gave in to sleep, which most times seemed dreamless. She always woke before Joseph, and got his breakfast ready, before preparing herself for market.

The days of summer were certainly not lazy, but it was the most wonderful time, and on days when Joseph did not take her to the market, she would wander along the beach and pick up shells which she kept in a huge bowl near the door. She would sit on a large flat rock at the far end of the beach for hours, and just dream, but in her reverie, there was always a bad part, when her mind ruthlessly flashed back to the scene of Martha and Alexi heaving the heavy body of her adoptive father away from the woodman's cottage to a place that she did not know. The face of her real father, kneeling in desperation at the graveside of a mother she never knew. Would these images ever fade, and would she ever in her life again have to face such awful times? Would that she could always stay here and look at a peaceful blue sea throwing its white horses at the sand, and seeing them gallop back to meet the next ones coming in.

At the end of the year, she would reach her fourteenth birthday. Where would she be? She had saved a little more money, after buying some small bits of food to go on Joseph's table for supper. How long would she be able to go on doing the same things that made her so happy, things that were so easy and simple to do, things that made Joseph laugh, and made him happy too. Making Joseph happy was one of her prime objectives. He saved her life, and he also gave her a life that she had never known. Her entire life up until the moment she ran away was spent around the woodman's cottage, and of course with her beloved Martha, but she had never had a friend, only the little boy who she used to race to school. The other pupils never made an effort to befriend her; they seemed to think that she was a little below them. Now she knew so many people, who all seemed to like her, and she them, and of course she had Joseph and Pip. She could not imagine life without them. When the realisation of this sad thought brought her back to reality, she would leave the rock, and start the return journey up the beach to the cottage, savouring the feeling of sand between her toes, and the soft wind in her hair.

Joseph for his part was a happy man. He had never had anything going on in his life, nor did he want anything particular. He was happy to be out on the ocean fishing for a living, and was too tired when he finally got back to the cottage to think about anything but preparing his nets and boat for the next day, and going to bed. Now he always looked forward to coming home to Katherine, to hear her stories for the day, and to sit and listen to her reading to him. She had taken to doing this, because Joseph had told her that he couldn't read. She had volunteered to teach him what little she could. Martha had been very strict, and made her read to her before she went to sleep. The vision of her bedroom came into her mind, and then the awful memory of that terrible night. She quickly put it out of her head, and concentrated on teaching Joseph a few easy words. She was surprised how quickly he learned, and was equally surprised that he had not learned at school. He told her that he didn't go to school much. He was quite young when he went to his grandfather, and his life was governed by him and that was to fish, which he loved, and so school was forgotten. Katherine could understand that and never questioned it again.

Every night now they would sit, and Joseph would read, slowly but perfectly with Katherine gently prompting him on the more difficult words. The only problem now was that, as he improved, the words began to mean something when they were strung together into sentences, and Joseph began to understand the story, and the story was the one that Katherine had bought from the market, which was without doubt a girls' book, with a small amount of romance within its pages. This became a bit embarrassing for Katherine, but Joseph was secretly amused as the plot became clearer. Katherine decided that the next thing she would buy with the money she earned at the market would be a suitable book for Joseph to learn by, and one that he would find interesting as a man. When the reading improved enough, in Katherine's opinion, she found an odd piece of paper and made him copy the letters, so that writing very quickly became part of his curriculum. He loved it. Sitting there with Katherine, life was fast becoming something he had never dreamed of. She was becoming so much a part of his life that being without her was almost impossible to think about.

Summer was fast becoming over, and they had agreed to discuss the future then. Joseph wanted her to stay, but how could he ask her when she had gone through so much to realise her ambition. Katherine was going through the same torment. Unbeknown to Joseph, she too was wishing she did not have to go, but she had her promise to Martha to fulfil, and she knew that Joseph could not afford to keep her here; even if she worked they couldn't go on living at the cottage as it was. She was getting older, and would need a room of her own. Neither could she ask Joseph to leave his cottage; he loved it too much. So there was little alternative, but maybe she could stay just a little longer until Joseph could read and write properly, and then she would be able to write to him after she left. Thus the summer drifted into autumn, the days mellowed, the beach was still beautiful, and the weather still warm enough to sit outside.

One evening, after their reading and writing lessons, which Joseph now excelled in, was over, Katherine sat in the chair beside the fire with Pip at her feet, and with Joseph in his rocking chair, and she decided that the time had come to tell him her story. Joseph sat quietly, never taking his eyes from her face, as Katherine related it slowly word by word, leaving nothing out. At the end, she sighed and said, 'now you must understand why I can tell no one. I can't allow the possibility of Martha being charged with murder when it was all my fault.'

Joseph, horrified, and deeply moved by her utmost bravery, said, 'Katherine, how could it be your fault? You were but a child, and that cretin deserved to die. I would have killed him myself had I been there.'

Katherine said, 'I can't write to Martha until I am in England and have somewhere to live, in case the authorities, or worse still my father, gets to hear and discovers my whereabouts. In spite of my hatred for my father for what he did to my mother, I think he may look after Martha, because of his involvement.'

It took some time for Joseph to take in all that Katherine had told him. For one small person to go through what she had, and still be as gracious as she was, he found quite unbelievable.

The story of Katherine's mother had intrigued Joseph; he had a vague recollection of hearing about the tragic death of a young famous ballerina in a riding accident. General news reached the area by virtue of newspapers, but to Joseph who couldn't read, news of this nature only came from visitors to the area discussing it around the market, or in one of the big towns where he occasionally had to make a special delivery to a hotel. Of course there would be no knowledge of the daughter that had survived. Only Martha, Katherine's father, Alexi, and the mother of Cordelia would know, and they all had their reasons for keeping silent. It was all such a burden to put at the feet of a young girl, and she had to find out by herself. Thank god for Martha, he thought.

He himself felt a great thankfulness for the selfless and unconditional love this woman had had for this child, raised as her own, and then to have her torn from her side, in the cruellest of ways. He felt he wanted to go and find her and bring her here to Katherine to carry on caring for her. All then would be perfect, because he too could be there and watch the rest of her life blossom into happiness. He knew he couldn't betray Katherine's trust in him, but she must be curious, and also she had the address in Milan that she knew nothing about. Could he possibly take her to Milan one day, and maybe take her to the theatre where her mother had once danced? Could they find the address, and find out who lived there? Would it help her, or make her upset? The only way to find out was to ask her, and if she said she would like to go, then he would take her.

When Joseph approached Katherine with the proposition, she sat for a while and thought. She would like to see the place that made her mother so famous, but, never knowing her, she had no reason to think that it would help her situation. She would feel no love, no sadness at her loss, just a simple curiosity as to the life that brought her finally to her death, due to her attraction to a man that felt nothing for her, or for the fact that he had made a child with her, and it meant nothing to him, and, worse than that, he had married her best friend and had babies with her. To Katherine this was the ultimate insult. Then she thought that there was a great possibility that she would be seen in Milan, as that was the place she had been making for when she ran away. She voiced this to Joseph, and he said that her appearance could be altered.

He would talk to Lena, and see if she could help. Maybe they could get her hair cut, and dress her in some modern clothes, which they could, between them, make or purchase at low cost at the market. She would be with him, and anyone looking for her would be looking for someone who was alone, and anyway it was a long time ago now, and probably they had all decided that the search for her was just not worthwhile any more. Katherine thought that it was a chance she would never get again. She would never be able to come to Italy once she was in England. She would be working hard to pay for Martha's passage home. She agreed to go with Joseph, and she offered all the remaining money she had saved to pay for the journey. Joseph would not hear of it. They could travel quite cheaply on the early morning train that carried mail and the people who worked in the city. The earlier they arrived the more they could see, and they could return on the same train at night, coming back with the workers and returning mail.

Lena never asked questions of Katherine. She knew that something bad had happened to her, and she trusted Joseph implicitly to keep her safe, so the change of appearance happened. Her hair, that had been left to grow without ever being cut, was taken up to her shoulders, and cut into a pretty shape that surrounded her face with a halo of soft curls. They found for her a smart looking dress, with a pleated skirt, short sleeves, and a little white collar that sat around her neck in a pale shade of green check, and with it there was a neat jacket with two pockets, and three pearl buttons to fasten it. Lena suggested that she tucked her locket, that she would never remove, inside her dress so that it was not visible. Milan, like all large cities, had its fair share of villains who could likely snatch it from her neck.

All this completed, and the day chosen, they said their goodbyes to Pip, who looked quite dejected as they set off on their adventure. Katherine, feeling quite nervous although excited, held on to Joseph's hand as the huge train pulled into the station. He opened the door for her, and she stepped inside. How different she felt from the day when she skulked in a corner, frightened to death, hungry, and surrounded by what she remembered as evil-looking people from whom she could not escape. Now feeling every inch a lady, she sat by the window, and idly watched the fields go by as they made their way to the big city.

The journey wasn't a long one, and soon the green fields gave way to large buildings and grey streets. The sun seemed to disappear into the haze that hung over the tops of the buildings, and everything seemed dull in comparison to her beautiful beach and sea, and the cottage that she had come to love.

Joseph had found in the market, a street map of the centre of Milan, and so they made their way toward the theatre that would be their first port of call. They would not be allowed in to the theatre, but they could look at it, and look at the pictures outside. On the way, they would have an ice cream in one of the parlours that only sold ice cream. They sat at a table and a young girl came and brought a jug of water, and two glasses.

Katherine looked surprised, and so did Joseph, but evidently it was normal for water to be served, as ice cream in great quantities could make you thirsty, and a great quantity of ice cream was what they got, served in a balloon-shaped glass, in five colours with two triangle shaped biscuits stuck in the top. Katherine's eyes nearly popped out of her head.

'Enjoy,' said the young girl smiling as she left them to the task of eating them.

Joseph ate as if there was a time limit in which to finish, and Katherine savoured every mouthful, but in the end they both got to the bottom of the glass at the same time. A glass of water was quite a welcome addition, and they both found it refreshing and thirst quenching. Now they made their way to the theatre and, as they approached, Katherine had a strange feeling, and touched the locket that was safely tucked under her dress. They stood outside and looked at the pictures of ballerinas, and notices as to the ballet that was at the moment being performed; it was *Swan Lake*. Katherine thought how lovely that sounded, and she would try and find out what it was about. She knew there was a story to each ballet, but had never before thought about them. They walked from one picture to another, staying a while at each, reading the captions underneath, and peeping through the doors at the lush red interior to the theatre. Katherine was enthralled, and Joseph was happy just to stand and watch her face, wondering what emotions were going on inside her head, realising that it was her mother who had danced here just before she was born.

As they stood quietly before the picture of the prima ballerina who would dance at today's matinee performance, a woman left the theatre, idly looked as she passed them, and then stopped and stared. They didn't even know she was there, but she turned and ran back into the theatre, straight to the stage door office, and into the arms of the old stage door keeper. Her face as white as a sheet, she said, 'Aldo, I am sure I have just seen Maria's child. She is her absolute double, her face, her hair, her eyes, definitely her eyes, please come and look.'

Aldo, grabbing his coat, ran as fast as his old legs could carry him to the outside of the theatre, but they had gone, not a sign of them. They walked back and forth, around the theatre, but they had gone. Zara burst into tears. 'I know it was her,' she cried. 'I know it was.'

Aldo put his arm around her shoulder. 'Maybe it was, but we will never know. We will always have our memories and we will have to be satisfied with those.'

The next stop for Joseph and Katherine was to try and find the address that had been on the piece of paper. Joseph enquired at the postal building, and they gave directions, but said some of the houses were no longer being lived in. Eventually, having walked for what seemed many miles, they found the road, and then they found the house. The whole place was filthy, and it had curtains at each window which were stuck to the glass with dirt. The front door was painted a sickly looking dark pink, and there appeared to be no one there. A couple of houses along, sitting on a crumbling old wall, was a woman who could only be described as a drunken old soul who was lost to this world, but not ready to enter the next. Joseph asked her if any one lived in the house, and she leered at him through eyes that were mere slits, surrounded by bruising. The whole picture made Katherine feel sick. 'No one lives there,' she said. 'I used to, but they threw me out. I haven't seen any one there for years. The door's open, you can look if you like.'

Joseph looked at Katherine, and she shook her head in disgust. Whoever was there, and whatever it was that related it to her mother, Katherine did not want to know. 'Please can we go home, Joseph. Thank you for bringing me and showing me the theatre; it was lovely, and I think that perhaps my mother was happy when she was dancing. I will keep her shoes and her locket always, and I think now that I would like to think of her in these her days as a dancer, and not as the mother who thought more of a man than she did of the child she held in her body.'

Joseph looked at the child that stood before him, and he felt a protective love for her that he had never felt for anything or anybody in his life. He couldn't quite come to terms with the feelings, but he knew they would stay with him for a lifetime, with or without her being there. She had planted an eternal seed of love in his heart that no one would be able to kill. As for Katherine, she just wanted to be back in her cottage, getting breakfast for Joseph, and waking up to Pip licking her awake, so that she would be ready for her lovely happy days at market with Lena.

In fact all her days were happy, the days at the market, where she was becoming known as the young lady who sews. Her days with Joseph and Pip were so happy that she just wanted to jump up and down with the sheer joy of living.

The long fingers of autumn were beginning to stretch across the land, the sky was a little less bright, and the sun a little less hot, but still it was so pleasant. Katherine had tended the garden, then she had scrubbed the path with Joseph's large broom that he used to sweep out the boat and clean the jetty with. He thought her efforts were a bit tough on the bristles of his brush, but he forgave her that. The flowers were blooming with her gentle care, and they formed a guard of honour down the path to the front door. She never got tired of looking at them, and felt proud of herself for creating the garden.

Talk of her leaving was raised many times, but always something was afoot to defer the decision, and every time both her and Joseph secretly and silently breathed a sigh of relief. Lena's husband was going to be at sea for much of the Christmas period, and it was arranged for Lena, the children, Joseph, Katherine, and Pip, to spend Christmas day together at Lena's house. They all gathered up as much food as they could. Katherine did the best, as most of the stallholders by this time, had taken to her, and they scouted around the market to pick up some very tasty morsels that would add a touch of luxury to any Christmas table. They all had a wonderful day, and hugged one another at the end of it, when Joseph, Katherine, and Pip, now the proud owner of a large lamb bone by courtesy of the local butcher, left to go back to the cottage.

Winter finally caught up with them, and Joseph would come home with the cold from the bitter winds penetrating his clothing. He would be soaking wet from the rain and the spray which raised the water into waves, and washed across his bow. Katherine would have hot water for him to wash in, instead of the cold to which he had become accustomed in his life alone before she was there. She could cook simple things, and all they had were simple ingredients, so that was never a problem. She had become adept at making stews and soups. Vegetables at the market were cheap, and Katherine would wander round at the end of the day, and beg a few leftover items. An odd piece of meat would find itself in her bag, and she would pop that into the pot with some of the vegetables, peel some potatoes which were always available, and they had a tasty meal.

Winter had always been Joseph's worst time. He hated the cold wet weather, the early hours to market, and the lateness of coming home in the dark, but now he whistled as he walked down the path to the cottage. The lamp was always lit. He made sure it had oil in it before he left, and had taught Katherine to light the wick very carefully with a long spill. She also managed to pull the lamp up on its chain, and secure it to a hook in the wall. They spent companionable time together reading or writing, or just sitting. Joseph would tell her stories of when he was young, and later when he spent his days with his grandfather. She gradually elaborated on the things that had happened to her, and her life with Martha. Winter turned to Spring, and Katherine realised that it was a year ago when all the terrible things happened that prompted her to run away, and when fortune had smiled on her, and miraculously brought her here to Joseph.

It was on one Spring evening, when Joseph came home and saw her sitting on the rock at the end of the beach, where she frequently sat to think, that he wandered over to find her crying. She would not talk to him, but begged him to fetch Lena for her as she needed to talk to her. He tried to placate her, but she could not be pacified, until, in the end, Joseph set off to see if Lena would come over while he sat with her children. He left Pip with her, and as he disappeared she buried her head in Pip's furry back and sobbed. Lena eventually arrived and came and sat by her, took her hand, and asked what was wrong. Katherine said that she was ill, and couldn't tell Joseph, because she was too frightened as to what would happen to her. Then she told Lena that she was bleeding, and couldn't move from the rock.

About half an hour later, Lena returned to a worried Joseph and told him that today his little Katherine had become a lady. She had explained everything to her, and told her all the possibilities of growing into a woman, so that she understood fully all the implications. She had made her change her clothes, and would take the soiled ones away to wash, and she had left her with plenty of protection. She would learn as each month passed that it really wasn't as bad as it seemed at the moment. She also pointed out to Joseph that the time had come when he should seriously consider what should happen to her. She would now need a little more privacy.

Joseph couldn't take it all in. She was no longer the child that he had come to love, as a child. She was an adult. How could he allow himself to love her? Now it was his turn to let the tears fall. When Lena had gone, and for a few minutes when he was alone, he succumbed to emotions that he never thought he would feel. A while later, when Katherine came quietly through the door, she walked up to him and put her arms around his waist, rested her head on his torso. For a moment, he stood there, and then his arms went around her and he held her tight, as they both cried.

As the year went on, and still no decision was made for Katherine to go, Lena was worried by the closeness of the two. Joseph she knew was an honourable man, and no scandal would be started. To all but her, everyone was sure she was his niece. Katherine was the worry. She had become a calm, happy young woman, and her eyes shone with happiness. Lena felt that Katherine was feeling the beginnings of a physical attraction to Joseph, and it worried her. Joseph had taken on board what Lena had said about Katherine's need for privacy. He had bought some thick material used for making sails, and had hooked it up outside of the nets, so that she still had the pretty drapes, but had the privacy on the outside. Her tent had also a large flap that could be pulled across, and tied on the inside.

Katherine reached her fourteenth birthday, as the end of her second year at the cottage came near. All her fears of being found were now forgotten, and the memories of her thirteenth year were fading fast. Living with Joseph was easy. He held her to no time limit. He never asked again for her to make a decision, and leave him for a new life. He was as ever content in her company, and her growing into a woman did not present him with any problems. She handled it just as he expected her to do, with down-to-earth acceptance. It had been a good year. His fish yield had been high, and he had gained a contract to supply fish to a new hotel that had been built close to the lake. Katherine had taken to making children's aprons and bibs for babies, and Lena had allowed her a corner of her stall to sell her goods for her own profit. For the first time in her life she felt as if she was a person in her own right, making decisions, and being able to contribute to the upkeep of the cottage, and supply some of the food that Joseph had been struggling to provide ever since she landed on his doorstep. Life was good, and continued to be as the year ended, and the next one began.

Katherine had grown in size, and was developing into a very shapely young woman, but nothing seemed to have any effect on the way she behaved and presented herself to her customers and, in spite of herself, how she acted in the presence of Joseph. She was still the child who loved to run along the beach, hair flying, and skirt above her knees so as not to impede the speed with which her legs could carry her. She loved to walk along with Joseph, and search for stones and shells to decorate the garden. She would sometimes take his hand, and swing his arm in a way that a child would, but sometimes she would be very shy, not stay too close to him, sit quietly and read a book on her own, instead of reading with him. There were many times when Joseph felt her nearness, and was disturbed by it. Then she would look at him and give that impish grin of hers as she passed and dug her fingers into his ribs, to send him jumping in the air. He would retaliate, and pretend to set Pip upon her, much to her delight, as Pip bounded toward her, jumped into her arms and proceeded to kill her with a hundred licks, as Joseph had instructed him to do.

The year passed by quickly. The summer that year had been very hot, sometimes unbearable, and sometimes with storms of great proportions, bringing torrential rain and thunder. One night, the rain had started early, washing away the heat of the day, and giving life to the parched earth, making the drooping flowers straighten their stems and turn their faces to the cool comfort of its wetness. Katherine had waited for the light from Joseph's boat to appear around the headland before she went and prepared some food. She knew he would be tired. The variations of a stormy day always took its toll on the fishermen, and Joseph was no exception. He pulled in the boat, removed the crates, and salted the fish before dragging them to the shelter of the boathouse ready for market in the morning. He entered the cottage and, as always, was thankful to see Katherine there, busy at the fire, and to see the table laid with the nice white cloth that she had found on a market stall, and given to Joseph for Christmas. He was tired, and said very little as he ate his meal before washing with the water that Katherine had placed by his bed for him.

Katherine went to her bedroom while he prepared for bed, and then as soon as he was in bed and lying facing the wall, she crept out and cleared the table, and quietly washed the pots and pans. She then took herself to bed. Pip had stayed in the boathouse; he sometimes liked it there in the heat of a summer night. Katherine drifted into a deep sleep. In the early hours, the beginnings of a storm had woken her. The lightning was vivid, and lit the room with its white light, followed seconds later with a mighty crash of thunder. Katherine had witnessed many storms, but this one was as bad as any she had seen. Soon Pip was yelping at the door, and Katherine opened it to find him shaking and wet from his walk from the boathouse. He scampered in and made for the fire, hiding under Joseph's chair. Katherine went back to bed and lay there, waiting for each flash, and then the thunder, and wishing it would all stop. It didn't stop, but got progressively worse. The sea was now roaring in and dashing itself against the rocks around the boathouse.

Joseph, woken by all the noise, got up, put on his oilskin and wellingtons, and went out into the night. Katherine was petrified. He had not said anything, just gone with a scowl on his face. He went round to the boathouse, and while it was safe from the sea, there was always a chance that some of the water could reach his crates of fish. With this in mind, he moved them further into the dryness of the space at the back of the boat, and returned to the cottage. Katherine, now fully awake, was frightened in case anything happened to Joseph. When he came in she was near to tears, and wanted to run to him, but the look on his face told her not to. He took off his clothes, and boots, and got back into bed. Katherine lay there, sleepless and frightened. The whole cottage seemed to shake, the one window loosened its latch, and the door rattled with the wind that screamed like a banshee. Katherine sat huddled in the bed. She pulled the sheepskin covers around her and put her fingers in her ears.

Now the storm was overhead, and there was no space between lightning and thunder. Pip howled, and Katherine put her head underneath the covers. It was the last straw when they heard a crash outside, and then a splash of water, and the sound of metal hitting the gravel near the house. Katherine screamed, jumped from her bed, and flew toward Joseph. As he leaped out of bed, she threw herself into his arms, cold and shivering, and to Joseph it was as if it were the night he found her in the water. He caught her folded her in his arms, and rocked her back and forth, stroking her head, and whispering, 'don't be afraid, I'm here.' Gently he pushed her away, and said, 'I have to go and see what has happened, stay here.'

She followed him to the door, and could see through the driving rain that the top of the well had come away. It had loosened the handle on the winch, to send the bucket falling out of control into the water below, and the handle had ripped itself away from the chain mechanism, and ended up landing on the ground, broken and useless.

Joseph shook his head, and turned back to Katherine who was now shaking, standing in the doorway. He walked to her, took her hands, and pulled her back inside the cottage. She was in his arms, and he was kissing her hair. She lifted her face to him, and kissed his lips. He moved his head, but kept a hold of her. Her young body did not move from his arms, and he held her close, his hands gently moving across her back, taking his own comfort from her closeness. She responded to his caress, and his body found itself on fire; the need for her was overwhelming, and he wanted her so desperately that every inch of him cried out in agony for the love of her.

He walked with her in his arms back to her bed and gently released her as he said, 'I can't do this, Katrina. I want to so much, but you are too young, and I don't want you to hate me in the morning. Go to sleep, and tomorrow we will talk. We will mend the well top, and believe me that you and I will be glad that tonight ended like this.'

The storm had abated, and Katherine and Joseph fell into their own sleep, and their own dreams. When Katherine awoke the next morning, she listened and heard nothing. Pip was not there, and Joseph had gone too. She sat up, realising that she had overslept so that now she would not be able to get to the market in time to spread out her goods for the first buyers who always came early. She was a little annoyed. Joseph had always said he would take her, but only if she was ready, which meant she could have a ride on the cart with the crates, but she thought that this morning of all mornings he would have woken her. Now she would have to find an excuse for not being there. Lena would ask questions, and she would have to lie, and say it was the storm that frightened her, and kept her awake half the night. The excuse of course would be the truth, but it was the underlying reasons that worried Katherine. What had Joseph said? He of course would not have told Lena anything, but he would have had to give a reason, as she had never missed a day since she started selling her own sewing. The baby bibs and aprons had become quite a success for her. Should she perhaps stay at home and just say that she didn't feel too well, and wait for Joseph to come back and clarify his story to her. She decided that this was what she would do.

The day was agony for her. She dwelled upon the events of last night, turned them over and over in her mind, until she felt quite sick. What had Joseph really felt? How was he feeling now? The feelings she had felt last night, frightened her a little, because she realised that she had encouraged him by kissing him, instead of just accepting his arms as a comfort against the terrifying ferocity of the storm. She remembered what had happened at the woodman's cottage, although she knew that she had done nothing then, it was all him, and she had fought and screamed for her life there, but with Joseph it was so different. She loved being with him, and now she was a woman she guessed that she could love him in spite of her young age. She would be prepared to stay with him as long as he loved her too.

With this in mind, she decided to wait for Joseph, and tell him what she thought, and see what his reaction would be. She thought about Martha, but decided not to do anything about her yet, until everything was settled here. She began to see her dream materialising. Thinking back to last night she remembered Joseph calling her Katrina, although she had always called herself Katherine to him, as that was what Martha named her, but she

liked Joseph's use of her name, especially as last night was the first time
he had used it. The day dragged on, and doing all the chores in the cottage
and garden only served to let her dream about Joseph, and the possibility
of a life shared with him. As the time drew near for his return, her bravery
wilted, and she began to fear that she had assumed too much in her
reasoning.

Joseph was having much the same day. This was the reason for his
early awakening, and his deftness of moving around quietly, as he watched
her sleep. His emotions were still running high. He had never in his life felt
this way; she had come into his life, a child close to the edge of death, and
now in less than two years she was turning his world upside down. He
knew now that a decision had to be made, and made quickly. He could not
live with her under his roof and be with her like the Katherine she was
until a short while ago. Now she was his Katrina, and whatever the outcome
of the next few days, she would live within his heart for ever. He had a
good day despite his mind being in turmoil. The fishing was excellent and
the catch had outweighed most of the landings for that day, so that it took
him much longer to salt and stack it than it usually did.

Finally, as he headed for the cottage, he caught a glimpse of her peeping
from behind the door, and then quickly stepping inside so as not to be seen
waiting for him. She smiled somewhat hesitantly, and then proceeded to
serve his dinner, which she had carefully prepared. A beef and vegetable
pot, with some diced potatoes, and an onion that she had grown herself in
the herb garden where Joseph used to grow his carrots. These she continued
to grow under Joseph's tuition, so as to ensure their sweetness was what
he had told her. Joseph ate, and she watched as she slowly and with little
relish ate hers. When it all was eaten, and Pip had been served what was
left over, they both sat in front of the fire, knowing that the time had come
to talk. Katherine waited for Joseph, as she thought it should be him to
have first chance to speak; it was his life, and his house.

'Katrina,' Joseph said quietly, 'I left without you this morning because
I was deep in thought, and had to sort things in my mind before I spoke to
you again. I told Lena that you were very scared last night, with good
reason, so that I left you to sleep this morning, and I didn't know whether
or not you would be coming to the market, but I was sure you would be
fine tomorrow.'

'Thank you, Joseph, yes I was scared, and I was frightened for you
when you went outside,' answered Katherine.

'How do you feel now about last night?' asked Joseph.

Katherine never had been one to hedge; she was always straight and honest with her answers, even when she had done something wrong and Martha had questioned her reasons for doing it, she always found this was the best way, as trying to wriggle out of something only got you in deeper trouble in the end, so Katherine straightened her back and said, 'Joseph, I love you. I know it sounds silly, but even if you feel it can't be a grown up love, I will still love you always. I would be so happy to stay with you, if you will have me, and if as I grow older, you could love me too, I would spend all of my life caring for you. I have been here two years now, and in another two years I would be nearly old enough to marry you. I would be so happy to do that. Two years has passed so quickly, and perhaps in another two I would be able to write to Martha, and perhaps she would consider coming here instead of going to England. My father would have no need for me by then. Please say you will consider what I have just said; you may have time if you want it to think. I understand, and I hope you are not angry with me for telling you. I have burdened you so much of late with the story of my life. Perhaps you would rather I left, and if so I will go, but I pray you will consider. One more thing Joseph, I loved you calling me Katrina.'

Joseph sat wide-eyed at her revelations. 'I will need some time by myself to consider all that you have just told me. I will go to the boathouse where I can be alone and go over all of it, section by section, and when I have done that I will give you an honest answer, just as you did for me.' He then got up to move and, with Pip at his heel, he made for the door. 'Katrina,' he said softly, 'The answer may not come tonight, or tomorrow night, but I will answer you, and the answer I give, I hope you will accept.'

Katherine had a tiny tearful smile on her lips as Joseph left the cottage. She looked around, and could not explain, even to herself, the way she felt about this place, and wanting to spend the rest of her life here. It shone now from floor to ceiling, and wall to wall and, as crude as its construction was, to her it was a magical place; to go away and leave it would break her heart, she knew that, but would not admit it to herself, and certainly not to Joseph if that should be his decision. He did not return to the cottage that night, and neither did Pip, who would stay with his master without question. Katherine felt restless. Could she dare to go to the boathouse, and at least ask Joseph if he would like a drink? No she couldn't, not under any circumstances, she thought, and so she went to bed.

She would be up in the morning early, and go to market with Joseph as if nothing had occurred. She wouldn't mention the conversation at all. It would be difficult to discuss ordinary things now like they used to. Katherine felt grown up. She had had to do adult things herself at a very tender age. She had made decisions that some grown-ups would not have had the courage to do. She had been terrified, and had had to carry on, and when she thought she was going to die, Joseph had appeared like a guardian angel and saved her from destruction. Yet still she knew she was a child, and had to take that into account when he gave her his answer.

The answer came on the last day of the week. Joseph had decided to take the Saturday off. He had managed to earn about twice the normal amount of money that usually came from his deliveries to the hotel, and he felt that under the circumstances a day off would be appropriate, come what may after the result of the conversation that would take place this evening after supper.

Katherine childishly washed and dressed herself. She wondered what to wear, and decided that Joseph might be embarrassed if she tried to look too old, so she wore her favourite trousers, and a white high necked jumper that suited her new shorter haircut. She sat quietly while he finished his mug of hot coffee that always ended his meal. He pulled up his chair to the fire, and bade her to do the same. This was where they always sat and had the conversations that they both loved.

'Katrina,' Joseph started, as he brought his eyes up to look directly into her eyes.

'Yes, Joseph,' Katherine answered, somewhat hesitantly.

'Katrina,' he repeated, 'there is nothing more wonderful that I can think of than to have you stay with me.' Katherine leaped up and made to go to him. 'No, Katrina, you must sit and listen until I have finished saying everything that I need to say to you. That would be simple, but it is not simple. If we lived together here in this cottage, feeling the way that we obviously do at this moment about one another, things could go terribly wrong. You could end up hating me by the time you are old enough to marry me. I, as a man, Katrina, have not had very much experience of the wiles and needs of a woman. However I do know the needs of a man, and for you that may prove to be the worst thing you have ever known. I may hurt you when my moods are bad, as they are sometimes. I may ask you to do things that you do not want to do, and you may refuse to do them, and make me angry, or you may do them to please me, and hate me for what you may call my inconsideration. Living with me now is easy because you are your own person, and doing all the things that you want to do, but living with me with the future prospect of being my wife, and with the knowledge that you will want a more intimate relationship than we have now, and the knowledge that I will not be able to live with my feelings for another two years at least, means the whole situation will be impossible.

'So, Katrina, I have a proposition for you. There are three options that could be considered; the third of which would be very hard for both of us, so at the moment I will leave that one out of the question. The first option is that you stay in the cottage and do exactly the same as you do now, the only difference being that I would take my sleeping area to the boathouse, and you would sleep here. We would spend time together as we do now, and talk, laugh, and play as we do now, and if, in two years, we both feel the same as we do now, we will discuss our future together. The other option would be, and I have to tell you that I have discussed this with Lena, and she is happy to help us, and happy that we are going to make a sensible decision for both of us, that life would be the same as the first option, but that you would go and stay with her, and look after her children in the evenings so that she could get on and do some work, and sleep at her house, getting up in the morning, feeding the children, and seeing them to school before going to the market. We would still have time together, and carry on enjoying our present relationship, with you still in charge of the house and garden, having plenty of time for yourself.

'The third option would be that you left me and the cottage, and kept to your plan to go to England. I would help you find a way of getting there. I don't know how, but I would do it. As you said to me likewise, I give you time to consider my proposition, and when you are ready I will accept your decision, but I will not enter into any other options. These I know are the right ones for you, more than for me, my Katrina.'

Katherine reluctantly agreed to take the option of going to Lena's for evenings and nights. She would of course have to go back to the cottage when Lena's husband was home from the sea, but that was not often enough for Katherine. Life once again had an air of contentment around the cottage, both for Katherine and for Joseph. Katherine spent her life living for the days that she could spend with Joseph, and Joseph for his part made many plans for days out whenever he could. The garden overflowed with flowers and vegetables. It gained a reputation, and

Katherine found herself having visitors who wanted to witness all the glory of a garden that flowered in spite of the saltiness showered on it by the winds from the shore. She was only happy because she held the dream that one day it would all be hers and Joseph's. They spent very little time alone together, and only now and then would they touch hands and smile at each other. Katherine's fourteenth year was fast moving on, and when it reached its end there would only be one year left until she was sixteen.

Her feelings had changed in the last few months. She knew now that she loved Joseph much more than she did when the night of the storm started all this. Joseph sometimes looked pale. He was working too hard, and she knew he was secretly missing her company, as she was his, but they kept to their pact and never mentioned that night or the repercussions. Lena was proud of them both. She knew all about young love, and how difficult it was to be without a loved one even for one day. She spent long hours talking to Katherine, and by now Katherine had told her everything, about her life, about her being witness to murder, about her days without food, about walking and running away from it all, until she landed on Joseph.

Staying with Lena was easy enough. The children were fun and she enjoyed doing little jobs for her; it sort of paid in some small way for the kindness that she had always shown her. She shared a bedroom with one of the girls, which to her was strange, but not as strange as not being in her beautiful tent, cosy in her skins, and surrounded by the very few treasures that she had amassed. She missed Joseph every hour of the day, she always did, but she knew that at sometime in the evening, the tiny white dot of light would come around the headland, and grow larger and brighter, and Joseph would bring home his catch for the day. Now she could only imagine him, and hoped that he had liked what she had left simmering above the flames on the old stove for his supper.

She saw him in the mornings when he brought his fish to market. Always he had a bright smile for her, but she thought he looked tired, and she wished she could go home to the cottage and sit with him one evening by the fire and read to him just as she used to. If she suggested it, he would just take himself off to the boathouse and spend the night there, she knew that, and so never made any such suggestion. Once when Lena's husband came home, the younger daughter who had been sleeping with her mother, had to return to the bedroom she shared with her sister, and Katherine, much to her joy, went home to stay with Pip and Joseph. She made each moment precious to herself, and she was sure to Joseph as well. They read, and talked, laughed a lot, and when the hour got late, Joseph would be the one to say 'Good night' and retire to the massive bed that took up a large corner space. He undressed in the outhouse, and quietly slipped under the covers when he returned without any further contact. They had agreed that he should not sleep in the boathouse which had been an option originally, and Joseph had been glad. The boathouse was such a cold, dark place, and his makeshift bed was uncomfortable to say the least. Katherine for her part was just so happy to sense his nearness, and just lay there listening to his breathing until she finally fell asleep.

The pattern of their lives changed little as summer turned to autumn. Katherine's time with Joseph made little difference to the decision that she had agreed to with Joseph. She was secretly hoping that he would change his mind after a few months of not having her around. The evenings that they spent together became rather more regular, as Lena's husband seemed to be spending more time at home with his family. Lena had to agree with Katherine that Joseph and her had kept to their agreement faithfully, but she was still worried by Katherine's feelings. Katherine would confide in her regularly, which Lena liked. It left her confident that at the moment all was going according to plan. Time was moving on and she hoped that they could both see another year through as this year had gone, and then Katherine would be nearly old enough to make a final decision whether to give the rest of her life to Joseph.

Lena felt that Katherine had already made her decision, but she felt that she had not given enough thought to Joseph's way of life, and whether it would accommodate a young woman, and probably children, without a lot of changes on his part. He was still a young man, and quite naive in his own way. He was undeniably kind, and it was obvious that he adored Katherine, but she had come to him in such a way as to bring out the protective and loving side in him, which in Lena's opinion would have been there if Katherine had stayed the child that he saw emerging from the drowning piece of flesh that he had pulled from the water. Lena, however, had misjudged Joseph, and the love he felt for her now was far removed from that which he felt nearly two years ago. The child had become a young woman whom he longed to hold in his arms, as he had done on the night of the storm.

The strength of the feeling sometimes frightened him, and it was one evening during their reading to each other, when Joseph got tangled up between his Italian and English, which sent Katherine unto uncontrolled giggles. It was totally infectious, and Joseph, caught up in the hilarity, took her face in his hands, and kissed her. She broke away quickly, and then seeing the frightened look on his face, she returned his kiss. He pulled her into his arms, and kissed the tears of laughter from her eyes; she clung to him, childishly to begin with, and then relaxing against him, kissed his face, and his tear-filled eyes. Her arms reached up and stole around his neck, until they were locked together in an embrace that felt as if it could never end. They found themselves on the pile of skins that she had arranged in her tent. They lay together, and shyly looked at one another; they hugged and kissed and confessed their feelings.

Joseph sat up and said to Katherine, 'I am so sorry. I shouldn't have started this, and now we must stop, because you are still too young.'

'I love you, Joseph, can't you see that?' cried Katherine.

'Yes, I believe you do,' answered Joseph, 'but I can't yet tell you how I feel. There are many years between us, and you, although you are the perfect woman, are still a child in years. We have to wait until our agreed time of consent is reached.' Joseph then kissed her tenderly, and rose gently from the bed, pulled her to her feet and said, 'wait a while longer, my Katrina, until all our decisions can be made together. It will be difficult for both of us until then.'

Katherine was now sitting in her chair, with Pip licking her leg and looking up at her as she quietly let the tears fall. Joseph in his turn picked up his bedding and made for the boathouse, turning once to Katherine to whisper, 'I'm sorry.'

She replied, 'Don't be.'

The next day, Lena noticed the red-ringed eyes, as Katherine quietly got on with her work behind the stall. She did not question her, and neither did she get any answers. Joseph, as well, seemed quieter than usual and looked tired and pale, Lena thought. The night was gradually forgotten, and life returned to the normal routine. Lena's husband was on a long trip again, and so the possibility of the times when Katherine and Joseph could be alone together at the cottage became few and far between.

It was winter now; Katherine's fifteenth birthday had been celebrated. She was becoming a beautiful young woman, the sight of which had not been lost on the local stallholders at the market. 'She is going to break someone's heart soon,' was the comment that was overheard by both Lena and Joseph one morning, who both looked at each other and smiled. Joseph had been working hard. He had gained more business from a new hotel that had been recently opened. He had been staying out on the boat much longer, and both he and Pip had been spending some nights at the boathouse to save more time by being ready to go earlier in the morning. Katherine was only seeing him in the mornings at the market, and was feeling unhappy. Lena, try as she may, could not make her see that Joseph was working hard so that they could afford a future together in another year. They still were able to have at least one day at the weekend together, but that was all of them, Lena, the children, Pip, and Joseph. This was not what Katherine wanted.

It was one morning, when Katherine felt particularly low, that Joseph didn't turn up at the market. He could of course have gone to the hotel first, but he did not usually do this on a Saturday. Midday came and still no sight of him, and when it was time to close down the stall, both Lena and Katherine were showing signs of worry. Lena, putting her arm around Katherine, said, 'I will go home and get the children, and I will come with you to the cottage to see if anything is wrong.'

Katherine knew that something was wrong, she could feel it. She was frightened, as she was the night of the storm when she thought Joseph was hurt. They arrived at the cottage to find it in darkness. The door locked. No sign of Joseph, or of Pip. They looked around the end of the sea wall, and there was no boat at anchor. They looked up at the boathouse, and that was all in darkness too, except for a tiny white light that was reflecting on one of the walls. Katherine called 'Joseph', but there was no answer, and then they heard a whine. 'That is Pip,' cried Katherine, who raced up to the boathouse, never thinking, as she did the first time she made her way up the slippery slope, that she might fall. Up she went. Seeing the boat there gave her a sense of relief, and then Pip came hurtling out from behind it, jumping and barking as he ran back and forth. By this time, Lena had reached the top, telling the children to wait in the garden. Katherine found Joseph slumped over the edge of the boat, retching, and shivering, and looking pale as death. 'Joseph, whatever is wrong,' she cried, cradling his head in her arms.

Lena came over to them and said, 'Katherine, he has a fever. We have to get him down to the cottage, and get him into bed, and warm. Can you manage to help me lift his body into one of the crates, and we can tie one of the ropes to it and lower him down the slope? Between them they pushed a crate under his body that was hanging from the boat, and then with Katherine holding on to it, Lena pulled on his arms until he finally was sitting in the crate, legs and arms hanging over the side, head falling down upon his chest. The weight of his body made the crate so heavy to move, and they knew if they let go, both Joseph and crate would go crashing to the bottom. Lena managed to pass the rope through one of the rowlocks on the boat, so that they would be able better to release it more slowly. With Katherine guiding the crate and Lena, leaning against the boat for support, holding on to the rope, they slowly lowered Joseph to the ground.

Once the crate had levelled out and Joseph was sitting in an upright, if slumped, position, Lena and Katherine, standing each side of him, each with one foot against the crate to steady it and taking an arm each, proceeded to try and lift him. This was an impossible task as he was just too heavy, and had little power in his legs to help them. They decided that they would have to leave him in the crate and somehow pull him to the door. Pip by this time was becoming impatient and was trying to take part in the operation and causing chaos by trying to nuzzle his way into the crate too. The two girls, in spite of the seriousness of the situation, began to see a funny side to it all and started to giggle. At this moment, Joseph, suddenly aware of what was happening, started to groan, and began to try and heave himself out of the crate. With little success, and weakened by the effort, he started to cough and retch again, but the girls had caught hold of his arms as he tried to lift himself and now had him in a vice like grip. Slowly but surely they moved toward the door.

Once there, it was easier as he could help himself by grabbing the sides of the door frame and levering himself inside. Katherine, managing to slip under one arm, stood in front of him and steadied him as Lena came through the door. Now all that remained was to get him to his bed. They didn't have time to throw off the covers before his body landed, and so they scooped up his legs and turned him so that he lay in a reasonable position. They both straightened their backs, and looked at one another, worried by what they saw, but knowing that he was a strong man. If they could get him warm and get some liquid down him, it would be a start on the road to his recovery. Lena brought in her children, and set them to task, getting more logs for the fire, and filling the pot to get some hot water, while Pip just sat at his master's side and looked hopeful. Lena went in to action, rummaging through the odd vegetables that were sitting at the side of the fire. 'Onions, I need onions,' she said, mainly to herself.

Katherine was frantically trying to remove some of Joseph's clothing which was wet and clinging to his fever-ravaged body. She thought the best thing to do, to start with, was to remove his heavy wellingtons, and his socks which were soaking wet. He had obviously fallen into the water in his effort to get out of the boat and pull it to safety. He was helpless; his arms and legs were too weak now to help. How he had ever managed to attach the boat to the winch, and pull it up to the boathouse she would never know, and she doubted that he would ever remember. Lena, seeing her difficulty and having already thrown some chopped up onions with some herbs, bacon, and some potatoes in to the pot, she came over to help Katherine.

'Grab his legs and pull him around so that they hang over the edge of the bed,' said Lena. With that done, Lena stood with her back to the patient, and, with Katherine facing her, they both took a firm hold on one of his boots and pulled and pulled to no avail. Joseph was moaning again. Lena looked at Katherine, and began to smile. Katherine in response let out a not very ladylike comment which sent Lena into more of the same until the two of them collapsed beside Joseph, trying to control their laughter, but ending up with tears of laughter running down their cheeks. This over and with an anxious look at Joseph, Lena said, 'you sit beside Joseph and pull his trousers from the boot and hold on to the top of his socks, then pull as hard as you can, and while you are doing this I will pull on his boot.' Lena ending up sitting on the floor with an upturned boot issuing water from its depths, and Katherine being able to peel off the sticking white socks from his feet. They cheered at the success of their plan, and repeated it on the second foot. Finally they were able to dry his feet and legs on a towel that Lena thoughtfully had hung in front of the fire.

While they had him half way between sitting and laying, the pair of them pulled the jumpers over his head, and for as much as Lena did not totally agree with what had to come next, between them they removed the rest of his clothes, rolled him over on to a clean warm sheet, and finally, drying him, and covering him with the covers that Katherine had used for her bed, laid him down to rest. He was now shaking uncontrollably. Lena went back to the broth that she was brewing. She had dealt with this kind of fever before, and it usually came from tiredness of overwork, and alternate coldness and overheating.

Joseph had been throwing himself into everything that he did in order to earn enough money to marry Katherine when she reached the legal age. It had all become too much, and his body had reacted badly, forcing a fever upon him that could last for a good few weeks if not treated properly.

It required bed rest, and liquid meals which needed to be taken every two to three hours He needed to be kept warm in spite of his feeling hot and wanting to throw off the covers. His covers would need changing regularly, and this would mean continual washing and replacing. He would also need to be sponged down and dried continually. The fever would get worse, and would reach a pitch that Lena warned would be quite frightening if you had not witnessed it before. Once the crisis was reached, only then would the fever begin to abate, and the patient would begin to recover. He was a strong young man, and should eventually return to full health. Katherine listened quietly, knowing that she would stay beside him day and night, wash him and feed him, if Lena would help with the supply of the necessary liquids that she said would aid his recovery. She would see that he drank every drop, even if it smelled most horrid in her opinion.

So began the fight to get Joseph well and back on his feet again. With all that was happening, the catch that Joseph had come in with that night had been forgotten, and was left on the boat until one of the local fishermen agreed to go and get rid of it, wash his boat down, and get it ready for him to return. He also agreed to supply the hotels that Joseph had gained trade with, until he was better. All this being agreed, Joseph just had to lie there and be waited on by Katherine and Lena. He was not a good patient, and got grumpy when Katherine would not allow him to sit up before she thought that he ought to. Katherine, on the other hand, was living her life in a way that she knew was all that she ever wanted. She tirelessly washed, and cleaned, and fed Joseph with his gruel, with alarming accuracy that even Lena was astounded. She would lay with him in the bad times when he was shivering, and shaking. He held her in his arms, and only let go when she insisted that the time had come to feed, or be changed.

When he slept, she sat and watched him and, when the crisis came, it was every bit as awful as Lena said it would be. She cradled him in her arms as his breathing became laboured, and she cried as her tears mingled with the sweat that formed in large beads on his forehead and face. She kept his body dry, so that it would not grow cold from the surrounding air, and she kept him warm with her own body until finally in the early hours of a Saturday morning, two weeks from the day that she found him, the fever broke, and his breathing eased. He opened his eyes slowly, and he smiled at her; a bedraggled picture she made, he thought, not so different from the child he had picked up nearly dead so long ago. Pip who had never moved from the side of Joseph's bed throughout the whole time, except when nature demanded, gave a little wag of his tail, and gently stuck his nose into Katherine's hand as if to say, 'Is it O.K. now?'

Katherine patted his head, and lifted him up so that he could sit next to his master, and witness his return to them. The terrible fever had left him, but the weakness of his limbs prevented him from moving from the bed. He slept most of the time, but now it was a peaceful sleep allowing his body to recoup the strength that had been sapped in the last two weeks. Katherine stayed with him, read to him when he was restless, and when the coldness invaded his body as it did often during the days of his recovery, she would lay down beside him and provide warmth and comfort. Lena would come by often, and together she and Katherine weaned him off the liquid diet, that had kept him alive, on to some soft solids. They would cook him a poached egg with small pieces of soft bread without the crusty parts, or some rice soaked overnight and made with the creamiest part of the milk which Lena would make and bring down to be reheated on the stove. Lena never questioned Katherine about her nights alone with Joseph; she assumed that he was too ill to even think about their previous relationship, and the promises that they had made.

It was a night after he had suffered a bad day. He was aching, and he was worrying now about his business, and how soon he would be able to get back to his fishing. Katherine sat beside him on the bed, propped up by a pillow with her head against the wall, listening to his ramblings. She gently put her arms around him, and pulled his head down to rest against her, she twined his thick hair around her finger and announced that tomorrow she would cut his hair, and trim the beard that had now grown around his chin, soft and curly. He laughed a deep throaty laugh, and protested with passion that no woman would get her hands on the hair that protected his face from the ravages of wind and rain. Katherine said no more, but she knew that it would happen, and that he would be far the better for it.

As he lay with his head encased in her arms, she let her fingers wander idly around his face, gently touching his ears and nose until just her index finger came to rest upon his closed lips. Placing a small silent kiss against her finger he raised his head to look at her. She matched his look with one equal in sensuality, and let her fingers continue to trace its way over his now aware body. She had no thoughts of doubt about what she was about to do, and she continued to gently allow her fingers to explore the body that she had nursed, and cried over for many days, until it responded to her touch. Joseph, shaken but beyond a time when he could gain control of his feelings, allowed his hands to touch her and know the innermost feeling of love of one human being for another. They clung together, each one in their own world of ecstasy, but with each giving joy and fulfilment to the other. The act of love for them was as if no one in the world had experienced the like before, and never would, and as dawn broke, the two of them, in one tiny corner of Joseph's enormous bed, lay curled up like two children who had just watched Cinderella walk away with her prince to live happily ever after.

In the real world of course this does not happen and, now as the sun crept in the window of the little cottage, the reality came home to them, and they would have to spend this day, which should have been the happiest in their lives, deciding what to do about the future which now could be fraught with problems. They stayed where they were for a long time, neither wanting to break the spell or deal with the uncertainty. Lena would be arriving with some food soon, and she would surely suspect that something had happened to the both of them. Joseph had a healthy colour in his cheeks, with still a tired look around the eyes, but for the main part almost better. Katherine for her part looked as if she had been given something more beautiful than she had ever seen in all her young life.

She had decided that this morning was better by far than any other to give Joseph a haircut, and that was exactly what she did, and as Lena walked up the path, Katherine was sweeping up a mountain of black curls, and Joseph was sitting with a grin on his face that had been hard to see in the past, and now that face looked as handsome as any young man could wish to own. Lena glanced at them both, said nothing but went and stood between them, held them both in her arms and said, 'God bless you both.'

Both of them now knew that life could not go on without them being together, but Katherine was still only just entering her fifteenth year. Joseph being ill had cost him financially, and he would have to make that up, and work much more in order to make enough money to take her as his wife as soon as she was old enough. No one must know that she was not the child of his brother. It was such a risk that they would be taking, but he could not live without her now, and she could not leave him to carry out her original plan to go to England.

In spite of all the problems, and decisions, life was as sweet as it could be. Katherine and Joseph both worked hard, and loved one another with a deep and unending passion. They ran on the beach with Pip, and their laughter rippled across the silent evening air whilst, likewise, the waves skipped and danced to meet them and join in their fun. Nothing could hurt them; together they were invincible, and their lives lay before them like a picture of sublime happiness. Joseph improved in health and became stronger as the days went by.

Going back to working on the boat was a giant step, and he took it all with ease. Katherine was back in the market each day, rushing home to cook for Joseph, waiting patiently for him to salt and stack the fish in their crates ready for market before she could spend time with him. Their evening meal held no embarrassment now as it had when they both had to hold their feelings in check. They still sat and read to one another, or, sitting with elbows resting on the table, told one another of the comings and goings of the day, Pip sitting at their feet, and now and then giving a contented yawn as the warmth of the fire reached his bones. At night they would lay gently wound in one another's arms, dreamily discussing the future when they would be known as husband and wife. They didn't want the time to pass too quickly, because each day was heaven blessed, but they yearned for the day when together would be a way of life instead of a state of mind.

Katherine talked endlessly to Lena about the things she wanted to do. When all was settled with her and Joseph, she wanted to write to Martha and ask her if she would leave the cottage where she presumably still lived, and come and live with them, and maybe one day when they had children, she would be able to look after them, as she had done for Katherine for the first thirteen years of her life. Martha knew nothing of all that had happened to her, because Katherine was still afraid that her father would find out where she was, and because of her age would insist she went into his care. When she reached the age of consent and married Joseph, he could not touch her, or have any influence on what Martha did with her life. Katherine wanted so much to know how she was, and to know whether or not there had been any trouble about the disappearance of her evil husband. So much had been left unsaid, and sometimes Katherine had terrible moments of guilt, even though it was not her fault. Joseph had to keep reminding her of what might have happened had he not been found out on that terrible night two years ago.

A month had passed now since Joseph's illness, and all was back to normal. Lena agreed, albeit with misgivings, that Katherine stayed at the cottage which meant that she had to spend more time at her house with her children. Her husband began to come home less and less, and so the burden of the welfare of the children fell on her shoulders, which meant longer days at the market in order to earn more money, and more time at home with them, because Katherine could no longer be there. When the days at the market were slow, these were the times that Katherine would talk to her, ask her questions, and tell her things that she would only have told Martha. Lena felt as if she already knew this woman who had been such an influence on Katherine, and whom Katherine had loved dearly, and would love for the rest of her life.

Joseph now had more orders than ever from new hotels that were springing up around the coast. One hotel in particular had impressed Joseph, and he told Katherine that one day he would take her there. The hotel, as the story goes, was originally a villa commissioned by an aristocratic family who lived in Milan, for them to use as a summer residence. It had marble halls and staircases, and chandeliers of sparkling beauty hanging from the ceilings. Outside there was a park, and a lake, and wonderful views of the surrounding mountains. Katherine thought that Joseph was setting his sights too high, and anyway nothing could be as beautiful as their little cottage and beach. She wanted no more than to spend the rest of her life there with Joseph, and she told him so in no uncertain manner, to which he answered, 'We will see!'

Summer and autumn passed with little excitement, just days of utter contentment for Katherine. She was happy. The money that Joseph was earning brought good wholesome food to their table, and Katherine's takings on her sewing brought extra comforts to the cottage. The size of the inside was increased by replacing some of Joseph's grandfather's old furniture for more modern styles. Katherine, in the spare time that she had at the market, had scoured every corner until she found things that caught her eye, and Joseph had collected them on his cart. Then, in turn, they had been lovingly placed in strategic places in the cottage, and polished until they shone. Her bed, of course, had now gone, but she had retained the nets that Joseph had so carefully hung to give her some privacy, and had hung them from a hook holding a picture of Joseph's grandfather, draping them to each side of it so that they formed a canopy over their heads.

She had made matching orange and green cushions which she laid on the bed during the day which made it quite comfortable for them to rest against to read or talk with their feet raised from the floor. The table she had moved to the area where her bed had been and which was scrubbed and set with a white table cloth with pretty lace edgings, thus leaving the space around the old stove empty enough to lay a brilliant coloured rug which she had made from small squares of cotton under the guidance of Lena. Thus the cottage that had been just somewhere to sleep for Joseph, had suddenly become a home that would be a pleasure for anyone to come to, which indeed it was for Joseph and Katherine, and Lena when she had a spare moment to visit 'her extra children' as she called them.

It was one afternoon, just after the turn of the year, when Katherine had left the market to go home and prepare some dinner for Joseph, that Lena decided to go around and see the cottage now that Christmas had passed and it was relieved of its tree and the little stars that Katherine had fashioned from cardboard and silver wrappings to festoon the windows and door with. Lena knocked, and Katherine opened the door. Although she greeted Lena with a hug as she always did, she seemed a little quiet, and looked pale, and not her usual happy self. When Lena asked if she was all right, she hesitated and then said, 'yes', followed quickly by a not so hesitant and quite a shaky, ' no'.

Fear began to rise in Lena's heart. 'What is it, child?' she asked.

Katherine, looking directly at Lena, asked, 'How do I know if I am pregnant?'

'What makes you think you are?' asked Lena, stalling for time to gather her thoughts.

'I should have bled by now; it is six weeks since I did,' Katherine said.

'You would have to see a doctor,' Lena said, knowing that it was not necessary. She had but to look at her to know that Katherine already knew she was.

Katherine sat down, put her head in her hands, and said, 'I've done it again, haven't I? I've turned a happy situation into one of threat and panic. You know I can't see a doctor, Lena. Everyone will know, and what will Joseph and I do then?'

Lena, now seeming to be calm, even though she was in turmoil inside, said, 'Let me think on this tonight, and tomorrow we will talk. I think it best you don't tell Joseph just yet. Can you do that, or will it be too difficult?'

It was too difficult for Katherine, and as Joseph walked down the path to the cottage, she opened the door and threw herself into his arms. Joseph caught her in mid-air, held her at arm's length, and looked into her face. Seeing her flushed and with red rimmed eyes, he was worried now. What was wrong with her? She couldn't talk because she was so upset, and then the words came tumbling out amidst sobs and incoherent sounds of distress. Finally Joseph caught the last sentence: 'I'm going to have our baby.'

They both stopped, and looked at one another, and then Joseph took her in his arms again, and whispered, 'It's my fault. I am so sorry, Katrina.'

'No,' sobbed Katherine, 'the fault is mine. I made you love me, and I was irresponsible.'

Now inside the cottage, Joseph pulled her toward him and they both sat on the bed, each of them desperately hoping for some solution to the problem to manifest itself in the next few minutes so that everything would go back to a day ago when they were so happy. They sat, arms around each other for some time before either of them spoke.

Katherine spoke first to say that nothing had been confirmed, and that Lena knew, and had said that she would have to see a doctor, but of course she couldn't because it would have to continue from then on, and eventually everyone would know, and they all thought that she was Joseph's brother's child. The implications of that alone were catastrophic. Joseph, at a loss for words, could only say, 'I love you Katrina, and I will do anything you want me to do. I will find somewhere to hide you, and people to help you until it is all over and we can all be together.' The words stopped and he realized that there was very little he could do, indeed he knew nowhere and nobody who could deal with the situation. The only person who might be able to help was Lena. The other one could have been Martha, but he knew that she was the last person they could expect to get involved. They were both sitting together on the bed when there was a tap on the door. Joseph went to open it to find Lena standing there with her two children.

'I'm sorry I had to bring them; can they play with Pip for a while?'

'Of course,' answered Joseph, who called a grumpy Pip from his slumbers to take a stick and go and play with the children. Lena came in and sat down. Starting to talk slowly, quietly, and calmly, she began to set a plan before them which they could accept or not. The choice was theirs but the decision would be the hardest that either of them had ever made so far in their lives. Also it could lead to further decisions that only one of them could make, and that one would be Katherine.

Lena knew the captain of a tramp steamer that would be leaving from the coast of Liguria in February. It would be sailing through many ports on its way to its final destination of Liverpool, England. It would take several months, and it would not be easy, but he had a couple of passenger berths, one of which had already been taken, and he was prepared to offer the other one to Lena's friend, but she would have to make her own way by train to Milan, and then to Genoa, from where she would be picked up and transferred to the ship. Her decision must be made immediately, as berths on these steamers were hard to come by, and cost relatively little compared to normal passenger travel. Lena had very quickly communicated with several people to put this plan into action should Katherine and Joseph agree to it. There was a place in Liverpool that cared for young people such as Katherine in the same condition as her, and she had all the necessary information and addresses.

When she had finished, both Joseph and Katherine looked at her and in unison said, 'No'. Then Lena stood up and faced them both, and firmly but sadly started to lay down the facts as they stood if they should agree to go it alone. Joseph, if as it had been noted that Katherine was his brother's child, and his brother was to wash his hands of it all and not agree to reject the statement, would certainly be taken away, and most probably hanged for the crime of incest or face a trial to protest his innocence. At best he would be arrested for having sexual relations with an underage child. In Italy this would be classed as rape and carried a minimum twenty years prison sentence. Katherine would not be able to give evidence, or make her feelings known on the subject. To the best of her knowledge, Lena believed this to be true, and as such she saw no other way of handling the problem, even if she at worst thought of abortion, she would first have to have a positive result of her pregnancy, and this would mean being examined by a doctor.

This was all too much for Joseph; he excused himself and headed for the garden. Lena, now alone with Katherine, spelt out in detail the only course that she believed was possible, and which in the long run would cause them only a separation of about two years. If Katherine could have her baby in England, and then spend some time there, she would eventually be able to return to Italy and to Joseph, be married, and spend the rest of her life with him. Her plans to go to England had been common knowledge around the market, and now would be a good time to go, as the berth on the tramp steamer had been offered to Lena for her friend who would be overjoyed at the opportunity. If by February, she discovered that she was not pregnant, then they would have to find some excuse for her not to go, but both of them knew that this would not happen.

As for Joseph, he would carry on working hard, and earning enough money to be able to care for a wife and child in due course. It would be hard, very hard, but the possible consequences of her staying with Joseph were unthinkable, and moving somewhere else in Italy would make her extremely vulnerable, with little money, and nowhere to go where she could be cared for. She would have a little time before the birth of her baby, and she would have addresses of contacts which Lena had gathered for her. She was clever, and hard working, and she could earn some money with her sewing. Liverpool was poor, as were many cities, but Lena, through her husband, had come to know some Italians who had travelled this way before to England, and had made their own way to a life across the sea, and fared not too badly.

Katherine by now was feeling quite sick, and allowing herself to be pushed into another situation over which she had no control. She thought her days of running were over, but now they were back, and twice as bad as before. At least then she only had herself to care for, only herself to starve if necessary, but now she would have a baby inside her that would need to be nourished. She was tired and needed to rest. She needed to feel Joseph's arms around her, and she didn't want to make a decision, not now, not tomorrow, not ever. She hugged Lena and thanked her for all her care and love, and then she asked if she would leave, and send Joseph to her. Joseph and Katherine spent that night in each other's arms, not talking, not moving, just locked together in sadness and fear, and in the morning they went hand in hand to the market, smiled aimlessly at Lena, and turned to their own chores.

The booking would be secured for the trip, and they would begin to count the days until they would have to say goodbye for a very long time. Lena told the regular stall holders who had become fond of both Joseph and Katherine, that finally Katherine was going to fulfil her dream and head for England's shores. She told them that hopefully she would return and see them all one day, when maybe if all went well she would be a rich lady.

During the day, the news went around the market, and in the late afternoon just before they all packed away their goods and closed their stalls, the lady from the material stall, who had been the first one to set Katherine off on her sewing, came and gave Katherine a little black velvet pouch. Katherine peeped inside it to find it was stuffed with notes and coins. *To send her on her way*, the little note read. Katherine wept all the way home, and she felt that she would never be more loved anywhere in the world than she was in this tiny community that had taken her to their hearts.

February loomed closer, and Katherine and Joseph shared every minute that they could together. They walked with Pip along the beach. They sat together on Katherine's rock, where she used to sit and dream of a life with Joseph. Katherine was suffering a few bouts of sickness, which confirmed to her that she was indeed pregnant. If the boat trip went to plan, she would be in England in good time to go to the address that Lena had given her, where her pregnancy would be confirmed and monitored.

It was now only one day until she would have to board the train that would take her to Milan, and then to Genoa. She had heard Joseph and Lena whispering outside the door, and that evening as they sat quietly at the supper table, Lena had come round to say her goodbyes, and Joseph said to Katherine, 'Lena and I have decided to come with you on both trains, and see you aboard the boat, so that we know you are safely on your way.'

Katherine, bursting into tears, protested that they could not all go as they did not have the money. 'Never mind about that; a little dip into our savings can be put back in good time for your return,' said Lena.

Katherine then went and did her final packing, tucking her little case with her treasures from the past down into the bottom of the large bag with handles that Joseph had bought her. She came back as Lena was leaving. She threw her arms around her and kissed her. 'Thank you,' were the only words that she could say as Lena left, and she turned to Joseph.

He took her hands and sat her on the bed, opened up her left hand, and placed in it an earring. It was Joseph's grandfather's earring that he always wore. The one that, he had explained, sailors wore to pay for their burials if they died at sea and had no relatives to bury them. 'Keep it, my darling Katrina, and if you need to sell it, it will ensure that you will never be without money to buy food, or to pay for somewhere to live. Gold will always bring a good price, so don't sell it carelessly. It is a good weight, so take care of it, but don't be frightened to let it go if you need to.'

'Joseph, you will have nothing for your burial,' cried Katherine.

'I will need nothing if I don't have you. Life or Death will not exist. So come back to me, my Katrina,' replied Joseph.

The three people who boarded the train for Milan, made a sad picture. The journey was not long, but there was another one to follow, before the moment that none of them wanted to happen. It was three thirty in the morning. The mists were clinging to the shoreline. Katherine raised her eyes to the heavens to see that rain was forming around the moon again, just as it had when she had run away on that fateful night at the woodman's cottage.

She had left Lena and Joseph at the quayside, and was walking alone to board the ship that would take her to England for a totally different reason than she had dreamed of so long ago. Lena and Joseph stood and watched as the mists surrounded her, and took her from them. They turned and, as the ship left its moorings, they could only hear the muted sound of the engine chugging slowly away, taking with it their most cherished possession.

Chapter Eleven

A Will to Live

Days and nights, at the beginning of Katherine's voyage, were dogged by sickness and loneliness. The cabin, although very small, was reasonably clean, the facilities meagre. A closet to attend to bodily functions was three doors down a dimly lit corridor, a bowl for washing was on top of a chest which had one drawer. The water was obtained from the tap in the closet, to be returned and emptied after use. The bunk was narrow, with side slats to stop its occupant from falling out when high seas rocked the ship, as it did almost all the time. A china chamber pot with a lid which was cracked and discoloured was hidden under the bunk. The serving of meals was carried out by crew members, and there was no choice. Presumably, passengers and crew were served the same food, but not necessarily at the same time, as most times hot food arrived at Katherine's door nearly, if not entirely, cold.

As travel sickness enveloped her, she laid in darkness on her bunk, sleep interrupted by bouts of vomiting. She saw and heard nothing, except for the clinking of dishes and glasses as they were delivered, and taken away. No one knocked to enquire as to her wellbeing, and she felt too weak to venture from her cabin. She lost track of time, and had no knowledge as to which way the steamer was travelling. Sometimes she would let her imagination take her to beautiful places with mountains and lakes, but most times she would just lay and wish she were back in her little cottage with Joseph.

One evening the sickness seemed to leave her. She had ventured to try some of the food that was left on the little ledge outside her cabin. It was not particularly pleasant, but it was filling and she felt a little stronger for the eating of it. That night for the first time she slept. Because the cabin was on the inside of the ship, no natural light was visible, but somehow the sounds were different at night, and the engines appeared to settle into a softer rhythm.

Katherine slept until the clatter of dishes outside her door heralded breakfast. She hadn't undressed properly to sleep since she had come on board, so after she had eaten a quite palatable scrambled egg on a piece of greasy bread, she took her bowl to the closet, filled it, brought it back, and washed herself. She brushed her hair, which she had had cut just before she left the cottage so it would be easy to handle. She returned to the closet with the bowl and emptied the water, attended to the needs of nature, and then brought the bowl back, tidied her bed, and, picking up her special little suitcase and the key to her cabin, she ventured outside.

She walked along the corridor to where a flight of stairs led to the next deck, she could see light at the top, and could feel a slight breeze. Interested now, she climbed the stairs; the sickness from the previous days had gone and she felt better. At the top of the stairs she found herself out on the deck, quite narrow it was, but it had a hand rail on top of the boarded side of the boat. Until she reached the rail she could see nothing but sky, but upon walking to the edge, taking the handrail and peering over the side, she saw waves of white foam as the ship ploughed its way to whatever destination lay ahead. A couple of crew members padded by in their soft soled shoes, and briefly nodded at her, but she was content to lean against the rail and watch the endless blue sea stretching into infinity.

Glancing away from the sea, and idly looking up and down the deck, she caught sight of an elderly gentleman. He had in his hand a sheaf of papers caught together by a red ribbon which fluttered in the breeze. Clasped in the same hand, while the other hand held on to the rail, was a walking cane, black in colour, and because he had it held by the middle of the cane instead of the handle, Katherine noticed it had a shiny silver top about three inches long, topped by an ornate knob, round in shape and just the right size for his old hand to hold, Katherine thought. Somewhere in her mind she thought that she had seen a cane somewhat like his, but could not remember where. Perhaps it was on one of the market stalls, she mused. She stood for a while, watching both him and the sea. He was engrossed in one of the sheets of paper, glancing occasionally from it out to sea, while the sea just kept throwing up its foam as if to open a channel for the boat to pass through.

Katherine wasn't aware of the time that she had spent standing there, but suddenly felt tired, and turned to return to her cabin. The elderly gentleman was still standing, utterly consumed by the papers that he held in his hands, as Katherine made her way down the stairs and back to the dull darkness below. A small light burned continuously, which gave a yellowish tinge to the woodwork. Katherine sat and removed her small case from under her coat, opened it, and took out the earring. She studied it now as she couldn't when Joseph had given it to her. It was beautiful, and she thought she would move hell and high water before she would sell it, and hopefully one day she would return it to Joseph to seal their love once and for all. She stayed in her cabin for the rest of the day and started to read the only book that she could find space for in her luggage.

As the days went by, she set herself a routine. She prided herself on the fact that she had been in a perilous situation akin to this one before. She had fought, albeit with the saving of her life brought about by Joseph, against all manner of hardships and deprivation, and with his love and help, she had found happiness beyond her wildest imaginings. She knew there would be no Joseph on this journey, but she was carrying his child, and she would die if that was what was needed to bring his child into a world where it would be loved and cared for. However, she had no intention of dying; she was going to be well, and when she finally got to England she felt that her problems would be resolved. How, she knew not, but solved they would have to be, for she could not keep up this running away if she had a child to be responsible for.

She had some papers that Lena had given her when they boarded the train which Lena said she must keep safe, and not let them get into any other hands but the authorities responsible for the safe passage of minors who, Lena explained, were young people who were under the age of being expected to manage their own affairs. What this truly meant, Katherine was not sure, but she trusted Lena more than anyone else, and she had got her a passage on this boat which was owned by a very good friend of her husband, and who had promised to see her through the voyage, and pass her into the care of the right people at the end of it. With all this in mind, Katherine thought that she would do her best to arrive in the best health that she could, so that she would be ready to face whatever befell her and the tiny life that she held so tightly inside her.

The captain duly knocked on her door most mornings now that she was better, and enquired into her health and comfort, to which she answered that she was well, and thanked him for the food that was regularly left for her. One morning she asked him where they were about to travel to, and how long he thought it would take to get to England, to which he replied in a gruff voice, 'first stop, Naples. England is a long way off, and many stops will be made before we reach there, so I do not know exactly how long it will be, maybe two, maybe three months, maybe less, maybe more,' and with a touch of his hand to his hat, he departed.

Slightly unsettled by this information, Katherine wandered up the stairs onto the deck above, where she stood watching the endless rolling seas, silently hoping that the captain knew the way. She stood by the rail and, no longer feeling sick in the mornings, she could enjoy the feeling of the fresh wind on her cheeks. Her head and ears were muffled in a warm wool scarf that Joseph had tucked in her pocket on the cold morning that she had left him on the quayside. She also had a fur muff that Lena had given her that last Christmas when they all knew that she would be leaving Italy for maybe much colder countries, along with a long coat that she had found herself at the market, and some warm socks and shoes. She was happy because it allowed her to go on deck, and not sit confined in her cabin.

It was quite a while since she had seen the elderly gentleman with the papers and the cane up on deck, but on this particular day he was there. He stood today, not immersed in his paperwork, but looking at her with a questioning look on his face. After a while, he walked toward her, and said, to Katherine's amazement, 'Am I not mistaken or do we meet again, young lady?'

Katherine stiffened and whispered, 'I do not think so, sir, for I do not believe that I have ever seen you before.'

'Think back,' he said. 'Were you not on a train travelling to Milan with, I think, some very dubious characters. Don't be afraid, child. I wish you no harm. In fact, I felt a need to offer you some help at the time, but you disappeared from the carriage, never to be seen again, and I did hear some conversation taking place on the platform between one of the persons accompanying you, and the driver of the train.'

The cane! Suddenly it came back to Katherine. She remembered where she had seen it now, and remembered how she had mused that this old gentleman might offer her some help. 'Sir,' she said, 'it was indeed me, and I was in grave danger, and had to get away. It is a very long story, and not one that I would wish to bore you with, but, sir, I am so pleased to meet you, and I do remember your beautiful cane. I watched you a while ago, and wondered what you were doing aboard this ship which will travel to goodness knows where. I wondered where you would alight in your quest to find or add to the information you hold in all your papers, so neatly kept together by the piece of red ribbon that I watched on the first day when I stood here feeling very sick and weak. I remember thinking how a piece of ribbon had no feelings and was free to just flutter in the breeze.'

The old man smiled now, took a step nearer, and said, 'Young lady, would you like to sit with an old man and drink a cup of tea? I have been very lucky, and have been given the courtesy of being able to use the captain's cabin during the day, and so have the facility for making tea at any time, which is rather nice, don't you think?'

'I do, sir,' replied Katherine, 'and I would like very much to join you in a cup of tea. Thank you.'

So it was that a new friendship was born between the old and young, and it was to create for Katherine a lifetime of loyalty. For the elderly gentleman, a reason for living, a joy of giving, and a person on to whom he could unload the knowledge that the years had bestowed upon him, knowing that it was being received with such a thirst for its content that it left him breathless. Each day of the journey now became a lesson. The old man, with a never ending explanation of what he was trying to achieve, and for Katherine a fountain of knowledge into which she could dip her feet whenever she wanted to, and someone in front of whom she could lay down her own incredible story.

They stood together on the deck as the ship docked in Naples. They heard the crashing and grinding of machinery as some cargo was off-loaded, but from their vantage point they could see nothing of the comings and goings. However, what they could see was a beautiful coastline in the mist on a winter's morning bathed in sunlight and with a multitude of birds circling overhead.

'This is why I'm here, Katherine. Part of my life is taken up with ornithology. I study birds, and note their habitats and their migratory systems. I am aiming to write the most informative book ever on this subject. An amazing amount of people find birds interesting, and I hope to fulfil their quest for knowledge on the subject. I have travelled to many parts of the world in many ways. Since my last and fleeting encounter with you, I have travelled the length and breadth of Italy using many modes of transport, and have collected some invaluable information which you have already noted is tied with a simple red ribbon. I have to explain that I have many parcels of notes, and every country that I visit has its own colour ribbon, thus I find it easy to refer to individual files, as I index each of them in their own colour code, and, with each ribbon hanging loose from its pile of papers, I have only to pull the end to retrieve the one I need, very simple but most helpful,' he concluded.

Night fell, and the boat was still standing in dock, its engines silent, and no sounds now of cargo being hurled about. Both the old man and Katherine had long since retired to their own cabins, and Katherine lay on her bunk and thought about the day. How interesting that she found this elderly man who was an absolute minefield of information, all of which she found absorbing. She enjoyed his company, and she was beginning to feel a trust in him. She wanted to confide in him all her life story, but she couldn't just yet. She was frightened to tell him about the baby in case he disapproved so badly that he didn't want to acquaint himself with her any longer. This she would find hard to bear.

It took an amazing two days and nights before the engines of their boat fired in to life again, and they left the beautiful bay in which Naples was nestled in tranquil waters. Amongst all the beauty, there was no evidence of their being there, no rubbish on the dockside, only a couple of men standing idly chatting, and giving a carefree wave in the direction of the bridge.

Adolphus Peregrine Fry, resting in his cabin in the late afternoon as the steamer gushing black smoke from its stack moved slowly onward to its next destination, reflected upon the last few days, spent mainly in the company of an extremely unique, intelligent and, to say the least, pretty young woman. Here he was, fast approaching the autumn of his life, with little or no experience of life outside of the walls of university and a never ending study of one subject or another. He found himself enjoying her company immensely, and if it only lasted to the end of this, probably his last journey of discovery in foreign climes, his life would be so much the richer for the experience. Pulling out the red ribbon gently, and adding a few more sheets of neatly written notes, he smiled; he had never even been aware of its fluttering in the breeze before.

Katherine, for her part, remembered with pleasure that day when he invited her for a cup of tea where they exchanged names, and sketched the outline of their lives, very vaguely, neither wishing the other to be bored, or find the information a bit too much to take in at such an early stage in their friendship. She liked to think of it as a friendship. Although he was an elderly man, he never treated her as a child, and he explained with patience and understanding his role in life. For a while she would forget her reason for being here, and then would suddenly see a picture of Joseph waving goodbye on that cold February morning, and she would feel her eyes stinging and a lump come in her throat, and a longing for the boat to turn around and head her back to him.

Katherine's days now began to form a pattern. Rising early, she would wash and dress. Having not brought many clothes with her on the voyage, she would always fold them very neatly, as she used to in the cottage when she first had her own little corner. She would wash a piece at a time in her small bowl after she had washed herself, and leave it hanging on the knobs of the drawer to dry. She always felt it was important to present a clean image to the world even if it wasn't the height of fashion. She completed her routine by brushing her hair (a hundred strokes, Martha had told her, would keep it shining and clean). When all this was completed she left her cabin and made for the deck.

Adolphus was not always there, and she would feel a little disappointed, but she would stand at the rail and watch for birds, try to remember what they looked like and question him the next time she saw him. The boat was now travelling closer to land, and she could see clearly the outline of sandy shores, and lush green vegetation. She had never seen anything more beautiful, and even in these days of winter the sun fought its way through the clouds to bestow its brightness on the land below. Little boats with billowing sails would sometimes be just visible around the coastline. Did they have a fisherman on board taking home his catch every night? she wondered. Adolphus would generally appear at sometime during the long day, beckon her to join him, and when all that he needed to note was finished, they would retire to the captain's cabin and 'partake in a cup of tea' as Adolphus would say. Katherine would laugh at his repartee and drop a mock curtsey answering 'delighted, sir'.

The captain's cabin, in the scale of things, was not much better than either of theirs, but it was larger, and there was a desk of sorts, where Adolphus could lay out his papers, and sort them into order while he answered Katherine's endless questions, with a quiet confidence and a touch of humour. He explained to her that he was a professor, a doctor of physics, and science, and that he was a governor of The University in Liverpool, England, so he still spent much of his time in that city, giving of his services to support the university in every way that was possible. He enjoyed it, but sometimes he just longed to drift off on an adventure like this one that would come to an end when this boat on which they were travelling docked at Liverpool in a couple of months' time. He lived in a small flat in the precincts of the university, but he had a home in the outskirts of London, to which he would head when he had the chance. London was where he was born, and as such he always regarded it as home. Katherine listened with the utmost interest as he described life in the capital city of England.

It was different from the countryside that Martha had described, when she talked of her childhood to Katherine. Perhaps before she returned with her baby to Italy, and to Joseph, she would have a chance to see some of England, and perhaps one day she would keep her promise to Martha and take her back to the land of her birth. She told Adolphus about her life with Martha, and how wonderful she had been to her, but at this time she could not explain to him about the train journey and what had led up to it. The boat had a long way to travel yet, and maybe as time went by she would be able to relive the memories and confide in him. She felt that he would have to know everything if he was going to know about her baby, because he may not understand about the baby if he didn't know all the story, and she would hate him to think she had been totally to blame for bringing such shame upon herself. She had to make him understand; she didn't know why, as she could just walk from the boat and never set eyes on him again, but she did not want to do that. She hoped that he would not ask too much of her, and in fact he didn't.

Life proceeded happily aboard the steamer as it headed onward toward the toe of Italy, stopping a couple of times on the way, just for a short while and with little fuss or bother, allowing its two passengers the luxury of watching a beautiful land pass before their eyes, and becoming firm friends.

Katherine, asleep in her bunk, awoke to the feeling of the boat juddering, and the engines whining as they slowed the vessel down. The constant note coming from the smoke stack, which became so much a part of the journey, now stopping as the final scrape of metal against solid ground told her that the boat had docked again. When it had docked at Naples, she was up on the deck, and so was Adolphus. She found everything about this journey so interesting, she sometimes felt guilty to admitting that she was quite enjoying it all. She was not uncomfortable, she was being fed, and she had met a delightful gentleman who showed equal interest in everything that was going on around them. She lay impatiently and waited for breakfast to be delivered to her door. This was the only way she had of knowing roughly what time it was, and when she could get herself ready to go up on deck. She stayed in her bunk until she could wait no longer, and decided that if she got washed and dressed she would be ready and could go on deck immediately after she had eaten.

She felt a little sick this morning, but decided it was just excitement, and maybe her baby felt the excitement too. Eventually it was time, and she left her cabin, taking with her as always her little case with the treasures of the past in it. Nothing would separate her from them whatever happened. Adolphus was already at the rail, busily jotting notes down, resting his papers on the board that had the most enormous clip that snapped the papers together safely, and gave him a hard surface on which to write. It was not always easy, he confessed, when the boat was bobbing about in a high sea. This morning, however, was perfect; the boat was still, and the weather was chilly but bright and quite mellow for the time of year.

'Katherine,' he cried, as he looked up and saw her watching him. 'Do come and see. We are in Sicily at a place called Messina, and just out to sea right in front of us there is a volcano. It is not active so you will see no fireworks, but it is there, on the island of Vulcan, and named after the Greek god of fire. If you look to your right you will see the very tip of the Italian coastline. Is that not just perfection? There are many birds here that you will also see in England. No one really knows why they travel so far during migration, and we do not know why they choose certain areas above others. This is why I study them, and this is why, for the last part of my journey, I have chosen to travel on this boat to get some sort of insight into their flights across the seas to coastal areas. I do hope I don't bore you with my talking about something that has become a lifelong mission. You do seem so interested in everything that it is a joy to have your company and be able to put my theories before you. I have to say, for a young woman who I suspect is not too worldly wise, you are a most intelligent listener, and always ask pertinent questions. Thank you, Katherine,' he concluded.

'No, sir,' contradicted Katherine. 'It is I who should say thank you. You are turning what would have been the most miserable journey into something quite wonderful, and very exciting. I actually feel like someone who is very rich, and is taking one of those world cruises that I have read about in the newspapers. I actually thought this morning, as I was waiting to come up on deck, that I should feel guilty for enjoying myself so much when the reason I am here is to get very far away from Italy for the time being, and at the end of my journey to face a frightening situation in which I will have to be extremely brave. So I am indeed most thankful for your kindness. The memories of this journey, and you, will give me strength and hope for the future. I would like very much to be in your company for the rest of the journey, if you feel that is possible without my becoming a nuisance to you.'

Adolphus Peregrine Fry, at that moment, felt something that he had never felt in his life before. He was worried about another person, which he had never done before. He had always had only himself to worry about. His parents had sent him away to be cared for when he was a mere child, and he had no siblings as far as he knew. He was lucky in as much as he was clever, and made the most of his learning ability to reach a very high degree of education. Friends had been few and far between, and of the same ilk as him. He made no friends outside of university, and had nowhere to go during holidays. Eventually, when he was adult enough in his opinion, and earning enough money, he travelled to London and bought himself a house which he spent years furnishing and renovating, but could find no one to share it with, so it had a cold feeling about it. It was left in the hands of a housekeeper, and he would visit it occasionally, as he would when he returned from this voyage. He would, if he had the chance, tell Katherine about his life, but at the moment he had a very deep feeling that all was not well in the life of this beautiful young lady who had graced his world for the past few weeks, and he hoped that the journey that they had both embarked upon would give them time to share confidences enough to count one another as close friends when it ended.

'My dear child,' he finally said after Katherine felt a rather long silence. 'My life has become the richer for your presence in it, and you will never become a burden to me,' Adolphus replied. 'We must find something that you can call me; I think 'sir' is a little formal when we are sharing tea in the captain's cabin, don't you? I have never had sisters, brothers, nephews, or nieces, and I would quite have liked to be an uncle. Would that be too forward of me to ask you to call me uncle?'

Katherine gave one of her irrepressible giggles that Joseph used to love and said, 'I would love to call you uncle. I never had one either, so you see we do have something in common.' So, uncle it was and would be for as long as they knew one another. It just remained for the time to be right for Katherine to deliver the news that might shatter the new found happiness that they both shared. Their stay in Messina lasted about twenty-four hours according to the captain who had become used to seeing the two of them, heads together, poring over maps and drawings.

It was good for him, as his life aboard the tramp steamer was a busy one, and to be responsible for a young woman was to say the least, worrying. Left to the old man, Katherine became almost no liability at all. As the captain passed by them, he tipped his hat to the old man and said, 'Going the long way this time, round the south of the island, to Siracusa.'

Katherine for one moment felt a pang of worry. How long was this journey going to take? she thought, as she was now in her third month of pregnancy. At the moment there was no evidence of any change in her size, but the longer the journey took, the more difficult it would be to hide her predicament. She was the only woman on board, so hopefully she would be able to disguise her enlarging torso with the couple of loose fitting items of clothing she had brought with her.

Adolphus, catching her in a moment of deep thought, stayed silent and watched a little protectively, and then said, 'Why don't we stop work for a while, and enjoy this beautiful scenery?'

Finding a place to sit, he quietly regaled her with some of the history and geography of what he considered to be one of the most beautiful sun blessed islands that had been host to visitors for centuries. It had been in its time invaded by Greeks, Romans, Arabs, and Normans, and all had left their own mark in a blend of temples and cathedrals, some of which were now mere ruins. If the boat sailed close to shore they may see the snow-topped Mount Etna.

Katherine, enthralled by his stories as they chugged on somewhat lazily down the coast, forgot her worries for a while and relaxed in the mild sunshine, and in his company. Siracusa, their last stop on the southern tip of Sicily was reached late in the evening, and so remained a mystery to Katherine. She had retired early to her cabin, bidding a polite but sincere goodnight to Adolphus, who had spent the whole day with her again, keeping her attention, but feeling her tenseness, and retiring himself with a restless mind, wondering just what had happened to this seemingly innocent and gentle child whom he had come to respect and trust beyond his powers of reasoning.

They now had a long journey to the next port of call, and Adolphus knew that he had to catch up with the logging of his sheets, which had been neglected for a while in his effort to keep Katherine company.

However, he decided that it had not been in vain, both for him and her. He would invite her for tea, but not go on deck for the next few days, for as beautiful as the coastline was he had to do some work before they left this island for a new destination, which he hoped would bring new knowledge of the habits of the bird population. His journey was now well under way, and with this trip on the steamer the final part of the realization of a dream, and the foundation of a book that would be so infinite in its content, it would be almost impossible to improve upon, in his lifetime anyway.

Katherine also spent most of the time during the next few days in her cabin. She felt extremely tired, and had no desire to read a book. She took her possessions from her case and laid them out on her neatly spread cover, and one by one picked them up and examined them. The ballet shoes, which she now knew belonged to her mother, who was a famous ballerina when she was not much older than Katherine was now. The locket on a gold chain, which she wore all the time tucked away under the layers of clothes, which also was her mother's, but now she knew that the old worn photo was of her mother, and the man in the other half of the locket she now knew beyond any doubt was her natural father. The earring, belonging to Joseph, passed down on the death of his grandfather to him, and passed on to her when Joseph kissed her and held her tight on that last night before she left. These, she concluded, were her whole life in one small parcel; a life of extreme misery, but also extreme happiness, and one day perhaps she would be able to gather her grandchildren around her, to tell them the story of their old grandmother, and smile as they listened wide-eyed and innocent at the revelations that she would lay before them.

The journey onward, although extremely interesting for Adolphus, would probably prove very tiring for Katherine. The first part would be much the same as they had just completed, as it was to take them around the southernmost coastline of Sicily, and with all their cargo in place from the stop at Siracusa, they would only need to top up the necessary coal bunkers, and wood for fuel, and take on board some provisions to see them through one of the longest parts of the journey. They would then head across to the North African coast, and hug the north shoreline to Alger, where they would change cargoes and continue to Tetouan on the tip of Morocco. This heralded good news for Adolphus as he would be able to complete his research on some of the largest areas of migratory birds known to him personally. Undoubtedly when his notes were delved into there would be some comments to the adverse, but he didn't mind that, because it would serve as a rich enlightenment that would hopefully add to the interest of those who read his book.

At last, Katherine, who had begun to take interest again after being a little unwell for the last few days, had come on deck and watched Sicily disappear and North Africa come into view. The land changed colour quite dramatically. The sparse brown land beyond the fringe of the green coastal area, replaced the lushness of Sicily. Although still bordering the Mediterranean, the harshness of the Sahara desert pushed its fingers of flying sand to the very limit of its existence and invaded all that surrounded it. Progress, to Katherine, was slow, because she had no idea of the distance covered by this terrain. Africa was an unknown quantity in her knowledge, and the only person who could help her understand this strange phenomenon was Adolphus, but at the moment he was spending every available minute with his telescope, busily creating sheet upon sheet of neatly written notes. Katherine would sometimes just stand by his side, and he would smile and say, 'Tea break soon'.

These days, without his full attention, laid heavily on her, and she realized just how much she had come to rely upon his company for her peace of mind. This part of the journey was going to take a while, he gently explained to her, and she should take some rest whenever she could. He found her a small canvas chair that had a nice long back to it, and he placed it for her in a sheltered spot that was quite warm, and sheltered from the winds that in their travels had collected a fair amount of sand from the desert, which could be irritating to the skin and eyes.

After settling her comfortably, he asked her if she would do some work for him. Agreeing, without a second's hesitation, she found herself reading from the beginning, the notes that Adolphus had carefully put together on this voyage, each with its own colour ribbon. At first she found it hard work, and some of the words she didn't understand, so she kept her own piece of paper, that Adolphus had readily given her, for the purpose of writing down the word, and then the explanation as he gave it to her. Thus it was that the days passed a little more easily for Katherine, and she began to enjoy the enthusiasm which she found in the work of Adolphus.

Finally, on a warm balmy day in early April, they steamed into Tetuoan. The captain explained that this was the last stop in the relatively calm waters of the Mediterranean, and they would stop here for a few days. Some of the seamen would take their leave from the ship, and some new hands would take their place. Some work would take place on board, and things would get quite busy. At certain times they may be asked to stay in their cabins, mostly for their own safety. Adolphus would still be offered the use of the Captain's Cabin during the day, and Katherine would be most welcome to accompany him. Their own cabins would be untouched by any one, so that their belongings would be quite safe during the day, and of course they would retire to them as usual at eventide.

On the day the steamer was making ready to depart again, Adolphus was standing at the rail wondering why Katherine was not there. He thought she would be excited at the thought that the next part of her journey was about to begin. He waited for a considerable time, and then decided to go and knock on her door to invite her to come on deck and witness the departure from Africa, and the arrival at a very important place in the scheme of things. On arriving at her cabin door, he raised a hand to knock when he heard sounds of crying coming from the other side. For a moment he hesitated, not sure what to do, and then curiosity got the better of him, and he knocked and called at the same time.

'Katherine, please open the door. I can hear you crying. What is it? Can I help?'

The sound of her crying lessened, but it was a long time before the door slowly opened, and a Katherine that he had not seen before stood in front of him, dishevelled, and tear-stained, saying not a word, just looking at him, tears welling up in her eyes again.

'Oh dear,' said Adolphus, not standing too close, putting out his hand and taking hers and saying, 'I think a cup of the Captain's tea is in order, young lady. Come with me.'

Taking the key from the inside of the door, ushering her gently out, and locking the door behind him, he proceeded to pull her gently with him until they reached the sanctum of the Captain's cabin where he steadied her with both hands and sat her down. Saying no more until two steaming hot cups of tea stood before them on the table, and then he said, 'I think the time has come for you to tell me everything I need to know in order that I might help you with your problems. I am completely out of my depth with this sort of situation, but I am sure that this is what an 'Uncle' would do. Do you agree, Katherine?'

Katherine nodded, but felt no confidence in what she had to tell him, for their precious friendship could end here in this room, on this day, and she would then have to face the rest of her days, not only on this journey, but forever without him. She didn't think that she could do that, in fact the panic inside her told her that she knew she couldn't.

'Sir,' she started, 'in order to explain my reason for being on this ship with the hope of reaching England, I have to tell all of my story which starts at my birth. It will include things that you may find you cannot accept, but if I start my story, please let me finish it, because then you may see that it was not all my fault. What you decide to do or not do, I will totally accept. I need to say now that these days that I have spent with you have been most rewarding, and I thank you from the bottom of my heart for being there at a time when the need for someone like you was almost unbearable in its being.'

Adolphus said nothing, but just settled himself back in his chair, and with a wave of his hand bade her begin.

Katherine, still with a catch in her voice from the crying that had suddenly overtaken her that day, began her story, and she told it without embellishment and without heroism. She just stated the facts from the earliest time of her recollection, and added to it the things that Martha had told her of her early days. As she continued, Adolphus never interrupted, but his eyes and hand movements showed his amazement and distress, mixed with a little touch of irony and amusement at the times when she had shown such alertness and self composure. As her story reached near to its climax, he reached out to touch her hand, and she held it like a child seeking the security and confidence of a much trusted adult.

She finally ended it as it had begun, telling him that all she loved and cared for seemed to be taken away from her by some cruel act of fate. She told him that she knew not what had happened to Martha, and she had no idea who had killed the woodman. She only knew that she saw her mother and her real father carry his body away. She told him how she loved Joseph, and would somehow take her baby back to him when it was possible. She finally ended her story, with a tearful smile, shrugged her shoulders with a resigned look, and raised her eyes to Adolphus to see tears running down his cheeks. He took her other hand as she wiped it across her face in a tired gesture.

'Come with me, Katherine. I think we should share the next part of this voyage, and if you so wish we will share the rest of our journey of discovery. It will give me the greatest pleasure, and I will be there for you any time you need me. I have to confess I know little of nature's miracles, but I am in contact with many people who will be able to get you help. There is no more time to be spent in tears; let us enjoy our time together, and let the future take care of itself. All will be well, you will see. Come, I want you to see Gibraltar; we will pass the big rock soon, and it is quite an amazing place, and then, my dear, we will have to prepare ourselves for some very heavy seas as we head through the straits of Gibraltar and toward Portugal, then along the northern coast of Spain, to France. We will have to face the Bay of Biscay, but we will hug the coast all the way, stopping a few times, I don't doubt. The captain is a good man and has taken this steamer around this route many times. He assures me that this little lady can ride any storm, much the same as you, Katherine, so be brave. Come on let's go.'

He smiled now as he let go of one hand, and led her out on deck. Katherine went willingly with him, although she felt exhausted, and would have liked to lay down quietly on her bunk, and go to sleep. She knew that tonight she would do that, as the majority of her fears had now been allayed. She knew that Adolphus would stay on the boat until it reached Liverpool, and as she had no specific place to aim for, she decided that she would accept his invitation to end her journey there too. It was a good city, he had said, and he would be there for a considerable time, so that she could rely on his help and company. So it was that their journey continued, Katherine still keeping all his notes in good order as they grew in proportion. They would work together in the Captain's cabin during the days when Adolphus was not busy on deck, which were few and far between as he said these waters were some of the most important to his research.

It was summer now, and the weather was set fair so Katherine was able to sit in her sheltered corner and just enjoy the beauty of the coastline being pummelled by the Atlantic Ocean. The next stop would be Lisbon, where they would stay a short while, and then make a stop at Vigo, almost on the borders of France. Katherine's geography told her that they were very slowly heading toward the dream that she had of visiting England. For all the wrong reasons though, she thought sadly as she sat and watched Adolphus, his grey hair blowing wildly in the wind as he struggled to handle the papers, and his telescope as he trained it on the land that they passed. He never seemed to tire. His enthusiasm for his work never paled, and each little note that he wrote, was with satisfaction. Katherine noted that there was never a crossing out or a correction placed in the margin. He was indeed a clever man, and she was sure he had more than earned the right to be a professor. She was indeed so proud to have known him, let alone have his company and friendship.

One afternoon as they were working, the captain entered the cabin and they both made a move to get up and go, but they sat down quickly again as the captain removed from inside his jacket a black and white cat. Katherine eyes lit up as the captain handed it to her. 'Found its way on board at Naples; they have been looking after it below, but this ship already has its cat, and it is giving this one a hard time so I thought that you might care for it during the journey. I can't just put it ashore. I will send up extra food, and we will decide its fate when we reach Liverpool.'

Adolphus smiled. He liked cats, he said. 'Very independent creatures.'

Katherine thought, not this one as it curled up on her lap and promptly went to sleep.

The captain departed, and Adolphus said, 'What shall we name him then?'

Katherine said without a second thought, 'It had better be Naples, don't you think?'

Adolphus roared with laughter, and Naples just stretched, let out a little meow and settled back to his nap. Naples proved to be the perfect companion, and followed Katherine everywhere. Adolphus suggested that they made him a collar and fix a piece of string to it, so that Naples wouldn't take it into his head to leap overboard. And so they were three, inseparable, all happy in their own way, all destined for Liverpool, where their lives would undoubtedly change, and where they may have to face a life without each other; but that was a long way off yet, and the living was good at present. Katherine, now well into the fifth month of her pregnancy, realised that time was going to be short to find a home and some work before her baby was born. There was nothing she could do but wait.

They had now left Vigo, and were to sail as far as Santander, where they would head out across the corner of the Bay of Biscay to Bordeaux in France. This done, the worst part of the journey would have been completed, and they would stop in Bordeaux. After that, there would be no more stops until they reached the Channel Islands where they would make a stop to take on produce and fuel before heading for England's shores. The next part of the journey for Katherine was difficult. The sea was rough now, and she was getting heavy with child. Moving about was not easy, and she admitted that it was easier for her to stay in and around her cabin; sometimes sickness invaded her sleep, and a terrible tiredness seemed to wash over her. Adolphus would bring his papers to her, and she would sit on her bunk and go through them. Naples slept at her feet, but the days dragged and she longed for the smell of fresh air and the feel of the wind in her hair.

The boat rocked back and forth as it forged its way along the North coast of Spain. The captain had said that they had sustained a little damage, and that it would have to be fixed in Santander before they headed into open seas across the Bay to France. This was a setback that Katherine had dreaded. She was not sure, but she thought that her baby should be born around September, and it was fast heading toward June. She would not bother Adolphus with her thoughts, but she prayed she would be off this boat long before that happened. She was the only woman aboard, and she could not imagine what it would be like. No! She would not even consider that; she would rest, and do everything she could to ensure that it wouldn't. The stay in Santander was longer than anyone expected. The damage to the boat had occurred during the loading of cargo at Vigo and, although not serious, it needed attention before the crossing to Bordeaux and the long trek north along the coast of France.

Adolphus had resigned himself to the situation. Santander was not his most favourite place, either on land or by sea. He decided that he would begin to collate the pages that Katherine had read. It would save time eventually, and keep him occupied, along with Katherine's company, for the few days that they would be imprisoned in their cabins. He was just thankful that the damage didn't require the boat to be lifted from the water, as this would have meant that the two passengers, along with some of the crew, would have to go ashore. In all, they were in dock for five days.

During one of those days, Adolphus suggested to Katherine that perhaps they should stretch their legs awhile, and that he would accompany her from the boat and take her to a tiny eating place that he had used before on his travels. He insisted that she took with her all her treasured possessions that she had carefully shown him when she had related her story, and all the papers that she had been given before embarking on the journey. This duly carried out, Katherine put on her coat to cover her now obvious condition, held his arm, and stepped on Spanish soil for the first time. It felt no different to the soil that she had last trodden on when she left Italy, but she was fascinated by the Spanish language, and by the way Adolphus conversed with every one that he met. They walked down a narrow street bedecked with flowers hanging from lamp posts and tiny wrought iron balconies which perched high upon the narrow houses until they came upon an eating house with a large striped canopy over its door and window.

Adolphus ushered her in front of him, and spoke in a soft voice to a woman who held a note pad attached to a chain which in turn held a pencil. The woman wore a black skirt with many flounces that swirled around her as she moved, a white blouse with a high lace neck, and shoes with pointed toes and little heels. Katherine was enthralled by the whole picture, and said as much to Adolphus who just smiled and bade her sit down and enjoy the meal that he had chosen for her.

When they finally returned to the boat, Katherine felt like a lady who had been escorted by a lord to a banquet of great proportion, held in a magical place that only the very best of people would know about. She could not stop talking about it, and made it her business to inform the captain about this wonderful place, and tell him that one day he must visit it too, to which he answered, 'Mademoiselle, I most certainly will, and thank you for telling me about it.' Then, giving Adolphus a sly wink, he carried on with his duties. The memories of that day stayed with Katherine for a long time, and she would think about it when the journey got rough, or when she felt tired and a little unwell.

The ship, now operational, got up a full head of steam and started to proceed across the corner of the Bay of Biscay making for the coastal town of Bordeaux in France. This was a piece of open sea, but, having lost a lot of time in Santander, the captain made a decision to do this instead of following the coastline which would take very much longer. This part of the journey was always going to be the most difficult for the passengers, for after they had docked, and departed again from Bordeaux, they would have to negotiate one of the worst stretches of water known to sailors, let alone passengers.

Katherine was going to stay in her cabin, but it was the turn of Adolphus to be ill, and indeed he was very ill, so much so the captain asked Katherine if she would consider sitting with him and try to get him to drink as he was getting seriously dehydrated. Of course she agreed, so taking her small case and her papers, she moved herself into his cabin. The captain had put in there an enormous chair that stood on two rockers, and he padded it with cushions and covers so that she would be comfortable. Adolphus dropped into bouts of delirium, and she gently fed him fluids, remembering when she had nursed Joseph with much the same symptoms. It took almost a week for him to sit up and take some solids. He couldn't recall what had happened to him, but he knew that Katherine had been there, and that it was her care and devotion that had brought about his recovery. He was still very weak from the loss of fluid, but he was lucid again and was gathering his senses. Katherine stayed with him until he was able to care for himself, and was ready to start back on his work.

As yet, the boat had only made it a short way up the coast towards the small offshore islands at La Rochelle. From there onward it would encounter numerous small islands, which meant taking a wider course out into the bay to stay clear of them and to avoid the risk of grounding. Safety from these hazards would not be over until the boat reached Brest, and there it would stop, giving the crew some rest before it finally headed into the English Channel, made for the Channel Island of Guernsey, and then to the southern coast of England. This part of the journey could still be fraught with danger, as the English Channel was not the haven of peace that you might like to think it was. Some of its tides were extremely dangerous, carrying cross currents which could pitch a boat off course. The captain explained all this to two avid listeners, one old man with an urgent desire to finish the work on the book that had taken much longer than he ever had thought it would to complete, and one young woman with a most urgent need to find a safe haven in which to prepare for the birth of her child that was now giving her many nudges to tell her that its arrival was not that very far off.

August was two weeks from its end. The boat had to make a stop at the rope-making town of Bridport, in the county of Dorset, to collect a large consignment of rope which would be packed and stacked, and waiting for them at the quay ready for delivery to Liverpool docks. This would be the last stop for the tramp steamer before it took on a new crew and started its return journey. This part of the journey for Adolphus Peregrine Fry was perhaps the most busy. He was looking to find offshore habitats that would slot neatly into the sections of his notes where such locations were vital for birds migrating from northern territories, and as a stopping off place for those whose journeys would take them far into the southern hemisphere. Thus his research would reach full circle, and his book would emulate its name.

Katherine was growing daily more tired as the weight of her unborn child laid heavily upon her. She was none the less in good spirits. She would pass each section, that Adolphus gave her in the morning, back to him each night after being thoroughly read, and tied with its relevant coloured ribbon, the ends of which were hung from each section with exactly the same length of ribbon hanging neatly. If the sizes of the piles of notes varied, she would make one end shorter to even up the length left. Adolphus commented continually on her neatness, and her ability to read English and comprehend it so well. He also found she had an almost faultless accent, to which she explained that Martha, being English by birth, had been determined that she would be fluent in it from the moment that she uttered her first words. He had said that he would like one day to meet the woman who had created this almost perfect human being, who stood before him with the utmost courage for one so young to face an unknown future with acceptance, and the will to succeed at whatever cost. She had changed his life without even trying. He knew that he would, if he possibly could, support her in all that she hoped to do. He was affluent, and he had influence in places that many people would have envied. Until the present time, he had had no call to use any of his privileges, but now he would push out all the boundaries necessary to help her. He would not tell her this, as he knew she would object, but help her he would.

The journey across the English Channel was by any standards appalling. The autumn tides were rough, the weather was unkind, and Adolphus had to abandon his plans for this part of the journey, for the visibility was poor, and standing on deck was not easy even when you had two legs to stand on and two hands to hang on to rails. Adolphus, with a slight amount of shock, realised that he was beginning to get too old for this kind of adventure, and resigned himself to drawing the circle together with a small amount of author's licence, and a good imagination. He spent many hours with Katherine, which was always a joy to him. They talked about his book, and how he would bring it all together in the next two months, so that it would hopefully be published by the New Year. Katherine would be a mother by then, and this led them to talk about her, and what she hoped for. All she wanted, she said, was for her baby to be in good health, especially as she had had no medical advice, due to her age and situation in Italy.

'All will be well, my dear,' promised Adolphus. 'I will see that you are cared for as soon as we land, as long as you are prepared to come to Liverpool with me. I have to go there and I can take care of your interests easier from there. You will be safe, and so will your child.'

'How can I ever repay you, sir?' she said. She still could not bring herself to call him anything but sir, and he didn't seem to mind too much.

They docked in the beautiful little town of Bridport on the south coast of England. The weather was calmer, and was still warm enough for Adolphus to take a now very large Katherine for a walk along the quayside, and along the picturesque seaside, where many of the local folk were taking a stroll. It was Sunday, Katherine worked out; time just didn't exist when you were sailing, so it was lovely to feel a part of the human race once again, and feel her sea legs gradually coming to terms with 'terra firma'.

It was another two days before the little steamer took to the seas for the last push that, with possibly one short stop, would take them to their final destination. Katherine had but one hope in her heart, that they would reach Liverpool before the final days of her confinement, at best she could still have five weeks, at worst she could be looking at less than three. The captain assured her that with a good following wind, and calm coastal seas, they would be docking in about two and a half weeks.

She rested in her cabin as much as she could; she talked to her baby, and sang it lullabies, much to the amusement of Adolphus who asked if he could talk to it too so that it would get to know his voice, and then perhaps it would know him when it was born. They had made their way slowly but steadily up the west coast of England, stopping on the north west coast of Wales. As they hugged this large part of stunningly beautiful coastline, Adolphus took to the rails again with his notes, and this time a yellow ribbon. Once again, he was absorbed into his lifetime mission, and feverishly jotted down page after page of his ever neat and concise writing. It was nearly over now, for him to fulfil a dream that had taken him around the world, and for her to head where ever life took her in an effort to work toward taking Joseph's child home to him, and spending the rest of her life in idyllic happiness in their little cottage on their own beautiful beach, and perhaps to see Martha once again. What a story she would have to tell her!

She began to pack away her clothes, and her little case with all her treasures was left in a prominent position so that it could be the last thing that she picked up as they left. Adolphus had told her to be ready, and that he would come to her cabin and escort her from the boat. A couple of times she had felt her baby move violently, and it had caused her to catch her breath. Now and then it made her feel quite sick. It was in the early hours of the morning when they were due to pull into Liverpool docks that the pain was quite bad; she laid back on the pillow, and talked to the little one that was giving her such a jolt. 'Be patient, my angel; please wait a while.' Lena had gone through all of this with her in the weeks before she left Italy, and what she had told her was happening to her now. The pains grew in intensity, although still a while apart, which Lena told her to note as and when they happened. She tried to stay calm but, with the thought that she had to walk from the ship when all she wanted to do was to lie down, it all began to take its toll on her.

Adolphus had already left his luggage at the exit point, complete with a black and white cat called Naples, who the Captain had asked him to take with him as he could not stay aboard the boat. They had fashioned him a basket made from an old crate to which they had fixed handles, and put a blanket in. Naples had settled quite comfortably as Adolphus headed for the staircase to Katherine's cabin. The Captain had already sent one of his crew, on Adolphus's instructions, to take both his and Katherine's belongings to the carriage that would be waiting at the end of the quay. Katherine, white-faced and clutching only her small case in her arms, was standing in the doorway, a look of complete relief upon her face when she saw Adolphus. Together they made their way down the gang plank, saying goodbye and thank you to the Captain, to whom Adolphus passed a large white envelope folded in half to secure its bulky content. The Captain grinned, and said, 'Thank you very much and good luck, sir, with everything!'

Katherine was now showing signs of feeling very ill; her steps were slow, and her breathing quite laboured. She stopped once, doubling up with pain as Adolphus put his free arm around her, and the crew member from the boat, who had just put the luggage aboard the carriage, ran across to offer help. Between them they managed finally to get her aboard the carriage as she collapsed against them, crying out as the pains came more frequently and were lasting longer. In fact, now the pain was continuous, and Katherine was helpless. Adolphus spoke briskly to the driver of the carriage, jumped aboard and they headed away with great haste. The streets were busy with the morning traffic, so negotiating the twists and turns was not easy for the driver, and was agony for Katherine.

'We are going straight to the hospital,' Adolphus told Katherine. 'I will see to everything, but it seems we have little time. I have sent a message ahead and they are expecting you. I will have to leave you in their care, as I have some important things to do, but you will be safe and I will come to you as soon as I can.'

Katherine knew very little as nurses and doctors surrounded her. She was frightened, but held on to the promise of Adolphus to take care of everything and return as soon as he could. Then the pain just took over, and she gave herself to it. Mixing screams with crying, and sometimes following an order that was being thrown at her as she floated in and out of labour. Eventually there was nothing. There seemed to be nothing for a very long time, just an occasional sound of floating voices way above her. She saw fields of flowers, and heard the voices urging her to follow them to where she would be happy. She fought with them because they were unrecognisable, and then she heard them say, 'we can't get her back.' She was not going with them, not without her baby, but still they were trying and still she fought them. She felt herself being shaken and she was getting angry, saying, 'Go away and leave me alone. I will not come with you.'

When at last she opened her eyes, she met the eyes of a nurse, who, without the slightest sympathy or understanding, said, 'I am sorry but I'm afraid your baby died; we did everything we could and at least we saved you, and you are young so you can have another baby when you are old enough.'

Katherine let out a piercing scream, tried to lift herself from the bed, fell back retching from the shock and, burying her head in the pillow, repeatedly screamed 'No! No! No!' as Adolphus walked through the door. The nurse waved to a second nurse to stay with Katherine while she dealt with the matter. She ushered Adolphus to a side ward and sat him down. He was also now in a state of anxiety seeing Katherine this way and asked what had happened. The nurse proceeded to explain to him what they had done.

'Everything has been taken care of, sir,' she began. 'We did what you asked and took care of her, and her baby. So, sir, you will have no worries now; the child will go to a good home. We had a couple waiting for such an occasion as this, and all the papers have been completed. We thought we had lost the mother, and so we acted quickly; you will now not have to accept the responsibility of paternity.'

'Paternity! Paternity! What in heaven's name are you talking about, woman?'

'Sir, we assumed, due to your concern, and your orders to us to look after her and the child, that you were the father,' answered the nurse.

'You think I am the father of the baby of this poor child next door, whose baby you have stolen, and to whom you have told the most outrageous lies. How much money have you made from this deal, and what do you think that I am going to do about it now? In fact, what are you going to do about it before I bring justice to bear on you as a nursing sister, and your hospital? It really warrants a lot of thought, doesn't it? I am not leaving that child in there, who I tell you has more courage in her little finger than you will have for the rest of your life in your whole being, believing that her baby is dead. Where is the baby now?'

'It has gone with a temporary wet nurse with the adoptive parents, and it has been arranged that it will stay there until all the paperwork is returned to us,' the nurse replied with trepidation as to the next question or comment.

Adolphus, who had been frantically thinking how he could remedy this terrible mistake, had no cares at his time of life about what people would think. 'Well, nurse, I will not be leaving this room until you come up with something acceptable that I can go and tell Katherine, or until I start proceedings which could well see you finished in your profession. This young woman, believe me, is no pushover, and she will fight for the right to have her baby back.' With this, he crossed his arms and sat staring at her without a flicker in his eye.

'Sir, I can only see one way that would assure her that she could see and hold her baby. I am afraid that the paperwork has been done legally now, and to reverse that would be very difficult indeed for someone as young as her, who has no abode and no means of caring for the child. The adoptive parents are not young, and the baby will need a permanent wet nurse at least for a while, but Katherine would not be able to admit to being the baby's mother and this could appear to be quite impossible for her,' the nurse said, realising that she was putting her life on the line if this went wrong and Katherine spilled the beans. 'Do you feel that this would be acceptable?'

'Acceptable? Nothing will seem acceptable to her; there could be no substitute for caring and raising her own child,' Adolphus replied. 'Nothing that you could say or do will ever undo the terrible wrong that you have just done, but I will think about what you have said, and I will go and see her. At the very least she has to know that her baby survived the birth. You will go nowhere near her, do you understand?'

'Yes, sir,' she replied.

'Just one more thing before I leave you to think on what you have just done. I would also like to see... No! in fact, I insist that the money that you have received for this transaction goes to the children's ward of this hospital. As I am patron, I will personally send a letter of thanks for such a generous donation.'

Leaving the nurse falling into the empty chair that he had just vacated, he picked up his cane and left the room. Exhausted, he wished that he had not had to spend the last four days at the university. He could have spent them near to Katherine, then none of this would have happened. He would somehow now have to make her sit and listen very carefully to all that he had to say to her.

The door to Katherine's room was open. She appeared to be sleeping, and the nurse was hovering around. Adolphus made a sign for her to go, which she did rather quickly, he thought. He quietly pulled a chair to her bedside and, while he waited, he rehearsed what he had prepared to say. He thought, as a writer, it would be comparatively easy, but it wasn't. He watched her stirring, and then whimpering. As she turned from her side to see him there, new tears streamed down her beautiful face, and he found it hard not to reach out and hold her. I could if she were my daughter, he thought. They sat for a while and looked at each other, neither knowing where to start.

Katherine finally said, 'I have lost my baby… it was a girl… she died… how could she die? I have loved and nursed her through all of these months, and now she has died. Why, Adolphus… did they tell you why? They wouldn't tell me... only that she was dead.'

Adolphus sat quietly and let her rant on until she had spent any remaining energy, and then, offering her a clean white handkerchief, he started to speak. 'Katherine, you must now sit and listen very, very carefully to what I have to tell you. Courage has been by your side almost all your life, my child, and never have you needed it as much as you are going to need it now.'

He took a large intake of breath, and held both of her icy cold hands in his and began. 'Please don't interrupt until I have finished what I have to say, and then we will talk. First, and this is going to be the most unbelievable part of my story, your little daughter is not dead!'

Katherine's mouth flew open, and he gently placed two fingers against her lips. Seeing her pale and wan, he gently set her back against the pillow. 'Stay a while, child, and listen. Your daughter did not die, but the nursing staff thought that you had died, and they arranged for your daughter to be taken away. Unfortunately, they believed that I was the father of your child, and they decided that some money could be made by allowing a childless couple, who were on their books, to adopt a child, be allowed to pay for having a new-born, and to relieve me of the responsibility of fatherhood. I know it is very bizarre, and a bit too much for you to bear, but, my dear, you must listen, and then you must make a choice.'

Katherine, now incensed, could listen no more. 'Where have they taken her? How dare they! She is mine and I will go now and collect her.' Screaming and crying, she tried to leap from the bed, but in a state of collapse she fell backwards screaming, and with great sobs, crying, 'I want my baby... she is mine... they have stolen her from me.' Adolphus once again gently pushed her shaking body back against the now soaking wet pillow. 'No, Adolphus, I will not listen,' she screamed. 'She is my child and they have no right.'

'She is your child, Katherine, and you do have a right to plead your case, but this is the hardest bit of all. You are under age and have legally no way of caring for your baby. If all had gone well, and you could have left the hospital with your baby, I could and would have provided for you both, but circumstances did not allow that to happen. What you now have to consider is that if you fight for the right to have your baby back, the law could step in and take your child from you, and you would never see it again.'

Katherine by now was nearing hysteria, pummelling her pillow, and screaming, 'I must find her... she will need me... who will feed her...? she will be crying. Get me out of here, Adolphus, and please help me find my baby.'

'Katherine, there is something more far-reaching than this for you to consider first. If you contest the adoption of your child, the authorities would ask for the father's name, and if you were to refuse to give it, you would find yourself in an impossible situation. If you gave them Joseph's name, then he could possibly be sent to jail. Even though he is in Italy, it would be pronounced as rape, and because of your age the British police would forward the information to the Italian authorities.'

All Katherine could say now was, 'I will not! I will not let them take her,' and turning into her pillow, she wept. All that Adolphus could do was wait. The nurse passed the door once or twice, and Adolphus shook his head and told her to go away. Eventually she raised her head and said, 'what do I do then?' she sobbed.

Adolphus, feeling more emotion than he had ever felt in his life before, started again where he had left off. 'The child will need a permanent wet nurse for a while, and probably from there on she may need a nursemaid. I can leave the nurse to arrange this, and I assure you that there will be no mistakes. This will be the only way that you will not only be able to see your baby, but you will be able to nurse her and care for her just as you would have if none of this had happened. I am so sorry that it did happen, and I will not forgive myself for it doing so. I will be here in Liverpool most of the time, and we can meet. This is one of your choices; the other is that you return to Joseph and carry on as if nothing has happened, but that would mean that you would never see your child. If you choose to do this, I will arrange for a much more comfortable journey home for you. I can't leave here today until you make your decision. I can go away and leave you for a while if you wish, but by tomorrow it may be too late.'

Katherine, sitting up now in bed, eyes full of tears but shining as she said, 'I can't desert my baby, and Joseph would not want me to, I know that, and yes the risk is too great to fight for my daughter's return to me, so, yes, Adolphus, I will stay and do whatever I have to do. I want so much to see and hold my little daughter. She may have a different name, and I know she will never call me Mama, but I will love her, and be there for her forever. Thank you, Adolphus. Please do whatever you have to do, and I will follow your instructions to the letter. Thank you for giving me so much of your life, when I know it is all so strange for you. I will never forget you, and I hope that my future will allow me to see you, and you to see my baby one day, for you and only you will know the truth. I love you much more than I would love an uncle, Adolphus,' she sobbed, throwing her arms around him and crying tears of submission, tinged with a tiny ray of joy, that she would soon hold her baby.

Gently she kissed him on the cheek, then slowly settled back against her pillow and closed her eyes. With this, he left her room, wiping away both hers and his tears from his cheek with the back of his hand, and made his way back to set the seal on the agreement he had reached with the nurse. At least now she had stopped calling him sir!

Chapter Twelve

A New Beginning

Katherine awoke early on a crisp autumn morning, gazing from the window in the hospital where she awaited the arrival of Adolphus who was to take her to the house where she would find the child that she had given birth to a week ago. He had promised to deliver her and her luggage, but then she would be on her own to make herself known to the family who were now, by the signing of a piece of paper, the parents of her baby. Adolphus entered her room carrying a large travel bag, and the small case in which he knew was Katherine's only link to her birthright. With a slight smile, he took her arm and led her out of the room that held so many bad memories, and along a corridor, where white clad nurses quietly got on with their duties. As they reached a large desk, a lady dressed in a dark blue uniform, came from behind it, nodding to Adolphus, and smiling at Katherine, as she handed over a large brown envelope and wished them goodbye. Adolphus held open the main door for Katherine and they stepped out together into the sunlight.

They walked a short distance to a carriage, and climbed aboard as the driver placed the luggage on the rack at the back. Once aboard, and sitting comfortably, Adolphus proceeded to instruct her as to her introduction. 'The name of your employers will be Mr James and Mrs Lavinia Elford, who are now the legal parents of your child. They live at Lacey House in Green Street, which is where we are now heading, Katherine. I am so sorry that all this must seem so difficult for you to understand, but it is the only way that you will be able to be in close contact with your baby. It is most unusual for this to be allowed, but I have negotiated with the hospital and, provided that you follow your instructions to the letter, I see no reason why it will not continue for the foreseeable future. I will leave you at the house, but I will be in touch, and will be checking on you in the capacity of an uncle from time to time. Then we will be able to make arrangements to meet, perhaps in the park, and you will tell me all about your new life, and that of your daughter, but, remember Katherine, no one must be aware of your relationship to the baby that you are about to care for. Work hard and do all that they ask of you, and you will I am sure settle in to a rather nice routine as a wet nurse, and who knows what will evolve.'

Katherine could think of nothing but holding her baby, and it was all she could do at the end of the journey to stop herself from leaping from the coach, and up the stairs to the enormous oak door that stood closed before her. She whispered her goodbyes to Adolphus, and taking her luggage in two hands from the driver, she took a deep breath and climbed the steps with some trepidation, set her luggage at her side, and pulled the large metal handle that rang the bell. Silently the door opened and the noise of a baby crying reached her ears, as a tall hard-faced woman stood in front of her. 'About time too,' she bellowed, 'you the nurse? The brat has not stopped yelling since it arrived. What they wanted a child for at their age I will never know,' she shouted as she looked disdainfully down her nose at Katherine. 'Get upstairs and try and stop that row as quick as you can. I will come up and sort you out when I have had my tea break. Second floor second door on the right; just follow the noise.'

Katherine needed no second bidding. She picked up her cases and headed with all haste toward the sound of her baby crying. Tears were forming, but she had to hold them back and act like the wet nurse that she had been employed as. She quietly knocked at the offending door, and a voice bade her enter. The first thing she saw was the pale face of an attractive woman, beautifully dressed. She was sitting in a large wicker chair surrounded by cushions, with her hand on a wicker cradle rocking it back and forth. From inside the cradle came the heartbreaking sound of a baby crying incessantly. The woman looked at her and pleaded, 'Please can you try and stop her crying; the previous nurses have not been able to. They have fed her ,but still she cries. I think she has something wrong with her.'

Katherine's heart took a leap at the last statement. She steadied herself, pulled aside the pink blanket which covered the baby, and for the first time set her eyes upon the child that had brought her here to England. Joseph's baby that he would probably now never see. The little wrinkled face, all red from crying, and the tiny body, enveloped in a cotton gown that was now soaking wet, looked a sorry sight as Katherine lifted it from its pillow. She took her across the room to where there was a window seat, then sat and let her nestle against her breast and, to her amazement, for the first time she felt her baby try to suckle her. She adjusted her dress and allowed her full access to her feed, at which her daughter stopped crying and nestled against her mother as if she had been there since the hour she was born.

Mrs Elford sat and watched in awe as this young girl fed the child, and afterwards changed her nappy, pulled a fresh gown from the pile that had been ironed, and sat there just holding her. There was no more crying, and it appeared that the child knew just how to handle her charge. Perhaps she would be the right wet nurse, and they would all get some peace and quiet. Katherine, not moving from her position near to the window, watched the baby as it now slept peacefully, its tiny face, although still a little screwed up, was pale and its skin so soft to the touch of her finger as she gently stroked her cheeks. She was still sitting holding her against her breast as the door flew open and the voice of the housekeeper came screaming across the space between them.

'Come along, girl, there are other things for you to do as well as sitting cuddling that child. Give it to its mother, and follow me.'

Katherine, following the instruction reluctantly, passed the baby over and received a grateful smile from its mother, who sat up to take the baby from Katherine. 'We have decided to call her Dorcas Louise,' she whispered, looking at the baby with an uncertainty that was not lost on Katherine.

'It's a beautiful name for a beautiful child, Madam,' Katherine replied, as she followed the housekeeper from the room. Down the stairs they went. The housekeeper setting a pace that Katherine found difficult to keep up with due to the soreness that remained within her body after the birth of her child that now seemed a lifetime away.

Once downstairs, they negotiated a narrow corridor which lead to a large room that was filled with linen, and then on through a door, and along another corridor which was adorned with an assortment of clothing hung on pegs, until they reached the door to the kitchen, which the housekeeper threw open and sniffed the air on finding two people busy with obviously important chores. 'Stop,' she yelled with force as the two occupants jumped to attention, and faced her. 'We have here yet another wet nurse, whom we will undoubtedly be saying goodbye to in the not too distant future. She will be referred to as "Nurse", just as you two are referred to as "Cook" and "Footman". Do I make myself clear? There will be no using of names, and you will only be allowed to have a conversation during your fifteen minute dinner and tea breaks which will be taken in the ante-room. All crockery will be returned to the kitchen, washed up, and put away. You will make yourself known to the maid when she returns to duty in a couple of days, but in the meantime you will take a share of her duties, along with Cook whom you will now stay with for the preparation of lunch for the mistress. You will of course be responsible for all the child's needs, and you will personally be in charge of the washing and ironing of all the bedding and clothes pertaining to the child. Any further duties that the mistress requires you to carry out will be done without question. Is that quite clear, Nurse?'

'Yes, ma'am,' replied Katherine, dropping the smallest of curtseys. The housekeeper, eyebrows shooting upward at the audacity of the girl, but choosing to ignore it this time, said, 'I am the one exception to the rule of using a title instead of a name during communication. My name is Miss Paris, and you will call me by this name in or out of my presence at all times, and the curtsey will not be needed. I will now leave you with Cook to fill in any further details that she may consider relevant to your position. You will then return to the mistress, who will, I'm sure, delight in showing you your room, which in my opinion is much too good for you.'

With this, she exited the room with a flourish, nose held high, and heels clicking loudly as she made her way back to the room she occupied just off the main hall. Katherine stood and waited for some movement to come from the two people who had remained silent throughout the whole episode.

The first to speak was the footman who stepped forward with a grin and introduced himself. 'My name is Charlie Orchard, and I do a lot more than just be a footman. I am at her beck and call day and night, never a moment's peace she gives me, but I sticks it because the Master is good to me, kind he is, and if I keeps quiet and gets on with the job, I gets a few perks that she don't know about. What is your name then? We all know each other's names. She thinks she has us scared, but she don't know nothing, so come on whisper, what do they call you?'

'I am called Katherine Anne,' she whispered, looking over her shoulder to be sure no one was eavesdropping.

'A pretty name for a pretty lady,' Charlie remonstrated. 'Shall I tell you a secret Katherine Anne? Her name is Trafina Paris. What an 'andle, eh!

Sharp by name, and sharp by nature, that's what we say. Tell her your name, Cook.'

Katherine turned expectantly to Cook and, reluctantly, Cook said, 'My name is Ruby Stone, and we need to get on with the mistress's lunch or we will be in trouble on your first day, so come along, Nurse, and we will get you back to the baby upstairs who seems to have responded to your touch already.'

With the preparation of the lunch complete, both Katherine, and Ruby the cook, made their way up the staircase. No sounds of crying could be heard, which in one way pleased Katherine, but in another way she wished that the baby had cried after she left so that she could take her in her arms again and comfort her. As they opened the door, they saw that Mrs Elford had been asleep, and that the baby had been returned to the cradle where it was sleeping, wrapped tightly in the blanket. Katherine thought that as it was so warm in the room, the covers should be loosened around the baby and hastened toward the cradle to attend to her. She found that her napkin was wet, and set about changing her while Cook arranged the small side table for the mistress to eat her lunch. This done, Cook bade them farewell and departed, leaving Katherine to care for the baby, and the mistress to eat her lunch and return to the book she had been reading when she fell asleep.

Katherine hardly noticed that the adoptive mother did not seem to mind that the baby she had so quickly taken from the hospital was being cared for by a stranger. So overjoyed was Katherine that she was able to attend to Dorcas Louisa, cuddle her, and see to her needs, the fact that the mistress had very soon put her down in the cradle after Katherine had left did not give her cause for questioning the real feeling behind the reason for the adoption of this tiny baby. Nothing registered in Katherine's mind at this early stage of her nursing except the overwhelming love she felt as she held her baby to her breast and felt her take her feed with an eagerness that amazed her. She appeared to have plenty of milk, so there would be no problems in the quantity required by this tiny scrap of humanity that had struggled for life along with her mother just a short while ago.

Lavinia Elford raised her head from the book that she was reading to notice how gently, yet confidently, this young girl was handling the child, and how contented the baby seemed to have become in just a short couple of hours or so. She was indeed happy, as the last few days had been becoming fraught. She herself found that having a real baby to care for was indeed very much more difficult than she had imagined, and while she could give it anything it needed in its life, she had no notion on how to give of herself as a mother. If this young woman could handle all the things that were needed to carry the child through babyhood, so that she could pay attention to the social life of her and her husband James, then they could all have a good life. Dorcas Louise needed a good home, and Katherine was heartbroken at the loss of her baby, and needed to give her love and attention to someone. She herself felt the need to be a mother and watch with satisfaction as the child who was now hers grew up into a beautiful young girl, and then finally to marry a well-to-do young man. She could accomplish all this with little effort.

She smiled at Katherine as she went about the business of taking Dorcas Louise toward the little washroom that was equipped with all the baby requirements. Katherine stopped as if to question her right to bathe the baby, and the mistress nodded and waved a hand in the direction of the little white linen cupboard where Katherine found the pure white towels and, underneath, the long white cotton nightgown embroidered with tiny flowers across its yoke. Katherine stopped for a moment in reflection and remembered the few tiny garments that she had brought in her little case all those miles across the seas for the baby that she could no longer call her own. At least she could hold and keep her safe from any harm, and with this lady who would provide her with the wherewithal do this, she felt at least a little blessed.

When Katherine returned with the baby cosily dressed in her night gown and wrapped in a shawl, she walked across to the mistress and laid the baby in her arms. Lavinia looked down at the now less puckered face and damp fair curls that stuck to the tiny head, and gently rubbed the curls with the towel that Katherine had given her until they were dry and fluffy, before returning her to Katherine for her to lay in the cradle.

All this done, Lavinia said to Katherine, 'Come and see your room. I have had your cases placed there.' She rose from her chair and led Katherine to the door next to the bathroom. She opened it, and Katherine gasped when she saw the room. It was beyond her imagination, and something that she had only seen in the books that found themselves on the market stalls where she had worked. Pale lemon walls lent themselves to the pictures of children that adorned them. A matching yellow carpet gave way to an enormous fur rug in front of a bed covered in a quilt of so many colours that Katherine thought it would take her at least five years to count them all as they sat in tiny squares edged with a narrow white lace. Two lace-edged pillows sat at its head and, leaning against the pillows, a large teddy bear took pride of place. There was a cupboard for her clothes whose space would never be filled, and next to her bed a table holding a pretty lamp. The window, adorned with frilled curtains, and a blind that would be pulled down at night, looked out upon a neat small garden, set with a lawn and with a graceful statue at its centre. The space on the other side of the bed would house the cradle which would be wheeled into the bedroom, so that Katherine could be on hand for night feeds, and to care for the needs of Dorcas Louise.

Katherine needed now to remind herself that all this could be short-lived, and her services could be dispensed with at any time, but at least not while the baby was still suckling, so for now she would devote her time to making sure that she never stepped out of line with the mistress, and as much as she had felt an instant dislike for Trafina Paris, she would answer to her call in any and every situation. Dorcas Louise was the be all and end all of her desire to live, and live she would, striving always to keep the household happy by caring for the child that had now become the daughter of very rich parents, whom she suspected would give her anything in the world, except perhaps the one thing that would nurture her throughout her babyhood and on through her young life, and that was love. Katherine felt that the mistress, as lovely and as gentle as she was, would never know the love a mother feels when she holds the baby in her arms that she has carried in her womb, and given birth to. She, Katherine, would substitute that love, knowing that she would never be able to claim that it was in fact her that had given Dorcas Louise the gift of life.

A few days passed, and things in the Elford household ran like clockwork. Even Miss Paris was bearable, although never lacking in the opportunity to call someone to book on some very feeble mistake. Katherine spent each day in the sheer joy of feeding, clothing, changing, and generally looking after Dorcas Louise, who had, according to the nurse who visited the house to check on the infant, gained weight, and was healthy. Mrs Elford was very pleased with Katherine, and in fact was becoming accustomed to having her around. She would cuddle Dorcas when Katherine put her in her arms while she went downstairs to attend to washing and ironing. Sometimes, in with the baby's washing, she would pop a couple of her own items of clothing, saying to Katherine that she preferred the way that she did them. Katherine never minded what she did, in fact she quite liked Mrs Elford, and they would sit and talk sometimes in the afternoon when Dorcas Louise was put down in her cot to sleep.

The household was now at its full complement of staff with the return of the young maid, who had introduced herself with the permission of Miss Paris, as Florence Petite. She was a bright, pretty young girl with spirit, and a cheeky attitude that caused some titters behind the back of the housekeeper. Katherine sometimes joined in, but always in awareness of the fragile position that she held. The master of the house had not been at home yet; business kept him away for long periods of time, the mistress explained. He had been at the hospital to sign the papers of adoption, and had seen the child then, but he would be quite surprised by her progress, she said, with a certain amount of pride. Katherine was finding the routine easy. She was sleeping well, and so was the baby. Almost every night she would have to wake her for her feed, which was taken with great relish to the delight of Katherine.

Often in the quiet moments, with her child at her breast, she would think of Joseph, and wish he was there to witness his daughter's beauty, and to feel the joy of holding her. She knew now that, for the time being anyway, she had no choice but to stay and care for Dorcas Louise. She could not under any circumstances leave her, so she would have to somehow write to Joseph and explain what had happened. She would so much like to speak to Adolphus, and ask for his help and guidance in the matter.

Perhaps, when the baby was a bit older, she would be allowed to take her for a walk in the beautiful perambulator that she had seen standing in the hall, and perhaps if Adolphus were to get in touch, she would, as summer approached, be able to meet him in the park and introduce him to the baby that had sent him scurrying across the streets of Liverpool in an effort to bring her into the world safely. All these things went round and round in her young head as she nursed this tiny child, who had found itself at the heart of a well-meaning upper class family, and who had not the smallest notion as to the great and exciting life that could be in store for it. Katherine could only give her love and attention, and this she did with unstinting patience and understanding.

The days and weeks hastened by, and Charlie Orchard became a champion to Katherine. He would run errands for her right under the nose of Trafina Paris, and in doing so would bring her little presents of fruit, and now and then some lovely toffee which was so sticky that she needed something exceedingly heavy to smash a small piece from the block. Thus she found herself in possession of a small hammer with a wooden handle, so that with a smart rap at its centre, it would send shards of sticky toffee across the kitchen table. They all found this amusing until the day when Miss Parris entered the room with her usual flair, and caught Katherine with hammer raised. A loud scream sent them all, including Katherine, scuttling to their allotted tasks.

'You, young woman, will come with me to the mistress, and we will see how long you last in the job you are supposed to be so good at, when in fact you are down here causing all my staff to put their jobs in jeopardy by your foolishness,' and turning on her clicking heels, she yelled, 'Follow me.'

Mrs Elford, having to listen to the housekeeper's view of the whole episode, had to hide a smile as she said quietly, 'I'm sure that Katherine is sorry for having shown a little childish foolishness, but she will stay on as a nurse for Dorcas Louise for as long as I need her. Thank you, Mrs Paris. I bid you good night. Katherine, would you please change Dorcas? She is a little fretful and you have such a gentle way with her.'

With this, feeling belittled and insulted, Trafina Paris took her leave, but she would not forget, and somehow revenge would be taken. Make no mistake about that, she fumed, as she descended the stairs, nose in the air. She did not see the three white faces peeping from behind the kitchen door, not knowing exactly what their fate would be, but the day ended, and the next morning began with not a further word on the subject from the tight lips of the housekeeper.

Katherine and Mrs Elford often referred to the time that Katherine was caught in an act of violence with a hammer, and Charlie Orchard now gave Katherine pieces of sticky toffee that he himself had smashed with the hammer when he was sure that Trafina Paris was not in the vicinity. After the episode of the sticky toffee, Katherine had a little cause for concern and was most careful, in or out of the presence of Trafina Paris, who obviously held her in low esteem, and who made some cutting remarks to her in front of the other staff in the house.

On one occasion, as Katherine moved around the kitchen preparing food for the mistress, Miss Paris, sitting in the high backed chair that was her domain when she was about to hold forth or issue some commandment, said haughtily, 'Why are you doing that? It isn't in your orders, to my knowledge.'

184

Katherine answered, 'Begging your pardon ma'am, but the mistress asked me if I could just prepare her a small repast as she was going out for a couple of hours to meet a friend.'

'Huh,' replied the housekeeper. 'She should be here caring for her child, and not leaving her in the hands of a little trollop like you. By the way, I have been meaning to ask, what exactly happened to the offspring of yours that you should be suckling instead of being here as a substitute mother?'

Katherine stepped back aghast at the onslaught of words, and had to think rapidly in order to answer. As it happened, she was so horrified at the words that had come from this woman's mouth that her flushed face and eyes bright with tears could act to her advantage as she answered. 'Ma'am, my baby died; I too almost died. I never saw my baby; they just told me she had died at birth.'

The questions went on. 'The father, what about the father? Where was he whilst all this was happening, eh?'

Katherine, in a quiet voice, replied, 'He was working many miles away, and could not be there.'

'I see,' the housekeeper said with a sneer. 'Bring it on yourself did you, many women do, saved you from being taken away, very clever that, but nearly killed yourself in the effort, did you? You should have been taken to the workhouse, plenty of babies there to feed, I've no doubt, women having babies all over the place with not a man to support them.'

Katherine by this time was distraught and, against her better judgement, lashed out at the old dragon she saw before her. 'How dare you. I wanted my baby more than anything in the world, and so did her father. We were all to be together as a family, but then how would you know about families? I'm sure that nobody would want you as a part of their life, and I would thank you to stay out of the private part of mine. I will work for you, and answer all your questions if you put them to me with respect. I will serve the mistress for as long as she needs me. You do not pay me, the mistress does, and therefore I am answerable to her, not you. However, because of your position, and in respect of your advancing years, I will treat you with the respect you deserve.'

With this she flung herself from the kitchen, and ran to the linen cupboard where she closed the door, leant against it and sobbed. She would not tell the mistress about this morning, so she could see what Miss Paris would do about it. If she decided to tell all, then Katherine hoped that the mistress would forgive her. If she took the side of the housekeeper, then Katherine knew that she had brought about something that she would regret for as long as she lived.

Time passed and all was quiet in the household again. The housekeeper rarely spoke to Katherine, but when she did, it was with disdain in her voice, and she never looked into her eyes, but aimed her comments way above Katherine's head. Katherine in turn was very polite, so as to give no cause for complaint. The baby was flourishing, and the relationship between Katherine and Lavinia Elford took on an easy companionship. The fact that Katherine almost completely took over the day to day care of Dorcas Louise didn't seem to cause the slightest problem with the mistress.

The bright new leaves appearing on the trees outside the windows heralded the arrival of Spring. Dorcas Louise, now three months old, gurgled as Katherine held her at the window and showed her the outside world. Unbeknown to anyone, Katherine reached her sixteenth birthday, and remembered the time when at fifteen she was too young to marry Joseph. Almost a year had passed; she missed him so much, and thought that now she should try and write to him and explain as gently as possible what had happed to her. She would have to go along with the story of her baby dying, in case the letters got into the wrong hands, but then Joseph would want her to go back to him in Italy, and how would she be able to explain the reason why she couldn't. She would try and contact him first; she would write in Italian of course, so that would be difficult for most people to translate. Then, after receiving his reply, she would decide what to do next. No one in the house knew of her contact with Italy so she could concoct a story, maybe with the help of Adolphus whom she missed too, and would love to see. Maybe one day he would visit the house in the guise of an uncle, and then perhaps they could meet in the park out of earshot, and she could enlist his help once again.

How lucky she had been to meet such a man, for without him she would now have no contact with the child who shared that endless journey tucked inside her mother. Katherine realised as she was musing here that she rarely left the house. She loved it so much, and her devotion to the needs of Dorcas Louise took pride of place; her own life faded into insignificance as a consequence. Now, as the warmer weather approached, she began to feel the desire to walk along a leafy street, to watch the people as they went about their daily tasks. She had no idea of the direction she could take, but being, she thought, quite self assured, she would find her way around the local area of Liverpool with little difficulty.

The mistress, she noted, began to go out more regularly now, and come home with a healthy glow. The master had returned for a few days, and had bustled around his wife, bringing her gifts, and taking her out to dinner. He had peered into the cradle, and commented upon the cherubic face of his young adopted daughter, but had made no attempt to lift her up. He had just gently touched her cheek with the back of his hand, and said, 'We are lucky to have such a beautiful little creature in our midst, are we not?' He directed his comment to Katherine and not to his wife, which Katherine found slightly embarrassing, but nodded with a smile, and went to her room in the hope that together Mr and Mrs Elford would bond a little more definitely with their child.

Katherine sat on her bed and began to read a book that Mrs Elford had lent her. She stayed as long as she thought was necessary, and then, upon hearing a whimper, she put down the book and entered the nursery. She stopped as she saw Trafina Paris bending over the cradle. She made a move toward her. Miss Paris on hearing her footstep stood up quickly and turned, face like thunder.

'What are you doing, Mrs Paris?' cried Katherine, checking quickly to see if the baby was all right.

'You had left her alone,' snapped the housekeeper.

'I had left her with her mother and father,' answered Katherine calmly.

'I saw them leave the house, and I came to take away any dishes,' the housekeeper claimed.

'As you see, there are no dishes,' and seeing that Dorcas Louise was fine, Katherine moved to the door, held it open, and Trafina Paris sailed through without further comment.

Katherine headed for the cradle, lifted out Dorcas Louise, placed her gently in a shawl, and laid her on a rug while she stripped the clothes from the cradle to make sure that nothing was amiss. Throwing the linen on to the floor, she replaced the bedding with clean, then changed the baby and made her ready for her feed. She shuddered at the thought of that evil woman touching her baby, and she could think of no good reason why she should be there in the room at all. What had she been up to, she wondered, but she knew she would never again let Dorcas Louise out of her sight when the mistress was not there. She also wondered why the mistress had not told her that she was going out.

The weeks followed uneventfully upstairs in the Elford household. The master had gone away again on business. Katherine did often wonder

187

what type of business he was connected with, to finance the kind of life lived in this lovely house, situated in such a pleasant area, and enjoyed by his wife and staff, and now by her own tiny daughter who for the foreseeable future was assured of the best upbringing that Katherine could have wished for. With this in mind she was determined to stay on good terms with her employer, no matter what, but she would always be aware that some sort of danger was evident from the ever present Trafina Paris. Dorcas Louise was still showing a healthy appetite for her feeds, and Katherine always seemed to have a plentiful supply. She ate and drank healthily with the guidance and assistance of the cook, and she hoped that weaning the child from the breast would take a while longer yet.

Katherine started to write a letter to Joseph. There was no real address to which to send it, but she hoped that, as the area in which they had lived was quite small, and had not many houses, Joseph eventually would be found. She would also write to Lena; how pleased she would be to hear of her final arrival in Liverpool. She assumed that the captain of the ship would by now have passed back through the port from where they had departed nearly a year ago, but whether or not he would have been in contact with Lena's husband was an unknown factor. She knew that to post a letter to a foreign country would cost a lot more money than one staying in England, and as she was not sure how to go about getting stamps for her letters, she decided to keep them in a safe place until she could ask someone; perhaps Charlie would go to the post house for her.

Spring now in all its glory, spread its magic around the house. The trees sprang into masses of pink and white blossom, daffodils grew in profusion around the borders of the garden, the grass became an unbelievable vivid shade of green, and every morning the birds sang their song of joy outside Katherine's bedroom window. She awoke one morning, and she felt happiness spreading throughout her body. Her baby, although no longer her own, was happy and healthy, and she cared for her every moment, catching the smiles as they lit up her darling little face, and cuddling away the tears when sometimes she had a reason to make herself known to all around her by wailing in discontent at having to wait a few minutes for a feed. She was now over half a year old, and beginning to show interest in all that was happening.

The master was home again, and it was on a Sunday morning that Katherine was summoned to the library. The mistress said that she would play a while with Dorcas Louise while Katherine went down to see the master. Mrs Elford could see that Katherine showed a frown and was more than a little flustered by the summons. 'Go, my child, there is little to be frightened of here. You can tell me about it when you come back.'

Katherine quickly removed her apron, smoothed down her black skirt, and tucked in the blouse that she had chosen as it was Sunday, quickly went to her bedroom and brushed her hair until it shone in the sunlight that reflected in the mirror. She washed her hands, dried them, and sprinkled a little of the rose water that the mistress had given her on to a tiny handkerchief that she had embroidered herself with a small K in the corner. The library, situated on the ground floor, was out of bounds to all staff, and so she felt extremely nervous as she knocked softly on the large oak door. She recognised the master's voice as he called loudly, 'Come in, Katherine.' She turned the brass knob, gently pushed open the door, and was greeted by a smiling Mr James Elford.

There was another gentleman who sat with his back to her, very elegantly dressed in a black suit. In front of him on the desk was a top hat, and laid on top was a pair of snow white gloves, by the side of which was a neatly wrapped parcel in brown paper. Katherine walking slowly toward the two men, wondering what all this was about, when she suddenly caught sight of a black cane with a beautiful silver top. Her heart leaped, and her footsteps faltered, as the gentleman slowly turned to face her. 'Adolphus,' she whispered. She wanted to run into his arms, but she just stood there.

The master's voice broke into her thoughts. 'I had no idea that you had such a famous man for an uncle, my dear. Your uncle and I frequent the same gentleman's club in the city. He has asked my permission to come and visit you here, and also to ask, if you were free, if could he accompany you to the park. The mistress has given her blessing, and if you wish you may take Dorcas Louise in her carriage with you. Katherine by this time was shaking with some relief and with a great deal of excitement.

'Oh, sir, it would be my greatest pleasure, not only to have the pleasure of the company of Uncle Adolphus, but to be able to show Dorcas Louise the park; she would love it, I know. I hold her at the window, and she shows such interest.'

Uncle Adolphus, now raising himself from the chair, turned to Katherine and said, 'Come here, Katherine, let me look at you; it is a long time since our journey together. I have been very busy, and I see that you have found a delightful position with this family, looking after their baby. I am told that both the master and the mistress are more than pleased with you. I am so happy. I have, I must confess, been quite worried at times. You were so unwell when I left you, but now I see you are blooming. If everyone agrees, I will call for you at two o'clock this afternoon, and bring you back in good time for you to see to the needs of your young charge, whom I'm sure is missing you at this moment. Just one more thing, and then I will bid you adieu until this afternoon. I have this little gift for you. I hope you enjoy it.'

With this, Adolphus shook the hand of James Elford as he walked with him to the door, leaving Katherine to make her way back up the stairs. So immersed in what had just happened, and the feel of the paper wrapped gift in her hand, she did not see the contorted face of Trafina Paris, who had to drop a curtsey for the eminent gentleman who had just left the library in the company of one Katherine Anne Carrera, whose name she had seen on the package that was placed on the hall table as he had greeted her master on arrival. She would have to be very careful, and somewhat devious, if she was to hatch a plan to remove the wet nurse-cum-nanny from her household, which up to now she had ruled with a rod of iron. Everything had changed for Miss Parris since the arrival of Katherine Anne.

The staff, although still very obedient and polite to her face, had developed a lighter attitude to their work, and sometimes she had even caught Cook humming a little tune as she prepared the vegetables. Charlie Orchard and Flo Petite had gained a rapport between them, and had been caught sharing a giggle on more than one occasion. She was losing her grip, and she knew it was down to the little goody-goody who reigned supreme upstairs, and influenced those who should be subservient downstairs. Katherine headed for the nursery as fast as her legs would carry her without breaking into a run. Opening the door, she saw the smiling face of the mistress beckoning her to sit on the stool beside her and recount her visit to the library, 'in every detail', she insisted as Katherine sat down, peeping as she did so at the sleeping Dorcas Louise in her cradle.

'Oh ma'am, it was my dearest uncle, and he is going to call for me and Dorcas Louise at two o'clock this afternoon to accompany us to the park, but only if you agree. He said that you had already, so please, is it all right?'

Lavinia laughed that tinkling laugh that Katherine liked so much. 'Of course it is all right,' she replied. 'In fact it will please me very much if you go with Dorcas Louise. You have both spent too much time inside the house; the weather is delightful, and you will both be fresh as daisies when you return. My husband assures me that your Uncle Adolphus is a man who commands great trust from all who enjoy his company, both in business and pleasure. I should like very much to meet him in the near future.'

Katherine, still holding tight to the parcel in her lap, said, 'I'm sure you will, and I am sure that you will find him as I do, a most gentle and caring man with an understanding of frailty in humans equal to that of the birds that are his joy to write about.' Her fingers were now playing with the string which held together the brown paper wherein lay the gift he had bestowed upon her. 'May I open my gift?' Katherine asked.

'Of course,' answered Lavinia Elford, fascinated by this young woman's obvious adoration of her uncle, who up to now had been the only person she had ever talked about. As Katherine pulled away the paper, it revealed the beautiful cover of a book which had as its illustration a stunning picture of a flock of birds, wings outstretched, hovering over a brilliant blue sea. Katherine, eyes alight, and lips slightly parted in breathless admiration, whispered, 'the book, he finished it in time as he said he would.' She opened the book to reveal the first page, and thereupon found these words:

To Katherine, I could not find one other person who could have lifted me to the utmost pinnacle of my talent, as you did in the days that you shared my thoughts, and sorted my writings during a very long and tiring voyage. Without you I would have been unable to bring this book to its ultimate end, and so it is, Katherine Anne Carrera, that I dedicate it to you with my love and thanks. Adolphus Fry.

Katherine, without lifting her eyes, passed the book to Lavinia Elford, who read the dedication with amazement, and then turned to Katherine and gently put her arm around her. 'Time is passing, my dear. Go and prepare the carriage for Dorcas; I will hold her until you get back, and then go and enjoy the company of your famous author.'

Katherine skipped down the stairs to find that the carriage was ready for the young Dorcas Louise. She looked around and saw Trafina Paris disappear into her room. Quickly she pulled back the covers and inspected the interior, even pulling out the little removable lid that covered a space for storage in the bottom of the perambulator. Suspicious, but satisfied that all was in order, she turned to go upstairs to carry Dorcas Louise down.

As she went, she pondered on how the housekeeper knew that she was taking the baby out, but then she accepted that probably the master had asked her to prepare the carriage, and she chastised herself for thinking badly of the old housekeeper.

Adolphus, good as his word, arrived at the door on the stroke of two o'clock, and with a wave from the cook, the maid, and Charlie Orchard, the little threesome set off on their afternoon adventure. Once out of sight, Adolphus asked Katherine to stop and let him see the baby that had caused him so many sleepless nights over the last few months. He bent over the carriage, gently folded the satin covers back, and took his first peep at Dorcas Louise. Katherine noted a slight catch in his voice as he said, 'She is exquisite; a tiny replica of her mother.'

Katherine looked at him and said, 'You are the only one who is able to say that to me.'

Adolphus smiled in a secret way, pleased that indeed he was the only one to have that pleasure. The afternoon went with a speed that enveloped them in memories, both good and bad, and enduring promises that they would always stay close and be there for each other whenever they could. Katherine's heart was full of the kind of love that you only reserve for a parent or a child. They decided to meet on Sundays when it was possible. Adolphus promised to purchase some stamps for her, for the letters to Italy, and to give her some special paper that was very light in weight. He thought Charlie Orchard sounded a very nice lad, and one that could be entrusted with the job of posting them for her. He was worried slightly by the stories of Trafina Paris, and told Katherine not to step out of line at all, and keep as much distance from her as she could, but at the same time not to let her see that she was frightened in any way by her presence.

She hugged him and thanked him for the book, and for the lovely dedication that she could not believe he would have written for her. Adolphus, as always, was enchanted by this young woman who had grown in stature and confidence since he had last seen her in a state of total distress at the hospital. She would cause him to spend more time in Liverpool than he would have under normal circumstances, but he would also have to travel to London to see that the property he owned was being cared for by his housekeeper, a trusted soul but advancing in years, which had made him wonder how long she would be able to cope with the large house on her own without any help. All this having been discussed, and noting that the time had come for them both to return to their own destinies, but now in the knowledge that they were intrinsically linked by a small chance in the scheme of things, never to be parted.

As the large oak door closed on the receding figure of Adolphus, Katherine felt a kind of sadness, but at the same time a bright feeling that would bring contentment and happiness whenever they met. She lifted a sleeping Dorcas Louise from her carriage, and carried her upstairs to the nursery, whereupon she woke and gave a toothless smile to Katherine and Lavinia as they stood above her.

The days went lazily by. Trafina Paris became less of a threat, as Katherine felt confident now that she could handle the situation should she try to intimidate her. She knew that she hated her because of the position she held that kept her close to the mistress. Charlie Orchard became her champion, much to the chagrin of the housekeeper. He would fetch and carry for her, and when she had to go to the kitchen to prepare morsels for the mistress, he would drop a few tasty titbits in her pocket. The house-keeper inevitably would appear and give that haughty look of contempt in their direction, but she kept her own council, which made Katherine slightly suspicious as to whether she was waiting for the moment when she could pounce on them, and deliver evidence to the mistress that might send them both packing.

Katherine, despite the fact that she had a soft spot for Charlie, tried to keep his concentration on his numerous jobs around the house so as not to arouse any more of Trafina's rages. Charlie had also whispered to Katherine of his feelings toward young Flo Petite, which had not surprised her a lot, for she had noticed the lingering looks that he gave her as they sat around the table and ate their lunch. They were both terribly young, she thought, and then remembered how young she was when she first fell in love with Joseph.

Katherine and Adolphus had met a few times now and talked about many things. He gave Katherine the paper he had promised, the envelopes, and enough stamps for four letters to Italy. 'Wait a while in between writing them,' he had said, as it would probably take quite a while before they found their destination. He was looking tired, but he revelled in the company of Katherine, and now they were very much at ease in each other's company. He had told her of the trip he had made to London, and that his house was being carefully looked after by his housekeeper of many years. 'She was a treasure,' he told Katherine, but now growing older and he felt that he should see to it that she had a nice little house of her own one day, so that she could retire and have someone to care for her, as she had cared for him. He said that he would love Katherine to meet her, and see the big old house that was to be his domain upon his retirement. The publication of his book would allow him to carry out his wishes if it sold well, and the first few months of sales had proved its worth, to his satisfaction.

Katherine thought what a fine, good man he was, and how honoured she felt to have played a small part in his life. She would love to see the house, but she knew that she couldn't leave Dorcas with the mistress for any length of time. She just did not seem to have the slightest notion of how to deal with a young baby, now growing fast and moving about, albeit in a somewhat crabwise motion. Katherine was left almost completely to look after Dorcas Louise, and although to her it was with the utmost joy that she did it, it made her almost indispensable, and the mistress made no bones about telling her so.

Dorcas Louise held her first birthday party in the nursery. Two of the young children from the nearby houses came bearing gifts. The daughter of the gardener came dressed in a bunny outfit with large pink ears. Everyone thought she was the sweetest thing, and Dorcas Louise planted a giant kiss upon her cheek, which caused the rabbit to cry, but only for a short time when Katherine picked her up and cuddled her until she smiled and waddled of in the direction of Dorcas Louise to retaliate, and thereby started a new friendship. Cook entered the nursery bearing a large birthday cake iced all over in pink icing with a giant candle, which was duly lit and placed on the table.

Katherine thought back to the first day when she had offered Dorcas her first little dish of solids. She should now only be fed once a day, the nurse instructed, and that should be before she was set down to sleep; the rest of the time Katherine would follow the weaning process, and feed her according to the paper that the nurse left her. Katherine was now living in her worst nightmare. The weaning of Dorcas Louise meant that her days as a wet nurse would be over soon, and this was what she was employed for. She sat one morning, holding the child that she had borne, and that had been her secret for one whole year, and tears ran down her cheeks at the thought that she might no longer be needed. As she sat there looking down on the golden head, she reached for a tiny pair of scissors that she kept in her bedside drawer, and she gently snipped a tiny lock of hair from the curls that surrounded the beautiful face of her daughter. Then she cut the end of the piece of ribbon that was threaded through the neck of her nightgown and tied it securely around the lock of hair, held it in her hand for just a minute or two, and then reached for her little case that was always close at hand and lovingly placed it amongst the treasures that were her life to this moment. She sat holding Dorcas Louise, gently rocking her back and forth, as the child, sensing Katherine's anguish, looked up at her and smiled, a smile that one only gives to the one who loves you, and in most cases that would be a smile from a child to a mother.

Katherine wasn't aware of the presence of Lavinia Elford in the nursery, and she had not been aware that the mistress had been there quite a while. 'What is it, child?' the mistress asked, seeing the obvious distress in Katherine's eyes. Lavinia had become very fond of Katherine, and realised that she could not raise this child without her; in fact she really did not want to. She was happy to perform the part of devoted parent, and in fact she adored the child, but in all honesty she did not want the job of raising her, and the thought of dealing with all the traumas of school days and teenage tantrums, sent a cold shiver of panic down her spine. 'Katherine,' she repeated, 'tell me if there is anything wrong. Are you not happy with your life here at the house? Do you not want to care for Dorcas Louise any more?'

At this point, Katherine looked into the questioning eyes of her mistress and said, 'Oh Madam, I love being here, and as for looking after Dorcas Louise, she has become my reason for living, but I am frightened that now she has nearly stopped feeding you will not need my services any more.'

'Katherine,' the mistress said, as she returned the questioning look with a smile. 'Would you do me the honour of staying on and being nursemaid, and later on nanny to my adopted daughter. She loves you, and I could not cope without you. You do not have to answer right now, but I hope with all my heart that you will accept, and if you do I will draw up an agreement that both my husband and I will sign, and then you will become a permanent member of our household.'

She rose as if to go and give Katherine time to think, but Katherine jumped up and stood in front of her, tears now streaming down her face as she replied, 'I accept with all my heart, and I will stay for as long as you and Dorcas Louise need me.' Of course, by finalizing her agreement to serve the family that had unknowingly taken her baby from her, in that second she had renounced her intentions of returning to Joseph, but she had made the decision unconditionally and without regret.

Katherine grew accustomed to the permanent position she now held in the Elford family residence. The news spread quickly to the staff, who all, with the exception of the housekeeper, greeted it with happy acceptance. Cook was delighted, and decided she would bake a special cake for the nursery tea to celebrate. Charlie Orchard was exuberant and quite spontaneously had picked up Katherine and twirled her round much to everyone's amusement. Flo Pettit was not there to join in the fun, but unfortunately Trafina Paris was, and it was with great relish that she regaled the incident to Mrs Elford as she came from the nursery to see what all the commotion was about, commenting that she had seen more than she wished to of Charlie paying much too much attention to the newly acclaimed nanny. She carried on to report that she thought in view of these observations, one of them should leave the employment of the house, and as it was not the wish of the Master and Mistress that it should be Katherine, in her opinion she would advise that it be Charlie Orchard. She concluded that his attentions being in question in the case of Flo Petite were enough to cause disruption to the household, but now the incident with the nanny would in her opinion place his reputation, and that of the Elford family, into doubt, and it would surely be better to deal with it now before it became a scandal.

Downstairs was in turmoil. Flo Petite had flown at Charlie Orchard in a rage, until Cook had pulled her aside, and told her exactly what had happened, and that they were all there at the time, and that the whole thing had been totally innocent. Flo was then reduced to tears of panic at the thought of Charlie being sent away and her not ever being able to see him again. Katherine was inwardly seething, but she knew that she had to keep quiet until the mistress had considered all the facts. The housekeeper, meanwhile, had disappeared red-faced and furious into her room, and had slammed shut the door. Charlie sat by the kitchen door, head in hands, waiting for the decision to come from upstairs, not understanding what he had done wrong. Katherine had made her way back to the nursery to calm down Dorcas Louise who had been woken up by the raised voices.

The mistress came back in to the room, and Katherine apologised for the disturbance. The mistress waved her hand. 'I will deal with the house-keeper. She does seem to be looking for trouble lately, and I know you better than to believe what she is accusing you or the young Master Orchard of. Please will you take Dorcas Louise to your bedroom, close the door, and I will call the claimant and the accused up here and end all this now.'

Once again, the housekeeper was not given the chance to cause a rift in the staff of the household of James and Lavinia Elford, who were both very satisfied with the way that everything in their domain was being managed. Trafina Paris was now obsessed by the notion of removing Katherine from the house. She had caused nothing but trouble from the moment she had set her tiny little feet on the doormat. She was obviously going to get nowhere with the mistress, who was now treating the little trollop as one of the family. She would find some way of catching her out, and she would use that stupid Charlie Orchard to do it. Somewhere, somehow, sometime in the future, she would set them up, and they would have no escape. She would kill two birds with one stone. The house would then be back under her control, and the mistress would have to look after the snivelling child that she had adopted, herself.

Katherine, once again, settled into life with Dorcas Louise. Spring had turned to summer, and Katherine had become used to finding her way around the outskirts of Liverpool. Adolphus, good as his word, came often and accompanied her to the park, and walked with her to the local shops where he guarded Dorcas Louise in her carriage, giving Katherine the chance to spend a little of her allowance on some personal purchases. She had told him that she had written to Joseph and Lena, but had heard nothing back from them. She had given the letters to Charlie to post for her. She told him that, until she heard from Joseph, and knew that he was well, she wouldn't tell him about the baby and what had happened. She was frightened that the hurt would be too much for him, especially the knowledge that she could not leave England, and also she was frightened that the truth would find itself in the wrong hands. Adolphus agreed that for the time being, she should keep the news of the baby's adoption to herself. He himself could not think of a way to handle the news at present, but he was sure he would be able to come up with a solution when once she had made contact with him.

Dorcas Louise, sitting up in her carriage now, and catching the eyes of passing walkers, was besotted with Adolphus, and opened her arms to him with a grin that now heralded the beginnings of one tiny white tooth, set in the middle of her little rosebud mouth. He lifted her from her carriage, and held her so that her feet wriggled to find somewhere to rest. His beard tickled her chin, causing her to sneeze, so that he could say bless you, which he did with great regularity. Katherine told him one day with great pride that Mr and Mrs Elford had asked her if she would be godmother to

Dorcas Louise, and would she swear in church that she would always care for her. 'What more could I ask for?' she said to Adolphus. It had been agreed that she would be christened at Christmas time; that seemed appropriate, as she would be approaching her second birthday by then.

It was when the invitations were being sent out that Charlie was on his way to the door with two letters that Katherine had asked him to post. Trafina Paris came along the corridor with an armful of post and saw Charlie with the two letters. 'What are you doing with those? Who are you writing letters to? I didn't think you could write,' she said scornfully.

'They are not mine. I am just posting them when I go to the shop for the master,' he said.

'Give them to me. I do all the posting of letters here,' she said, snatching them from his grasp. She looked at them, said nothing, but tucked them at the bottom of the pile that she had in her hand.

Katherine's days stretched endlessly before her, now that she was secure in the knowledge that she would always be able to care for Dorcas Louise. In fact, she found herself almost entirely seeing to her needs, while Lavinia took on the tasks of entertaining guests, and ensuring that her staff, under the orders of her housekeeper, were keeping a well-run household.

Trafina Paris, on the other hand, was vexed to say the least. The idea of the wet nurse now becoming a nanny, and gaining more and more responsibility and respect from the mistress, hit hard upon her confidence. She had been in the household for many years, working for Mr Elford's parents as a housemaid, before being given the position of housekeeper. Lavinia had come to live at the house after her marriage to their son James. It was not a marriage of young love. James had been serving in the armed forces, and had met Lavinia at a local gathering during one of his service breaks. His parents were happy to see him settled, but Lavinia had always been very quiet. Trafina herself had always silently thought that the girl needed a good prod in the back, or she would never make a good hostess for James whose job entailed many an evening of entertaining to lay out the plans for his business associates to see, and be prepared to bring his plans to fulfilment.

It was not until after the death of his parents, when Lavinia became mistress of the house, that James could see that, although she never complained, she was not the happy, supportive wife he needed. Life at the Elford house was dull, and James Elford spent much of his time away from home which made the housekeeper's job very easy. She worked hard to keep the house running smoothly in his absence, and received his praises regularly. She engaged her own staff and had them performing their individual tasks completely at her behest. It was therefore a great shock when the master informed her that he and the mistress were looking to adopt a child. The mistress felt that she was missing out on the most important part of a marriage and, as she was not now of child-bearing age, she felt that it would be a wonderful thing to offer a child a life that otherwise it would never know.

Trafina would carry on in the way that she did now, and the baby would not be in any way her responsibility. The mistress felt that she would be quite capable of nursing a tiny baby, and she would learn as she went along the why's and wherefore's of its growing up. Her friends had raised children so there was no reason why she shouldn't. Trafina's proverbial nose had however been put out of joint from the moment the screaming child had been delivered into her quiet contented life. Even more so when the sweet-faced little wet nurse had appeared and performed her miracles of turning a screaming brat into a gurgling, smiling infant. In honesty, she couldn't say that Katherine had deliberately caused her any grievances, but her presence brought a sense of unease to Trafina that she could not accept. She had worked hard for the family for many years, but now she felt that her advancing years may go against her, and the master may find her position as housekeeper unnecessary. Her inner anger was unfortunately brought to bear on the staff that she had had no problems with until now. Katherine was not under her supervision, and so could not, as she had found out, be held responsible for the wrong doings and upheavals in the kitchen. She would certainly never lose her job, as the mistress obviously relied upon her totally for the upbringing of her adopted daughter, and who also had a very personal liking for the girl.

Charlie Orchard, however, was another kettle of fish. He was also, she thought, besotted with the nurse, and was getting involved in running her errands, and bringing her gifts. She had seen with her own eyes the little parcels wrapped in a lacy napkin that he had slipped to Katherine. She was not convinced that there was not some sort of liaison going on between them in spite of his amorous advances to Flo Petite. Through him, if she was careful, she may be able to bring Katherine down in the estimation of the mistress, and if it happened often enough, she may just find a way of causing the dismissal of the nurse. Her mind in so much confusion, she could not see that she was almost bringing about her own downfall, but her bitterness was such that reason did not come into the equation. Her obsession with getting Charlie into trouble manifested itself on more than one occasion.

The booming voice of the master came reverberating down the corridor one morning to summon Charlie to the library, where he was accused of getting black shoe polish on the inside of his master's shoes, which had rubbed off upon a pair of white silk hose that the master only wore on important occasions. Charlie protested his innocence by informing the master that he always wore white gloves when cleaning his shoes, so that any slip of the polish would immediately be obvious, and would be removed. The master, confused and surprised by his quick answer, sent him packing with a warning, but was left questioning the reason behind what appeared to be a deliberate act.

On another occasion, the baby carriage was left outside the kitchen door, and it had rained upon it, although the hood was up, and the rain cover on, it was still something that never should have happened. As soon as Dorcas Louise had been taken to the nursery, the carriage would be brought in and put in the small alcove in the hallway; its covers, pillows, and toys removed, and returned to Katherine. Again, Charlie was blamed, although he swore to Katherine that he had brought in the carriage, but was called to the kitchen by Trafina on some matter of little importance before he could remove the covers. He was also adamant that he had taken down the hood, thus raising some suspicion in Katherine's mind that someone was out to bring trouble down on Charlie's head.

Katherine, although worried by the incidents that involved Charlie, could see no way that she could help without causing trouble for herself, and she had no desire to do this. She was so happy with her life, and that of Dorcas Louise who was now crawling about and causing chaos in the nursery.

Adolphus loved her, and the three of them spent many happy hours during the bright days of summer, walking around the leafy lanes and parks, in this, an elegant area on the utmost outskirts of Liverpool. The only worry that played on her mind was the fact that she had received no answer from the letters that she had sent to Italy. She had now decided to stop writing for a while, as she could not recount to Joseph the joys and laughter that his daughter brought her. She was sad in case her letters had not reached him and he thought that she no longer cared. When she recounted her thoughts to Adolphus, he sat and quietly took in all she said, then he told her to wait a while longer, and not to lose hope, and that one day there would be an answer, he was sure. When Katherine had finished confiding in Adolphus, he turned to her and said, 'I hope you will be pleased to hear that Mr and Mrs Elford have asked me if I would kindly perform the duty of being Godfather to Dorcas Louise. It goes without saying that I am overjoyed at the invitation, and it also means that I can support you in your role of Godmother. How do you feel about that, Katherine?'

'Oh, Adolphus, how perfect. Dorcas adores you, and I can't convey my happiness. It rather points to the fact that Mr and Mrs Elford are happy to draw you into the family, and that can only be good for us all.'

To Katherine, Adolphus was like a father, grandfather, favourite uncle, and best friend all tied up in one package, and she did not hesitate to tell him her thoughts, at which he threw back his head and roared with laughter. Dorcas Louise, watching them from the confines of her carriage, began to giggle, and they both stopped in amazement. They turned to see her, head on one side, with one hand over her mouth as if to stifle the new sound that she had made.

'I think it's time to take this young lady home,' said Adolphus firmly, 'or we will all be told off for laughing.' Thus, Katherine had spent another day in the happy state of adoptive motherhood. Reaching home and bidding farewell to Adolphus, she lifted Dorcas Louise on to her shoulder and carried her triumphantly to the nursery, where Lavinia was sitting writing some more invitations to the christening which was still a few months away, but, as she pointed out, there would be many guests and she would need to know as soon as possible the numbers that they would need to cater for.

Summer drifted into autumn, and little disturbed the happy atmosphere of a family preparing for a celebration. Dorcas Louise had made a couple of tottering steps with Katherine supporting her. Lavinia had watched with pride, and not more than a tiny moment of envy as Katherine whooped with joy at her progress. Katherine never took a day off, and never wanted to, but Lavinia insisted that she went to town, and bought herself a nice outfit for the christening. She gave her an extra ten pounds in her wage packet, and said that she would take great care of Dorcas Louise, and Katherine was not to worry. Katherine would worry; she would always worry, but she knew that sometimes she would have to put her trust in someone else. So, one afternoon when lunch was over for the mistress, and the young Dorcas Louise was popped into her bed that had replaced the now too small cot of her early days, and in the company of her favourite pink, long-eared rabbit, Katherine headed for the shops she had walked to with Dorcas and Adolphus, past the glowing windows, but had never looked more than just idly at the contents therein. Now she felt nervous at the thought of going in and asking to see something of her choice. She glanced inside one of the smaller shops and noticed a pretty young girl standing gazing into space next to a row of pretty dresses. She had a pin on her dress, with a little label that said Charlotte. Katherine approached slowly, and the young girl said, 'Can I help you?' Katherine explained what she needed and why, and Charlotte smiled and said, 'How nice.'

The two of them then started to create an outfit which turned out to be just perfect. A beautiful shade of delphinium blue, which was a perfect foil for her hair colour, Charlotte said with the confidence of a first class sales lady. With it they found a short jacket with long sleeves edged in a darker shade of blue velvet. In a moment's reverie, Katherine remembered the lady on the material stall at the market in Italy, all that time ago when she had, with the lady's help, made a dress to wear for Joseph. Tears momentarily sprang to her eyes, and Charlotte looked at her.

'Oh,' said Katherine, bringing herself back to the present. 'This is absolutely beautiful; its mine,' she sighed. Charlotte moved away out of sight for a moment, and returned with a pair of shoes which matched exactly, and, unbelievably, fitted Katherine as if they had been made for her. Finally, fully dressed, she twirled in front of the mirror. She paid her young sales lady a little more than the extra ten pounds that the mistress had given her, actually quite a bit more, as she had very little left from her wages, but she didn't care, she sailed home, head held high, holding the bag like she had seen the ladies of Liverpool do, and swinging it back and forth.

Everything at the house seemed to be quiet as she climbed the stairs to the nursery where Dorcas Louise was sitting on her mother's lap, listening to a story that she was reading. Lavinia smiled as Dorcas wriggled free of her arms to be placed on the floor where she crawled to rescue rabbit and sat and chewed on an ear while Katherine showed her purchases to a very impressed Lavinia. Another exciting day over, thought Katherine, as she picked up discarded toys from the rug, and prepared Dorcas Louise for her last little meal of the day before she put her into her pretty new bed, with her covers festooned with Teddy Bears and balloons. In spite of all her heartbreak, Katherine had to admit that this was one very lucky little girl who would want for nothing.

The Master was home now, as the days rapidly moved toward Christmas, and of course the christening of Dorcas Louise, which was to be the Sunday before Christmas day. Plans were being hatched, and everyone in the household was entering into the spirit of things, with the slight exception of Trafina Paris who informed everyone that she had quite enough to do with the normal running of the house. The mere preparation for a christening could in her opinion be coped with easily by Cook, with the help of Flo and Charlie, who were, it has to be said, rather pleased to take their orders from Cook, which they would follow to the letter. Cook had baked the celebration cake, and Flo had been sent to town to buy some sugar icing to decorate it. Charlie was to make sure that there was plenty of cloakroom space for all the guests to leave their travelling apparel, and to be sure that those who were staying in the guest rooms had plenty of hot water, towels, and anything that they would need to make their stay comfortable.

The Christmas tree had been delivered, and was standing outside the kitchen door, waiting for the gardener to place it into a large pot, and deliver it to the lounge where Charlie and Flo would put on all the baubles. Katherine had taken Dorcas Louise out for a short walk, while Mr and Mrs Elford retired to the library to put the final touches to the table that had been prepared to receive the christening presents.

Katherine had noticed in a shop window, when she was searching for her outfit, the tiniest silver heart on a silver chain. It was more than she could afford, but she had some savings that she swore she would never touch unless it was absolutely necessary. This, she thought, was probably the most necessary thing she had ever done. Asking permission from the mistress, she left Dorcas in her care, and took off to purchase what she hoped would be a treasured possession of a little girl who would never know how hard it was to give it without being able to say who it was really from.

The christening gown was to be made from a length of pure silk that had been left over from Lavinia's wedding dress. It arrived from the dressmaker, and Lavinia eagerly opened the package which had been sent from London.

'Oh my goodness gracious me.' Katherine heard her cry as she entered the nursery from Dorcas's bedroom where she had been tidying the freshly ironed clothes.

'What is it, ma'am?' asked Katherine, looking at the clouds of tissue paper surrounding the box that held the gown.

'This will never fit,' she cried. 'I gave her all the right measurements and she has made it far too small. It's too late now to return it. I will have to go and purchase a ready-made gown from the shop.'

Katherine moved to look at the creation that had caused her mistress so much distress and, thinking quickly to the days when she used to make her own dresses, she thought that if there was a large enough piece of matching material anywhere she could probably make a reasonable job of altering it to fit Dorcas Louise. Putting the suggestion to the mistress caused a little more distress than finding the mistake in the first place.

'The only place where there is a piece of material equal to this is actually a part of my wedding dress, which was made by the same dressmaker ten years ago. Can you do it, Katherine? If you can I will allow you to remove the train from the dress and use it. If however you fail, I will never speak to you again.'

Katherine stared at her, only to see her smiling. 'I will do my very best, ma'am,' she answered with the lowest curtsey she could manage. Katherine, with Lavinia's help, carefully removed the train from the dress so as to not cause too much damage in case the dress was needed for a future wedding. Mentioning this, Katherine brought a grateful smile from the lips of Lavinia, who was thinking what an amazing person Katherine was, more than half her age but with an inner knowledge and talent she had rarely encountered in anyone. The scissors slid with accuracy across the silk. Three pieces in all were cut, one the length of the gown, and two twice the length of the gown, all five inches wide; the two outer pieces were gathered and attached to the inner piece, and Katherine very painstakingly made tiny silk roses, and stitched them to the seams on either side of the inserted piece which would then be stitched to the centre of the gown where a split had to be made down the middle, thus making the size that was needed for Dorcas Louise to fit in to it. The final alteration was for the neck to be slightly gathered, and a narrow piece of satin ribbon fixed around it topped by a tiny bow with long ribbon streamers with a tiny silk rose at the end of each one. When all the cut seams had been neatened on the wrong side, the gown was gently ironed, and placed back in its tissue until the day when it would adorn one Dorcas Louise Elford on her christening day.

The day dawned bright and clear. Katherine took Dorcas Louise out for a short walk around the park in the morning while all the hubbub of preparation was in progress. Cook, red-faced and bright-eyed, was hurrying to and fro with silver dishes bearing all kinds of elegant snacks. She had not had a day like this for a very long time, and was relishing every moment, accepting praises from the master and the mistress with all the dignity she could manage on such an exciting day. Following the afternoon buffet, which would take place on the return of the guests from the church, she would have to clear the tables, and make ready for an evening meal. This would all have to be strategically planned, and both Florence Petite and Charlie Orchard had been given important roles to play in the process.

The only person keeping out of the limelight, by her own choice, and not that of Cook, was Trafina Paris who had professed to be very busy ensuring that every room was pristine, and that nothing was left out to cause clutter. Everyone bowed to this, as the house was her domain at the end of the day, and she was responsible for the final face it showed to the world. It was thus that she was seen, feather duster and dustpan in hand, scuttling about, shaking her head and mumbling under her breath about dust and untidiness. Finally, disappearing into her room and shutting her door, she would emerge during the celebration, scrubbed and dressed immaculately in a long black dress, hair scooped into a large bun on the top of her head, secured by a sparkling comb.

The day went like a dream. Dorcas Louise looked like an angel, her beautiful face creased by an everlasting smile, as everyone patted her head and tweaked her cheek. The rocking horse that James and Lavinia Elford had bought for their daughter was magnificent. It stood in the hallway, decked in pink ribbon so that it would be the first thing that Dorcas Louise would see as they returned to the house after the christening had taken place. As she was lifted by her father, and held in position with the reins tightly clenched in her hand, she let out whoops of delight as she gently swayed to and fro. She was then passed to Katherine, and they all made their way upstairs to where the buffet was laid out. The table of presents was now overflowing in masses of pink ribbons, and neatly wrapped parcels. It was decided that these would be opened later, and just a couple at a time so that Dorcas Louise would not become too overwhelmed by it all.

Katherine said that she would stay in the nursery with the now sleepy child, while the rest of the guests enjoyed the repast that was laid before them. She took Dorcas Louise, and together they sat in their favourite place by the window. Dorcas cuddled into Katherine in silent contentment, and it was this perfect picture that Adolphus Fry was presented with, as he silently stood in the doorway with a plate full of sandwiches and cakes that he had rescued, in his hand.

'Lavinia thought you would be hungry,' he said quietly as he peeped at the sleeping Dorcas Louise.

'Oh, please sit down,' said Katherine. 'I will have to go and get her tea in a while, and then give her an hour's playtime before I put her down. Has it all gone well, do you think?'

'It has gone wonderfully, and you have been incredibly brave but then I knew you would be,' he answered. 'Lavinia has decided that Dorcas Louise will be kept awake this evening. She has arranged for a high chair to be put at the head of the table, with her food being served along with ours, and you are to sit next to her, and if she cries you may hold her, but you are not to disappear to the nursery. She asked me to make that very clear to you. I will be sitting on the opposite side of the table, so that between us perhaps we can keep her happy. By the way your outfit is delightful, and it should not be wasted, so I suggest that you cover it while you attend to Dorcas Louise before you present her to her guests for the evening, and maybe you should remove her gown for a while, and replace it when it is time for her to go.'

All this was accomplished, and the evening was a great success. Dorcas Louise was a prima donna in the making. Adolphus was the perfect guest, endearing himself to everyone there, and the cause of great amusement as he pulled faces at Dorcas, sending her into giggles. She lasted throughout the meal, and well into the evening, before she surrendered to the comfort of Katherine's arms and slept. Lavinia Elford proved to be a first class hostess, much to the pleasure of her husband, whose eyes rarely left her during the evening. He had never seen his wife so sparkling, not only in herself but in her dress. She was wearing a gown of the palest pink lace, encrusted with pearls and sequins. It had a top of delicately pleated silk caught at the shoulder with a magnificent brooch, which he had bought for her on his return from America just recently. She looked absolutely stunning, and he made no bones about telling her so quite publicly, which made her blush profusely.

Katherine said her goodbyes to Adolphus, and graciously wished the guests that surrounded her good night. Gently cradling the sleepy head that was laid on her shoulder, she climbed the stairs to the nursery once more and took Dorcas to her bedroom. Slowly, she removed her beautiful gown that had been the subject of many a compliment during the day, laid it amongst the tissue paper, and quietly whispered, 'a wonderful day, my darling, but will you ever remember it?' Lavinia came to say good night and to thank Katherine for her contribution to its success, bent over her nightdress clad daughter, and planted a gentle kiss upon her cheek.'

'We will open your presents tomorrow when the rest of the guests have departed,' she said to the non-responsive Dorcas Louise.

The morning dawned in chaos; guests who had remained up late were slowly making their way down to the breakfast room where Cook had been catering for the last few hours in relays of assorted plates of food. The master and the mistress had been up early to receive their guests and wish them safe journeys home. Some seemed to want to linger in the ambient setting of this lovely house that many of them had never seen until the occasion of the christening of the cherished daughter, who it seemed had brought warmth and joy to her new parents which had radiated to each and every one of them. Many a comment had been made about the nanny that had been found for them, and what a little treasure she was, and how they wished that they could have found one like her when they were raising their off-springs.

Katherine had kept to her usual routine of preparing breakfast for herself and Dorcas Louise. Bright as a button, the young Miss Dorcas Louise Elford set about her day with gusto. After breakfast, Katherine dressed her in a new coat and bonnet, and took her downstairs to where Charlie was getting her carriage ready for her daily ride. 'Mornin',' he said cheerfully to Katherine. 'How long do you think this one is going to want to be seen in this then. I reckon she will be trying to stroll round the houses before long,' he chuckled.

'You could be right, Charlie, but for now she will have to be content with the ride,' Katherine retorted with a smile.

The housekeeper, entering her room with a pile of letters and some papers, turned and said icily, 'Hopefully there will be better things to do than idly standing about chattering, and walking around the streets. I suppose I will now have to go and clear up everything that should have been seen to last night by the people who took off to bed when they should have been tidying up.'

Both Katherine and Charlie ignored her innuendos and carried on getting Dorcas Louise safely into her reins in the company of rabbit. Katherine then winked at Charlie, and set off on another morning of adventure. Carriages were in the drive, drivers collecting luggage, and guests lingering with their last goodbyes. James and Lavinia Elford, on the doorstep waving them on their way, came over to kiss their daughter. Katherine thought they looked more happy and relaxed than she had ever seen them since she had arrived at the house when Dorcas was just a few days old. Where had the time gone, and how could she have dreamed that she would still be here two years later?

The house was quiet on her return. She left Charlie to see to the carriage, and took Dorcas Louise, as she did on many a morning after her walk, into the kitchen to see Cook. Cook always found a tiny biscuit, or cake in her pantry, which she gave to Dorcas Louise as she fussed over her telling her what a beautiful girl she was. Flo and Charlie came into the kitchen whispering.

'What are you two up to now?' said Cook in a gently scolding voice.

'We wanted to tell Katherine something,' Flo said.

'What is it?' said Katherine.

'Well it may be nothing, but as I was going to pick up the breakfast dishes, I saw Trafina leave your bedroom. I waited behind the nursery door until she had left, so she didn't see me. I couldn't think why she would need to go to your bedroom, as you care for it yourself, everyone knows that, even the mistress don't go in there, does she?'

'No she doesn't,' answered Katherine. 'Thank you, would you not say anything outside of the kitchen? I don't want to cause trouble if there is no reason.'

Katherine was slightly annoyed at Trafina's nosiness, and also a little curious as to why she would go into her bedroom. There was nothing there belonging to Dorcas Louise, or for that matter anything of any interest to anyone but Katherine herself. She and Dorcas went upstairs to the nursery where Katherine sat her in her little rocking chair, which she loved, and backwards and forwards she would go, making little singing sounds. So, with her happily settled, with rabbit of course, Katherine went into her bedroom.

She had carefully shut the nursery door, so that she could leave her bedroom door open to keep a watchful eye on Dorcas Louise. Nothing was awry. All the doors and drawers were shut as she had left them. The bed was tidy and unruffled. She opened a couple of drawers, and their contents were undisturbed. She looked into her writing case and there was no evidence of prying eyes there. She walked around the bed to her little table where she had her night light, and that was all intact.

With nothing left to search, she turned her attention to Dorcas Louise who was still sitting happily trying to remove rabbit's coat. As she went to walk away she noticed a corner of her little case of treasures poking out from under the quilt that didn't quite reach the ground. Nobody had ever touched the case. She knelt down and pulled it gently from its hiding place, opened it up, and to her heart's relief she found everything that should be there had not been disturbed. Fingers shaking, she went to close the clasp, and then she spied something glinting. Gently reaching down the side of the case, her fingers closed on a pin which pricked her finger. Pulling at the pin, she found it was attached to the beautiful brooch that the mistress had been wearing with such pride at the dinner last night. Panic set in now with a vengeance.

What could she do? If she took it to the mistress, she may think that she had stolen it. Katherine didn't have any doubt at all who had stolen it, but why plant it on her. She had no time to wonder why. She had to get rid of it now. When once she had done that, whatever happened she would not be under any more suspicion than anyone else. She held the brooch tightly in her hand and opened the nursery door; this would cause no problem if anyone saw her. Outside on the landing, past two doors that led to more laundry rooms, and in a corner under a window, was an enormous aspidistra plant. Katherine slipped quietly and quickly toward it, reached deeply into its roots, and placed the brooch as tightly as she could in the middle of it.

This done, and fright taking over her heartbeat, she raced back as quickly as her legs would carry her to the serenity of the nursery where Dorcas Louise, blessed as she was with an inner contentment, sat with rabbit finally minus his coat. Katherine sank into the chair, and began to think of what she could do. The realisation hit her that Trafina Paris had made a last ditch attempt to get rid of her. Well, she might just live to regret it for the rest of her life, because somehow Katherine would turn the tables on her, and if she could do it before the brooch was found missing, Trafina Paris's dirty deeds were surely about to come to an end.

Katherine had to act very swiftly. Some of the guests were still wandering around the house. Mr and Mrs Elford would stay downstairs until the last ones had departed, of this Katherine was sure. Frightened now by the possibility of the housekeeper doing something extremely dangerous, she had to be sure that Dorcas Louise was safe and not left alone for a minute. Picking her up from her chair, she walked from the nursery and closed the door. She made her way downstairs and headed toward the kitchen. The housekeeper was nowhere to be seen; normal sounds were coming from the kitchen, and nothing would be seen as odd if Katherine was visiting the kitchen staff again. Once inside, she closed the door and beckoned Cook, Flo, and Charlie, silently to her side.

'You will need to move away from me to your tasks quickly if the door opens for any reason,' Katherine warned. Then she proceeded to tell them what had happened upstairs, and said that Flo was right to suspect that something was wrong, and how grateful she was that she had the presence of mind to tell her. They stood there open-mouthed as Katherine breathlessly told them exactly what she had done with the brooch, but now she had no idea what to do next. She just knew that she had to get it out of her room, so that no finger of suspicion would point at her. Charlie pointed out that she couldn't be allowed to get away with it. If she did then heaven knows what she would think of next. All four of them swore an allegiance to each other that together they would see that the brooch found its way into the possession of the person who stole it, and that they would do it now. They hatched a plan that was sophisticated in its entirety, but could they carry it out.

It was decided that the kitchen door would be left open, and Cook would be seen to be busy clearing up the pots and dishes, and making sandwiches, while keeping a close eye on the movements of Trafina Paris, who seemed to have an air of agitation about her this morning. Flo would be sent about her tasks, complete with arms full of clean towels, but would stay in sight of the culprit at all times. Katherine would wait for a signal from Charlie, who would take one of the trays full of champagne glasses and walk with it to the foot of the stairs, where he would stop near to a small table that stood by the wall. At this moment, and with all the speed she could muster, Katherine would take the brooch from its hiding place and make her way to the housekeeper's room where she would plant the brooch. They all decided that they could think of no better place to hide it than in the drawer of the writing desk, which would be an obvious place to look when the theft was discovered and a search of the house was ordered. Dorcas Louise was safely left out of sight in the kitchen with cook.

They all took their places. Flo was to shout 'Charlie', if Trafina Paris was seen to be making her way back to her room, and Charlie would then cause a diversion that would send the housekeeper into a rage, and straight to his side. It was time for the housekeeper to go and collect the mail that was left in a tray on the desk in the library. Charlie had already checked that it was indeed there, and he noted that there was a substantial pile that would take her a while to collect and take back to her room to put on the stamps which were always left in a little tin box just inside the door. With military precision, he gave the housekeeper two minutes to get past the stairs, before he moved out, tray in hand, to the bottom of the stairs, and stopped. Katherine, shoeless, fled to the plant, retrieved the brooch and headed down the stairs, past Charlie, glancing at the kitchen, and making for the door of the housekeeper's room. It was ajar, so she only had to push it open, pass through it, and pull it to behind her. With deft but trembling fingers, she opened the drawer, and placed the brooch as she had found it in her case, pin upwards and tucked down the side toward the back of the drawer. She closed the drawer and made a move toward the door, when she clearly heard Flo shout, 'Charlie,' followed by a terrific crash of glass, a shout from Charlie, and a scream as Trafina Paris hurled abuse at Charlie.

She froze, not knowing what was going on out there, but she certainly couldn't stay where she was, so she eased open the door, where she had a clear view of the scene. Charlie was on his knees trying to pick up broken pieces of glass, and the back of Trafina Paris was bending over him, with a pile of letters scattered in a trail behind her. Katherine slid silently out of the door, and crept unnoticed to the kitchen, where Charlie and Flo found her five minutes later after they had both been read the riot act by the housekeeper, who was now picking up her letters as Charlie made his way back to the site of the accident complete with dust pan and broom, and a contrite look of guilt upon his face. Trafina Paris was in such a rage that she did not even look at Katherine as she walked with Dorcas up the stairs to the nursery.

The guests finally had all departed, and the house was quiet again. Charlie had offered his apologies as he cleared up the mess in the hall, which were accepted by the mistress. Not so the anger of Trafina Paris, who kept Charlie on his knees until each tiny scrap of glass was removed from the floor, and then she insisted that he get the tin of wax polish, and re-wax the whole of the hallway. Her anger was intensified by his smile as he set to work polishing away until he could see his reflection, and that of her as she stood over him, hand on hips, foot tapping relentlessly until she could stand it no longer and she retired to her room.

Now all they could do was wait. Katherine tried to be calm and not show her nervousness to the mistress when she came into the nursery to see Dorcas who was happily playing on the floor. 'We thought we would bring in some of the presents, Katherine. Would you like to fetch yours and give it to Dorcas? Katherine, who in spite of what she had just done, showed remarkable calm as she sat beside Dorcas, and helped her undo the wrapping paper and ribbon from her gift. She lifted the little silver heart from its box and passed it to Dorcas who promptly decided to eat it. Lavinia jumped up and rescued it from her daughter, looked at it and said, 'It is exquisite', as she placed it around her daughter's neck.

Katherine smiled and said, 'I liked it.'

At that moment, James Elford appeared, and the opening of the presents started in earnest. There were silver rattles, and tiny silver shoes; there was a silver cross on a white ribbon, and a silver holder in which to place the christening certificate. Adolphus had left her a substantial amount of money to be held in bonds until she reached her eighteenth birthday, unless she married before that date in which case she would receive it then. James and Lavinia Elford were overwhelmed with the kindness and love shown by Adolphus to their daughter. Katherine was just secretly very proud to have known him. When all the presents were unwrapped, and Katherine had taken a note of all the bearers of the gifts, so that thank you notes could be sent, Dorcas Louise sat contentedly in her rocker chair with rabbit and a couple of new friends who had miraculously appeared from odd-shaped pretty paper. A yellow-haired dolly, in a red spotted dress, now shared her chair with her, and a white dog sat next to rabbit who appeared to be quite happy to make his acquaintance.

James Elford came and sat next to his wife, and put his arm around her shoulders. 'Darling, I was so proud of you yesterday, and you looked so beautiful. I would like to take you out somewhere special to dinner tonight, so why don't you go and put on that exquisite dress for me once again. Our daughter will be well looked after here, of that we have no doubt. Thank you, Katherine, for all your hard work, not only for yesterday, but for every day that you have spent here. I really don't know what we would do without you.'

Katherine smiled and showed more confidence than she felt inside. 'It's a pleasure, sir,' she said quietly. Left alone with Dorcas, Katherine heaved a large sigh; it would be just a short time now until the whole household would erupt, because she knew that when the mistress put on her dress, she would look for the brooch. Had she done the right thing, she thought, or should she just have said she found it, and returned it to the mistress, but then, rightly so, Charlie had said that Trafina would only try again, and again, until finally she might have caught Katherine in an impossible situation. She hated doing this, but Trafina had to be stopped.

A knock came at the door. It was only Flo with tea for Dorcas Louise. Katherine told her about the mistress being taken to dinner, and that she would be wearing the same dress. They both sat there for a few minutes, holding their own thoughts as to what might happen at any moment now. 'I had better get going back down to the kitchen and warn Cook and Charlie,' said Flo.

Alone again, Katherine could not settle. The palms of her hands were damp, and her heart was thumping, but there was an almost hushed silence about the house. Time passed, and Katherine gave Dorcas her tea and played with her for more than an hour. It was as she started to undress her ready for bed, that the shout was heard. There was a clattering on the stairs, and raised voices. The master's voice, loud and clear, came above the animated whisperings of everyone else. 'Everyone to the library, instantly please. Katherine, you must come too, you will have to bring Dorcas with you.'

At this point, Dorcas Louise started to whimper. Katherine quickly wrapped a shawl around her, as there was a chill in the lower corridors. She held her close and began to descend the stairs. Once in the library, the atmosphere was strained. The mistress stood in her evening gown, the master beside her, pale-faced and clearly angry. Cook and Flo came scuttling in after Katherine. Charlie followed, bringing in the gardener who had been at that moment dragging out sacks of potatoes from the cold store, and an extra cleaning lady who had been hired for the day to help clear the remnants of last night's party. The last to enter the library was Trafina Paris, who walked in haughtily and took her position next to the master. All stood there silent now, not knowing what to expect.

The master spoke, slowly at first, thanking every one for acting quickly to his request, and then he said, 'My wife unfortunately has mislaid the brooch that she was wearing last night. We have looked in all the places where it would likely be. We know it was on her dressing table this morning before breakfast, because we both saw it there. Very few of the guests who were at the dinner last night would have been in the area of our private rooms, and they would be above suspicion. I am very sorry to have to say this but, saving that it was accidently swept up by one of you while executing your duties, it has to be said that we have to assume that someone here has to be in possession of it. Therefore it is with great regret that I have now to perform a search in every area in every room of the house until I am sure that it is not here, thence I will inform the police.

'Miss Paris, I must ask you as housekeeper to accompany me on my search, and I must offer my apologies to all of you when I say that I may have to search personal and private areas of your rooms and places of work. I intend to start at the top of the house, so that means, Katherine, that your rooms, both the nursery, all rooms connected to it, and your private bedroom will be searched, so in order that you may witness the search would you please now return to the nursery, and of course you may make Dorcas Louise comfortable in any way necessary.'

Katherine, shaking now, held Dorcas Louise tightly, and ascended the stairs in front of the master and the housekeeper. She didn't look left or right, but kept her head firmly down, focusing on the stairs, and reached the nursery without a flicker of emotion showing on her face. The search took over half an hour, and no space was left unturned. As they were about to leave the room, with the master satisfied that nothing was found there, the housekeeper put out her hand to stop him, and said, 'Sir, the nanny has a personal case under her bed that you may not know about. She keeps her secrets in there. Should you not check to see if she had anything in there that should not be?'

'Indeed I should, Miss Paris. I apologise Katherine, but this has to be done.' Katherine nodded, wanting so much to ask the housekeeper how she knew she had a personal case under her personal bed, and in her personal bedroom. The master pulled out the case, clicked open the lock and carefully removed each item from the case, surprise flickering across his face, and humility showing in his glance at Katherine. 'I am so sorry,' he said as he returned each item as carefully as he had removed them. 'Nothing untoward there,' he said with a sharp scowl that was not lost on Trafina Paris, as her face showed horrified amazement. 'That is enough here. We will now search every corner of this corridor, and that of the floor below, before we attempt the downstairs rooms and kitchens.'

He had decided that this would be the end of his planned outing, but he was determined to get to the bottom of this if it took all night. 'Thank you, Katherine,' he said as he left her to go back to the child that was now showing her frustration by wailing loudly. A further half an hour found them in the kitchens, where the task was enormous. Cook volunteered to move pots and pans under the supervision of him and the housekeeper, providing him at the same time with a much appreciated cup of tea.

Cupboards were emptied, brooms and brushes were removed from their relevant hooks in their cupboards, and even their bristles and heads were searched in case the brooch had been secreted amongst them. Food that was being prepared was checked, even the inside of the chicken that was ready to be stuffed and cooked for lunch tomorrow. Cook went out of her way to help, also suggesting places that even the master would not consider. Charlie, who had been standing in waiting for his turn, watched carefully, and gave a sly nod to Cook when the two detectives had their heads stuck in a drawer, and cupboard.

Trafina was now showing agitation and a slight suggestion of fear as she followed the master with nowhere near the same confidence as she had when the search began. She of course had no idea where the brooch had gone, or in fact who had found it and moved it. It was with much trepidation as they neared the end of their search that she wondered what the master would do, and indeed what the police would do if they were called in as the search failed to produce the missing brooch. The kitchen search over, and the downstairs hallway searched; even the baby carriage was stripped of its clothes and every corner looked into.

The master once again called them all to the library. The mistress, having remained there the whole time, so as not to cause added unrest to the situation, now stood at the side of the desk as the master spoke. 'Thank you all for your co-operation in this serious situation. It looks as if I now have no alternative but to call in the police for further investigation. Katherine was frozen to the spot, also Charlie and Flo. The extra lady brought in for the day had been sent home, as it was confirmed that she only cleaned in the dining room. Cook finally was the one to step forward. Taking a large breath, she said, 'Sir, we have all been searched, our rooms and our private belongings also have been searched. Begging your pardon, sir, but would it not seem fair to also search the office and the housekeeper's room. In this situation, should anyone be above suspicion?'

The housekeeper, at this outburst, cried, 'I am in a position in this household to be considered as above suspicion. What would I do with the brooch anyway? I have no reason to be afraid of what you may find in my room, not like some people who secrete things under their bed. Go ahead, I will even help you.' The search proved to be more difficult than even the master had expected. There were untied piles of papers, which were supposed to be filed, tucked under tables, and on bookshelves. The master insisted that they all be removed, placed on the floor, and filed properly tomorrow when this search had ended, or gone to another level. They moved to the desk. 'There are some of my private letters in there,' the housekeeper protested.

'There were private things in the nanny's room, which I recall you made no bones about pointing out,' the master retorted. 'Everything out, please.' Trafina Paris, not worried, but annoyed beyond belief, began to scoop the contents from the drawer. The master's eye caught sight of a few letters on airmail paper, held securely by a rubber band, and some more letters which he picked up, and placed in his pocket. The housekeeper's face turned a dark red, as she plunged her hand back into the drawer, only to yell, and pull it out to find a finger profusely running in blood.

'What caused that?' said the master, as he carefully ran his hand along the side of the drawer where the offending spike had struck. 'I think I have found the cause of your injury, Miss Paris,' he said slowly as he withdrew the diamond brooch from its hiding place. Trafina Paris screamed with disbelief, as well as total fear.

'What is that doing there. I never put it there, it was...'

'It was where, Miss Paris?' asked the master.

'I don't know. I never saw it until now,' she cowered, and stopped her defence speech there.

'I think we will all return to the library, where we will discuss this matter, and if you or anyone else can throw any light on this ugly matter I will be happy to listen, but I'm sure, Miss Paris, that even if you can convince me of your innocence regarding the theft of the brooch, there will still be the matter of the un-posted mail, which I'm sure you were aware that I confiscated during our search.'

On returning to the library, the master asked one question of all who remained there. He asked, 'Do any of you know or have any idea how the brooch found its way into the office?' His question was answered by silence, and all of them, including the housekeeper, were asked to return to their duties. James Elford passed the pile of letters to his wife, along with the brooch. 'Leave the business of the letters until later when we have decided how to deal with all of this.'

It had worked, but somehow Katherine felt sad now, and a little sorry for Trafina Paris in spite of all the things she had done to try and get rid of her. She was getting old, and was probably scared of not being needed any more. It must take a very sad and insecure person to act in such a way, thought Katherine as she finally settled down Dorcas Louise, and took herself to bed, thankful that this day was over.

Trafina Paris however was pacing the room downstairs, racking her brain as to how the brooch that she planted in the bedroom of the nanny found its way into the drawer of her writing desk. For the first time in many years, she sat down on her bed and cried.

The next morning, as Katherine was clearing away the breakfast ready for Flo to come and take away the dishes, Lavinia Elford entered the nursery, bade Katherine come and sit awhile, and took the hands of Dorcas Louise as she made her slightly tottering advance toward her mother. She lifted her on to her lap, and planted a kiss upon her head. Katherine drew up a chair and sat opposite her mistress, looking at her enquiringly, anxious to hear the result of last night's events. Lavinia Elford began to explain.

'My brooch, as you know, was found in the desk that our housekeeper used. She is adamant that she does not know how it got there, but my husband assures me that he feels beyond any shadow of a doubt that it was her who removed it from my table, as she was the only one who yesterday morning would have been on the landing where our bedroom is, and also there was something else that made him feel that there was no alternative than to give her orders to leave the property. The alternative would be that we call the police and ask them to do a complete investigation which would mean taking the questioning to a much higher level, and the result could be far worse than her leaving the household.'

Katherine, feeling a pang of guilt now at playing Trafina Paris at her own game, thought that perhaps she might be able to influence their decision a little in her favour. Why she should, she did not know, but that was what she felt, and it would do no harm to put forward a little defence on behalf of the housekeeper.

'I have to say ma'am that for quite a while now Miss Paris has been acting rather strangely, both Charlie and Cook will agree to that, I'm sure. Do you not think that is rather sad, and it may be due to her age and a feeling of insecurity, especially since you have had Dorcas Louise, and I have been kept on as nanny. She feels possibly that her services aren't needed as much as they used to be. Your staff now are quite young, and perhaps it is difficult for her to accept. Could you and the master reconsider her going, and offer her the chance to stay on the promise that this will never happen again? I do feel very sorry for her now, and I'm sure that the rest of the staff feel the same.'

The mistress, gently lowering Dorcas Louise to the floor, got up from her chair, and walked to the window. She stood for a minute and then turned to face Katherine and said, 'I do not think that the master will reconsider, and you may feel a little differently when you see these.' Lavinia Elford slowly pulled from her pocket a pile of letters secured by a rubber band, and gave them to Katherine. As Katherine saw the envelopes, she knew what they were, and she sank down on the chair and stared at them, not believing what she saw. All her letters, every one that she had sent to Italy, complete with their stamps that Adolphus had given her. She couldn't speak, her legs felt like jelly, and tears flowed uncontrolled down her cheeks. Lavinia crossed the room, and put her arms around Katherine.

'I g-gave my letters to Charlie,' Katherine stuttered. 'How did they come into her possession?'

'I don't know,' confessed Lavinia, 'but we will ask Charlie, and I will call the master to come and discuss all this with you.'

Charlie, duly called, had confirmed that the housekeeper had caught him with some of the letters, and berated him for doing her job, threatening him not to post any mail under any circumstances without first passing it to her. He was scared to go against her instructions, although tempted once or twice to slip out before she saw him. He apologised to Katherine, hating to see her so upset.

'It's not your fault, Charlie, I should have saved them until I saw Adolphus, but I wanted them to go quickly as they were for my family, you see, and none of them know where I am, or how I am, and now it's been so long they may have given up hope of ever hearing from me.'

At that point, the master came into the nursery, and his wife explained the conversation that had gone on before she had passed on the letters. He smiled at the tearful Katherine and said, 'It is very commendable that you show compassion for the housekeeper, but I'm afraid it was not only your letters, but some very important ones of mine that she had in her possession, also she has not been keeping up with the important paperwork that she has been paid to do. The stealing of the brooch was her undoing and therefore I am afraid I have no alternative but to end her employment at the house, but in consideration of your comments I will give her a reference, which up until now I had no intention of doing.'

The master then left the nursery and made his way to the office where a crumpled Trafina Paris awaited her fate. Gazing around the office at the confusion, he said, 'I am afraid that as a direct result of the events of yesterday, I have to inform you that your services will no longer be needed by this household. However, it is because of the kindness and loyalty of your staff, and the person I employ to look after my adopted child, that I am prepared to offer you one week's wages for every year that you have spent in my employ, which I calculate to be about thirty five years. This is because of the early years when your conduct was very acceptable, and with this you should be able to live a reasonable life. If you do have a problem with my decision, I will have no alternative but to call for further investigation which will involve the police, and I will have no control over the consequences.'

Trafina Paris offered no apology, just a nod of the head, and as she went to her bedside and pulled out a battered old suitcase into which she slowly started to fold and place her belongings, she cried bitter tears of regret. The master then called once again for all staff to be present in the library in fifteen minutes. Dorcas Louise made the journey in Katherine's arms; nothing would be left to chance where this child was concerned. The letters were now in Katherine's pocket, and the shock of what had happened had left Katherine weepy and sad. She had no idea what to do now; she would have to open the letters, and see what she had written over the last eighteen months. Charlie, Flo, and Cook all reached the library together. As Katherine came through the door, they looked at her tear-stained face, and without exception felt her unhappiness in their own hearts.

The master stood before them and spoke quietly but firmly, telling them that the housekeeper had to go and at this very moment she was packing her bags and would be out of the house within the hour. He told them that on their behalf he had seen that financially she had been more than fairly treated. They all sat and wondered what they had to do next. The mistress, sitting at her husband's side, smiled as she looked at their anxious faces. James Elford, who was quietly happy with his young staff, began to lay out his plan before them. 'I would very much like you all to carry on with your duties as you are at present if you are happy to do that. Katherine, I know from my conversations with Adolphus Fry that you are very capable of dealing with paperwork and I would like you, if you feel you could manage it along with your caring for this young lady, to try and make some inroads into the mess that has been building up in the office for quite a while. I was rather hoping that we could manage for the present without employing another housekeeper, so with that in mind I was wondering, with the help of Cook, and the co-operation of you, Charlie and Flo, if we could run this house competently between us. My wife I know would be very happy for that to happen, and of course you would all receive a financial increase in keeping with your extra duties. I would like you all now to adjourn to the nursery, discuss it with the mistress, and I believe that we can have once again a happy well run house. All of you enjoy Christmas, and let us put this incident behind us. Just think about this house as a family home in which we all play a part in its being. Thank you all for your loyalty. With a smile, James Elford left the library, and his family and staff, not quite sure of what had just occurred, were left with a feeling of togetherness and security which had been missing for a while.

Chapter Thirteen

Lost and Found

Christmas came in a whirl of white. Snow fell like a magic carpet on Christmas Eve, and a hush descended as if the world was waiting in silence for the gladsome morn. Katherine, with a fur clad Dorcas Louise, ventured outside the front door to watch Charlie and Flo build a snowman. Cook found him a chef's hat to which she had fastened some holly and bells. The gardener brought a carrot from the store room for his nose, and some small pieces of coal for his eyes. Three red baubles borrowed from the Christmas tree made his buttons, and a pair of old boots that Charlie had found in one of the outhouses was stuck at his base, so that he now had feet to stand on. Dorcas Louise stared in amazement, and laughed as Katherine made her a snowball, and pretended to throw it at Charlie, at which Charlie returned the favour, and promptly hit Katherine on the head, causing a cascade of ice crystals to rain down upon Dorcas, which made her scream in surprise and delight. Unfortunately she had nothing substantial to wear on her feet, so Katherine could not let her kick snow, but it was a happy scene that the master and mistress of the house beheld as they came down the stairs to see what all the hubbub was about.

Christmas would be different for them all, but the radiance and happiness of their adopted daughter, her nanny, and their remaining staff, brought a warmth to them both as they reached for each other's hand. 'Happy Christmas, darling,' James Elford whispered to his wife. More gifts were bestowed upon Dorcas Louise from Santa Claus who stood by the tree on Christmas afternoon. Although the ceremony had little influence on Dorcas, she gleefully ripped the wrappings from the gifts, sat in the middle of the pile of paper that was left, and chewed on a piece of apple that Katherine had carefully peeled and sliced. Thus Christmas day finally came to an end, and an exhausted cook made her way through the snow to her cottage just a short way from the house. Charlie and Flo lingered under a huge ball of mistletoe that hung from the light outside the front door, until Katherine bade them come in as the draught from the open door was cooling the house. Reluctantly they stole a last kiss, and made their way to their own rooms. Katherine managed a sly smile, remembering the times that she so longed to be with Joseph, and someone for the very best reasons had called her away.

The rest of the holiday passed quietly for Katherine. She cared for Dorcas Louise while James and Lavinia Elford entertained guests. James was astounded at the change in Lavinia; how bright she was, in fact the perfect hostess that he had looked for in the beginning and never thought he would find. Cook worked hard, but well, under the mistress's instructions. Charlie and Flo were always there to give support above and beyond their normal duties, and were duly rewarded as the master had promised. As for Katherine, she was as happy as she could possibly be, with the cloud of the un-posted letters still hanging over her. Her time spent with Dorcas, as always, was the joy of her life, and the mistress was pleased to leave her upbringing to Katherine, while she attended to her husband's requirements.

The mistress, sitting with Katherine in the nursery on Thursday afternoon, the week following the New Year celebrations, thanked Katherine for the work she had done in such a short time in the office, and echoed the assurances that Adolphus Fry had given her, that Katherine would in time have it all efficiently under control. Following that, the mistress informed Katherine that Adolphus had accepted an invitation to dinner with her and her husband, and yesterday they had met for lunch at a local hotel. Her husband had some business to discuss with the professor, and afterwards over a glass of mulled wine, which Adolphus had promised would keep out the cold, she had broached the subject of the missing letters. Adolphus, she said, was extremely angry, and had asked if he could come to the house and discuss the matter.

'Katherine,' said the mistress, 'I hope I haven't done the wrong thing in discussing your business with him, but I can tell how fond he is of you, and he would have been worried if he had seen your distress when I gave the letters to you. If you agree, he would like to come here tomorrow at two pm to speak with you. I feel that when I spoke to him he was working on a possibility of being able to get your letters on their way to their destination. He knows a lot of people, and over some he has a great influence, so all may not be lost; keep your hopes up, and I will look after Dorcas Louise tomorrow from two pm onwards, so that you can spend time with your uncle.'

Katherine liked Lavinia Elford very much, and knew that she would never make any promises until she was sure that they could be carried out. She had put the letters in her little case, not knowing what she could do. It was no use posting them all now, there would have to be a letter explaining why they had not been posted, and also the risk of losing them all together was just too much for Katherine to consider. Maybe tomorrow Adolphus would have a solution, though what he could possibly do she could not imagine. Adolphus as always arrived on the dot of two pm. Flo let him in and, with a smile, dropped a tiny but sincere curtsey. He passed her his hat and coat, and asked her to pass on his greetings for a happy new year to the staff. Katherine, making her way down the stairs, welcomed him with a smile and a gentle hug, to which he responded with a light kiss upon her cheek. 'My dear, it is good to see you again, and to see you looking so well. I trust the young Miss Elford is being good, and has had a rewarding Christmas.'

'Oh yes, Adolphus, Dorcas Louise has had a wonderful time, as have we all in spite of the unhappiness, and the sad result that we have had to endure'.

Walking toward the library, with fingers crossed and hand resting on the letters that she had in her pocket, Katherine said. 'I find it hard to believe that someone would do a thing like that without thinking of the possible heartbreak it could cause, not only to the sender, but to the people to whom they were sent, and to add to that, to steal the brooch from the mistress for whom she had worked for so long. I can only think that she must have been desperately unhappy.'

Adolphus answered her quietly, but in certainty. 'You are right, Katherine, and it is gracious of you to feel sorry for her, but at the end of the day she committed a crime, and but for the sensitivity of her employers she could have ended up in a very serious situation. Now you must forget, and we must find a solution to your problem.'

Once inside the library, where Mrs Elford had arranged for a tray of tea to be left, Katherine and Adolphus sat at the desk. Katherine pulled the pile of letters from her pocket and passed them to him. 'I have not been able to bring myself to open them and read them, for if I do I may feel that some of the things I wrote then I would not want to say now. Does that make sense to you Adolphus?'

'Only you know how you feel, my dear, and I can only imagine how much you are hurt, but the past is past, and we have now to look to the future.' With this comment, Adolphus poured them both a cup of tea and said how much it reminded him of the days on board the old steamer. He sat back, stretched his legs, laid his cane alongside the chair, bade Katherine to make herself comfortable, and then he began. 'It is most fortunate that I had made arrangements a while ago to return to Milan. It was going to be in the late spring, but that is neither here nor there. I can change my plans with very little effort, and have in fact, in view of your predicament. My visit to Milan will take a while as I have some important business to complete there. While all the things that need to be done are being worked on, I will be able to be absent from the proceedings for a few days here and there. I know several people on whom I can rely to help me, and I am fairly familiar with the surrounding areas.'

Katherine, by now, was sitting open-mouthed, but uttered not a sound. 'I will go, Katherine, and I will find Joseph, and I will also try to find your stepmother. This may be more difficult as she may have found it necessary to leave, due to the circumstances at the time of your departure. I will go by the addresses that you have sent your letters to, and move on if necessary from there. Is there anything else I should know? I will not be in touch often, but be assured I will do everything within my power to find a satisfactory end to all of this. No information will be passed to them relating to what has happened, but I will make sure that they can communicate with you after they have read your letters. I will just assure them that you are well, and being cared for in the best possible way. Does that meet with your approval, Katherine? It will give me the greatest pleasure to reunite you with your family, if only by letter.'

Unable to speak, Katherine stood up, walked around the desk, and placed her head next to Adolphus's. She put her arms around him, and just stayed there for a long time before she whispered, 'Why would you do this for me? I will never, never be able find the words to say thank you properly, but for all my life I will never forget this moment, and for all my life I will always love you. Please, please be careful in your travels and, if all fails, please come back to me without sorrow for I know that you will have done your best.'

Releasing her gently from his grasp, he said, 'It hasn't been a lifetime since you left, Katherine, although it must feel like that. It is under three years, and in the scheme of things life should be much the same around the fisherman's cottage, and at the market, so at least I have a good chance of finding someone. Be patient, my child, and I will do my very best. It will be three to four months before I return, and I hope that I will bring glad tidings to you. Now I must go and prepare for my journey. Go back to Dorcas Louise, and give her a kiss from me.' He raised himself elegantly from the chair, picked up his cane, kissed Katherine on the cheek once again, and bade her goodbye.

At the bottom of the stairs stood the lovely Mrs Elford, with her equally lovely adopted daughter in her arms. Adolphus smiled at her and nodded, to which she said, 'thank you,' as she held his hand tightly. Dorcas Louise made a concerted effort to be taken into his arms, but her mother restrained her, allowing her tiny arm to wind itself around the neck of Adolphus, causing them all to laugh, including Katherine who had joined the threesome heading for the door. It was past tea time for Dorcas Louise. Adolphus had been there for two and a half hours, and had given Katherine another ray of hope in her life. He seemed to be in the habit of doing this, Katherine thought, as she remembered the nightmare journey across Liverpool to have her baby, and then the support he had given her when they told her that her baby was dead. The incredible way that he had found her the job of wet nurse, when unbeknown to her he was a friend of the family. In fact the whole being of Adolphus Fry was very close to being a guardian angel, thought Katherine as her mind took her back to the boat, and the black cane that had jarred her memory of the train journey where she came close to almost losing her life. Adolphus had been there it seemed, a stranger in every way, and yet a part of her very being.

She now had to settle down into her life here in the Elford household where she hoped she would always be, but Dorcas would soon grow up, and then the decision would have to be made by her parents as to what sort of education she would have. Katherine could only hope that her services would be required for the intervening years at least. At the moment, that was all she could hope for, and so she would take one day at a time, do her best to ensure that Dorcas grew to be an obedient and loving child, as well as one of character and charm. She would serve Mr and Mrs Elford to the best of her ability, and most of all she would enjoy the child that no one but Adolphus knew was hers.

Life in the house was much calmer now without the worry of Trafina Paris. Strangely enough, if a little sadly, no one missed her. Every one happily got on with their chores. There was no one to shout at them when they stopped for a word or two in the passage, or laughed at a mishap that got quickly put to rights. Charlie still brought Katherine broken up bits of her favourite toffee. Cook would do what she called her special days, when chocolate cookies would appear on a plate in the kitchen, and one day even the mistress popped her head around the door, and sneaked two away, one for her and one for the master she said as she headed for the library. Flo and Charlie were inseparable but both worked hard, and never did anything to put their jobs in jeopardy.

Katherine for her part had a calm, happy existence. She walked Dorcas Louise in the park, even on the coldest of days. She wrapped her up in a warm hat, scarf, and gloves, which she had knitted herself, much to the interest of Lavinia Elford. The perambulator had been modified by removing the centre pad from the bottom of the carriage, thus making a square hole in which her feet could dangle, and she could sit up straight, supported by reins. Katherine tucked a warm blanket around her legs, and off they set, to watch and feed the ducks on the near frozen pond. Rabbit and Teddy would accompany them on their travels, but would more often than not find themselves on the path, sometimes run over by the carriage wheels while a laughing Dorcas waited for them to be returned, only to repeat the performance until Katherine drew a halt to it all by placing them in the basket housed underneath.

The master and the mistress threw an occasional dinner party which was always a success. When the master went off on one of his business trips, Lavinia Elford spent a lot of time sitting in the nursery engaged in conversation with Katherine. They both enjoyed each other's company and shared many a tale of their early lives. Katherine resisted the temptation to reveal her secrets; she knew she couldn't, and therefore stuck to ordinary everyday stories that could happen to anyone.

The cold windy days of winter slowly gave way to trees showing tiny buds waiting patiently to burst into blossom as the warmer winds of Spring gently shook the countryside into action. Katherine waited patiently too for the news that she so desperately wanted to hear from Adolphus on his return. Dorcas Louise had now discovered that one foot placed in front of the other allowed her to propel herself across the room. The first time it had happened caused her mother and her nanny to raise their hands and cheer. Dorcas, in her excitement, lost concentration and landed unceremoniously on her bottom. About to cry, she turned to see her mother holding out her arms to her and laughing, at which she forgot her walking steps, and crawled with great speed toward her to be scooped up and hugged.

Life at the house carried on happily. Katherine was able to gather the paperwork in the office in to good order, and with some help from Cook began to learn about the ordering and storing of food. Cook found her a delight to teach, and began to leave her with some of the work that she herself had done, so that she could organise her kitchen, and make it more efficient. The master, when he was home, began to have many more social events, which his wife hosted to his great satisfaction. Dorcas Louise was such a happy child, she was easy to care for, and Katherine used to take her into the office sometimes. Her rocking horse had been moved there from the hall, and she would love to sit on its back, arms around its neck, and rock back and forth until Katherine would remove her, and sit her on the large fur rug that formed a circle in the middle of the room. Then she would remove all her toys from the toy box, and place them with amazing neatness all around her.

One morning, upon opening the door, Charlie Orchard was faced by an elegantly dressed middle-aged man who asked to see the master. Charlie bade him enter, offered to take his coat and hat, and left him while he went to the library to advise the master of his visitor.

'Thank you, Charlie,' the master said, raising himself from his chair. 'That will be the butler from the agency that I was expecting; will you show him in, please?'

Charlie, shaken and surprised by the revelation, moved slowly back to the hall, and politely pointed the man in the direction of the library. The man stayed about an hour, and Charlie escorted him from the premises, as he had welcomed him, with politeness. The day dragged on for Charlie, who was feeling low and very worried. He was likely going to lose his job here at the house, a job he loved and a job that he thought he had done to the best of his ability, especially since the housekeeper had gone. He had taken on more responsibility, and the master had seemed pleased with him. He liked the master, and he had been very kind to him when he first came to the house. Then there was Flo. How would he be able to see her? Perhaps that was why the master was getting rid of him, because of his friendship with the maid, but they had been so careful not to show affection during working hours; in fact they behaved with the utmost decorum at all times when their duties threw them together.

At four o'clock that afternoon, the master called Charlie to the library. 'Sit down, Charlie,' the master said, with what Charlie thought was a very serious note to his voice. Charlie duly sat on the chair opposite the master, straightening his jacket, placing both feet together, and resting his hands clasped together in his lap, his eyes meeting the master's in question. 'Charlie,' began the master, 'the gentleman that you brought to me this morning was from the agency which sends competent and first class butlers to people like us who need them to train a member of their staff in every aspect of being a butler, and that, Charlie, is what he is going to do. If you see yourself in the future as a well-respected butler, and can also carry out other duties, mainly in the direction of running an efficient household, I am going to employ him for three months to put you through a very stringent course of everything that you will need to know, and at the end of that period, he will account to me on your progress. After that, if you prove to be of the best material, then there will be something else for you to consider. I deliberately placed you in the situation of meeting him this morning for him to form an opinion of you at first sight, and I am pleased to tell you that you passed the test most favourably. So how do you feel about becoming official butler to this household, Mr Orchard? Am I to continue, or are you not interested?'

'Sir, I am not only interested,' answered Charlie breathlessly, 'but I am most honoured, and will do everything that is asked of me. Thank you, sir!'

'That is fine then,' said the master. 'Of course, as soon as you have your position officially, you will be fitted with a uniform to be proud of, and will wear it all the times that you are on official duty. You will have a space of your own in the dressing room next to the laundry room, where you will keep your uniform always in pristine condition, and when you are performing menial tasks, you will of course wear your normal clothes. That is all for now, Charlie, well done, you have worked exceedingly hard since you have been in my employ, and in my opinion no one deserves this more than you.'

Charlie left the library with these words ringing in his ears. He felt like leaping in the air, but decided that this was not the sort of thing that a well respected butler would do. Once in the kitchen, he caught hold of Cook's ample waist, and waltzed her around the table. 'What next, young man, behave,' she admonished with a concealed grin. When he told her the news, she in turn almost picked him up and returned the compliment. She always had liked Charlie Orchard, a more honest young man she had never known. He would try hard, and do well in anything that was asked of him. The only small thing that worried her was his obvious feelings toward Flo. It had been commonplace for most of her life in service that members of the staff did not fraternise with other members, and sad as it was this could cause Charlie a lot of problems in the future. They were still young at present, but she would have to have a quiet, kind word with them on the subject, and see what their reaction was. Better sooner than later, she thought.

The moment came sooner than she had expected when she caught them hand in hand walking in from the garden, Charlie pulling the wheelbarrow with one hand, while Flo held a large bunch of daffodils. Once Cook had their attention, after she had called them into the kitchen and given them a cup of tea, she related her feelings to them, and to her amazement they said that they had both realised the dangers of the situation, and anyway they would not have enough money to settle down for a very long time yet. Cook had to be content with their reactions, and hoped that they would be strong enough to carry out their intentions to wait that very long time. She had many a doubt about that, but would not worry for a while at least.

Spring, with its magnolias and daffodils, gave way to the magnificence of roses and sweet peas in the garden beneath Katherine's window. Every morning, she never tired of looking from her window to see rows of rose bushes laden with blooms whose perfume spiralled its way up to her open window. She felt a contentment that almost outweighed the longing, and waiting, for news from Adolphus. She had not heard from him since he left, but he did warn her that maybe he would not be in touch, and so she tried not to linger in melancholy thoughts, instead she revelled in the growing up of Dorcas Louise.

She knew now that she would never go back to Joseph, but she wanted him so much to understand why, and she could not tell him until he had read the letters that were in the care of Adolphus. Three months had now passed. When he came home he would see such a change in Dorcas Louise, she was becoming a beautiful little girl, half way to her third birthday, and walking now.

One morning just after her breakfast, Katherine had heard her say Mama; she turned in delight, only to see her daughter run into her adoptive mother's arms. She quickly turned away in time to hide the tears that sprang to her eyes, but it was not lost on Lavinia Elford.

Another month passed before the letter dropped into the post box, and Flo brought it to Katherine who was working in the office. She stayed and played with Dorcas for a while to leave Katherine free to read her letter. Fingers trembling, Katherine carefully slit open the envelope with the silver opener that the mistress had bestowed upon her on Easter Sunday, as a thank you she had said. She slowly pulled out the thin paper, and read its contents. Adolphus wrote that he was still in Milan, the business problems with the publisher who was dealing with the Italian distribution of the novel was taking longer than he expected so he had made no further headway with her letters. However, in a day or two, all should be completed here, and then he would start his search. When this happened he would not contact her anymore, until he met her in person at home in Liverpool. He was so sorry for the delay, but he could do nothing about it. He hoped she was well, and of course Dorcas Louise; he begged her to be patient for just a while longer, and he sent his love and best wishes to the Elford family. Katherine, desperately disappointed, but happy that Adolphus was safe, turned to her duties once again, took a giggling Dorcas from the clutches of the maid, and got herself and Dorcas ready to go for their daily walk.

Charlie was a new man now, getting prepared for his entry into a new world of learning and studying. Katherine passed him on the stairs, and gave him a rapturous slap on the back; turning quickly he jumped away, and said, 'Mistress Katherine, you must learn to treat your butler with respect,' to which they both resisted the temptation to retaliate, and just smiled and passed by. Katherine was thrilled for Charlie. He had been her champion in the days of Trafina Paris, and she would never forget that. She would give him all the support that he needed to attain the coveted position of butler in the Elford household.

Lavinia Elford and Katherine were becoming closer than would usually befit a mistress with her child's nanny, but she remembered the days that Katherine had given her help not only in the ways of becoming an adoptive parent, but in building her own self-confidence. Lavinia was almost awestruck by the way that Katherine, still in her tender years, was capable of holding, not only herself high in the esteem of everyone who met her, but in lifting her to heights that she never thought she could accomplish, thus bringing the adoration of her husband down on her like a shower of stars. He needed her now at every function; he had in her now the perfect hostess, and was talking about her travelling to America with him in the near future. Dorcas Louise, she knew, would be perfectly all right with Katherine, and so there was no reason why she couldn't go. Confirming the fact that Katherine would have no difficulty in caring for Dorcas Louise, it was planned that they would travel in the autumn.

For Katherine it would be lovely to have Dorcas Louise all to herself, and with the master and mistress away, she would have time to talk with Cook and Flo, and of course Charlie, to discuss anything that was considered important to the running of the house that they had all come to love.

It was June when Lavinia Elford came into the nursery to find Katherine. Dorcas Louise was trying to build bricks into a tower, and yelled each time they fell down. Katherine, putting them back within her reach, saying 'again Dorcas' to which Dorcas replied 'again Kat'. Dorcas had difficulty in saying Katherine. As much as she tried, she could get no further than the first three letters, and it was left at that; from now on she would be Kat to Dorcas Louise.

Lavinia sat by Katherine and said, 'I have had a visit from Adolphus, and he would like you to go to his apartment today if you can. I know nothing Katherine, but I think you should go. I will care for Dorcas all day, so you may have all the time you need.'

Katherine jumped up, sending the pile of bricks flying across the nursery. 'Again Kat' Dorcas shouted with glee.

'I will deal with her ladyship,' promised Lavinia. 'I have arranged for a carriage to take you to Adolphus, and I'm sure he will arrange for your return here. Go and get yourself ready, the carriage will be here very shortly.'

For Katherine, the next hour went in a blur of expectation, trepidation, and an unrelenting need to be with Adolphus.

She rang the doorbell to the apartment Adolphus owned in the precincts of the university. He had spent many years here and was known throughout the area, being held in great respect by all who had come into contact with him. He answered the door to her, and stood there smiling as Katherine put her arms around him, happy just to see him home, with or without news. 'Come in, my child, and sit down. Help yourself to some iced orange juice, and please try some of my special chocolate cake.'

Katherine looked at Adolphus, and had a feeling that he was more than a little upset. His usually bright eyes seemed dull, and his step was not as light as when he left her four and a half months ago. 'Are you well, Adolphus?' Katherine asked, 'you seem tired.'

'I am tired, Katherine, and I have been trying very hard to decide where I should start regarding the news that I have for you.'

'You have news,' Katherine said excitedly.

'Yes, I do have news,' said Adolphus, 'but I must start by telling you that the news will not be what you expected.'

'Please,' begged Katherine, 'tell me, whatever the news may be, it will be better than having no news at all.'

Adolphus stood up and moved toward Katherine, put his hand upon her shoulder and said, 'I am so sorry to tell you, Katherine, that Joseph died just a few weeks after you left Italy.'

Katherine let out a strangled cry, and then just sat with her head in her hands. 'He can't have, not my Joseph,' she whispered.

Adolphus just stood quietly by her side and waited.

After a considerable time, she cried, and cried, tears of disbelief and desperation, until finally she asked. 'How? Why? Adolphus, what happened?'

Adolphus took a slow breath and began. 'Evidently there was an accident aboard a brig which had been caught in a terrible storm. A large hole was gouged from its bow, and it sank in less than fifteen minutes. Local fishermen, including Joseph, set out to rescue passengers who had jumped or been thrown into the water. Many were saved and brought ashore, but one of the fishing boats got into difficulty with people still on board, and Joseph set out again to help them. The story gets a bit vague here, but it is believed that the people panicked and tried to climb from the beleaguered boat into Joseph's, and in the process turned over his boat. Both fishermen in the boat that they were leaving, went into the water and tried to save those who were floundering. A larger boat came to their rescue, saving some but not all of the passengers, and unfortunately losing sight of Joseph. The other fisherman was hurt, but rescued. Joseph's body, and those of the other lost passengers were found a few days later. Joseph died a hero, Katherine, and his brother came forward to claim his body, and gave him a burial fit for such a hero, to which all the village turned out as a mark of respect. I have since arranged for a memorial to be erected in memory of Joseph and the lost passengers in the market square.'

Katherine, crying unashamedly now, said to Adolphus, 'I should give you his earring as part payment.'

Adolphus replied, 'Keep the earring, Katherine, and treasure it. Joseph would have wanted you to have it, and by the way I have something else for you.' He reached into his pocket and brought out a somewhat screwed up piece of paper which he handed to Katherine who unfolded it to find the drawing that she had done all that time ago as she sat on the beach outside the cottage.

She looked at Adolphus, and questioned him. 'How did you find this?'

'I found Lena, Katherine, and spent a long time with her. She has never stopped worrying about you. I told her all that I could, and now you will be able to write to her yourself. She has Pip in her care but says it breaks her heart every morning when he makes his way down to the cottage and sits by the boat house waiting for his master. He comes home to be fed, and then back he goes. She told me that the cottage remains empty, but Joseph's brother has left it for her and the children to use whenever they want to, so it is kept clean, and the children love being there, just as Katherine did, she said wistfully. She sends all her love to you, Katherine, and your sorrow she shares, and says her life was made so much the happier for the times that she had with you and Joseph.'

Katherine waited for Adolphus to finish his story, and then she said sadly, 'So all of my letters were written in vain to Joseph. He never knew he had a beautiful daughter, and he never knew that I would not be able to return to him. How strange.'

They both sat in silence for a while. Katherine trying to take in all that Adolphus had said, and still finding it hard to believe. Standing up and moving to the window, watching the people getting on with their daily lives, not knowing of the terrible things that had been visited upon her.

'Thank you, Adolphus, for all you have done. I will be in your debt for ever. Is there any more news? Tell me about your journey, and how you managed to find Lena.'

'Number one, Katherine, you owe me nothing,' said Adolphus. 'You have given me more than I could ever have bought and, number two, there is some more news, but before I tell you we will have a cup of tea. I think we both need one, and it is generally our destiny to drink tea at the important times in our lives, isn't it?'

'Is the news important then?' enquired Katherine.

'I think so,' Adolphus replied, 'but I will leave you to decide after tea.'

Katherine, still gazing from the window, turned as she heard tea cups rattling on a tray being delivered for Adolphus. The tray was placed on the table, and Adolphus said 'thank you' to the maid who turned to leave, and in leaving said, 'Hello, my darling.'

Katherine's eyes flew to the face of the woman. 'Mama,' she whispered almost inaudibly. Martha held out her arms, and Katherine threw herself into them. Both of them stood clinging to each other as Adolphus said, 'I take it you approve of my new housekeeper then?'

Katherine pulled herself away from her mother, and reached for Adolphus, nearly bowling him over. 'Hey, steady girl, remember my age,' he said laughing.

The three of them now hugging one another, two of them with so much to say, and one who was about to leave the other two in each other's company to say all that they wanted to. 'I have something to attend to that will take a couple of hours, and then I suggest we all have something to eat before I send you home, young lady. Martha knows nothing of your life since you left her, so I think you owe her one or two explanations, Katherine Anne Carrera.'

With Adolphus gone, Katherine and Martha sat together on the old leather couch, neither knowing quite what to say. Martha started by saying that life for the last four years had been unbearable. She had lost the child that she had loved above all others, and she knew not where she had gone. She had played a part in a crime that, although still undiscovered, came back to haunt her each day and night. She had walked the land endlessly looking for her, but to no end, and finally had given up hope, and just prayed that she didn't hate her for what had happened to her on that fateful night.

Katherine broke in there, and told Martha how she believed that it was all her fault, and that she couldn't stay and see her hurt or taken away. She told her how she had seen everything, the body being borne away by Alexi and her, and that she thought if she ran away Martha would be able to hide without having her to worry about. Then, as Martha just sat and listened, she told her the whole story, every single bit, and it was like a cleansing of her soul to tell her mother all the things that she had yearned to tell her for so long. As she came to the end of the story, and the news she had heard today, she told her darling mother that one day quite soon she would meet her granddaughter.

Adolphus returned on cue as usual. He sat between them and told Katherine of his plan to take Martha to London, where she would care for his house until the time when he would move there permanently, which would not be too long now. His life at university was virtually over, and he was looking forward to a lazy life being looked after, and looking forward, he hoped, to regular visits from his two best girls in the world.

Martha had, with the help of Adolphus, and not informing Alexi, left the cottage without a trace of her identity anywhere. Adolphus thought the chance of her ever being traced was unlikely, as no one had ever enquired about the disappearance of Vittorio, and even if the body was discovered at some point, the local people would deny any knowledge of his existence. However, just as a precaution, he thought it would be prudent for the connection between her and Katherine to be kept a secret just for a few more years.

'Please,' begged Katherine, 'may I see you again soon, and could I one day bring Dorcas Louise to meet you?'

'I'm sure, with Adolphus's blessing, that could be arranged, and we will for sure never lose touch ever again. Is that agreed, my Katherine?'

'Oh, so much agreed,' said Katherine, as she hugged her mother and headed for the carriage that was waiting to take her back to Dorcas Louise and her life at the house.

Katherine's journey back to the house was filled with the utmost emotions. The terrible, hopeless sadness of the news of Joseph's death that she would in some way never get over, and yet the ultimate joy of finding her mother again, after what had seemed a lifetime. She had been but a child when she took flight from that awful scene at the woodman's cottage, and now she was a woman, and the mother of a child that she could never call her own, who would never know the wonderful man who was her father, and to whom Katherine owed her life.

She opened the door quietly, and walked quickly up the stairs. She felt that she needed some time to reflect on her day before deciding what explanations, if any, to give to the mistress, and her friends below stairs. They were indeed her friends and she loved them all equally, but she knew she could not betray her mother's identity to anyone. As for Joseph, it mattered little now, for he was no more, and to all intents and purposes her baby had died. Nevertheless, she felt that she would like to hold on to his memory for a while longer, whether that happened or not would depend on how she bore up to the conversations that always arose when one or the other was away from the house for a day. It was commonplace to discuss the happenings; even the mistress was interested and spent many an hour chatting to Katherine, always glad when she was back 'in the fold', which was her favourite expression.

The two of them were developing a strong friendship, which was very unusual between mistress and servant, but it never seemed to affect the feeling of respect of one for the other. Lavinia Elford was sitting in her favourite chair with Dorcas Louise on her knee listening to her mother reading nursery rhymes.

'Kat,' squealed Dorcas, sliding down her mother's leg, and heading for Katherine as she entered the nursery.

'Hello, darling,' Katherine said as she scooped her up to sit in the crook of her arm. 'How are we all? Being good, I hope,' as she winked at Lavinia.

'We are just waiting for our tea. We have been for a walk. Dorcas took me to see the ducks, and showed me how to throw them some bread. I really got quite good after some practice, and some very good advice from Dorcas who managed to land most of it on the path, causing the ducks to heave themselves from the water to retrieve it, and it appears that it was the correct way to do it, and much more fun than throwing it in the water.'

Katherine smiled, and explained that it was Adolphus who conjured up that idea, and of course Adolphus could do no wrong. 'Talking of Adolphus,' Lavinia ventured, 'how was your day? Adolphus asked me to ask you how you felt about his new housekeeper, and whether you would be kind enough sometimes to allow her to accompany you on your walks. He explained that she hailed from the South of England originally, and although he had been lucky enough to meet her when he was in Italy, she had every intention of returning to England, eventually, and he had just made it easier for her by offering her a job here. He said he was very pleased indeed with her, and hoped she would stay, and finally return to London to work for him there looking after his house, and in fact him too. So, can I pass on to him your decision, Katherine? Are you happy to have her join you occasionally, perhaps on your visits to the shops? It would be nice for you to have some company other than that of Dorcas Louise.'

Katherine thought what a clever man Adolphus was. Only he could have thought of something so ordinary to allow them to share each other's company on a regular basis. She answered as casually as she could that it would be a pleasure to have the lady's company, who she had found very friendly, and very kind to her uncle Adolphus.

The plan hatched meant that she could spend some very special moments with her mother. They still had much to talk about, and nearly five years of separation to catch up on.

Katherine's shield was now down at this point, and she was not ready for Lavinia's next question. 'What happened about your letters, Katherine? Did Adolphus find out about your family?'

She looked up at Lavinia's concerned face, and crumpled. The tears came without warning, and Lavinia was at her side, putting a comforting arm around her shoulders. 'Do you want to tell me?' she said quietly.

Katherine raised her tear-stained face to Lavinia and said, 'Joseph died... Joseph was loved by everyone in the village, and he died trying to save other people's lives. He drowned, and they said that everyone was sad, and that they missed him terribly... but I miss him most... he was my Joseph, Lavinia, and he was the father of my baby.'

Lavinia stepped back. The shock of Katherine's revelation, not only took her by surprise, but filled her full of sadness and sympathy for this young girl who had devoted her life to Dorcas from the day she arrived at the house. She had lost her baby, and now she had lost the man to whom she had given herself, obviously at great risk due to her tender years. What had happened to her, she wondered, for all of this to evolve. Maybe she would never know! Katherine, since her life here, had grown into a very astute person with great potential. Lavinia knew that from this moment on she would protect and nurture this young woman, who in fact had played a great part in giving her the encouragement she needed to handle the social life that her position demanded. She had indeed become very fond of Katherine, and could not imagine life without her around.

She took both her hands in hers, and said, 'I am so sorry, Katherine. I cannot imagine the hurt that you are feeling. Please accept my sincerest sympathy, and please be aware that there will always be a place for you here, even when Dorcas has grown beyond the need for her nanny 'Kat'. I will always be happy to have you in my house in any capacity. I have actually been thinking down the line of Housekeeper. Would that be acceptable, do you think, when the time is right?'

Katherine, now crying like a baby, sat head in hands. Lavinia waited, handing her a large handkerchief. 'I always keep one of these handy, one of James's, it helps to mop up a lot of tears, and in the past I have shed many. One day we will talk, Katherine.' Lavinia moved to the bell, and rang the kitchen for some tea to be sent up, raised her daughter into her arms, sat her in her chair, and gave her a plate and spoon to play with until some food arrived. When Katherine's tears abated, she thanked Lavinia for her kindness, and her offer, which she accepted gratefully.

Gradually over the next few weeks she began to accept Joseph's death, and came to realise that in spite of the horror of what had happened, she could now devote all of her life to The Elfords who, unbeknown to them, held the only other reason for her living. She would be able to see Dorcas Louise grow up, and now she had yet another secret in her life. The knowledge that her darling mother would always be within easy reach of her, and that they would be able to see each other often. Adolphus would see to that. In fact they had already met. Adolphus had given Martha an advance in her salary, and told her to meet Katherine, and go shopping.

Martha had left the cottage with very little. She could not afford to be seen carrying a suitcase, and anyway she had very little to put in it, so she had filled an old shopping bag with just a few essentials, shut the door on her past, and walked out. Slowly, she had put distance between her and the village to a spot where Adolphus was waiting for her in a carriage. Now she was going to meet her daughter, who this time was alone. She would have to wait to meet the child, born to her beautiful Katherine, until next time, as shops were not the place for an inquisitive, lively toddler.

Katherine had asked Lavinia if she would care for her while she took Adolphus's housekeeper out to buy some new clothes. Lavinia was pleased to see Katherine with a little colour in her pale cheeks, and a light of interest in the eyes that had looked so sad for the past few weeks. So it was arranged, and Katherine met Martha half way between The Elford house and Adolphus's apartment. Adolphus had walked a little way with her, and then left her with instructions that would take her with no difficulty to where Katherine was waiting.

They hugged like two old friends, and laughed as Katherine took her mother's arm and said, 'We will go and see what we can find you, and then we will go to the tea shop, where we will indulge in something extravagant and very sweet.'

Her mother raised her eyebrows, and she smiled. She would have to get used to the grown up daughter that she now was looking at. Shopping with Martha was not easy, Katherine discovered. She remembered that her mother had never bought anything. All the clothes she owned were made from bits of old material, cardigans were darned at the elbow, and fell unevenly around her body. The only money that she ever spent was on Katherine. She remembered her dress that her mother made for the concert at the school, and the coat that she loved, which had been ruined in the water. Now she was here and, thanks only to Adolphus, could afford to buy at least two outfits, and some shoes. Was there no end to the kindness of this man, and why had she been so blessed by his presence in her life? Shopping finally done, and complete with boxes and bags, they headed for a well-earned cup of tea and a piece of rich fruit cake. In spite of the two hours spent on their first day together at the apartment, they both still had so many questions to ask.

Katherine asked about her father. She really didn't want to know anything about him, but felt duty bound to ask because of his involvement in the demise of her stepfather, and the help that he evidently gave to her mother after the incident. Alexi, her mother said, had become a broken man, and although he had supported her financially for a time, the payments had long since ceased, and she had to live from the meagre supplies that could be harvested from the land, mainly vegetables, with an odd rabbit or two that she caught in the traps that were set in the surrounding woodland. She said that Alexi was often to be seen kneeling at the graveside of her mother, no longer the nobleman who rode so proudly across the fields that connected the big house and the woods where he had lived with his wife Cordelia. He was now poorly shod, and the news spread around the village that his wife had left him, and the children had been put into private education at the expense of their grandmother. Martha said that she had made no attempt to approach him as she was frightened that it may raise suspicion, and that if it did, questions may be asked as to the whereabouts of the woodman.

Therefore there was no connection at all with anyone for Martha, and she lived a lonely, sad life at the cottage until the day that Adolphus knocked on her door. At first, she hid behind the curtains, frightened as to who this well-dressed, elegant man was, and what he wanted. Not to be put off, he leant on his stick and waited, continued Martha, until she had no choice but to open the door, 'and my darling, the rest you know' she said with such a sigh of contentment that it almost set Katherine's tears flowing again, but not quite, because she was so happy that she wanted to get up and shout at the top of her voice, 'This is my mother,' but decorum reigned, and she just said, 'I love you; I always have and I always will, and now I will pay the bill.'

Together they left the tea shop, and headed back toward the part of the town where Adolphus had deposited Martha all of four hours ago. He was standing there resting once again on his cane. He couldn't help smiling at the two people walking toward him, one of which he loved beyond his powers of understanding, and one who he hoped would be his companion for the autumn of his life. They took their leave of one another with a promise to meet again very soon. Katherine gave a little skip as she turned and headed back to her life, which now held a degree of certainty that sent tingles of joy through her body.

Summer days, now in all their glory, were made up of happiness and contentment for Katherine, and a time for adventure for a little girl now growing up enough to appreciate the things around her as she learned to walk supported by reins. Trying to catch a squirrel as it darted across her path to disappear up into leafy sanctuary of the tree. Rabbits too with their fluffy tails fascinated her, as they hopped here and there in the magical place that Kat called the park. They went there often, and other children would stop and say hello, which delighted Dorcas. Martha, having grown accustomed to the walk through the streets of Liverpool to meet Katherine, came often and accompanied Katherine and her new darling granddaughter. She soon had Dorcas Louise winding her around her little finger, and doted upon her like a true grandmother.

Since settling in to the apartment, and looking after Adolphus, she had become a different woman. She now dressed nicely, and made the most of the new clothes she had bought. Adolphus had also made her buy some work clothes, so that she could save her others for going out. Her hair had been cut into a short curly style which made her look so much younger, Katherine thought. Thinking so many times that one of her dearest wishes was to have Martha with her had now come true, and Katherine sometimes had to pinch herself to know that she was here. When she had, at her lowest and most frightening times, cried for Martha, now she could reach out and touch her, and talk to her, and when she moved to London she would ask Lavinia if she could take Dorcas Louise to visit her and Adolphus. Lavinia gave her permission for Katherine to take Dorcas anywhere she wished; she knew that she would be safer with her than anyone else in the world.

In the autumn, James and Lavinia Elford were to visit the United States of America. Adolphus suggested that it would be a good time to take Martha to see the house in London, and he would be delighted if Katherine and Dorcas Louise were to join him. They could spend a few days at the house, meet his present housekeeper who was going to stay until the new housekeeper was moved in, and then she would be able to move to her new little house and enjoy her well-earned retirement. He was hopeful to have Martha settled by the end of the year, and then tie up all the ends of his profession at the university, moving himself to London about the same time. Katherine was sad that she would be losing her darling mother again so soon, but at least this time she knew that she would be safe and happy with Adolphus, and that she could go at any time and see her. She would save a part of her wages every week so that she could afford the fare on the train. She would also have to think to the future, when she would be full time housekeeper at the Elfords, and that she would have to give Dorcas part time to a governess, and watch her grow up.

She had lost her dearest Joseph, but she had found a mother who had given her life, and had loved her selflessly for thirteen years until the dreadful night that had wrenched her away and put her in terrible danger. Sent her halfway around the world to give her a child, and so soon to take it away. Now somehow life had amended the ills that it had bestowed upon her, and had given her a chance to grasp once again the happiness she deserved.

Chapter Fourteen

Times Of Change

Over the next few months, Katherine began to come to terms with the loss of Joseph. When she lay in her bed at night her mind would meander slowly across the memories of her life with him. They were like clear pictures that danced in front of her eyes. The growing to know him, from her initial meeting when he presented quite a wild impression, and then feeling the beginnings of love and the joy when she found that Joseph felt the same; seeing Pip, as he jumped for joy when the tiny boat pulled in to the boat house, and he saw her waiting for him and Joseph to come in to dinner. Her life with him had been happier than she ever could have dreamed. The cottage was a magical place, and it was Joseph who made it so. She was back again, sitting on her rock and watching the blue water slowly licking at the white sandy beach, her feet digging deep into the grains, and feeling its coolness as it ran through her toes. Her hand moved under her pillow to touch the earring that she had put there on her return from Adolphus, whilst her drawing, bad as it was, now rested on her little table at the side of her bed. One thought haunted her. What if she had not become pregnant?

Pushing that to the back of her mind, she thought of the wonderful times when they had loved one another, and afterwards when they skipped down the beach chasing each other, and she knew that she would not have had it any other way. She had known Joseph, and loved him above all others, and now there was her child, a secret to everyone except Adolphus and Martha.

There was also Martha, who was a secret to everyone except Adolphus and her. How could so much happen to one person, she thought, and how did I become that person? With that self question she gave up thinking, and sleep became the only thing left, until Dorcas Louise awoke her with a toothy grin that melted her heart. How Joseph would have loved you, she whispered only to herself and Dorcas.

For all the sadness and excitement that had come together, Katherine never stinted on her tasks, between her caring for Dorcas Louise, and trying to keep the household accounts and paperwork in order, she went to Cook as often as possible, and learned more about the meals that had to be prepared and served, and how the dinner parties, and evening business meetings in the library, were dealt with. Cook, as far as Katherine was concerned, was the centre of this household, and she held her in great respect. Cook for her part admired Katherine, and thought that she had a head on her shoulders that was far advanced for her years; she also had a genuine soft spot for her, and would give her all the help she could.

All in all, life was good at the house. Charlie and Flo, although closer than two peas in a pod, worked extremely well together, and Katherine had not a single worry that they were not completing their duties, each one to the best of their ability. When on the odd occasion she espied them leaving one of their rooms together, she closed her eyes and prayed that they wouldn't get caught, and if they did she hoped that the master and mistress would look upon them favourably. She also prayed that their fate would not be the same as hers, and that babies would come in the years following a marriage, something she hoped desperately would befall them one day.

Charlie would soon now be entering his time when he was to learn to be a butler, and for that he would have to put all other things aside, and give himself to hard work. Roger Cloverleaf arrived at the Elford residence at 8am on the morning of the 15th August 1904, carrying a smart carpet-bag. He was casually dressed, but smart in a jacket fashioned in a small black and white check, with a white shirt and a check tie to match the jacket. He wore grey trousers and a pair of highly polished black shoes. He wore no hat, and his hair was slick, and neat, with sideburns. Charlie answered his knock, and opened the door with a flourish.

'Good morning, sir,' he said, as he stood to attention in front of him, and then swiftly moved to one side, holding the door open wide so that he could pass through. Flo was standing ready in case she was needed, but Charlie had it all under control as he said, 'May I take your valise, sir, and may I show you to the master?'

'Indeed you may,' the butler replied.

Charlie headed with measured step toward the library, knocked on the door, and at the master's command opened it; half turning to the butler, he said, 'Please enter, sir,' and at the sight of the back of the butler taking the seat that the master had offered, Charlie quietly closed the door and headed back to the kitchen.

Cook had a cup of tea at the ready, and said to Charlie, 'Sit down, lad, and drink this, you did right well I reckon.'

'Thanks, Ruby,' he said, drifting into the use of first names which they all did at times of stress, and out of earshot of the master or mistress. 'That's only the beginning; I reckon I shall be after lots more cups of tea before this is over.'

Roger Cloverleaf sat and discussed with the master the kind of teaching that would be required, as different situations and different houses made for some changes in the method of his approach to young would-be butlers. 'When there was a need to cater for a large amount of guests at a dinner party for instance, the butler would be required to carry out many duties, and in this respect he would have other staff to call on to do behind stage duties, so that he could always be in sight of the guests, and at their service. Here, sir, with respect, you do not employ that amount of staff, and while I can see by the way the house looks, the staff that you have are very efficient, a great deal of strain would be put on Mr Orchard.'

'I respect your comments,' replied the master, and if an evening dinner party required more staff then I would certainly acquire them, but I would want them to work under the command of Charlie Orchard. Therefore I would ask you to treat his training as you would someone who was likely to be moving to far higher places than this. I have known this young man for about four years now, and have every reason to believe in his ability. He is honest, hard-working, and is a very likeable character. I think you could turn him into a first class butler, without stripping him of his good nature and popularity. Do you think you could do that, Mr Cloverleaf? If you do, I will leave him in your hands and, at the end of three months, we shall see. For the last month of your stay here, my wife and I will be travelling abroad, so you will be able to see for yourself how he fares without a master and mistress in the house. Do you not think that would be a very good test?'

Roger Cloverleaf had always been one for a challenge, and this was going to be quite a challenge, he thought. 'I will do the very best I can for, and with, the young man, sir,' he concluded. The master then called for Charlie, and asked him to escort Mr Cloverleaf to his room, and arrange for breakfast to be served in the dining room in twenty minutes. Charlie took a deep breath, and proceeded up the stairs to the room where his tutor would probably write up a report each night on how well or how badly he was doing.

The following day started with quite a jolt for Charlie. As he descended the stairs at 8am, as he had always done, Mr Cloverleaf was standing by the closed housekeeper's door, waiting. He gave Charlie a cursory glance, looked at his watch, and moved to greet his charge.

'Today, Mr Orchard, we will start as we mean to go on in the matter of preparing yourself for a life as a butler. First, I have two gifts for you. The first is this clock, within which is a mechanism which at a given time will ring an alarm bell, and this alarm will always be set at 6.30am so that you will be washed and dressed, and ready to serve your master by 7am, unless of course he decrees differently, and then you will adjust accordingly. You will always dress in your chosen uniform for day use. I always advocate tails and black tie, and this is what you should adhere to in your time of training with me. I will make myself responsible for attaining your uniforms with the master's agreement. The second gift is this black notebook. I trust that you will keep it in good order and always write neatly. I assume that you can write competently, and I will want it to be kept not only until I leave, but as a constant reminder of the proud profession that you are about to enter in to. The pencil that accompanies it should always be kept sharp, and should be sharpened by the blade that is with it, and not by one of Cook's knives. I will read your notes at the end of each day, and you will make any adjustments that I think fit, before we close our tuition. As you are the only one here at present to act as butler, you will have to carry out your normal duties as well so that the family feel no inconvenience. Are you ready, Mr Orchard?

'Lesson number one, Mr Orchard. From now on you will be known to me, the staff here, and the housekeeper, as Mr Orchard, and to Mr and Mrs Elford, as Orchard, or possibly another name chosen by them. I will be known to you, and be addressed as Mr Cloverleaf. I will go on now to list some of your duties, all of which I will address individually as we progress, adding or dismissing some in accordance with our needs. You would be well advised to take a note of each one, as I will not repeat them, and you will certainly need them daily. Your notebook, Mr Orchard, is designed to fit the inside pocket of your jacket so that you may discreetly refer to it in times of insecurity.'

Mr Orchard obediently took up his notebook and pencil and proceeded to write. He had always liked writing, and copied some articles from the papers before they were discarded, so he had little difficulty in producing a nice script for his first day's notes. Mr Cloverleaf, he noticed, also had a black notebook, but the cover was quite worn. He wondered how long he had used it before he remembered every single thing that had to be done. At this moment, Katherine descended the staircase and opened the office door. 'Would you care to have the use of this room, sir,' said Katherine.

'Thank you. I have not yet been introduced to you,' Mr Cloverleaf said, throwing a quick glance at Charlie, standing slightly embarrassed at Katherine's side.

'I am sorry, sir... um... Mr Cloverleaf, sir. May I introduce you to Miss Katherine Carrera; she is our housekeeper, and nursemaid to the mistress's daughter, Dorcas Louise.'

'I am pleased to make your acquaintance, Miss Carrera, and I hope we will meet often in our duties here,' Mr Cloverleaf said.

'I am sure we will,' answered Katherine with a smile. 'Please excuse me now, I must go and see to the needs of Dorcas Louise.'

Mr Orchard led the way into the office, followed closely by Mr Cloverleaf. Sitting at the desk, one talking, one avidly writing, the morning began in earnest. Mr Cloverleaf started to dictate.

'Your first duty of the day will be to iron your master's newspaper...' Ignoring the beginnings of a comment, he continued, 'You will then arrange for the breakfast table to be laid in the dining room. Before breakfast you will deliver a tea tray, the newspaper, and any early morning correspondence. Servants' breakfast will then take place, and afterwards you will see what the master needs, and attend to it. Prayers should then be held, and attended by all in the household. You will need to liaise with the housekeeper for this arrangement, and of course follow the wishes of the master. After this stage, you should announce breakfast, and wait on the family. The clearing up of the dining room should be undertaken when all persons have left, around 10.30, or at a time agreed by the mistress of the house. The housekeeper should discuss the menus for the day. I understand that the lady in question is not yet ready to take on full responsibility of housekeeper, and therefore you will carry on as you usually do, but be aware that this is what should happen in a properly run household. You should also take orders from the master, and then relay the said orders to the staff. After all this has been accomplished, at approximately 11.30, you should take your morning tea with the rest of the servants, and staff, and then you should prepare to lay the dining table for the family luncheon. This completed, you should arrange midday dinner for the servants and yourself, and possibly to follow, share coffee or tea with the housekeeper. By this time, you should have passed on all the necessary orders to the cook and staff, as required by the master. How does the end of your morning duties seem to you, Mr Orchard? We will take a short break now, while you go and catch up with your normal duties. I will see you in two and a half hours. Thank you.'

'Thank you, Mr Cloverleaf,' said Charlie, with a lot more confidence than he felt. In his two and a half hour break, Charlie managed a quick visit to the kitchen, to find Cook, Flo, and Katherine assembled, each playing their own little part as they always did in the running of the house. Charlie tried to explain that a few things were going to alter due to his promotion, but he hoped that in spite of these changes he would still remain their friend. He would not be able to bear it if they could not, when they were out of sight of the master and mistress, have their little laughs and friendly conversations which had helped them all along to carry out sometimes quite hard and strenuous duties. Both Katherine and Cook placated him, and assured him of their undying friendship, and Flo just snuggled under his arm, gave him a kiss on the cheek and said, 'Let them try and stop us, Charlie.'

Returning finally to the office, he found Mr Cloverleaf browsing through drawings of uniforms. 'Ah, Mr Orchard, back again, slightly late I fear. I will overlook it at these early stages of your training, but it must never happen when you are on duty. Never. Do you understand, Mr Orchard?'

'I understand... um... Mr Cloverleaf,' Charlie stuttered.

'Right then, we will now go into your afternoon schedule when first you will check that the dining table is set for lunch. I notice that the household does not have a gong in the hall, Mr Orchard. How do you inform the family that luncheon is served?'

Charlie answered with confidence. 'We, Mr Cloverleaf, have everything standing ready and tables set, so that the master or the mistress, or both as the case may be, can eat at any time it suits them.'

'I see,' said Mr Cloverleaf. 'Then my task here is going to be a little more difficult. I will have to either teach you what is right and proper and leave you to work your way around your employers, or I am going to have to discipline them as well as you. For the time being, I will go through the duties that should be applied, and I will speak with the master and mistress later today. After the family has eaten their lunch, I will allow you to leave the dining room while they are busy with their dessert course. This will give you time to have some refreshment yourself. After lunch you will clear the table, as you obviously already do. You should organise one of the servants, which should be a footman and, which of course at present you are yourself, to answer the door so that you may take a rest before you partake of tea with the other servants around four o'clock. After this, you should return to duty, and serve afternoon tea to the family when and where they desire.

'Now to the evening duties, Mr Orchard. I hope you have concise notes on all that I have been talking about.' Mr Cloverleaf had in fact been watching closely as Charlie's pencil moved with alacrity across the pages of his new notebook.

'The evening, Mr Orchard, starts when you are washed and shaven, and changed into your evening uniform. Then you will place out the plate and glass, and go to the wine cellar to select the table wines. You would be advised to consult the master on this before your visit to the cellar. We will discuss wines at a later date. This all completed, you will make yourself available for any help that the master may need. If there are extra guests, you should wait on the gentlemen after dinner. You will go through your inventories every day to ensure no damage has occurred to plate or glass, and remedy the situation immediately. The remaining part of the evening, provided you have made sure that nothing is needed, or that another member of staff is available to attend to the family, may be spent at your leisure. At the end of the evening, you will wait until the master tells you that you are no longer needed and may retire. First, you will proceed to see that all the lights and fires are damped out, and all the outer doors are secured. You and you alone will be responsible for the keys to the house, and it will be your duty to lock up. If at some time you should deem it possible for someone else to do this final duty of the day, and should some error occur in so doing, you will be held totally responsible, not the person who has done the chore for you. Finally, Mr Orchard, I should comment that you should have a footman to clean your shoes for you each night, so that you may step into them in the early hours to perform your first duties of the day, but as at the moment there is no footman, only you, I am afraid that you will have to perform that chore yourself. That, Mr Orchard, is all I have to impart upon you this day. I now have to make my own notes, and present myself with them to the master this evening. You will be called, so I would suggest that you keep yourself alert until after this has happened. Thank you, Mr Orchard.'

With that, Mr Cloverleaf shut his notebook, rose from the chair behind the desk, and briskly walked out of the door, leaving Charlie wishing that he could curl up in bed and go to sleep, but he now had to carry out the duties that had seemed relatively easy until now. He would have to go and beg cook for a nice cup of tea first, and maybe have a little chat with Flo. Today he had felt that his old familiar world had been thrown out of the window. He wasn't quite sure that he liked it.

Mr Cloverleaf duly submitted his notes to Mr and Mrs Elford in the library after supper as they had suggested. On the subject of uniform, Mr Elford explained that he had already made enquiries, but if Mr Cloverleaf would like to take the responsibility of carrying out the task, he would be most grateful. The subject of employing another footman was a little harder for Mr Elford to accept. He explained that, although the increase of dinner parties and business soirees were high on the agenda, he felt that the household at all other times was well within the capabilities of Charlie to handle. Mr Cloverleaf, a little taken aback at the statement, felt that now was the time to point out the reason that he had been employed here. 'Charlie! Mr Elford.' Mr Cloverleaf bristled at the use of his first name. 'Charlie, while he is under my instructions and tutoring, should in future be called Mr Orchard by the rest of the staff, and myself, but you and your Lady wife would call him Orchard, or possibly Charles. Would that be acceptable, Mr Elford?'

'Yes of course,' answered the master contritely. 'I apologise, and bow to your superior knowledge regarding the rise to a butler from a footman, but how does Orchard feel about it?'

Mr Cloverleaf countermanded the question, and replied, 'If Mr Orchard wishes to join the ranks of one of the most prestigious positions in this country today, he will accept with humility the road on which he has to travel to reach the end. Do you, sir, wish to ask me any questions before I present my first report? If not, I think it would be pertinent to ask Mr Orchard to join us at this stage.'

'Go ahead,' answered Mr Elford, not being able to think of anything more to say, much less to ask any questions.

Charlie Orchard was thus summoned to the library. He was ushered quickly from the kitchen, where he gave Flo a fleeting peck on the cheek, which heralded a severe 'Now then' from Cook. On entering the library, he stood facing the desk where Mr Elford was sitting. The mistress stood at the master's side, with her hand placed gently on the back of his chair. Mr Cloverleaf stood to the left hand side of the front of the desk, and Mr Orchard took his position at centre front. Mr Cloverleaf cleared his throat and looked toward Mr Elford who nodded his approval for him to begin.

'Mr Elford, Mrs Elford,' he said, with just the slightest hint of a bow. 'Mr Orchard,' he said, inclining his head toward the trembling Charlie Orchard. 'I will start by saying that I have been suitably impressed by your concentration on all the things that I have pointed out to you this day, and although it is too early to give a genuine report upon your conduct and general bearing, I have reason to believe that it would be worth carrying on with your tutoring. You will need to pay attention to certain areas of your daily routine, and improve considerably if you wish to attain anything like the high standard that will be required of you to become a fully fledged butler.'

Continuing, now directing his conversation to the master, he said, 'I have spoken to you, sir, of employing a footman, and I do believe this is necessary for menial tasks, for instance the cleaning of shoes and helping to clear tables, to mention just two. If Mr Orchard is to become your butler, it would be seen as beneath him to be doing these things, and I am sure there are many more tasks that could be handed to a footman. However, if you decide against my request, I will have to ask that at least when you have dinner parties, or are entertaining more than a dozen guests, you obtain some help, and do not rely on your already hard working staff. With reference to the purchasing of uniforms, I will take the opportunity of escorting Mr Orchard to a tailor recommended by my employers, and have him properly attired. I do believe that a man is more efficient in his job if he is perfectly dressed at all times, and this will be one of my most important lessons for Mr Orchard. Now as I mentioned before Mr Orchard entered the library, from this moment he will be called Mr Orchard at all times by the staff; this will also apply to your cook, who should be known as Mrs Stone, or Cook at any time; your maid may still keep her name, but she will also bestow the correct title to Mr Orchard. Your child's nanny should be referred to as Miss Carrera. The position of butler in any household is one of prestige, and it is the right of the person who attains that position to be treated with respect at all times. With your permission, sir and madam, I will leave you now; and you, Mr Orchard, I will see in the office at 8am. Thank you and goodnight.'

Mr Orchard, almost glued to the spot, now compulsively made for the door to open it, and let out Mr Cloverleaf. He turned half apologetically to the master and the mistress, who both smiled, and the master said, 'You may go now, Orchard, you will not be needed any more tonight, goodnight and thank you.'

'Good night, sir,' answered a bewildered Mr Orchard. As he left the library he wondered if he would ever end up like Mr Cloverleaf, and he rather hoped he wouldn't.

Mr and Mrs Elford looked at one another, and decided that they would have to call the rest of the staff together tomorrow and pass on the instructions of Mr Cloverleaf. Lavinia looked at her husband and said, 'I'm not sure how "Orchard" feels about Mr Cloverleaf, but he frightens me to death.'

Her husband, with a suspicion of a smile, returned, 'Me too, darling, shall we retire?'

With that, the Elfords took one another's hand, and left the library. The reactions of the staff, the following morning, were varied. Flo hooted with laughter. 'Me, call my Charlie, Mr Orchard when I'm going to marry him one day. Never.'

Katherine smiled at her and said gently, 'Do it for Charlie, Flo, he will need all the support we can give him, and if it means calling him Mr Orchard, then so be it.'

Cook decided that she would rather be called Cook than Mrs Stone, and Katherine was happy with whatever they wanted to call her. Cook said to Katherine, 'My son could do with a bit of extra work; they have a little'un on the way. I wonder if the master would consider him for a few hours here and there.'

'I will mention it to him if you wish,' said Katherine. 'It could be the answer to the extra footman the master was considering employing.'

Charlie Orchard's tuition started in earnest the very next day. The wine cellar was traversed for what seemed to be most of the day. Labels were checked, and it was arranged for the local wine merchant to bring some new wines for the master to taste. Mr Orchard would be present at the tasting, and would listen and learn about the properties of every bottle that was considered to grace the table at the next dinner party, which was to be just before the master and the mistress left for America. Business for the master was doing extremely well, and this would be reflected in the food and wine that would be offered to the guests. Mr Orchard would be prepared very carefully for that night, and Mr Cloverleaf would be standing in the wings to see that the butler performed as near perfectly as he could make him in such a short time. Help would be at hand. Cook's son would be on duty to handle tasks that Mr Cloverleaf had made sure he could do without hesitation.

Adolphus Fry, being one of the guests for the evening, had offered the help of his housekeeper to assist Cook in the kitchen. The offer was hastily taken up by Cook, who let out a sigh of relief at the thought of vegetables being cooked and side dishes being arranged, leaving her to concentrate on massive joints of meat that all had to reach the end of their cooking at the same time, which sometimes exasperated her. The big black range, absolutely bulging, and the pots that hung from the hooks over the heat, belching steam until the whole kitchen was like a cauldron, was what she called being close to Hades. Cook was the calmest individual, and never let anything get beyond her control, but sometimes these dinner parties pushed her to the limits of her endurance. Katherine then would be her runaround. In between looking after Dorcas Louise, she would fetch and carry for cook, bringing her dishes as she called for them, keeping an eye on the time, and keeping Flo up to scratch. Katherine loved every minute, she was so happy, even her sadness about Joseph was slowly diminishing, and she was remembering the happy times she had with him instead of mourning his loss.

Autumn was nearly here, and both Dorcas and her would see another birthday pass before the master and the mistress returned from their business trip. Then there would be Christmas, and the beginning of a new year. Charlie would have finished his training, and be the butler. Cook's son would have the job of footman whenever he was needed. Dorcas Louise would be heading toward a governess entering her life, and Katherine herself would take over full duties of housekeeper to the Elford household. Changes were indeed heralded. Katherine, for the very first time in her life, felt secure and happy about the future.

To his own amazement, and to that of Mr Cloverleaf, Charlie, now getting used to his new title, took to the tasks that he was set like a duck to water. He now had his new uniform, and wore it with pride. Slowly, Mr Cloverleaf was gearing him toward the night when the Elfords would entertain more guests in the house than ever before. Rooms that had been left unused for a long time were opened up, and cleaned from top to bottom. They were furnished with new bed linen, and curtains, and Katherine was left to choose what the mistress called fripperies to make them all look inviting for the guests who would stay overnight. Katherine was able to meet Martha on her shopping expeditions, and they had a wonderful time choosing all kinds of things like cushions to place on the beds, and vases into which they would put fresh flowers, new jugs and bowls which would be filled with hot water in the morning, for the use of the ladies. New towels they would buy to put close to the bowl. A carriage was put at their convenience to carry all their purchases back to the house. Martha had met Cook, and they instantly liked one another, much to Katherine's pleasure. Mr Cloverleaf insisted that Martha should comply with the rest of the staff, and be called Mrs Wilkin.

It had been decided by Adolphus that Martha should adopt her maiden name, just as a precaution, and both her and Katherine had agreed that it was a good idea. Life thus, although changed somewhat, seemed to be settling into an almost perfect state for Katherine, Martha, and Adolphus, who was a very happy man at the outcome of his eternal plan, for the future of the girl who had given him a reason for living. From the moment he found her, after losing her on that train so long ago when the memory of her haunted him until he found her again on the boat, he believed in destiny, and he knew that somehow his would be entwined with hers for the rest of his life.

The last days of summer were idly passing by, the roses starting to fade, except one red rose that bloomed below Katherine's window, and seemed to last until all the others had gone. How beautiful it was, thought Katherine, and on one particular day when incessant rain caused it to bend and droop, she went down and plucked it from its branch, took it to her room, and gently placed it in a small white vase that she had brought with her from Joseph's cottage. It seemed to hold a message for her. There had been a rose exactly the same as this one in her little garden that she had tended and loved. 'I feel you there, Joseph,' she whispered; the rose lifted its head, and she kept it until the last petal had fallen.

The master and mistress were busy planning their trip to America. It was the first time that Lavinia had been there and, although a little nervous, she was excited about travelling with her husband on business. It would mean that she would be involved more than she had ever been in the world of commerce. Her husband had discussed certain aspects of his work with her, but had never included her in any decisions. Now he had handed her a large file of papers to read, and had asked her to comment on them.

She had been a good scholar, and was in fact very intelligent, but upon marrying James, she had been rather turned toward motherhood and wifely duties. The motherhood of course had not been possible, and that had caused a setback in their relationship. The arrival in their lives of Dorcas Louise, and ultimately the presence of Katherine Carrera in their family circle, had created a change in Lavinia that her husband found miraculous. This being so, James Elford looked forward with relish to the dinner party. He had invited every important person he could think of, knowing that if he made a good impression, it would push his business into the realms of financial greatness. He was already in a position to use the stock market to his advantage, and was doing so with good results. He would take the opportunity of showing off his beautiful wife in the knowledge that she could now hold her own in any conversation with the ladies, and not be too shy to answer any questions that the gentlemen may throw at her. She would of course be the perfect hostess, and stay at his side until he bade her to entertain the ladies after the meal was finished, and the gentlemen indulged in their cigars and after dinner drinks.

Charlie Orchard was being pushed on quickly through certain aspects of his training in order to cope with this special night. Mr Cloverleaf explained that things would return to their normal pace when the evening was over and, while the master and mistress were away, they would have the time to go through everything without the worry of looking to the duties of their welfare. Roger Cloverleaf, without showing any encouragement to Charlie, was secretly very pleased with his progress. He showed a lot of dedication in all that he did, and he never seemed to get tired of learning, just the opposite in fact, he sometimes asked questions that his teacher found difficult to answer. At the end of the day, he found notes meticulously written and totally relevant to the teachings that he had given. If there were any complaints, it was the trouble that Mr Orchard seemed to have with rising at an early hour. Always the hurried footsteps in the corridor heralded a breathless but perfectly attired butler entering the office with a guilty look on his face. Charlie would always be Charlie to Katherine, who every morning gave a quick but quite loud rap on his door, and a loud whisper through the keyhole, 'Shake a leg, Charlie'. To which she would hear a gruff 'O.K. O.K.'

She showed a very different face in front of the rest of the staff, and bade him a very smart, 'Good morning, Mr Orchard', to which he would reply, 'And to you, Miss Carrera'.

Dorcas Louise, now almost three years old, was chattering away as Katherine got her ready for her morning constitutional to the park. 'Ducks, Kat, please feed ducks.' Once in the park, Katherine would let her get out of her carriage and walk holding the handle with upstretched arms; she could just reach it. Katherine would hold her tight on her reins, especially when she reached dangerously close to the edge of the water in order to throw pieces of bread. The thought of falling into the water, still after all the years since it had happened to her, gave her nightmares.

Adolphus had asked permission of the mistress to take Katherine and Dorcas Louise to London, along with Martha, to stay for a couple of days at his house while she and James were away in America. His housekeeper would still be there, and would look after them, he had told Lavinia in case she was worried about their welfare, but in fact she was very happy for them to go.

'Katherine does not get out enough,' she told Adolphus, 'and it would be lovely for Dorcas Louise. Perhaps she will find some more ducks to feed.'

'I'm sure she will,' he laughed. 'I will see to that, and I will take care of them all.'

Lavinia answered, 'I have no doubt whatsoever on that score, Adolphus.'

Travel plans throughout the household were put into action, and it would leave Cook, Flo, Mr Orchard, and Mr Cloverleaf, with the welfare of the Elford house in their hands.

The last day of September moved ever closer, and the house buzzed with the preparation for the farewell dinner party. Cook and Katherine, sitting together at every available moment, planned everything down to the last detail. Over the last few months, since Katherine knew she would soon hold the position of housekeeper, they believed that they had developed a very efficient system of stocking cupboards and buying food. They had what they described as a stock control. The cupboards would be kept immaculate, and everything would be at hand with the minimum amount of disturbance. Flo had been trained to return all that she used to the same place as she had taken it from, and when each item reached its end, the container would be left in a mesh basket until the next shopping list was created. Once upon the list, the container of the said item would be sent to the rubbish bins. The same system applied to mostly all of the food, except a little more thought went into the organisation. They decided that in order to avoid massive amounts of wastage, they could roughly account for each person's requirements by weighing the individual portions that made up the meal of one person, and multiplying it by the number of people eating. This seemed a tiresome and difficult pursuit, but it had paid off and indeed there was very little food that found its way to the compost heap. A dinner party, such as the one that they were about to embark upon, seemed to be the ideal situation to prove their system would work, but they would account for ten more people than were actually listed.

'For the ones who took a rather larger portion of caviar,' said Cook with a sarcasm unusual in her vocabulary. Most of the meat and poultry that cook ordered could be served cold for supper the following day, so no expense was spared, as the master had insisted that she brought on the fatted calf. She would do exactly that. The butcher, knowing what was good to serve at such a banquet, sent a collection worthy of any royal table, and all Cook had to do was what she was paid for, not only to cook it, but present it in such a way that it would be the talk of the town for many a day to come.

The day had dawned, and the household was awake. Martha had arrived, along with the milk delivery, and quickly on its heels, local grown vegetables came tumbling from the back of the cart. Katherine was going to take Dorcas Louise for her usual early morning walk, but before that she would help Martha and Cook stack the vegetables ready for preparation. Once peeled and perfectly cut into their relevant shapes, they would be plunged into large containers of ice cold water to preserve their texture and colour until they were ready for the pots. For the time being, Flo would entertain Dorcas, as her duties would not need attention for a couple of hours yet.

James and Lavinia Elford, as always on the days when they held a large gathering, stayed well out of the way. They had both given their personal instructions, and wishes, and now they left it all to their trusted staff. Mr Elford had reconsidered the request for another footman, and had employed cook's son on a temporary basis until he could decide whether the need for a permanent footman was warranted. Mr Orchard was with Mr Cloverleaf receiving last minute instruction, before he was plummeted head first into probably the most important moment in his life. The things that he had to do would not stay still in his head. They kept jumping around until he didn't know whether he was on his head or his heels. Mr Cloverleaf took him by the shoulders, stood him still and said, 'Think only of the next fifteen minutes, and then when that has gone, think of the next. I want you to do this, and believe me I think that you can. I can help you no more than that at this moment, but I will be here if the going gets really tough.'

Katherine tried to keep Dorcas Louise occupied until late into the afternoon in the hope that she would settle down and sleep throughout the evening and then through the night. This was rather more wishful thinking, than a certainty, for Dorcas Louise was now a very inquisitive child with an aptitude for dance, that she did in her somewhat wobbly state at every opportunity. Katherine hoped with all her heart that she would not end up in the world of theatre. The mistress loved to see her hop from one foot to the other, and often commented that she could become a dancer. Little did she know of her ancestor, and from Katherine's point of view, she never would.

The tables were laid and looked magnificent. Some of the guests had arrived and were in the drawing room, where three young waitresses that the master had requested be sent for the evening, were handling silver trays laden with glasses of the best champagne for the guests to avail themselves of, along with exquisitely decorated trays of bites strategically placed around the room on small side tables. In the kitchen, an air of exaggerated calm was apparent. The main courses were on their way to completion, the smell was drifting overhead, making everyone except Cook suffer a mouth watering experience. Martha had the fish dish under control and ready to follow the soup that was now simmering gently on the hob. Flo was hovering, waiting for the time when she would carefully load the soup tureen and bowls on to the trolley that would start Charlie off on his first visit to the tables. It would all go in relays, and as the last table was served the soup, the first table should have finished and be ready to be served the fish dish. This was the procedure, and they had practised it with Mr Cloverleaf timing each section to the second. They had carried the dishes minus the food with precision, and were now poised to carry it out to perfection.

The time had come for Mr and Mrs Elford to come down and join their guests who, except for a few stragglers, were all in the drawing room. Katherine, standing quietly at the bottom of the stairs, caught her breath as she saw a beautiful Lavinia Elford descend in a gown of white satin encrusted from the left shoulder down to the ground in pearls and sequins. The skirt swept away behind her and slithered down the stairs like a waterfall. Her hair was caught in a diamond clip beneath a circle of curls that overflowed at the back, and fell to her neck in ringlets. On her ears she wore a matching pair of diamond earrings. Her satin slippers peeped from beneath the dress to complete a perfect picture of loveliness. Mr Elford walked in front of her and turned to take her hand as they reached the bottom of the stairs, and the look on his face said it all. He walked with the utmost pride, and to a round of applause as they entered the drawing room.

Mr Cloverleaf had decided that it would be just too much for Orchard to welcome the guests and act as master of ceremonies as well, so he would, just this once, take it upon himself to enact this part. He was standing now outside the dining room. There would be half an hour for the guests to be seated and the short speeches of welcome to be made, before the first course would start to be served. The sign would come from Orchard, who would be standing by until Cook gave the word that all was in order and ready to go. Cook took a swig of the cooking sherry, and nodded to Charlie, who headed for the door and nodded to Mr Cloverleaf, who in turn nodded back and disappeared into the dining room and closed the door.

Charlie turned, and was about to say 'here we go', when Flo turned and tripped on the wheel of the trolley, sending a wave of dark brown Windsor soup out of the tureen and straight down the leg of Charlie's brand new black trousers, on to his shiny shoes, and across the floor. Flo screamed and burst into tears. Cook grabbed the trolley to stop its momentum sending it into the wall and smashing the bowls that were perilously close to the edge. Charlie just stood there in a state of shock.

'What am I to do?' he cried. 'Where is Mr Cloverleaf? Oh god, he is inside... what can I do?'

'Come with me quickly,' said Katherine, gathering her wits around her, and thinking, please don't wake up, Dorcas, as she hauled the hapless Charlie up the stairs. 'You will have to borrow a pair of the master's,' she said.

Charlie was now in a state of complete distress. 'They will be too big and too long for me,' he panted.

'Pull yourself together, Charlie,' Katherine said. 'I will do something with them, but first we have to go into his dressing room and find a pair. We have twenty five minutes so look sharp and get going.'

Once inside the dressing room, they searched the rails until they found a pair of obviously very new trousers, but they were perfect. 'Take off your shoes, and clean them,' Katherine said, 'and don't get anything on your shirt sleeves. Then put on these trousers inside out, and I will get my sewing box.'

Leaving him doing this, she raced to the nursery, and thankfully a sleeping Dorcas was not disturbed by her presence. She returned to find Charlie in his underpants. Grabbing the trousers, and helping him into them, she started to pin and to sew with as much speed as could be mustered with a fidgety Charlie not helping too much. With ten minutes left before the call for the first course, which would be made by Mr Cloverleaf, Katherine and Charlie crept down the stairs and back in to the kitchen. Cook had everything back on course. Martha had placated Flo, and they all stood ready and waiting for the meal to begin. From that tremulous moment on, the evening passed with no more incidents, and Mr Orchard performed to absolute perfection, whilst the support he gained from his staff was without doubt faultless. Flo held on to every plate and glass as if it were gold dust, and looked at Mr Orchard as if he had given her the last star from heaven.

Mr Cloverleaf stood smugly in the corner. Every now and then his gaze fell upon the lower half of Mr Orchard, but he decided not to ask questions until after all the celebrations were over. Mr Elford, giving his hand to his wife, as the ladies retired to the drawing room, and drawing her close, as if to plant a kiss on her cheek, whispered to her, 'Do the trousers that Orchard is wearing look remarkably like the ones I had delivered from the tailor this morning?'

'Yes, James, they do,' replied his wife, 'they have the same edging around the pockets.'

'Hum,' replied Mr Elford.

Katherine came down to the servants' room, to join them for some food, after the tables in the dining room had been cleared by Arthur the new footman and Flo. They all agreed that the evening had been a success, and the master and mistress appeared to be satisfied with their work. Katherine told Charlie to run upstairs quickly, and put back on his own trousers which were now pristine, and leave the borrowed ones in the nursery. 'Please try not to wake Dorcas Louise,' she said. She omitted to tell Charlie that in her haste to get him back downstairs she had left her sewing box in Mr Elford's dressing room. She had not remembered until she had also come downstairs, and had thought about removing all the stitching and pins. She would now have to hope that the master did not return to the room before she had a chance to retrieve it, undo all that she had done, and return his trousers to the cupboard.

Charlie's part in the deception now over and with his own trousers back on, he returned downstairs to be confronted by Mr Cloverleaf who looked curiously at the now immaculate trousers that during the meal seemed a slightly odd fit. His not to reason why, he thought, as he stood facing Orchard and said, 'Well done, I was very pleased with the way you executed your duties tonight, and with no reference to your notebook. I did think that your trousers were a little creased so please make sure that does not happen again. I see that they are now perfect, so you must have noticed it yourself, and done something about it. A little more care in future before you come to the table. Now you may go and finish your duties and look after your guests. Well done again.'

Katherine was about to go and find her box and the master's trousers when a knock came at the door, and she opened it to see a tall young man in a chauffeur's uniform standing there. 'I have been told that I may have something to eat here. I am Mr Fitzgerald's chauffeur, Thomas Moreton, and drive the carriage that you see outside.

'Of course,' said Katherine, standing aside to let him pass. 'Please sit down. This is our cook, Mrs Stone, and this is Mrs Wilkin who is a friend and housekeeper to my uncle Adolphus. Mr Orchard, our butler, is still on duty, and Flo our housemaid is also on duty. My name is Katherine Carrera, and I am at present nursemaid and nanny to Dorcas Louise, the daughter of Mr and Mrs Elford, but in the near future I will become housekeeper here.'

Katherine stopped for breath, realising she had been very forthright, which to her was strange. She asked him to help himself to as much as he wanted, and offered him a hot drink, to which he promptly nodded before taking a bite from a large chicken leg.

Mrs Stone and Martha looked at each other and winked as Katherine took it upon herself to make him a steaming cup of tea, with two spoonfuls of sugar, to warm him up for the journey home, she commented. Thomas Moreton then began to regale her upon the merits of the motor vehicle that had replaced the horse driven carriage that he used to drive. The establishment from where the horseless carriage had been purchased had given him lessons, and now he had become a fully fledged chauffeur, and was very proud to become one of the first of the people he knew to manipulate the many levers and handles that propelled the vehicle at alarming speeds across the countryside.

Katherine sat enthralled by the tales of only just missing a horse as it shied at the noise that the engine made, and annoying an elderly gentleman who walked in front of him by giving a loud toot on the horn. In fact, she had sat so long that she had forgotten the trousers, and worse than that she had not looked in on Dorcas for more than an hour. She jumped up. 'Please forgive me,' she cried. 'I have to go, I'm afraid.'

Thomas replied, 'I will have to go too, and wait for my master and mistress, but I hope I will see you again in the not too distant future, Miss Carrera. Good luck with the housekeeping,' and to Cook and Martha, he said, 'Thank you for my supper; it was excellent.' Both looked at one another and said in unison, 'You are most welcome, Thomas.'

Katherine looked at them both, blushed, and ran through the door. Up the stairs she went as though needing to reach the top as quickly as possible, stopping at the nursery door and hearing nothing she entered to find Dorcas Louise still fast asleep with rabbit tucked under one arm. She looked at her chair to see the pair of borrowed trousers carefully folded awaiting her attention. She looked at the clock which read close to midnight. Would she reach the master's dressing room before any of the guests that were staying started to wander the corridors?

She decided that she had to try. She really had no option if she was to put the trousers back to their original state and back in the cupboard before the master caught her. She made it without trouble, and headed back for the nursery, but she didn't notice that her measuring stick had fallen behind the chair, and she left without it. The call from the master came for Katherine early in the morning, requesting her presence in the library. As she entered, the master sat at the desk waving in front of him the elusive measuring stick that Katherine had discovered was missing when she started on the job of putting the trousers back to how they were before dinner the previous evening.

'Do you wish to explain to me why Orchard was waiting at my table in my trousers last evening, or should I maybe ask our butler myself?' said the master.

'Sir,' answered Katherine, 'I am so sorry, but I could not think of any way that I could avoid the ruination of an otherwise perfect evening, and I hoped that you would understand. It was an accident, and it wasn't Mr Orchard's fault. We had just twenty minutes to find a way of presenting him at your table in the best possible way that we could, hopefully without any of your guests noticing the slight disarray of his clothing.'

At this point, the master arose from his chair and said, 'Thank you, Katherine. Would you ask Orchard to come and see me now?'

Katherine left the library feeling guilty at having to disclose the goings on of the evening and, finding Charlie still tidying up some of the last remnants, sent him with a sad heart to the master. 'Orchard,' began the master in a very serious voice, 'I have it from a very reliable source that you took it upon yourself to borrow a pair of my trousers last night. I do have to comment that you picked the best and most expensive pair in the cupboard. I don't want to know the details of what happened, but I do want to say that in view of the fact that you performed with excellence your duties of butler last evening, I am prepared to overlook the whole episode. I suggest that you pass on to Katherine your grateful thanks for her quick thinking and even more her imaginative skills in tailoring. Also, I think that in the circumstances you should pay from your wages the cost of cleaning my trousers, and then keep them in a safe place, as a spare pair for any further accidents that may occur in the future.'

Mr Elford rose from his chair, and made for the door, turning once to say, 'Well done, Orchard, the evening was a success, and much of the credit must go to you, thank you.'

Charlie Orchard floated back toward the kitchen, not quite able to believe his good fortune. Katherine was waiting for him, and when Charlie related Mr Elford's words, she said, calmly as always, 'Oh I think if I finish off the job properly, Charlie, you will have an excellent pair of trousers, and I really don't see the need for cleaning them. I will use my iron with a damp cloth between it and the trousers, and press them until you will see no sign of the alterations that were so obvious last night. Well done, in the circumstances your behaviour in front of the master's guests was impeccable, and I'm sure Mr Cloverleaf would agree. He told me to tell you that he would be out for a while this morning, and to carry on with your normal duties, and study your notes if you have time.'

Flo, coming into the kitchen, received a massive hug from Charlie, which led her to believe that she had been forgiven for her gross carelessness which had nearly ruined the most important evening in Charlie's bid to be the most perfect butler.

The day following an evening of entertainment such as they had all witnessed the previous evening, tended to be a rather quiet affair. Katherine spent the whole day with Dorcas, playing and reading to her, taking her on her regular visit to the park, where today she found Adolphus sitting on a bench idly reading a newspaper. It was quite a while since she had spent some time with him. Martha had come back into her life, and she ached to be with her. Adolphus understood completely and had allowed them that privilege at every available moment. Now he was here alone, and Katherine made haste toward the seat, to sit with him while he dangled the adoring Dorcas Louise from his knees.

Katherine asked so many questions. How had he found Martha? How had he known it was her mother? Were there any sightings of Alexi?

'So many questions,' he sighed. 'I can't answer all of them, but what I remember most was the look on your mother's face when I asked if she knew a young girl called Katherine Carrera. The decision to bring her back to England was made easily, but the actual carrying out of the deed was not so easy. There had to be no trace of her left in and around the cottage, and I couldn't risk being seen loitering nearby, so your mother very bravely set about wiping out her existence, and making her way, somewhat as you had done before her, Katherine, to meet me at an agreed spot in the country and a fair distance away from the village. The rest you can talk to your mother about soon when I take you, Dorcas Louise, and Martha to London to visit my house there. I have permission to allow you to stay a few days, and I will be able to show you around the big city. There is of course something that I have to ask you to do in return for my hospitality.'

Katherine interrupted at this point as Dorcas Louise was now jumping up and down on Adolphus's lap to gain his attention, so it was decided to return her to the carriage and continue their conversation on foot, while Dorcas concentrated on trying to remove her shoes and socks, and use them as missiles to aim at passing walkers. They found it amusing, usually picking them up and laughing at the irresistible child being impossible.

'Anything I can do for you, I will, Adolphus, you know that,' said Katherine.

'It is difficult to describe my house,' started Adolphus. 'You will have to see it for yourselves and then you will understand. It has two halves, and at the moment I am only living in one, as my stays there have been infrequent, but now I would like to give it what it deserves in the way of decoration, and spend the rest of my days enjoying it, and being cared for by Martha.

'So this is what I want from you and Martha, Katherine. I want a plan of action, colour schemes, and furnishings, that I can leave with the company that I have chosen to carry out my instructions before I finally leave Liverpool for southern climes. I hope that you will have a little spare time from your housekeeping at the Elfords to come and visit regularly. Next year, Dorcas will have a governess, and will start to prepare for her schooling, and I'm sure when the household is quiet, Mrs Elford will be glad to let you have some free time. She has already commented to me that you work far too hard, and too long, but you and I know the reason for that, and I would not want or expect you to change. Dorcas Louise will always need you, even when she grows up, but you must also make a little space for yourself in your busy times, and with that little bit of advice from an old man who may have seen a lot of life but has never lived it in the way he now wishes he had, you and I should head back toward our homes. Take care, my Katherine, and always stay as you are. Never let the cares and woes of the world change you; believe that you can change them, and it will happen, believe me.'

Katherine left him as she found him, on the park seat neatly folding the newspaper and tucking it under his arm, picking up his cane, and waving at Katherine and Dorcas Louise as they left the park and headed for home.

The days now moved on, back in the normal routines for the Elford household. Lavinia and Charles Elford, preparing for the important trip to America, Lavinia trying to collect a wardrobe together of every conceivable article of clothing. There would be lunches to go to and of course evening dinners with business associates. There would be places to visit, and advice to be given and taken. There would be deals to be done, and plans to be made for when they returned to England where both sides of the Atlantic would join hands in unity, which would considerably strengthen each of their financial dependencies and business successes.

It was with all this in mind that Mr Elford had plans for the running of his household. He was secretly proud of the little band of employees that were keeping the wheels turning in the house that he loved, and he had no plans to alter that, but he had plans that would maybe make their lives a little easier in the future.

November had arrived, and Katherine had now passed her 18th birthday, whilst Dorcas had been a three-year-old for quite a while it seemed. Charlie had six more weeks to follow Mr Cloverleaf's unstinting efforts to leave him as a fully fledged butler. The Elfords were ready to go and face the journey across the Atlantic. The day finally came for goodbyes to be said, with the arrival of Thomas Moreton in the new horseless carriage that the Fitzgeralds had sent to take them to Liverpool docks, from where the ship would depart. All of them stood on the steps to marvel at the shiny carriage with its white wheels, and hood that could be taken down when the summer weather arrived. Thomas proudly showed off the vehicle that was now his responsibility to look after.

He took Katherine to the step that the passenger stood on in order to enter the vehicle in a stately manner. 'Hop up quickly before the master and mistress come down,' he said, holding her arm protectively, 'isn't she just beautiful?' Katherine stepped aboard, and agreed that yes she was beautiful, but how did he know that the vehicle was a woman. Thomas laughed and said, 'All cars are called she, that is the way it is. Perhaps one day I will be allowed to take you for a spin, if you would like to come.'

Katherine, taken aback and slightly embarrassed, answered that she would like to, but was very busy at the moment. Thomas, appearing a little crestfallen, said quietly, 'Well maybe one day soon then.'

Mr and Mrs Elford were about to leave, Flo called, and Katherine headed for the nursery to bring Dorcas Louise down to say her goodbyes. Amid shouts of 'good luck' and 'goodbye', Thomas helped them aboard and stowed away their luggage, while Katherine held Dorcas up for a last kiss from her mother and father. The little cavalcade started to move, with a pompous toot from the horn, and everyone stood back. Mr and Mrs Elford were on their way.

Dorcas Louise, wriggling to be let down, grabbed hold of Katherine's hand and said, 'Let's go see ducks and Dolphus, Kat.' Katherine had a little secret thrill passing through her as she thought, she is mine for a whole month. She allowed herself to be pulled into the hall where Dorcas's carriage awaited her. 'Why not, my angel,' she said in a whisper.

The house settled down, but was a strange place without a master and mistress. Cook had decided that she would take apart the kitchen and clean it from top to bottom again. Charlie was occupied with the final bringing together of all his information, and the knowledge that Mr Cloverleaf would be giving his final report very soon after the Elfords' return. Cook's son, Arthur, Mr Elford had decided would be very useful during his absence to give a hand to two workmen who he had employed to construct a building adjacent to the house. While it was common knowledge that this would happen, no one knew what it was for, so there was much speculation on the subject. Thomas Moreton returned to the house the following day to report on the safe embarkation of Mr and Mrs Elford on to the ship that would take them to New York.

He seemed to be the only person who had any idea as to what the new building would be used for. 'I am only guessing and I will not say anything more in case I am wrong, so no more questions please!'

Katherine appeared to like the company of this young man, but hastily denied any underlying feelings for him. 'Stuff and nonsense,' she admonished cook when she teased her 'I have responsibilities and a child to care for, and have no time for such flippancies. Thomas, however, visited quite often on the premise of enquiring after their wellbeing without the master and mistress to run the house, to which he was set straight in no uncertain terms as to their absolute capability to run and care for this property at any time, but he would be welcome to come and check whenever he wished.

Adolphus arranged for the visit to London to take place during the second week of December, which would bring Katherine and Dorcas back before the preparation for Christmas started, and before the return of the Elfords. Dorcas held tightly to Katherine's hand as they boarded the train. Adolphus had arranged for a baby carriage to be made available when they arrived at his house, but until then Dorcas would walk or be carried by one or the other of them, to which she had no complaints at all. It was a long journey, but Dorcas was fascinated by the pictures that she saw through the windows of the train of cows and horses, trees, lakes, and at one stage, a river that was crossed by a bridge, and under the bridge there were 'Ducks'! Dorcas squealed with delight. The arrival at the sooty London station she found a bit frightening, especially when a very big engine let out a great cloud of steam accompanied by the loudest noise she had ever heard in her young life.

Adolphus held her and explained that the engine needed a tummy full of steam so that it could move. She really wasn't that convinced but as long as Adolphus had her in his arms, she knew that she was safe. Martha and Katherine, arm in arm, followed in procession with a porter trailing behind dragging all their luggage on a trolley. A carriage was at the kerbside as they left the station, and they were bundled in, luggage and all, and set off on another leg of their journey that would take them to the house where Adolphus would spend his remaining years, and where Martha would start a new life that would bring her the joys that she so much deserved.

The smoky, narrow streets of London eventually gave way to leafy avenues with large houses like the one that Katherine had left in Liverpool, but when the carriage pulled into a drive of yellow shingle, Katherine caught her breath. She had never seen anything more beautiful, she thought. The front of the house consisted of two gables made of slats of wood painted white, and in each of them sat a large window made of tiny panes of glass sealed together by a metal strip. Above them, the red roof followed their shape with a chimney at each end topped by a long chimney pot, one of which at the moment had smoke issuing from it. Below the wooden top of the house was a wall of bricks, which housed another two large windows, also fashioned in tiny panes of glass below which continued the wall, until it became divided in the middle of the house by a square arch supporting a glass atrium which stretched across between the two windows on the first floor and passed beneath them. In the centre of the atrium, was an oak door of magnificent proportions, and to each side of the atrium a window which matched the atrium in length, and was as wide as the building would allow.

The circular drive finished the whole picture, as it circled around a grassed area with neat bushes trimmed and shaped to perfection, and two magnolia trees that Katherine thought would be quite beautiful when they came into bloom at Easter time.

'You are both very quiet.' Adolphus's voice broke the silence. 'Do you not approve of my humble abode?'

'Oh, Adolphus,' Katherine said, 'It is the most beautiful building I have ever seen.'

'Then you must come inside, and I will explain to you its complex content, and you will see that the back of it is really just as lovely as the front.'

'I'm coming to see too,' came the excited voice of Dorcas Louise.

'Of course you are,' laughed Adolphus.

As they all descended from the carriage, the door opened. 'Martha, come and meet your predecessor,' Adolphus invited. 'This is Mrs Green who has looked after me for many years, and now is going to have a well-deserved retirement, but she has agreed to stay until all the alterations that I want to be done are completed, which I hope will be in the new year.' As they entered the house, behind the atrium was a long corridor with just one door on each side of it.

Adolphus explained, 'The house at some time in its existence has been divided in half, and probably occupied by two different families. Unfortunately, I do not know its history beyond the person from whom I purchased it, and he insists that it was exactly as it is now when he purchased it many years ago. I have always lived in just the one side, for obvious reasons. I spent most of my time in Liverpool, because of my work with the university, but now I want to turn the house back into the beautiful building that it was, and this is to be the project for my old age, but I need the touch and flair of the female sex to give it light and texture. Katherine and Martha, I hold you both responsible to furnish me with the ideas, and I need samples to back up your decisions. I am not saying I will use every one of them, but it will be of great help when I am grappling with colour charts, and upholstery textiles. I want a format for each room, and Katherine you can colour code them if you wish in the same way as you did my notes on the compilation of my book.'

As they reached the door on the left hand side of the corridor, they opened it and passed through it to another passage, but this time it had more doors and a staircase to the upper floors. Adolphus led them back toward the door, stopped, and said, 'This is the one room that you will not touch in any way. This is the only room in the house that is mine and mine alone.' As he opened the door, both women stood in amazement. It was a library, and was furnished in dark oak with shelves from floor to ceiling, housing hundreds and hundreds of books all neatly stood in rows, with their spines in perfect symmetry. At the corner of the room was a ladder made of the same dark wood that had wheels on each foot, so that the top shelves could be reached along their length without descending the ladder.

In the middle of the room was an enormous desk, also fashioned in dark oak, with intricate carving to its edge and legs. In the centre of the ceiling hung a chandelier of sparkling crystal, and on the desk a brass lamp with a green shade that, when lit, gave a bright light to the pages of the books. 'I think,' said Adolphus, 'that we have seen enough today, and I note a very sleepy young lady is leaning on your shoulder, Katherine. Mrs Green has all your rooms ready for you, and dinner will be served as soon as you wish. I think she had a little special something for Dorcas Louise, so I will see you all in about half an hour or so.'

The days with Adolphus flew by. Dorcas Louise was happy running up and down the corridor that divided the house. Katherine and Martha spent hours together poring over colour schemes, wallpaper, and furnishings. All of them travelled into London, Adolphus to place orders in the most modern and fashionable shops, Katherine and Martha just to revel in amazement at the clothes in the exclusive shops of the west end of the city, forgetting for a while that they were here to supply suggestions to Adolphus on the renovation of the house.

It was suggested that Martha should choose two rooms, one as a bedroom, and one a sitting room, both of which would be near to the kitchen, and while she was here, she was to be given her choice of furnishings and decoration. This would leave Adolphus free to arrange for the rooms that would be his, to do the same. That would take care of the ground floor. The upstairs rooms would be made into guest rooms, and bathrooms would be available on both floors. A linen room and laundry would be made on the ground floor near to the kitchen, which to Martha's amazement and some trepidation, would house a new gas cooker, and also a gas water heater which would make washing clothes, and oneself for that matter, very much easier.

The other half of the house, it was decided, would be equipped in the same manner as the one in which Adolphus lived now. Not only would it mean that, if his financial position ever warranted it, the adjoining part of the house could be classed as a first class residence available for rent, it would also mean that he could entertain as many friends as he wished without disturbing his own privacy. So thus it was done, and after four days he was armed with all the details he needed to set the process up, and bring in the workmen.

There was just one thing that Katherine had an idea about, but this would only be possible if the whole house was to stay as one property. She put it to Adolphus that the corridor which divided the house could be turned into a beautiful art gallery, which could house pictures of the birds that he so dearly loved. He could commission an artist of some repute, and there could be some eight paintings along its length, and they could be lit from above by the now common electric light, or large candles in floor standing holders for special occasions. The effect would be wonderful if the walls were white, and Adolphus could have a nice shiny wooden floor, and maybe a couple of small gilt chairs strategically placed so that visitors could sit and enjoy the paintings. At the end of the corridor was a great window arched at the top, which looked out upon a garden, which albeit needed attention, but would add such splendour to this already magnificent property. Adolphus sat and mulled over this suggestion made by this oh so young lady with an oh so mature head on her small shoulders.

'I will do it,' said Adolphus, 'but only for you, Katherine. If it will make you come and see me often, it will all be worthwhile.'

'I will come and see you as often as I can,' replied Katherine, 'with or without the art gallery; just you try and stop me.'

The journey back to Liverpool was filled with chatter about the house, and all that was going to be done. Martha was bemused by all that Adolphus was going to do for her. No one had ever cared for her enough to do anything, except of course for Katherine who had adored her from the moment she was old enough to see her. Her life now was like a new beginning, and she held her breath in case she woke up one morning and found that she had been dreaming. Katherine for her part knew why Adolphus was going out of his way to make Martha happy. He had taken her life in his hands and moulded it as best he could under the circumstances, and he had given her back her child in a very unusual way. How he had done it, she would never know, but she would never spend a day without thinking of him and his unending kindness to her.

She had no worries now. Her job at the Elfords was secure, she would see her daughter grow up, and she had a friend in Lavinia which made for a perfect existence. The Elford residence had survived without her presence. Charlie was near to the end of his training. Dorcas Louise was getting excited as Christmas drew near. The tree had arrived, and was in the big pot just outside the front door. The construction that had caused so much speculation the week before she left was nearing completion. To all intents and purposes it looked like a large barn that had been propped up against the side wall of the house. Preparation was going on in the kitchen for the Elfords' return.

Finally all back together again, the Elfords celebrated Christmas with all the usual trimmings and far too much food. Mr Elford decided to quell all the speculation on the evening of Christmas Day, when he called on all the staff to join the family in the drawing room. First, he announced that Orchard had received an excellent report from Mr Cloverleaf, and therefore he had great pleasure in announcing that as from January 1st 1905, Mr Orchard would become butler in the Elford household.

As for the construction to the side of the house, 'This,' he exclaimed, 'will be for a brand new horseless carriage that I will be purchasing from the Rolls Royce company.' He went on to explain that as the butler of the house usually had the pleasure of driving the mistress to town, he would now be sent for lessons freely given by the company on not only how to drive the vehicle, but also how to maintain it correctly, and keep it in pristine condition.

'Close your mouth, Charlie,' whispered Katherine from behind him.

'Have you anything you would like to ask me, Orchard?' the master said, smiling at the astounded look on the face of his newly appointed butler.

'No, sir… th-thank you, sir,' Charlie stuttered.

With that, all the present company applauded, and Charlie, now a little overcome, made an effort to bow. Everyone laughed, not least of all the master and mistress of the house. 'There is just one thing, Orchard,' said Mr Elford with a grin, 'remember that there are no trousers in my closet that are suitable for a chauffeur.'

Chapter Fifteen

Revelations

It was Saturday morning, and Katy Louise Brown had spent a sleepless night. Her husband had tried to fathom out the discoveries that she had made in the box given to her by the solicitor who was dealing with her godmother's will. 'This was left for you, Mrs Brown,' had been what the small bespectacled man had said when he had left the small private room where the mourners had gathered for coffee and biscuits. 'She had had no children, and there was no next of kin, just a few friends, and of course you, Mrs Brown. I will be in touch with you later to settle further details, but I thought that this may be personal, and there was no reason why you shouldn't have it now as it has no bearing on the late Miss Carrera's will.

Stephen Brown was one of nature's gentlemen, and he adored his wife. Katy considered herself to be the luckiest person in the world to have him for a husband. Before they said good night and fell asleep last night, he had promised to take the children for the whole day, so that she could just sit and read the book, the last item that she had pulled from the box yesterday. He would take them to the zoo, and that was met with whoops of delight from their two small daughters to whom nothing was greater than a day out with Daddy.

Armed with a cup of coffee, Katy sat at the table and picked up the book that had lain there throughout the night, just asking to be picked up and its pages to be turned. It was nine o'clock, the house was quiet, and Katy started to read. At four thirty that afternoon, when Stephen and the two girls arrived home, they found her surrounded by dirty cups, some half-filled with coffee. She was also surrounded by all the items that she had found in the box. The ballet shoes, now out of their tissue paper, the locket sitting open in front of her, the earring, and the lock of hair. Her tear-stained face was red and sore from the constant wiping of her eyes, and soaking wet handkerchiefs, one of them belonging to Stephen, were crumpled in her lap.

Her children, clearly distressed by the sight of their Mummy crying, were gathered into her arms. 'I am so sorry, darlings, but I have been reading a very sad book, and I could not stop, but now I will, and I will get you some tea.' Looking at her husband, she said, 'We will talk after tea.'

He nodded, and said lightly, 'The girls had a lovely day at the zoo. We saw all the animals, but the bit they liked best was… what, girls?'

'Feeding the ducks,' they both said in unison.

How very strange, thought Katy Louise, regaining some of her poise, but visibly shaken by what she had read. Feeding the children and getting themselves some soup and bread seemed to take a long time. Katy wanted so much to sit and talk to her husband. Eventually the moment arrived, the children tucked in their beds, and Katy reached for her husband's hand, and led him downstairs.

'What did you find, Katy,' Stephen said a little tremulously. Katy began, 'I can't take in any more for the moment, Stephen, in fact I can hardly take in what I have read, and I cannot imagine what I am going to find in the following pages of which there are many.'

Tears began to surface again, and Stephen put his arms around her and said, 'Tell me, darling.'

'Oh! Stephen,' she whispered. 'Kat was my grandmother. All those years when she cared for me, when I loved her so much, and she couldn't tell me that I was her granddaughter. You will have to read the book, and I will have to read it again to be sure of its content. It is the most amazing story, sad, and wonderful at the same time. I know now what all the items mean, and what she went through to keep them close to her along with the secrets that they held.'

'Tell me,' he repeated, 'slowly and from the beginning.'

'I can't tell you the whole story. I can only tell you what I now know about my darling Kat, and about each of the items that she kept and left to me, only when she knew that no harm could come to anyone who was involved in her story. She was my grandmother, and only two people knew it until she told me today. She was born to my great grandmother who was a ballerina; the ballet shoes were hers. My great grandfather was an Italian nobleman, who would not marry my great grandmother because she was of peasant birth, and he a nobleman. On the night that Katherine, my grandmother, was born, her mother, Maria, was killed in a riding accident, and she was given to a peasant woman who was married to a woodman where they lived deep in the forest in Italy. My grandmother was raised for thirteen years by this woman who loved and cared for her very much. A tragedy then happened and my Kat ran away.

'After narrowly escaping death, as you will read, my Kat's life was saved by a fisherman, and after about a year they fell in love. The earring was his. She fell pregnant with my mother when she was fifteen years old, and had to run again, finding herself in England, and helped by an elderly gentleman called Adolphus. My mother was taken away from her as soon as she was born, but thanks to Adolphus, Kat found herself in the house where her baby had been taken and became her wet nurse, and ultimately her nanny. The lock of hair was my mother's, and finally the locket was my great grandmother's, and the pictures were of her and her lover, the Italian nobleman.

'The story goes on to tell us of the life she had, and of the people who became a part of her life. She was such an amazing person, and I thought she was just my lovely Kat who cared for me for the whole of my life. I never knew much of my mother, and so I don't know what happened to her. I have vague recollections of her, but she was always away with her husband. I think he was an American, but that was just what Kat told me. It was she who fed me, saw me through my life as a child, and a schoolgirl, and when I met you. I remember how happy she was, and when I said I was going to marry you, and when the girls were born, she was so, so happy.

'Oh Stephen, so much comes back to me now, and one of the strangest things is that she described the house that Adolphus owned and to which the lady called Martha was brought, to look after him. Stephen! Martha was the lady she was given to the day she was born, and the one who cared for her for thirteen years. I can't bear to tell you what happened when she was thirteen; you will have to read it yourself. The house she described, Stephen, was this one, the one in which we live now... I'm sure it was. It has changed, I know, but I remember being brought here as a child. I need now to take all this in and read it again; perhaps we could read it together, I would love that. When I am completely able to understand it all, I will continue to read the rest. Oh Stephen, I have just buried my grandmother, and placed a red rose on her coffin. Now I know why she asked me to do that once long ago when we were talking. There are no more items in the box, so what else has she to tell me, do you think?'

'I don't know, darling, but it is all there for you to treasure, and finally she will rest knowing that she has told you all that you wanted to know.'

It was three days later when the book was once again opened to reveal to its reader the life story of one Katherine Anne Carrera, and the people whose lives she had touched with such infinite love and wisdom.

Chapter Sixteen

The Troubled Years

The Elford household had settled into a peaceful, happy mode. It was now 1911 and the last few years had seen Mr James Elford become one of the most respected and admired businessmen in the area. This gave credence to the confidence of those who worked for him, and the mistress. Cook, to her delight, was now the proud possessor of a brand new gas cooker, and the whole house now benefitted from the installation of electricity, and the bathrooms from hot running water.

The construction that had been built to house the new motor vehicle was Charlie's pride and joy. He kept it all tidy, including the little loft above the building that housed all his tools that he needed in order to keep the wonderful Rolls Royce that the master had bought in 1905, in perfect working order. Thomas had given him some good working tips, and had added to the lessons that the garage had provided, which would prove to be invaluable in the years to come. He had also proved to be an excellent butler, and often met Mr Cloverleaf for a drink and a chat, on even terms these days, although they still referred to one another as Mr Cloverleaf and Mr Orchard.

Katherine had now assumed the permanent position of Housekeeper, as Dorcas Louise had become less and less dependent on all of her time. Although sad, Katherine had seen the beautiful child turn into a very intent pupil and, now into her 11th year, she had survived a couple of governesses, and was now on her third. At night, when the house was quiet, Dorcas would creep into Katherine, sit on her knee, and ask her numerous questions, all of which she tried to answer with complete honesty; some she couldn't, which she always admitted to, and Dorcas would say with a giggle, 'Never mind, Kat, I will take you to feed the ducks tomorrow,' which had always been Katherine's answer to everything.

Katherine would retaliate with a smart rap on her behind, and say, 'You, young lady, are still not too grown up to receive a smack.'

Dorcas would look at her with a pretend look of horror and cry, 'No! No! please not a smack,' then she would put her arms around Katherine's neck and hug her tight.

Responding to the child as any mother would, Katherine hugged her back and said, 'Away to your bed.' Dorcas planted a kiss on her cheek and headed for her bedroom.

Flo, of late, had been getting a little involved with the new governess. A lady in her early thirties, with some strong views that Katherine thought should be kept to herself. Governesses had been somewhat of a problem in the household, so much so that Katherine had suggested that maybe a daily tutor would be more acceptable. One of the governesses had made rather obvious tendencies toward attracting Mr Elford, and although he was quite amused, though definitely not interested, Mrs Elford was seriously offended, and not at all amused. Therefore the governess was informed that her services would no longer be required. The second one was extremely strict, and frightened Dorcas Louise, to say nothing of Flo, who would do anything, or take avoiding action in the house, in order not to come into contact with her.

'Gives me the creeps, she does,' complained Flo to Cook.

'Keep your head up, girl, and don't let her see that she bothers you,' advised Cook.

The present one had lasted the longest, and seemed to be making inroads into the education of Dorcas Louise. Katherine herself had been responsible for Dorcas Louise being well ahead with 'The three Rs'. She had had an excellent teacher in Martha, and had adopted the same technique with Dorcas, likewise as she had done with Joseph, when he could not read anything, either in Italian or English.

Adolphus had told Katherine that there were very few young ladies that were bilingual to the standard that she was, and her English was impeccable. He had suggested many times that she wrote a book about her extraordinary life, perhaps one day when the things that mattered now, had been relegated to history. She had said that there was no time in her life for such luxuries as writing; maybe in her dotage when there was nothing else to do, she would reconsider.

The governess was so impressed by the fluent reading and legible writing of Dorcas Louise that she had pushed her further into the realms of literary accomplishment than she would normally do for a child of this age. The Elfords seemed very pleased, and Katherine only had a few reservations, one of which was the woman's strong political tendencies, and interest in the social reforms that would bring equality to women. She would talk about the movement called the Women's Social and Political Union, which had been founded by Emmeline Pankhurst in 1903. Thousands of women had joined the Suffragettes, she explained, and it would have been easy if the Liberal party had not been returned to power, and Herbert Asquith had not become prime minister.

Katherine was somewhat worried about Flo's obvious interest in all that Miss Oldberry preached, and she could see the light of adventure and excitement in Flo's eyes. She had a quiet word with Lavinia Elford, who agreed that her leanings toward the violent actions of the suffragettes were, to say the least, worrying, but she was a very competent teacher and she was reluctant to end her employment. She mentioned that militant action by the suffragettes had been suspended until November, and suggested that they should wait until then before becoming too anxious. In the meantime, she would mention it to Mr Elford, whom she said would in no way encourage violence of any kind, although he had sympathies toward the women fighting for equality through the law, especially in education and employment.

Outside of her time in service to the family, Flo was at liberty to befriend whoever she cared to but Charlie too was concerned at the influence that Miss Oldberry was having on Flo and he told her in so many words. Flo threw his advice back at him, and said that Miss Oldberry was teaching her politics, and that was important for a woman in these modern times. These times may be modern, thought Katherine, but these women were suffering antiquated torture to further their cause. She had read of the force feeding that the prisons had inflicted on these women when they went on hunger strike. This had been happening for a good couple of years now, and it appeared that it would carry on until the battle was won, or that there was no one left to fight it.

Katherine, trying to throw some doubt into the mind of Flo, told her the story of an upper class lady who went on hunger strike, and was released after two days due to a weakness in her heart, but who believed that it was because of her status. She changed her name and rejoined the Women's

Social and Political Union, and was subsequently arrested outside Walton gaol, sent to prison, and forcibly fed eight times. It was said that the pain was unbearable. The jaws were forced apart, and a tube was pushed violently down into the stomach, making the person choke, until it was finally swallowed, and then the food was poured into the tube, thus producing vomit that caused the body to writhe in pain, whereupon the wardress would push back the head, and the doctor administering the food would lean on the knees. The horror was indescribable, when it happened once, but eight times all but caused death, and the lady in question never fully recovered. She received a medal of valour, as did many hunger strikers, but what a terrible price they paid.

Flo appeared to be suitably horrified, but as the year passed, political stalemate left a very small opening for women of property only to be allowed on the electoral role. With a wide divide between the Tories and the Liberals, each one gave a little to benefit their own election status, but it had no effect on the main body of women fighting for their rights.

Christmas came and went, and by March of 1912, a militant body of protestors, feeling angry at the politics of the parties, started to smash windows in the West End of London, and prison sentences once again began to reach massive proportions. Force feeding was reinstated on the hunger strikers, and almost anyone appearing to be causing a disturbance was scooped up, and landed in the already overcrowded gaols. Miss Oldberry was becoming pedantic and began to talk of violence in front of Dorcas Louise, and was told by Mrs Elford that this would have to stop, and that her daughter was in no way to become aware of any militant gatherings that were likely to develop in the City of Liverpool, or for that matter the reason why they were happening. There would be time enough when she was older to learn of such things.

Katherine had been relieved that the mistress had spoken so sternly, and been adamant in her address to the governess. However there was still a doubt in the mind of Katherine as to the extent of this woman's involvement in the movement. She had also seen Flo entering into serious discussion with Miss Oldberry, and this worried her. Flo was still only sixteen, and quite naive, very easily led when she was being goaded into something mischievous or adventurous. Her worst fears were realised one evening in early March, when the governess came from her room in black hat and coat, stating that she was going to meet friends, and was in a hurry, as she brushed past Katherine at the bottom of the stairs. Nothing particularly suspicious in that, thought Katherine, but as she passed the governess's door, that in her hurry to get out she had left open, Katherine noticed a large sheet of paper folded in half on the floor near to her desk. Feeling guilty, but urged on by her feelings of great doubt, she stepped inside the room and picked up the piece of paper, unfolded it, and to her horror read the neatly written letter.

> *Dear Oldberry,*
> *So glad you have found your scapegoat, we all have*
> *one now, and so we can go tonight. Does yours know*
> *exactly what she has to do? If there is a police*
> *presence, stay clear, and give her the ammunition. If it*
> *gets nasty, leave her and get out of there. If all goes*
> *well we will use them again for as many times as we*
> *need to get our message across. Remember if any of us*
> *get caught, keep silent.*
> *Good Luck, and God Bless You*

Katherine, knowing exactly who the scapegoat was, flew to the kitchen where Charlie and Cook were sitting having a cup of tea.

'Where's Flo?' Katherine yelled.

Charlie jumped up. 'What's wrong, Katherine? Flo has gone out to see a friend tonight.'

'Did she say where?' said Katherine, now beginning to fret.

'No, only that she was going to a friend, which she does occasionally, and that she may be a bit late back. She asked me to wait up for her and let her in.'

Katherine dropped into a nearby chair and said, 'Oh god, I knew this would happen,' and she passed the letter to Charlie.

'Silly little fool,' Charlie said through his teeth, 'I knew that woman was trouble. What do we do now? We have to get her back.'

'We will have to tell the master and mistress; we dare not go it alone,' said Katherine.

Cook just sat there not believing what she was hearing. 'How could Flo be so stupid as to get involved with these people? Do you need mine or Arthur's help?' she volunteered.

'Let us see the master and mistress first,' said Katherine, 'and then we will make a plan. This could be very dangerous indeed for us all.'

Charlie and Katherine went upstairs, and rang the bell that communicated with the Elfords in time of any trouble that may befall the servants or the household in general. It was not used under any other circumstances.

Mr Elford responded to the call, and seeing both Katherine's and Charlie's agitated faces, said, 'Whatever is wrong? Is someone hurt?'

At the sound of his voice, the mistress appeared at the door. 'What is it, James?' she cried.

Katherine passed them the letter. 'Dorcas Louise,' screamed Mrs Elford, 'where is she?'

Katherine, realising what Mrs Elford was thinking, quickly reassured her. 'Dorcas Louise is fine. She is in the nursery reading.'

'Then who...?' Mrs Elford started, and then said, 'Oh no, not Flo, stupid child. Where is she?'

'She has gone out, and I let her go, never suspecting what she was up to,' Charlie returned.

Mrs Elford then said, 'Perhaps it is not her and perhaps she has just gone out, and the scapegoat is some other poor child that Miss Oldberry has involved in this dangerous mission.'

Charlie replied, 'I don't think so, I have seen them of late whispering and nodding to one another on the stairs. Flo is in great danger. What can we do?'

Mr Elford, who had been silent during the exchanging of comments, said, 'Go, Charlie, take Katherine, and take the automobile. Use physical pressure if you have to, but get her back. Be as careful as you can, and let us hope that you get there before an affray takes place. Leave me the letter, and I will see that it reaches the proper place as evidence of your being there in case you get caught in any of the violence that appears to have been planned for tonight. Go now quickly. Wear sensible clothes and sturdy shoes. We will take care of Dorcas Louise, Katherine, so don't worry about that. Just work as a team, and hope to god that you can rescue this silly young girl, who will have me to answer to for tonight.'

Katherine and Charlie, passing a quick message to Cook, made for the automobile, and Charlie made a deft but fast exit from the drive heading toward the city. The night was damp and misty, with a slight drizzle of rain that made seeing things clearly very difficult. The outskirts of the city were nearly empty of people, just a few couples walking without haste along the quiet roads. Not knowing exactly where the planned mayhem was to take place, Charlie had to try a number of routes, all of which up to now had given no clues. Katherine suggested that the main shopping area might be the chosen place if the breaking of windows was their mission. They heard the noise before they reached the corner. The crashing of glass as the missiles hit the large windows of the stores in the main shopping area, the angry high pitched voices that shouted 'Votes for Women', and the sound of pounding boots which foretold of an army of policemen throwing themselves into the middle of an angry throng.

Charlie stopped the automobile. To go in to the middle of the crowd would be foolhardy, but to stay on the outside would be fruitless in the quest to find Flo. He edged the motor slowly forward and around the corner. A missile caught the fender with a loud ping. The view through the windshield was hampered by the mist, and by the laboured breathing of Charlie and Katherine, as they caught sight of the milling crowd bearing down on them. Another window on their right hand side exploded, sending shards of glass across their path, catching the faces and hands of some of the marchers causing them to scream and run away. The crowd seemed to be getting larger. Women were running with a brick in each hand, toward anything that they thought they could damage. There was no fighting, they all seemed intent on causing the maximum amount of damage they could to property, especially property whose end product produced money for the government. It was becoming impossible; their vehicle was sustaining damage, and the likelihood of finding Flo in this crowd was beginning to look very doubtful. They could move neither forward, nor backward, and they were both feeling more than a little frightened, when Katherine caught sight of the governess. She was standing, arms raised holding a banner, and a few feet in front of her was Flo.

'Let me out, Charlie, I can see her,' screamed Katherine.

'I can't leave the auto,' cried Charlie, voice strangled in fear.

'Stay there and get ready to grab her,' shouted Katherine as she hurled herself from the automobile and headed for the angry mob. Just as she got within reach of the governess, she saw her, dropped her banner and ran. Katherine turned just in time to see Flo raise her hand to throw the brick that she was holding into a nearby lighted window. Katherine lunged at her, grabbed the brick, and as she did so the nightmare began. They were surrounded by policemen beating them with large sticks. The crowd dispersed in panic, sending some of their mob sprawling to the ground. Flo was grabbed by a policeman, and Katherine was pushed to the ground brick in hand, and then lifted by the armpits and dragged away in the wake of a screaming Flo.

Charlie, holding on to the steering wheel as if it were a lifeline, saw it all. He was helpless as he sat there with tears streaming down his face. Katherine, Flo, and about one dozen more kicking and screaming women, were bundled aboard the police wagon and driven off at high speed. The road that had been a battleground just a minute ago was now almost empty. The crowd, beaten back by the law, walked away bedraggled and forlorn. Banners were strewn across the road, along with glass and the remnants of missiles. Charlie started the engine and, turning around, drove away shaking with fear, back to give the terrible news to the master and mistress, and Cook.

Katherine and Flo, along with a handful of the violence seekers, were dumped unceremoniously in a large cell which was already full to over-flowing. The door slammed with a resounding clang. Flo flew into Katherine's arms sobbing, while the inmates who had gone through their initiation laughed and jeered. 'Soon have something to cry about in 'ere,' one of them sneered. 'That 'air will go, that's for sure,' another one chipped in.

Katherine just stood there, back against the wall, still reeling from the shock of being arrested.

Charlie arrived at the Elford house, wanting the earth to open up and swallow him whole. He got out of the lovely Rolls Royce to see a large dent in the fender, and scratches down the side from the shower of glass. One of the marchers had vomited on the bonnet while begging Charlie to get her away from the violent scene. He put the automobile away, and went into the house. Mr Elford listened quietly as Charlie told his tale. Mrs Elford went to Dorcas Louise who, realising that something was terribly wrong, could not get to sleep. She cried in her mother's arms at the thought of Kat spending time in that awful place. Lavinia held her and comforted her, and said that Daddy would do everything possible to bring Kat back to her. She didn't tell Dorcas that her governess was the instigator of the trouble, and that her time here was limited to the time it took her to return.

The morning dawned damp and misty as the night before had been. Charlie was to drive the master to the gaol, and would accompany him as a witness to try and release both Katherine and Flo. Nine of the defendants would come before the magistrate this morning, amongst them would be Miss Carrera and Miss Petite. This was a move in the right direction, thought Charlie. Katherine was fourth in line to come to the dock; two of the others had been sent down, and one had been released due to ill health, but on a caution that should it happen again no mercy would be shown. Katherine stood before them, white-faced, and clearly frightened. Charlie was asked to give evidence, which he did to the best of his ability under the circumstances, realising that the slightest mistake could send Katherine down. Mr Elford then produced the letter, and told the magistrate that he personally had sent both Mr Orchard and Miss Carrera to the scene of the riot, to stop Miss Petite from acting in such an irresponsible manner, and that he would give his assurance that no such thing would happen again. The magistrate asked for the letter to be kept in the files, in order to apprehend Miss Oldberry immediately. Katherine Carrera would be free to leave the court as soon as all necessary details had been taken, and she was aware that any further incident of this manner would be handled most severely.

Three more cases were heard, and all went down. It was Flo next, who stood like a tiny child scared beyond belief in front of the magistrate, who had already had the assurances of Mr Elford that this would never happen again. Charlie was sure that it would all be all right, and he would give her such a telling off when he got her back. It wasn't all right, and Flo, who the magistrate said had committed a serious crime of wilful damage to property, and danger to life, would spent one month in Walton gaol.

Charlie, frozen to the spot, was helped away by Mr Elford, as Flo went down accompanied by a grossly large warder to spend the most horrendous month of her young life amongst some of the lowest specimens of humanity. Katherine was waiting at the door, after her release, as Charlie, now unashamedly weeping, walked toward her, and held her in his arms. 'We failed, Katherine, we failed,' he sobbed. 'They will hurt her now. I know they will.'

Mr Elford, also feeling the shock at what had happened, tried to keep up his bearing, and ushered them to a place of quietness, before they went home leaving the young Flo Petite to wait a month for her release.

Flo did in fact suffer. She was placed in a cell with two local prostitutes, and a suffragette who had spat in the face of a policeman, and kicked him in the groin. They had cut off her hair in one piece that left it jagged and sticking out all around her tiny face. Her tears were met with jeers, and unsympathetic jibes, which Flo in her young innocence didn't really understand. The rough language and the attitudes of both her fellow cell mates frightened her somewhat, and they would not leave her alone. When they left the cell to go to eat, they would push her, jostle her, and when her plate was nearly full, one of them would jog her elbow, and send the contents of the plate spilling on to the floor, at which the warder would shout at her and tell her to be more careful or they would feed her. Flo remembered all that Katherine had told her about the force feeding of the suffragettes, and so she would eat with as much relish as she could the horrible slop that was served. She would eat bread in whatever quantity it was given to her, and drink water at every available moment. This she figured would keep her alive. Her moments of joy came when Charlie was allowed to see her. Just fifteen minutes was all they allowed, but to Flo it was a lifeline.

Charlie, Katherine, and Mr Elford had arrived home to find Cook in some distress wondering what had happened, and overjoyed to see Katherine, but cried when she heard of Flo's fate. Mr Elford was about to search out the governess, but Cook said that she had seen nothing of her since she left the house on the previous evening. Mr Elford had gone to her door with the intention of 'sending her packing'. He found the door locked. He rapped loudly upon it and called Miss Oldberry, but there was no reply.

He asked Katherine to bring him the master key, and to accompany him as he opened the door. They found the room empty and devoid of any of her belongings. They opened cupboards and drawers to find no evidence of her presence therein. They wondered how she had escaped without Cook noticing, as she would have had to pass the servants' room and the kitchen on her way out. There was no other key, so that had presumably gone with her, and then they noticed that the curtain although drawn, was moving slightly. On pulling back the curtain they had found the window had been opened as wide as the sashes would allow, and outside under the large cherry tree were many broken branches, and a couple of pieces of torn petticoat. She must have thrown out all her belongings, and then climbed down the cherry tree. When and how she had done it, no one knew, but done it she had, and escaped for the time being from the clutches of the law.

Mr Elford had had to give a description of her when he delivered the note that had put all of his staff and family in jeopardy; now he would have to report her missing and let the law take its due course. Dorcas Louise ran into Katherine's arms, and begged her not to make her have another governess. They had all been bad she had remonstrated, and she did not wish to have anything to do with the suffragettes if that was all they were going to try and make her do.

'Hush, child,' soothed Katherine, 'they are not all bad, you just seem to have had the worst ones, I will talk with your mother, and see what she wishes for you, but I think under the circumstances you should have a few days off from your teachings, and we will arrange some little pleasure outings for you.'

Dorcas looked at Katherine with a wicked look in her eye, and a wide smile, and said, 'We could go and feed the ducks, Kat!'

'We will do just that, madam,' Katherine replied as she ushered her into the nursery, closely followed by Lavinia Elford who had witnessed that little conversation with a smile. As they sat and enjoyed the tray of delicacies that cook had brought them, 'as a treat' she had said, Katherine broached the subject of the further education of Dorcas Louise. 'Do you think that perhaps it would be better at this stage if she were to go to a proper school where she would meet other young ladies, and start to be introduced to a foreign language, and maybe learn deportment, things that would benefit her in the adult life that really isn't too far away now.'

'I have actually been thinking down the same lines for a while now,' answered Lavinia, but I have made some enquiries, and have not quite found anything that I hoped I might.'

Katherine, looking at both Dorcas Louise and Lavinia Elford, then said, 'I was thinking of going to London for a few days, and I was wondering if you both would like to accompany me. I have not seen Adolphus now for a few months. Both he and Martha have been extremely busy with the work that has been going on at his house. It seemed that there were some problems with the actual building that had to be addressed before the cosmetic refurbishment could be done. Now it appears that it is reaching completion, and would not cause any disturbance to visitors. Adolphus may have some ideas, or indeed know, of a good school in Liverpool where the best subjects for a young lady could be undertaken.'

Lavinia sat up in interest, and Dorcas Louise's eyes lit up with the promise of seeing Adolphus again. 'James is away for one week, in two week's time. Could we possibly go then? I would very much like to see Adolphus, and his house. Could you arrange it, Katherine?'

'I see no reason why not; that would leave only Charlie and Cook to look after things.'

Charlie had not stopped working on the automobile since the night of the battle in Liverpool's main street. On close inspection, there had been considerable damage to the paintwork, and a few more dents that had not been apparent at the time. Between his duties in the house, and walking to the prison for his fleeting visits with Flo, he had spent every available moment in an effort to return the beautiful Rolls Royce to its original splendour. Thomas had been a grand help in his off duty times. He had come with some tools that Charlie did not have, and had set to work gently teasing out scratches and dents while Charlie washed and polished. Thomas had become a good friend to Charlie, and also to Katherine who was always happy to sit awhile during her rest periods and chat to him.

They had found a sort of contentment in each other's company, which pleased Cook. She always felt that Katherine should have a personal friend that she could call her own. She had given so much to everybody else and asked nothing in return. Thomas was a nice lad and would never take more than was his due, so she would encourage the friendship as much as she could without causing embarrassment to either party.

One week of Flo's sentence was over. She found that her cellmates had become tired of bullying her, and because she had not complained to the wardens, they had started to talk to her and tell her some amazing stories of their lives. They even made her laugh on odd occasions, and the suffragette had tried, albeit in vain, to do something with her hair, which of course she could not see herself because there were no mirrors. They had said it was pretty awful, but that it would grow again and then she could have it cut properly. The suffragette had said that it was what she did on the outside, but of course here they would not lend her any scissors, but every day she would brush it with her own brush until it began to shine. Even Charlie, who in the beginning was horrified at the sight of it, had commented on its shine, and said that by the time she came home she would be a 'right little beauty'. Flo had cried then, and had said that she didn't think that day would ever come.

'It will Flo. It will,' promised Charlie.

Mr Elford had called Charlie to the library one morning, and asked what he thought should be done with Flo. He knew that they were close, but in view of her behaviour, and the damage that had occurred because of her, he felt that he could no longer keep her in his employ. Charlie was devastated, and begged Mr Elford to reconsider. She was indeed very foolish to be tempted by the excitement, and the encouragement of that awful woman, but he was sure that her term spent in the gaol would be enough to frighten her off for ever, and he promised to guide her along all the right roads in future.

'Are you thinking of marrying the lady in question, Charlie?' asked Mr Elford.

Charlie, taken aback, said quickly, 'I am, sir, but not yet. We could not afford to rent somewhere to live even with my position as butler here. It would take a while to save enough money to take such a big step.'

Mr Elford thought about Charlie's answer and then said, 'I could not allow you to live in this house as a married couple, but, if by marrying this girl you can keep her out of trouble, I will arrange for the loft in the building where the automobile is housed to be converted into a sleeping area for you both. Your rooms that you have in the house would be kept only for your working hours, and each one used separately by you both. How do you feel about that, Charlie?' enquired Mr Elford.

'Sir, I don't know what to say,' mumbled the stunned Charlie.

'Well you had better decide. I need to know whether Miss Petite stays or goes,' Mr Elford insisted.

'Yes, sir. Yes indeed, sir,' Charlie gabbled. 'Can I tell her next time I see her?'

'No, I think I would like a word with her first, if you don't mind. I want to know that you and her know what you are about to let yourselves in for. You, Charlie, will have to keep your news to yourself for a while longer and, if it gets out, you and your Flo will have me to answer to. Do you understand, Orchard?'

'Yes, sir,' said a strangely elated Charlie, who would walk on air for the next three weeks.

Katherine duly made her arrangements with Adolphus, who wrote back to say how both he and his housekeeper cook, Mrs Wilkin, would be delighted to have the company of her, Dorcas, and Mrs Elford for a few days. All would be made ready for them, and Mrs Wilkin would see to all their needs.

Cook and Charlie were happy to keep the running of the house in order, and they would prepare for their return, along with Mr Elford's, and of course it would coincide with the release of Flo. With that in mind, Cook asked permission to make a little celebration dinner for the master, mistress, and Dorcas Louise, and also for the servants to have a little celebration of their own to welcome back Flo into the fold. Charlie at this point was bursting with the longing to spill the beans to Cook, but thought better of it, remembering Mr Elford's words of warning. So the plans were laid, and the Elfords, with their respective staff, went their separate ways, each one with a mission to complete, and hopefully, a more settled and happy household to return to.

Charlie, still in the process of repairing the automobile, took time out to take Mrs Elford, Katherine, and Dorcas Louise to the station, and see them off on their journey to London, where Adolphus would arrange for his personal driver to pick them up. Dorcas Louise, now feeling very grown up, sat quietly and glanced through the morning paper that her mother had brought from the house. She remembered travelling to London before with Adolphus and Katherine, but that was a long time ago, and Adolphus had spent most of his time still in Liverpool since then, but now he was going to be in London all the time, so she had to show him that she would soon be grown up enough to travel and see him on her own. The station in London was still noisy and full of smoke, but it wasn't frightening to her now as they made their way to the exit, and to the awaiting transport which whisked them at great speed through the London streets until the smoke gave way to the trees that heralded the suburbs.

The horseless carriage took on a slower pace, and its passengers were able to enjoy the lovely houses set in leafy streets. The driver apologised for the speedy trip through the city, but explained that there had been a lot of unrest due to the suffragette movement, and he didn't like to be seen to be loitering. His passengers decided to change the subject and spoke of the house which Adolphus was having renovated, and how excited they all were about seeing it.

'A fair mansion it is and no mistake,' the driver exclaimed, pleased to be able to sing its praises, and pleased to be able to announce that Mr Fry had offered him the chance to be his personal taxi as and when he needed transport, at an excellent rate of pay, which was very acceptable, as the garage across the street where he worked had little need for a driver. They mostly dealt with damage to vehicles sustained through lack of experience in the drivers of these new fangled machines. They had but one carriage that was used for passengers, and it was this one, he explained, and not many people trusted them. Their arrival at the house put a stop to the driver's ramblings as he jumped from his seat to open the door. Doffing his hat, he wished them a pleasant stay, and would call for them for their return journey to the station.

Martha came down the drive to greet them, ushering them to the door where Adolphus stood, leaning on his cane and smiling as he always did at the sight of Katherine. The house had changed enormously since her last visit, and Katherine hesitated before entering the door and taking Adolphus's hand.

'Welcome to my new abode,' he said.

'What has happened to all the glass?' Katherine said in amazement.

'Come inside and enjoy a cup of tea, and then I will explain, and take you all around,' he said, taking hold of Lavinia's hand, and putting the other arm around Dorcas Louise. Once settled in the beautiful drawing room, Martha wheeled in a trolley and set up a small side table with afternoon tea. Adolphus then started to explain the problems that had faced them as they had progressed through the renovation. 'The walls that supported the glass atrium had become unstable, which had rendered the atrium unsafe, and so it had to go along with the great oak door that stood in the middle of it. It took many weeks of planning and preparing, but eventually they came up with the frontage that now stands complete in all its glory and its practicality,' said an obviously satisfied customer. 'I now have two houses, one of which I will either rent or, better still, keep for the times when I can entertain all my special guests that I hope to see much more of in the future,' he said, winking at Dorcas Louise who nodded excitedly. 'There is just one part of it I would like you to see Katherine, before Martha does the rest of the tour, and shows you your rooms.'

He took her hand and led her down a carpeted passage to a door on the right hand side that she recalled led to a large passageway. He unlocked the door, and ushered her inside, reached for the electric light switch, and then stood back. He had done what he had promised and created an art gallery. There were paintings of birds, and of places, including Italy. All the places that they had visited on that fateful journey so long ago, beautifully depicted on canvases, some big, some small, but all incredibly beautiful, framed in gold against a background of the palest blue walls. On the opposite side there were bookcases full of neatly stacked books whose spines sat in perfect symmetry against the dark wood. The middle bookcase was special, he had said, as he walked toward it. The middle book on the middle shelf was the book he had dedicated to her, but, upon touching it, the whole bookcase slid out to reveal a door, and upon turning the key and opening the door, Adolphus and Katherine were able to walk into the other house. Adolphus smiled at Katherine's astonishment.

'My promise to you is fulfilled, and that is why at this moment I will not rent this half of my property. If in the future I decide to change my mind, then I will have the doors bricked up, and incidentally the reverse action is available from the other side, except that the bookcase is moved by key, and not by touch. Well, my Katherine, does it please you?'

'It pleases me, Adolphus. Oh yes, it pleases me. Could I have just a few minutes to look again at the paintings before we return to the others?'

'Indeed you can, but you have a few days when you can sit in here on the chairs that you suggested would be perfect, whenever you wish to.'

Katherine had not noticed the little gold cane chairs that were placed strategically along the gallery. She just stood in adoration of the elderly gentleman in whose life she had played such an important part. Before returning to the others, Adolphus, taking her arm, gently stopped, turned toward her and said, 'I have something to ask your opinion of while we are out of earshot of our guests. I have to tell you that I am so very pleased with Martha; she is a gem, and has made my life so much easier, especially here in London when the going has been quite tough as the building work progressed. She managed the situation with apparent ease and efficiency. I feel that my housekeeper and servant would be worth a little better title. I would like her rather to be a travelling companion. We already share time together in conversation, and while I do not want in any way to insult her, there are times when I need someone to accompany me on invitations to dinner, and also on my travels. It has been my greatest desire to visit India, and now my work is virtually finished at the University, I find myself thinking down the lines of a possible voyage to what I believe is a wonderful country. So therefore Katherine, do you think that Martha would be offended if I asked her to accompany me? She would have the best accommodation everywhere we went, and I would take great care of her. I know the love that you feel for her and I would do nothing to endanger that.'

Katherine, feeling the tears rising in her eyes, gave him the answer to his question, taking his hand in hers. 'You, Adolphus, have been more to me than any father, grandfather, uncle, or any other relation could possibly have been, and I love you dearly, and there is no one in this world that I would trust with the safety of my wonderful Martha more. I hope that the time will come one day when the need for all the secrecy that I have brought upon us, will no longer have any bearing on our lives. Ask her, Adolphus, and I will be by your side should she show any doubt.'

They were both smiling as they passed back through the bookcase, to where Dorcas Louise, Lavinia, and Martha were engrossed in conversation. Dorcas was holding forth on the question of her education, and Martha was looking at her animated face and remembering how Katherine had been when she had been asked to sing at the concert at school when she was just about Dorcas's age. Dorcas jumped up and dragged Adolphus into the circle, bemoaning the fact that another governess was just too much to endure, and why couldn't she go to school every day, and wear proper school clothes.

Adolphus looked at Lavinia, who shrugged her shoulders. 'I have searched through the possibilities, and there are not that many. Those that are available are very difficult to gain entry to unless you have a sibling there already.'

'I do know of one,' Adolphus said. 'You would need a sponsor, but I would be prepared to do that for you, but Dorcas, you would have to study very hard, and the subjects would not be anywhere as easy as those you have been used to with a governess. You could attend daily if you wished, and it is situated on the same side of the city as your dwelling, so, at a later date, you would be able to walk there; it would not be too far. I would make enquiries for you, if you wished,' he said to Lavinia. 'Talk to James and let me know if you wish me to do so.'

Dorcas threw her arms around Adolphus's neck, and said, 'Thank you, thank you.'

Adolphus continued, 'It is in no way settled yet, and in the meantime I suggest that you revise on all that your governesses have done their best to instil in you. If you are lucky enough to gain a place there, you will be at least a little ready to act like a responsible young lady, because the aim of this school is to produce the best, not only in educational studies, but in deportment, and self respect. If you achieve highly in all that you are taught, you will be able to walk into your adult life with confidence. Does that sound like what you want, Dorcas, because if not we need go no further now?'

Dorcas had never heard Adolphus speak in such a way, and was now a little nervous, but she thought that anything was better than another governess and so she committed herself to all that Adolphus had promised her. Their few days in London passed with speed. Lavinia had enjoyed the company of Katherine and Martha, and of course as always, Adolphus had been the perfect host.

Katherine had stood by while Adolphus had put his proposition to Martha, and had revelled in the look on her face when he had suggested the trip to India. How a life can change. Katherine thought of the years of drudgery and abuse that Martha had suffered at the hands of her husband, and how now she was entering a phase in her life that she had only read about in the few books that had been available to her. Now she had a library which Adolphus had, a little reluctantly, given her permission to avail herself of whenever she wished. Her working days, spent caring for him and the house, were just delightful and she wished, nor wanted for anything.

Their transport arrived at the door, and they all said their goodbyes with promises that they would return often. Dorcas Louise skipped along, head in the air. Katherine loitered a minute to say a special goodbye to Martha, who could not resist a small hug, hoping it would go unnoticed by Lavinia, but she need not have worried as Adolphus had Lavinia by the arm and was ushering her into the automobile.

'I love you, Mama,' whispered Katherine as she slowly released her hand from Martha's.

There was a hum of activity in the Elford household upon the return of Mrs Elford, Dorcas Louise, and Katherine. They found an exuberant Mr Elford who had had an exceptional success in an investment that had led to an affiliation with an American company of great repute. He waited with bated breath to converse with his wife and regale her with the future possibilities for all of them should the venture prove to be as exceptional as was expected.

Downstairs, the atmosphere was also tinged with a high powered buzz, but for a different reason. Today was the day that Flo Petite was to be released from gaol. Charlie had been allowed to go to the gates and wait for her. She was the only one today to gain her freedom, and she was more than a little nervous as the great door shut behind her, and she looked into the sunlight for the first time in four long weeks. She felt a little sick, and weak from long hours of doing very little in the way of exercise. Adjusting her eyes to the brightness, she finally saw Charlie. She wanted so desperately to run into his arms but she felt ashamed and shy, so she stood hesitantly gazing at him as he stood there looking so handsome in the new jacket that he had told her he was going to get. Then he waved and started to walk toward her. She ran then, tears running down her cheeks, into his arms, whispering, 'I am so sorry, Charlie.'

He put his cheek against hers, then hugged and kissed her. 'Come on home,' he said.

Flo tried to tidy up her hair that had persistently stuck out in all directions this morning when she had tried to make it look a little respectable.

'Leave it,' said Charlie. 'You look lovely to me, and it will grow quickly when you are home and happy.'

Flo looked at Charlie and said, 'I am happy now I am with you.'

Mr Elford had allowed Charlie to borrow the now pristine Rolls Royce to bring Flo back to the house. She took in every road and tree on the way as if they had all been put there while she was away. She had changed from the little scatterbrained maid that had crept from the house that night, into a serious young girl, well aware of her stupidity, and also aware of her vulnerability in getting involved in something that she had no understanding of. She was sure that the reasoning behind the suffragette movement was for the betterment of women. After her initial introduction to the suffragette who shared the same cell as her, she had found her to be a very special person who believed implicitly in her mission to gain the rights of women to vote, but she knew that she had neither the commitment nor the courage to involve herself. However, she was very much in awe of those who gave of their services without any doubts, and who knew that their possible fate would be of an horrendous nature, and that some would not survive the battle.

Upon entering the house, and receiving welcoming hugs from Cook, Flo was summoned to the library. Mr Elford sat at his desk, a stern look on his face. Flo stood in front of him, now feeling extremely tired as the excitement of her release, and the journey home with Charlie, faded at the sight of Mr Elford. 'Sit down, Miss Petite,' said Mr Elford, waving a hand at the chair placed in front of his desk. 'Have you anything to say for yourself?' Arms crossed, he waited.

'I can only say how sorry I am to bring such disgrace to you, sir. I was stupid,' was all that Flo could think of as she lowered her eyes from his intent gaze.

'Yes indeed, you were stupid, and far too young to get involved in things that you know nothing about, and I am afraid that I can no longer employ a Miss Petite who now has her name on a criminal record sheet. This would not bode well for my reputation. I therefore suggest that you go and speak to Mr Orchard who seems to have a suggestion whereby you could gain employment in the future. Thank you, Miss Petite.'

Mr Elford rose from his chair and left Flo Petite completely devastated and unable to move. She sat until she heard footsteps outside the library. Feeling utterly miserable and ashamed, she rose slowly from the chair and walked to the door with thoughts of packing her belongings and leaving the house and Charlie. It was Katherine who was outside the door. Seeing her distress, she put an arm around her shoulder, and led her to the kitchen where Cook stood, a questioning look on her face. Flo, now inconsolable, sat on a chair weeping uncontrollably, her hair now sticking out all around her pretty face. As Charlie entered the kitchen, he smiled, which caused all present to show amazement on their faces. Flo just looked at him, now too desperate even to acknowledge his presence.

'What is it dearest?' said Charlie, kneeling at her side. Flo repeated Mr Elford's words in rasping sobs, and then just sat there, not looking at anyone, or making any attempt to move. Charlie lifted her chin and said, 'Flo, will you marry me?'

Everyone in the room gasped, and Flo for the first time looked up. Charlie repeated his question, and Flo still just sat there unable to take in what Charlie had just said. 'Will someone get this girl to answer my question, please?' said Charlie.

Cook shook Flo by the shoulders and said, 'Say yes, Flo, before he changes his mind.'

Flo, now realising what was happening, and through a mist of tears, laughed out loud and said, 'Oh yes, Charlie, I will.'

Everybody cheered, and then Charlie took her hand, kissed it, and led her from the kitchen to the library where Mr Elford was back at his desk, but this time with a suspicion of a smile on his face.

'Yes, Miss Petite?' he said.

Flo, still in a state of confusion, could not utter one word, but the gallant Mr Orchard explained that Mrs Orchard would have no criminal record, and would be an upstanding member of society, and as such would make a perfect employee of this respectable household. Mr Elford could now no longer keep up the pretence, and so instructed Miss Petite to dry her eyes, and never do anything as stupid as that again. He told Charlie to go to the cellar and find an appropriate toast to celebrate, with the rest of the household, the happiness of the future Mr and Mrs Orchard.

All the excitement over for a while, the Elford household began to regain its quiet eloquence. Flo drifted through her duties with an unusual serenity. The surfaces of the furniture gleamed as she rubbed away, smiling at her reflection in its shine. The whereabouts of Miss Oldberry were still a mystery in spite of regular calls at the house by a member of the constabulary, which sent cold shivers, not only down Flo's back, but down Katherine's and Charlie's too.

Thomas visited often with the excuse of giving Charlie a hand, but with the ultimate aim of setting eyes on Katherine, and sometimes being allowed to share a cup of tea with her. Cook went out of her way to ensure that this happened as often as she could arrange it. The alterations to the space in the loft above the housing of the Rolls Royce were ongoing, and no one but Charlie knew what they were for. Mr Elford had sworn him to secrecy until it was finished and ready for him and Flo to turn it into comfortable sleeping accommodation. Flo kept repeating to Charlie that they would not be allowed to sleep together in the house, and Charlie repeatedly answered, 'Something will turn up', to which Flo would get annoyed and moan 'When? That's what I would like to know'.

Finally, after a few weeks, all was revealed, and Charlie led Flo up the wide-stepped ladder that had been installed, to the place under the eaves that would become their bedroom in the future. She was enthralled; the walls had been washed in a pale pink and the window that had been built into the end of the loft nearest to the garden, let in the golden light of the late afternoon. Thomas had made for Charlie a screen of slatted wood which had been secretly lifted into place in the dead of night. It stood between the bed and the rest of the room, which now had two small armchairs with a table in between them and a large cupboard which would hold their own clothes, and at the end of the cupboard was a door which opened to reveal a shelf that held washing facilities for them to use before returning to the house for their duties.

Flo hugged Charlie, and asked who had done all this for them. Charlie answered that Mr Elford had been responsible for it all, and Thomas had helped to put the whole thing into operation. Now all that was left was to set a date. It was now approaching August, and it was decided that a little time would be needed to prepare for the event as it could not clash with either 'Orchards', or for that matter any of the staff's duties which would need to be performed for some important dinner parties in the Autumn, and then Christmas tradition must be upheld as it always had been. Neither Charlie nor Flo wanted to be married in the winter time, and so it was decided that April of 1913 would be earmarked for the celebration.

Katherine, who had offered to make Flo's wedding gown, needed some time to collect all that was needed for the task. She would be a perfect bride, Katherine promised, looking at the hair that, in order to tidy it up, had had to be cut very short, and thinking that it would grow considerably in the coming months. Charlie was thinking of asking Mr Cloverleaf if he would do them the honour of giving away Miss Petite at the service that he hoped would be performed in the tiny village church. They met quite regularly, and Charlie still asked Mr Cloverleaf's advice on several occasions, which he gave of freely. The young man, that he thought might be a difficult pupil, turned out to be one of the best that he had had the dubious pleasure of teaching. It was Thomas who accepted with great joy the invitation to act as best man to Charlie. It not only gave him the greatest pleasure to do this for Charlie, it also meant that he would be in the close company of Katherine for the whole day.

Dorcas Louise, upon hearing the news, cried out to Katherine that please could she be a flower girl. She had seen pictures in one of Kat's books of girls in pretty dresses scattering petals on the ground in front of the Bride and Groom; could she please do that? Katherine, after careful consideration, offered to ask her mother if it would be possible, but that she could not promise. She had always tried to not let Dorcas be too aware of the gap between servant and family member, while a servant was always there to do whatever the master of mistress required of them. Katherine always implied that a servant should be treated with a certain amount of respect that befits their position. Dorcas had always liked Flo. She had got down on the floor and played with her when Kat was busy.

Katherine did put the question to Lavinia Elford, who very diplomatically said that both her and the master would be out for the day, and as long as Katherine looked after Dorcas, and kept her teenage tendencies under control, she could wear a pretty dress that Katherine would choose for her, and she could scatter some petals, but the title of flower girl would not be mentioned in the invitations to friends of the pair. Katherine thought the consent of Lavinia was very acceptable, and she would see that the wording of the invitations would be in the best taste.

'Thank you,' said Lavinia, 'I will leave it in your hands.'

Thus the plans were put into action. Six months seemed ages away for Flo and Charlie, but they were so happy to be here in this lovely house, working together, and with the prospect of being a respectable married couple, and still being allowed to stay here was unbelievable. This was always uppermost in both their minds, as they toiled away at all that they had to do, and were always at hand if things got tough for Cook or Katherine. It was a band of very happy workers that suddenly found Christmas looming just around the corner. During all the excitement of the forthcoming nuptials, Dorcas Louise had been accepted at the Academy that Adolphus had recommended, and had faced her first day with some trepidation. She had donned the uniform of navy blue. The jacket had a bright yellow edging around its collar, and down its front edge. The skirt had pleats all around, and underneath she wore a white blouse with a bright yellow tie, and to top it all off, she wore a navy blue velour hat with a yellow and navy blue band around it.

Katherine watched as Charlie drove Dorcas, accompanied by Mr and Mrs Elford, out of the drive to the school that it was hoped, would, at the end of six years, produce a young woman who would grace the annuls of society with a charm and intelligence that would be worthy of its reputation. Katherine found it hard to realise that the tiny baby who had caused her so much pain and heartbreak all those years ago, was now facing her first steps into adulthood, and that she had herself nearly reached her twenty-seventh year.

She had written to Lena recently, and she in turn had written back. It had given Katherine a chance to recall her Italian language, and to translate the news that Lena's children had grown up, and had gone away to work in the hotels out on the coast where visitors were chasing the sun, and spending days lazing in chairs, and wandering around the bright streets that always welcomed them. The memorial to Joseph and the people who lost their lives in the water that dreadful night of the storm, was a permanent reminder of the times that she had shared with him and Katherine. She wished her every happiness and said she thought of her often. Katherine smiled a sad smile, and remembered also the life that had become so precious in that wonderful place next to the sea, with Joseph, and Pip. Lena had not mentioned Pip, and Katherine wondered if he had gone to meet his master.

Leaving her memories behind, she turned to the tasks awaiting her attention. She now ran the household with great confidence, along with Charlie who was always by her side to give a helping hand. Office work was easy and enjoyable to Katherine. Everything was filed neatly, and her system was easily understood by all who had access to it. Questions were answered swiftly and with accuracy; her timing was perfect, and so the rest of the staff, being continually informed of the master's requirements, followed her lead and were always ready for any eventuality.

The end of any year, as always, brought a whirl of excitement. Parties were numerous, and Christmas spread its own magic on the household. Katherine, now with a little space in her life, with the absence of Dorcas

Louise during the day, found time to read and do small things for herself in between her duties as housekeeper.

She studied the magazines that the mistress passed on to her after reading them herself, and began to draw some designs. Thinking of the wedding of Flo and Charlie, she thought of a style that might suit Flo. She was a tiny girl, very pretty, and now that her hair had started to grow again it framed her face in a halo of curls which rather suited her better than the long tied back style that she had favoured before the prison wardress had taken a pair of scissors to it. She found that sitting with a pencil and sketching was very therapeutic, and remembered the time when she had drawn the picture on the beach for Joseph. Her talent was obviously lost on that because the childish picture that she had produced at a very tender age bore no comparison to the images that appeared on the paper in front of her now. Skirts flowed from tight bodices; some fell into long trains that would sweep along behind the bride, and others fell in soft gathers to the ankles where a frothy frill would bounce around the hem. She completed a large selection in a very short time, and later, when Flo had finished her duties, she would show her, and let her choose what she would like to finally walk down the path to the small local church in.

Flo never knew her parents. She believed that she was one of many, and that her mother had no means to feed or look after her, and so she had spent her young life in a convent, which had been hard to say the least, but the scrubbing of floors, and washing dishes, had in fact set her in good stead for the job that was given to her by the Elford family when she was thirteen years old. Katherine felt an affinity with Flo, and took her welfare very seriously. Flo, along with Charlie, looked upon Katherine as sort of family, and in spite of her position over her, Katherine felt the same. Now with their wedding arranged, she wanted so much to make their day as happy as possible. Mr Cloverleaf had agreed, and said that it would be an honour to give away the bride, and also on this special occasion he would be willing to act as master of ceremonies and toastmaster. Thomas had almost too willingly accepted the part of best man to Charlie, and so plans were going ahead in a way that left Flo speechless.

She sat for hours turning over the pages of designs that Katherine had sketched, selecting a skirt and then a top until she had collated a dress that would put all others to shame, she said, eyes sparkling. Katherine had saved some money for what she called 'something special', and this to her was something very special, and so she would go and purchase the fabric that she knew would bring the design to life. Also she would make a dress for Dorcas Louise in a colour that would complement the bridal gown. With her colouring, blue was a good choice, and Katherine picked the richest dark blue she could find, and some lace matching that of the trimming on the bridal gown. The bridal gown itself was to be made of a rich white taffeta that would rustle as she walked, with lace insets on the bodice and a matching lace cap to cover her head, leaving tendrils of hair peeping out on her forehead and around her ears. A veil of the finest white tulle would cascade from the back of the cap and fall to the ground.

The day of the wedding dawned, with pale sunlight filtering through Katherine's window and casting its beam across the array of dresses that hung from her wardrobe. She sat up in bed and gazed at the completed dresses with a feeling of achievement. The lady at the stall in the market where she had spent happy hours learning to sew, would, she was sure, be proud of her at this moment, and she allowed herself to feel that pride too. Dorcas knocked on her door as she often did, and came and sat on the bed.

'Oh! Kat, they are so beautiful... you are so very clever,' she said, giving her a hug.

'Thank you, darling,' said Katherine, unthinking.

Dorcas raised her head and said, 'That was nice.'

'What was?' answered Katherine.

'You called me darling, like you used to when I was a baby.'

'You are a darling and I love you,' said Katherine, feeling that she was allowed a little informality on a day like today.

Flo was let off all her duties for the day. Cook arranged and served breakfast for the staff, but Charlie insisted on carrying out his own duties until the very last moment when he would leave for the church, accompanied by Thomas. It was nearly time for Flo to leave. Charlie had ordered two carriages to be sent. The one that would take him and Thomas would return and take Katherine with Dorcas Louise, and the other would be for Flo and Mr Cloverleaf, who, it has to be said, was quite nervous. He had his little notebook tucked in his pocket, to which he had frequently referred to throughout the morning, much to the silent amusement of Charlie. Dorcas Louise looked beautiful in her blue dress, carrying a posy of lemon daisies.

Flo took Mr Cloverleaf's breath away when she came down the stairs. A vision of loveliness, he thought, dressed in her taffeta gown which billowed out around her, its lace sleeves and high necked bodice clinging to her tiny figure. The cap upon her head, that held a cloud of white tulle at its back, had been studded with shiny glass beads which glittered as she moved her head. A tiny posy of white lilies completed the picture. Mr Cloverleaf stood at the bottom of the stairs, and held out his hand, and led her through the door to the awaiting carriage.

Mr and Mrs Orchard stood at the front door together and welcomed their guests back into the house. The service had gone without a hitch, and Mr Cloverleaf had only looked at his notebook one more time just before he handed Flo over to Charlie, in answer to the question, 'Who gives this woman', he stated with resounding clarity, 'I do'.

Cook had excelled, and the dining room was prepared, with the tables decked with ribbons, and a wonderful arrangement of food for the guests to enjoy. Mr Cloverleaf, now feeling that he could cope with anything, made an excellent speech, and proposed a toast to what he referred to as a perfect young couple at the beginning of a great adventure. The guests all applauded, and Mr and Mrs Elford made an appearance and wished the happy couple every success in their life together. Mr Elford, turning just before they left, said with a wicked grin, 'I will expect you at 7am in the morning then, Orchard.' Mrs Elford smiled and just wished them happiness.

As all the guests finally left, Katherine walked to the door with Thomas, who turned, took her in his arms, kissed her, and said, 'Thank you, Katherine.'

Chapter Seventeen

Torn By Conflict

'How did we get here, Charlie?' said Thomas, as they bumped and jolted their way across the rough and dusty terrain of Northern France. The Ford truck that was used for transporting men, food, ammunition, and equipment to the Allied front, was not designed for comfort, as had been the motor vehicles that they had both become accustomed to before following in the footsteps of thousands before them. The year 1914 began with the disbelief of the declaration of war, and the call for all able-bodied men to volunteer their services in the fight against the onslaught of German armies forcing their way into Belgium and France.

Both Charlie and Thomas had held back, hoping that the war would end, as some of the politicians had suggested, in a very short time. In fact, things got decidedly worse, and finally at the call of Lord Kitchener for another 500,000 men to sign up, they both succumbed and became recruits. They were promised that there would be good training, and accommodation, and many of them after training would be allowed to live at home until their services were required.

Many tears were shed in the Elford household. Charlie and Flo had entered in to married life with joy and love. They had proved that they could work together as a married couple, as well as they had before. They loved the private space that they had been given in the loft above the building that housed the Rolls Royce, and they spent many a golden hour together there after their working hours. Katherine too had spent some happy times with Thomas, much to the satisfaction of Cook, who had worked out some very careful plans toward that end. Dorcas Louise had settled into school, and was doing very well. The early days of the war seemed not to have had a great effect on Liverpool and, according to the news from Adolphus, London too was not suffering any obvious disturbance, only the loss of many of its young men to the front.

Charlie and Thomas had been recruited together, which was often allowed when friends joined at the same time. Because both of them had driving experience, they were prepared to serve in the area of field transport. Their early days were not only geared to driving, they also had to enter into the basic army training under the evil eye of one Sgt. Major Taylor, who according to Charlie had a very dubious parentage. In 1915, their training was finished, and their uniforms issued. To their utter delight, they were given seven days leave before they were to embark on one of the troopships leaving Liverpool for France. They were both welcomed with open arms at the Elford household. Thomas, only receiving a cursory acknowledgment from his employers, also made his way over to spend some time with Katherine, who he felt had softened a little toward him in the months following Charlie's marriage. Cook's son, Arthur, had now also gone for recruitment, but had been sent to a different training area to Charlie and Thomas. His departure had been taken very badly by Cook, as he not only had to leave her, which was terrible enough, but he also had to leave a wife, son, and a new baby daughter not long since born.

Still there was little evidence of the war in Liverpool. A Zeppelin had crossed Norfolk in a night raid, dropping bombs on unsuspecting towns, killing some civilians. Some bombs had fallen near Sandringham, which was the home of the King. The population lived in a sort of permanent fear, but with the belief that by carrying on and helping out where help was needed, the worry could be borne more easily. Many women, now without their menfolk, turned out to work in factories, or at local hospitals, helping the wounded who were being sent home in their hundreds.

Flo clung to Charlie each night, eventually crying herself to sleep. 'Why do you have to go?' she asked time and time again.

'I just have to,' he said, 'it is my duty. I will write as often as I can. Just look after yourself, and Katherine, and be a good girl for the master and mistress, and Miss Dorcas, and when I return all will be well again, you will see.'

Katherine, trying to keep up a calm appearance, felt inwardly sick at the thought of Thomas going into battle. One evening as they sat quietly in Katherine's office, Thomas had asked her if she would consider acting as his next of kin. He had lost touch with his mother after some family rift, and his father had left them when he was just a small boy. He had no siblings, and he felt the need to have someone who could be notified if anything happened to him. Katherine cried, and said, although she would be happy to be his next of kin, she was unhappy at the reason for his asking her.

'Nothing will happen to you, Thomas. I couldn't bear it,' she said, thinking, 'Please, not again.'

'I hope not, Katherine, but no one knows what is out there, and I would feel so happy to know that you were close to me wherever I was. I am falling in love with you, Katherine. I think you know that. I would love to ask you to marry me. Would you ever consider it?'

Katherine, with no heart to rebuff him, knew that she would never marry him, but how could she tell him without explaining her reasons, and without hurting him. She couldn't do it now, not at this time. She had to send him away with at least a hopeful heart. 'Now is not the time, my dear Thomas. We all have to keep strong and see this through… just go, take my love with you, and come back safely.'

Mr Cloverleaf arrived at the house one morning. The news of Charlie and Thomas, and now Arthur, had reached his ears, and he came to offer his services to the family during their absence. Charlie had become fond of his tutor, and looked upon him as he would have an elder brother, and so he was relieved and very grateful to him for his kindness.

'I shall be honoured to serve in any way I can,' said Roger Cloverleaf to Mr Elford when he came personally to thank him, and accept his most welcome offer. 'Sir, it is but a small chore in comparison to what these brave lads have to face. I feel humble in their presence, and think that maybe both Charles and Arthur should be relieved of their duties here for the short time that they have left as civilians. I will gladly take over, and I trust that the Fitzgeralds will see fit to offer the same civility to Thomas.'

The Fitzgeralds did not see the situation in the same light, and unfortunately insisted that Thomas worked until the last day, whereupon they would allow him time to prepare for leaving. Arthur was allowed to go and spend his days with his wife and children.

Charlie decided to take Flo away for three days. They would go to Blackpool, and walk along by the sea, he proudly told Flo, who was so excited at being given the time off as well that she could hardly contain herself. Katherine helped her to pack, and with Thomas by her side she stood on the steps and waved them goodbye.

Thomas spent every minute that he could at the house. Lavinia Elford had noticed the change in Katherine, and gently commented that it was nice that she was there for Thomas, to make his last few days in England happy ones. Katherine smiled, but made no other comments. Lavinia didn't pursue the conversation; she hoped that Katherine would not keep all her secrets inside her forever, but she respected her right to do so if she wished. She had grown so fond of Katherine that she almost looked upon her as a close friend, and not a servant.

Flo and Charlie returned from their break looking refreshed and happy. They all had one more day before the boys would have to leave. Katherine had asked if she and Flo could go to the ship to say goodbye, and Lavinia said that she too would like to go and say her farewells. Dorcas Louise was at school until 4.30 so there would be plenty of time to get back for her. Cook would be going to the ship to see her son off; his wife had admitted that she could not face saying goodbye in front of hundreds of people, and so she would stay with the children, and their goodbyes would have to be said at home before he left. Thomas had been allowed the last afternoon off, and had packed all his belongings into his haversack, locked his door at the Fitzgeralds, and walked through the quiet streets to the Elfords. Cook had said that he could spend his last night at her house, so that he could have some time with Katherine.

That night the house had a restless quietness about it. Mr Cloverleaf had served the evening meal, and had retired into one of the guest rooms. Katherine had told Charlie to go to Flo, and she would lock up. Cook whispered to Thomas that she would leave the key to the front door under the stone pot in the garden.

At 7 o'clock, the following morning, she found it exactly where she had left it, and upon entering her kitchen she found a sleepy-eyed Katherine and Thomas sitting in front of her fire which had been lit by a thoughtful Mr Cloverleaf. They sat like two young children waiting for something to happen, they knew not what, but they knew it was not what either of them wanted. Cook made them some tea, neither wanted to eat, and Katherine had to see that Dorcas Louise got up and had her breakfast before leaving for school. Thomas, looking guilty, thanked Cook, and made his way to her house to pick up his luggage, and put on his uniform that she had laid out carefully for him on the bed.

At 9.30, the little party left the house, the men in uniform, proud but sad, and the women just openly sad. They arrived at the docks amidst such turmoil that they could hardly take in all that they saw. There were of course all the new soldiers in their equally new uniforms milling around, trying to work out which way to go, but also there were the wounded who had just left the very ship that would turn around and take the strong to a place where being wounded was probably inevitable. The sight of the wounded was a terrible shock to all who stood there, the bloody bandages, the missing limbs, the cries and groans of those in pain, and the look of helplessness in every pair of eyes.

Before they knew it, a call to board was issued in a loud booming voice, and the witnesses of the horror now became the victims, tearing themselves apart from their loved ones. Flo clung to Charlie, weeping, and Thomas held on to Katherine as if to take her with him was the only answer to his prayers. Arthur stood quietly, resolutely pushing back the tears as he hugged his mother, and asked her to take care of his children. Katherine, with a multitude of feelings churning in her stomach, reached up and kissed Thomas gently on the mouth, and whispered, 'Come home safely.'

The uniforms merged into one mass now as the men all surged toward the gangplank. The womenfolk, all trying to discern their own man in the crowd, had to give up in the end and just wave aimlessly, in the hope that the men recognised a hat or a scarf in the crowd. After an hour of massive movement, the troops were almost all on board, but the wounded were still there waiting for transport to take them to hospitals, or home, depending on the seriousness of their wounds.

Lavinia Elford suddenly said to Katherine and Flo, 'I feel that we ought to do something to assist in the welfare of these brave men. I would hope that someone would help ours in the same circumstances.'

Katherine jerked herself back into reality and, listening to Lavinia, thought what a wonderful tribute that would be to Charlie, Arthur, and Thomas, but at this moment she felt so exhausted that all she could say was, 'I will do anything, anything at all, anything.' They all nodded in agreement, and then walked in silence away from the abhorrent sights that in the next few years would become commonplace.

The theatre of war was anything but a picture of brave men marching to victory, or horses galloping toward their enemy carrying on their backs men in bright, coloured uniforms. Here it was drabness, men dug into ditches, living in fear of the shells that screamed overhead, missing their target and finding one of them. It was cold, wet, and muddy underfoot.

The uniforms that were so new a few weeks ago, were now stained and crumpled. The brave smiles for their loved ones as they left were now worried frowns and tight lips set in dirty, tired faces.

The old Ford truck that had been issued to Charlie and Thomas, was used mainly to get supplies to the front. One of them drove while the other was lookout. They thanked their lucky stars that they had been given the chance to ride together. Their missions were dangerous, and their driving skills were looked upon favourably by the company sergeant major. Speed and dexterity were called for in the effort to reach the front with their cargo, and then to drop it where it was needed, to escape without being caught or shot, and finally to get back behind the lines to prepare for the next run. It seemed only yesterday when they had sailed out of Liverpool, and yet they had been here in this place of terror and death for the last six months. Letters home had been written, but as yet none had found their way back to them.

At home in Liverpool, life was dreary for those who just sat around and mourned their existence, but the Elford family had taken it upon themselves, each and every one, to do what they could to help the sick and wounded. Mr Elford had agreed to finance a tea wagon, which was made by converting the back of a model T Ford belonging to, and donated by, one of his associates. Lavinia Elford herself ran this, and both she and Katherine agreed that Dorcas Louise was now old enough to learn about the tragedy of war. She was allowed to help her mother on Saturday afternoons when the wagon would be at the hospital near to the main entrance so that families visiting the wounded and sick could stop a while and discuss their problems with others in the same situation.

It was not at all usual to find women driving, but both Katherine and Lavinia had taken to the wheel. Katherine would now drive the Rolls Royce to take Dorcas Louise back and forth to school. There was no great reason to fear for her safety, but it was decided that she would not walk. Though the distance was not long, Katherine would take her, and two of her friends who lived a little further away. The school had, with the consent of parents or guardians, planned to continue teaching until such time when it was considered to be dangerous.

The never-ending lines of soldiers, some with the most terrible injuries, continued to pour from ships, and from trains which had tried to get the wounded as near to their home town as possible. As if all the death and injury of the war was not enough, the morning papers on May 8th 1915, had reported the sinking of the Cunard line ship 'The Lusitania'. It had been hit by a torpedo from a German submarine, and had sunk off the coast of Ireland on its return to Liverpool. It was feared that possibly 1,400 people had lost their lives. Just three years before that, in 1912, the White Star line 'Titanic' was lost, striking an iceberg on its maiden voyage. The loss of life then was estimated to be around 1,200. Two great ships that would have probably now been ferrying these poor souls away from the horrors of war-torn France.

The year of 1915 was nearly at an end, and for Thomas and Charlie, one day just drifted into another with sights that neither of them would have dreamed of witnessing. Friends they had made were no longer any more. They both had days that, if it were not for each other's company, they would have lost the will to survive. They ran the gauntlet of enemy fire, dodging flying shrapnel, and hitting potholes in the now non-existent road that they had to travel daily.

Sometimes on the return journey, they would have to pick up men who had sustained injuries that, although not serious, were enough to render them unable to carry out their instructions. They would clamber into the back of the truck, glad to be returning to near sanity for a while. They soon found that driving the truck needed nerves of steel, and a little foolhardiness sometimes had to be faced, whether or not it achieved the result that it aimed at.

The war dragged on into 1916, and in July the battle of the Somme depleted the British army by 60,000 men in a few days. Charlie and Thomas were now operating a near daily service, carrying ammunition to the front, and it felt like they were fighting a losing battle. The fatigue was growing across the land. They couldn't let it get the better of them because alertness and speed was the essence of their success, and they began to scratch the successful runs on the side of the old Ford truck which also now showed signs of battle scars.

Back home, where the women heard little of their menfolk, it was hard to understand why. Newspaper headlines told of massive losses in what seemed to be a never-ending battle. How many had to die before this futile war ended, and when it did, would the victors be able to say it was worth it?

Katherine received her letter first from Thomas who reported that both he and Charlie were unharmed and working together as a team. He said that there was not time to write all that he wanted to, but hoped that his being alive and well was good enough for the time being. He sent much love, and hoped that life in England was not too difficult. News travelled very slowly to where they were, and came very often from unreliable sources. He personally had received no mail, and hoped that it wasn't because Katherine hadn't written. He was sure that she had, and so would wait patiently. Katherine ran to the kitchen to tell Flo, who immediately burst into tears. 'Why hasn't Charlie written?'

'I'm sure he has,' Katherine said. 'It must be very hard to get every letter from every soldier, and send them all at once. At least you know that he is alive and well, and I'm sure that you will receive your letters soon.'

Cook also said that she hadn't heard from Arthur, and neither had his wife, which was a very great worry, but we just keep on hoping.

The tea wagon was a great success, and was now bringing a few extra volunteers who would take trays loaded with anything that could be spared, into the hospital and distributed amongst those who were well enough to eat. Lavinia organised anyone who could cook to keep up a regular supply of simple snacks that could be served cold. Cook was happy to turn out as many titbits as were needed, her pantry well stocked from local suppliers who knew her, and who admired the fortitude of the women doing this great service for the poor men back from the front.

Katherine, as often as she could get away from the chores of the house, went to the hospital, and visited some patients who had no relatives to sit by their side. She would read to them, or sometimes write a letter from them to a loved one miles away from where they were. She would listen to the tales they had to tell, sometimes funny things that happened, and sometimes so sad that she had to fight back tears. She learned of the horrendous conditions under which they had to exist, and the moments when they had to move forward into the unknown, and see the man beside them drop to the ground, to be picked up by a stretcher bearer, or just left there if the soul had already departed. There was a place called No Man's Land where, for a time each day, the stretcher bearers were allowed to go in unmolested to pick up the dead and dying, and return them to their own lines.

Each day that Katherine spent there was a little more harrowing than the one before, but the looks on the faces of the survivors who saw her coming was enough to boost her morale, and keep her returning.

One morning, Flo received, not one letter but two from Charlie, one telling her much the same as Thomas had told Katherine. The second was a little more personal, and she placed it in her pocket until she could sit alone in the bed upstairs in the loft, and read each line over and over. Charlie had also said that both he and Thomas had now received letters from her and Katherine, and they both had them next to their bodies, tied with pieces of bandage around their torso. Katherine smiled when Flo told her this and said, 'Silly dear fools that they are.'

Cook had received news from Arthur, which followed on from the one he had sent to his wife and children. 'It appears that he has been given the job of chef,' laughed Cook. 'I reckon with his cooking he could finish off the troops quicker than the Germans could.' His son would heartily agree with that. The moans and groans when he was left to serve breakfast could have been heard in the city centre. His daughter was still a mite young to give her opinion, but his wife rarely left him in charge of the oven, and no one could blame her, Cook remonstrated. Everyone laughed, but they were all so pleased that Arthur was well and, although at the front, would not have to meet the enemy hand to hand.

The winter had been especially hard, and Christmas had left them all less than optimistic. Neither side had gained the breakthrough that they had hoped and fought for, and the cost in lives had been immense.

Thomas and Charlie had a few bumps and scratches, but had survived many a close encounter that had caused some damage to the old faithful truck. They had in their few spare moments, kicked and pummelled at the dents in the old girl, spat and polished her, and sent her back into battle like the old war horse that she was.

The ammunition at the front line was getting low, and their trips from the arsenal, were now almost doubled in their frequency. The danger of collecting it and taking it to where it was needed was indeed high. Just one spark and they would be gone, but their cover was guaranteed by ground forces causing a diversion long enough to allow them to push through. The coming back however was a different dimension. They had no choice but to make a run for it with little or no cover, because no one knew exactly how long it took for them to unload their cargo and make their departure. The idea was to start very slowly, hardly making a shadow on the horizon, and then as the land in front of them opened up, to get their heads as low as they could, without obscuring their vision, give the old girl her head, and go like hell.

The shells that exploded around them, lit them up, and they were like sitting ducks. Now the whole thing was down to luck, and at the end of it, if they reached safety and still had all their limbs, they would leap from the truck with a whoop, and hug one another; one more success to chalk up on the old girl's bodywork.

At home, the Elford family carried on much as usual. For Mr Elford, the business associates that he had in America were reporting a prosperous 1916, and were putting their expertise into aircraft engine manufacture as well as ship building and the manufacture of munitions, with the intention of helping the war effort. This had created more foreign trade, and Mr Elford had invested heavily, ignoring those among his fraternity who were expecting the bubble to burst. His shares in the stock market had reached a new high, and his outlook for 1917, he said, was very favourable.

The caring for the sick and wounded was still a prime objective for his wife. Her daily visits to the hospital were always received with a genuine gratefulness, and her ladies, who ran around with trays of specials, as they called them, were given a hearty greeting from the recovering soldiers, and a smile from those who were not so well, but who loved to see someone from the outside world.

Dorcas Louise was enjoying her last year and a half at the school which she had grown to love. She had excelled in her subjects, and had received glowing reports from her teachers. For her, personally, the war had not invaded her life too much, although she hated to see Kat so worried about Charlie and Thomas. Flo, who used to love to sit with her when she was young, now didn't seem to want to stop and say hello, her eyes were always red from crying. On Saturdays, when her mother took her to the hospital, she would look at the poor soldiers who were so hurt, some of them crying for their mothers, and would sometimes go to them and hold their hands, and that made her want to cry too.

Cook was receiving mail more often than either Katherine or Flo, and they assumed it was because Arthur had stayed in the same place the whole time. Cooking was becoming easier now, although the day to day living was a nightmare. He had complained in one of his letters of, 'Mud up to your knees, stretcher bearers sinking trying to get the wounded to safety'. The picture he painted was indeed a sorry one, but at least it was a picture. It was four months now since a letter had come from Charlie or Thomas. They all assumed that they were still together on the battlefield, and that afforded them a little comfort.

News had been received from Adolphus that London had suffered its first bomb attack. It centred on the East End and had killed more than 100. There were about 15 aircraft, and they had encountered anti-aircraft fire from the ground, but had managed to drop a bomb on a school, and one on a railway station, hitting a train. Among the dead were ten children. He reported that he and Martha were well, and hoped to see Katherine soon, and of course said he would like first-hand information from Dorcas Louise on her education. He had heard from the head of the school, and had been suitably impressed at his god-daughter's success.

The battleground at Flanders had turned into a quagmire, and it was virtually impossible for men or vehicles to move. There were almost continuous rainstorms. Enormous craters were formed by large shells, and soon filled with water. By September, the allied forces had gained but a few hundred yards. The highest amount of shells was being unleashed and that, together with double the average rainfall, meant the mounting toll of missing persons became almost impossible to record. It was never absolutely positive whether those missing had been taken by the enemy, killed by enemy fire, or sucked in by the invading mud.

Charlie and Thomas had been given a mission that HQ had said was without a doubt the most dangerous run that had been undertaken, but it had to be made, and on information that they had received, Private Orchard, and Private Moreton were the two that could carry it through. The ammunition had been depleted at the front, and a large amount was available to be collected before sundown.

They would have to drive along the ridge to avoid being bogged down in the mud. There would be machine guns in pill boxes that could not be damaged by any amount of battering shellfire. Charlie and Thomas had done it hundreds of times before, but not in these conditions. They had been told that this would be the last run for the old Ford truck, as she had sustained some damage dangerously near to the petrol tank, and would be withdrawn from service after this run. There was no replacement vehicle ready, so the risk would have to be taken.

They set off as always quietly and slowly, not awakening much awareness of their movement. Eyes always alert, ready for a quick evacuation of the vehicle if the necessity became urgent. Making good progress, they could now see the vague outline of the building that was their destination. Shellfire seemed to be a little lighter than usual, or was it wishful thinking, or the unstinting energy that they built between them to accomplish the mission, and return in the shortest possible time. They had made it, and suddenly like black panthers, men crawled toward them, and relieved them of their cargo with just an acknowledgement of the hand.

Not speaking or leaving the vehicle, Thomas and Charlie turned around to head back the way they had come.

The shellfire was increasing and they decided this was not the time or the place to dally, so Thomas, now in the driving seat, hit the throttle hard; they both put their heads down and went. The blinding flash came first, before the Ford flew into the air. Then the crunching of metal, and the smell of burning, and finally the flames, and the voice of Thomas screaming 'Charlie'.

Chapter Eighteen

The High Price of Peace

Katherine was the first to see the boy on the bike riding slowly up to the front door. She knew the pale envelope held a telegram. Today there were two. The boy separated them from the pile that he held in his hand, all the same size, all the same colour. 'One for Carrera, and one for Orchard', he said in a matter of fact voice. Katherine took them from him without a word, and softly closed the door as the boy rode away. Hands shaking, she took them to the kitchen where Flo was preparing lunch. Gently she laid a hand on Flo's shoulder and passed her the telegram that was hers. Flo's eyes flew open, and she screamed 'No'. Katherine showed her the one that she had, and they both sat down together at the table, neither one wanting to be the first to open hers. Cook came in waving a letter from Arthur that had just been delivered, opened her mouth to speak, but stopped dead at the sight in front of her.

'Oh no,' she cried. Both girls, paper white and shaking, looked at her holding her letter. She quickly put it in her apron pocket and said, 'I'm so sorry.' In the end it was Flo who opened hers first and, with trembling voice, read aloud:

> *It is with great regret that I have to inform you that I have received a report stating that Private Charles A. Orchard is missing, feared dead, while on army duty in his country's service. I am to add that any information received following this report will be forwarded to you as soon as possible.*
>
> *I am your obedient servant. Officer in charge of records.*

Katherine then opened hers, and found that it read exactly the same. They clung to one another in disbelief.

'Both of them together, side by side, they must have fallen,' said a now desperate cook. 'We don't even know exactly where they were. A field somewhere in France, is all we know.'

Katherine had to go and tell Mr Elford. Her legs would hardly carry her upstairs; she had no tears left to cry. Angry inside, she thought bitterly, just another person that she had loved snatched from her. Mr Elford wrang his hands in desperation as he read her telegram.

'This bloody war; how many more of our young men are they to slaughter before they find an end to it? I am so sorry, Katherine.'

'Flo has one too, sir, exactly the same.'

He looked at her and said, 'Not Charlie. Oh no, not Charlie.'

'Yes, sir, I am afraid so.' Katherine faltered a little on the brink of tears that a moment ago would not come.

'I need nothing today. I have a business meeting,' said Mr Elford, 'and Cloverleaf is around if you need him. If you do see him, ask him to come and see me this evening if he will. Thank you, Katherine.'

Dorcas Louise was at school, and Mrs Elford came with words of comfort for both Katherine and Flo.

Cook went into the garden and read her letter from Arthur, who had suffered a few bruises from flying objects when a shell hit part of the food store just as he was entering, but he sustained no permanent damage, and was only tired of the torrential rain and the continuous sound of bombardment. He was however becoming quite a good cook, and would be surprising the kids when he got home. 'Please God,' whispered Cook, as her son's words seemed quite empty after the news that had just reached them about Charlie and Thomas.

The day dragged by. Katherine spent a lot of time with a devastated Flo who just kept repeating, 'Feared dead, feared dead.'

Dorcas Louise, arriving home from school, dreaded the moment when she would have to face Kat. Now nearly sixteen, and learning about life, and love, and all the traumas that both bring, she climbed the stairs to where Katherine was doing what she always did at this time of day. She was warming Dorcas's slippers in front of the fire, and putting a ready prepared light tea on the table for her. Dorcas slipped to her side, put an arm around her shoulder, and whispered, 'I'm so sorry, Kat, and would you tell Flo that I feel for her too?'

Katherine turned, and took her darling Dorcas in her arms, feeling her young and tender body warm and trembling against her. 'It's all right, darling. Thomas was a good man, a very close friend, and he would want us all to carry on and not be sad, and so would our wonderful Charlie. I think we will all be allowed to call him Charlie now, don't you?'

Dorcas replied, 'I always thought we should, but Mr Cloverleaf was always very strict, wasn't he?'

'He was indeed,' said Katherine, 'but he has also been extremely kind to us when we most needed someone, and his opinion of Charlie was without doubt the very best.'

That evening, after Mr Elford had spoken to Mr Cloverleaf, Flo, Cook, and Katherine were called to the library. Mr Elford sat at his desk, and Mr Cloverleaf stood by the side of the small table on which stood a bottle of champagne and seven glasses. Mrs Elford and Dorcas Louise entered the library and stood beside Mr Elford, as the rest of the staff gathered round, sad faces brushed aside for what it appeared was going to be a speech.

At the nod of consent from Mr Elford, Mr Cloverleaf moved one step forward and looking at each one of them slowly, and with a reverence befitting a man who had to deal with such a delicate situation, began, 'Mr Elford has asked me this evening if, in the circumstances, I could stand in for a while to replace Mr Orchard. I have agreed with no hesitation, and I will honour his absence in the best way that I know how. However, I am not here to take his place. I came to know the man very well, and knowing him taught me that he was a man of great courage and fortitude. I do not wish to raise false hopes in the heart of his wife, but I have a belief in my own heart that the fear talked about in the telegram may be only a fear. Read it again; it does not say "killed in action", or "died". No one knows that for sure, and until we have news to that effect, I think we should all have faith, and think positively, and in our hearts bring them home. They are undoubtedly together, Charlie and Thomas, and if the worst is realised, then at least we have the comfort of knowing that. I am going now to pour you all a glass of champagne. It is the one that Charlie... um... Mr Orchard always chose for the best occasions, and we are going to drink a toast. Yes, to absent friends, but to their strength and friendship, and to the health of their loved ones at home here tonight, and to their return. To Charlie and Thomas!'

Everyone raised their glasses, not only to the missing boys, but to the man who tonight endeared himself to all of those who stood beside him.

No one seemed to want to move, and even the Elfords stayed and talked. It was a special night, and somehow the sorrow of the day had lifted slightly, and a tiny spark of hope began to manifest itself in the hearts of them all. Time alone would tell, but if hope and faith could bring them back, then the Elford household was hanging on to them with every fibre of its being.

The days stretched endlessly, the sorrow eating into the very bones of Katherine and Flo. Lavinia kept up her support at the hospital, and now had quite a following of local women helping her. They had worked out a shift scheme so that it enabled them to have longer breaks, without depriving the patients of their services. Dorcas too gave of her time freely when she was not at school, and was beginning to show a responsible caring side to her nature that gave Katherine a special pride in her. Katherine, without fail, took Flo to the docks each day, and searched for hours amongst the sick and injured, for even the smallest clue to the fate of Charlie and Thomas, and with the undying hope that one day those dear familiar faces would be there patiently waiting to come home.

Instead of the shiploads of men returning getting less as the war progressed, they seemed to be increasing. How many men could there possibly be still out there somewhere in a muddy field in France who still had the strength to stand up, let alone fight. It had been a month now since the telegram, and Katherine was showing signs of exhaustion. Lavinia would sometimes find her quietly weeping in the nursery, sitting in the chair that she first sat in when she came to be a wet nurse for Dorcas Louise. One day she sat beside her and suggested that she took a few days off and went to see Adolphus. She had been working on a scheme that would appear to be a good excuse for Katherine to go without her thinking that she was being sent away.

'I want to give Dorcas Louise a surprise, and I need her out of the way for a few days. I was wondering whether you would take her with you. She will be so happy to go and see Adolphus. I don't think that they are in any great danger, any more than us, and I know that Martha will look after you both. I would be pleased if you would also ask them if they would do us the honour of spending Christmas here with us,' Lavinia concluded.

Katherine, although overjoyed at the prospect of staying with Martha and Adolphus, was terrified of not being there if word came through about Thomas or Charlie, and she was also worried about leaving Flo who continuously clung to her for comfort.

'We will take care of Flo, and there is Cook too who knows what it feels like to have a son fighting out there; she will look after her,' answered Lavinia, looking at a Katherine now near to collapse. 'There is no need to worry about the house, or us, and if any news, good or bad, arrives we will get it to you immediately, and deal with anything necessary straight away. Say yes, Katherine, and I will tell you of the surprise that I have in store for Dorcas Louise, and when you have agreed, I will go and tell her that she will be going with you.'

Katherine sank among the pillows in the chair and, in an almost inaudible whisper, said, 'Yes please.'

'Good,' said Lavinia, standing up and looking around the nursery. Dorcas would never allow her to touch it, only to replace the little bed for one that her feet didn't fall over the end of, and that she could turn over in without hauling herself back from the edge. Lavinia said, 'I am going to have two rooms and a bath closet turned into a small apartment for her. She is fast reaching the end of her education, and I don't know what she is going to do with herself, but I feel that she should have a little independence, and be able to entertain her friends. I will do nothing to the nursery, or your room, unless you would like to change your bedroom for another, and that could be done with no trouble at all. I just ask that you mention none of this to Dorcas, so that if she hates it when it is done, then she can stay where she is for as long as she likes. How do you feel about it, Katherine?'

Katherine raised her head, a little colour coming back into her cheeks with interest in Lavinia's plan. 'I think it is a wonderful idea, and Dorcas Louise is a very lucky young lady indeed to have parents such as you and Mr Elford, and yes I would love to go to Adolphus, and take Dorcas with me. Shall I make the arrangements?'

'No, I will, after I have spoken to her,' said a relieved Mrs Elford, who now had to put the rest of her plan into action. She was waiting at the door as Dorcas arrived home from school, waving goodbye to her friend whose mother had driven them both home.

Lavinia took Dorcas by the arm and led her into the library. 'What is it Mother?' Dorcas said, concerned that there may be bad news.

Sitting her down with a cup of tea and a biscuit, her mother proceeded to say, 'I want you to do something for me. You know that Katherine is feeling very low at the moment, and I am quite worried about her. I am going to send her to London to stay with Adolphus for a while, and I would like you to go with her. I don't want her to travel alone, but also I don't want you to mention the conversation that you have just had with me. I need her to think that it is because I want you to go during your break from school to give Adolphus a full report on your achievements. Will you do this for me, Dorcas?' Lavinia asked.

'Mummy, I would love to,' exclaimed Dorcas, 'and I will look after Kat, I promise.'

'I know you will,' said Lavinia with a smile. 'I will arrange it for next week.'

Plan accomplished, Lavinia set the arrangements into motion and patted herself on the back.

Martha was of course delighted, but worried at the same time that Katherine, once again, was to suffer the agony of loss. This time, seemingly, it had shaken her self confidence which shocked Martha, knowing what she had coped with in the past on her own a great deal of the time. It would be good to cosset her for a while. Adolphus too was concerned and desperately wanted to see Katherine. She had always been the joy of his life, since he had found her on the boat all those many years ago. Old age had treated him kindly, and he still had the air of a well-to-do gentleman, but when his thoughts strayed to Katherine, he thought of the days when, lost in the contents of his writings, she had been by his side, unfaltering in her commitment to his unknown success, not caring what he looked like when he was unshaven, and trusting him with the story of her life. He loved her, he imagined, as he would have loved a daughter, and now she had given him the chance to share the life of another child, not as beautiful as her, but with her own special personality that he found enchanting.

Also, he now shared his existence with the woman who had given life to Katherine, and suffered intolerable violence because of it. He wanted to have them all together here more than anything in the world, and if it was only to be for a few days at a time, so be it. He would enjoy every moment, and he would hopefully send Katherine home a little better for his love and Martha's care. The train arrived on time, and Adolphus as always was there waiting. He stood at the edge of the platform, hatless, cane in hand, impatiently tapping the ground. Dorcas Louise, leaning from the window, saw him first, and frantically waved her hat that her mother had insisted she wore.

'All elegant young ladies wear hats when they travel,' she had said with a quick glance at Katherine who quickly snatched hers from the hall stand and placed it at a rakish angle on her head.

Adolphus caught sight of her and returned her wave as the train strained on its brakes and stopped. Opening the door, she jumped from the train and, then remembering Kat and their luggage, climbed back aboard, ushered Katherine out, and struggled out herself with two valises.

'Go ahead, Kat, I can manage these,' she said, making a face at the indulgent Adolphus, who was now at Katherine's side, taking her arm and gently leading her from the busy concourse.

'Good girl,' Adolphus cried, 'follow us.'

Once aboard the waiting automobile, he planted a kiss on both of their cheeks and said, 'It is wonderful to see you both, and looking so beautiful too.' He glanced at Katherine, thinking she is indeed beautiful but she is tired and worried. He had seen that look before and he knew she was suffering, as she had suffered the loss of her child, and the loss of Joseph, so was there more to this young man called Thomas than met the eye. He was aware that he had spent a lot of time at the Elfords but was not sure how close a friend he had become to Katherine. He would speak to Martha and ask her opinion.

In the meantime, he meant for his two girls to have a good time in London, and in spite of the war and its restrictions, he was sure he could arrange some shopping trips, and some outings that would hopefully take their minds off the constant reminder of the fighting, and their unstinting work with the returning troops, both sick and wounded, as had been described to him by Lavinia when she arranged their stay with him.

Martha was at the door, drying her hands on her apron as they arrived. Adolphus, taking Katherine's hand, helped her from the vehicle. She flew to Martha's side and buried herself in her arms, neither speaking, both just holding one another as if the strength of one could overcome the weakness of the other.

'Oh mama,' Katherine whispered, out of earshot of Dorcas Louise. 'It is so wonderful to be with you.'

'It is always wonderful to me too, my darling,' Martha whispered back.

Dorcas Louise then came running up the drive like a young gazelle with legs and arms going in all directions. All three of them stood there like statues while Adolphus looked on thinking, perhaps he had three girls to care for now. He secretly thought that he could never want or ask for anything more in his life than he had at this moment, standing here with luggage at his feet in the middle of his drive that up to now had witnessed no one but himself, and his old housekeeper walking to and fro. Normality regained, the driver brought the luggage to the door. Martha stood aside and indicated for him to take it into the hall. Adolphus, joining them, agreed that a pot of tea and some sandwiches would be most acceptable, and thus they all entered the lounge where Martha had laid a small table with delicate china cups and saucers, two silver pots, one with tea and one with water, a plate of delicious looking cucumber sandwiches, and in the centre a cake stand full to the brim with tiny iced cakes. Their stay with Adolphus started here, and for an instant, the trauma and worry was lifted from Katherine's brow as she looked at Martha, smiled and said, 'Thank you'.

Responding to the loving kindness bestowed upon her by Adolphus and Martha, Katherine began to feel a little less hopeless. In the days that followed their arrival at the now finished house with two front doors, Katherine and Dorcas Louise were escorted by Adolphus to some of the finer shops and restaurants in England's capital city. The residents of the sprawling area of the north and the city limits were only too aware of the ensuing war, and moved around with a certain awareness of a possible air attack as had happened not so long ago when women and children were killed. Adolphus commented wisely that life had to carry on, and we could not allow the enemy to frighten us from our own streets.

Dorcas Louise regaled Adolphus with stories of her life at the school for young ladies, and continually thanked him for being responsible for her being sent there. She spoke to him in French, and was amazed when he answered her. She walked serenely around in front of him to show off her deportment to the best of her ability, to which he applauded with great enthusiasm. She confided that she found maths a little difficult, but Katherine was helping her by giving her little jobs to do from the office that required a certain amount of mathematical skill. Adolphus smiled at that, remembering how Katherine had cringed at the sight of his expenses accrued in the months of travelling by sea. She would pore over them for hours, until finally she realised her success, and presented a perfect sheet of figures to the ever patient Adolphus. Dorcas gave her final report about the friends that she had made, and her work at the hospital which, in spite of the horrors she saw, she loved.

Adolphus was indeed very impressed with the young Dorcas, and said that as a reward he would take her shopping to the West End of London, and she could choose some clothes which she would soon need for her initiation into the social life of a young lady of her standing. Katherine was to stay with Martha, as Adolphus wanted to spoil Dorcas just a little, without seeing a look of disapproval on the face of her beloved Kat; besides he wanted Katherine and Martha to spend some time together.

Off they set the next morning, each one in their own personal bubble of excitement. Adolphus had never been near the ladies' departments housed in the recently completed Selfridge store. Dorcas, eyes popping at the beautiful colours and feminine designs that presented themselves before her, gripped his arm tightly. She dragged him through display after display of exquisite gowns, shoes, and delicious handbags, until finally he begged her to take a break and join him for a relaxing cup of tea. It was approaching the afternoon and, following a light lunch, Dorcas decided that she just could not manage another bag.

Adolphus laughingly said, 'If you can't carry it, young lady, then I'm afraid that you can't have it. So, let us go. I have one more purchase to make, and it will not laden you down with its weight, but I hope that it will outlast all these fine clothes that I have had the pleasure of buying for you today.'

They left the department store, and took a short walk to a jewellery shop whose windows shone and sparkled from every angle that Dorcas Louise looked at them. Adolphus rang the bell, and a gentleman in a uniform came and opened it for them to enter.

'Good afternoon, Mr Fry. I trust you are well,' he said with a slight bow.

'Very well, Mr Gordon,' Adolphus answered. 'This is my god-daughter whom I told you about. She is about to finish her education, and as I mentioned I want her to have something special as a memento and a reward for her hard work, and for growing into such a delightful young lady. Have you been able to complete my commission?'

'I have indeed, sir, and I think you will agree that it will be something very special indeed for such a young lady, and I hope it will give her many years of pleasure, and that she will carry with her as she wears it the memory of an extremely generous and loving godfather.'

Dorcas, standing amidst a pile of bags and boxes, could hardly contain herself as the jeweller reached beneath the counter, and withdrew a small velvet box with a gold clip. He passed it to Adolphus, who turned away from Dorcas Louise, and opened it, and with a look of total approval, he turned, closed the box, and gave it to Dorcas Louise. With trembling hands, she opened it and gasped at the watch that lay upon the velvet cushion. It was fashioned in gold, not small, but not too large. It had a pale face with gold hands that had a tiny diamond set in the points of both hands. Diamonds encrusted the surrounding edge of the case, and at each side they formed a cluster which held a heavy but delicately decorated gold bracelet. The clasp that held the bracelet was also of diamonds that had a tiny chain linking the two ends, so as to safeguard it against falling from the wrist, should the bracelet come undone. Dorcas, tears in her eyes, turned to Adolphus and said, 'It is more beautiful than anything that I have ever seen; even Mummy's jewellery will never be as beautiful as this.'

'Turn it over,' said Adolphus. Dorcas followed his instruction and read the message engraved neatly on the back of the watch.

For Dorcas Louise Elford.
From your godfather
Adolphus Fry
London 1917.

Dorcas Louise handed him back the watch gently and said, 'Please look after it until we get home. Thank you, Uncle Adolphus.'

They bade the jeweller goodbye, and returned to the bustling street. Dusk was beginning to enfold the few shoppers still gazing into the bright windows. Adolphus promised that their driver would be here very shortly to take them back to the house. Dorcas slipped her hand into his and moved close to him, trying to remember just when this elegant, wonderful elderly man entered her life, and wondering how Kat had become so much a part of his life before she had. She was still musing quietly on the subject when Adolphus bundled her and all her possessions into the motor car, and they were on their way home.

It was a rare and precious thing for Martha and Katherine to spend time together, and today they cherished every moment, exchanging snippets of experiences that they had had in the last few months. Katherine had asked how Martha was finding life back in the country of her birth, and spending her days looking after Adolphus.

'Life,' Martha said, 'was what it was.' She had never known what life was until Adolphus lifted her from the squalor and horrible memories of her life in Italy, and she was still unable to talk about the days after the terrible event that took Katherine from her. The nightmares returned only occasionally now, but when they did, they were vivid and violent. Adolphus was kindness itself. She told of the trip that they had taken to India, and of the profound effect it had had on Adolphus. It was as if a kind of peace had descended upon him and embraced her in its serenity. She would, if it was what he wanted, serve him until the end of her days, and be happy to do so. She told her that Adolphus had admitted that she, Katherine, had been the sole reason for his success, and for his book becoming famous worldwide, much to his amazement and utter joy. Katherine, sitting comfortably in the big old sofa in the lounge with Martha, began to feel herself wind down; her hands that had been two clenched fists for the last few weeks, now sat in her lap gently folded.

Martha sat and looked at her and said, 'Do you want to talk to me, darling? You always came to me when anything was worrying you, and I feel that something is now. I know you are terribly upset about Charlie and Thomas, and I fully understand that; not knowing for sure what has happened is worse than the worst news. You must just keep hoping, you and Flo, and if the time comes when hope is lost, then you must comfort each other. Has Thomas any family? They must be feeling much as you do. Have they been in touch?'

Katherine, now clutching at the smallest straw to tell Martha everything, she looked at her, and saw her as she was when as a small child she sat and nestled into her ample body, and poured out her troubles to have them wiped away along with the tears. She took a deep breath and replied to Martha's questions.

'Thomas has no family, Mama; his father left them when he was small, and he lost touch with his mother, when at twelve years old he started to look for work, and finally landed up in the employ of Mr and Mrs Fitzgerald who have shown little interest in his wellbeing. I have allowed myself to become his allotted next of kin, which I am more than pleased to be. He has proved to be a great friend to Charlie, helping him with the motor carriage, and helping out Mr and Mrs Elford. They seem to have taken a shine to him.'

Martha, having let her proceed on the subject of Thomas, now asked, 'And you, Katherine dearest, have you too taken a shine to him?'

Katherine, turning to Martha, eyes bright with tears, replied, 'Yes, Mama, I was beginning to like him very much, and we happily spent time talking to one another when he often spent his off duty hours in the company of Cook and the rest of us. He asked me just before he left to go to war if I would consider marrying him. Mama, I couldn't say "No" at that moment, it would have been so cruel, but I could never marry him, not with all that has happened to me in my past. I would have to tell him everything, and I can't do that. I can't risk him knowing that Dorcas Louise is my child, and worse still it would implicate you if I confided in him. Those are the two most important reasons why I would have to say no, but my story doesn't end there, does it? There is my real father, probably still alive, and then there are the terrible happenings between you and my stepfather, and lastly, but by no means least, there is Adolphus and his reputation to consider. No, it would have to be "No". Can you see, Mama, throughout my life, I have in some way been a part of a destiny which has befallen the people who I have loved, and who have loved me, and if Thomas is dead, then destiny has stepped in again and stolen a love from me. I am so happy at the Elfords, looking after Dorcas, and being almost a part of their family, but I am so terribly sure that in some way I have visited death upon Thomas, and in doing so I have dragged Charlie down too. I do love Thomas and I hope and pray with all my heart that they are alive somewhere in that carnage over there, and if they are I will have to find a way of letting Thomas know I love him, and hope that he will accept my refusal of marriage for what it is, and not because I have no feelings for him.'

The front door slammed, and a delirious Dorcas Louise flew into the lounge, planting an enormous kiss on the cheek of Martha, and throwing her arms around Katherine, followed by an equally delirious, but much quieter Adolphus, who entered with his usual decorum, placing a pile of boxes and bags carefully on the floor in front of the sofa.

'Please, Martha, would you kindly bring me a cup of tea with three sugars? In spite of the shortage, my need is very great at this moment to sit down and drink until the last drop has gone.'

Martha smiled, turned to Katherine, ran her hand down her cheek, looked at Adolphus, and said sweetly, 'Of course, sir, with pleasure.'

Adolphus sank back into his cushions and took refuge in the tray which Martha planted on his lap with his favourite biscuits, and his much longed for cup of tea. Dorcas Louise, by this time, was becoming desperate to show off all her purchases, but most of all her watch that Adolphus still had in his possession. She would wait until he had finished his repast and then she could hold it once again, and place it on her wrist so that the world could see it.

Meanwhile, sitting on the floor in the middle of all the brightly coloured bags, and square boxes which were suddenly issuing forth tissue paper, Dorcas started to pull the contents randomly from their packaging. There was a dress, a coat, a pair of shoes, and some silk underwear.

Adolphus at this point stated that he had nothing to do with the selection; he had merely paid the bill. There was an evening dress, and a tiny fur cape caught at the neck by a pearl clasp. Katherine sat still, not quite believing what she was witnessing.

'Adolphus,' she said. 'Do you not think that you have been a little too extravagant?'

'I knew you would say that,' retorted Adolphus. 'That is why I left you at home. I needed some practice so that when I take you I will know what to buy, besides, if I can't be extravagant with my god-daughter then who can I be extravagant with?'

'I rest my case,' said the defeated Katherine, smiling at her beloved Adolphus.

Finally, when the fashion parade was over, and Adolphus was resting in his chair completely satisfied, if not a little smug, he said to Dorcas, 'Would you not like to show Martha and Kat the final gift that I have bought for you on this special day?'

'Oh, yes please,' said Dorcas, jumping up and going to Adolphus. He removed the box from his pocket and handed it to her. 'Shut your eyes,' she demanded of them both as she undid the clasp. Martha and Katherine duly obeyed her, and then she said, 'Open them.'

They both gasped in amazement as she held the watch before them. 'That is so beautiful,' said Katherine, as Martha just sat open-mouthed.

'Turn it over,' said Dorcas, 'and see what Uncle Adolphus has written.' They both read the inscription, as Dorcas said in a most emphatic voice, 'I shall wear it until I die.'

Adolphus smiled and said, 'It may not last that long.'

The days with Adolphus and Martha went too quickly for Katherine. She felt better for telling Martha about Thomas, but now had to face the fact that she may never be able to tell him how she felt. She knew that Martha would discuss it quietly with Adolphus, and she had given her permission to do so. She felt stronger now in body and in mind, and she, like so many women who had lost their loved ones in this war, supposedly to end all wars, would carry on and care as best she could for those who survived and needed help. As they said their goodbyes at the door, and promised all to be together at the Elford house for Christmas, Katherine realised that it would be so different this year with no Charlie, no Thomas, and possibly no Arthur, for although the news from Arthur came with great regularity, there was no guarantee that he would be home. She would do her utmost to see that they all had the best time that they could, and at least they were lucky enough to have a roaring fire to sit by.

It had been decided by Mr and Mrs Elford that the rules of the house would be discarded, and that on Christmas day they would all spend it together. Martha would be there to help Cook, and Flo would lay up the tables. Mr Cloverleaf would officiate, and then they would all drink a toast to each other, and to those who could not be there with them. Going home now seemed more acceptable.

The train station was crowded, and there were many young men in uniforms mingling with the civilian passengers. It was hard to tell whether they were going away, or coming home. Their uniforms looked smart enough, and their kit bags seemed tidily packed, but their faces looked pale and sad. Katherine's eyes, as always, scanned the crowd for those one or two familiar faces, but they were not there. They passed over their tickets and boarded the train for Liverpool. Dorcas now had an extra valise that Adolphus had lent her to put all her new purchases in. She jumped aboard first, and then took Katherine's bag from her, and helped her lift it onto the rack above their heads. Her own two bags followed, and then they sat opposite one another, both in a seat nearest to the window.

Dorcas glanced at Katherine and thought that she looked a little better than when they left a few days ago for London. She loved Kat, and hated to see her unhappy and unwell as she had been lately. Now that she had finished school, perhaps she would be able to spend some time with Kat, and help her. What would she do with her life now, she wondered. She did like going with her mother to the hospital but that would soon stop when the war was over. Christmas was a couple of months away, so she would wait until after the holidays, and see what her mother had in mind. She settled into her corner and thought of all her lovely clothes, and when she could wear them, and she thought of showing off her beautiful watch to her mother. Katherine's thoughts were of a far different nature, but watching Dorcas she had no doubt where her thoughts were heading. Katherine could see the beginnings of a confident, beautiful woman, and that gave her a pleasure that she would never have dreamed of.

Lavinia Elford was halfway down the stairs when her daughter flew past Mr Cloverleaf as he opened the door for the returning travellers. She hugged her mother and, words falling over one another, began to tell her of the day that she had spent with Adolphus. Managing to guide her upstairs and into the nursery, Lavinia sat her down, as Flo arrived with afternoon tea. Katherine arrived eventually, after talking to Mr Cloverleaf and confirming that the house had run without problems while she had been away. She never had any doubts on that subject, but thought it was nice to ask, and to thank Mr Cloverleaf for everything that he had done. It had, she commented, made her recovery very much easier knowing that the house and its occupants were in safe hands.

Lavinia welcomed her back with open arms, and said how much she had missed her, and of course Dorcas Louise, who by now was bursting with excitement. She just could not wait any longer and, nearly sending her cup of tea flying across the table, she held out her wrist for her mother to catch the first glimpse of the extraordinary timepiece that peeped out from beneath the frilled cuff of one of the silk blouses that had found itself tucked into her purchases from Selfridges store in London. Her mother gasped, and looked at Katherine who shrugged her shoulders and said, 'A doting godfather.'

She then proceeded to remove the watch and pass it to her mother in order that she may read its inscription. Following on from that, all the parcels had to be undone one at a time, and passed to her mother for her approval. She commented that this was in fact the first time she had been allowed to shop for herself, and she believed that she had done really well. Uncle Adolphus had not interfered in any way, except when it was time to go to the jewellers' shop. Having reached the last package, she heaved a great sigh, and said, 'That was the most wonderful day of my life.'

Her mother, after inquiring as to Katherine's wellbeing, and noticing a big improvement which she had no hesitation in commenting on, stood up and said, 'Well, I really don't know if I can compete with Uncle Adolphus, but I do have a surprise for you, Dorcas Louise.'

Katherine shot a quick glance at Lavinia, and smiled as Lavinia nodded in her direction. 'Follow me, both of you.' She led them to the end of the corridor where the large window looked down on to the courtyard beyond the building that had been erected for the motor vehicle, and for Charlie and Flo's sleeping area, then opened the door just before the end which had been one of the best guest rooms that the house boasted. She bade Dorcas Louise to step inside. The room had been divided by a large book case that reached across the room, leaving just enough space for a door, which had shelves above it. The shelves were full of books on varying subjects, some with dust covers, some without. The door opened to an exquisite bedroom, decorated in the palest shade of blue, with a white ceiling, which had at its centre, a circle of darker blue around which tiny gold cherubs held gold chains that looped into the centre of the circle and held a small but perfect crystal chandelier. Matching cherubs also adorned the corners of the room.

The bed was large, and was covered in a white silk throw that flowed to the ground. The furniture was elegant in its entirety, and included a wardrobe that would house many more outfits than those which she had brought back from London. This thought passed through Lavinia's head at the same time as the thought that Dorcas had not yet realised that this was to be all hers. There was also a chest of seven drawers, all neatly adorned with gold handles. A dark blue carpet completed the scene.

Once back through the door, their eyes encountered the highly polished wooden floor which housed a beautiful cream coloured rug sitting at the feet of those who would grace the dark red couch. A small gilt armchair with matching red seat was placed at the side of a perfect round table, just large enough for afternoon tea, or drinks for guests as required. Against the wall behind the main door stood a desk, not large in its proportions, but with all the necessities for the writing of letters, or for use as an office desk should it be needed. The decor of this room, although not pretty like the bedroom, was tastefully done with walls of cream and adorning a white ceiling, another beautiful chandelier.

One more door to go, at right angles from the connecting door from sitting room to bedroom, housed a bathroom in gleaming white with gold trimmings. Towels had been carefully folded and hung on a rail beside the bath, and a little white cupboard placed to house the toilet needs of its owner. A vase of white chrysanthemums that sat on its top had been the final touch. As they all turned to leave, the fire crackled in the grate set in the white fireplace on the only remaining wall. None of them had made any comments throughout the viewing, and Lavinia was the first to speak.

'What do you think of it?' she addressed her audience expectantly.

'Absolutely beautiful,' said Katherine, turning and waiting for comment from Dorcas Louise.

'It is most beautiful,' said Dorcas Louise. 'Which of your guests will be lucky enough to stay in these rooms, Mother?'

'Well, I was rather hoping that my daughter would like it enough to move from the nursery suite into here,' said Lavinia, looking straight at Dorcas Louise.

'Me,' said Dorcas. 'Me… have this all to myself?'

'Yes,' replied Lavinia, 'if you would truly like it, if not, you may stay where you are. It doesn't mean that you have to be in here, and not visit us or Kat in the nursery. I know you have always loved it in there, but I feel that you should have some independence now, and entertain your friends if you wish in the privacy of your own apartment. Does it appeal to you?'

'Oh, does it!' Dorcas cried, eyes shining. 'Oh, yes please.'

'Did you know about this, Kat?' she accused.

'I cannot tell a lie,' Katherine admitted, knowing that the ruse had worked, and not only for Dorcas Louise, but for her too. Lavinia was indeed a very loving and kind person, and she had been extremely lucky finding herself, against all the odds, being here with all the good things that were attached to her life because of the extreme kindness and forethought of a man met in extenuating circumstances who had become the centre of her being, and the lifelong friend of this her extended family.

Katherine and Lavinia left Dorcas Louise staring in amazement at her new domain, and they headed back to the nursery.

'Katherine,' asked Lavinia, 'are you happy in the bedroom that you have? If not, I would be pleased to give you another room. As you will see, when you have a chance to look, I have taken the liberty of directing my decorators to freshen up your room, and have purchased as a gift from me to you some new linen for your bed. I do hope that you approve. For the time being I have decided to leave Dorcas Louise's room as it is. She will want to move things from there to her new room, and I thought that I would leave her bedroom as it is. It may come in useful in the future if we have any children staying with parents who are our guests. It would be nice for them to have you to care for their children during their stay. Would that be acceptable to you?'

Katherine answered, 'It's a lovely idea, and one that I would happily agree to, and, no, I would not like to change my room. I love it there, it has so many memories, and I am happy when my work is done to relax here in the nursery.'

Lavinia smiled, her job accomplished. Dorcas Louise, by the end of the day, had the entire contents of her old bedroom happily removed to her new quarters. Clothes hung in neat straight lines in the wardrobe, drawers were packed to capacity and, because she just couldn't leave them behind, bear and bunny now had pride of place upon the bed quilt. Her bookcases were a little devoid of literature, but in time she would fill them to capacity, she stated.

Katherine went to her room and came back with a book. She passed it to Dorcas Louise and said, 'This book is one of the most precious things that I have ever owned. You were too young when I was given it, so you will not be aware of its importance. Your Uncle Adolphus wrote it, and gave me the first copy, which you will see if you open it. I made a long journey and found myself in his company, and I, in some small way, helped him to keep his writings in order. As you know, he is now the most special person in my life, and he has touched your life too because of it. Your father knew him before I did, and so he really has become part of this family, and you are indeed lucky in the extreme to have him as your godfather. I want you to keep and treasure this book, even if you are not interested in its content. One day it will be important that you have it.'

Dorcas took it, ran her hands over its cover, opened it and read its inscription. To Katherine's great surprise, she reached for a handkerchief and wiped the tears from her eyes. 'I will treasure it always, Kat,' said Dorcas, as she placed it gently to one end of an empty shelf on her bookcase. Tonight she would spend her first night as an independent young woman, sleep in her new large bed, and in the morning arrange her own bathing schedule, and try and arrive on time for breakfast.

Katherine for her part would miss her early morning conversations with Dorcas, but had to accept the fact that now she was an adult, and would soon be appearing on the social circuit with all the trials and tribulations that would ensue from that. She herself had never known what that was like. At Dorcas's age, she had already borne a child, and faced things that she knew Dorcas would never have to face. With that blessing understood, she prepared herself to return to the duties of the household, and start to make inroads into the preparations for Christmas. She would go and see Cook, and see how Flo had been keeping up with the agony of each day without any news from the front. It had been nearly a month now since the telegrams had shattered their lives.

Cook was still receiving mail from Arthur, and it told of the terrible conditions out there, still little headway for the allied troops, and battles being fought now across borders in other lands which the poor soldiers who had spent months in ditches didn't understand. They thought that the war was there where they were in that one damned field from which there seemed no escape, except to be carried out by stretcher, and so many of them were doing exactly that. The ones left wondered if that was perhaps the only answer, but none of them wanted to go there.

Flo still cried a lot, and would not sleep upstairs in the barn, as they all called it. 'I will sleep there when my Charlie comes back, and not before,' she said adamantly. She would go quietly to her little box room each night, and settle on the mattress there, as she used to before she was married.

The house was quiet. Mr Elford would hold no parties, partly because of all the serving men being absent, and also the restrictions on food. His business aspects were thriving, and the stock market shares, especially those of the United States of America, were flying high. He was looking ahead to doing great deals across the Atlantic when this war came to an end, yet there seemed no visible signs of that happening at present.

Katherine spent time with Mr Cloverleaf, discussing how thrifty they would need to be with the Christmas fare. It was decided that, as there would be so few of them present, and there were no plans to invite guests, only Adolphus and Martha, who were really more family than guests, they could afford to buy the best that was available, and make the days as happy as they could be under the circumstances. There would be the usual gifts under the tree, and all the trimmings on the table. There would be brandy poured over the Plum Pudding, and set alight. They would invite the local carollers in for mince pies and mulled wine. Dorcas Louise was upset when she was told that there would be no hanging up of her stocking on Christmas Eve, so they all relented with a chuckle, and allowed her the honour just one more time.

Flo and Katherine still trudged daily down to the docks and searched the rows of waiting injured and sick soldiers in the vain hope of finding at least one of the dear faces of their loved ones, but with each day the hope and resilience became harder to endure. They visited the hospital to see if any prior notice had been given of injured or sick troops being sent home, but all to no avail. Each time they returned with a heavy heart, and the beginnings of a horrible truth being realised.

October passed, and November brought the ugly dark fogs that descended without warning, turning the street lights into faded halos of light that did nothing to brighten their paths home. For something to do, Katherine suggested that they bring the Christmas decorations down from the loft, and place them in the office, where they could at any time begin to sort them out, and do repairs on those that had suffered damage at their last airing. They all, at some time or other, took time out, and sat by the fire in Katherine's office, gently teasing out the paper decorations into recognisable shapes. As each one was finished they were gently placed behind the sofa in long lines. The boxes of precious glass ornaments were emptied on to the floor and carefully wiped with a soft cloth until they shone, and then replaced in the box ready to be hung on the Christmas tree on Christmas Eve, as was the tradition. The tree would be delivered during the first week of December, and stand in the porch outside until it was planted in the giant tub that would be repainted. Mr Cloverleaf had volunteered for this job in the absence of Arthur.

A letter from Arthur had brought the news that he would not be allowed leave for Christmas; he was needed to cook for the men who had little enough to celebrate. At least he would be able to put a little something special on for them, depending what was on offer of course. He was fine, and gaining quite a reputation for 'doing good grub' they all said. His wife and Cook of course were disappointed, but at least they knew he was all right, and had access to sending mail without any trouble. He always asked for any news of Charlie and Thomas, as he was not in the area that they were, and no news got to him. He relied on contact with home for any information, though sadly there was none.

In early December, there was a light dusting of snow, just enough to give the garden that magical look that the mind always associates with Christmas. It didn't last very long, and the cold days just passed by with very little enthusiasm for those who had part of their families missing. The Elford house began to look a little festive with holly and mistletoe decorating its doors and hallway, and the paper decorations, tenderly prepared, now being hung in the drawing room. All was completed, and the house awaited the arrival of the tree, which was being carried with considerable difficulty by Mr Elford and Mr Cloverleaf to be stood in its place of honour in front of the window. It was the night before Christmas Eve and the tree would stand in waiting until the morning, when each and every one of the household would place bauble after bauble on its branches. In spite of themselves, they all felt a little of the feeling of excitement that Christmas always brings.

Katherine, unexpectedly, awoke a little later than usual and found Dorcas Louise sitting in her old chair in the nursery. Smiling sweetly at Katherine, and looking freshly scrubbed, she told her that she had already asked for breakfast, and that her mother, sitting at the dining table with her father downstairs, asked her if she would like to join them, and that she had declined the offer in favour of sharing breakfast with Kat. 'I am truly honoured, darling,' said Katherine. 'I always enjoy our breakfast chats, as long as your mother does not object.'

'She doesn't,' said Dorcas, 'and after all it is almost Christmas.'

'That is true,' answered Katherine, 'and when we have finished here, I would like nothing more than to walk with you to the park. Will you go with me, Dorcas?'

'I certainly will, but only if we can feed the ducks,' giggled Dorcas.

Katherine laughed. 'Of course we will, and then we must start to decorate the tree. The two of them set off, Dorcas holding on to Kat's arm. The morning was cold but bright, the sun pale in the winter sky. A bag of bread clutched in her other hand, Dorcas was humming 'Away in a manger' as she walked in quiet contentment with her Kat. They sat on the seat that Adolphus used to like to sit on when she was a baby. She could now throw the bread quite easily into the water, and she turned to Katherine and laughed as the ducks came to the water's edge to snatch a quick meal. Katherine put an arm around her, and said, 'I would have been very proud to have had you as a daughter, Dorcas. Don't let anyone change you.'

Dorcas looked at her and said, 'Have you ever loved anyone more than anything in the world, Kat?'

Stunned, Katherine found it hard to find words to answer her, so she simply said, 'Yes, darling, I have, a long time ago, many years before you were born. Why do you ask?'

'You have been so sad lately, and I have been thinking that you need someone to love.'

'I love you, Dorcas, and I love your mother, and father, Flo and Cook, and of course, Charlie, Thomas, and Arthur, not forgetting Adolphus and Martha. I love you all, and I don't need anyone else if I have all of you.'

Dorcas smiled, not completely satisfied with the answer, but it would have to do for now. Perhaps it was not the right time to pry. Loving Kat was easy, everybody loved her, but finding someone for Kat to love might prove difficult.

They headed for home, and work began on the Christmas tree. They all stood around it, dipping in to boxes and hanging baubles. Mr Cloverleaf was standing on a high pair of steps, placing tinsel on the highest boughs. It was a grand tree, and took a long time to fill its branches. At lunchtime, Cook and Flo went to the kitchen to prepare some sandwiches. Dorcas Louise went to find the angel that sat on the top of the tree. It lived throughout the year in the cupboard near the front door where her perambulator used to stand; she could remember as a baby peeping inside the cupboard to see the angel.

The scream reverberated through the house, as Dorcas ran, angel in hand, toward the drawing room. 'It's Charlie,' she screamed as Katherine leaped to her feet, and Mr Cloverleaf wavered dangerously on the top of the ladder.

'It's Charlie,' she screamed again as she reached the drawing room. 'It's Charlie, and he has Thomas with him.'

By this time, they were all on their feet, and heading for the front door, but as they opened it, no one was there. They all looked at Dorcas Louise with disbelief. 'How could you?' exclaimed Mrs Elford.

'It is true,' said Dorcas Louise, 'I saw them. I opened the door and saw them turning into the drive. Thomas was in a chair.'

With that, they all headed for the kitchen, threw open the door, and there was Cook with her arms about both of them, tears running down her face. They all just stood there, shocked and silent, as Charlie raised two bandaged hands, and Thomas waved one leg; the other one was partly missing. Katherine was the first to move. She ran to them, knelt in front of Thomas, and sobbed. Then she looked at Charlie, to see the side of his face badly burned, but the cheeky smile fought its way through what was left of the bandages that had come loose in transit.

'Where's Flo?' she asked suddenly, realising that she was missing.

'I sent her on an errand,' said Cook, drying her eyes on her apron. 'She will be back soon.' Everyone started to talk at once now, and the boys looked startled and tired.

Mrs Elford stepped in and said, 'I think we should give them a little time before we start to question them. Charlie, you stay here and wait for Flo. We will take Thomas and sit him comfortably, and when you are both ready you can tell us what has happened. We have all been so worried, and are overjoyed to see you both.'

At this moment, Flo came through the kitchen door with the contents of her errand. She stopped dead, dropping the items she had purchased on the floor.

'Charlie,' she said uncertainly, 'Charlie,' she said a little louder, 'Charlie,' she screamed, and ran into his arms. It was his turn to scream then as his body encountered pressure from Flo's advance. Flo jumped away startled, and said, 'What is it, Charlie?'

'My chest has burns on it, Flo. I am so sorry, I didn't mean to frighten you, but the pain is bad at present. It will get better, but it will be slow. I am so sorry.'

Flo, with a feeling mixed between anger and remorse, then said, 'Don't you dare be sorry, it's them bastards over there who should be sorry, not you. You're never going there again, never, do you hear?'

'Yes, I hear,' said Charlie, 'but we will all talk together soon. Poor Thomas has worse to cope with than me.' He gently gave his wife a hug, and kissed her cheek and said, 'I was frightened to come home in case you would not want me with the scars I am going to have when all this has healed.'

'Want you? Of course I want you,' cried Flo. 'Every hour of every day, so don't be thinking such things.'

'Come, let us go and find Thomas now,' said Charlie, suddenly feeling very tired. 'He badly needs a friend just now.'

Thomas had been taken gently from his wheelchair and lowered in to a comfortable armchair near the fire, facing the half-finished Christmas tree. Mr Elford had asked how they got here, and Thomas told him of the kindness of the driver of a hospital vehicle, who had been ferrying patients, who were well enough, home to their families for Christmas day, and had related how Charlie had stayed with him while he went to his employer's house, but on arrival the footman had told him that the Fitzgeralds had closed the house for the duration of the war, and would not be needing him as a chauffeur on their return. Charlie had insisted that he came back here with him. 'I trust that Charlie has not taken too much for granted, sir, and if so I will return to the hospital. We only arrived in Liverpool last night, so it is all a bit strange for us, and for so many more, sir. I do apologise.'

Mr Elford, horrified at the attitude of one of his trusted business associates, said to Thomas, 'Young man, you are most welcome to stay here for as long as you wish, and most certainly for Christmas. I will be most honoured to have both you and Charlie under my roof, and it is I who should feel that I am taking too much for granted, but I would like here and now to offer you a position here on my staff. I need a footman and, while you can't drive, you can still help with the maintenance of my vehicles. Anyway, we will not discuss this for the time being. We will talk to you both together, after we have arranged for you to refresh yourself. I am sure that Katherine can arrange a room for you, and Flo is obviously dealing with her husband's needs, so while the rest of my staff and I sort out this Christmas tree, we will leave you in peace until later.'

With the hustle and bustle over for a while, and Cook left preparing the evening meal, Mr Cloverleaf and Mr Elford found themselves, along with a now placated Dorcas Louise, putting the finishing touches to the tree. Dorcas, feeling that she deserved a little more than a 'sorry' for her mother doubting her sincerity earlier, insisted that she placed the angel on the top of the tree. Mrs Elford, standing back, decided that her daughter was not about to be refused anything at this moment. She agreed to stand at the bottom of the steps and hang on with eyes closed until the task had been completed. Dorcas Louise did the job with aplomb, and descended as gracefully as the angel herself would have, looked up, and nodded, satisfied and justified.

Amongst the apparent lighthearted goings on in the Elford household, Adolphus and Martha arrived at the front door. Mr Cloverleaf welcomed them in, smiling, which for Mr Cloverleaf was not a common occurrence. Adolphus enquired as to his wellbeing, to which he answered, 'Well sir, very well now.'

Adolphus, sensing an underlying note of excitement in his voice, said, 'Is there a special reason for your being very well now, as opposed to being not so well yesterday?'

'Yes, sir, indeed, but I feel that it should be the master to explain my outburst, but yes, sir, there is a very good reason.'

Adolphus, now beginning to feel impatient, made his way to the library where he thought he would find Elford, but no, it was not Elford he found, it was Katherine collecting some books. He held out his arms, and she ran to him. He could see the slight traces of tears on her cheeks. 'What now, my Katherine?' he said.

Katherine raised her eyes to his and said, 'It's Charlie and Thomas; they are home and they are here, Adolphus.'

'Thank God,' he whispered.

Katherine then explained. 'They are both badly hurt, and will need a great deal of treatment before they recover. Thomas has lost part of his leg and his foot, and they are both badly burned, but in spite of that and all that they have gone through, they are in good spirits. They are both resting at present, but they will make it down for dinner, and will spend Christmas day here with us before they have to return to hospital.' Katherine then said, 'Can we please go and tell Martha who must be wondering what is going on.'

Martha was overjoyed, and the look on Katherine's face was enough to tell her what she wanted to know. Charlie and Thomas were helped to the table, refreshed and thankful for the time they had been given to lie down and rest. They knew that during this evening they would have to relate their months of suffering, but tonight they would be able to sleep without the interminable sound of war ringing in their ears, and with the knowledge that they, unlike so many of their comrades, would be safe and cared for and would be able to celebrate the joy of Christmas amongst a close and loving family. Their wounds would have to be professionally tended to, but Katherine and Flo had made them at least comfortable and clean by wrapping strips of pure linen torn from old sheets around their existing bandages, not daring to remove them for fear of doing the wrong thing. That would be dealt with on their return to hospital.

After their meal which was served impeccably by Mr Cloverleaf, they all gathered around the fire in high spirits, but with a certain respect toward Charlie and Thomas who were at the heart of their gathering.

Mr Elford spoke first, and asked, 'Are you both in the right state of mind to tell us your story, or would you rather leave it for another time, and just join in a traditional Christmas Eve free for all?

Thomas spoke. 'We feel we owe you some sort of explanation, as we understand that you received no information, only the fact that we were reported missing. We did in fact leave messages everywhere that we could, but obviously things got so bad out there that nothing was getting through. I need first to tell you that, but for Charlie, I would not be here now, in fact not ever. We had driven the truck back and forth to the front line for months on end, hundreds of journeys, and we thought that we were invincible. This night was to prove the exception. The old girl had done one too many journeys. She had always seen us through, but on this night she didn't make it. A shell exploded in front of her, just missing the bonnet, and with a blinding flash she was lifted into the air. I saw Charlie disappear out of the door, and then the truck landed, crushing my foot between the pedal and the sharp metal of the damaged cab. The truck tilted half on its side and I couldn't move. Then the fire came, and choking black smoke. I heard myself cry for Charlie, but I didn't know where he was. I felt something tugging at my foot, and the pain was incredible. I felt myself drifting in and out of sleep, and then I felt my foot come free, and I knew no more, until I saw the vision of a man draped in bandages calling my name, and saying, "Time to wake up, Thomas".

'I had evidently been unconscious for quite a while, and Charlie had insisted that he would not leave me until I could walk from the hospital. Charlie was hurt too. He had climbed into the cab to try and free me; my clothes were on fire, and he tried to rip them off, and finally, although how he did it I will never know, he managed to pull me and himself from the cab, and roll us both in the mud until the fire was quenched. The rain evidently was ceaseless that night. Charlie said it was as if heaven had sent it to cool our red hot agony ridden bodies. How long we were there, I have no clue, and Charlie said he ceased to care, as he lay against me and thought I was dead.'

Thomas stopped there, and Charlie took over. 'I knew that we were both terribly hurt, but I heard not a whimper from Thomas. I was so tired, I wanted to sleep. I knew I shouldn't, but I wanted to so much. I closed my eyes, and I saw my Flo, and I heard her calling me, and I knew I had to get back somehow, someday. The voices grew louder, and I heard someone call, "Over here". I felt them lift me away from Thomas and I remember screaming "bring him too", and then I was taken from the stinking land, and I saw a white room, where angels smiled at me, and said, "Come on, you can make it." I felt my body being immersed in something that felt like acid, and I felt as if my skin was being peeled from me. I felt no more until I was laying with hundreds of others in a makeshift bed hurting like hell from my head to my toes, but I discovered that I was alive. I called at the top of my voice for Thomas, and a nurse came to ask who I was, and who I wanted. I told her I was Charlie, and I wanted my friend Thomas whom I had been with since the beginning of time. The nurse enquired where Thomas came from. The same bloody field as me, I answered. He is burned like me, and he has hurt his foot. It took me a week to find Thomas, but he was there in the same makeshift hospital as me, and I was told that he had lost his foot, and part of his leg, but that he knew who I was and was asking for me.

'We were reunited one night when the gunfire was still raging around us. Fires were always a hazard, and water was always at hand to deal with them. The cries of the men never completely stopped, for one lot followed another in and out of this hospital. Arrangements would be made eventually to get us out of there, and on a ship for England. I made it very clear that I would not leave without Thomas, and I think they agreed in the end just to keep me quiet. Thomas was quite ill for a while, infection set in around his wounds, and he became delirious. I could only sit and wait. I talked to him all the time, to keep him conscious, and in the end the fever broke, and after another week or so Thomas sat up and started to take notice. Eventually our turn came, and we were embarked on a troop ship heading for England. Unfortunately, it made for Tilbury, which meant we couldn't be sent to a Liverpool hospital. We were hospitalised and the war had its effect on the treatment and hospitality we received, but we were together, and that counted for everything in my book. We compared our pains and our injuries, and decided that we were about even, and that we would just hold on and wait to see what else fate had in store for us. Again we left messages for someone to send on, but again it seems that did not happen. It was just yesterday when they took us to London and put us aboard a train for Liverpool, me walking, Thomas being pushed in a wheelchair, and it is from the Liverpool hospital, where they left us, that we have come here today. They will come and collect us after Christmas day, and take us back to the hospital, where we will continue our treatment until we go before a medical board who will issue papers confirming that we are no longer fit to join the fighting services. May we both say to you, Mr and Mrs Elford, thank you for your great kindness in accepting us back in to the heart of your family, especially at Christmas time.'

They were all settled comfortably now. Mr and Mrs Elford, and Dorcas Louise, all happy it seemed to sit and relax with each other, and with their servants and staff. Cook was last to join them, and Mr Cloverleaf stood hesitantly in the doorway. Mr Elford beckoned him to come closer, and then stood up and spoke.

'Tonight I believe is a night for families to join together. There can be no distinction between me, my family, and all of you, who grace our drawing room. You have each played a part in our salvation, helping our wounded and suffering, and returning from battle. I am very proud of my wife and daughter for their kindness and devotion to their tasks, which have at times proved very harrowing. There are no words that come to mind when I now turn to the two young men who, by the grace of God and their courage, have been returned to us today. They come back with their bodies scarred and broken, but look at their spirit as they sit there. Their eyes tell us that, against all the odds, they have made it, and what is more they have managed to stay together, which I find quite amazing. The strength that they gleaned from each other will take them on to full recovery, I am sure of that. When that happens, we as a family will ensure that for the rest of their lives they will be secure in the knowledge of our unending support. Their infinite friendship will be up to them.'

A round of applause for that speech set the trend for the rest of the evening, with everyone talking, listening, and each giving their contribution to the conversations. The hour was getting late, and Charlie was the first to ask to be excused. The day had finally taken its toll, and he needed some rest. Flo gently helped him, and together they walked to the door, and made their way to the sleeping quarters that Flo had kept clean, but not stayed in, since Charlie went away. Once up the stairs, Flo, with great care, removed his clothes, and settled him in the large bed. She covered his top half just in the sheet, and left his hands resting over the top. She put a warm blanket on the bottom half of the bed where at least his legs and feet would be warm. When he was settled, she eased her way into the space left, and lay without touching him.

'I am sorry, Flo, I dearly want to love you, but I can't bear the pain of any pressure on my skin. The doctors say it will get better, but I have to be patient. Can you be patient too, my love?'

Flo, turning her head toward Charlie, answered, 'Don't be daft, Charlie, two years without you has been hell, but I can wait a bit longer now that I have you by my side. I will care for you, and help to make you better if I can, and at least when I come to the hospital I will be able to sit with you now, as well as the poor boys coming and going every day as they do. I love you, Charlie, now you rest and sleep, and tomorrow we will share the most wonderful Christmas day together. Then a new life will begin for both of us. At least now they can't make you go to war, can they?'

'No, my darling, they can't; but anyway let's hope the war will be over soon.'

Katherine's task was a little more difficult. She had prepared one of the downstairs rooms for Thomas, and Mr Cloverleaf had offered his help, which both she and Thomas accepted gratefully; also he had told Thomas that if he needed help in the night he was there nearby, and all Thomas had to do was ring the little bell that Mr Cloverleaf had given him. Thomas was still reeling from the offer of a job at the Elford house, and this made him determined to get better as soon as he could. In spite of all his injuries and discomfort, he felt at this moment that life could not get a lot better.

The year 1917 passed into history, and 1918 saw the war still raging on the continent. Men still died in their thousands in some foreign field. Arthur, it seemed, would be there until the war ended. The only home comforts that the troops had, was someone to cook them hot and sustaining food, nothing fancy, but something to fill the gnawing pain of emptiness, and bring a little warmth to the bodies that were cold, damp, and weary. Arthur, it seemed, did this to everyone's satisfaction, and it had to be said, in spite of the terrible loneliness of life without his wife and children, he had grown to accept his lot, and enjoyed the camaraderie of his fellow soldiers.

Charlie, once back in hospital, was put under the care of Dr Fortesque, who in turn had introduced him to the nurse who would be seeing him through the treatment that would follow. Nurse Janet had told him that the treatment that Dr Fortesque had considered to be the best that he could offer would be difficult and painful, but that the result could be very successful. She would be there for all of the sessions, and she alone would change dressings, and administer his medication. Charlie looked at the pretty young nurse, with the shiny dark hair, and matching dark eyes, and thought how lucky he was. His stay in hospital would be for quite a while, but during the respite periods he would be allowed home, where she would come and change his dressings. The thought of a long stay in hospital did not please him, but at least he could see Flo, and to get his hands working again would be wonderful. His chest burns would eventually heal themselves, but would leave some permanent scarring.

Thomas was also back at the hospital, where the stump that remained from his amputation was being prepared for a false foot that would be made and fitted as soon as the open wounds healed and hardened. He would be allowed home too, and the burns that he suffered would also heal, he was told, with careful dressing and medication. His burns were not quite as deep and penetrating as Charlie's, as his body had been outside the cab of the lorry, only held by the trapped foot that now was no more. Most of Charlie's burns had been sustained by his climbing into the cab to try and release the shoe that held Thomas fast. The inferno meant that Charlie didn't have time to act slowly; he had to get Thomas out or he would have burned to death, not realising that not only the boot was left in the cab but half of Thomas's foot too. In the end, Thomas would be the first to say that the foot was a small price to pay for having his life saved by Charlie.

At the Elford house, Mr Cloverleaf had agreed to stay and continue with Charlie's duties until he was well and fit enough to return and take over once again. Thomas too was to be employed permanently. There were many jobs that had fallen by the wayside, because of the wartime circumstances, and Mr Elford would be glad of Thomas's knowledge regarding motor vehicles, as he would be purchasing at least one more as soon as the industry recovered from supporting the war effort.

Fate had a way of turning things around, and Mr Cloverleaf was no exception to its rules. Adolphus had been involved in conversation with him on the subject of what he would do after he had completed his duties here. Mr Cloverleaf had confessed that he thought his days as a butler would end from the last day here as an employee. There seemed to be little call for butlers now, and the agency that used him had folded, so he would, it seemed, be wise to make a decision and retire.

Adolphus had been thinking down the lines of finding someone to care for the garden, and be some general help in the house. It was a large house that Adolphus himself lived in, and where Martha had her quarters, but there was also the house next door that at the moment stood empty. Adolphus had no wish at present to offer it for sale or rent, but rather wanted to keep it for visitors.

It would be, however, quite acceptable to him to allow someone like Roger Cloverleaf to occupy the top floor, which could be turned into a pleasant flat. He had quite enjoyed his company over the Christmas period, and his interest in stamp collecting, he thought, offered a good topic of conversation interacting with his own love of birds. Martha too showed interest in the idea. She too had found Mr Cloverleaf a very interesting man, and in spite of his aloof appearance, he had a good sense of humour, and the way in which he had stepped into the breach while Charlie was away warmed her heart.

The proposition was put to him that, in return for duties around the house and garden, the rooms upstairs in the second house would become part of his salary. Roger Cloverleaf was astounded by the offer, and accepted with great pleasure. He had always wanted to go to London, and had never had the courage or the chance for that matter. Now he could go and live there. Adolphus was the kind of man that he could discuss things with, and sharing the work with Martha would indeed be a pleasure, such a kind lady, and so devoted to Miss Katherine, whom he had always found to be delightful, as well as very clever. He would miss this house, but he knew that Katherine visited Adolphus often, and perhaps once in a while Charlie would come and visit too, and perhaps bring Flo, who always, against his better judgement, made him smile.

Katherine went to the hospital as often as she could, and sat with Thomas. The pain sometimes was unbearable. He said that he could often feel the pain in his toes on the foot that was missing. The doctors had confirmed that this did happen sometimes, but that it would eventually disappear. The wound was beginning to show signs of improvement, and some days the bandages would be left off to let the skin breathe, he was told. His burns were now healing too, and when Charlie was allowed to come and visit him they would compare, he told Katherine, who thought that this was a little gruesome, but she could understand their curiosity getting the better of them.

When she visited, Thomas would always say, 'Please sit on the bed; sitting in the chair seems so distant, and I do like to hold your hand, it makes me feel better.'

Katherine fought to keep her feelings for Thomas on a rather more friendly basis than a loving one, just until she could find a way of dealing with the question that Thomas had put to her the night before he went away to war. Although she hated him being hurt and suffering such pain, at least it gave her a little space and time to get the words ready, and to say them in such a way that Thomas was not made to think it was because of his disability that Katherine was declining his offer. She did want him and, against all the odds, she found herself loving him more every time she saw him. Sometimes she would put it down to his vulnerability that made her feel like this, but she knew it wasn't, and she would soon have to tell him that she could never marry him, and would not at the moment be able to tell him why.

Charlie and Flo had no such difficulties, and were always billing and cooing. When he had his respite days, and came home, he would wander around the house during the day. He would prop a book up against the washing basket in the laundry and read, while Flo did some ironing. He would chat to Katherine when she came to see Flo about some chore or other, and he would spend time with Mr Cloverleaf whenever he could. They now had a good friendship, and with the need for exemplary politeness between them gone, they could talk on equal terms.

Charlie was so pleased to hear the good news of the new life that Mr Cloverleaf was to be given on his return to duty, and he hoped that it would not be too long. He had already received some treatment, and they were right, it was extremely painful, and at the time seemed to make little difference to the flexibility of his hands, but with the determination of his doctor, and the deftness of the hands of his nurse, and last but not least, his own determination, slowly but surely an improvement became evident. The burns on his body remained sore, and tender to the touch, and only the small amounts of the orange liquid that was dropped around the burnt area gave some relief. Flo was sweetness itself. She never moaned or became anxious, except on the days when nurse Janet came to the house to change his dressings, and administer some medication, though she did think that her attention to him was a little more keen than it needed to be. She would then walk by and say, 'How much longer, nurse? His tea is almost ready.' Charlie would just smile, and think how nice it was to have two women eyeing one another over him.

Chapter Nineteen

An Englishman's Home

It was to be nearly another year before Mr Cloverleaf could make his move to London. Charlie had had to undergo many more difficult treatments before he finally achieved the approval of Dr Michael Fortesque, who had been determined that the young man who had risked his life for a comrade, would be returned to as near normal as he could make him. With the help of his assistant, Nurse Janet, he gave far and above the call of duty to make it possible. Charlie, in spite of being chided by Flo, had become fond of the dedicated nurse, who had tended to his burns with the utmost gentleness, and had showed such compassion when he had screamed in agony, if not with his hands, then with his chest, which remained sore, and needed continual attention. At the end of it all, when the time came for Charlie to leave their care, he cried as he took hold of the hand of his surgeon and shook it. The pain now was bearable and would soon fade to insignificance. Nurse Janet hugged him, and confessed that she had been so proud to have known him, and then whispered in his ear that she and Doctor Fortesque were to be married.

Thomas, whose burns had been easier to deal with than Charlie's, had had to learn to walk again with the false leg and foot. At first it was frustrating, and many times he felt like giving up. The rails that he had to use for support hurt his hands on which the burns were still sore. The part of the leg where the strapping held the false part in place continually rubbed the skin, causing blisters which were also painful. The doctors and nurses, who attended him, were as wonderful as Charlie's, but because of the time he had to spend in rehabilitation, he had many of them, rather than the one to one treatment that was Charlie's.

Finally, with much help from them all, and the care that Katherine gave him back at the Elford house, he too was fit enough to work. He could not drive, but he was a good mechanic, and his experiences during the war with the old tank of a vehicle that he had nursed through so many perilous expeditions, held him in good stead. He would be able to keep the Rolls Royce in tip top condition, and Charlie would now be able to drive it again. Charlie would also, thankfully, be able to resume his duties as butler, thus giving the redoubtable Mr Cloverleaf the freedom to begin his new life at the wonderful home of Adolphus Fry, which he had seen and fallen in love with at first sight.

The war had dragged on until November of 1918. Three quarters of a million men from Britain had died before peace came, but when it came it brought jubilation to the nation. Church bells rang, and people rushed on to the streets waving flags. Adolphus, with Martha, had joined the throng, and jumped on a bus to join the already singing and shouting passengers heading for the city. The streets were now ablaze with lights, people were dancing in the squares, and shop girls were cheering from the rooftops of the department stores. Flags were hoisted on every available post, and Big Ben was heard striking for the first time in four years.

Arthur arrived home to great celebrations just a week before Christmas. The Elford family house once again hosted a Christmas like no other. It was bursting at the seams, not with elegant guests sipping champagne, but with what seemed to have grown in to a large, happy family, and strangely enough it was the Elford family themselves who seemed to gain more satisfaction from their part in it than any of the joyful participants who stood and raised their glasses to each other, and to the peace of a nation that war had left torn and ragged, but with a spirit undaunted and with the courage to face whatever the future held for them.

The year 1920 saw the return of some normality to the household. Mr Elford was planning a business trip to America, and this time he suggested that Dorcas Louise joined him and Mrs Elford on the trip. Katherine felt a little anxious at the thought of Dorcas Louise travelling across the Atlantic, but she knew how excited she was, and was swept along with the tide of preparation. The business contacts that Mr Elford had in America offered more than a passing interest in forming a sister company in England, and if this were to happen, the financial gains would be enormous for both sides. With all this in his sights, Mr Elford was prepared to invest heavily in the project, and this was his main reason for the intended visit. He knew that most of the time Lavinia would have to be left to her own devices, and he thought that the company of Dorcas Louise would be an ideal solution. Now a very sophisticated nineteen-year-old with the world at her feet, Dorcas Louise wasted no time in creating a wardrobe for the trip, to be taken on one of the newest liners which would sail from Liverpool to its destination in New York.

There would be days spent strolling around the decks, and of course there would be the evenings when she would be able to wear the beautiful dress that Adolphus had bought her. Now she would probably need at least another three, she told Katherine, as she primped and posed in front of the long mirror that was inside her new wardrobe. Katherine by this time had forgotten the misgivings that she had felt, and gave in to the euphoria of it all.

The great day arrived in due course, as did the Rolls Royce that would convey them and the considerable amount of luggage to the docks. As Katherine waved goodbye to them, she thought of the months that they had all spent at the docks, and the hospital, caring for the poor souls that landed bereft of luggage, and with little hope. Now these very docks would be festooned with streamers as the ships left on a very different mission.

She closed the door with the realisation that another stage in her life had been reached. The child that she had borne, had now reached adulthood, and was hardly in need of her. A shiver passed along her spine, and as it did so, the light touch of a hand brushed her shoulder. She turned to find Thomas there, standing now finely balanced on both feet, albeit one having a rather large boot on. It was always good to see him handling his disability with confidence and acceptance.

'Is there time in your busy schedule to come and have a cup of tea with an old soldier?' he asked hopefully.

'There certainly is,' she replied as she followed him into the servant's room. 'We all have nothing to do except look after ourselves and the house for the next few weeks.'

Thomas looked at her expectantly and said, 'Does that mean that you could perhaps spend a little time with me? Could I take you out somewhere? Maybe we could walk in the park; it would be good practise for me. Would that be possible, Katherine?'

'It would be very possible, Thomas,' said Katherine, but for the next couple of days I will be busy clearing up the remnants of the tissue paper, boxes, and bags, discarded by Dorcas Louise, as she paraded her outfits for my benefit. Thomas laughed and agreed that the young Miss Elford was fast becoming an alluring woman who could easily break the heart of some unsuspecting young man who may find himself in her company. Katherine pushed that thought to the back of her mind, but half knowing that it was very much on the cards. She just hoped that it would not be too soon. To spend a while seeing what the world had to offer seemed to Katherine to be a far better option. Her hopes were to be dashed, and her worst fears realised in a very short time.

Unaware of the devious planning of Mr Elford in that direction, Katherine was at present thinking only of her own problems. Tom was very attentive, and the unnerving thing about it was that Katherine was enjoying his attention, and was putting off the moment when she would have to tell him of her decision. She would for the time being, until he made his intentions clear, enjoy his company, and allow him the privilege of enjoying hers. The house was quiet without the family, and it allowed Katherine to clear up old outstanding paperwork and file it neatly. With Flo's assistance, she would also make an inventory of all the linen used, and replace as necessary.

During the day, Tom and Charlie would work on the car, and tidy its workshop, and then Tom would head for the garden, which he had grown to enjoy over the last few weeks. It was winter, so nothing could be planted, but he tidied the ground, and cut back dead foliage, swept the paths, and generally kept everything spick and span. He loved the house, and of course he was near to Katherine.

In the evenings, when all the tasks had been completed, with Cook returned to her cottage, and Flo and Charlie tucked up in their little nest, Tom made the rounds of the house, shut the windows, and locked the door. He would sometimes head for his own room and read a book, but most nights, armed with a tray upon which sat two cups and saucers, a teapot of tea, some milk and sugar, and some of Katherine's favourite biscuits, he would arrive at the nursery door and tap upon it. Most nights it would be ajar, and he would see her sitting with her sewing box on her knee, embroidering little samplers which she said put her mind at rest.

Tonight she was there, but there was no embroidery. She sat with hands laid gently in her lap, head bowed as if in sleep. As Tom tapped on the door, she jumped and said, 'Come in, Thomas, I was deep in thought, and you startled me.'

'Sorry,' said Thomas, as he entered and placed the tray on the small table. 'Could you use a little company?' These were the words that he used with great regularity, as if an excuse to visit her was important.

'That would be nice,' she answered as she always did. They sat in companionable silence as they finished the biscuits and drained their tea cups to the last dregs.

'Wish I could read the tea leaves,' said Tom.

'You must never read your own leaves,' warned Katherine, 'it is unlucky.'

'What if I read yours then; would that be all right?'

'It would be if you could read them, but you can't,' teased Katherine.

'That is true,' said Tom. 'If I could read them, would they tell me that you would marry me, Katherine?'

'Dearest Thomas,' said Katherine, 'they would not. They would tell you that, with all my heart I wish that I could, but the leaves know that I can't, and they know that neither can I tell you why I can't. It has nothing to do with you, I want you to know that beyond anything else. It has to do with something that happened in my past that was partly my fault, and for the foreseeable future I have to live with the knowledge that marriage for me is out of the question. I would dearly love to have you in my life forever, but that would not be fair to you. You should find someone to love, and have children with.'

Thomas sat in silence and digested what Katherine had said. He looked into those wonderful eyes and said, 'I could never love or want anyone but you, Katherine. I have known it for a very long time. It carried me through those terrible years of battle, and the moment I saw your face as I walked through the door of this house, I knew that I had made a lifelong commitment to you, with or without your love, with or without marrying you, and with or without children. So on those terms, Katherine, will you have me?'

'Yes, Tom, I will have you, but it will not be easy, so think very hard. I will not hold you to your commitment. I will always love you, but we will not be able to be seen together as a couple in this house, and neither of us has any other way of earning a living or having anywhere to live. Together we would be frowned upon anywhere, and I could never risk getting pregnant, so you see what the future would hold for us.'

Katherine sat while Tom considered her words. He reached across the table, took her hands in his and whispered, 'There is no future without you.' He lifted her up, and put his arms around her, held on to her for what seemed an eternity, then he kissed her lips, probing gently until they parted, and she wrapped her arms around his neck, and returned his kisses with a passion that surprised them both. It was with some reluctance, much later, when Katherine wished Thomas goodnight. With much more reluctance, he made his way to his room with little or no chance of sleeping, he thought. Katherine lay sleepless too, remembering the evening and going through all the reasons once again why she could not marry Thomas. If they were to share some sort of life together, they would both have to make great sacrifices, and she could just see no answer to it. They would remain close friends under any circumstances, there was no doubt about that, but anything more as far as she could see was impossible.

Adolphus, by this time, would know about Thomas, and Martha would be totally in favour of the relationship, but Katherine knew that the more people who knew about her, and about Martha, made the possibility of her identity vulnerable. Also, there was Dorcas Louise, and for one other person to know that she was her child, would make the risk of the Elfords finding out the truth even greater, and would put them in a very difficult position. They may have no alternative but to send her away, and she just could not bear that, not now when she would almost certainly see Dorcas Louise finding love, and making a life for herself, as she would have if she had lived with her as her mother. Why did this have to happen at this time when everything was back to normal? The boys were home, and the war was over; all should now be peace and contentment. She wondered if she could marry Thomas and not tell him anything about her past, but she knew that she couldn't, and that would put so much pressure upon their relationship.

As Katherine fell asleep, she decided that she would take Thomas to see Adolphus and Martha, and maybe they could come up with some solution, although in her mind there was only one answer, and that would break Thomas's heart.

She left Cook, Charlie, and Flo to look after the house on a promise they could all take some time off when she came back. It would be a good time while the family were away, and she would take care of things with the help of Thomas. With all that settled, they set off for London. Katherine, now being familiar with the journey, sat in her favourite corner seat with Thomas next to her holding her hand. Adolphus sent the motor car for them as he always did, and they arrived with only a small amount of luggage, to be welcomed by Roger Cloverleaf who shook their hands in his usual impeccable way, and led them to the drawing room where Martha was arranging a table ready for them to enjoy a lunchtime snack. Adolphus, joining them soon after, apologised for being caught up with something he was completing in the library. He hugged Katherine, and shook Thomas's hand warmly.

'We will eat now,' said Adolphus, 'and then I will take you, Thomas, to see the work that Mr Cloverleaf has done in my garden, while the two ladies spend some time together. The midday repast passed pleasantly with general conversation. Thomas gave Mr Cloverleaf a written message from Mr Orchard, which was greeted with great appreciation and a certain amount of humour. This amused both Katherine and Adolphus, as they both saw a different side to the man who had once filled them with dread, and a great deal of sympathy for Charlie. Adolphus offered an invitation to both Charlie and Flo to come and visit him whenever it was convenient. Both Martha and Mr Cloverleaf agreed that it would indeed be a pleasure to see them, and so it was agreed that Katherine would pass on the invitation, and make it possible for both of them to be absent from the house in the very near future. With that happy conclusion, Martha and Katherine settled in the easy chairs, and Adolphus took Thomas's arm and led him to the garden.

On their way around the large garden that fitted snugly inside a ring of chestnut trees that separated them from the bustle of the main road, Adolphus proudly pointed out all the improvements that Roger Cloverleaf had completed, and indicated the areas for further work that had been planned. He told Thomas how Cloverleaf had proved to be an excellent choice, and that he found him to be an interesting man with a wide knowledge of many subjects, as well as showing great interest in his life's work on ornithology. It was a joy to converse with him on many subjects that he had always had to work on alone.

With this out of the way, and Adolphus far enough away from the house to talk to Thomas, they found a convenient bench to sit on. Adolphus's approach to Thomas was cautious, as he didn't know whether Thomas was aware of Katherine sharing a confidential conversation with Martha, and giving her permission to relate it to Adolphus, he thus started quietly to talk to him.

'As you are probably aware, Thomas, Katherine means more to me than life itself, and I believe that she has begun to mean a lot to you. She has you in her mind continually, this much she has confided in me, and it is with great respect that I ask you if this is all true, and would it be intrusive of me to ask you to tell me how you feel?' He stopped tentatively to wait for Thomas's reaction.

Thomas, looking at him nervously, said, 'Sir, I know that I am not a great catch, with my disability, but I am learning fast to conquer the inconvenience of it, and, sir, I have fallen in love with Katherine. I feel that she could equally fall in love with me, but there is an evident problem which she is not prepared to tell me about, which worries me so much. I have asked her if she would consider marrying me, and she answers that she would never be able to do that. I cannot imagine how this could be, unless she is already married, in which case surely it would not be difficult to tell me. We enjoy each other's company, and I think we would both love each other very much given the chance. The problem of living in the same house could be resolved, not easily, but it could be resolved if she would agree to it. Sir, I cannot sleep, or eat properly, until I can have some sort of decision or explanation from her. Can you, with your obvious past connection with her, and the closeness that you have, give me any hope for our future together? If not, I may have to reconsider my present situation in the employ of Mr Elford, which I have absolutely no wish to do.'

Adolphus, satisfied with what he had heard, turned and with a sigh, said to Thomas, 'Indeed I agree with you that your love for Katherine is reciprocated, but you will now have to make a decision that may be far from that which you would like to make. Katherine has very bravely had to come to terms with the fact that she may never marry. She, let me first point out, is not responsible in any way for the reason behind this state of affairs, and until now it has never caused her any worries, but loving you has been for her like falling into a well that she had always been sure to keep the lid on, so that she wouldn't be able to fall in. You, young man, removed the lid and she finds herself falling in. I am afraid that I can tell you nothing that will help you. She will tell you nothing either, at least not for the foreseeable future, but what I will tell you is that if she were to marry you, and publicly announce it, she could be putting one person's life in great danger, and ruin the future of another. If you love her, Thomas, as I see it the only way you could be together would be secretly, and I mean secretly, in a way that you young people today call a relationship. She will never marry you, but she will love you, and I know that because she has a great capacity for love. You would be most welcome to spend some time here together at the house if you so wished. I can offer you no more help than that. All I would ask of you is that you please do not hurt her. She has had more than enough hurt in her life, and she deserves so much better, so if you believe that she is worth all of the love you can give her, without her being yours legally, then I am sure that you will make her very happy. The last and most delicate thing that I have to ask, for me is very difficult, and I can only say it in a direct and honest way, Thomas. Katherine must never become pregnant.'

Adolphus stopped suddenly, looking at a crestfallen Thomas who had the merest trace of a tear in his eyes, and said, 'Well, Thomas?'

Thomas answered, standing up and facing Adolphus, 'Whatever the reason, I will always love her in any way that she wishes, and I will not put her under duress to enlighten me, neither will I mention this conversation to anyone, and one more thing, sir, may I say that I envy you so much, you who can love her totally and without fear of losing her. I would give a lot to be in your position, but I am honoured to have known you and your honesty, and I will honour your Katherine too for the rest of my life.'

They strolled back to the house together, as if a walk in the garden was the perfect solution to a thousand problems. Thomas's decision was made. He would never ask Katherine to marry him again, but he would spend his life in her service and her protection.

Katherine and Martha looked up to see the two men walking toward the house. Their conversation had really been along the same lines. Martha had relayed the discussion that she had had with Adolphus, and Katherine knew that she could do no more. The decision had to be Thomas's. Mr Cloverleaf had come into the drawing room to discreetly remove all the trappings of lunch, and brought them a fresh pot of tea neatly set on a silver tray with some of Martha's cake. Katherine felt the quiet contentment of the house, and enquired of Martha how it was all going with Mr Cloverleaf now that he was settled in to his new abode.

It is all rather wonderful, Martha had answered. Adolphus is very impressed with him. He is a clever man with many talents, and has excellent powers of conversation which has seemed to bring a new light into the world of Adolphus. Katherine then posed the question of how Martha felt about another person sharing the life that she had become used to since her rescue from her previous existence. I like Mr Cloverleaf very much, she confessed. My whole life in this house with my two gentlemen is a joy each day that I live. Katherine was indeed happy with that result, and it ended once more a conversation with Martha that Katherine put into her treasured memories.

They all smiled as they sat together once more in the drawing room. Thomas took Katherine's hand and nothing was said, but they both knew that somehow they would share a lifelong love. Katherine spoke first and said, 'This house is so beautiful; it responds to its inhabitants with an almost jealous protection, and it has become now a true Englishman's home. I would like to say thank you, Adolphus, for sharing it with us, and giving of your time to me and mine. I will always be in your debt.'

Adolphus looked at her and remembered the frightened child that had taken his heart with her as she disappeared from the train on that fateful day. He said, 'An Englishman's home is said to be his castle, but there will be no locked turret here, my Katherine. You and yours will be free to come and go as you please. I have issued an invitation to Thomas on that score, and I hope that both of you will take advantage of it. Martha and Mr Cloverleaf will prepare us an evening meal, so please spend the rest of the day as you wish. Take Thomas around, and show him all the rooms, and of course the gallery.'

Adolphus turned to Thomas and said, 'The gallery was Katherine's idea, and it has given me the greatest pleasure in its existence. I hope that you will like it too. I am going to the library for a while. Come and find me there when you are ready.' With his cane to steady him, he walked with unfailing elegance from the drawing room.

Thomas excused himself and left the room, giving Katherine a chance to say to Martha, 'Adolphus is looking slightly frail these days. I hope we are not tiring him with our constant presence here.'

'You, my darling, could never tire him; you are the light of his life. Remember he is eighty-two years old now, and you have known him for twenty years. Time takes its toll on all of us, but be assured he is loving every day of his life here in this beautiful house, and Mr Cloverleaf and I will see to it that he always does. Go and be happy darling. I realise that I am the cause of your worries, and one of the reasons for you refusing Thomas's request for marriage, and I feel terribly guilty about that. I would take the risk of my identity being discovered if I thought it would make everything right for you, but there is the child, and I understand your reluctance to risk the chance of her identity being realised. Oh my darling, what did we do to make you deserve all of this, and, if we had known, what else could we have done?'

'Mama,' Katherine whispered, as she put her arms around Martha, 'you did what you thought was right, and I could not have chosen any one to be my mother who would have been better than you. My love for you is unconditional and always will be so please don't worry, I will be happy with Thomas by my side.'

Thomas returned to find them hugging one another, and Martha held out her other arm to embrace Thomas as well. 'Take care of her, she is very precious.'

'I will,' said Thomas, and they all laughed. The rest of the day passed with an easy co-existence between them, and later in the evening Katherine and Thomas took their leave. As the motor taxi whisked them away, they watched the cameo at the door of the Englishman's house, and felt fulfilled in their own love for one another, and with the love of Adolphus Fry and Martha Wilkin, not forgetting Roger Cloverleaf who now seemed to balance the scales perfectly between them.

Chapter Twenty

Cause For Celebration

It was late when Katherine and Thomas finally arrived back at the house. Charlie was waiting to close the windows, and leave the front door for Thomas to lock, and the landing lights for him to put out. Katherine went to the office, and picked up a pile of mail which she quickly scanned, putting down those which would be dealt with in the morning. Charlie stuck his head around the door before he left, wishing her good night. 'Goodnight, Charlie, and thank you,' Katherine replied.

Amongst the pile of mail there were two that would not wait until morning. Katherine tucked them into her valise and made her way upstairs. Sitting in her chair close to the window, where outside the moon spread its light from behind the clouds, she thought there's rain around the moon tonight. She never knew where that expression came from, but somewhere in her childhood she thought she had heard it. Martha had never used it, but to her it heralded bad news.

Quickly she ripped open the letter from Dorcas Louise, and, far from it being bad news, it was in fact the happiest of letters. She was having a wonderful time, and was spending it with the most beautiful young man called Nathan. He was the son of her father's business partner, and was taking her to the most romantic places, buying her wonderful gifts, and generally treating her like a princess. The best part was that her father was going to bring him to England, and teach him the rudiments of the business from this side of the Atlantic. At this part of the letter, Katherine's heart started to sink.

Dorcas was being allowed to drift into this friendship with the total approval, not to say encouragement, of Mr Elford. Hoping that Dorcas

357

Louise was being over dramatic, Katherine opened the second letter which was from Mr and Mrs Elford. On the contrary, the letter only served to endorse the first one, and Mr Elford was asking Katherine to prepare one of the best rooms for Mr Nathan Applebee, not on the upper floor, but the one on the ground floor that overlooked the eastern side of the garden. They would arrive in less than two weeks, and Mr Applebee would be staying at the house until he was completely satisfied that he could uphold this part of the business. Katherine held no doubt in her mind that Mr Elford would make sure that he did, and that his daughter would have ample opportunity to keep company with this young man. She was suddenly very tired, and the day that had turned out so well, now faded into insignificance with this unwelcome news.

A knock came at the door, and Thomas came in with a tray bearing two cups of steaming hot milk, and some biscuits. The look on Katherine's face told him that something was wrong, and as Katherine passed him the letters to read, he too saw what was happening.

'Dearest, there is nothing that we can do until they all come back. We may be jumping to conclusions, and this may all be a flash in the pan.'

'I do hope so,' said Katherine. 'She is too young, and only just finished school. What is he thinking about? She should have time to grow and meet other young men from whom she can draw some sort of comparison.'

The letters put aside, Katherine and Thomas sat in silence, each lost in their own thoughts, draining their cups as if to prolong the moment. Katherine was fidgety, and kept touching the letters. Thomas sat by her side until he found himself losing the fight against sleep.

'I have to go to bed, Katherine; Charlie needs my assistance in the morning.'

Katherine rose from the chair and walked with him to the door. Thomas bent to kiss her; she put her head on his shoulder and said, 'Would you stay with me tonight? I don't want to be on my own.'

Thomas shut the door quietly, and together they climbed into the cool sheets. Thomas loved her, not with the fierce passion that she had experienced in the days of her first love, but with a slow, gentle possessive love that ended in an explosion of mutual feelings that left them exhausted as sleep surrounded them in infinity.

Dawn spread light around the room as it found the chink in the curtain of Katherine's bedroom. She awoke, turned to see Thomas's head next to hers, and was glad that after all it had not been a dream. He had felt her movement, and raised himself on one elbow so as to plant a kiss upon her head.

'Time for me to go, I think,' he said. 'I must unlock the door before Charlie finds out that he can't get in.'

Katherine, giving a small giggle, replied, 'I must go downstairs too before it is discovered that we are both missing. I'm sorry Thomas but this is going to be the way of things if we are to be together. Does that spoil it all for you?'

Thomas thought for just a moment and then confessed, 'Nothing could spoil it for me, darling. I would rather shout it from the rooftop, but I will settle for a hideout in the attic as long as you are in it too.'

'I will be there, always,' said Katherine.

They parted quietly, each to do their own chores, until the next time they could share the sweet honest moments of just a few hours ago. Katherine picked up the two letters that had been forgotten for a short time, and read them through slowly and thoroughly. Dorcas Louise was obviously smitten by this young man, and Mr Elford was obviously revelling in its possibilities. Mrs Elford's input was short and rather vague, merely commenting on the preparation of the room. Katherine wondered if the part she had played in the visit was a little disappointing, and overshadowed by the meeting of her daughter with this young American. Dorcas Louise had ended her letter with the words, 'Just can't wait to show him off to you, Kat.'

Katherine's doubts were already beginning to well up inside her. She wanted to talk to Adolphus, but she just could not bring herself to worry him yet again. She would wait, and do everything she could to make the young man welcome, and then maybe she could at least allay some of her fears. She would pass the letters on to Cook, and of course Charlie and Flo. The world of the Elford family was about to change again, and her world had already changed to a great degree with the love of Thomas bringing a new joy into her life. With his help and support, she could more easily face any turbulence that may occur.

Charlie and Thomas had polished the Rolls Royce until their reflections in her bonnet were crystal clear. It was the morning of the return of the Elford family, and their young American visitor. The house was busy. Cook had excelled in her cooking, even though the war had left the amount of food available low, and the prices high. She had meat for roasting, and had been to the market extremely early to claim good vegetables. She had baked cakes, made jam, and was prepared to supply endless cups of tea to the young American. It was Charlie who drove the horseless carriage to the docks, and it was Charlie who sat and waited and watched the well-dressed travellers disembark. The whole scene denoted opulence, and Charlie thought of the men who just a few short months ago waited here too, cold and hungry, hurt and lonely, some waiting to be shipped to who knows where, and some returning from places that they never really knew, and waiting to be hospitalised or sent home. He had been one of them, and it was all too easy to remember how it felt.

It was a long time that he waited, and then suddenly there they were, smiling, and waving at the waiting relatives of people that they had met on the voyage. They said their goodbyes, and exchanged good wishes, and then were on their way, searching for Charlie amongst the hundreds waiting for loved ones and friends to walk down the gangplank.

Charlie raised both hands, one holding his cap, and waved frantically. It was Mr Elford who saw him first, as he gathered his family and visitor to his side. They made their way toward him, followed by a porter pulling a trolley which held the luggage. Charlie hoped desperately that the straps he had brought with him would be large enough to hold all of it in place on the lowered back of the boot section of the vehicle. Polite greetings were observed, and Mr Elford introduced Charlie to Nathan Applebee, as Mr Orchard, my personal chauffeur who has just returned after sustaining serious injury in the war.

'Nice to meet you, Orchard,' said the brash young American, as he brushed past him to climb into his place next to Dorcas Louise.

Charlie jumped into the driving seat, and manoeuvred his way out of the docks and away toward the outskirts of the city. The rest of the journey was left to Mr Elford to document, and soon they came to a standstill outside the door of the Elford residence. Thomas was at the door in his capacity as footman today. He welcomed home all of them, one by one, took coats and hats, and then left them to Katherine and Cook while he made his way to the dining room where a welcome breakfast would be served. Katherine stood reverently at the bottom of the stairs, and acknowledged each of them, but not moving until the mistress bade her to. Cook was ushering Flo into the dining room with a trolley which held a large silver lidded bowl containing soup, which she would serve immediately, with crusty bread. There would be a light buffet to follow from which the guests could select for themselves.

Dorcas Louise was far too excited to eat. She clung to the arm of Nathan Applebee until her father made both of them sit down, her with her mother, and Nathan next to him on opposite sides of the table. The sulky look that Dorcas gave her father went unnoticed by everyone, and was totally disregarded by her father. The meal eventually coming to an end, and Mr Elford taking the young Mr Applebee with him to the library, Dorcas Louise, a little disappointed that she could not do the introductions that she wanted to do, made her way to Katherine's side.

'What do you think of him, Kat? Isn't he just beautiful? I have had the most wonderful time in America, and Nathan has promised to take me back again after he has done the work that his father wants him to do here.'

Katherine replied with caution because Dorcas Louise obviously wanted to hear nothing but praise for the young man who had made such an impression upon her. 'It is so grand to see you home safe and happy, and, as for the young man who is your father's guest, I really don't feel that I can comment yet, as I have not had the pleasure of meeting him properly. When I do, I will give him my undivided attention, and then I will report to you. If you will settle for that, then in the meantime I would love to hear from you all about your holiday, and the places that you visited, and see some of your souvenirs. Should we perhaps share a cup of tea, and then I can listen properly?'

The meeting with Mr Nathan Applebee came sooner than Katherine expected. The following morning, as she made her way to the office, she overheard the conversation with Thomas.

'Clean the car, Moreton, I have to be out by 10am.' Nathan Applebee was issuing his orders to one of her staff in a tone of voice that had never been used in the Elford house up to now, and as far as Katherine was concerned, would never be used again. Thomas had answered with due respect that he already had a job to complete for the master, to which the brash young American had retorted, 'Leave that, and leave him to me. My car is new and needs cleaning, so do that first, and then you can complete your other chore.'

Turning away from Thomas, he came face to face with Katherine who, by this time, was a little more than rattled by Dorcas's beautiful young man. 'Good morning, Mr Applebee. Could I ask you to step inside my office for a moment? There is something that I have to discuss with you before I start my day.'

Mr Applebee found this woman a little daunting. He had seen her watching him from the doorway of the drawing room last evening, and had felt a mite uncomfortable. 'Please sit down, sir,' Katherine said, pointing to the leather armchair. 'You have a new car, I hear, how very nice for you. What kind of car is it?'

'A Mercedes,' answered Nathan Applebee, somewhat startled at the line of questioning. 'My father had it shipped for me so that it would arrive the same time as I did.'

'And you wanted to drive it this morning?' said Katherine.

'Yes I did,' answered the young man, clearly confused at Katherine's comments.

'Well, young man, I see no reason why there should be any difficulty with that, except for the way that you approached one of my staff without my permission, and ordered him in no uncertain manner to clean your vehicle. I am not well read in the manner with which you treat your servants in The United States of America, but here, Mr Applebee, especially in this household, we the servants treat Mr and Mrs Elford and their family with the greatest respect, and carry out our duty, and their requests with the utmost speed and efficiency. They in turn show their respect and trust in us and, Mr Applebee, we have a very happy household here, where orders are given and received with the same politeness on both sides. I would ask you therefore, with the greatest respect, to please conform while you are here, and I think you will find that my staff will be only too happy to look after your interests. Now, if you wish Thomas to clean your car, I am sure he will be only too glad to do so after he has completed his chore for the master. If you need desperately to have your car cleaned, and choose not to wait, I am sure that Thomas will be able to find you some water and a piece of cloth, and you may with pleasure clean it yourself. Finally, Mr Applebee, I welcome you here, and assure you of my attention at all times. I hope that your stay will be very enjoyable. If you would like to follow me now, I will introduce you to the rest of my staff. The two young men, who have been in the employ of Mr Elford for a very long time, have both served in active duty during the war, and as a result have both sustained very serious injuries. Mr Moreton has unfortunately lost a limb. They are indeed two very special young men who, by their bravery along with thousands of others, have earned us our peace. Thank you for listening to me, Mr Applebee. Come now and meet my staff, and then I will leave you in the very capable hands of your hosts.'

Not a word of the conversation was passed on by Nathan Applebee. He had, he decided, been slowly and steadily put in his place by the efficiency of the housekeeper, and he was not about to tread on her toes. In fact, his charming, if a little brash, attitude was happily accepted by Cook and Flo, and the boys decided that they would accept him for what he was, 'One of those crazy yanks,' said Charlie with a dramatic raising of one eyebrow.

Dorcas Louise finally had her moment, and brought a rather sheepish Nathan Applebee to be introduced to Katherine. 'This is Kat,' she said, 'who has looked after me since I was born, and I would really like it if she could look after you as well while you are here.'

Nathan replied, placing a careless arm around Dorcas Louise's shoulder, 'We have already spoken, sweetheart, and I know that we will get on famously. Do you think that we will, Kat?'

'I am sure that we will both do our best, Mr Applebee,' Katherine answered, with the suspicion of a smile playing around her lips. 'Perhaps, Dorcas, you could take Mr Applebee to the park. It is the ideal weather for a walk.'

Playfully, Dorcas Louise added, 'We could always feed the ducks.'

The days and weeks, after the confrontation, passed pleasantly enough for Nathan Applebee, and Katherine. Although apprehensive about his intention to take Dorcas Louise to America again, she softened to his ways, and they met somewhere about the middle. She could plainly see that Dorcas adored him, and if it was him that made her happy, who was she to argue. Nathan worked alongside Mr Elford most days, and his progress was evident in the way that he was left to negotiate on many occasions the financial commitments made by one company to the other. On completion, Mr Elford would read them through carefully, and place his final and binding signature upon them. Nathan would then be responsible for the safety of the papers, and would take them personally with him when he returned to New York to place them in front of his father, and witness his signature alongside the one from Mr Elford, thus making the transfer of funds complete. The merger of the two companies would be for Mr Elford, and for Mr Applebee senior, the biggest that either of them had ever committed to, and would put them into the realms of unknown greatness.

Dorcas Louise spent her days going through her wardrobe, preparing for the evenings when her father would throw the kind of parties that he used to before the war. She would now be present at them, and hopefully

Nathan would be at her side. Sometimes she remembered the times as a child when she would peep through the banisters and watch from upstairs as the beautiful ladies in sparkling dresses, arm in arm with their respective partners, and see her mother sweep down the stairs to greet them while she was whisked away to eat a special supper that Kat had said was for a special princess who would one day be there in the middle of all those ladies, and shining like a star.

Well now that time had come, and she would shine like a star, and Nathan would be so impressed that he would take her in his arms, kiss her and tell her that she was the most beautiful lady of all, and that he loved her. He would then lead her into the garden, and they would kiss again. Everybody would stand aside as they walked back into the house, and Nathan would wave an arm to gain their attention as, holding her hand, he would announce their engagement and present her with the most amazing diamond, which he would slip on to her finger.

It didn't quite work out like she had dreamed, but it did happen. On one September morning as they walked in the park, Nathan told her that he had asked her father for her hand in marriage, and he had consented happily, so would she please do him the honour of becoming his wife. Dorcas felt very vulnerable now that it had happened; she dreamed of it so often, but now she felt a little frightened, and she wanted to run to Kat, and nestle into those comforting arms and tell her before anyone else so that she would know that, with Kat's approval, all would be well. She couldn't do that because Nathan wanted an answer, and expected one immediately and without hesitation.

This was Nathan; decisions were made, and there was no going back, so Dorcas Louise that morning committed herself to a life with Nathan Applebee. The ring would be placed on her finger at a celebration party that he himself would arrange for next weekend.

Katherine, walking into the nursery later in the afternoon, found a pale-faced Dorcas Louise curled up in her chair with a scruffy rabbit and bear tucked under her arm. 'What is it, darling?' she said, looking upon her with concern.

'I am going to be married,' whispered Dorcas as Kat came toward her.

'What, so soon?' exclaimed Katherine

'Yes, Father has consented,' said Dorcas.

Katherine sat heavily on the window seat, looked at her and asked, 'Is it what you want, and what does your mother think?'

'I haven't seen Mother. I wanted to come to you first and, yes, I suppose it is what I want but I just didn't think it would all happen so quickly. I wanted everyone to know that we were in love, before a wedding was planned.'

Katherine, for once in her life, did not have an answer for Dorcas Louise. All she could do was sit with her, hold her hand, and remind her that, at the end of the day, the decision was still with her and, if she had any doubts, she could ask Nathan to wait a while.

'I don't feel that I can do that,' said Dorcas Louise. 'The plans that Nathan has made are already being put into action.'

Katherine, feeling inwardly annoyed once more by the impudence of this young man, wondered why Mr Elford had agreed to the plans without first consulting Dorcas Louise. She needed to talk to Mrs Elford. Giving Dorcas Louise a hug, she told her to wait quietly for the moment, enjoy Nathan's company, but not to get involved in the preparations until it was certain that her parents had approved.

Finding Lavinia Elford in the library, Katherine knocked gently on the door, and Mrs Elford invited her in. 'I was going to call you in, Katherine, but I just haven't had a moment to myself. Has all gone well while we have been away?'

Katherine said swiftly that everything had gone well, and that the boys were improving every day, and coping very well with their chores, in spite of their physical disabilities.

'Good,' said Mrs Elford. 'Have you spoken to Dorcas Louise?'

'Yes I have,' answered Katherine. 'In fact, I have left her in some confusion as to the speed with which plans are being made for a wedding that she only agreed to this morning. Surely she could be afforded a little time to get used to the idea before rushing into pre-nuptial preparations.'

Lavinia Elford looked at her, a little shocked by her outburst. 'Dorcas Louise will never have a chance like this again in her life, Katherine. She will never want for anything, and she will marry into one of the richest families in The United States of America. We all want what is best for her, and Nathan Applebee is a very handsome young man who will make her a perfect husband.'

'Does she love him?' Katherine threw back at Lavinia Elford.

'Love him?' Lavinia laughed. 'They have been stuck together like glue for the whole of our stay in America. Have you asked her if she loves him?'

Katherine had to admit that she hadn't, and by now felt that she was losing the argument rapidly, and so apologised for her interference, and thanked Mrs Elford for her time. She returned to the nursery to find a totally different Dorcas Louise arranging a massive bouquet of red roses in a large glass bowl.

'Isn't he just amazing, Kat, and aren't I the luckiest girl in the world?' Katherine sat down wondering what she had been doing for the last twenty minutes, and slowly answered, 'I hope very much that you will be, my darling.'

The following morning, all the staff were summoned to the library by the master and the mistress, and were told of the plans for a large party to be held the following weekend to celebrate the engagement of their beloved only daughter to Mr Nathan Applebee. It was agreed that Mr Orchard would once again be butler, and that Mr Moreton would be footman, and that Katherine, as always, would be in charge of all the arrangements. Dorcas Louise, now caught up in the euphoria, was being called upon by friends who had learned of her fate, and who gazed starry eyed at the prospective bridegroom. Her days as a princess had arrived in due haste, and it seemed that Katherine was the only one who harboured some serious doubts.

Nathan Applebee's parents and two brothers were already on their way. It seems that they had booked the trip while the Elfords were visiting, having already had advance warning of a possible celebration. They would arrive the day before the party, and so Katherine duly set Flo the task of making four of the first floor bedrooms ready for the most important guests. Cook was thrown into activity, not only for the night of the party, but for the culinary wellbeing of all those guests who would be spending the whole weekend at the house.

Martha, as always, was asked to help with the party evening, and of course Adolphus would be there in his capacity of godfather to the young lady who would be centre of attraction for the weeks ahead. Adolphus asked permission to bring Mr Cloverleaf with him as, due to his ascending years and some difficulty in moving his joints, which according to the medical profession was acceptable at his age, he needed some assistance to dress. Charlie was very happy with that decision. It would indeed be very nice to see his old tutor again. He had missed him since his departure for London.

Dorcas had dragged Katherine to the shops to see her try on at least twenty dresses. The final one that she chose was not Katherine's choice, but Katherine had decided that to agree with her would save her further confrontation, as if there had not been enough already. The dress of purple satin, in Katherine's opinion, made her skin look extremely pale. The style of the dress, however, was beautiful and enhanced her already perfect figure. Invitations were hastily written and delivered locally, mainly by Charlie and Thomas. Katherine, who along with her everyday paperwork, helped with the addressing of the envelopes. This young man certainly has no time to waste, she thought, as she stuffed the last invitation into the pile on her desk ready to be taken by Charlie.

Cook had mentioned to Katherine that Arthur would be home for a few days, and would be glad to help if he was needed. Arthur had decided to stay in the Army. He had been offered the job of staying with the troops until the whole of his division was finally repatriated. He had for his services been promoted, and given a good raise in pay. He would have to stay in the field canteen to cook for those left to clear up the mess after the fighting had ended. The job at times was harrowing, but the men left were in high spirits, knowing that eventually they would be sent home, and they would run no more risk of being injured, and quite possibly killed. Eventually he would return to England, and continue to serve as chef in the army canteen. He was due some leave, and would be coming home to his family, before embarking on his new career.

Nathan's family arrived with due pomp and ceremony. Mr Elford was waiting at the door, and greeted them enthusiastically, ushering them to the drawing room while their luggage was to be taken to their rooms by Charlie and Thomas. Thankfully, Arthur, who had just set foot in the kitchen before their arrival stepped in and grabbed the largest pieces, tucking two under his arms, and carrying another two. 'Thanks, mate,' said Thomas who was grateful not to have to put an extra amount of strain upon the false foot, which still gave him problems on occasions such as this. Charlie too, in spite of the great improvement, still had tender hands, and was thankful not to have to carry the heavy valises.

Dorcas Louise and Nathan came into the drawing room hand in hand, and were gathered into the circle of their two families. Katherine, coming from her office, caught sight of one of Nathan's brothers who appeared to be staring at her. Keeping her head high, she nodded and passed by and up the stairs to the nursery. Her day ended with her being able to spend a while talking to Thomas. Indeed, life was every bit as difficult as they had expected. Spending time together was virtually impossible, and the return of the Elfords, bringing with them all the fuss and excitement of a wedding in the not too distant future, merely added to the problem.

Katherine, who was clearly anxious about the whole procedure, was happy that Thomas could spend some of his time with her trying to help her accept the inevitable.

The day of the engagement party arrived, and Nathan appeared to have everything under his control. Katherine was having none of it. This brash young American maybe taking Dorcas Louise from her, but he was not going to rule the roost in her domain. When trying to organise her day, he was in receipt of a smart rap on the knuckles, and the comment that her duties were listed and approved by the mistress before he had raised his head from the pillow this morning. Despite the rancour between them, there was a certain amount of respect each for the other that was recognisable.

The evening got under way when guests started to arrive. Both sets of parents stood at the door to welcome them. Mr and Mrs Elford on the right hand side, and Mr and Mrs Applebee on the left. Nathan and Dorcas Louise, took their positions in the centre of the room, arms linked. As the guests gradually filled the room, champagne was offered from silver trays neatly carried by Thomas and Charlie, now looking spectacular in their new evening attire that Mr Elford insisted they should both wear. He had also insisted that Thomas should share the duties on nights such as this when staff was hard to come upon.

Adolphus finally arrived, impeccable as usual, leaving Martha to find Cook, and keeping Mr Cloverleaf close by his side should he need help, he said, under his breath, and with the slightest wink in Cloverleaf's direction. Dorcas Louise gave Adolphus a kiss on both cheeks, and introducing him to Nathan, said, 'This is my godfather, and he is wonderful.'

'Nice to see you, sir,' replied Nathan. 'I hope you enjoy your evening.'

'Oh I will indeed,' answered Adolphus as he turned to take a glass of champagne, and then make his way to the dining room where he had spied Katherine hovering around Flo as she completed the floral decorations.

'Good evening, ladies, how very lovely it all looks. I hope that the young couple appreciate it,' said Adolphus.

Katherine gave him one of her very worried smiles, and Adolphus knew that all was not well in the house of Elford, and he would have to corner her and talk about it. He would do that just as quickly as he could without raising any eyebrows belonging to the ecstatic crowd of guests who would be expecting an invitation to probably one of the most talked about weddings for a very long time.

The war was over and spirits were high. Businesses, that had been suffering setbacks, were now gaining financial ground again, and these two families now merging could hold the highest ground on both sides of the Atlantic. It was certainly a happy Mr Elford who proudly presented his daughter and future son-in-law to the gathered audience who applauded, and cheered.

The feast that they were served was indeed a banquet. Cook had excelled, with the help of her son, whose talents amazed her, considering that before he joined the army his wife and children refused to eat even the toast that he had prepared. Katherine had organised the evening with her usual flair, and her staff, as always, worked for her to perfection. She was proud to have them all by her side.

After the coffees had been served, Katherine stood just behind the door where she could watch as Nathan Applebee placed a diamond ring on the third finger of the left hand of her darling Dorcas Louise. Tears welled up in her eyes, as Dorcas stood on tip-toe and placed a chaste kiss upon the lips of her future husband as she answered his question with a tremulous 'Yes'. She had agreed to be the future Mrs Nathan Applebee.

While the party drifted on into the small hours, Adolphus came and found Katherine. Roger Cloverleaf, who had accompanied him upstairs, now asked permission to go to the kitchen and wait for Charlie to finish his duties which he commented had been carried out with the utmost discipline, and refinement. Adolphus was absolutely happy with the company of this man at his house in London, and made no bones about saying so in front of him, and to Katherine.

Left alone, Adolphus plied the question, 'What is bothering you, Katherine, apart from the fact that your precious daughter has now grown up, and is going to leave you to start a new life with the man she loves? Is that it, or is there something more?'

'Oh, Adolphus, she has seen no life yet, and that young man is so irritating in his manner. I wonder how she will be married to him, and under his control which she surely will be.'

'He is young too, Katherine, and America is so different from England. Here we are slower at making decisions, and are more polite in our approach to one other. She will, I'm sure, be well looked after, and she is certainly not a little mouse. She will be able to look to her own morals, and she will use them if the need arises, I am sure.'

'I do hope you are right, and thank you for listening. I probably am being over protective, but at this time I am finding it very difficult to forget she is my daughter.'

Adolphus placed an arm around her shoulder and said, 'I sometimes find it difficult to accept that you are *not* my daughter, and like you, all the wishing in the world cannot change the facts, and we have to live with them, as much as sometimes we hate to. Don't be too hard on the boy, he has to show the world that he has status, and that comes from his parent's position in life. Dorcas Louise has made her decision. I hope that with not too much parental influence she will see it through to a good marriage. Now, do you think we could possibly partake in a good cup of tea? It was always a good leveller in the days of our adventures.'

Katherine smiled, one of her adorable smiles that Adolphus found irresistible. 'Yes, sir, I will see to it immediately, and may I please join you.'

'Indeed you may, my Katherine.'

It was the following morning when Dorcas Louise came to find Katherine to proudly show her the ring that adorned her delicate hand. Katherine hugged her, and wished her every happiness, and promised always to be there if she should want her. They descended the staircase together, where Nathan's family were ready to leave. They had to return to America to finalise the first part of their agreement with Mr Elford and, as they were here for the party, Nathan could pass them the completed papers that he was responsible for instead of travelling out himself. He would be able to stay here and start the next stage. He came to stand by Dorcas Louise who was chatting to Kat. Mr and Mrs Applebee said their goodbyes, and Nathan's brothers both came to offer theirs. Looking at Katherine, and then at Dorcas Louise, Nathan's eldest brother exclaimed, 'My goodness, you two could be sisters, you are so alike. Did you not notice it, Nathan? Miss Carrera would pass for Dorcas Louise's sister anywhere.'

Katherine froze and, for a minute no words could be spoken, then she managed to gather her wits enough to say laughingly, 'Well, they do say that you become like the person you live with. It evidently is the same with animals. I can assure you, sir, that I am definitely not her sister, although I am very flattered if you think I look like her, for she is very beautiful, and I would never put myself in that category.'

The moment passed without further comment from either side, and Katherine was glad to slip away from the families, finding her legs refusing to move her body as quickly as she would like them to. Last night, Dorcas Louise had sparkled in her purple gown with her short hair cut, which she announced was the new bob, and very fashionable; she had the exquisite beauty of a young aristocrat about to step into a world of untold wealth. Katherine could only wonder at the magic of it all, and how she had escaped a life beyond imagination, to bring her child to this, for if the series of events that preceded this moment had not happened, both she and her child would have lived a life of deprivation, torn apart, neither knowing the fate of the other.

Katherine shivered, remembering the words of Nathan's brother, and praying that he would accept her trite explanation, and accept Dorcas Louise for what she was, a beautiful, intelligent young woman whom his brother had chosen for a wife. There was no further mention of the conversation, nor any comment on the likeness in looks of the Elford's daughter and her nanny.

Katherine did manage to catch a quick word with Adolphus before he left, but as always he seemed to be able to allay her fears. 'There are far too many things on the minds of the young couple, and their respective families, to pay any attention to a flippant comment from the groom's brother,' said Adolphus in his wise old owl way.

Katherine settled back in her routine, eventually letting the fear of discovery fade into insignificance. It was only brought to mind again when Nathan's parents sent an invitation for the couple to visit. They had a gift for them, but not one that could be given or sent. They would have to go in person to receive it. Eaten up with curiosity, Dorcas Louise could not wait, but she had to for a while as Nathan was dealing with an important client who would be the mainstay of the British office of the company. All this, to Dorcas, was beyond her comprehension and, in fact everybody, except Mr Elford who seemed to be pushing ahead on everything that Nathan was advocating, felt the same.

Finally the tickets were booked, and once again the ship sailed for America with Dorcas Louise aboard, but this time with only Nathan as her companion. Nathan, in the space of the last few weeks had, with her parents' consent, arranged for their wedding to take place in London on the fifth day of the fifth month of 1921. Katherine was once again stunned by this young man's race against time.

It would be Christmas again before they returned to England, and then they would once again be buried beneath a mountain of paperwork in which of course Nathan would play no part. He would expect it all to be done without a trace of dust, and then he would sail down the aisle as if he had arranged every tiny flower that decorated his path. He would, Katherine groaned, turn their beautiful little butterfly into a dragonfly, who would flit about with not a minute to spare to see the world pass by. She sat with lists of dressmakers, hat shops, shops which catered for the mother of the bride, and those which specialised in the menfolk. There was one saving grace in all of this, she thought, the wedding taking place in London meant that the house would not be overflowing as most of the guests would be staying in a hotel near to the wedding venue.

Mrs Elford spent a lot of time sitting with Katherine, discussing the wedding. In fact, Katherine's company was a great comfort to Lavinia Elford now that her husband was so caught up in the high-powered business race. She became quite frightened at times, she confessed. James seemed to be swept along with the young Nathan, and Lavinia was not sure that he wasn't sometimes a little rash in his decisions.

Katherine was secretly pleased that Lavinia felt a little like she did, that there may be no stopping Nathan, when the need was there to stop and take into account certain pitfalls that may be overlooked in the effort to get to the top. She of course had no right to put this to Lavinia, but she was pleased to see that at least one of them still had their feet on the ground, when all around her were flying high. Katherine felt quite safe with Lavinia by her side, and she knew that, whatever happened, they would both be there to assure the wellbeing of Dorcas Louise.

Christmas, once more, was looming up, and the old tradition of decorating the tree and the house came up on the agenda. This year, for the first time, there would be no child to cater for, and while they would follow the tradition to the letter, the season would not be the same ever again, well not until there were perhaps some grand children. Katherine wondered if there would ever be time in their busy lives for children.

Dorcas Louise and Nathan returned just one week before Christmas. Looking stunning in a dark red velvet suit, and matching hat, Dorcas entered the drawing room which was strewn with boxes of glass baubles ready to adorn the tree which already stood in waiting in front of the big window. Nathan followed, looking around the room without comment. He sat on the only open space on one end of the sofa, and waited for Dorcas to tell everyone what his parents had bought them. Dorcas, bright-eyed and sparkling, reached into her bag and withdrew a long cigarette holder. She deftly removed a cigarette from a silver case, and pushed it into the holder, much to Katherine's disapproval. Nathan jumped up and casually took it from her, lit it from a taper placed in the fire, and passed it back to her.

She stood in front of the fireplace, like a star from a silent movie, and said, 'Nathan's parents have bought us a beautiful house in the state of Florida. It is not ready yet, but it will be by the time we are married, and we will spend our honeymoon there. We would like to stay here in this house for the times when we are in England, which will be for quite a while even after we are married, if that is convenient to you?' She directed her question to her mother and father, who of course had no option but to agree.

'We will extend your suite of rooms to meet your requirements and your wishes,' Mrs Elford replied to her daughter, feeling a little ruffled by her approach and thinking that Nathan's influence was beginning to take hold of her daughter.

She cast a quick look at Katherine, who had a look on her face which said it all to Lavinia. 'Welcome home,' she said as she put her arm around Dorcas's shoulder. 'Go and make yourselves comfortable, and Katherine will arrange some food for you.'

Leaving the room without comment, Katherine headed for the kitchen, where cook was already waiting for instructions. 'Could you manage a large portion of good manners, and perhaps, as a sweet, a bowl of good common sense?' Katherine said with a certain disdain to Cook, who without a word started to pour her a cup of tea.

'With a wee drop of brandy, me thinks,' she said, as Katherine slammed the cutlery down on the serving tray.

'You mark my words, Ruby, that young man will be the downfall of her, and if we are not careful he will take the rest of us with her.'

Cook had not seen Katherine quite so angry since the days of Trafina Paris. Nathan was certainly putting his mark on the family business, but to be fair he had always treated her politely, and since Katherine had spoken to him soon after his arrival he had not harassed any of the staff, not even Katherine if she were to be honest.

'Give him a chance Katherine, he is young, and has suddenly acquired a high powered position in his father's business, which of course is now linked to the Elfords, plus he has found himself a future wife who is extremely beautiful, and obviously adores him. He is flying high, and wants everyone to recognise that. Accept it if you can, and if he falls in the process, give him a hand to get up, and I think you will find that there is a reasonably human person under that facade.'

Katherine looked at her, shrugged her shoulders and said, 'Maybe', and as she took up the tray, and went out of the door, she turned, smiled at Cook, and said, 'I will give it a try.' Give it a try she did, and after a few days Dorcas Louise was her old self again. She came to the nursery when Nathan was out or busy, and sat as she always did in her chair and chatted away to her Kat about her feelings for Nathan and her forthcoming marriage. She admitted that at present she could see no further than her big day. She could not see herself in the role of Nathan's wife, and behave like her mother did toward her father. She would always have to have her say, and she wouldn't agree with him if she thought he was wrong. This went down very well with Katherine. She after all raised a child with a little touch of a rebel, and with a spark of independence.

Lavinia too would join in the conversation, and the three of them began to build a common bond which caused many a giggle when they were discussing things like seating plans for the wedding breakfast, and the top hat and tails that would be mandatory for all the men. It was agreed that some had the body for the tails, and some would look remarkably like a penguin. Dorcas would, it seems, have eight bridesmaids, starting at the tender age of five, and ranging up to adults. They would walk in pairs and the tallest would be at the front, and the smallest at the back, so that any stragglers could be rescued and put on the right path without upsetting the whole procession.

The marriage service was to take place at a large church in Westminster, and the reception would be held at a magnificent hotel in the heart of London, famous for its celebrity weddings. Dorcas Louise was not to be told where it was, or that she and Nathan would arrive in a glass coach pulled by four grey horses. She would be taken to the church in a landau, accompanied by her father, who would give her away to Nathan, when they finally arrived with their attendants at the altar. The dresses were to be made by a well known bridal manufacturer in London, which would involve many trips to the city for fittings, and with the need to travel with some young children, Katherine was called upon to be chaperone, along with the bride herself.

First, they would have to pore over designs sent by the dressmaker who would be in charge of the whole procedure. She had sent hundreds, ranging from sleek and shiny to flimsy and frilly, to just plain beautiful.

Dorcas Louise was mesmerised. She sat on the floor surrounded by drawings, gradually sifting out the definite failures, until the pile was reduced to half a dozen. Her choice finally was white satin, high necked with the tightest bodice whittling in her tiny waist, until the whole thing ballooned out into an amazing skirt which flowed and rolled with every movement. The back of the bodice would be tied with white satin laces down to a large bow that would be encrusted with pearls and diamonds, and flow to the ground meeting more pearls and diamonds at the hem to form a small train. The sleeves would be tight fitting, and would end in a point which would sit exactly at her third finger on her left hand where her wedding ring would be placed.

There would be a selection of headdresses given to her later, when the dress was finished, and a veil had been chosen. Her bridesmaids would, she decided, wear very pale gold dresses, also in satin. Flowers and headdresses would also be chosen along with the bride's at a later date. The important thing now was to concentrate on the dresses, as the time that they had been given was very short in comparison to most of the aristocratic weddings, which were arranged much earlier.

Arrangements had been made for all the guests and the wedding party to be picked up at the hotel where they would stay overnight, but Dorcas Louise had other ideas, and begged an audience with her father to discuss it. 'As it will be the most precious day of my life, Father, I would dearly love to leave from Adolphus's house. I could stay there with Kat the night before, and you could come and meet me at the door when it was time to leave for the church. That way there would be no chance of me seeing Nathan before I marry him. Do you not think that would be a perfect idea?'

Her father looked at her. He could refuse her nothing; it had always been that way in spite of his long absences from home. He had little control over granting her wishes. 'If that is what you wish, my dearest, I will see to it, but I suggest you ask Adolphus first. He may not want that much fuss at his house.'

'Oh he will, Father, I know he will. If not for me, then certainly for Kat.'

Of course he did. Adolphus, overjoyed at the prospect of seeing his god-daughter as a bride before anyone else, gave consent without hesitation. During one of the trips to London with Dorcas and two of her bridesmaids, Katherine had agreed to meet Adolphus while the girls were having fittings. She told them to stay where they were, and she would return for them.

Adolphus met her at a little restaurant that he frequented, which was small and quiet, and where they could enjoy a light but filling meal, along with some intimate conversation. Katherine, as always, felt at her ease and happiest when she was with Adolphus. She looked at his dear face, and saw a wonderful elderly man whom she adored with all her heart. She could talk to him, ask him, or tell him anything in the complete confidence that he would understand, and help her whenever he could.

He had asked her here today for a special reason. He said that he thought the wedding was going to be the hardest day that Katherine had had to deal with since that day long ago when she had to make the decision of looking after her daughter, but never disclosing the fact in the knowledge that she would have a good life, or taking her into a life that would give her nothing but doubt and fear. She had, Adolphus said, made the most wonderful job of being just a nanny, when she should be playing the part of a proud mother. With this in mind, Adolphus had made up his mind that, for one moment in the most special day of Dorcas's life, Katherine should have a special moment too. He had decided to buy for Katherine, the most beautiful diamond tiara to give to Dorcas as a present from her Kat to wear on her wedding day, and then to keep it to pass on to any daughters that she may have, to wear on their special day. Katherine had no words to say to Adolphus. She wanted to jump up and throw her arms around him, but couldn't, so instead she just let her tears fall into her lap, as he held her hand and kissed her fingertips.

'It gives me the greatest pleasure in the world, my darling girl. Now let us go and choose the diamonds and the style, before you return to your duties.'

Dorcas thought that Kat looked a little upset when she returned to meet them, but Kat just brushed it off by saying, 'Weddings always make me sad, but I will be happy if I know that you are happy, darling. You will be, won't you?'

'Yes, I will, and all the happier for knowing that you will be there.'

The house, once again, was in a state of upheaval. Dorcas Louise's little domain that she had used for such a short time, was now undergoing another radical change in order to make it a live-in residence for both her and Nathan after their marriage, and in between trips to America. Katherine was convinced in her mind that once the merger of Elford and Applebee was complete, the whole operation would be transferred to the American side. This would mean that Dorcas would make her home there, and she would lose her forever. Nathan still succeeded in annoying her, as much as she tried not to let him, and occasionally when he cornered her, she practised the art of conversation with him on the topics that she knew he could not hold court on. Each time he fell into the trap, and each time she had a sense of satisfaction at being able to bring the ball down into her court, and take the point. Her love of Dorcas Louise made her keep her aggravation under strict control, and they as always had a loving relationship.

Mrs Elford, Katherine thought, felt much the same as her, and worried about Nathan's brash approach to everything. Dorcas obviously felt nothing but adoration for the handsome, clever, and rich young man who would soon become her husband, and at present was thinking only wedding dresses, shoes, flowers, and the venue for the wedding reception, which her father had taken her to see. It was such an opulent building, with its mirrored walls and crystal chandeliers which sent myriads of light into each corner, the tables with their gold chairs, and the red carpet that spread across the whole area, only leaving a small dance floor which would house an orchestra to play throughout the five-course meal, and later for the guests to dance. All this for her, and she would finally become the princess of her childhood dreams.

Days flew by relentlessly. Katherine had written and sent four hundred gold-edged invitation cards. She had travelled to London on five occasions, each time with different charges. She had decided that she would not see the dresses, so she would wander around the shops, and return in time to escort them all home again.

She met Adolphus twice in those five visits, and once went with him to pick up the tiara that had now been completed. The salesman came to the counter with the white box held reverently upon a white velvet cushion. He laid it down, and opened the lid, gently peeled away the flimsy paper that covered it to reveal the most delicate coronet, with spears of diamonds ascending from its circle, which held pear-shaped stones separated by tiny diamonds set in clusters around the base of the precious metal rim that had narrow ribbon loops through which were passed diamond studded clips that would hold the whole thing to the veil, and keep it steady upon the head of the bride.

Katherine announced her disappointment that Dorcas Louise had had her hair cut into this so called modern bob, when her long fair curls would have been a perfect foil for this most beautiful object that was now hers to give to Dorcas Louise. Nothing however could detract from the beauty of this piece, and nothing would ever replace the joy in her heart that Adolphus had thought of doing this wonderful thing to make her feel special on the day that her daughter would walk down the aisle with no knowledge of her mother standing in the crowd watching her.

She returned to the shop, and waited for the final fitting of Dorcas's dress to be completed. She came from behind the screen, and to Katherine's amazement, had on her dress. 'I wanted you to see it, Kat. What do you think?' Katherine, fighting the lump that was rising in her throat, just stood there and stared.

'Well?' said Dorcas Louise, twirling around in front of the long mirror.

'It is beautiful beyond words,' said Katherine. 'Have you chosen your veil yet?'

'There are two that I like, but I can't decide,' said Dorcas.

Katherine, now recovered from the sight of her in the dress, placed the box on the little table by her side, and said, 'Perhaps this will help.'

Dorcas, looking curiously at the box, bent to open the lid and gasped, 'Where did this come from? It is beautiful beyond belief,' she said as she gently touched the diamonds with her finger tips.

'It is my present to you, my darling, for what you have been to me for the last twenty years. You have been a joy to raise, and I will never be able to thank your mother enough for allowing me to do so. I hope that in future years, when you look at it occasionally, you will remember me, and know that I have grown to love you as I would my own daughter. So please wear it and enjoy it on your very special day.' Tears began to gather in Dorcas's eyes, and Katherine grabbed the tissues. 'Please don't drop tears down your dress. Choose your veil, and let me see it on your head, and then we will collect your bridesmaids and head for home.'

The veil that she chose was perfect, a mass of sheer tulle that fell from the tiara like a mist. Both Dorcas and Katherine decided that Lavinia should not know that Kat had seen the dress. She would have to know of course that the tiara had been a gift, and that Kat had given it to her, and been there when she chose her veil.

One more visit to the shop saw the bridesmaids' dresses completed, and it was arranged that they would all be delivered by special couriers three days before the wedding; the wedding dress to Mr Fry's house, and the bridesmaids' to the hotel. All would be hanging, and ready to step into. Martha prepared the rooms for the wedding party guests who would be staying with Adolphus, and set aside another room in which the dress could be stored safely, and where Dorcas could have everything that she needed on her wedding morning.

The day dawned with gentle sunlight on the house of Adolphus Fry, on a morning that in his wildest dreams he never thought would happen to him. Here he was, the professor and ornithologist, playing host to the most beautiful girl on the morning of her wedding. He had in his house also the woman who had made all this possible, and who he loved more than life itself, and she in turn had brought to him a lady who now cared for him with a quiet but sure positivity that afforded him a life of serene contentment.

Mr Cloverleaf had also in his final years brought him companionship together with his excellent ability to cope with all the needs of the house, along with Martha. Life really was worth the living for a man who had always been a loner immersed in his quest for knowledge, and now surrounded by people who really cared for him. He felt very blessed at this moment as he gazed from his window and watched his beloved birds that seemed to know there was a joyous day ahead, as they sang and flitted from tree to tree feeding their young, and generally having a social get together with their neighbours.

Inside the house, Mr Cloverleaf served all the party a special wedding day breakfast, and there was laughter and warmth in the old house as they all sat together and discussed the day. At eleven o'clock, Dorcas Louise descended the stairs with Katherine in her wake. Adolphus, Martha, and Mr Cloverleaf, standing in the hall, silent now as the vision of loveliness, who a few months ago was scampering around the house as a normal teenager, floated down as perfect as any bride could be. At the bottom of the stairs, she stopped, put her arms around Adolphus, and said, 'Thank you, Uncle Adolphus for everything,' and raising her cuff showed him that she was wearing the watch that he had bought for her. 'I will wear it forever.'

As if on cue, the landau with her father on board arrived at the door, followed by another carriage to take Katherine and Adolphus to the church. Mr Cloverleaf opened the door, and ushered the bride through, passing her the bouquet of pink roses that she had chosen. Her father, in wonderment, looked at his daughter, moved forward to escort her to the landau, and as he gently placed her in her seat and sat beside her, he said, 'This is quite the proudest moment of my life, and Nathan is the luckiest man in the world. Thank you, my darling.'

The bridesmaids were standing in waiting, looking wonderful in their golden dresses, with white roses in circlets on their heads, and tiny posies to match, carried in front of them with trailing gold ribbons fluttering in the slight breeze. Thomas stood quietly by to help the bride from the carriage, and as Mr Elford nodded to him, he stood aside and left him to walk with Dorcas Louise toward the church. Katherine and Adolphus arrived and, with Thomas, slipped into the church as the bridal procession made its way to the altar. Dorcas Louise Elford was married with due ceremony to Nathaniel Applebee, and the young couple walked into the sunlight with the sounds of the wedding march echoing in their ears.

Chapter Twenty-One

Seeds of Doubt

Katherine awoke early the following morning, with Thomas by her side. The comfort and contentment of his being there with her in the room that Martha had made ready for them was sullied by her thoughts of the events following the wedding ceremony.

She had waited just inside the vestibule of the church for Thomas to return after he had seen Mr and Mrs Elford, and Mr and Mrs Applebee safely into the carriage which would follow the bridal procession to the hotel for the wedding breakfast. In the throng of people, Katherine saw a young woman, distinctive in a brilliant red dress, make her way to the bridal couple. She then saw her provocatively straighten the tie of the bridegroom and, reaching on tip toe, whisper something in his ear followed by a kiss on the lips which Katherine thought to be a little more than friendly. She dismissed that thought, but wondered who she was.

Her curiosity was soon to be satisfied when she moved outside the door to get a closer view of Dorcas Louise and Nathan as they boarded their carriage. A voice from behind her was saying, 'Who was the woman in red?'

Another voice answered, 'That's the secretary, came over with the brothers evidently. I have heard from a reliable source that she has a reputation for being much more than a perfect secretary.'

Katherine, now feeling quite sick, and with no courage to turn and see who had uttered such obscenities, quickly moved away. Seeing Adolphus waiting with Martha, she headed for them, just as Thomas saw her and made his way to her side. Once inside their carriage, she started to tremble. Martha took her hand, and Adolphus reached into his pocket for the tiny flask of brandy that he always carried. Thomas watched, but sat silently opposite, and saw the face that he loved so much regain some of its colour as Katherine sipped from the little silver cup, and allowed the brandy to work its magic.

'I'm so sorry,' Katherine said at length. 'I don't know what came over me. I'm fine now, so please stop worrying.'

Her fellow travellers, accepting what she said, but not completely satisfied, all kept their eyes on her for the rest of the journey to the wedding reception. For her the evening was torture. The woman in red was not there, and Nathan's two brothers seemed to be at ease. Katherine began to wonder if it was all in her head, but she knew it wasn't, and she would have to find out who this woman was, and more importantly what she was to Nathan Applebee. She would not, at present, worry either Adolphus or Martha. Thomas was different, and she had mulled over for a long time as to whether she would tell him everything, but as yet she felt that she couldn't. There was still so much at stake. He would just have to trust her, and if he loved her as much as he so often expressed, then he would accept her as she was, secrets and all.

He kissed her tenderly as she rose to bring in the tray of tea that Martha had left outside the door, after tapping quietly, and then moving away.

'They are such lovely people, your Adolphus and Martha, and I feel so honoured to have become a part of your life,' said Thomas.

'I too feel honoured to be loved by you,' answered Katherine. They sat, heads together resting against the pillows, and discussed yesterday. 'Something happened, Thomas, and I will tell you, but not here and not now. I hope that it is not what I read into it, but I have a very uneasy feeling which may be unfounded. I pray that it is.' Katherine turned to kiss him, and he took her hand.

'I love you, and you need not worry if you do not wish to tell me. I only want to be there for you and if I can do that, and ease your pain at any time, then that will be enough for me.'

'You are a very special person, Thomas Moreton, and one day I will be able to unburden myself upon you, and what a day that will be.'

Katherine smiled at him, wrapped her gown around her, picked up her clothes and departed for the bathroom, leaving him to watch her in amazement at her beauty. Upon her return to the bedroom, she found that Thomas had used the facilities in the room, washed, dressed, and gone, presumably down to join Adolphus. Katherine, gathering her, and Thomas's, belongings together, and placing them in the travel bags, opened the door to leave them for Mr Cloverleaf to pick up. She found him outside the door waiting. Katherine bade him good morning, and thanked him, and went to pass him to make her way to breakfast. He hesitated before he picked them up, clearing his throat as if to say something.

Katherine said, 'Is everything all right, Mr Cloverleaf?'

'Well…' Mr Cloverleaf stuttered, and then said, 'Oh yes, it's nothing, Miss Katherine.'

'It doesn't look like it's nothing, Mr Cloverleaf, can I help?' said Katherine.

'Could I possibly have a word with you, sometime, not necessarily today, but sometime please?' he answered, words tumbling quickly from his lips.

'After breakfast,' promised Katherine, 'I will think of an excuse, and meet you in the gallery.'

Katherine whispered to Thomas when they had finished their breakfast, 'Can you keep Adolphus busy, Mr Cloverleaf seems a little agitated and wishes to talk to me.'

Thomas shook his head, smiled and nodded, looking at her and thinking 'everybody's angel', that's what she is. Roger Cloverleaf stood in the gallery, twisting his handkerchief like a small schoolboy about to confess a crime. Katherine drew up two of the gold chairs, bade him sit, and she waited.

Eventually, he spoke, hesitantly. 'I find myself in a very difficult position, and one that I have never been in before. I find myself experiencing a feeling of fondness toward Mrs Wilkin, and I wondered if you thought it would be in order for me to invite her to join me for an evening out. I do not wish to anger or upset her, and I wondered if you could enquire as to her thoughts on the subject without giving away the knowledge of my feelings.'

Katherine found herself wanting to laugh, but thought that if she did it would be very unkind to this man who on the surface appeared to be full of disciplined confidence, but was now as unsure as a young boy.

'Mr Cloverleaf, I feel that you should now pluck up every fibre of your courage, and go and ask the lady yourself. Look upon it as you did when you walked into the Elford household to teach a young frightened Charlie to become a first class butler. Whatever her answer is you will feel all the better for having the confidence to ask. Martha is a very loving, and kind person who would never let anything that you said affect the respect that she has for you already. Go and talk to her, and I think that you will be pleasantly surprised by her answer.'

Katherine left him looking blankly at the pictures on the wall. Thomas and Adolphus were waiting in the hallway. She walked toward them to say her goodbyes to Adolphus, who as always was sad to see her go. Martha came from the kitchen to see them off, and Katherine casually said as she left, 'I've just seen Mr Cloverleaf, he was looking for you.'

The chauffeur had brought the limousine to the door, stepped out and was handling the luggage into the compartment at the rear of the vehicle. Adolphus moved forward to hand him the payment for his services, which he placed in the inside pocket of his jacket. He stood up straight, his face looking strained, and addressed himself to Adolphus. 'Sir, I will not be able to carry on serving you for very much longer. The owner of the garage is going to put it up for sale and at the moment I am running the business, and doing all the driving. This is not a problem, I can easily manage but of course I have to close when I am taking a fare. My business partner has decided to leave and look for alternative employment, and so that will leave me in an impossible position. I can't afford to buy the premises, and who knows what the new owner will want to do. I was so hoping that I would be able to work here for at least another seven years. That would bring me to the age when I could retire. I wanted to tell you, sir, so that on occasions such as today you can make other arrangements. I am sorry, I have been very happy to drive you, and you are my best customer. I will be sorry when it all comes to an end.'

Adolphus, thinking for a moment, said, 'Go and take these good people to the station, so that they do not miss their train, and then come and see me on your way back to the garage.'

'Yes sir, I will sir,' said Evan Pugh.

Adolphus took both of Katherine's hands in his, and kissed her on both cheeks. 'Don't make it too long before you and Thomas come back and stay with us again.'

'We won't,' said Katherine. Thomas shook hands warmly with Adolphus and Martha, and said his thanks to both of them. Martha had stayed instead of running off to see Mr Cloverleaf. Whatever it was, she was sure it would keep. They both stood and watched as Thomas and Katherine sped away. They looked at each other, and smiled in the knowledge that both of their young charges would be happy in each other's company whichever way fate decided their future.

Adolphus shut the front door, and made his way to his library. Martha headed toward the kitchen where she knew that Mr Cloverleaf would be waiting for the cup of tea that she always made him at this time of day. Mr Cloverleaf, who always sat relaxed at the table, today was standing nervously in the doorway. Easing past him, and picking up the teapot, Martha said, 'Did you want me, Mr Cloverleaf?'

'Um, yes, I think so,' gabbled Mr Cloverleaf. Martha looked at him in expectation. He was usually so confident and outspoken in their conversations, of which they had had many over a cup of tea sitting at this very table. What was different about today, Martha wondered, beginning to feel a little apprehensive.

'Well?' said Martha.

'I have been thinking of late,' began Mr Cloverleaf. 'I would sometimes like to go out in the evening to see a show in the West End, or visit a nice restaurant.'

Martha sat, chin resting on her hands supported by her elbows placed one each side of her cup of tea, which was sending swirls of warm steam up her arms. 'I'm sure that would be very nice,' she condescended.

How does one carry on this conversation, thought Mr Cloverleaf, now trapped between offering a direct invitation, or hedging a bit more in hopes of gaining some encouragement. 'Do you ever feel that you would like to do the same, Mrs Wilkin?' he ventured.

'I have never had any thoughts in that direction, Mr Cloverleaf, but I suppose if I had someone to go with it would be very pleasant.' Martha, now beginning to see the way that the conversation was heading, was going to lead him into a situation that he had never been in, and was enjoying every moment.

Mr Cloverleaf, handkerchief suffering mutilation under the table, began again, 'I think too that it would be so much nicer if one had company to do this sort of thing; it could be embarrassing for one to be alone in either a theatre or a restaurant, so perhaps I should reconsider.'

'Mr Cloverleaf,' Martha said, now looking at him directly, 'if you are considering asking me to go with you, then could you perhaps do it sooner rather than later, and if you are not, then I think that you should find someone as soon as possible, who will fill your need for company in your quest for entertainment.'

Mr Cloverleaf, handkerchief now beyond repair, asked, 'Mrs Wilkin, would you do me the honour of accompanying me one evening to the theatre?'

'It would give me great pleasure, Mr Cloverleaf, to do just that. I will look forward to your confirmation with great anticipation.'

Mr Cloverleaf left the kitchen, his tea cup still in his hand, the tea in it now cold, and headed toward the library where he would ask permission from Mr Fry, thinking that possibly he should have asked him first, but too late now he mused, head in the clouds at the thought of an evening spent with Mrs Wilkin. Martha sat at the table relishing her second cup of tea, and wondering how long it would take to bring this most correct and perfect person into the realms of the real world. It would be a while, she thought, but how she would enjoy it.

'Come in, Cloverleaf,' shouted Adolphus from behind the door. 'Sit down, I want to talk to you.'

'And me to you, sir,' Cloverleaf countermanded.

'You first then,' said Adolphus. He liked this man, and felt quite at ease and comfortable in his presence.

'Well, sir, I have just done something that I had never considered in all of my fifty odd years. I hope that you will approve, and I apologise in advance if it does not meet your criteria regarding my being here.'

'Get on with it, man,' said Adolphus.

'Well, I have asked Mrs Wilkin if she would consider accompanying me on a visit to the West End, possibly to a theatre, or to a restaurant, and she has accepted. I spoke to Miss Katherine, and she seemed to be very much in favour of it, so I hope that you will be too.'

'I see,' said Adolphus with a very straight face. 'Well, if Miss Katherine has given her blessing, then I see no point in saying otherwise. Of course I approve, very much; go ahead and enjoy yourselves, but there is one stipulation that I have to make. If you steal my cook, and wonderful housekeeper, you will be in my black book for ever. So think on that, Cloverleaf. She stays here, which means that you have to stay here too, so if that meets with your approval, then it's a deal.'

The two men shook hands, and Adolphus started to plant the seeds of an idea in Mr Cloverleaf's head. 'The garage across the road is evidently on the market, which will leave Evan Pugh, and his assistant, in the unenviable position of possibly ending up unemployed. The man obviously can't raise the money to buy the business, and there is no guarantee that the buyer will want to carry on with it the way it is now. I was considering it as a possible venture that you and I could enter into. We all have the need of an automobile. I would not consider driving one myself, and the availability of transport on our doorstep is something to be desired, especially when we have our visitors, which I hope will be often. Does the thought of running a business appeal to you, and do you think you could manage the financial side? Pugh and his assistant are, I know, responsible people, and they have an unquenchable desire to give their time and experience to the running of a garage. Pugh has about seven years until he wants to think about retiring, but that doesn't necessarily mean that he will, and by then we would be fully in touch with the success or failure of the business. What do you think, Cloverleaf? When Pugh returns from the station, he is coming in to see me, so do you think we could stop him from making a decision to lose his partner while we delve into the possibilities regarding my purchasing of the garage, and him renting from me?'

Roger Cloverleaf thought that for the second time today, he would make an amazing decision, and his life would maybe change forever. 'I think that it would be the most exciting thing to do, and I will go with you to whatever level you wish to reach, Mr Fry.'

Adolphus then, with total assurance and speed, made a space on the desk for Cloverleaf to set out a plan for his investigation into the viability of the whole project. The knock at the door came at just the perfect moment. Martha answered it and brought Evan Pugh into the library. Cloverleaf pulled out a chair for him. He sat nervously in front of Adolphus, and waited for him to speak.

'Mr Pugh, I can't at this time offer you any absolute assurance of your future in the garage, but I may be able help you. I will need a little time, but if you can trust me you may find the result will be to your advantage. Also if you can persuade your assistant to stay for the time being, and continue paying your rent to the owner as you do now, it would be a great help to me. I will, I assure you, be in touch with you just as soon as I can, and you will see Mr Cloverleaf here looking around the garage from time to time. Don't be alarmed; he will be under my instructions.'

Mr Pugh left the house, a little bewildered but with a tiny spark of hope, and made his way back to talk to his assistant. He put away the limousine before going home to his wife to relate what had happened that afternoon. Mr Cloverleaf set to work with a passion, and the report that came back to Adolphus was quite astounding. The garage was found to be in need of some attention, and some of the tools that were being used were in his opinion antiquated, and in need of replacement. The two main cars were fine, but there were three at the back of the building that could stand some restoration. Charlie and Thomas came to mind, and wouldn't they just love the chance to take the job on. If the garage were to become a garage where customers' cars could be repaired, as well as providing a taxi service, then they would benefit from installing a petrol pump on the forecourt. The asking price for the premises was high, but Mr Cloverleaf hastened to point out the areas lacking in repair, and facilities.

An agreement was finally reached that was acceptable to both sides, and Adolphus Fry became the proud owner of The Corner Garage, with Evan Pugh and his assistant offering, not only a good chauffeur service, but a repair and general maintenance service, with the added attraction of a petrol pump given pride of place on the forecourt. Adolphus sat back, and smiled at the thought that now he had moved on from his life built around the university of Liverpool, and his love of birds, to be an owner of a garage, when he knew nothing of the mechanics of it all. He only knew that he would always have the necessary transport for his weekly visits to his club.

Katherine and Thomas had arrived home to a quiet house that was still showing signs of a forthcoming marriage. Mr and Mrs Elford had been away for a few days, to recover from the turmoil. Katherine set to work to tidy up. Flo had cleared up all the prenuptial decoration, and had washed, scrubbed, and made beds. Charlie had restocked the wine cellar, and put all the china and glass back in their pristine condition in the relevant cupboards. Katherine followed up, and in a short time the house looked as if nothing but the day to day living had taken place.

It was two days later when Charlie answered the door to a young woman smartly dressed in a black dress, over which she wore a white jacket. She wore black high-heeled shoes with a sequined bow across the toes. 'May I see Mr Charles Elford?' she said. Her American accent bearing witness to the connection between her and the Applebee family who as far as Charlie knew, were still in London.

'I am afraid that Mr and Mrs Elford are not at home,' Charlie said, as she edged her way toward the doorway.

'I need to have some of the paperwork that Mr Elford is working on at present. If I may come in, and you show me to his office, I can collect it. I know exactly what I am looking for,' she exclaimed.

'I am afraid that I have no instructions to allow that,' Charlie stated. 'I will call the housekeeper, Miss Carrera. She may be able to help you, if you would kindly wait here in the hall.'

'I do not have much time, and if Mr Elford is not here then I will have to insist that I retrieve the paperwork that I need.'

Katherine came to the head of the stairs as she heard the voice that drew her attention. Her heart leaped at the familiarity of the woman. It was her, the woman in red, the secretary, the one who had ruined her day at the wedding.

'May I help?' She heard her voice come out utterly calmly, and with a certain authority that the anger inside her provoked. 'I am Katherine Carrera, housekeeper, and person in charge during any absence from the house of Mr and Mrs Elford. What is it that you require? You are already aware that Mr Elford is taking a few days away with his wife, after the wedding of his daughter to Mr Nathan Applebee, who I assume you are employed by.'

The woman looked at her with disdain, and said, 'I am Mr Nathan Applebee's personal secretary, and as such have the right to access all things relevant to his business.'

Katherine, now beginning to feel angry, replied, 'You may have the right to access Mr Applebee's business effects, but you do not have the right to enter this house without the permission of Mr Elford, and you certainly do not have the right to enter his private residence in which he has all things relevant to his side of the business. In addition to which, I have no means of entry to his office, neither does any of my staff, so unless you have a way of contacting him in my presence, I have no choice but to ask you to leave, and return when Mr Elford is here. Would you please show this lady out, Mr Orchard? Goodbye, Miss…?

'Lucinda Hepworth is the name,' the woman answered, 'and you will be hearing much more from me in the future, Miss Katherine Carrera.' She flounced out of the door, held open by Charlie, and into a waiting black automobile, which hesitated for only a minute and then drove away.

Katherine stood shaking as Charlie closed the door and looked up at her. 'Who did she think she was, coming here unannounced, and being so rude?'

Katherine moved into the kitchen to sit down, and Flo came to her side, placing an arm around her shoulders. Cook, as usual, was on hand with the mandatory cup of tea to calm the nerves. 'She,' said a furious Katherine, 'was the private secretary to Mr Nathan Applebee. She was present at the wedding of Nathan and Dorcas Louise, but not at the reception, which in my opinion points at the fact that she was uninvited. I saw and heard something that I found most upsetting about her, but I will not repeat it at present, because it may have further repercussions, and I do not want it to be me that reported it. I hope you understand, and I think it would be prudent not to mention this visit for the moment. I will be relating it to Mr Elford upon his return.'

Finally, they all settled down and returned to the tasks that they had set themselves in the absence of Katherine, Thomas, and the Elfords. Katherine was very proud of her staff, and the way that they worked together when the house was left in their care. She could trust them implicitly, and for that she was truly thankful. Charlie had acted with the utmost discipline and without hesitation as the strange woman had forced her way into the house. She would see to it that this had a mention when reporting to Mr Elford.

Sitting down later with Thomas in the nursery, she swore him to secrecy and told him what had happened at the church. He was mortified, and confessed to not seeing her at all. Katherine said that she must have slipped away from the crowd directly after her little display, and observed that Mr and Mrs Elford probably would not have seen her, as they would be making their way to the carriage that would follow the bridal pair to the reception. Her little exhibition, which would have been observed by the remaining crowd, had taken possibly three to four minutes, Katherine concluded. Therefore, would both sets of parents, and the occupants of the carriages that were waiting in line, notice the delay of the bride and groom who were expected to be in their carriage first to head the procession to the reception?

Thomas, by now more than a little impressed by Katherine's astuteness, and obvious suspicion of the motives of the disappearing woman in the red dress, began to think that there was something not very nice going on. The lovely day, the evening, and the night spent at the house of Adolphus, now began to be overshadowed by the happenings, not only on the wedding day, but today also, which to Thomas seemed to have added an even more sinister side to the actions of this woman. They talked long into the night, and Katherine told Thomas about Mr Cloverleaf and Martha. Thomas commented that Mr Cloverleaf had also dropped a gentle hint to him, and he thought it was a wonderful idea, and hoped that maybe a little more than a friendship would develop between them.

They both arose before the rest of the household, so that Thomas could make his way to his own room unheard, and unseen. Katherine had lain in his arms for what seemed a very short night, and Thomas had made love to her gently, until finally she rose in passion to meet him. For a short while, the worry and gnawing pain that had powered anger within her, abated, and she let the love of Thomas fill her heart and mind. He took her in his arms, held her tightly, and kissed her once again before he left. Almost always she would eventually come up with an answer, not only with her own problems, but with everyone who sought her help. This time it was not to be. She would tell Mr Elford what she had done as soon as he arrived home, and if he said that an apology was needed, then she would submit, and offer one to that horrible woman.

It was a week before Lavinia and Charles Elford returned home. They looked rested as Charlie took their coats, and ordered Cook to prepare a tray for them. Katherine decided to wait until the morning, when Mr Elford would be picking up the threads of business once again, to broach the question of Nathan's secretary.

Lavinia Elford came to the nursery, and Katherine felt pleased to have her around again. They had almost become friends, and both were happy in each other's company. The wedding was of course on top of the list for conversation, and Lavinia had obviously not been able to talk about it while they were away, for as soon as she sat down, she began to compare notes with Katherine. Dorcas's dress, and headdress, the little flower girl, the cake, the carriages, everything she wanted to relive again.

Katherine sat quietly and listened, nodding, and putting in a word or two. Finally, both agreed that it had been the most perfect wedding. Katherine was thinking and fiercely praying that it would stand the test of time, but she had more doubts than she would care to admit. She forewarned Mrs Elford that she had something that she had to tell Mr Elford, which she felt to be of great importance, and she hoped that Mrs Elford would be present in the library to hear what she had to say. Mrs Elford shot her a questioning look, but Katherine insisted that it had to be directed to Mr Elford, and that she would understand why when it was told.

Morning came, and the moment arrived. Katherine was nervous, but Mr Elford could not imagine anything that Katherine could say would shake his faith in the good feelings that he had about his life at present. He stood smiling as both Katherine and his wife entered the room at the same time. He had chairs ready and waiting for them, and wasted no time in enquiring as to what it was that Katherine was obviously so worried about.

'Sir,' Katherine started, a little nervously, 'I have to report that I have dealt rather heavily with a lady who came to the door, and introduced herself as Mr Nathan Applebee's secretary. I, rightly or wrongly, totally disliked her attitude, and asked her to leave when I couldn't furnish her with the details that she requested. She was in my opinion extremely rude, and very demanding of Mr Orchard, whom I thought dealt with her with excellent composure. She was also threatening to me.'

Mr Elford stopped her at this point, and asked, 'What was it she requested, Katherine?'

'She did not ask specifically for anything, but wanted to enter your office, and look herself for the details that she said she would recognise easily, and would take away to work on.'

At this point, Mr Elford showed some signs of concern, and said, 'Thank you, Katherine, you did exactly the right thing, albeit with a little more attitude than I would have given you credit for. I would not normally discuss my private affairs with anyone, sometimes not even my wife,' and turning to his wife, he said, 'I am sorry, darling, but that is true, only because secrecy is sometimes absolutely necessary.' He returned his attention to Katherine and said, 'Just in case this ever happens again, I am telling you now, Katherine, that there is nothing in my private office here that anyone but me would need to know about. All paperwork that involves my connection with the Applebees is within the walls of the office in London, belonging to them, and obviously where this young woman is at present working. I have no knowledge of a secretary, and I seriously wonder what it was that she wanted. Until Nathan and Dorcas return, there is nothing that I can do to find out, but be sure that I will find out, and you have my authority to deal with her or anyone else who tries to enter this house without my permission. Thank you once again, Katherine, for your insight and common sense.

Lavinia Elford, who had been sitting quietly during the conversation, now said to her husband, 'I believe that there should be some way of contacting us quickly if something like this occurs when we are away. We should have a telephone. I believe that calls between London and Liverpool are quite commonplace now, and we should be able to speak to you when you are away on business. Also, Katherine could contact Adolphus if she was concerned about anything in our absence. We have so many reasons now for the need to communicate. Our daughter will not always be here, and she may need to talk to Nathan when he is away.'

Mr Elford, convinced by his wife's reasoning, agreed to have a telephone installed in the hall. Not for chit chat, he ordered, only for important calls.

All these new fangled inventions were expensive. In spite of these reservations, the order was placed, and the Elford household would now be on the telephone network.

Katherine, keeping silent about the events of the wedding day for the present, carried on with the running of the household, not however being able to forget the smug look on the woman's face when she fronted her in the house. She thought of Dorcas Louise continually, and felt sick inside when she considered the possibilities of a personal relationship between Nathan and Lucinda Hepworth. Giving them the benefit of the doubt, she thought that if there was evidence of a liaison before Nathan's marriage to Dorcas Louise, then the past was not her business, but Nathan's very attitude to life gave her cause for concern. The return from their honeymoon was not due for a couple of months, and the possibility of hearing any news from Florida was indeed very unlikely. Katherine pushed the whole thing to the back of her mind, and just said a silent prayer for the child who she loved with a passion rarely found in parents, much less in a nanny.

The memories stirred again when Lavinia Elford came into the nursery with the box which held Dorcas's wedding regalia. She gave it to Katherine, saying that she thought that she would like to pack it carefully away and keep it where it would be safe in the hope that one day there would be a daughter who may like to wear it on her wedding day. Katherine took it from her, and placed it on the chair until later when she could give it her full attention. Lavinia stayed a while and seemed to want to talk, so Katherine, placing aside the linen that she had been folding away, sat beside her. She called for Flo to bring them some tea, and looked at Lavinia Elford whom she thought looked very tired, in spite of her last few days spent lazing at a lakeside resort in Switzerland. Katherine waited for the tray of tea and, upon its arrival, poured a cup for the mistress and one for herself, and offered a biscuit which Lavinia refused. Then, turning to her, she said, 'Please excuse my impertinence, but it seems that you are worried by something; can I help?'

Lavinia answered with a slight tremor in her voice, 'I do need to talk to someone, Katherine, and I would rather it be you than anyone else. I know I can trust your discretion, and I have also seen the concern in your face of late.'

Katherine looked at her in surprise, and said, 'I have a number of concerns, but they are purely in my mind, and I doubt that they have any connection to those which you have. However, as with your trust in me, I also have trust in you, so shall we share our worries and concerns in the knowledge that they will remain only between us, unless any future situation calls for them to become public?'

Lavinia fought with a persistent smile that hovered around her serious face, and said, 'Yes, Katherine, that would be such a relief, but who will go first? I think I would like it to be you, because I believe that it has something to do with Dorcas Louise, and possibly the woman who obviously caused you some distress. Am I right?'

'Yes, you are perfectly right,' answered Katherine, 'and in order for you to understand my grief, I will have to go back to the day of the wedding and tell you exactly what I saw and heard.'

Sitting bolt upright now, and with full concentration, Lavinia listened as Katherine repeated word for word the whole episode. Lavinia, her pale complexion now showing signs of stress, nodded her head as if to confirm an answer to a question that she had asked herself on the day. She looked at Katherine and said, 'I wondered at the delay in Nathan and Dorcas Louise arriving at their carriage, and I also had a fleeting view of a woman who was dressed as if she were a guest standing beside the carriage. She was blowing a kiss toward the bridal pair as they departed, and then hand on hat running across the road between the bridal carriage and the one that James and I were in. I looked for her at the wedding breakfast, and then I watched all evening for her, but as far as I could see she did not return.'

Katherine exclaimed, 'You can imagine now how I felt when I saw her at this house, trying to gain entrance, and being extremely rude in the process. I am scared, Mrs Elford, very scared that Dorcas Louise's marriage is going to be marred by the presence of one Lucinda Hepworth.'

Mrs Elford, now with a very strong voice, stated, 'If she is still in London after the return of Nathan and Dorcas Louise, and I find that she is causing any problems at all, I will personally see to it that she is sent back to the United States where she came from. I think that we will bide our time on this, Katherine, and review the situation when Dorcas Louise is at home here with us. Do you agree?'

'I feel happier now that you know,' said Katherine, placated for the time being. 'Would you like now to unburden your worries on me, Mrs Elford?'

It was Katherine's turn to sit and listen. 'First,' Mrs Elford fidgeted, 'do you think that in our private personal moments, you could call me Lavinia? We have lived in close harmony, and raised a child between us for the last twenty years. I think each from the other has gained respect, and I would feel more at ease in disclosing some of my innermost thoughts if we could address one another as friends.'

Katherine answered with a smile, 'I would find that very pleasant, and most comforting to know that you are a friend. Thank you, Lavinia.'

'I don't quite know where to start,' Lavinia interrupted, 'and lately I have been drifting between what I know is fact, and what I am imagining. After today's revelation, I am beginning to think that it may all be relevant. I truly believe that my husband is getting far too tied up in this deal with the Applebees. It worries me greatly, and I think that deep down it worries him too, but he would never admit to that, so I just have to hope and pray that I am wrong. I hope also that I am wrong when I think that the marriage between Dorcas Louise and Nathan might have been not wholly their decision, but with a little push from here, and another from there, and the two young people found themselves in the glitz and glamour of a heady romance, with the backing of two of the richest families in the land.'

At this point, Katherine began to tremble and wonder if all her fears were justified, and where did the woman at the wedding figure in it all? They both sat in silence now, each gathering their own thoughts. Lavinia was first to speak. 'I think we should now hold on to what we think, and wait until the honeymoon is over, and they are back in England, then I think we should keep a very close vigil on all the happenings that may bear any resemblance to our suspicions. Together, Katherine, we can and will protect Dorcas Louise from any badness that could come from all this.'

The day of the return of the honeymooners was earmarked for a small celebration. Nathan's parents and brothers had returned to New York soon after the wedding, and so the young couple were returning to Liverpool on their own. Nathan had hinted to Dorcas Louise that he would like them to find somewhere to live in London, as it would be easier for him to work in the London office than to share the space belonging to his father-in-law in the Liverpool house. Dorcas Louise had agreed to go if that was what he wanted, but he then decided that perhaps it would be better if he stayed in London when it was necessary, and then Dorcas Louise would not have to leave her family. Later on, of course, he would hope that the whole business would be transferred to America and that Dorcas's father would be the only contact in England. Then all the dealings would be done through the American market. Dorcas Louise, not really understanding all the high finance involved, had readily agreed with everything that Nathan suggested.

Charlie and Thomas had cleaned, polished, and made ready the Rolls Royce, and Charlie would drive it to the docks to meet the ship. Dorcas sailed down the gangplank, looking a million dollars in a yellow polka dot dress, with a cute little head hugging hat also in yellow. Nathan followed her, looking dapper in his dark suit and carrying a bowler hat. Charlie moved out of the dense crowd waiting, and made himself visible to the couple who raised hands and made their way toward him. A little man pushing a trolley, a little bigger than himself, and the familiar looking luggage was deposited at the Rolls Royce. The little man, clutching a silver coin in his hand, disappeared into the waiting throng.

'Good afternoon sir, madam,' Charlie said as he opened the door for them to climb aboard.

'Good afternoon, Orchard,' replied Nathan. 'Get out us out of here as soon as you can; I can't stand crowds.'

Charlie deftly swung the Rolls Royce around, people in his path quickly hopping out of the way. Clearing the dock area with amazing speed and heading out of town, they were soon on their way. Dorcas Louise was secretly excited at the thought of going home with her new husband, and seeing her parents, and Kat. She also wanted to show them all the lovely clothes that Nathan had bought her, and the jewellery that he had showered upon her. She would forget the nights when he had been a little rough; he hadn't hurt her, not really, but she had felt a little embarrassed and sad when she hadn't reached the height of excitement that he had. She would improve, and then he would really love her, and the things that he bought for her, she would feel that she deserved.

They were all there at the door, her mother and father, and Kat standing behind them. Cook was at the kitchen door, as always wiping her hands on her apron. Flo stood, tray in hand, smiling, remembering her day when she had returned to the house as Mrs Orchard, and she remembered feeling that she never wanted Charlie to leave her side. Dorcas Louise, however, forgetting for a moment her new status, leaped from the carriage, and ran to her mother and father, hugging them, and in turn, Kat got a big hug and a whisper in her ear, 'I missed you.'

Katherine, choking back the tears, just nodded and smiled, and gently said, 'Welcome home, Mrs Applebee.'

Mr Applebee was still easing himself from the seat next to Charlie, where he had sat to accommodate the enormous amount of luggage that had been placed on the seat next to Dorcas Louise. The romantic picture of them arriving home hand in hand had been abandoned in favour of bringing home expensive presents for the family, which had been Dorcas Louise's wish. Mr and Mrs Elford waited for their new son-in-law to make his way to the door, and greeted him warmly.

Katherine slipped quietly into her office, thinking that she would greet him later, a little less warmly, but with all the sincerity that she could muster. Hopefully, he would be with Dorcas Louise when they met, and that would make things a little easier for her. She would try desperately not to let her feelings get the better of her. Dorcas Louise looked beautiful and happy, and she could settle happily for that, and would react accordingly.

The meeting came after they had all had a celebration meal. Cook had once again excelled, and had served a fish course followed by a succulent lamb roast, and to follow, a wonderful concoction of strawberries and cream, topped with pink and white hearts made from sugar. They had all retired to the drawing room to have coffee served with mint creams. Katherine came in to pass to Mr Elford some greetings that had been delivered after the couple had left for their honeymoon. She said that it might be nice if he read them, as would have been done at the wedding feast. Nathan, in his usual brash way, rose and, clasping Katherine's hand rather too tightly, said, 'How nice. Thank you, Miss Katherine.'

Katherine, half turning to face both him and Dorcas Louise, said, 'Not at all, welcome home to both of you.'

Over the next few weeks, the house took on a normal air of quiet confidence from all its inhabitants. Katherine settled to her office jobs, and Dorcas spent some time re-arranging her apartment, which had now been extended to a comfortable suite of rooms to accommodate the newly married couple. Nathan and Mr Elford, ensconced among the vast amount of paperwork, were rarely about until later in the day, when they joined their respective wives for a pre-dinner drink, and some light conversation that steered clear of anything financial.

Some days, Nathan would leave very early in the morning for London, and the house always seemed a little more relaxed without his powerful presence. Mr Elford would still spend a lot of time in his office, but now and then would venture out and sometimes take his wife out for a trip to town and a quiet lunch. Lavinia would come home much happier for his attention and company.

The year was gaining momentum once again, and the autumn leaves were leaving their golden red carpet along the roads and alleyways around the house. No mention was made by Katherine, Lavinia, or James Elford, regarding the untimely visit of Miss Lucinda Hepworth, or the comments that were made. It seemed that it would be forgotten and pass into history. Katherine would never forget it, and would never cease to worry about her existence in the life of Nathan Applebee.

It was in October that Nathan announced that he would be bringing his secretary back to the house with him when he returned from one of his trips. He would be instructing her further in the running of the business, so that on her return to the United States of America, she would be fully conversant with both sides of the merger until it was finally one. She was, he concluded, to be given full assistance, and access to all paperwork held here in the house. Mr Elford, in the circumstances, had no choice but to agree. However, he had in his mind more than a little doubt, and would be very careful as to the papers that he would leave available to her.

It was agreed that she should stay at the house for one week, and that Katherine would prepare a room suitable to her requirements. She would of course be the personal guest of Nathan and Dorcas Louise, and in consequence, Katherine would take on the same responsibilities as if she were a guest of the master and mistress. The room that Katherine selected was situated on the floor directly below the suite of Nathan and Dorcas Louise, and at the opposite end of the corridor. This did not escape the notice of Lavinia Elford, who passed a knowing smile of agreement to Katherine when she inspected and gave approval of the choice. The evening of her arrival, sitting next to Nathan in his American car, gave cause for some comments in the kitchen.

'Madam has arrived wearing a gown of antique cream, which matches perfectly with her antique cream complexion,' snorted Flo, who had witnessed the exchange of conversation between her and Charlie when she last made her appearance at the door.

'Quietly,' scolded Katherine, smothering a giggle at Flo's comments.

She left the kitchen to be at the door in the welcoming position, and noticed how closely Lucinda was sitting next to Nathan, her hand against his arm as he opened his door to get out, and then waiting for him to come round to her side of the automobile, so that she could grasp his hand as she gracefully slipped out of her seat. Mr and Mrs Elford by this time had arrived at the door to welcome them, and Dorcas Louise, a little shyly, hung back and waited for her introduction to the woman whom she had see planting a kiss on her husband's lips so frivolously on their wedding day. Nathan had followed her in and proceeded to introduce her to the family. It was obvious by now that he knew nothing of her previous visit to the house and, to their credit, none of the staff showed any recognition. They reached Katherine, who, with a blank expression, hands at her side, dropped her eyes, and gave the slightest impression of a nod of the head.

'This is Lucinda Hepworth, Katherine, my secretary. Would you be kind enough to see that she has everything that she needs during her stay at the house?' Nathan said in his usual flippant manner.

'Of course, sir, that is my duty, and I will carry it out as always to the best of my ability,' Katherine said, eyes now firmly fixed on those of Lucinda Hepworth. 'If you will follow me, Madam, I will show you to your room,' and with a flick of her skirt, and a determined stride, Katherine headed upstairs with the house guest in close pursuit, finding it difficult to keep up in her tight skirt and high heels.

Dorcas Louise, who waited for her husband, was sent ahead by him to prepare for dinner while he followed his secretary up the stairs behind the athletic Katherine, who by now was turning the lock in the door, and waiting to usher in the guest. Standing in the doorway, thus blocking the path of Nathan, she said, 'Your luggage is on its way, Madam, and the master and mistress will be waiting in the drawing room where drinks will be served in half an hour. Your host and his wife will welcome you and ask you to accompany them to the dining room for their evening meal and join them for the rest of the evening.'

Turning to Nathan, Katherine said, 'Sir, with respect, you will need to make haste as your wife will be waiting for you to join her. If you require my further services, do not hesitate call me, or send a member of my staff to find me. Thank you.' With the utmost composure Katherine quietly shut the door, and waited for Nathan to turn away and head for his own suite where Dorcas Louise was waiting for him.

Nathan, being unaware of the reasoning behind Katherine's attitude, was distinctly annoyed, and unfortunately Dorcas Louise bore the brunt of his anger in complete innocence. He slammed from door to door, and pulled things from drawers, leaving a trail of unwanted underwear in his wake, as he bathed and dressed. Dorcas Louise, who had already dressed, waited patiently, going behind him and picking up the things that he had rejected, and placing them back where they belonged. He looked at her and, thinking silently how beautiful she looked, he muttered, 'Dinner will have to wait. I've been rushed enough today.'

Dorcas Louise, showing no emotion at all, said, 'I'm sure everyone will be happy to wait for you, Nathan.'

Dinner did have to wait. Mr and Mrs Elford were left to entertain Lucinda Hepworth, Cook was holding the presentation of vegetables, and Charlie was poised, carving knife in hand, waiting for the signal to go so that the meat could be placed carved under the silver lid of the meat dish, hot and ready to serve, following the soup that was steaming on the range, with Flo hovering ready to place it on the serving trolley. It was forty minutes after seven o'clock when Dorcas Louise on the arm of Nathan came serenely down the stairs to join the waiting family. No apology was given, and none was asked for. Lucinda Hepworth, looking faintly guilty, and to be fair, slightly nervous, waited to be shown to her place next to Mr Elford. She shot a fiery gaze at Nathan, who gave a slight shrug of the shoulders, hardly noticeable except to the one to whom it was directed.

Katherine stood outside the door and watched with glee as the secretary had little choice but to sit and make polite conversation with Mr Elford. He would far rather be talking to his wife, who as usual looked the most beautiful hostess, serene and sure of herself in an awkward situation. How he loved her, and always would. It was quite late when all the chores had been done, and the tables emptied, glass and china washed and returned to the shelves. Katherine, satisfied that all was tidy, shut the drawing room door, and went to the kitchen for a much welcomed cup of tea, shared with Cook and Thomas. Charlie and Flo had retired, and Thomas was waiting for the silent house to tell him that its inhabitants too had retired for the night, so that he could check the lights and lock the door.

The next couple of days saw Mr Elford, Nathan, and Lucinda Hepworth, locked in the office. Occasionally, the haughty secretary would appear, and order refreshment to be served with haste. She would look at Katherine in total distaste and, with a warning look in her ice-cold grey eyes, she would taunt her, dropping Nathan's name into a command that Katherine knew was nothing to do with him. As much as she didn't like the young man, she knew the kind of words he would use, and the ones that Lucinda spoke were not from his vocabulary. What was she up to she wondered.

Dorcas Louise would come and sit with her, and tell her of the worries she had, and that she thought that Nathan was already tiring of her company, and much preferred that of the flighty Miss Hepworth. Katherine assured her that he loved her, and that it was just the business deals that were getting complicated, and consuming his thoughts. As for his secretary, she told her, 'Bright lights like her burn out very quickly, my darling, while softer beautiful rays of sunshine last a lifetime.'

The week in which Lucinda Hepworth was supposed to complete her time in the house was at an end. Katherine, Dorcas Louise, and Lavinia, were heaving sighs of relief, until Nathan declared on the penultimate evening of her stay that all that he had hoped for had not been attained yet, and so Miss Hepworth would be asked to stay, possibly for another ten days or so. His statement was greeted with total silence from all at the dinner table, except for Mr Elford, who, apparently with some reluctance, agreed that it was possibly a good idea.

He suggested then that it may be prudent to remove all the relative paperwork to the London office, and that he travelled there for any future collation that may be needed. He would prepare all relevant papers that he had in the house to this end, and would be prepared to meet Nathan on a regular basis. He felt that this residential environment was not conducive to efficiency.

Mr Elford had sensed an atmosphere, and it was making it hard for him to concentrate. His mind kept returning to the earlier visit of Miss Hepworth which added to his concern, as nothing had been mentioned by her or by Nathan about the outcome of the visit, neither of her leaving the premises. The staff had kept quiet, and Mr Elford marvelled at their diplomacy.

A couple more days had passed, and the lady in question had been a nuisance, Lavinia had told him when they were getting ready to retire. She seemed to have a desire to anger Katherine, and it was beginning to upset her, which in turn angered Lavinia, and frightened Dorcas Louise, who by now was beginning to suspect that there had been something between Nathan and her, maybe before she had met him. She had no proof, except the kiss at the wedding, but that was really of little consequence.

It was Wednesday morning, and Katherine was in her office. Lavinia had taken breakfast with Dorcas Louise, as Nathan had an appointment with the manager of the bank in London, and had breakfasted early in the company of Lucinda Hepworth. She evidently was not needed by him, and so was left to carry on with her own work in the office in the presence of Mr Elford. Lavinia had suggested that she and Dorcas Louise should spend a little time together, as she had missed her company a lot since she had been married to Nathan, and she thought that they could go to town, and maybe have some lunch, and treat themselves to a little something. Mr Elford, pleased with that decision, gave Lavinia the wherewithal to do exactly that. 'Have a good time, my darlings,' he said, as Charlie opened the door for them and waited for them to climb into the car.

The morning was uneventful, and at lunchtime Katherine made her way to the kitchen where Flo was finishing the trays that had been requested by Mr Elford. He wished to have a light lunch in the office so as not to waste time, and they could all meet tonight for an evening meal. Katherine ate with Cook and Thomas. Conversation for these three was never difficult, but today Katherine was quiet, and just smiled and added a word here and there.

'What's wrong, Katherine?' asked Thomas. 'You seem lost today.'

'It's that woman,' said Katherine. 'I just feel her eyes boring into my back wherever I turn. I have done nothing to her, except to refuse her access to Mr Elford's private papers when she forced her way in last time. This morning, she made a comment as she passed by me in the hall, and I couldn't catch what it was, but the sneer on her face told me that it was something unpleasant. Her very presence here worries me.'

Katherine made her way back to her office, taking with her the orders from Cook for the replenishing of the kitchen cupboards. The shrill ring of the telephone made her jump from her chair. She was nervous of this new acquisition of the Elford household, and the fact that Mr Elford was insistent that it be kept in her office rather than his own left her in trepidation as to its use. There was no one here but her, so she had no choice but to pick it up, which she did very carefully, placing it to her ear and saying what she had been instructed to say, 'This is the Elford residence. How may I help you?'

A soft, gentle, and familiar voice said into her ear, 'You may help me by saying hello, Katherine.' There was a long pause, and then the voice said, 'It's Adolphus, Katherine, and now I too have a telephone, so my dear we will be able to talk to one another. I will call you, so that Mr Elford does not have to bear the cost.'

Katherine could have cried. 'I knew your voice but I couldn't believe that you could talk to me all the way from London.'

Adolphus answered, 'I know, it is wonderful, but what is more wonderful is that I can hear your voice too, and I have the peace of mind of knowing that if you need me, I am here. Just dial the number that I am going to give you, and I will be able to talk to you.'

'Oh, Adolphus,' cried Katherine, 'you just don't know how happy that makes me feel.' She was wishing that she could tell him how worried she was, but she couldn't, not now, she just had to pretend all was well.

Adolphus, the old wise owl that he was, knew that all was not well, but against his better judgement he left it alone, and chatted to her about Martha, and Mr Cloverleaf, and all the good work that was being done in his garden. 'Life was good,' he confessed. 'I will talk to you again soon, Katherine. Pass on my respects to Elford, and Lavinia, and give my love to Dorcas Louise. I would love to see you all again one day soon.'

'Oh you will, Adolphus, you will,' said Katherine. 'Goodbye for now. All my love to you too, and of course Martha.' Katherine replaced the telephone on its cradle, and returned to her order book. She had left the door open as she had returned from the kitchen, and she didn't hear the footfall of Lucinda Hepworth behind her. All she heard was the high pitched whine of her voice as she demanded, 'Does Mr Elford know that you have been fifteen minutes talking on the telephone? I'm sure that he would not allow it if he knew.'

Katherine, annoyed by her attitude, but perfectly in control, answered, 'No, Mr Elford did not know, but I am quite happy for him to be informed. The person on the other end of the telephone line called me, and for your information he is a personal friend of Mr Elford, and would be pleased at any time for him to be contacting me.'

'Little miss perfect, aren't you?' Lucinda challenged. 'I want to use the telephone now if that is not too much trouble.'

'It is no trouble to me, but if it is a personal call I need to know if Mr Elford has sanctioned it.'

Furious, Lucinda snatched the telephone from its cradle, dialled a number unknown to Katherine, and said in a stilted voice to the recipient, 'Haven't you finished yet? I am here waiting for you.'

Katherine could not but hear and recognise the voice of Nathan Applebee as he answered her question. Lucinda Hepworth put down the telephone, turned to Katherine and said, 'There, I will not tell on you, if you do not tell on me.'

Katherine looked at her in disbelief and made to move toward the door, but Lucinda was there barring her way. Katherine said, 'Excuse me please, Miss Hepworth, I have work to do.'

'Oh dear, work is it?' retorted Lucinda. 'How does a poor little peasant like you get work to do? I have been wondering since Nathan's brother mentioned the fact that Dorcas Louise showed an uncanny likeness to you. Not her sister, you said to him, then I think maybe you and old Elford got together. Is that it, Miss Carrera? Got that snivelling little beauty from him, did you? Took Nathan away from me, she did. Only married her because her old man is ultra rich, Nathan told me. Get that pretty gold locket from him, did you? Is it his picture inside, let me look.'

She reached for Katherine's locket, but Katherine was too quick for her, and raised her hand sideways in an effort to bring it down round Lucinda's face. Her hand was grabbed from behind, and held firmly by Mr Elford. 'Don't do it, Katherine, don't bring yourself down to her level. Go now and pack her bags, and place them in the hall. Find Charlie and ask him to transport this lady from my house.'

Lucinda screamed, half in rage, and half in panic, 'You can't throw me out. I work for Nathan, not you. I can bring such scandal to your life that you will not be able to stay here either.'

'There is no scandal in this house, madam. Only what you have concocted, to which I bore witness outside the door. I was curious as to where you were going when you left a cigarette in the holder burning on the corner of my desk, which now has a permanent mark for which I will hold you responsible, and Nathan will have to attend to it in your absence.

'Katherine, when you have finished clearing the room that Miss Hepworth has been staying in, will you please wait here for Nathan, and send him immediately to me in the library when he returns. I will keep this young lady under my supervision until she has finally departed from this house. Also, will you tell Lavinia and Dorcas Louise kindly not to interrupt me when they return. Charlie will collect them on the way back from the station where he will leave Miss Hepworth to make her way back to London, and hopefully from there back to the United States of America.'

The house was quiet when the American car sped to a halt outside the door of the Elford House. Lavinia and Dorcas had arrived home safely, and were ushered by Katherine to the nursery. Dorcas Louise wanted to run to Nathan, but Katherine begged her to stay until her father called her. Nathan was quite all right, but it was vitally important that he spoke with her father before seeing anyone else. Dorcas Louise trusted Kat implicitly and sat with her mother, who shot an enquiring glance at Katherine, receiving only a slight nod in return.

Katherine met Nathan at the door, and showed him into the library, where a now cool and composed Mr Elford faced him. 'You, young man, sit down, and do not speak or move until I have finished. Do you understand?' A silent Nathan remained standing. 'Do you understand?' Mr Elford repeated, 'Or do I have to make myself understood in a much more physical way?' He moved toward Nathan and, hand on shoulder, pushed him on to the chair. 'I said, sit down.' Nathan sat.

Mr Elford, pointing to the burn on the table, said, 'Your girlfriend is responsible for that, but then she is responsible for so much more, isn't she? I have today experienced the most disgusting, flagrant piece of behaviour that I have ever witnessed. I understand from her that you married my daughter only because of my financial status. Well, let me tell you, young man, that I can and probably will withdraw every penny of my investment in the company that your father and I agreed to. Make no mistake, in one fell swoop I can bankrupt you. If you do not wish that to happen, you, young man, will go to my daughter, love her, and treat her as she deserves to be treated. If I find out, and be sure I will, that you are philandering with anyone, let alone a foul-mouthed liar of a woman with whom you have obviously been laying since you married my daughter, I will hit you so hard that your backside will not touch the ground until you are on the other side of the Atlantic. Is that clear?'

'Yes, sir,' answered Nathan in a whisper.

'Also, I think that you should know what kind of woman you have been loitering with. She forced herself into my house a while ago, verbally abusing my staff, and ordering my housekeeper to furnish her with the key to my private papers. Think on that before you try to contact her. You will not visit the London office again until I know for sure that she has left, and I will know, because you see, unlike you, I have trusted friends who will look out for me. Now, Nathan, I am going to make a phone call to your father. I am sorry but I have no alternative, and how he deals with the situation will govern how I continue with this merger. I have a great deal of respect for your father, and hope that his decision will be the one that I would make. I will leave you to decide what you think that may be, but in the meantime I suggest that you, BOY, go to your wife, and treat her as if you love her, even if you don't. One last thing, if she ever finds out about any of this I will deal with it in a way that you would never believe possible. Good night, Nathan. I will see you in the office here at nine o'clock in the morning, and from now on you will treat me, my family, and my staff, with the respect that they deserve. You, BOY, will have to earn yours.'

The phone call to Nathan's father brought the sort of reaction that Mr Elford had expected. One of remorse, and of anger, and one that Mr Elford had feared. An almost panic-stricken plea for the agreement not to be terminated. This told Mr Elford that, without his investment in this business, the result could be disastrous for the Applebee half of the company. On that assumption, could it be possible that the marriage of Nathan and Dorcas Louise had been encouraged for mercenary reasons. The tone of voice changed with the following sentence.

Mr Applebee continued, 'If you feel in your heart that you can no longer accept that all our hard work is worth completion, I will understand, but I do believe that Dorcas Louise and Nathan could have a wonderful life together, and I will personally take my son apart when I get to talk to him face to face. He has absolutely no excuse for the way he has behaved, and the only thing that I can say in his defence is that he is young, and perhaps the power over finance, and inevitably over a certain kind of woman has gone to his head. As for her, I am not quite sure at the moment how to deal with what she tried to do. I think she is very dangerous, and I do have certain people whom I can easily reach, and who would be very happy for a price to keep tags on her. I can assure you that she will find gaining the sort of employment in which she would like to be involved will be very difficult, and just in case you have any doubt, believe me, there will be no contact between her and Nathan, not even for her to give an explanation of the events that led to her departure.

'Now I am going to make arrangements to come immediately to England in the hope that I can restore some of your faith in me, and that we can once again bring all our plans to fruition. In the meantime, please keep my son from any further indiscretions, and assure him that he had better have some very good reports from both you, your wife, and last but not least, your beautiful daughter, who must have suffered most in all of this. I will, I promise, make it up to her, and she will have all the happiness that she deserves for the rest of her life.'

The morning began for Nathan Applebee once again in front of the desk, this time in the upstairs office where the remnants of the day before were still lying around. A cigarette holder, still on the wooden surface, next to the burn, with the inch long ash attached to the remainder of the cigarette. Flo had been told by Katherine not to touch anything until she was told to. There were a couple of crumpled notes on the floor, one was office work, one was private, and it was the contents of the private one that compounded Mr Elford's suspicions that Nathan and Lucinda had been having an affair right up until the day before last. Nathan was made to read the offending note, and a crimson glow began to show above his collar.

'Read it very carefully, and then pass it to me, and put it from your mind,' said Mr Elford. 'It will be the last note of that nature that you will ever read. Now, Mr Applebee, your first assignment this morning will be for you to go to my kitchen, and find each and every one of my staff, and apologise, not just a simple sorry, but a deep in-depth apology for being a crass idiot who has caused havoc in my house. When you have done that, you will then go to Katherine, and I don't know quite how you will deal with her, but I am going to let you use your imagination and your obvious prowess in the handling of women, to decide what would even touch the surface of the hurt that you indirectly caused her. After that, you may send Katherine to me here in the office, and then for your last and probably the most difficult assignment, you will go to your wife, and without divulging any of what happened yesterday, you will make her feel like a princess, because that is what she became the day she married you. You may take the rest of the day off, not for yourself, but for her, and you will give her a day to remember. If, when you have done all that, you have any time left, there is some paperwork here for you to complete, and then you may come with my daughter, and join my wife and I for dinner.'

After Katherine had sat and talked to Mr Elford, explaining her grief and worry for Dorcas Louise, and receiving his praise for standing up to that terrible woman, she went back to the nursery to find Lavinia sitting in the old chair that she always sat on when Dorcas Louise was a baby. She was drawn and looked weary.

Katherine sat beside her and said, 'I think it is over, Lavinia, and I don't think that Dorcas will be wholly aware of all the implications. It would be more than Nathan's life is worth to cause her even the slightest worry, and I see no reason why he can't find a good excuse for firing his secretary. That would set him high in her esteem, and she would need no further explanation. I assume she has now left with him for a day of indulgence, so we will see the result of that when they return.'

Lavinia said, 'I can't tell you how sorry I am for what you went through. James and I discussed it last night, and I was horrified. It was a miracle that James was there at the door, and heard it all, otherwise she could just have denied it, and heaven knows what would have happened.'

'I know,' replied Katherine. 'It was when she went to grab my locket that I lost control. I am going to tell you, Lavinia, it is only part of my story, and the rest for the time being I cannot tell, but the locket contains the picture of my mother and my father. It was all so long ago, but my memories still hurt and haunt me, and I think I might have hurt her badly had Mr Elford not been there.'

Lavinia came over to her and put her arm around her shoulder. 'I will never tell your secret to anyone, Katherine. Thank you for confiding in me, and I will always be here for you, I think you know that.'

'Yes I do,' answered Katherine. 'Now we have to prepare for a further battle. When Nathan's father arrives, I think I will shut them in my office. It is far enough away from the rest of the house, not to let the clash of swords be heard.'

Katherine did offer them the office, and Mr Applebee senior wasted no time in laying down the law to his son, who in spite of everything had shown a contrite side to his character, and had behaved impeccably from the night of the declaration of his sins. The report from the household was one of great improvement. His father laid his cards on the table, and told Nathan in no uncertain terms that the termination of the agreement by Mr Elford would mean the end for them. 'Elford has the largest portion of the shares, and still more personal investments. Do you realise that you, and that stupid little tart, could have ripped the heart out of everything, and Elford, had he a mind to, could put us in the bankruptcy court quicker than you could hop into bed with your mistress. I had hoped that you would find an everlasting love with Dorcas; she is a beautiful girl, kind, and I am sure she loves you. You never complained, and you readily married her. Of course I knew nothing of your infidelity then, but I do now, and you, my son, if you want to remain in the position in our company that will bring you both riches beyond your comprehension, then you had better knuckle down. Be a good husband, be a competent partner in the business, and all will be well. If you don't conform then you will find yourself in the gutter, where your ex-girlfriend is probably wallowing now.'

Mr Applebee senior departed the Elford household leaving an invitation for Dorcas Louise, and Mr and Mrs Elford to travel with Nathan to America, to spend Christmas with them in Florida. It would, he said, cement their friendship and family relationship into something permanent and worth having. They all happily agreed, and Dorcas was enthralled with the idea of showing off her house near the beautiful lake to her mother and father.

Christmas without the family at home would seem most strange to the loyal staff, who always gave of their time gladly for the traditional family gathering. Christmas Eve was always packed with excitement, as the last few decorations decked the halls and rooms. The last twenty years had seen Dorcas Louise turn from a baby gazing at the baubles in amazement, to a woman, now with a new husband, looking forward to putting the decorations on her own Christmas tree, which Nathan had promised would be waiting on the doorstep when they arrived. Nathan had undergone a major change in his attitude, both to his wife, and to his position as financial advisor, and partner to his father. Over the last couple of months, with the episode with Nathan and Miss Hepworth now firmly pushed out of his mind, Mr Elford, good as his word, had found another secretary for Nathan and himself, domiciled in Liverpool, but available to travel if the need arose. A lady of middle age, extremely smart, and with a very sharp wit that even left Nathan speechless at times. She was excellent with the finance, and commanded respect, but by the same token gave it in abundance. Nathan was bowled over, her word was law, and to the joy and thankfulness of Lavinia and Katherine, she encouraged Dorcas Louise to talk to her, on many occasions, and Dorcas found in her a great champion, especially when she needed to influence Nathan.

It was this calm state of affairs that prompted Katherine to ask Adolphus if she and Thomas could spend their Christmas with him in London. The answer of course came back with a resounding yes!

Mr and Mrs Elford, reluctant to leave the house empty, especially at this time of festivities, asked Katherine if she would sound Cook out, and see if she would like to invite all her family to stay here at the house, along with Charlie and Flo, for the duration of Christmas and New Year. With the family private apartments shut, she could arrange the rest of the house as she pleased. The Christmas tree was a permanent order, and so would be delivered as usual. She could order whatever food she wished and charge it to the household account. The decorations would be brought down from the loft by Charlie, and he would have use of the Rolls Royce, if he needed it. The rest would be up to her. Cook was overwhelmed, and began to plan, thinking of the children, and how excited they would be to be spending Christmas at the big house, where Daddy used to work. Arthur, unfortunately, would have to share the shifts in the army restaurant where he now had a full time job that he enjoyed. He would however have Christmas Day off, and would also be home early on Christmas Eve.

All of this arranged, Katherine started to tidy up her office, and make ready for the journey to London. She was so looking forward to seeing Adolphus, and now she would only have to tell him of the trauma of a few weeks ago, and not have to ask for his help and advice. She wanted too to talk to Martha as she had a little niggling worry about the reference to her likeness to Dorcas Louise. No comment had been made by either Mr or Mrs Elford, but in her mind she kept thinking of what she could say, should the subject be raised again. She rather hoped that neither of Nathan's brothers would cross her path very often. Confidentially, Mrs Elford had told her that the relationship between the brothers and their parents was not very good, and consequently Nathan had been given the prime position in the business over both of them.

This, thought Katherine, did not bode well for future negotiations that might involve a fight for financial gain over Nathan, him being the youngest, but standing to gain most as an inheritance. She decided that this was not her worry. Mr Elford must be perfectly aware of the pitfalls. She was now going only to plan and enjoy her Christmas holiday, that could stretch into New Year if Adolphus felt able to cope with them. Adolphus liked Thomas, and was full of enthusiasm.

Martha was given the enviable task of choosing the food, and Mr Cloverleaf was sent to the market to find a big tree that could stand in the hall. He had also to buy the paper things that pulled out into the shapes of bells and balls, and hang them all around the house, along with shiny tinsel, holly and mistletoe. Every day there would be a roaring fire in the drawing room, and he would open up the doors to the gallery, and light it with candles placed in the large brass candlestick holders, set at an even space down the length of the corridor; he knew how Katherine loved his picture gallery. He couldn't wait to see her lovely face again, and wake up to face her at the breakfast table. He would go and see Evan Pugh, who had now regained his status at the garage, along with his partner, and was now answerable to Adolphus Fry. He would ask him if he would take them all to Midnight Mass on Christmas Eve, at the small but beautiful church on the outskirts of the city. Adolphus loved to sing carols, and to smell the incense as it was swung in its ornate container on its long chain, up and down the aisle as prayers and blessings were said, and then see the congregation walking in reverence to join in Holy Communion. Finally, he loved the crisp cold air that clung to you like a naughty child begging for comfort, as you left the service and headed for home.

Katherine and Thomas arrived the day before Christmas Eve, leaving a happy house in Liverpool, with the sounds of children's laughter ringing out as they took turns to ride the rocking horse, that after twenty years still stood in the hall. This house needs children, Katherine thought as they all waved when the car, loudly sounding its horn, left for the station. The trains were full of good humoured travellers, all ready for at least a few days with their families. Thomas took Katherine's hand, and tucked it into his pocket until the warmth reached her fingertips, and she could feel them once again. Lulled by the movement of the train, and the warm comfort of Thomas beside her, she fell asleep. They were drawing close to London as Thomas gently shook her. She smiled a long, lingering smile at him, thinking how he had changed from the days when he used to sit at the table with her, as he waited for his employers to call him to duty. He had suffered a great deal in defence of his country, and so too had Charlie, but with eternal thanks to Mr and Mrs Elford, they had always had a job, and a job that they both loved.

Christmas, for the first time in twenty years for Katherine, had split them all up. She had grown to love her adopted family, both those who worked below stairs, and those who had looked down from their rich existence with an extremely caring attitude. Dorcas had gone to make her own life. Never would she be gone from Katherine's heart, and mind, but Christmas, and the intervening drama of her young husband, had taken her across the sea to share the celebrations with her in-laws. Ruby Stone, their loved and respected cook had been left in charge of the house, but with the love of her family around her, and Charlie with his adoring wife, were to be left to share their happiness together at the house where their love had first blossomed. Katherine, for the first time in all those years, was destined to share Christmas, not only with her now beloved Thomas, but also with Martha who had given her life when there was none, all those years ago, and who subsequently nurtured that life, only to have it snatched away to leave her devastated and devoid of any feelings, until that glorious day when a handsome, gentle, elderly man came and rescued her from her angry solitude, and reunited her with her Katherine.

Adolphus, of course, last but by no means least, would be there for her always, and every day felt like Christmas when Katherine shared his company. Each little group then were to spread the joy of Christmas around them, and all of them would spend it differently, but each and every one of them, for one small moment, would stand and drink a toast to all those whose lives and hearts had become intrinsically linked. Roger Cloverleaf, one of the latest to become a part of this family, was spending the latter years in the company of Adolphus Fry, and strangely for him, fate had dealt him for the first time in his life an amazing and wonderful piece of good fortune. Martha had agreed to walk out with him, and it was on Boxing Day when all was said and done, and when they were all seated comfortably in the drawing room, that he took his very frail courage in both hands, and dropped on to one knee in front of Martha. It took him a few minutes in this position, and with all around him waiting with bated breath, before he uttered the words, 'Mrs Wilkin, would you please accept this trinket that I offer you, in the hope that in the not too distant future, you will become my wife?'

Martha stared at the diamond, glistening in competition with the lights that sparkled from the chandelier above their heads, and in spite of her hardy character, and with a suggestion of the onset of a tear, answered, 'Mr Cloverleaf, I thank you for your wonderful offer, and with the greatest honour and pleasure I will wear this beautiful trinket, especially on the day when I say "I will", Mr Cloverleaf.'

Katherine threw her arms around Martha, who in turn, held Mr Cloverleaf's hand as he rose from his lowly position, to kiss the hand of the lady who had made him the happiest man in the world. 'Thomas,' said Adolphus, 'I think this would be rather a good moment to pop the cork on the bottle of champagne that is sitting there in the ice bucket, and each of us raise a glass to the future happiness of us all, who today have witnessed the coming together of two people who have made our lives so much the richer for their presence.'

The rest of the holiday passed with unbelievable speed, and it was with Martha standing with Mr Cloverleaf at the door, that Adolphus escorted Katherine and Thomas to the car to bid them farewell, and express the wish that they both return soon. His eighty-four years were bearing slightly heavily on his limbs, but his love of life, and especially of Katherine, shone in his eyes, and lit up his lovely old face. She felt a knot in her stomach, thinking of his rapidly advancing years, as she held him close. Thomas held his hand tightly, as he said goodbye, and promised to take care of Katherine. 'I know you will, Thomas, and she you. I am most sure of that. Be happy and return soon.'

Mr and Mrs Elford arrived home, leaving Dorcas Louise and Nathan to enjoy a while longer on their own in the house that had been given by Nathan's parents as a wedding present. While they were there they would visit New York so that Nathan could keep in touch with the business that was now beginning to thrive on the injection of the considerable amount of the Elford fortune. James Elford, now satisfied that he could make inroads into the stock market on this side of the Atlantic, was anxious to finalise the very last section of the merger.

Lavinia came home with comforting news for Katherine. Nathan had become a changed man, and they had all agreed that the past should now be forgotten. Dorcas Louise confided that at last she felt that she was giving her husband the kind of love that he needed, and was so happy. They spent hours together discussing their hopes and desires for the future, which both of them felt would definitely be spent in America. Katherine's heart sank a little at that statement, but if Dorcas Louise was happy, she could ask for no more than that, and she would be happy for her. She longed to see her, and talk to her, and be satisfied in her own mind that Nathan was giving her the love that she deserved, but she would have to wait a while yet. It was good to have Lavinia back, and to know that the trauma of the secretary was now over.

In their conversations, Katherine had asked Lavinia if she had any intention of telling Dorcas Louise that she was adopted, and Lavinia had told her that she had discussed it with James, and they had come to a decision that was in a way difficult, but it was they felt best for Dorcas Louise to always be known to be their daughter. She would become a very wealthy woman, and a stable background of coming from a financially secure family would stand her in good stead. Nothing was known to any of their associates, about the need for a wet nurse all those years ago, and their implicit trust was put in Katherine to keep it that way. They knew beyond a shadow of a doubt that she would always keep the secret. If the unthinkable happened, and some outside force used their knowledge to break that secret, then they as a family would have to take whatever measures were needed to quash both the scandal and the person who perpetrated it.

Katherine, in a few quiet moments, reflected on the last few months. Dorcas Louise married in June, the terrible days when Lucinda Hepworth nearly broke her spirit, and angered her so much as to cause her to raise a fist against an enemy, which she had never even thought about, much less put into action. She thought of the days when she worried about the attitude of Nathan Applebee and the consequences which could have so easily broken the heart of her darling girl. Christmas with Adolphus, which saw her dear Martha happy in the elegant company of one Mr Roger Cloverleaf, being assured by Adolphus that the chances of Martha being traced now were absolutely nil. She would still keep her relationship to Martha a secret. The worry of Nathan's brother's allusion of her likeness to Dorcas Louise still sent a shiver down her spine, but that would have to be dealt with as and when any future reference was made. Katherine settled down once again to the duties of housekeeper, and with her loyal staff around her, and the Elford family once again, it seemed, on an even keel, all that she could hope for was a future of success and happiness to all those who had had a hand in her now wonderful life.

Chapter Twenty-Two

Joy and Sorrow

It was the end of April when Dorcas Louise and Nathan finally returned to Liverpool. They both looked extremely well, and happy, and greeted the household with an exuberance that was reminiscent of the old Dorcas Louise in her early teenage years. Nathan hugged Mrs Elford, and shook the hand of Mr Elford firmly. Dorcas Louise just threw herself into her mother's arms, and held out a hand to her father to draw him into the circle. This was the picture that Katherine saw as she descended the stairs. She felt very humble, but at the same time very proud of the tiny scrap whom she had heard crying somewhere above the door at which she was waiting all of twenty years ago, and now she was watching a beautiful woman, full of confidence, and with a secure future.

Dorcas Louise looked up from her mother's embrace to see Katherine watching, and eyes shining she released herself and ran up the stairs to give a hug to her Kat. 'Welcome home, darling,' said Katherine.

Nathan, on the heels of Dorcas Louise as he climbed the stairs two at a time, said, 'Am I allowed to hug you too, Miss Katherine? This girl talks of you every day, and I need to make recompense for my previous behaviour.'

Katherine, gently pulling away from the hug, said, 'There is no need for recompense; I can see that you have paid already, and Dorcas Louise's happiness is all that I need to see, so welcome home, Nathan. Please be happy here, and every one of us will be at hand if you need us.'

Katherine made her way back to the office, and the happy pair headed for their apartment, followed by Thomas and Charlie weighed down with luggage. Cook had prepared a welcome home supper, and was busy putting the finishing touches to the pudding. Flo was her usual little busy self, humming away as she laid up the tables, and set the new candles in their holders. Candlelit suppers were always a favourite, nothing ostentatious, just a pleasant family evening with an appetising meal, some good wine, and gentle happy conversation. The family would all be left to rest as they wished until 7.30pm, when they would all congregate in the dining room for pre-dinner drinks and small delicious nibbles, as Cook called them. As a child, Dorcas Louise would creep into the kitchen on these occasions and ask cook for a 'nibbie' which usually ended up with a carefully selected tiny plateful.

The evening passed in a cacophony of sound. Voices raised in laughter or in animated description of happenings at the house in Florida. Nathan held Dorcas Louise's hand as she described the house in raptures. How it was among the new and very few houses that were owned by Americans who saw and loved the beauty of the area. Nathan's mother and father also had a house nearby, and so Dorcas would not feel lonely while Nathan was working. To Katherine it sounded idyllic, and it caused her sometimes to remember her cottage on the beach in Italy, where she shared her love with Joseph. Dorcas would catch her faraway look, and wondered where her thoughts were taking her. She told of the house, and how it stood, with a wooden balcony overlooking a lake, and how it had a white painted front door opening onto a beautiful high arched hallway. Rooms along its length all had windows with different views of a lush garden, which would, when once established, show a wonderful array of flowers and tropical shrubs. Upstairs, the light airy bedrooms had massive windows that led on to verandas, again dotted with beautiful pots containing more exotic plants. Nathan's mother loved flowers and plants, and had furnished the whole area to a high standard, and Dorcas Louise loved it.

Mr and Mrs Elford of course had seen all this, but wanted to give Dorcas the pleasure of regaling everyone with its splendour. At last, Katherine felt that all was settling down again, and she went about her business of running the household in a much happier frame of mind. There had been a minor hiccup that Lavinia had confided in Katherine. Mr Applebee senior had made a phone call to James Elford to warn of some mischief being caused by the disgraced secretary who had made her way back to America, and had tried without success to contact Nathan. Mr Applebee had intercepted a couple of letters, upon recognising the writing, and from their content he had decided to notify the police, who had in turn traced her place of residence and issued a severe warning of serious repercussions should this harassment continue. There had been no further incidents to date, he assured Mr Elford. Katherine, who was just beginning to relax, and think that all had finally come to a satisfactory end, was now edgy again. Dorcas Louise knew nothing of the story, and that was how it should be, her mother and father agreed. Katherine too wanted her to have no blot on her happiness, and so it was left to Mr Applebee to deal with it, should it once more raise its ugly head.

The nursery became the most favourite place, once again, for Katherine, Lavinia, and Dorcas Louise to meet on a regular basis, and on one such morning in early June when Lavinia and Katherine were enjoying a cup of tea while arranging the day's programme, and the requirements for their meals, Dorcas Louise came in with her usual flair, and sat on her favourite chair at the side of Katherine's. How beautiful she looked, both her mother and Katherine thought, as she sat there in repose. 'I have a little secret to tell,' Dorcas said. 'Nathan will be cross if he finds out that I have told you, so you will have to act surprised. Tonight at dinner, Nathan will tell you that he and I are going to have a baby.' Katherine and Lavinia just sat there transfixed. 'Well, aren't you pleased?' Dorcas laughed. Lavinia and Katherine jumped up in unison and rushed to her side.

'When?' squealed Katherine.

'Early January 1923, a new young Applebee will join us, and I wondered if you, Kat, would be her nanny. You, of course, Mama will become a doting grandmother I am sure. Does that appeal to you both?'

Once again in unison, Lavinia and Katherine said, 'Yes.'

'Now,' said Dorcas Louise, 'you had both better remove those smiles from your faces until you hear the news from my doting husband.'

Dinner that evening was planned as usual to be a normal quiet affair, but the news sent a ripple of excitement throughout the house and, upon hearing the glad tidings, all the staff came quietly to the door after the meal was over to offer their congratulations to the young couple. From this day onward, it became the sole topic of conversation for Katherine and Lavinia. They discussed where they thought it would be best for Dorcas Louise to give birth, and Katherine suggested that they transform her old bedroom into a birthing room, which could then with little difficulty be turned into a baby room for Katherine to place the baby to bed and look after it when her mother was not there. Lavinia agreed that this was a wonderful idea. Dorcas Louise would feel totally at ease in a familiar environment, and they would employ her own midwife and nurse. As it is with the news of a newborn, tiny clothes started to appear from all corners.

Adolphus, hearing the incredible news, wanted to do something really special, and left the decision with Dorcas Louise. He couldn't quite bring himself to realise that his involvement in the path that the life of this mother-to-be had taken at its very beginning, had brought him to such a simple decision, as to what he could buy for her offspring. As for the mother-to-be, she blossomed like a rose, and her husband worshipped the ground that she trod upon. Nathan had cast the memories of the past from his mind, and was giving heart and soul to his marriage, and the part he was playing in the business of both his and Dorcas Louise's father. His wife's pregnancy would keep them here in England for longer than he had hoped, but the prospect of becoming a father outweighed the disappointment. He had discussed the subject with his father, and Mr Elford, and had agreed that maybe they would settle here for a while after the birth of their baby. It would be good for Dorcas Louise to have family around her if she had to stay with the baby while he travelled back and forth to America. Also, Dorcas Louise wanted to have Kat around, as she had had for every day that she could remember. She wanted her baby to know the love of her nanny, as well as the love of her mother, as she had known it.

Katherine was overwhelmed when Dorcas Louise, now in her fourth month of confinement, had made such a comment to her in the nursery, as she patted her growing baby. 'I'm sure that your mother and I will be there for both you and your baby for as long as you need us, darling; be assured of that, but also be aware that your decisions will be the ones that will be followed. As your child grows up, there will be many decisions to be made, some nice, some not, but decide you will have to, along with Nathan, if you wish to be good parents. Loving and caring for a baby is of course essential, but there are no standard lessons that teach parents how to handle the complex problems that arise inevitably. Those who have had the experience can only pass on what they have learned. You, as parents, will have to add to it or take away, as you feel necessary.'

Dorcas Louise rose from her chair, and put her arms around Katherine. 'Thank you, Kat,' she said, repeating the same to her mother, as she drifted out of the door. Amid baby clothes, new baby linen for the cradle that had been hers, new towels and bathtime needs, new covers and rugs, and a complete renovation of the baby carriage, for which Charlie volunteered with relish, the months of her confinement passed in a haze of happiness, good health, and speed. Christmas, it was agreed by all, would be spent very quietly, with just the family and Adolphus there. Martha would be at home with Mr Cloverleaf, and Katherine would visit in the New Year, before the birth of the baby.

In spite of Christmas being a quiet affair, life in the kitchen and the house was still busy. Charlie now held most of the responsibilities of the household, along with Katherine. The food was selected, and the rooms given an extra going over, so that everyone could relax and enjoy the few days of the festive season together. One morning in early December, Katherine heard a scream, and the sound of running feet coming from the kitchen. She hastened from her office and headed toward the noise. In the kitchen doorway was Flo laid on the floor.

'She just passed out,' cried Cook, kneeling at her side and raising her head.

'Put something under her feet, and raise them,' said Katherine. 'Where's Charlie?'

'Gone with the post,' cried Cook.

Flo began to show a flicker of her eyelids, and Katherine gently dropped some water on to her lips. Slowly she began to come round, and was sitting up, steadied by Katherine, as Charlie arrived at the door. Rushing to her, Charlie tried to lift her up, and she was violently sick at the sudden movement.

'I think we should get her to the hospital,' Katherine said, getting up and making ready to inform the Mistress. 'I will go with you. Leave her with Cook for a minute, and go and get the Rolls Royce and bring it to the main door.'

About an hour later, Katherine and Charlie were sitting in the consulting room while a nurse and doctor took Flo into an adjacent room for examination. The area was quiet, and they seemed to be gone for a considerable time. Hushed voices only could be heard. The doctor was first to leave the room, and Charlie's face paled as he stood in front of them.

'Is it serious?' asked Charlie.

'A little,' answered the doctor.

Charlie, now in a state of panic, asked, 'Will she get better, and how long will it take? She will get better, won't she?'

'It will take a while, but yes, she will get better,' answered the doctor with a smile. 'The sickness may last a while, but I think with your help she will be able to cope with the rest of the situation. Flo came from the room, assisted by the nurse, still obviously very unsteady, and looking as pale as Charlie. The doctor now turning toward them both, announced, 'Mrs Orchard, it seems that you did not have the slightest notion that you might be pregnant. Is that a fact, because from the answers you gave me to my questions I feel that I have to take that for granted? You are in fact around eight weeks into your pregnancy although I can't be more explicit because you are somewhat hazy about your dates. You are going to be parents in approximately seven months from now.'

Charlie, now jumping up, cried out, 'I can't, they told me I wouldn't be able to father a child, due to my injuries and trauma in the fighting.'

'Well,' said the doctor, 'these things have a habit of making fools of us all sometimes but I can assure you that your wife is definitely pregnant.'

Flo, just sitting slumped in the chair looking as if she was about to be sick again, looked at the nurse who quickly passed her a bowl. Recovering enough to face Katherine and shake her head. 'It's over then. I won't be able to carry on with my duties, and Charlie and I will have to leave the house. Where will we go? No one will want us with a baby.' Then she began to cry. 'Charlie said that we would never be able to have children, and I was sad, but as long as we had one another it would be all right. It has been all right, but now my sadness has doubled, because we can have children, but now we will have nowhere to live, and Charlie will lose his job because of me.'

Katherine, soothing her, said, 'It will be a little while yet, so give yourself time to get used to the idea of being a parent, and wait and see what happens. I can find no solution at present, but maybe something will turn up for you both. I am a strong believer in fate. It has found me wanting often, and has stepped in on my side, so have faith, and think positively for the tiny life that you hold inside you. Cook had been concerned and had waited patiently for news. She looked at Flo's crumpled face, and went to her side, holding her in her ample arms until she calmed down again long enough to tell her the tidings.

'My word, and such sad faces at such joyful news,' she said, now raising her eyes to Charlie's worried face.

'There is no future for three of us, if two of us can't work,' said Charlie morosely.

'You mustn't look on the black side,' said Cook. 'We all sat here when you were missing in France, and we, each and every one of us, believed that you would be given back to us, and you were. This little one will be given to you two, and you will care for it and love it every single day, and somewhere, somehow, help will come to you, believe it.'

Charlie and Flo, still with wan faces, hugged one another for the first time since the momentous news was delivered. They moved toward the door, and followed Katherine who was taking them to the mistress to pass on the result of the visit to hospital. Mrs Elford, upon seeing Flo's drawn and tearful face, decided that perhaps the library was not the place for confidentialities, and directed Katherine to take them to the nursery.

Sitting quietly, and listening to the outpourings of doubt and fear from the young couple who had proven to be fairly indispensable to the needs of the household, she waited patiently for them both to put their case before her. Finally, after some serious consideration, the mistress offered her comments. 'I cannot speak for my husband, and obviously I will have to fill him in on all the details that you have given me. You will of course be aware that I will not be able to offer you full employment after the birth of your child, Mrs Orchard. However, I really do not want to lose your services, Mr Orchard, especially since you have acquired such a high standard in your position as butler of this household. I would be prepared therefore to let you both continue for the time being. After the birth of your baby, if you can manage to look after the child in your present sleeping accommodation, I can see no reason why Mr Orchard can't carry on with his duties. I will have to think about the necessity of employing another maid, but I would be prepared to hold you in reserve, so that if and when we needed extra help, we could arrange for your baby to be cared for. Would this be a solution to your worries, if Mr Elford agrees?'

Flo and Charlie could not believe how gracious this lady was and just how lucky they were to be part of this family. They went back to the kitchen, heads and hearts high and feeling the first pangs of excitement in the knowledge of their forthcoming parentage.

Katherine went back and sat with Lavinia, and told her how her kindness had changed three lives forever. Lavinia confessed that there was a tiny ulterior motive in her offer. She thought it would be rather nice for Dorcas Louise's child to have a playmate now and then, and she knew that Katherine would have no objections on that score. Life was nothing in this house if not interesting, commented Mr Elford, when his wife forwarded her proposal to him. I see no problem, he had said, as long as my days aren't plagued by two young hooligans playing cowboys and Indians around my plant pots. I expect you and Katherine to keep them on a tight rein, and teach them good manners. Of course darling, Lavinia had agreed. James Elford watched his wife depart from his company, and thought how much he loved her, and how much he would be prepared to give to keep her happy.

One happy event was enough to cause speculation, but now there were two to consider. Flo, not having any family, had clothes and toys bestowed upon her from the most unexpected quarters. The consultant who had dealt with Charlie's injuries, had in fact married his nurse Janet, and both of them had sent gifts and effusive good wishes at the news. Dorcas Louise, being within a few weeks of the expected birth of her baby, was feeling well and happy at the prospect. Nathan had spent a few days with his parents in Florida, and they had sent back with him more clothes for their grandchild, and a promise that they would make the journey across the Atlantic after the arrival of the newest Applebee.

The year 1923 arrived, cold and damp, and it was on the seventh day of January that Katy Louise Applebee decided that it was time to face the world. She was born, with little fuss, and with a determination to make herself known to the world as quickly as possible. Dorcas Louise was taken to her room, as her contractions became rapid, until finally a continuous pain brought forth her baby in less than three hours. Nathan, James, and Lavinia Elford, and also Katherine, at the request of Lavinia, waited in the nursery. The baby appeared at long last, held by the nurse, and was duly passed to her father, who unexpectedly shed a small tear as he held his tiny daughter in his arms. Lavinia nodded in the direction of the birthing room, for Katherine to go and see Dorcas Louise, while they awaited their turn to have a close look at their granddaughter. Dorcas Louise held out her arms to Katherine.

'How did I do, Kat?' she asked.

'My darling, you did wonderfully,' answered Katherine, now filled by an emotion that was indescribable, as her own baby had just brought another generation into her world.

Dorcas smiled and said, 'I so wanted a daughter, and I wanted her to have your name, but I couldn't really do that, and not use Mama's, and so Nathan and I both decided to shorten her name to Katy, and used Mama's and my second names. Have you seen her?'

'Not properly yet,' answered Katherine, 'but I will soon. Has she taken a feed? She is very quiet. When I came to help your mama, you were yelling your head off.'

Dorcas Louise smiled. 'I have always been demanding, haven't I?'

'Yes,' said Katherine, 'but in the nicest way. Now I am going to see if the proud father and grandparents will let me see Katy Louise, and then I am going to use the telephone to tell Uncle Adolphus the good news. So you must rest, and then you must hold your baby as much as you can, love her, and talk to her, she will understand.'

The baby had been placed in the cradle, and was being hovered over by the nurse. Nathan had gone in to see his wife. Lavinia and James were sitting quietly by. 'May I see her?' asked Katherine.

'You may hold her for a minute while the mother's parents go and see their daughter,' the nurse said brusquely as she lifted Katy Louise from her cradle.

Katherine took her in her arms and, gently moving aside the shawl, looked at the little head covered in fair damp curls. Her eyes closed in contented sleep were fringed with dark lashes, with a fleck of gold at their tips, just exactly as Dorcas Louise's had been the first time that she had picked her up. She held her tenderly, and whispered, 'You will be loved little one, always.'

Mr and Mrs Elford joined her, and both gazed at the child, with the uncertain belief that she would now be a part of their lives forever. The nurse then came and took her back to her mother, and asked for them to be left for a while in her care, to rest and to start the routine that she would set for them, and be in charge of for the next few days. Katherine asked permission to give the good news to Adolphus, which she did with the knowledge that he would understand her innermost feelings at this moment, and of course he did, wishing that he could be there to witness for himself the joyous feelings of them all, but most of all that he could perhaps give some comfort to Katherine who once again had to stand back, and watch as others took the praise. He was so proud of his god-daughter, and so delighted that the choice of the baby's name was given to her, because of Dorcas's love for Katherine, which had always been evident to him.

Katherine, now with very little to do, went back to the nursery, quietly listening for the least little whimper that might come from the direction of Dorcas's old bedroom where she would stay with the baby within calling distance of Katherine should she need her, when the nurse was not there. She lifted the box from the shelf that held Dorcas's wedding dress veil and headdress. It had not been touched since the day when Katherine had brought it back, her heart heavy with fear from the incident that she had witnessed between Nathan Applebee and the evil secretary. Now that was all dealt with and over, she could forget the bad, and remember the vision of loveliness that descended the stairs at Adolphus's house, and moved like an angel toward the marriage, that in turn had now given her a perfect little daughter.

She opened the box, and removed everything, finding tiny silver roses that had been strewn on the wedding table. She carefully collected them, rolled them in a lace handkerchief that was her own, and placed them in the corner. Then she laid out the beautiful dress on the floor, and with some of the masses of tissue paper that had been left and that she had saved, she carefully folded it with the paper inside each fold so as not to cause any discolouration as the years passed by. Lastly, she picked up the tiara that Adolphus had bought for her to give Dorcas. It was still as it had been, removed from her head with the veil still attached. Gently with a fine needle, she unpicked the stitches that held it, and separated it. Folding the veil in the same manner as the dress, padded with the tissue paper, she laid it in the box on top of the dress, and finally wrapping strips of paper around the diamond tiara, she carefully placed it in the middle of the box with a last sheet of paper covering it all. She closed the box, and with a length of white ribbon that had adorned the carriage, and that Adolphus had rescued for her, she tied it as she would a present, and replaced it on the shelf.

As she stepped down from the chair, she silently dreamed of the day when maybe Katy Louise would walk down the aisle in her mother's dress, and wear on her head the beautiful diamond tiara. It was nearly two weeks before the nurse decided that she could leave mother and child to begin their lives together, with the help and knowledge of the nanny, whom she had found to be fully competent, and to have the complete trust of the new mother and her family. Dorcas Louise truly loved her baby, and entered into motherhood with the same enthusiasm as she had in everything that she had ever entered into. Nathan adored his daughter, and cooed over her when time allowed him to.

Lavinia, as she had with Dorcas, left most things to Katherine who was as contented as she could possibly be when Dorcas left her to care for the baby when she felt like pampering herself, which she did often. Katherine, although sometimes thinking that she should perhaps want to care for her more than she did, but selfishly she was so happy that she did not question Dorcas. She just accepted that the job of nanny was, as Dorcas herself had remembered it, when it was always Kat who bathed and changed her, cuddled her, and put her to bed. Katy Louise was such a happy contented child. Eventually, when Dorcas moved back into the apartment with Nathan, the baby had her own little nursery in a tiny room leading off the main bedroom that Nathan and Dorcas Louise occupied. Katherine missed listening for the hungry cries in the night that heralded a feed, and consequently the quiet when, with a full tummy, she was put down to sleep again. Now she could hear nothing, but the baby was thriving, and Dorcas showed no signs of tiredness, so Katherine assumed that all was well, and the parents were handling the situation.

The days when she was summoned to the upstairs nursery to handle all but the feeds, which Dorcas Louise insisted on keeping up for as long as possible, were a joy and delight to Katherine. The system seemed to work perfectly, and all the family, including Nathan, seemed to be in complete sympathy with the situation. Spring came with its usual joyful brightness, and Katherine once again found herself pushing the perambulator to the park with a beautiful baby snuggled in blankets. Katy Louise, like her mother all those years ago, was fascinated by the movement of leaves dancing in the wind upon the trees. Her eyes would follow their movement, and now and then a toothless smile would appear, causing Katherine to chuckle, and gently pinch the tiny pink cheek. Life was sweet, and the house once again was happy.

As Dorcas Louise came through her pregnancy and the birth of Katy Louise, with few problems, so Flo struggled with hers from the beginning. Sickness plagued her for longer that it should have. She suffered acid pains when eating certain foods, and she felt continually tired as her body continued to grow in size. She was a tiny girl, and by the time she had reached her full time, according to the vague dates that she gave to the doctor on her first visit, she was nearly as round as she was tall. The summer months were proving to be hot, and the last few weeks of her pregnancy had seen Flo exhausted and spending a lot of time resting on her bed. The coolness of the sheets she found comforting, and Charlie had been an angel, bringing her cold drinks, and little snacks. Eating a whole meal was just too much for her, and so cook would prepare lovely tasty soups, and some thin bread and butter, which Charlie would deliver, and while he was on his break he would sit with her, and tell her funny stories.

It had been decided that she would have her baby in hospital. Mr and Mrs Elford had made all the arrangements, telling Charlie not to worry about a thing, just to be there for Flo when she needed him. It was 3.30 on the morning of the 19th July 1923, when Flo woke Charlie saying that she was in pain. There didn't seem to be any breaks between the pain so it was difficult to assess whether or not it was the baby coming, or just a pain caused by something else. Charlie was up and dressed in no time, and had the Rolls engine roaring. Katherine, hearing the doors opening and shutting, got dressed quickly and went downstairs to find Charlie waiting for Flo. He was shaking, and Katherine thought that it would not be wise for him to go alone with Flo, so she took it upon herself to go and help Flo get ready and bring her down from the sleeping quarters. 'We will soon get you to hospital,' she said, as she took the small case that was already packed, and helped Flo down and into the motor car.

The nurses helped her into bed as soon as they arrived at the hospital. Flo was now flushed by the pain, and the motor journey which had made her sick. Charlie and Katherine once again found themselves sitting together in the outer room waiting for news of Flo. They waited for what seemed many hours, as nurses and doctors went to and fro, none of them giving any indication of what was happening. It was 7 o'clock in the morning when the doctor came to tell them that in fact Flo had started to go into labour. There had been a slight problem, but now all seemed to be in place, and it was just a case of waiting for the baby to arrive. Charlie suggested that Katherine returned home while he stayed, but Katherine would not hear of it.

'Everything will be fine at the house. I have left a note for the mistress, and Katy Louise is safe with her mother.'

Midday came and went, and still they waited. At 2pm, the doctor emerged, and said to Charlie, 'You have a fine boy.'

Charlie jumped up, but the doctor stopped him and said, 'We have a slight problem so if you can be patient for a while longer, I will get back to you.'

Charlie sank into the chair, and looked at Katherine with a helplessness that nearly broke her heart. She had been there where Flo was now, and had known nothing until they gave her the devastating news of her lost baby. The next ten minutes were never ending, and Charlie now was feeling quite ill, as the door opened and once more the doctor walked toward him. He didn't look worried or strained, in fact he was smiling as he said, 'Mr Orchard, you have another fine boy. He was curled up behind the first one, and that was causing some if not all of your wife's problems. We weren't aware of a second baby during examination, but this sometimes happens. However, I have to tell you that not only are you the father of identical twins, both babies and your wife are well, and you can see them in ten minutes.'

Charlie was now sweating profusely as Katherine gathered him into her arms. 'Congratulations, sweetheart. Make yourself respectable, and go and see Flo and your babies. I will wait here for you.'

Charlie, not even answering Katherine, staggered to his feet, and went to the door where Flo had been taken nearly 12 hours ago. As the nurse bade him enter, Katherine heard a lusty cry, quickly followed by another. Brothers! She thought, how wonderful. The house will now have the children that it needed, but in abundance. Katherine and a very proud father returned to the house to spread the news.

'How wonderful,' Mrs Elford proclaimed. Mr Elford sent Charlie to the cellar for a bottle of champagne to wet all of the babies' heads.

Two weeks later, the twin boys came home, with Charlie holding one in his arms, and Flo the other. Two tiny bundles wrapped in shawls, both with a mop of black curls, and faces that were an absolute carbon copy of each other. Cook ceremoniously held out both arms, 'I want to hold both of them please.' Charlie and Flo promptly deposited one baby each into her arms. Charlie introduced his baby first, 'This is James Charlie, our eldest son.'

Then Flo introduced hers, 'This is Jack Thomas, our youngest son.'

Katherine was enthralled by their choice of names, knowing that they had deliberately chosen James for Mr Elford, and Thomas for her Thomas. Dorcas Louise brought Katy Louise down to also be introduced to the boys, and Mr and Mrs Elford added their own greetings. Flo would now have to make more space in her already slightly cramped conditions, but she didn't care, she now had the two most beautiful babies in the world, and she would wonder for the rest of her life how she got to be so lucky. Charlie was her pride and joy, and she would love him forever. Between them they would nurture and raise their boys to the best of their ability, and they would love them, and give them everything that was within their power to give.

The year passed in a never ending pile of nappies. Three babies can between them send the laundry into turmoil without even trying, and yet sometimes the smiles that came with the obvious need for a clean nappy left parents and staff in no doubt that all three of them were trying as hard as they could. They were all becoming bonny, and were a constant delight to the whole household. Occasionally, even Mr Elford was caught using an amazing vocabulary in order to communicate with his granddaughter. The result of her blowing bubbles at him was reward enough for all his studying of baby language.

Katherine, often being left with Katy Louise, much to her delight, would send for Flo and her two babies to join her and Katy in the nursery. Flo loved her babies, and wanted nothing more than to be with them, but she was worried about not being able to work, and so putting all the stress and strain on Charlie. Katherine put her mind at rest, telling her that with Mr Elford being so busy working on company business, she thought that possibly there would be no major entertaining done for a while, and she, Charlie, and Thomas could manage all the normal running of the house. If there was to be a special occasion that needed Flo's presence, then she would see that the babies were safe, along with Katy Louise, in the nursery where they could all pop in and out constantly. She gently reminded her that she had managed to keep Dorcas Louise quiet and safe when Mr and Mrs Elford threw the big parties that they used to. Flo, suitably placated, turned to watch her babies as they lay on the large blanket that Katherine kept for such occasions. She was indeed lucky.

Adolphus had not yet been able to see the children, much as he wished he could. His advancing years were taking their toll on his agility, but determined as he always was, it was decided that, with the help of Mr Cloverleaf and Martha, he would maybe make just one more visit to Liverpool. They would come, all three of them, and spend the weekend as guests of Mr and Mrs Elford. Everyone loved Adolphus, but no one more than Katherine, and she was overjoyed at being able to spend some time with him, and of course Martha. Dorcas Louise was excited at the thought of Adolphus seeing her darling baby girl. Charlie was looking forward to seeing Roger Cloverleaf, and catching up with all the news, and Thomas was just so happy to be spending his life near to Katherine. He offered to take as many duties as possible in order for them all to have time to spend with each other. Katherine hugged him, and promised that she would make as many spaces as she could to be with him.

The weekend dawned on the Saturday morning with intermittent sunshine and showers. Charlie, poised with an enormous umbrella, waited at the station forecourt, engine ticking over quietly. He saw Adolphus slowly walking toward him, leaning heavily on his cane, and supported the other side by the strong arm of a smiling Roger Cloverleaf. Martha followed behind, keeping a watchful eye on a porter who was trundling alongside with a trolley holding their luggage. Finally, safely aboard, Adolphus sighed, 'It's nice to be back to see old Liverpool again, but only because of this special reason for coming.'

They all agreed that it was indeed a special reason, and they were all so looking forward to the weekend. Charlie drove with care, slowly through the old streets of the city, and then to the outskirts, where tree-lined avenues replaced the confined city streets. The journey had seemed long for Adolphus, and he would be glad to slip into the luxurious comfort of one of the Elfords' large cushion strewn chairs that welcomed the travel-worn visitors to enjoy their comfort. It was Thomas who stood at the door to receive and pass to Mr and Mrs Elford the first guest. Adolphus, ignoring protocol, shook Thomas's hand warmly, and said, 'Nice to see you Thomas, and looking so well.'

With all three guests safely inside, and greetings duly made, beverages were offered, and Cook had as usual excelled with trays of deliciously tempting bites. Katherine had waited politely until Mr Elford beckoned her in to say hello to the guests. Adolphus tried to raise himself from the chair, but Katherine hurried to his side, and bent to kiss him tenderly on the cheek, and then in turn to take the hand of Martha, and place it gently against her face. She shook the hand of Mr Cloverleaf, who beamed at her. So unlike him, she thought, but nice just the same. Katy Louise made a triumphant entrance in the arms of her mother, dressed in pink frills, and hugging a very much worse for wear pink rabbit. Dorcas Louise knelt in front of Adolphus, and placed Katy Louise on his lap, supporting her so that he didn't have to bear her weight on his arm. Right on cue, the baby delivered one of her best smiles, and Adolphus was smitten.

The weekend passed in smiles, and tears. Adolphus confessed that he would not attempt the journey to Liverpool again, but he hoped with all his heart that each and every one of them would continue to visit him in London. After meeting Jack and James Orchard, at his own request, his invitation was extended to include them and their parents to pay a visit to his London abode. This was welcomed by Martha, and of course with the ongoing friendship of Charlie and Mr Cloverleaf, the family just tended to keep on growing. Katherine was sad to see age reaching out and touching Adolphus; she always thought that he would be indestructible. She would go and see him just as often as she could.

Dorcas was tending to leave Katy Louise with her rather more than Katherine thought she should, but she loved looking after her, and Katy Louise seemed to be as contented with her, as indeed her mother had always been. Perhaps, Katherine thought, she should be a little less enthusiastic when Dorcas Louise brought her to the nursery and placed her on Katherine's lap, saying, 'I can't do anything with her after she has been with you, but will you look after her while I go to have my hair cut, or go to the shops, or meet a friend for lunch.'

Once she was weaned, Katherine thought, I will probably be left with her for rather longer periods, and so she sat and made a list of dates that she would travel and see Adolphus. At least once a month, she thought, she would ask for a weekend off for that purpose. Dorcas Louise readily agreed, but did make the comment that she hoped that Katherine was not finding the position of nanny to her child too much to cope with. Katherine, angry at the inference, stated quite categorically that she loved caring for Katy Louise, and would be there for her whenever she was needed. Dorcas retracted her comment, and gave Katherine a hug, saying that she would trust the life of her daughter into no one else's hands but Katherine's. Thus the days of Katy Louise's childhood became full of Katherine's nurturing, and teaching, and the name of Kat was passed to another generation, without explanation or choice.

Dorcas Louise made sure that Katy Louise's first words after Mama, and Papa, would be Grandma, Grandpa, and Kat, followed closely by ducks, and bunny. As the first year of her life was nearly at its completion, and the Orchard boys were close on her heels, a birthday party was on the agenda. Grandpa Elford, when he was not enclosed in his office, was constantly caught with Katy in his arms waltzing down the once sacred corridors. He was without a doubt besotted by his little angel, and was going to give her the best party ever. Party they did, with little presents for all the young guests and a doll for Katy Louise that was bigger than the child itself, but beautiful beyond belief. At six thirty, all the little partygoers were taken home, and the Orchard boys, now sitting up, were transported on the shoulders of Charlie and Thomas to their beds. Katy Louise, full of life and smiles, was reluctantly scooped up by Grandpa, singing a song of sixpence as he ascended the stairs to pass her over to her mother.

Katherine had made her prior arrangements to have one weekend per month free, with the sole intention of travelling to London to see Adolphus. This she did throughout the following year. Katy Louise, rapidly leaving behind her baby days and becoming a bright happy toddler, spent many hours with Kat. The words Mama and Papa, she found difficult to come to terms with, but Kat was easy. Filling her days was easy. The perambulator became her favourite place to be. Kat would laugh and talk to her as she pushed her round the lake, and introduced her to the ducks. She would squeal with delight as Kat threw bread, and a whole lot of them would fight and splash the water. She would nearly always eat in the nursery with Kat, and sometimes Jack and James would be invited to share tea with her.

The happiness stacked up for Katherine, and offered a buffer for the weekends when she would travel to London, and find Adolphus becoming extremely frail. It upset her tremendously, but she had to hide her feelings when she sat by his side, held his hand, and read to him in the calm quiet of his library. Mr Cloverleaf had made for extra comfort by bringing in a large leather sofa, and opening up an old fireplace that had been made redundant. Once up and dressed, Adolphus spent his days there, contented, and surrounded by the books that he loved. Martha constantly poked her head around the door to see if there was anything he needed. Mr Cloverleaf would sit for hours, enjoying the company of Adolphus who still had a wonderful gift for words. They would read the papers and discuss their content in great detail. Adolphus, who had developed a great interest in Mr Cloverleaf's stamp collection, would weave stories from the countries where the stamps had originated.

He had been a widely travelled man and had encountered many strange and varied communities. His journey with Katherine, he confided in Mr Cloverleaf, had been the most inspiring of his life. It had brought him insight into a human situation akin to no other that he had ever experienced. When he first had set eyes on her, she was a mere child, but she had in her an inner strength and beauty that brought out in him an infinite joy of life. It gave him the power and incentive to complete a vision that had eaten away at him for all of his years as a professor. The book, he concluded, was the precious result of her unstinting devotion, and to see him achieve the almost impossible dream. That done, he only had to see her once in a while and his life was worth the living.

Now going into her second year of monthly visits to Adolphus, for Katherine they held no stress or reluctance, but only a fear that one day she would not have him, and that left her shaken inside, and unable to think of a future without his love and protection. Martha and Mr Cloverleaf had decided that they would like to get married. They wanted no fuss, only the presence of Katherine, Martha said, and Mr Cloverleaf would like Charlie to be there. Adolphus insisted that he was going to be there too, and he would like to give Martha to Mr Cloverleaf in marriage. While his general health had showed no further deterioration, and his mind was as sharp as ever, Martha was worried that it would all be too much for him.

'Nonsense,' he replied, 'These old legs will see me through this last honour, I'm sure.'

With this statement, all was decided, and they would marry in the beautiful little church that Adolphus attended, in April of 1926. Katherine was to leave Katy Louise, who was now in her third year, in the care of her mother for a few days while she went to be with Martha. Katy Louise was not very happy that Kat was going away again. The times when she wasn't there weren't any fun. Her grandma would read her stories, and Grandpa would play hide and seek, but she could always find him because he would sing in his hiding place. Her mother would kiss and smile at her, and take her out to buy a new dress, but she had plenty of dresses, and she would rather play with the boys, but Grandma always said that they were too noisy for her, and that when Kat came back she would be allowed to have them up for tea.

The wedding took place, and Adolphus was amazing. The happy couple returned to the house, and carried on with their duties as if nothing had changed, except that they now had smiles on their faces that indicated that the marriage was indeed a successful one.

Katherine returned home, and Katy Louise was happy again, but only for a short while. It was Mr Elford who had taken the telephone call from Mrs Cloverleaf, asking if Katherine could manage to come to London as soon as possible, as Adolphus was really very unwell, and had taken to his bed. Mr Elford, passing on the message to Katherine, instructed her to pack a bag, and leave immediately, and stay as long as she was needed. Katy Louise burst into tears when Katherine told her that she had to go away again for a little while. Katherine took her in her arms and told her that she would be back soon, and that if she was good she would talk to her on the telephone that was in her office. So she would have to listen for it ringing around six o'clock, after she had had her tea. Katherine, true to her word, placed a call to Liverpool at six o'clock on the dot, asking first to speak to Katy Louise, and Mr Elford passed the telephone to his granddaughter without question.

'Bye Kat,' came a little voice over the wires.

'Night night, darling, be a good girl for Mummy, and I will see you soon.'

'Bye Kat,' repeated the little voice.

Mr Elford took the phone, as the little voice disappeared into the distance. 'How are things?' he asked in a concerned voice.

'Not at all well, I'm afraid,' whispered Katherine who was in close proximity to Adolphus.

'Please let us know. Take care of yourself, and stay for as long as you need. Everything here is under control,' answered Mr Elford who quietly replaced the receiver on its cradle.

Katherine settled in a chair next to Adolphus's bed. He held her hand tightly, and at 3am on the following morning he passed away peacefully. Both Martha and Mr Cloverleaf were there with Katherine, and they all held each other close and cried for a long time. At 5am, Mr Cloverleaf gently led Martha and Katherine from the room, and began carefully and with great reverence to wash Adolphus, put on a clean nightshirt, and change the sheet on which he had lain. He put another over the top, and finally he closed the old man's eyes, as if to place him in his last sleep. He went to find Martha and Katherine who were sitting silently together in the kitchen.

'He is ready to go now, and we should call a doctor, and an undertaker,' he said.

'May we see him again?' said Katherine.

'Of course you may, if you wish,' he replied.

Another four hours passed until finally the doctor had been and made his report, and allowed the undertakers to take him. Mr Cloverleaf handled everything with perfect precision, and great sympathy. Adolphus Peregrine Fry, in his ultimate wisdom, had made all the arrangements, both for funeral and burial, and Mr Cloverleaf had in his possession all the relevant paperwork regarding payments, solicitors, and his last will and testament, which had been completed just a short while ago, and duly signed and witnessed, with his executors named as his own solicitor and the manager of his personal accounts at the bank.

Mr Cloverleaf had one more thing in his possession, a letter written in Adolphus's own hand and addressed personally to Miss Katherine Anne Carrera. Katherine, as much as she loved Martha, could not sit and read the letter in front of anyone. Martha, in full understanding and agreement, suggested that she take the letter, and sit in the gallery to read it. She would bring her a pot of tea, and a small bite to eat. Katherine just then realised that none of them had eaten since tea time of the previous day. She could not face eating anything, but a cup of tea would be wonderful. Once seated on one of her little gold chairs facing a beautiful picture of birds in flight disappearing into a gold-edged cloud, Katherine opened her letter and read.

My Dearest Darling Katherine

I will not be with you when you read this letter. It is the most difficult one that I have ever written, but I have to try to put into words my deepest feelings for you. I was never lucky enough to have a daughter, but I believe that had I been that lucky I could not have produced one such as you. I realise now that my life before you was like a grey sky that never saw sunlight, and then there was you , as if by magic painting it bright blue, and placing a ray of sunshine at its midst. From the moment I found you again, when I believed that you were just a figment of my imagination that appeared on that awful train journey for a fleeting second and then disappeared, you made my life not only worth the living, but gave it an urgent need to survive. Without you I would probably not have gained the success that I did with the book, and without you I probably would not have cared either way. I now truly feel that I have a family, and what a wonderful family they have turned out to be.

My dear Martha, whom I thank from the bottom of my heart for raising you, my love, and then my own dear goddaughter, who has really felt like a granddaughter, and who at such a young age has now presented me with a great granddaughter. Lastly, there is my dear friend Cloverleaf, with whom I have spent so many enjoyable hours, and who yesterday I gave Martha to in marriage. I would ask you when I am gone to take care of them all, but I know that you will without my asking, and please my darling, let Thomas love you, he does you know with all of his heart. I have taken the liberty of telling Cloverleaf our secret. I trust him implicitly and you should too. One day, and you will know when it is right to do so, you will tell Thomas, and then he will understand.

Now my darling girl, I am guessing that you are sitting in your gallery reading this letter. Knowing you as I do you will probably be weeping quietly, but please don't, because for twenty six years you have been my salvation, and now in my ninetieth year I have found that it has all been worth the waiting. From my final day on earth whenever it is my dearest one, your gallery will truly be yours, along with the rest of the house, and all my worldly goods I gladly leave to you. The business of the garage will totally be Cloverleaf's to do with as he wishes, the rest my darling is yours. You can now tell your beloved Martha the news that she will love to hear, that she may live out her days here in this house, because I know my dear Katherine that you will never sell it. Be happy my darling and I will be watching you, hopefully from somewhere beyond this earth. Mr Cloverleaf will furnish you with all the legal documents, and the solicitor that you will need to visit. Take Cloverleaf with you, he is a good man and will see you through anything that you may not understand.

Lastly, my own lovely Katherine, I leave you a love that I never thought that I could feel. Not the common love of a man for a woman for I am much too old for that, but the love of one person for another, a so special love that even in death I know it will go with me.

Yours for ever Adolphus Peregrine Fry.

Katherine sat perfectly still, her tea still in the cup, and the food left untouched. She looked at each and every picture, and the dear face of Adolphus smiled from them all. She read the letter twice more, before she rose and walked from the gallery, quietly closing the door. Letter in hand, she went to find Martha. Silently, she passed it to her, and sat at the kitchen table while she read it. They were both sitting side by side when Mr Cloverleaf found them. Katherine passed him the letter, and he nodded, folded it, and passed it back to her. He looked directly at Katherine and said, 'My dear, I do not need to read the personal and private words that Adolphus wrote to you. I know the content therein, as I was at his side when he completed and signed the letter. I also know how deeply he felt for you. He told me during one of our conversations. He also told me of his intentions, but bound me to silence, even from you, my darling wife.' He turned to Martha and took her hand. 'Before we turn to the future, we have to take this unique and wonderful man to his last resting place. He has in the last few months made all the necessary arrangements for his departure from this world, and all we have to do now is accompany him and bid him farewell.'

The arrangements were made for four days' time, and until then he would lie in a chapel of rest. It was agreed at the Elford house, that Flo would care for Katy Louise, and that Nathan would stay at the house. Charlie would stay there too. Mr and Mrs Elford, Dorcas Louise, and Thomas, made their way to London, and joined the little band of people who followed the glass carriage, pulled by four black horses tossing their plumed heads, to the tiny church. White lilies covered the top of the coffin as it was gently lifted on to the bier and carried to the graveside. The mourners standing silently, each lost in their own thoughts, as the words, 'Ashes to ashes, dust to dust', were spoken. Adolphus was slowly lowered to his rest.

Katherine raised her tear-filled eyes, when, just for a moment, a white dove fluttered to rest on the branch of a nearby tree, and then circled above them before flying upwards toward the heavens. 'Goodbye, Adolphus, may you fly with your beloved birds in freedom,' she whispered quietly to herself.

Chapter Twenty-Three

The Heart Rules the Head

The house seemed so cold and empty without the charismatic figure of Adolphus at their midst. The little family sat and recounted their memories of the man, some with laughter, some with tears, but all with an affection known to very few. Martha and Mr Cloverleaf recalled the day of their wedding when he had stood there between them, silver topped cane supporting him, looking every inch the splendid old gentleman that he was. Dorcas Louise remembered somewhat tearfully the day he had stood in the jewellers' shop, and given her the box that contained her watch, which she promised that she would wear forever; she would never break that promise. Thomas thought that he was the most caring man, and had only a short time to get to know him, but he felt that he had been there for always. Mr and Mrs Elford knew him only as an acquaintance of Mr Elford, before his connection with Katherine, but held him in the very highest esteem, and would remember always his extreme kindness to their daughter, and in turn their daughter's obvious love for him.

Katherine sat and listened, but her heart was too heavy to add any comments to those that had already been spoken. Her love was fathomless, and no amount of words could explain how she felt at this very moment. Losing Joseph had been dreadful, but Adolphus had been there to wipe away her tears. The tears that she would shed for Adolphus were hers and hers alone, no one could share them, no one could wipe them away, only time could lessen them.

As the day ended, and they all made their way to bed, Katherine picked up the silver-topped cane, and carried it with her to the room she normally shared with Thomas.

Tonight she felt that it would be inappropriate as Mr and Mrs Elford were present. Thomas agreed to occupy the adjacent room, and Katherine, propping the cane against the wall near to her head, eventually dropped into a fitful sleep. When she awoke early the following morning, she reached to take the handle of the cane, and realised that she had never held it before last night. It was quite a strange feeling; the etching around the silver top ran across her fingers, and caused the skin to tingle. She looked around in wonder, as she realised that the bed and the room, and in fact all of the house would be hers. She would be able to live here with all her memories of Adolphus for the rest of her life.

She washed and dressed, and made her way to the kitchen where Martha was preparing breakfast. She went to her and hugged her. 'Where would we be now, Mama, if it were not for Adolphus?' she said.

Martha, sitting down, replied, 'In places that no one would want to be in my darling, but we are here, and it is what Adolphus wanted, so we must now live our lives happy in his memory; he would have wanted that.'

Mr Cloverleaf came into the kitchen, took Katherine's hand, kissed his wife's cheek and said, 'Good morning, Mrs Cloverleaf.'

'Good morning, Mr Cloverleaf,' said Martha with a smile.

To Katherine, Mr Cloverleaf said, 'After our guests have departed, we will talk, Katherine. You have some business to complete, and solicitors to visit, before you return to Liverpool. I will be very happy to support you, if you so wish.'

'Please, Mr Cloverleaf, I would like very much for you to accompany me; I really feel quite nervous, and it all seems so sudden after Adolphus's death.'

'It is sudden, but unfortunately solicitors do not count time, only money, and therefore wish to complete their obligations as soon as possible. The sooner you comply with their wishes, the sooner you will be able to decide upon your future, and enjoy all that Adolphus has given you.'

Later in the morning, after the departure for the station, and the return to Liverpool of the Elford Family and Thomas, Katherine sat with Mr Cloverleaf at Adolphus's desk. A file neatly tied with a blue ribbon that trailed from its sheaf of papers, sat between them.

'Katherine,' Mr Cloverleaf started, 'I do know some of the contents of this file, but the details therein are held by the solicitor. I have taken the liberty of making an appointment for tomorrow morning, as I knew you would want to get back to Liverpool, and your duties there. You will know from the letter what Adolphus left for you, and that you and you alone will inherit all of his estate. That includes this house in its entirety, and all incoming royalties from his books, of which there were more than just the one that you played such a great part in. The business of the garage, he has bequeathed to me, and I will need to talk to you later on that subject. Any monies that he has, and I can reveal that there is a considerable amount, your solicitor will be able to give you all the information that you need to access that. It will all take upwards of a year to complete. To you and to me it seems quite simple, but by law there are many avenues to go down, and many ends to tie up before it is all completed. You in the meantime, my dear, will have to think clearly and carefully what you intend to do with your life from now on. You will be a rich woman, and will have no need to continue working if you do not wish to.'

Katherine, listening very carefully to everything that Mr Cloverleaf was saying, asked him tentatively, 'How much did Adolphus tell you of my life? He told me he had confided in you, but can you tell me exactly what he told you please.'

'He told me that Dorcas Louise was your own daughter, and he told me of your bravery in handling the situation as you have across all the years. He also told me of the part that Mrs Cloverleaf played in your life, and how much you two mean to one another. I am very proud indeed of both of you.'

'Is that all he told you?' countered Katherine.

'Yes,' answered Mr Cloverleaf.

'There is more to my life, and one day I will tell you, but at present I can't,' said Katherine.

'Do not feel in the least bit pressured, my dear,' he answered. 'I know that both your's and my beloved wife's lives have held secrets, and I would not dream of prying. I think I know you both well enough to know that you have dealt with them in the best possible way that you could, and if Adolphus held you as highly in his estimation as he did, then that is good enough for me. Now, have you thought at all about your future?'

'No, I haven't,' whispered Katherine. 'I will need some time, and if the solicitors are going to take a year, then I will be able to take that time too, won't I?'

'Yes indeed,' said Mr Cloverleaf.

Katherine, standing up and thanking Mr Cloverleaf for his kindness, asked if they could now go and talk to Martha together. Bringing in the silver tray, with the usual supply of cakes and biscuits that Martha had become so used to carrying into the drawing room around this hour of the day, they sat around the little table with its neat white lace cloth on, and talked. Katherine started by asking them both if they would please stay in the house, and care for it. She knew that they would, but thought it was right to confirm it in each other's presence. They both agreed that it would be a joy to do so. Katherine then explained that she would stay in Liverpool until the family eventually made their lives in America. She would then come and live in the house.

'As you are aware,' she explained, 'with Dorcas Louise being my daughter, in Katy Louise I also have a granddaughter, and while I really have no lawful reason to care for her, I feel in my heart that she needs me. That sounds a very contrite statement, I know, but something inside me tells me to stay and care for her for as long as I can. I love my daughter, but her marriage to Nathan has given her very grand ideas, and I hope with all my heart that she remembers that she has a child who is still only three years old. When they take her with them to America, then I will relinquish my responsibilities and retire here to this lovely house where I will spend the rest of my life in your company, and hopefully with Thomas too.'

Mr Cloverleaf then raised the subject of the garage. 'I have,' he said, 'agreed that Evan Pugh will retire as he wishes when he completes his seven years which will be in approximately two years' time. I was wondering if Mr Orchard and Mr Moreton would consider taking over the running of the place for me. There is a large residential area over the top of the workshop that could be converted into an ideal home for Florence and the children. It may mean that they would have to leave the service of Mr and Mrs Elford earlier than they may want, but the choice would be theirs, and I think under the circumstances it would be a very good decision to make for all of them. What do you think, Katherine?'

Katherine answered that she thought it would be perfect, and would leave it for Mr Cloverleaf to put the suggestion to them both. After lunch, Katherine and Martha found a little time to share with each other. Katherine had been thinking hard about how to handle her new found wealth and security. She held Martha's hand and told her of her plan to tell Thomas as much information as Adolphus had imparted to Mr Cloverleaf, and at present she would say no more than that. She did feel that he should know at least part of her story, and while she had no doubt that he would keep it to himself, there was always a small risk of it accidentally leaking out. Martha thought that it would be correct to trust him, now that his life was becoming daily more entwined with hers.

In respect of her inheritance, she would not mention any of it to Mr and Mrs Elford, because, she explained, they would realise that she no longer needed to work for them, and would perhaps become suspicious if she were to say that she would stay to look after Katy Louise until they moved to America. There had already been the comments about her likeness to Dorcas Louise, which she had shrugged off, and so she would say that the outcome of Adolphus's estate would take a year before details were passed to any beneficiaries, and she hoped that Mr Cloverleaf would if necessary back up her statement. Martha said she was sure that he would, and she fully understood Katherine's reasons for wanting to be with Katy Louise for as long as possible. Mr Cloverleaf would state that both he and Mrs Cloverleaf had been asked to stay until further notice, to which they had agreed.

The day passed relatively quickly, and all the discussions had been successfully completed. Financial arrangements for the upkeep of the house were to be organised by the bank. Katherine retired early, wanting to look her best for the appointment with the solicitor in the morning. Mr Cloverleaf arranged with Mr Pugh to take them, and to pick them up and return them home. In the event he had to wait a considerable time, as the solicitor was about to send Katherine into the realms of disbelief.

Her inheritance was to be above and beyond anything that she could have imagined. Adolphus had set it out in such a way that she would have to do nothing, except call at the bank when she needed money. They had under their control all the monies that had been invested, mostly in government bonds, which were totally safe, and which could be used should she need any large amount. She would have the same personal adviser that Adolphus had had, and he would furnish her every six months with a complete set of figures, relating to each component of the investments, and a total balance of her account. One by one, he ploughed through the balance sheets, and, one by one, Katherine was lost in total amazement. It took all of three and a half hours before the signing of papers began. Another hour on, and the sheaf of papers were now sorted into their individual slots, each containing her signature, along with Mr Cloverleaf's as her witness, and the solicitor himself. She was advised that from time to time she would have to come to London as the process continued, and give some more signatures. The solicitor thanked her for her patience, and thanked Mr Cloverleaf for the work that he had done toward the preparation of Mr Fry's last will and testament. It was a perfect example of planning completion, he had said. He rose from his chair, and came around to the front of his desk to shake their hands, and to say that if there was anything that he could help with he would be only too glad. Katherine, pale-faced, smiled and said thank you as she held on to Mr Cloverleaf's arm and walked from the office.

They sat in near silence as they were driven back to Adolphus's house. Not Adolphus's anymore, Katherine thought, but mine. She looked at the front door, and the tears fell then. Martha came quickly to her and took her in her arms, and they walked back inside the house that she had loved from the moment Adolphus had taken her into it with Martha, and given them the task of choosing decoration and furnishing. She sank into the chair, and Martha sat beside her.

'Did he know what he was going to do, Mama? Did he have it all planned all that time ago?'

'I do not know, darling, but he was a man of great integrity, and he would not want it any other way. He loved you more than any father, or grandfather, let alone an uncle, whom he assumed the role of to allay any suspicion regarding his relationship with you. Now somewhere up there, there is an angel who is heaven's gain and our loss. Be happy, my darling, and live your life in the way that you want to. I know that you will always bring love to everyone that you touch, but save a little for yourself, because you deserve it more than anyone on this earth.'

Martha held Katherine, remembering nearly thirty years ago, when as a new-born orphan she had come to her as if from heaven, wrapped in an old blanket, cold and hungry, and so nearly taken as dead. The secret would remain hers and Katherine's, until Katherine decided herself that it was time to tell. That may be never, who knows, she thought.

Katherine stayed one more night, and then returned to Liverpool.

Katy Louise, Lavinia confided, had been naughty, and had had some tantrums, and was now in the nursery with her mother who was trying to read to her.

'Perhaps I had better leave her for a while,' said Katherine. 'I do not want to step on Dorcas Louise's toes. I will clear up the mail, and go upstairs later to see them both'.

It was unusual for Katy Louise to be difficult; she was always happy, and an easy child to entertain. When Katherine finally went upstairs to the nursery, the sight before her made her smother a giggle, as she found Dorcas Louise sitting on the floor playing with rabbit, and Katy Louise with her head firmly planted in the linen basket, removing the clothes that Dorcas Louise had just put in there after changing her daughter into her night clothes. Dorcas Louise saw her first, and gave a guilty grin, as Katy Louise removed the last item in time to look up and see Katherine. Squealing with delight, and scattering her bounty around her feet, she flew into Katherine's arms.

'Kat's home, Kat's home.'

Katherine scooped her up into her arms, and cuddled her. Dorcas Louise, halfway between relief and frustration, said, 'Yes, Kat's home.'

Katherine thought, Yes, Kat is home and will be for a little while yet, I think.

Dorcas Louise kissed her daughter, and said, 'I think you would like to sleep in Kat's nursery tonight.'

'Yes! Yes please,' the answer came sweetly.

'If that is all right, Kat? I would be grateful. My nights have been a bit fraught since you left, and I have a few things that I need to discuss with Nathan before he goes to New York next week.'

Katherine answered kindly but firmly, 'There is absolutely no problem with that, my darling, but please make sure that you spend as much time as you can with your daughter. It is very important that you are the person that she runs to when she is in trouble, and not me. When you take her to America, she will need you much, much, more than she does now. It will all be strange, and she will not have any other familiar face to turn to.'

'Would you consider coming to America with us, Kat?' Dorcas Louise asked.

The question took Katherine by surprise, but she answered with complete honesty and conviction. 'No, my darling. When you all go to America, it will be without me. As much as I love you, I believe that a new start must be made by all of us. You will, as Nathan's wife, be a wealthy woman, and if you find that caring for your child, or maybe even children by that time, is not what you wish to do, then you will have to employ a nanny. I would like to think that being a mother to Katy Louise would be a joy rather than a chore, but that decision must be yours, and I will not make it too easy for you by always being there. I am sorry if that sounds very hard and uncaring, but I believe that being a mother is the most important thing, above all else. Go and make your preparations for Nathan, but think upon what I have said and please act upon it wisely, for in many years from now you will look back on your decision as the most important one that you ever made. I love you, and always will. I will miss you more than you will ever know, and the day that you leave for America will be almost too much to bear, but bear it I will, in the knowledge that you are happy, and that Katy Louise will be happy.'

'Good night, darling,' Dorcas Louise cooed to Katy Louise.

'Good night, Mummy,' came a little voice from somewhere around the skirt of Katherine.

'Good night, both of you,' said a thoughtful Dorcas Louise.

Katherine's words must have had some impact on her as she daily spent more time with her daughter, watching the things that Katherine did to keep the child happy and occupied, and suddenly remembering how she had lingered around Katherine's skirt, as her daughter did now. Did her mother not spend as much time with her as she should have? She thought, Kat was always there, when she hurt her knee, or felt sick, or even just needed a cuddle. Could she now, before it was too late, draw her daughter toward her, she would try, but there would be times when she would have to rely upon Kat. She knew that she would always be able to do that.

Katherine settled once again into the routine of running the household. Paperwork was at a premium, and so long hours were spent in the office. Sometimes Katy Louise would appear, and say, 'Katy stay with Kat.' The box of toys that were once Dorcas Louise's were placed on the circular rug that still had pride of place in the centre of the room. Katy Louise, like her mother used to, placed them all around the edge of the rug, and sat in the middle, having the most interesting conversation with them all. Dorcas would return and sit with her daughter on the floor. The two heads together, lost in their own world, tore at Katherine's heart, as for a short while just sat there and watched.

One evening when Thomas came and sat with her, they drank their cup of tea together in comfortable companionship. Katherine was looking at Thomas and thinking how much she cared for and loved him.

'What is it, my darling?' said Thomas.

'I have something that I want to tell you,' said Katherine. 'You have been so good and kind, especially in my reluctance to accept your proposal of marriage. Dearest Thomas, I truly can't marry you, as much as I wish

I could, and I can't offer any reason, not now, maybe not ever, but I am going to tell you a part of the story of my life. It is not my reason for not marrying you, but it does have a bearing upon it. When I tell you, I will need a promise from you that you will never disclose the knowledge of it to anyone. It is so difficult to know where to start, as so much went before, but what I am going to tell you will make you understand why it must remain between us. Dorcas Louise is my daughter, and therefore Katy Louise is my granddaughter. Mr and Mrs Elford were given my baby to adopt. I was under age, and I have to tell you that it was because of my dearest Adolphus that, with my secret unknown to Mr and Mrs Elford, I became her wet nurse, and subsequently her nanny, finally attaining the position that I now have in their household. The other part of my story has to remain with me, possibly forever. I do not know at present, but I do know I love you, Thomas, and if you can love me, knowing what you do, I will spend my days in happiness. Martha, who has a special place in my love and my heart, knows also that which I have just told you, and because of her marriage to, and the involvement of Mr Cloverleaf in Adolphus's house, he also knows, and that is it, Thomas; can you live with it?'

'My darling Katherine, I can not only live with it, but I can also tell you a secret. I have known in my heart for a long time that Dorcas Louise was yours. I have many times, when we lay together, wanted to ask you, but I decided that your answer would not be as important as your love for me, and so I tried to protect you as much as I could from the hurt and constant worry in your heart. I do not need to know the rest of your story, but if you ever feel that you can no longer face the memory alone, then I will be there for you, and I will hold your secret to my heart, and take it with me to my grave.'

Katherine was stunned. 'Do you think anyone else guesses as you did, Thomas?'

'I don't think so, darling. No one sees you with the eyes of love as I do. All of their lives will change when they go to America, and I think that Mr and Mrs Elford will eventually move there too. The whole business will evolve around the American market, and that will be the obvious place to be. They will all miss you as you will miss them, but memories will fade, and life goes on, as yours must. We will all be without work and a place to live, when it happens, and so we should all be preparing for that, I feel.'

Katherine, then for the second time that evening, had to reveal a secret. 'Thomas,' she said, gaining his attention with the excitement in her voice.

'Again I am going to tell you only half a story, but this one is a good one. You will not be out of work, and neither will Charlie, and I will have a place to live, and so will Flo. You will be hearing from Mr Cloverleaf in a very short while with an offer that I believe you should take with both hands, and I will be able to tell you one other thing that will have to remain a secret for a while. Again, my Thomas, you hold my future in your hands, and now, my darling, do you think you could spend tonight holding me in your arms, as both my mind and my body need your love and comfort to face tomorrow. I love you.'

Thomas, full of questions now, had as many secrets as Katherine to hold on to, but he could manage that with ease, as long as she was by his side.

The news that came from Mr Cloverleaf was addressed to Charlie. Mr Cloverleaf had a great deal of affection for the young man who took to his teachings wholeheartedly, only to find himself on a bloody battlefield before he had completed many months as a top class butler. The two of them had remained friends, and they missed one another's company, and so the next few words that were about to be spoken caused Charlie to sit on the floor, cross-legged with his back leaning against the office wall. Katherine watched as she waited, her face soft with the gentle love that she felt for the boy who became a man in the most horrendous conditions. Likewise Thomas, who only knew about the forthcoming conversation, but not its content. Charlie mouthed to Katherine, 'Please get Thomas', and get Thomas, Katherine did. He came to see a collapsed Charlie, with Katherine standing over him, and a telephone dangling on its cord between them. He just stood there looking blank. Charlie looked all right, slightly flushed, but all right.

He waited until Katherine had taken the telephone and was concluding the conversation with Mr Cloverleaf, promising to telephone him back when she could get a little sense from the two men who now stood before her open-mouthed.

'Goodness, Charlie,' she said. 'Put Thomas out of his misery, and repeat the words that you have just heard from Mr Cloverleaf.'

Charlie, standing now, told Thomas how the two of them had been offered the chance of running the motor car hire and repair garage, across the road from the house where Mr Adolphus had lived, and where now Mr and Mrs Cloverleaf were housekeepers until further notice. Evidently Adolphus had passed the business over to Mr Cloverleaf, and so it would not be affected by the future of the house. Charlie went on to tell Thomas that, above the garage, was enough room to make an elegant residence for him, Flo, and the children. Also he had said that Thomas would be able to stay at the house with the Cloverleafs for the foreseeable future. Stopping to take a breath, Charlie continued, 'We have to talk, and make a decision, and if we agree then he would want us in London before the end of the following year. His present manager has agreed to stay until the last day of December. Just over a year from now. We would have to give Mr Elford good notice, but then he would probably be going to America, and it would be a perfect choice for us. What do you think, Thomas?'

Thomas looked at Katherine, and she nodded. Charlie danced around Thomas, and said, 'All of our dreams, wrapped up and given to us as a present. Say yes, Thomas, we could do incredible things there with a little luck, and Mr Cloverleaf is not such a bad fellow, in fact he is quite a gentleman.'

Thomas looked once more at Katherine, and remembering what she had said a few nights ago as they talked secrets. 'Yes, Charlie, yes,' said Thomas.

'Yippee,' cried Charlie, 'can I go now and tell Flo to start planning for a new home for us and the boys?' Charlie then turned to Katherine, and a little solemnly said, 'What about you Katherine, what will you do when everyone here goes to America?'

Katherine smiled and said, 'Well, Charlie, I have in fact had a yearning to live in London for quite a while, and I will find myself somewhere to live, don't worry on that score. I have to stay here and help care for Katy Louise until her mother and father are ready to take her with them. Mr Elford is still busy with his investments in the business, but as soon as he and Nathan have tied up all the ends, I am quite sure that he and Mrs Elford will go too. It does make sense, don't you think?'

'Yes, I do think so. Then there will only be Cook and you left, and Cook is around retiring age, and has her husband, son, and his family to care for her. Yes, it does all seem to fall into place.'

All of this was decided, and Mr Elford duly advised of Thomas and Charlie's intention to give one year's notice of their employment here in the Elford household as from this day. Mr Elford, although thinking how sad it would be, like the coming to the end of an era, when he would lose two very special young men, one of which had been in his employ from the tender age of thirteen years, he was glad for them, and also slightly relieved that he may have been saved the problem of telling them that their services would not be needed should he have to take his part of the business to America in order to gain further success from its yield. That was indeed a great possibility. Mr Cloverleaf was overjoyed at the news. He would now have those two very bright and likeable young men working for him, and he would see to it that they had every conceivable chance to make the motor business, that they would eventually inherit, a great success.

Katherine for her part was playing a waiting game. In a few days' time, she would go to London to meet Mr Cloverleaf, and be taken to the solicitor for more signatures. She had also been advised that she would be given the final figure of her inheritance, subject to fees and charges that would be taken before the transfer of the money would be effected. The meeting again was quite drawn out, and Katherine was left speechless at the final amount that she would benefit from. The loss of Adolphus had been such that she found all of this just too much to comprehend. She could not grasp the fact that in a very short time she would be a very rich woman. There would be, the solicitor said, money placed in the bank immediately for her use, and that Mr Fry had insisted that all monies pertaining to the running of the house would be available to Mr and Mrs Cloverleaf, and this he was sure would be totally agreed to by Miss Carrera. This section of his instructions, would need her signature if she so agreed to it. Katherine placed her name on all of the necessary papers, and left the office, once again holding on to Mr Cloverleaf's arm as if it were a lifeline.

With apologies to him, and a promise to telephone both him and Martha as soon as she could, she hastily left him at the station, and jumped aboard the train, sat in her usual corner, and shut her eyes tightly, as if to squeeze out the thousands of thoughts that scurried through her brain. Upon returning to the house, she played the whole thing down. The day, she had said, was extremely tiring, and she had not been able to see Martha which had left her feeling sad. There had been many papers to sign in order for Mr and Mrs Cloverleaf to be able to continue to live at the house, and pay for its upkeep for the foreseeable future. She made no mention of herself being a beneficiary, let alone the only beneficiary. She thought that this would have to be yet another secret that she would have to bear, until she no longer had the responsibility of caring for Katy Louise. When that happened, she would miss her daughter, and now her granddaughter, more than she could ever imagine, but as long as they were happy, then she could finally go and live in the house that she loved, with Martha, and her beloved

Thomas, and stay there for the rest of her life. A life, she thought, that at last would be hers to do with as she wished. She would leave the Elfords who had given her, without knowing, the chance to see Joseph's and her baby grow to beautiful womanhood, and produce another generation. She had never been able to acknowledge her precious bairn, but she had loved her with a mother's love, unselfish and pure, and always would.

The rest of 1927 passed in relative ease. Nathan spent a few more weeks in New York, and while he was there, he visited the house in Florida, putting some more final touches to the property with the help of his mother, who was urging him not to leave it longer than necessary to move over permanently. There could not be much more to complete in England, she would prompt. They would in all probability make the move early next year, and then it would be down to Elford to decide whether to stay in England or to pull up sticks and move over to the United States. It was decided when he returned to England and put it to Dorcas Louise, that they would move early next year. They elected not to tell Katy Louise for the present, as they were not all together sure how she would react, and in fact how they would tell her. She knew nothing of travel, nothing of the reasons why her father disappeared all the time, sometimes taking her mother with him. She was happy to be left with Katherine, and always waved them off with little remorse when they went away.

'Mama gone to Merica again?' she would question.

'Yes, darling, but she will be back soon,' Katherine would say.

'Let's go feed the ducks; take rabbit, he likes the ducks,' she would reply, without concern for her departing parents.

Mr Elford, although still not completely sure that their plans were watertight, allowed Nathan to tie up the remaining ends, and with a massive boom in the American market, he was feeling very secure in his investments. Plans were made for him and Mrs Elford to remain in England for a while. Nathan would go, because there was little more for him to do on this side of the Atlantic. Dorcas Louise would go too, and she would set up schooling for Katy Louise who would be five years old when they came back to take her with them.

Lavinia was the one who most of all did not want to go and live on the other side of the Atlantic, but she would go for her husband's sake, and she would see that Katy Louise was cared for. Being without Katherine, for her, would be extremely difficult, but having put the idea to her that she travelled with them, and having received a gentle but definite refusal from her, she accepted her fate.

Mr Elford was just being swept along on the tide of success, and therefore could see no reason why Lavinia should not enjoy a life of luxury in America. They could, Mr Elford offered, leave the house in the hands of the servants, replacing Charlie and Thomas when they left, and then if Lavinia, or any of the family, wanted to return occasionally, they could without problems. Katherine had not yet made public the fact that she would be leaving when her time for looking after Katy Louise was over, and she had joined her parents in America.

The household seemed to be drifting along in a veil of uncertainty. Charlie and Thomas looked to their duties with their usual loyalty, and Flo was always available when she was needed. Katy Louise enjoyed the company of James and Jack when Katherine looked after them on the odd occasion. Still, there was an undercurrent of excitement when the forthcoming move was mentioned. Flo just lived for the day when she would have more than one room in which to raise her boys.

The turn of the year, for Katherine, brought her riches that she had never even dreamed of in her lifetime. Also it made her the sole owner of a beautiful house, in an elegant area to the North of the City of London. Still her life brought her restrictions, and her dream of living in Acacia Avenue would have to wait to reach fulfilment until her responsibilities came to an end. She would have to bear a great sadness before the dream came to fruition. Her darling Dorcas Louise would again be taken from her, and this time her little Katy Louise would go to, and in time they would both forget her.

The first part of the family departures came when Nathan and Dorcas Louise left amongst smiles and tears. Katy Louise, holding Katherine's hand tightly as Dorcas Louise knelt to hug her daughter, and Nathan from behind his back drew a large teddy bear, giving it to her as he too dropped to his knees, and told her to be good until he came back to collect her. Charlie drove them away from the house. Lavinia disappeared in tears to her room, and Mr Elford, putting on a brave face, picked up Katy Louise and held her tightly in his arms, telling her that soon she would be playing in the sunshine with Mummy and Daddy.

Katherine, with the usual solution to days of stress, dressed Katy Louise in a new outfit that her mother had bought for her at Christmas, and took her out into the chill winter sunshine. She pulled her own scarf around her neck, and tucked it in to her coat. She pulled the red woolly hat that Katy Louise had on, down around her ears, and wound her matching scarf around her, allowing the bobbles at the end to jump up and down as the child skipped along. Katherine watched, and her heart felt leaden as she thought of the few short months that she would have to share with this beautiful child. She would make the most of every moment, and when the time came she would pray for her safety in that foreign land of which she knew nothing.

Thomas, brought from a dreamless sleep, hearing the ringing of the telephone, made for the office as quickly as he could. Reaching to pick up the handpiece, and sleepily reciting, 'The Elford residence. How may I help you?' he looked at the clock, to see it read 4 am.

The voice said, 'Let me speak to Mr Elford. By the time he turned to go and find the master, he was there by his side saying, 'What is it Thomas?' Thomas passed the telephone to him without saying anything.

Mr Elford sat heavily on the chair, and Thomas could hear the agitated tone of the caller's voice. He had not recognised it, but he knew that something was terribly wrong. Mr Elford's face was ashen, and then his body crumpled with a stifled scream, followed by gasping sobs. 'Get the mistress quickly, but don't disturb Katherine or Katy Louise,' he said between racking sobs, the like of which Thomas had not heard, not even in his time during the war. Lavinia was at his side in seconds, but could make no sense of his ramblings. Katherine had heard all the commotion, and had crept from the nursery, quietly shutting the door so as not to disturb the sleeping Katy Louise.

Finally, Mr Elford, between his agonising moans and sobs, managed to get out a few garbled words. Thomas had gone to the kitchen and had brought some brandy. He passed a glass to Mr Elford, but he pushed it away, and then in a sudden moment of calm he whispered. 'There has been a fire, five people have been found dead inside the house, and a badly burned body has been found in the garden.' He stopped there, and looked at his wife, who by now had grabbed a chair and fallen into it. Mr Elford collapsed into tears once again.

Katherine had arrived at the office door, and looked at Thomas who shrugged his shoulders helplessly. Lavinia, seeing Katherine, held up her hands, as Katherine went to her side. 'What has happened?' she asked, with a sudden cold shiver enveloping her.

Mr Elford continued, his voice hardly audible now. 'Four people upstairs suffocated by fumes. One person downstairs burned to death, and one unidentified body in the garden, at present unrecognisable. They say that the bodies upstairs are believed to be that of Mr and Mrs Applebee senior and of their son and daughter-in-law. They need someone to go and identify the bodies.' With this, Mr Elford could take no more. He ran from the room, and along the corridor to the library where his sobs could be heard penetrating the walls.

Lavinia was now shaking uncontrollably, her arms and hands, her legs and feet, and her head, were moving like a puppet being controlled by a stick in the hands of its puppeteer. Katherine had not made a sound. She now took Lavinia's hand and guided her from the chair, gently manoeuvring her from the room, and up the stairs, never stopping to see how she was. Katherine continued until she reached Lavinia's bedroom. She took her inside, placed her on the bed, and then left.

She returned to the nursery, and sat without moving by the side of Katy Louise until the light of day crept through the window on a day that she didn't want to see the beginning of. Katherine felt numbness in her limbs that she had never felt before. Mr Elford's ramblings had not said that it was Dorcas Louise that they had found in the burning remains of the house. He had not said who had made the call. Everyone had assumed, but of course they all knew who it was, but did they. Katherine could not cry; she tried but the tears would not come. She would not believe; she would dress and go right now. No she couldn't. There was Katy Louise, sleeping the innocent sleep of a child, not knowing that maybe her mother was dead and she would never see her again. She must not be told, not yet, shield her, protect, her, but don't tell her. She repeated those words to herself over and over again, and then she felt angry. She wanted to know, and know everything. A glib statement across the telephone wires from someone without a name or a face. Where was Thomas? He had taken the call, so why was he not here to explain?

Katherine looked at the clock. It was 8 o'clock, and the house was quiet. I was dreaming, she thought, I am still in my nightdress, I was dreaming. Jumping up from her seat next to the child who would have been awake on any other day, she grabbed the nearest clothes, and with shaking hands pulled them on, brushed her hair, and returned to Katy Louise who had just opened her eyes and stretched her little body in anticipation of the day ahead. Katherine, with amazing will power, washed her, dressed her, and sang the little song that they always sang together in the morning before breakfast.

It was Thomas who knocked on the door. Katherine opened it, and he just stood there, eyes red-rimmed.

'It's true?' asked Katherine.

'Yes, it's true,' answered Thomas. 'I have come to take Katy Louise to stay with Flo and the boys. They know nothing; does Katy?'

'No,' answered Katherine, 'and that's how it will stay.'

'Yes,' said Thomas, 'I will be back immediately.'

Katy Louise, happy to go and play with Jack and James, had not picked up on the strangeness in the air. Collecting rabbit and a couple of toys, she went easily as Thomas held her hand, saying, 'You would like to play with the boys today, wouldn't you? Flo will take you all to the park.'

'Feed the ducks,' said Katy Louise as she negotiated the staircase, holding tightly on to rabbit.

Thomas returned to find a crumpled Katherine on Katy Louise's bed, her body heaving in great cries of grief. She pounded the pillow with her fists, shouting, 'Not again. No, not again.'

Thomas sat beside her, tears streaming down his face, as Charlie came to the door to see what had happened. Charlie did not know. He had not heard anything, not even the ringing of the phone. Thomas looked at him, and Charlie looked at Katherine as Thomas put her gently back against the pillows.

'Whatever is it?' questioned Charlie, moving toward Katherine. Thomas was sitting beside her and gently lifting her into his arms. She was not able to speak.

It was Thomas who told his old friend the happenings of the early hours of this morning. The telephone call had come from the county sheriff's office. That was all Thomas could tell him. The rest of the message was taken by Mr Elford, and they would have to wait until he was able to give them any information in addition to that which he had gabbled out in his incoherent state of disbelief. Thomas repeated Mr Elford's words as closely as he could to Charlie. He clung to Katherine, rocking her back and forth, as her tears soaked his shirt, and ran, together with his own, down his face into his mouth, where he could taste their salty deposit. There was no comforting her.

Charlie then left her with Thomas, and went to the kitchen where Cook would have arrived, also unaware of the terrible tragedy that had befallen this family. It was late in the morning when Lavinia Elford came to see Katherine. The tears had slightly abated, but as Lavinia walked through the door, she collapsed again. Thomas, not wanting to leave her, hovered as the mistress sat on her other side.

'Leave her for a while, Thomas, I will take care of her,' said Lavinia gently, her own tears welling up again at the sight of Katherine. Lavinia gently raised Katherine's head, and looking into those deep beautiful eyes, now red and sore, with huge swellings underneath, said, 'Darling, I know she was your child. I knew from the moment you took her in your arms and she stopped crying. That's why I would never let you go, and now we have both lost her, but somehow, together, we have to care for and raise her child. 'Do you think we could do that, Katherine, together?'

Katherine nodded silently, and putting her arms around Lavinia, they let their tears sate their bodies. Charlie came and brought them a tray from Cook, who he said was devastated at the news, as was everyone. Mr Elford, Lavinia said, had summoned every ounce of courage that he could muster, and had asked her to leave him alone while he contacted the number of the sheriff's office, where the call had come from. He needed to be calm in order to obtain all the information, and make any arrangements necessary to go and identify the bodies. Lavinia had pleaded with him not to ask her to go. She couldn't face the thought, although she felt guilty about it.

Katherine jumped up. 'I should go,' she cried.

'No, my darling, you can't,' Lavinia gently pleaded. 'Mr Elford has no idea that you are Dorcas Louis's mother, and I feel that I can't allow him to be faced with that now. Also I need you here for Katy Louise; how are we to tell her?'

'We aren't,' Katherine said. 'She is too young to be faced with such horror. In fact, I think that maybe she should never know.'

Lavinia, sensing Katherine's grief was clouding her judgment, left it there. The two of them stayed together, sharing each other's sorrow for the rest of the day. Each one thinking that the other one's tears were subsiding until suddenly without warning new floods issued from their eyes, one and then the other. Katy Louise came back at the end of the day, telling Katherine and her grandmother that the park was good, and that tomorrow Charlie and Flo were taking them to the zoo. Katherine and Lavinia looked at one another and smiled through new tears at the pure innocence and beauty of children. They both played a little while with her, and then put her to bed. She raised her arms for a hug from them both, cuddled into rabbit, and was asleep before they left the room.

Mr Elford, very unsteady and clearly traumatised by the news, called Katherine, Thomas, and Charlie to the library, where he and Mrs Elford stood holding hands by the desk. 'I will try and relay to you the events that led to last night's telephone call, as clearly as I can manage. The circumstances under which it all happened are still being investigated, but it appears that there is a possibility that the fire was caused by an arsonist. Until identification of the bodies has been completed, there can be no absolute confirmation as to who they are, but from certain objects upon the persons, it is conclusive that it was Mr and Mrs Applebee who died in their sleep from inhalation of toxic fumes, and it was Dorcas Louise and Nathan Applebee who also died in their sleep from inhalation of toxic fumes. These four people were in the bedrooms on the first floor gallery, which would offer them little protection from the rising fumes. Downstairs was the body of a young man assumed to be the son of Mr and Mrs Applebee, and the brother of Nathan. Apart from being badly burned, he had bruises and a wound to the head, and finally the body of a young woman was found in the garden, again badly burned. The coroner's reports have been received, but they are unable to release them until all the bodies have been identified. There was just one point that can be disclosed. The wife of the younger man was in the early stages of pregnancy.'

At this point, Mr Elford could not go on, and Katherine dropped to her knees with an agonising cry. Thomas lifted her up and held her to him, as Mr Elford excused himself and asked Charlie to give him half an hour, and then return to the library. Night was again closing in. Katherine would not even lie down. Thomas stayed with her and held her hand. He wrapped both her and himself in the blanket from the bed, and held her like a child frightened of the dark, until she finally succumbed to sleep. He lifted her feet gently and placed them on the nursery chair, put a pillow behind her head, and settled himself on the floor next to her.

Katy Louise woke them both up, saying, 'Zoo today, Kat, get up, zoo today.'

Katherine, aching in every limb, raised herself, and shook Thomas. They both looked at one another, and made the effort to keep Katy Louise happy at all costs.

Charlie had returned to the library, and Mr Elford had told him in great detail everything that he would need to know. He was to travel to America with Mr Elford to witness the identification of the bodies. It would be the hardest thing that they had ever done. Charlie, Mr Elford thought, would be the person who he would like to have with him. He had witnessed the horror of war, and seen the results of burning at close quarters, witnessing the pain himself, and it just seemed right to have him by his side. Early that morning, he had made arrangements to secure all the necessary papers for himself and for Charlie. Under these extenuating circumstances, the authorities had issued orders for uninterrupted travel from Liverpool to New York. The bodies had been transported from Florida to where all the enquiries could be dealt with properly, and quickly. They would have to leave today, and the rest would be dealt with by the American authorities.

The house was in turmoil, and Charlie's promise to go to the zoo with Flo and the children, had to be reneged upon, so Cook's son, Arthur, stepped into the breach, and with his wife, his two children, Flo's two, and Katy Louise, they all took off as soon as they could muster the children.

Katherine was relieved that Katy Louise did not have to witness the tears at the departure of Charlie and Mr Elford. Thomas stayed at Katherine's side, and put on a happy face as they wished the little band of children a good time. Lavinia collapsed in tears at the door as her husband kissed her goodbye. Flo had said her farewell this morning before the boys got out of bed. Katherine hugged Charlie and said, 'Thank you so much,' and to Mr Elford she said, 'I'm sorry it had to be you, but Charlie will take care of you.'

There was nothing now that could be done; they had to sit and wait, possibly for a good few days. Lavinia was going back upstairs to lie down; her head was pounding, and her body ached with an overpowering agony that nothing could quell. She had taken some of the medicine that she used to take in the days when she found it difficult to cope with some of the things that life asked of her. Now life had not asked, it had just taken, and there was no cure for that. She removed her clothes, put on a warm nightdress, and climbed into bed, burying her head under the pillow and pulling the bed clothes around her ears.

Katherine and Thomas went together to the nursery, and Katherine had just lain in Thomas's arms, and let the tears go. There were no screams now, nor were there agonising moans, but just a quiet continuous weeping that she had no control over. Thomas sat silently, and thought how glad he was that she had confided in him just the other night. To lose Dorcas Louise, after all she had been through to keep her, was beyond his imagination. To lose a child under any circumstances must be the worst thing that could happen to anyone, but to lose one in such a horrendous way has to be beyond imagination. To lose a child that has been raised by you, without being able to admit to its birthright, is something that no woman, however she had wronged, should have to face. Katherine, exhausted and all cried out, turned to Thomas in the afternoon, and suggested that, with Lavinia's permission, she would ask Flo to move into the house with the boys for the duration of Charlie's absence. It would be better for Katy Louise to have the boys around all the time, and not so lonely for Flo. The house was not going to be in any sort of order for the foreseeable future. They would all just have to pull together, and keep one another alive as best they could.

Cook was being a gem, and feeding them whenever they needed it. She made endless pots of tea, which always seemed to be accepted gratefully. Katherine went to Lavinia, and sat with her. She was wringing her hands in a kind of desperation, and when she separated them they were shaking.

'They won't stop,' she said, looking at her hands.

Katherine gently took them and held them. 'You are in shock, Lavinia; the news has hit us all in different ways, and as much as we all want to give up and run away, we can't. You and I especially have a little girl to care for who no longer has the mummy that she knew was hers. She must never be made to feel that we haven't the time to look after her. If we have to sacrifice our lives for her, so be it.'

Katherine then put her suggestion to Lavinia, and she agreed without question to bring them in by all means, make them comfortable, and let the boys spend as much time as they can with Katy Louise. The house, as it was, changed overnight. The children ran about unchecked, and their laughter rang throughout its corridors. Dorcas Louise would be happy with that, thought Katherine, suddenly remembering that another pair of tiny feet would have been pattering about, if it hadn't been for... She could not bring herself to say the words that would relate to the tragedy.

A few days had passed and, in New York, the news that faced Mr Elford and Charlie was of the worst kind. The fire had been started deliberately. Under the staircase in a small utility room, there was found a can which had held gasoline, paint cans, and remnants of bottles which had held flammable liquids. The fire trucks had been called by a man who witnessed the start of the fire, but by the time that they had quelled the flames sufficiently to make an entrance, and an ambulance had arrived, the person on the ground floor had been engulfed in flame, the stairs had gone, and by the time the rescuers had reached the upper floor, it was too late for the occupants who had died, it appeared, while sleeping. The smoke was dense and the fumes were extremely toxic. The fire had spread with utmost speed through the ground floor of the house. The windows had exploded, and what appeared to be the main run of the fire, which had taken purchase to each side of it as it ran, followed a line through the glass doors at the back of the house, which had sent flying glass in all directions.

It was as the fire crew continued extinguishing the flames into the garden that the sixth body was discovered, badly burned and bleeding. The body was of a young woman, and the coroner concluded that she probably was the last to die. The smell of gasoline lingered around her, and from the position of her body it appeared that she had been running away from the burning house, but could not escape until the glass blew out of the window, and by this time her clothes would have been alight. She had no identity that could be found on her body, and as yet no one had reported a missing person. From all the evidence gathered, it appears that the man who was downstairs put up some sort of fight, and was hit over the head which knocked him out, but it was the fire that had killed him. Enquiries had supported the fact that the man was the brother of Nathan Applebee, who had been visiting with his parents the house of Nathan and Dorcas Louise Applebee. There was, according to records, another brother, but as he was serving in the American navy, it would take a while to contact him. All that taken in by Mr Elford and Charlie now led to the worst part of all.

The coroner suggested that they took it very slowly with a break between each one. All that they would see would be the face of the person, and they would all have been cleaned as much as was possible. Nevertheless, the sights that they were about to witness would be very harrowing. In their own time, one by one, they looked at the people that they once knew. The body of Nathan's brother, without hair, and only a little skin, was almost unrecognisable, and yet the profile of the bones still had the shape of his brow and nose. Both Charlie and Mr Elford agreed that yes it was him. The next drawer was to bring them Mrs Applebee. The fire had not touched her at all, but her face was contorted as if it had struggled for breath before being overcome. Mr Applebee was next, and with much the same result. There was no doubt about their identities, and so they moved quickly on. Nathan Applebee had his head to one side. They had not moved it deliberately when they did the autopsy, as they believed that he was trying to say something to his wife as he was overcome by fumes. The coroner now suggested that they took a break before the next identification, as they knew that it would be the most terrible thing that they would ever have to do.

Mr Elford turned to Charlie and said, 'Shall we get it over with?' Charlie agreed. Dorcas Louise, as beautiful in death as in life lay before them. Mr Elford gasped, and Charlie began to falter. The coroner just asked the question, and all they needed to say was yes. They turned and walked from the room. Knowing what they had just suffered, the next question sounded impertinent to the coroner, but he had to ask it. He asked if they would consider looking at the final body in the room. It was unlikely, but it was an outside chance that it may be someone that the family had known, someone who meant them harm.

Reluctantly they agreed, and the sheet was removed. Mr Elford's face was a blank. She was badly burned, but apart from a gash on her face, and the fact that she had no hair or eyelashes, he had never seen anyone like her. Charlie's face looked twisted, as he said under his breath, 'Lucinda Hepworth.'

The coroner looked up in amazement, as Mr Elford supported himself against the adjacent wall. 'You know the identity of this person?' he addressed Charlie.

'Yes sir, I do,' Charlie replied, waiting for the next question.

'We will need to go to my office, if you would both be so kind as to follow me,' said the coroner, replacing the white sheet over the face, and closing the large drawer that held the terrible answers to the fate of the five people who had died so tragically just a few days ago.

For Charlie and Mr Elford, the shock had been intense. Mr Elford was visibly shaken to a point of near collapse, and Charlie was eaten with a feeling of anger such as he had never felt for anyone at any time in his life. Charlie related the whole story to the coroner, from the wedding day, until the day when he had had the instruction from Mr Elford to remove her from the house. The coroner took all the notes, and asked some relevant questions of both Charlie and Mr Elford. He then offered his condolences and his apologies for having to subject them to such a vile experience. The details would now all have to go to the courts, and as there were apparently no witnesses to the dreadful crime, the decision to let the burials take place would be taken by the coroner's office in conjunction with the high court of law. Had the perpetrator of the heinous crime not also died at the scene, she would certainly have met her death at the hands of an executioner.

It was Charlie who had the harrowing task of making the telephone call to Liverpool, and it was Thomas who Mr Elford suggested should be given all the information. It was thought that he would deal with passing on to Mrs Elford the outcome of this terrible day with the inevitable wisdom of words that he had come to expect from him. From the time that Thomas received the call, it took him an hour to come to terms enough with the news to make his way to Lavinia's room, and make the request that he be allowed to sit with her for a while. He related as best he could the terrible happenings of one week ago, when a part of this wonderful happy family was wiped out through the jealous insanity of woman scorned. Lavinia sat slumped in her chair as Thomas disclosed the enormity of the crime committed by Lucinda Hepworth, and the resulting wholesale sacrifice, and destruction of her child, and her new found family, and of an unborn baby. As Thomas stood before her, witnessing the agonising look that she gave him, she said, 'Go to Katherine, Thomas, she needs you now.'

The nursery door was open, and the sounds of children's voices that issued from it felt like a balm upon the soreness in Thomas's heart. Flo was there with Katherine, and as she saw his face, she jumped up and involuntarily asked about Charlie. 'Charlie is all right, Flo, and he asked me to tell you that he would telephone you soon, and he will tell you everything then, but for now could you take the children and give me a little while with Katherine?'

'Of course,' replied Flo and, taking the boys hands, with Katy Louise gently pushed on in front, she said, 'We will go to the park.'

As they left, Katy Louise turned and with upturned face, asked, 'When will my mummy be coming home?'

Thomas quickly said, 'You will see her one day, darling, but she has a long way to travel first.'

Satisfied by his words, Katy Louise skipped ahead, and the boys followed, while Flo turned away to wipe her eyes, before she uncertainly waved to Katherine, and left. Thomas held out his arms to Katherine, as his emotions erupted, and he burst into tears. 'Tell me Thomas,' said Katherine. 'I know the news is going to be bad, just tell me. It's better to know than to sit and wonder about what happened over there so many miles away.'

Thomas once again summoned all the power within him, and went through it all. The clarity of it sometimes blurring in his mind as, word for word, he told the story as it was told to him by Charlie. Katherine, sitting quietly by his side, winced as the details of Thomas's description brought pictures into her head. Her baby, the child that she had brought into the world with so much pain and difficulty, had suffered the ultimate pain as her life was finally extinguished. When Thomas told her that the fire had been deliberately started by Lucinda Hepworth, it brought Katherine to her feet screaming, 'I will kill her, I want her to die. I want to set the match that will burn her slowly to death, and I want to hear every piercing scream that emits from her mouth, and as she dies, I want to be there laughing. Where is she? I want to go and see her, and I will surely die for the pleasure of seeing her burn inch by inch.'

In delirium, Katherine continued to rant as Thomas held her tightly, her fists pummelling his chest, until he too cried out in pain. He held on to her, his eyes never leaving her beautiful face, now contorted with pain, and anguish, until she stopped screaming, and dissolved into heaving sobs. He sat her down gently , and knelt before her, gained her attention, and holding her hands tightly said, 'Darling, she died in the fire too; hers was the sixth body that was removed from the house, and Charlie identified it as being her. She was evidently trying to run away, after hitting Nathan's brother over the head with the heavy tin that had contained gasoline. Some of the liquid had run on to her clothes, and as she reached the back doors into the garden, they exploded causing her to be caught in the resulting fireball. She was found lying on the ground badly burned after all the other bodies had been discovered. She died at the scene.'

Katherine would never recover completely from the shock. Her tears now silent, her eyes dull, and her head bowed in disbelief, she stood up and slowly walked away heading toward Lavinia's room. Thomas let her go, knowing that she would be all right with Lavinia, and he headed to the kitchen, where Cook was waiting for news. It was Thomas's turn to be cared for, and Cook was the one to do it. She sat him down at the table, and held his trembling hands until he calmed himself enough to relate the news to her.

In America, Charlie and Mr Elford waited in the hotel room for further news and instructions. They took time out to go for walks, leaving the hotel receptionist to take any messages. New York was pleasant, and but for the terrible cloud that hung over them, they found comfort in each other's company. All that they could discuss over and over again was the whys and wherefores of the happenings in Florida. It was to be a new beginning for all of them. Houses built for the affluent white people seeing potential in the surrounding land, were few and far between. The Applebees had taken stock, and believed that with investment the returns and possibilities of having a residence in the state would bring great rewards. Mr Elford becoming involved had boosted the realisation of a dream. The stock market had reached a strong upward move in 1927, increasing investment from all directions, and at the beginning of 1928 the boom had begun.

Mr Elford could not talk or think at the moment of anything beyond the torture of the loss of not only his daughter, but of Mr and Mrs Applebee and their two sons. Slowly as he sat in reverie, during the evenings when conversation lapsed, as both men turned their thoughts to their families at home and their future lives, Mr Elford's thoughts drifted to his future. Where did he go from here? His investments were intricately joined to those of Nathan Applebee senior, and a large percentage of them were now held in The United States of America. There was also another son of Mr Applebee who would now become next of kin to him, and therefore automatically inherit the business if no last will and testament had been made. How would he go about retrieving that which was his, and how long would it take? Had the final signatures reached their destination before the tragedy happened, and had Lucinda Hepworth somehow, without anyone's knowledge, wriggled her way back into Nathan's company here in America? Could she have once again tried to wreak havoc in Nathan's business only to be put down and sent away by a now reformed Nathan? Thus, would she then vow vengeance and try to destroy them?

James Elford, suddenly dragging his mind from his thoughts, heard the ringing of a telephone call being diverted from reception. The confirmation from the coroner's office that the bodies were to be released for burial seven days from today brought him back to the reality of the task in hand. Lavinia could now make arrangements to travel. There would not be much time. He would in honesty have preferred to have Dorcas Louise taken back to England, but she was to be buried with her husband and his family in New York.

Katherine and Lavinia had spent many hours together. They had gone over and over it, again and again, with little or no reasoning. Katherine would of course stay with Katy Louise; she could not bear to leave her, and truthfully Lavinia was not fit or strong enough to care for her. How long they could keep the truth from her, they did not know. Martha had suggested that Katherine should bring her to London for a while, and maybe while Lavinia had gone to the funeral it would be a good time. The hope that she would soon be able to leave the house in Liverpool, and move to London would now go on hold for as long as was needed, certainly for the foreseeable future. Caring for Katy Louise was now Katherine's prime obligation, and she would see it through. The house would wait for her. Martha and Mr Cloverleaf would look after it. Charlie and Thomas would go, along with Flo and the boys, at the end of the year, and she would then discuss the future with Lavinia, regarding Katy Louise's education and her upbringing.

The news of the forthcoming funerals set the seal on Katherine's decision to go to visit Martha. Lavinia was happy. In fact, Lavinia was happy that Katherine was prepared to raise Katy Louise. She would of course be there as legal adoptive grandmother, and there was no one on Nathan's side of the family that could claim custody. The thought of going through another generation of school days, and teenage years frankly left Lavinia wanting. The plans for the journey to America were made, and Lavinia was soon on her way.

Charlie was very tired now, and a bit traumatised by it all. Mr Elford seemed sometimes to be lost in a world of his own, and the waiting for Charlie seemed to be a lifetime. He had spoken to Flo, who missed him so much and worried about him.

The night before the funerals were about to take place, Katherine, having tucked Katy Louise in with rabbit and told her a story, wandered into the garden. The clouds were heavy and rain leaden. There were no stars to see, and the moon struggled to find a space into which it could spread its light. The old saying came to Katherine's lips, as it had before when something bad was about to happen. 'There's rain around the moon' tonight she said to herself, but this is England, the sky may be clear in America. The rose that grew beneath her window was not in bloom, but she noticed a tiny bud had tucked itself behind a leaf as if in waiting. 'Wait for her Joseph,' she whispered into the night air.

The next day she had no wish to stay in the house, and so she packed a small case for Katy Louise, and one for herself, bade goodbye to Flo, and told the boys to be good. Mr Cloverleaf was waiting at the station, while Mr Pugh sat in the motor car ready to drive them home. Martha, as always, stood at the door, arms outstretched, as Katherine with Katy Louise holding her hand ran toward her. Martha, scooping a young excited Katy Louise into her arms, led them into the drawing room where the usual tray of delicacies and tea stood on the small table. Nothing had changed, thought Katherine. Martha, as always, had kept it all shiny and clean. She wished secretly that she was home to stay but that was not possible, not now. Katy Louise sat contentedly on the couch with rabbit, saving the last little bit of cake for him, but of course he didn't want it, and so Katy ate it herself. Martha, seeing the terrible sadness in Katherine's eyes, made no comment, but she had the feeling that telling Katy Louise was weighing heavily on her. Perhaps between them they could think of a way that she could be told.

Later, as bedtime approached for Katy Louise, Martha said that she had prepared Dorcas Louise's old room for her, as there were remnants of her childhood left in there. Katherine nodded, but found it hard to accept that Dorcas would never see it again. When Katy finally dropped off to sleep after three stories had worked their magic, Katherine sat with Martha and went through it all again. Martha, with her arm around Katherine's shoulders, listened in horror. She commented to Katherine that it was such a blessing that Adolphus did not have to face all of this. Katherine just nodded, feeling now the pain of losing them both in such a short space of time.

The mourners, following the five hearses that bore the coffins one by one to the church, sat in stunned silence as they watched the limousines ahead of them all in line, all carrying their precious cargo with reverence to their last resting place. Passers-by stopped and bowed their heads in respect, most of them not knowing the significance of the mass burial. The service completed, the gathering of mourners now increased by inquisitive followers, walked the short quiet road to the burial ground where each and every coffin received its own blessing, and its own little corsage of flowers strewn across its top. Nathan's brother had not made it to the funeral. It had proven difficult to locate him. Relations of Mr and Mrs Applebee, friends, and business associates were in attendance, but all seemed to keep their distance. Charlie, in the role of Mr Elford's butler, attempted to make an introduction, and invite them to meet his employers, but the offering of hands was weak, and the sympathy was meagre.

They very soon returned to their own circle, leaving Mr and Mrs Elford feeling lost and very much alone. If they had been in Liverpool, there would have been many mourners of their own circle of friends, and those of Dorcas Louise also, but it was deemed impossible for them to travel at such short notice to America. Many offerings of sympathy had been received by mail. Visitors had come from all around to give their support and sympathy, but on this day when sorrow was so deeply forged in their hearts, in a foreign land and saying goodbye to their darling daughter, it was indeed the loneliest and saddest day of their lives. Most of the mourners had already gone to a reception that Mr Elford had personally organised. The two of them and Charlie stayed behind, just for a short while to be alone with Dorcas Louise. Lavinia gently dropped a rose that she had been holding until that moment on to the coffin bearing her name. Mr Elford, choking back the tears, took her hand and led her away to board the last limousine that had waited for them. They insisted that Charlie stayed with them, and that is how it was; nobody talked to them, only the solicitor who was present in that capacity. Weak and drawn, they left after a very short time, returned to their hotel and sat together wondering why they had been treated as virtual outcasts. It was over.

Mr Elford would now set about the impossible task of unravelling his part of the business. He would have to stay for a while in America so as to have contact with the solicitor. Nathan's brother would also have to be contacted, and attend some meetings. The whole thing was now a mess, and to have to cope with it in the aftermath of what had occurred was daunting to say the least. Mr Elford could not afford to let things slide, he had to be ahead of the market, but would any of the finances be released, or would they be frozen by the law until the position of Nathan's brother was made clear in regard to his inheritance. As far as Mr Elford was aware, it was only Nathan who would inherit, as his father had stipulated it that way when Nathan became his partner.

Lavinia, with great regret, would leave America and leave her husband there to cope alone. Mr Elford had insisted on this, because of the time that he would have to spend locked away with the paperwork. He would send for her if it were possible before he left for home. He intended somehow to do that as he had no wish to stay in this land. He would work, and if necessary forfeit some of the financial benefits, in order to fulfil that decision. Charlie and Lavinia left America just three days after the funeral.

They arrived home with worried and heavy hearts. Charlie was welcomed with open arms by Flo and the boys. Lavinia was taken by the hand by a serious little girl who knew something was wrong, but had no idea what. She knew that her mummy had been away longer than she had ever been before, and Kat had loved and taken care of her, but she couldn't remember her mummy's face. She saw pictures of her dressed in her wedding dress, but that was not the mummy who came and kissed her goodnight. She would not go near her bedroom upstairs where Mummy and Daddy lived. She would stay with Kat forever. Kat always came home to her, and Kat took her to places that Mummy never did. Lavinia stayed with her and Katherine in the nursery until she went to sleep that night, and they decided that the next time she asked the question about her mummy not being there, they would tell her together.

From that night, as Katy Louise fell asleep whispering, 'Love you, Kat', she never mentioned her mother, or indeed her father, again. Lavinia was there and played the part of a doting grandmother, but it was Katherine who once again took on the role of motherhood. Lavinia and Katherine moved the playthings out of the upstairs nursery, and placed them in the old nursery, which thankfully Katherine had opted to stay in after Katy Louise was born, and she was placed with her mother and father in the upstairs apartment. Flo's sons were always allowed to play with Katy Louise, and so she had no difficulty in sharing toys. Flo moved back into the attic flat with Charlie. The boys often stayed overnight, especially when Flo started to collect items that would furnish her new flat that she and Charlie would move into at the end of the year. The attic became like Aladdin's cave, and Flo could not resist showing Katherine, and then apologising because she knew that Katherine would also like to live in London. She had often commented on how she would love to move, but would not entertain the idea all the time that Katy Louise needed a nanny.

In America, Mr Elford was struggling with the relentless pages of figures which had, over the months since the merger had been agreed by him and Mr Applebee, grown out of all proportion. His own investments, which fortunately were doing very well, and had at no time been touched by the merger would, he hoped, withstand the time lapse until he could regain his half of the American business, and return to England with most of his fortune intact. Martin Applebee, Nathan's brother, had at last been given permission to leave the ship for as long as he was required to straighten out all that was needed. To get to the funerals had been impossible in the time that he had. He apologised most humbly to both the solicitor and Mr

466

Elford. At least he was communicative, which was more than the relatives who had been there were, thought Mr Elford, as they waited together in the ante-room for the solicitor to arrive. He asked again for an explanation from Mr Elford as to the situation that led to the loss of his parents and of his brothers. Mr Elford, politely pointing out that he also had lost a daughter, went ahead once again with the harrowing story from beginning to end. Martin Applebee confessed that he too had noticed the woman in red at the wedding, and of her obvious attraction to Nathan, but he thought no more of it, and had not been aware that she had been his secretary. Mr Elford was impressed by the young man's openness, and hoped that he could spend some time with him while he was available.

The solicitor opened up the meeting by addressing both men, and by informing them that Nathan Applebee senior had in his last will and testament bequeathed the whole of his estate to Mrs Applebee, who would be responsible with Nathan Applebee for the running of the business. Upon her death, if it would be within thirty days of his own, the whole of the remainder would be passed to his son Nathan Applebee, who would continue to run the business, and would pay to Martin and Daniel Applebee a percentage according to the profit for the continuing lifetime of the company. No mention or provision was made in the will for Mr Elford's infusion of a vast fortune into the business. The solicitor asked if Mr Elford had the figures ready for him, to which he answered that the merger was only just at the end of completion, and that the signed documents were left in the hands of Nathan Applebee. Therefore it would be a fair assumption to think that every relative document was under lock and key in the New York office. Mr Elford, in a moment of panic, hoped beyond hope that none of the papers had been taken to the house in Florida. The solicitor then instructed that any movement of finances should be stopped immediately. He would need to obtain the key to the office, and would confiscate all the documents found therein. The untimely deaths of the family members mentioned in the will left the only surviving member as the sole beneficiary. Martin Applebee therefore would receive any remaining monies after debts were paid, and as there was no obvious interest in the business on his behalf, there would have to be an extensive search into the relevant documents, for concluding the business of the company.

Mr Elford would of course, when all his documents and investments in the company were passed to the solicitors for inspection, receive full compensation. This process would take some time, but if Mr Elford was able to present all of his papers in good order as soon as possible, the time factor would be lessened and the whole business brought to a satisfactory end. Mr Martin Applebee would not be required for at least a few weeks, so he could return to his ship as long as he kept the solicitor advised of his whereabouts. Mr Elford would be notified of all documents found at the New York office as soon as possible. The solicitor rose from his seat and bade both men 'Good morning', and left with a doubt in his mind as to the speed with which Mr Elford could provide the necessary papers which would bring to an end this unpleasant and difficult case.

Martin Applebee and James Elford parted company outside the solicitor's office. They would keep in touch, and be as much help as they could to one another. James Elford walked back to his hotel, not really knowing where he was going, but figuring that eventually he would find it; if he didn't he would call a taxi cab. He arrived with very little effort at the entrance to the hotel. In reception, he asked for a telephone call to Liverpool to be arranged and to be taken in his room. He made his way to his room, threw the keys on to the bed and, sitting in the armchair, he wept. Head in hands he wept like a child. He was still sitting there, eyes tightly closed as if to push out the visions that would invade his thoughts for the rest of his life, when the knock at the door brought him back to reality. A bell-boy brought in the trolley with the telephone, and James Elford dialled the number.

Katherine answered the call to hear Mr Elford struggling to keep his voice even as he asked if she could bring Lavinia to talk to him. In fact, Lavinia was close behind Katherine, with Katy Louise tugging at her skirt. Katherine took Katy's hand, and gently ushered her out of the room, closing the door securely behind her as Lavinia took up the telephone. Lavinia and James spoke for a long time, both intermittently lapsing into tears. James would need a few days more to organise his own solicitor to act for him in America, and then he would return home to collect every item that he could find to serve his case. He asked if Katherine, in the meantime, could put any existing papers relative to the merger in some sort of order, and if Lavinia could help by searching every corner of his upstairs office, and work with Katherine.

It was going to be a long time before it would all be sorted, and he just hoped that the papers that Nathan had in his possession had found their way safely to the New York office. James confessed to Lavinia that with each day that passed he blamed himself for all of this. He had unwittingly pushed his daughter into a marriage that he believed would be good for her, and would make, not only her, but all of them among the richest people in the land. Lavinia just said, 'Don't feel badly, darling, it's done now, just come home and we will face it together.' In her heart, Lavinia felt that he was correct. He did push the marriage, and she had said so at the time to Katherine, whom she thought probably felt the same as she did.

At the end of that telephone call, James Elford spoke to the solicitor who had been handling the legal side of the merger in America, and asked if he would please be present when the solicitor acting for the Applebees, searched and confiscated the papers that were in the New York office, which he believed was imminent. He then asked if he could continue to act on his behalf so that he could return to England and attend to his affairs there. This confirmed, he then spoke to the Applebees' solicitor with whom they had dealt that morning, and reiterated that he wished for his solicitor to be present from now onwards, until it was brought to a satisfactory conclusion.

All that could be done at this point was done. James Elford began to think in terms of going home. He was now a very worried man, and for the past few days the trauma of it all had haunted him unrelentingly. He knew that he had private finances upon which he could rely, but he had invested heavily, and had eroded a considerable amount. He would have to now work toward a plan to run the house economically, but he could not at this moment think any further ahead than getting the merger untangled, and then rethink his investments.

The irony of all this was that the stock market was booming, and he knew that now was the time for big investments. He was sorely tempted, but knew that he would need every penny to keep his home and family safe and secure. The day before he was due to leave for England, there was a message from reception to say that someone was at the desk asking to see him. Locking his door, he proceeded down the stairs to find Martin Applebee dressed in uniform standing waiting for him. He approached and shook his hand, after which the young man ushered him to a table where he had ordered some drinks and a few snacks. It was pleasant to see him, and his face held no defiance or malice, so James Elford sat down and, to be honest, it was a moment of light relief to have someone who had been through the same torment to sit and talk to. They held a quiet and reserved conversation for a while, and then Martin confessed that there was a reason for his coming. James looked at him with a little trepidation, but the young man smiled gently and produced from his pocket a small bag which he passed to James, and said, 'I was given this when I returned from duty. These are some of the personal effects retrieved from the bodies of our two families. Those of my mother and father, I have kept, and the watch that was Nathan's I have kept, but I thought that you and your family should have those that were found on Dorcas Louise. Anything that may be found at a later date within the precincts of the house will be retained by the solicitor until the final estates are realised.'

James, not quite believing the honesty and caring nature of this young man, opened the bag. There was a tiny gold cross on a chain, a wedding and engagement ring, and a watch which Martin had noticed was engraved in a way that said it was very special to Dorcas Louise, and that she was wearing it when she died. Had the fire reached them of course there would have been nothing left of the metals, and the stones would have been lost in the rubble. James Elford felt very humble in the presence of the young officer who sat opposite him, and he could find no words to say. He took his hand and held it in a firm grip, and said, 'I hope with all my heart that when we meet again it will be as a satisfactory end to all this, and I hope that we will at some odd time during the rest of our lives meet in happier circumstances, and be able to remember our loved ones with happy memories, and not with the dreadful pictures that we carry in our minds today. Thank you and god bless and keep you safe.'

James Elford arrived home, exhausted, unhappy, and with a biting dread of the near future. He wanted to shut himself away until all of this was over. He wanted a miracle to happen, and to wake up and find it had all been a dream. None of this would happen, he knew, but it was such an escape to dream that it might. Normally on his return from a business trip, he would greet everyone, family and staff alike, but this day even Katy Louise was given a perfunctory kiss, and a promise to play later. Katherine bundled her off to the nursery, saying that Grandpapa was very tired, and feeling a little sick, and that he would come and see her later on. Katy Louise, at the very tender age of five, was becoming used to people disappearing from her life. She didn't like it but grew to accept it.

As soon as James reached the sanctuary of his own apartment, and in the company of his wife, he drew a great sigh, and said, 'I am so sorry, darling, but I do not know what to do. I may not see my investment cleared for a year or more. The business in the United States is about to be wound up. There is no one left to run it. Nathan's brother has his own career in the navy, and wants no part of his father's business. I am too old to run it alone, and really have no wish to. There are many who will support house construction, and car sales will always survive. They were the businesses that Mr Applebee and I had mainly invested in, and while I am sure that someone will be willing to take on the well-established Applebee set up, I personally want to get out. I have made mistakes, many of them, but Applebee spurred me on with promises of big returns. I am floundering now, and I am not sure how long I can survive without returns from the invested monies.'

Lavinia listened with sympathy, but with little knowledge of her husband's financial plight. She sat there looking so sad that it cut into James Elford's heart like a knife. He passed the little black bag to Lavinia, which she opened, a questioning look in her eyes. She pulled the watch from its depths, and the rings which had been threaded on to the bracelet for safe keeping. The tiny cross fell out as Lavinia shook the bag. She held the precious objects in her hands and with a gasping sigh placed them on the table.

'Nathan's brother brought them to me at the hotel. Dorcas Louise was wearing them when she died, and they were held at the mortuary until Martin could collect them. He thought that we should have them. He is such a nice man, Lavinia. I liked him very much,' James told her.

Lavinia, running her fingers gently across each piece, looked up and said to James, 'I would like Katherine to have the watch if that seems all right to you. Adolphus was so close to her, and she loved Dorcas Louise. The cross, I think, would be nice for Katy to wear, although she knows nothing yet of her mother's fate. Maybe Katherine could give it to her, and then she would accept it without question.'

Thus it was agreed, and later in the day Lavinia went to Katherine and handed her the watch. She sat in the chair and looked at it for quite some time before she said in a whisper, 'How?'

'Nathan's brother was given the personal effects that were actually on the bodies when they were taken to the mortuary. I have both her wedding and engagement rings, and I thought that you could give this to Katy Louise as a present from you, and then we have no need to worry about questions.' She handed her the cross.

Katherine said to Lavinia, 'She had them on in bed, all of them?'

'Obviously so,' answered Lavinia.

Katherine, looking at her, eyes brimming with tears, said, 'Dorcas Louise promised Adolphus that she would wear the watch until the day she died. She did just that. Oh Lavinia, thank you. I will keep it close to my heart for ever too, and it's a lovely thought to give Katy Louise the cross. Such tiny objects to replace the life of someone so special, but they will be immortal.' Katherine made an involuntary movement of her hand to touch the locket that had always stayed around her neck, reminding her of a mother that she had never known. The watch she placed with the letter that Adolphus had written to her, and safely put it in her little case of treasures.

Mr Elford sat at his desk, and in desperation hoped that the solicitors would work with all the speed that they could. Katherine had collected all that was left of the paperwork that the solicitor would need, and Mr Elford was preparing to send it now with a covering letter on its way to New York. He was frantically working out the budget that he would have to set in order to keep this house running. Charlie and Thomas had offered to stay on in view of the now drastically changing circumstances, but Mr Elford had insisted that they go when the time was right for them. He would not stand in their way. Secretly he was glad that they were leaving the house, as paying them would be a massive strain on the finances. He would not for the near future need a butler, chauffeur, or an assistant butler. He could drive himself, and Katherine could drive, and between them they could, with Cook's help, survive the daily routine. There would be no more dinner parties, or evening soirees until all of this had sorted itself out, and he was financially secure once more. The strain of dealing on the stock market at the moment filled him with dread instead of the excitement that he used to feel.

Katherine was feeling a little uneasy, as the estate of Adolphus had finally been executed and delivered into her hands, making her a very rich woman. She could offer to help, but if the Elfords knew the extent of her inheritance, they would know that she no longer needed employment. She would however, if things became impossible, offer to continue to care for Katy Louise, and do the housekeeping for no payment save that of accommodation and food. She would also, without their knowledge, be able to buy clothes for her, and the things that a little girl growing up needed. Now that going to America was no longer an issue, Mrs Elford would have to start thinking in terms of education. After she had prepared the paperwork for Mr Elford, Katherine, realising the situation, and being aware for a long time that he had invested in the stock market more heavily than perhaps he should have, took it upon herself to talk to Martha and Mr Cloverleaf with the view to planning a slight deception.

She thought that she might advise Mrs Elford that Adolphus had arranged for an account to be set up solely for the education of Katy Louise, and that she, Katherine, would have the task of administration of the said account until Katy Louise's education was finished. Would they fall for the deception, or was she making a foolish mistake? Martha thought that with all that Katherine had achieved in the past, a little deception would not be out of order. Mr Cloverleaf would be prepared to write a letter to Mr Elford stating that he was aware of the wishes of Mr Fry, and that for the time being he was left in charge of certain areas of his estate, and of the running of the house in London. The account for Miss Applebee's education was within his dossier, and he could pass the reins over to Miss Carrera at any time. This was perfect, thought Katherine, and she would leave Mr Cloverleaf to commit his instructions to paper, send them to Mr Elford, and await his decision.

She imagined that in his state of mind, he would welcome help of any kind. How right she was. Mr Elford was struggling at every step. The actual available money left to him would not be enough to cover the day to day living of the household for a whole year, or maybe more. At some point, he would have to borrow from the bank. A short while ago Mr Elford had been riding the crest of a wave, with investments on the stock market that were returning massive profits, and millions of pounds were changing hands as the fervour to buy stocks reached fever pitch. He had not a worry as his merger with the Applebees doubled his availability. Now his whole life would go on hold for the next year. If the market held, he would survive and be in a very enviable position, albeit on his own and without the backing of the industries that had been the backbone of the Applebee business. He spent hours in his office, but in the end all he could do was wait. The papers sent, and the figures set on paper that should be the final result of the separation of him from the Applebee partnership would blur before his eyes, as he fought to find a way to escape, but there was none. The acceptance that Katy Louise would, by the untold generosity of Adolphus Fry, have an education comparable to any that he could have afforded, gave him one small shaft of sunlight in his dark and dreary existence.

The lengthy days of summer looked toward autumn, as Katy Louise prepared to enter a beautiful little school that was fairly close to home. It was privately run, and had an excellent reputation as a preparatory school for five to eleven-year-olds. All the children wore uniform which was unusual in the past, but the general outlook of the country had improved as the 1920s moved toward their end.

Flo and Charlie's boys, it was decided, would not enter school until they moved to London. They were seven months younger than Katy Louise, and so it was thought not advisable to settle them down only to move them in a couple of months. Charlie and Thomas would be needed to go and receive the necessary training, ready to take over the running of Mr Cloverleaf's business in early October.

Flo could hardly contain herself, and but for the sadness of leaving Katherine and Cook, and for that matter the house where her employers had been so kind and forgiving when she almost brought them all into disrepute during her experience with the suffragette movement, she could not wait to go. London awaited her with all its shops and famous places. It was where she could be mistress of her own house, eat and sleep in the same building, and give the boys a bedroom of their own. Katherine would be sad to see them go, and secretly sad that she would not be going with them. She of course would have her hands full, with the running of the house coming completely under her wing, and the traumas of early schooldays which would surely bear some problems. Mrs Elford had taken to leaving most things to Katherine. She would be there if she was needed, but would rather just wander from place to place, meeting a few close friends having afternoon tea, and discussing the latest trend in fashion.

National news from the Unites States of America was slower in reaching its wider public than maybe it should be, and the telephone call that reached Mr Elford at the beginning of October was to be another stunning blow. On the 26th September, a hurricane pitched itself into Florida taking with it whole towns, and killing between 2,500 and 3,000 residents. It wiped out generations of families with no one left to identify the dead. Three quarters of the dead were black migrant workers, but the houses of the few white people, the tourists' resorts and their occupants, were not spared. The house that was Nathan's, already unstable due to the raging fire that consumed its lower storey, would have been taken and broken like a wooden box. That of Mr and Mrs Applebee would have suffered much the same fate. It would therefore be safe to assume that anything salvaged from the beleaguered house would now have been blown into oblivion, and therefore offer no compensation to either of the beneficiaries. To send a representative into the area at the present time would be foolhardy to say the least. The papers needed by the solicitors had been received, and appeared to be in good order. Work would continue, and Mr Elford would be notified in due course of any further developments. Mr Elford wondered if there could be anything more to scupper his chances of regaining the life he was used to living.

Katherine, upon hearing the news, just thought that either way Dorcas Louise would have died in the 27th year of her life, in a violent and horrific way. Please god that now she was at peace, and in a place where no one could hurt her ever. The year passed finally, with Christmas and New Year being wholly and totally organised for the love of Katy Louise who had the best toys that money could buy, the biggest tree that could be found, and with Mr Cloverleaf playing a very believable Santa Clause, arriving in a Rolls Royce disguised as a sleigh, motor-driven but with bells, holly, mistletoe, and ribbons festooned around its body, and parcels galore of all shapes and sizes falling from its inside as the doors were opened by Mrs Clause, alias Martha Cloverleaf, with rosy cheeks, and a rather large behind adorned by a bow that read A MERRY CHRISTMAS.

The New Year brought little joy, and much more worry to Mr Elford. Katherine was now giving of her services free. Mrs Elford was getting more irritable. Katy Louise, by contrast, was enjoying her life at school. Katherine took her, and returned to pick her up. She was always full of stories, and in her school bag she carried pictures that she had painted. She looked so grown up in her green and white uniform, with her little white hat with the green band. On rainy days, she wore a mackintosh with a warm hood that pulled right over her head so that her hair never got wet. Katherine, for all her disappointment in not being able to go to London, was revelling in these days when Katy Louise was almost all hers.

It was May when Mr Elford decided that he could not sustain the expense of running the house, and in order to keep it he would have to borrow money. The house would have to be used as collateral and, with no other choice, he asked for Lavinia's signature to put with his own to gain the financial boost that he needed to carry him through until his financial return was realised. The application would take a while, and then at least they could live a near normal life for the next few months. The release of the loan coincided with a phone call from his solicitor in America to say that all the papers were now in order, and they were only waiting for the other beneficiary to be present. Martin Applebee, unfortunately, due to an important rendezvous involving many high ranking officers of the American Fleet, would not be allowed leave until the end of November. The monies would be left invested as they were at the moment they were frozen. As soon as Mr Applebee and Mr Elford could arrange to be in the solicitor's office to sign the final agreement, all the monies would be released.

James Elford sat back in his chair. Five months, that's all it would take. He now had the money from the loan, and if he was careful he could make up for some of his losses by November. From June until August, stock market prices reached their highest level to date. Without Lavinia's knowledge, once again James Elford took a risk. An economist stated that stock prices appeared to have reached a permanent high, which was what James Elford needed to hear, and he once again invested heavily. On September the 5th, the market started dropping. Prices fluctuated until October 24th, when stock prices plummeted. In New York, people waited outside the Stock Exchange on Wall St. There was an infusion from bankers who invested a large amount back into the stock market, which stopped some people selling. The market recovered, and people, including James Elford, started to buy again. Four days later the stock market crashed, taking with it all the investments that James Elford had made, now leaving him with a debt that would never be paid.

On the morning of the 30th of October 1929, the final strain and the realisation of his extreme foolishness resulted in James Elford suffering a major heart attack; he was found dead in the hallway, by Katherine. Clutched in his hand was a letter from the bank demanding instant repayment of their loan.

Chapter Twenty-Four

All Together At Last

Early in the morning of a bright spring day, the curtains of the upper stair window moved slightly to the side as Thomas watched the love of his life walking in her garden. She was leaning rather heavily, he thought, on the silver-topped cane that morning. He was seventy-five now and she seventy-six. The garden at her house in Acacia Avenue was her pride and joy. She had been living in the house for nigh on thirty years now. She had dreamed about it since she had known that Adolphus had left it all to her in his will, but her love for her natural granddaughter had kept her in the employ of Mr and Mrs Elford. The terrible happenings of 1928, when the child's mother had died in a house that was set alight by an act of arson, and then followed by the death from a heart attack of Mr Elford, her employer, and adoptive father of her natural daughter, started a chain of events that finally brought her to the only real family she ever wanted.

The Wall Street crash, that not only caused the death of Mr Elford, took every last penny that he had. Taking risk after risk, buying and selling on a crumbling stock market, he lost everything. The bank foreclosed on the loan that he had just recently taken, and the investments that he held in America dropped out of the bottom of the market. He died before his house was claimed in repayment, and before his family were given notice to quit. Every fixed asset would also go, the cars, the furniture, everything that would bring in enough money to pay his debts. Lavinia went into a sort of coma, saying over and over again, 'Where can I go? What can I do?'

Katherine took the reins, and asked Martha and Mr Cloverleaf to come and help her clear up all that they could. They were given twelve days to vacate the property. Cook would retire, and for her personally it would be a good move. Katy Louise clung to Katherine, not understanding any of it, only knowing that she would be leaving the school where she had just started, and that she would stay with Katherine in the house in London, and would have another school every bit as nice as this one to go to there. Lavinia would go too. Katherine would see to it that she was cared for, for the rest of her life. She was told to go and pack all her clothes into the boxes that Katherine had put out for her in her bedroom. She was in a state of great shock, and went about the task slowly, but eventually, in a sort of realisation, she completed it, and went to help Katy Louise, who was sitting on top of one of the packed boxes hugging rabbit and the raggedy eared bear, and telling them that they had to be good, and that Kat would look after them. A large amount of their belongings went ahead of them, and on the day that they left the house, it was all but empty. Katherine had told Cook to take the big rocking horse that was Dorcas Louise's for Arthur's two youngest children, one of which was just a few weeks old. Martha and Mr Cloverleaf had a couple of valises each, and Katherine carried her little case in one hand, holding Katy Louise with the other, while Lavinia followed with not a backward glance toward the house that had promised her so much, and that now would stand empty until someone rich enough came along to buy it.

That was how Katherine's dream finally came to fruition. She walked into her house, with her little retinue of followers. She was home. The house, the garden, everything, and she would be forever with her darling Martha, dear Mr Cloverleaf, and Thomas who deserved so much more than she had given him. Each day became more precious than the one before. It took a while to make everyone comfortable. Martha and Mr Cloverleaf would take care of her now. They would cook and clean, and make her life as easy as they could. No one deserved it more, they said with gusto, as they fussed and bustled around her, and she revelled in their indulgences.

Katy Louise was soon settled into a local school that Katherine would privately pay for to ensure that she had the best that education could offer, and being the happy child that she was, she made friends with amazing speed. Also, she whooped with joy when she found Jack and James living across the street. Flo, with great importance, invited the young lady over for afternoon tea at the first opportunity. Charlie and Thomas had settled in extremely well, and had taken to the motor car business with a great enthusiasm.

Lavinia was not in the best of mental health, and Katherine, on Mr Cloverleaf's advice, had visited the solicitor with a view to becoming the legal guardian of Katy Louise. He had agreed and prepared the necessary papers which he had suggested should be signed as soon as possible by Mrs Elford, while she could still be classed as of sound mind. Lavinia showed no emotion, and signed the papers without question. Katherine could now have complete control of the life of her young granddaughter, who reminded her so much of Dorcas Louise at that age. She would grow into a fine young lady.

Looking after Lavinia was not really difficult; she was never to be as she once was, but she was comfortable, and shared her days with the family. Katherine never shut the door on her, or was cross when she spilled her food, or wandered around in the night sometimes. She insisted that she took full responsibility for her. She would never forget how she had known about Dorcas, and kept her secret, always to the end. The end came two years after the move. It came quietly in the night after she had cried herself to sleep. Lavinia's body would travel back to Liverpool. Katherine decided that it was the last thing that she could do for her in respect of the past. The burial would be arranged to coincide with the arrival of the coffin, and Lavinia would be laid next to her husband in the quiet church yard close to their old home.

Katherine and Mr Cloverleaf would travel on the same train, and it would all be carried out with reverence, assured the undertaker in London. The service and the burial were conducted quietly, which would have been Lavinia's wish, and Katherine and Mr Cloverleaf took rooms in a hotel nearby for the night, returning after breakfast early the following morning. For Katherine, a little sadly perhaps, the links with the Elford family were now finally broken, and she could look forward to a new and happier life.

Katy Louise was waiting at the door as Charlie drove the limousine up the drive, bringing home her Kat and Martha's Mr Cloverleaf. Katherine expelled a great sigh of relief as, arm in arm with Katy Louise, she walked into her house to meet a smiling Martha, who opened the doors leading into the garden. Katherine loved to sit at the little table under the shade of the Linden tree, which seemed to survive happily in its sheltered environment in this London suburban garden. Katy Louise sat with her, enjoying a glass of cold fresh lemonade and neatly cut sandwiches, while in complete contentment Katherine sat and listened as she chatted without stopping for breath about her school, her friends, and lessons. Katy Louise was growing up, now eight years old, and with a delightful temperament. She was popular at school, and the reports from her teachers had been very rewarding for Katherine.

The extent of Katherine's inheritance remained unknown, and no one questioned it. The fact that Adolphus had left her the house, and its contents, and enough money to ensure its future maintenance was enough. Katherine really wanted for very little. Charlie and Thomas were there whenever she needed transport. Fresh fruit, vegetables, and meat were all delivered by the little dark green van from the large London store that Adolphus had always dealt with, and bread, milk, and any other commodities that were needed, came from the local stores who also had a good delivery service in this affluent part of the North London suburbs. Katherine had decided that she would leave the house as Adolphus had arranged it for the time being at least. Martha, Mr Cloverleaf, Thomas, Katherine, and Katy Louise fitted easily into the one half, and Katherine loved it.

She loved the library most of all, and kept it exactly as Adolphus would have expected. Any books borrowed or taken from the shelves, would be dusted and replaced as soon as the user had finished with them. If the book was to be kept out from the shelves for any length of time, it would be placed on the long table every night, unless special permission was given for the book to be read in bed, and then it would be placed in a brown paper cover, and kept in it until it was replaced on its shelf. Wanting desperately to have some sort of memorial in the name of Adolphus placed somewhere in the precincts of the house, Katherine liked the idea of a plaque attached to the outside wall, near the front door. She went to the stone mason who was responsible for the headstone that was erected at the head of the grave where Adolphus was laid to rest, and he agreed to take on the task. On the day that it was finally finished and fixed to the wall, Katherine found herself emotionally moved by its eloquence. It was an oval of the palest blue, with a fluted white edge. It read:

ADOLPHUS PEREGRINE FRY
1837-1926

On the topmost edge, a kingfisher was fashioned with wings outstretched as if to fly, like one of the birds that Adolphus loved. A halcyon, a bird fabled to calm wind and sea, a kingfisher, quiet and peaceful. The following years of the 1930s were halcyon years.

Mr Cloverleaf, as well as running the taxi cab service and the garage across the street, with Thomas and Charlie, kept the garden immaculate. Martha encouraged him to start his own patch of herbs, and small special vegetables like extra tender young carrots, and spring onions. He even managed to grow a marrow that won first prize at the local garden show.

Katherine spent some of the colder days in the cosy library, where a fire would always be crackling away. She had taken to writing a few lines every now and then about her life. Adolphus had spurred her on to do this, but she had neither the time nor the inclination until now. She would take Dorcas Louise's watch and place it on the inkstand in front of her, and using the old fountain pen that Adolphus had always insisted upon using, she would write as neatly as she had always done. She would write slowly and with deliberation, as she did not want to make any mistakes that would spoil the appearance of the note book that she had found in the bottom drawer of Adolphus's desk. To remember, sometimes, was not only difficult, but sad, hurtful, and frightening. If she was to do it, then she had to do everything, so perseverance was a lesson she had yet to learn. At the end of each session, she would lock the drawer in which the book was kept. There would be a time for revelation, but it would not be yet.

The late 1930s were to cause the dark clouds of war to cross Britain. Katy Louise was fifteen, and turning into a beautiful young woman who had it in her mind to become a nurse. Her exam results were well in keeping with those needed for her application to be accepted. If that was her wish then Katherine would support her throughout. She would go to college if that was desired and study, and she would do some practical work in local hospitals.

The mid 1930s had seen the death of King George 5th, followed by the abdication of Edward the 8th, renouncing his crown for the woman he loved, and the coronation of King George the 6th.

Living in London proved to be exciting for Katherine, and Katy Louise was her shadow wherever she went. In spite of all the pomp and ceremony of the capital city, there was an undercurrent of agitation and worry among its inhabitants.

As 1939 approached, the fears and doubts began to raise their heads, as the government implemented plans that would form a defence against possible bomb attacks on the capital. Air raid shelters started to be provided to homes in districts where it was thought that bombing would be most likely. One or two appeared in the north London area, but to Katherine's delight, her house had not been chosen. Evacuation of children from Britain's cities was started. Schools had become reception areas, and parents would have to leave their children to be taken from mainline stations to unknown destinations, and would be told as soon as possible their eventual location.

Under no circumstances would Katherine allow Katy Louise to be taken; they would stay together what ever happened. She would not risk losing her to any stranger, especially in a war-torn environment. As it turned out, at fifteen, Katy Louise would probably have been outside of the age bracket to be considered. War was finally declared on the 3rd September, and Britain was ready for a wartime winter. Hospitals had been prepared, a multitude of home defences were issued, and rules and regulations were the only things that bombarded the waiting public. Blacking out windows was compulsory, so Mr Cloverleaf set to and created movable black screens, made from frames of wood covered in thick black cloth. These would be mounted on small wheels that Charlie and Thomas acquired, and they could be moved in front of the windows each night, as the lights were put on. The blackout was total, and included all transport headlights and interior lights on trains and buses. This of course carried its own problems, and there was an increase in road deaths, and many minor accidents to vehicles due to them not being visible to other road users.

The house in Acacia Avenue carried on with its life with very little change, except for the shortage of food that was beginning to bite. Martha scored greatly here, as her life back in the days that she would rather forget served her well. She could produce the most amazing results with very little content. Katherine would smile at her in their private moments, and comment on how good her memory was for concocting 'special dinners', as she used to call them when Katherine was hungry and there was little in the way of food in Martha's cupboard. And what there was would be grabbed by the horrible man, as Katherine used to call him. Martha would hug her and say, 'All that is past now, my darling.'

The blitz of 1940 started with a vengeance in October. German bombers attacked London with a terrible ferocity. The glow from the fires could be seen across the city night after night. The 'home guard' was formed by men who were not presently engaged in military service. The age gap was wide. Any man between 17 and 65 could give of their services, but it was mainly the older men, usually veterans from the First World War, that took part with pride and enthusiasm. They performed a fire watch, and worked with other public services in an effort to release regular units for more important duties. Charlie and Thomas both volunteered. It was not likely that they would be called upon for military service, but there were no guarantees in a situation such as this. Mr Cloverleaf also offered his services, and to his extreme pride he was offered a place as a liaison officer, and would work closely with the fire and ambulance services in order to get help to those who needed it most, and to get it there as quickly as possible.

Charlie's twins were too young for call up, for which Flo was eternally grateful. Charlie had discussed the idea with Mr Cloverleaf of giving them a chance to learn the business, and get their 'hands dirty', he had laughingly said. Mr Cloverleaf was very happy to agree to that, as long as Thomas was happy. He would give them a small remuneration, just for the hours that they put in, he stipulated. He couldn't afford to pay them if the work was not available. They were still only 14 years old, and so it would virtually be just a small amount of pocket money, but he would place it in a proper wage packet. Charlie was overjoyed.

The blitz raged on night after night. Thousands were made homeless, and thousands more killed or injured. Thousands of people spent the nights in the underground stations, coming out into the light of day in the morning, never knowing whether they still had a home to go to. Some families just took a chance and stayed in their own homes, huddled all together in what they thought might be the safest room in the house, covering theirs and their children's heads and faces, as bombs exploded all around them. Mr Cloverleaf had noticed, when visiting areas of devastation, that nearly always, the staircases were left intact when the rest of the building was reduced to rubble.

With this in mind, he set to build an area underneath the structure of the staircase in the house, where they could all fit into, albeit in extremely squashed conditions, to escape the worst of any blast. He would, with Charlie's help, use a panel off an old vehicle that was beyond repair, and place it in front of the space, as a protection from flying debris. It may be crude, but it could just be their salvation. Martha and Katherine were so proud of him, and Katy Louise called him her hero, to which he blushed and shushed her away.

It was a bleak, cold Christmas in the year of 1940. Coal was being transported by rail. Food shortages were at their worst. Martha made her Christmas puddings with carrots replacing the fruits that she usually used. There was also a shortage of milk. All of this added to the constant threat of bombs dropping. The German bombers were now attacking the provinces in the effort of crippling British industry. This gave London a small respite, but a couple of nights before the New Year they decided to set fire to the city of London. It was timed perfectly, and at low tide thousands of fire bombs were dropped. With hardly any supply of water available from the river, the fire engines became almost unable to pump water. With what was described as an unbelievable piece of luck, the raid ceased, and it was assumed that the weather over Germany must have deteriorated to such an extent that the aircraft were grounded. Fire watching was increased after that night, and business premises were to be fined for not enforcing their duties.

In the early morning of a freezing January day in 1941, an ambulance came to a halt a hundred or so yards from Cloverleaf's garage. Its driver leaped from the cabin, ran to the garage and, hammering on the door, shouted, 'Please can you help us?'

Charlie, hearing the commotion, looked from the window and seeing the ambulance raced down the stairs to open the door. 'What is it?' he cried.

'We have broken down and we have a seriously injured patient on board. Can you help us?' the driver said, half running back toward the ambulance.

Charlie grabbed a bag of tools and followed. Fingers stiffened with the cold, he opened the bonnet and could see a broken fuel line. 'Five minutes,' he yelled as he headed back to the garage. It took a little longer than five minutes, but Charlie did it, and then shut the bonnet, started the engine, and waved the driver away.

'I owe you, mate,' shouted the driver as he continued his journey to the hospital.

The following day there was a phone call for Mr Cloverleaf. Charlie took the call, and asked the person to hold while he fetched him. Mr Cloverleaf picked up the receiver, and a woman's voice said, 'I have to thank you, sir, for the way that you dealt with my emergency yesterday, and to let you know that the patient's injuries have been dealt with successfully. I would like to make my way to the garage to thank you personally, and to pay the bill.'

'Madam,' replied a confused Mr Cloverleaf, 'I have no knowledge of the incident. I have to assume that it was dealt with by my manager who lives above the garage. His name is Orchard, Charles Orchard, and it would certainly have been him, as my other manager lives in the same house as I do, and would have called me.'

'Charles Orchard, did you say Charles Orchard... Charlie?' asked the woman, 'and you are Mr Cloverleaf... Roger Cloverleaf?'

'Yes, that is correct, madam, what is all this about?'

'Sir, did you and Charlie live in Liverpool at some time,' asked the woman in a now excited voice.

'Yes madam, we did.'

The woman then said, 'Mr Cloverleaf, may I please come over, and then all will be clear, and this will be the most amazing coincidence.'

Mr Cloverleaf, now in a state of complete confusion, just said, 'Yes, please come over, and I will meet you. How long will you be?'

The woman laughed and said, 'As long as my motor car does not break down, I will be there in half an hour.'

Mr Cloverleaf, in his usual way of keeping calm under all circumstances, refused to be caught up in her exuberance, and waited patiently for the arrival of the mystery woman who obviously knew both him and Charlie. Both Thomas and Charlie had their backs to the door, as the voice said, 'What have you been doing to my ambulance, Charlie Orchard?'

Charlie turned and looked into the face of Nurse Janet who stood there in front of him in a smart suit, a few years older than when he had last seen her, but with a face that he would never forget. 'My God,' he uttered, and made a move toward her.

Mr Cloverleaf stepped in and said, 'Not with those dirty hands, you don't, Mr Orchard, just say it's wonderful to see you, and then go and wash. Come to the house, and you Thomas, shut the garage for a while, leave a note on the door for any customers to find me at the house, and don't forget to tell Flo where you are going.'

The reunion was wonderful. Janet Fortesque, as she now was, since marrying her surgeon husband and acquiring two sons, had not worked full time. She had become a sister, and had continued to work in Liverpool after the end of the war. Her husband had then been offered a consultancy post in a main London teaching hospital, and they moved south. She had taken leave to raise her boys, and then returned to work at the same hospital as her husband. As the war started, she had agreed on a voluntary basis, during her rest days, and whenever she could in the evenings and throughout the night if necessary, to work as a liaison officer between hospitals and ambulance services.

This was where the coincidence materialised. In her records, she found the name of Cloverleaf cropping up time and time again, and she knew the name from somewhere, but could not, however much she racked her brain, remember where. Then the incident with the ambulance driver, who had contacted her to sing the praises of Cloverleaf's garage, had been the ideal opportunity to see if the name fitted anyone that she knew or had known. The rest as they say is history.

She stayed and chatted to them all, and it was with a great interest that she met Katy Louise, and learned of her desire to become a nurse. She could, and in fact would, put out some feelers, and she felt that she could probably help in that direction, thinking that she could maybe keep her from being amongst the women likely for call up if the war continued in the same vein as now. The hospital had its own training school, and nursing was amongst the most needed careers in the country at this time. Even novices could be of great assistance with the thousands of victims of the bombing passing through the hands of the medical fraternity. 'It would be discussed tonight,' she promised, and an extremely relieved Katherine thanked her. Katy Louise was eighteen, she was determined, and Katherine knew that she would put her heart and soul into her chosen profession, and at least she would be reasonably near to her, and be spared the ordeal of conscription.

It was Janet's turn next to ask a kind of favour from Mr Cloverleaf. 'Our ambulances are suffering damage, and misuse due to extenuating circumstances, and I wondered, in view of Charlie's handling of the situation yesterday, and with such an excellent result, whether you would consider taking on a few of the fleet, repairing and servicing the vehicles, and being on call in any breakdown emergencies.'

Mr Cloverleaf answered for himself, Charlie, and Thomas, and accepted with no doubt at all that they could handle it.

London continued to suffer the never ending blitz on the capital. It had been nine months now of unrelenting pounding of bombs. There were reprisals for the bombing of residential German towns, especially Berlin. The loss of civilians was high. The emergency services were stretched to their limits. Hundreds of people remained buried for hours under tons of rubble before rescuers reached them.

Janet Fortesque was good as her word and brought Katy Louise into the world of caring for the sick and wounded. For a young woman who had led quite a protected life, it was hard at first, but she came from tough stock, and stood up to anything and everything that was thrown at her, and she loved it.

Katherine was bursting with pride at the sight of her in nurse's uniform. Always there was the worry of the hospital being hit, but then everybody who lived in Britain, with very few exceptions, took the same risk.

Charlie and Thomas, revelling in their new found skills, were performing almost impossible repairs on beleaguered ambulances. They were also called to scenes of destruction where ambulances, and sometimes fire engines, were caught in the centre of an area that had suffered indiscriminate dropping of hundreds of highly explosive bombs and incendiaries, in a short space of time. They would take a new ambulance to recover the injured, and leave the damaged one until that too could be recovered, unless of course, as sometimes happened, it was damaged beyond repair. The two Orchard boys were now becoming indispensable. As each one of the repaired ambulances was topped up with fuel, the boys would set to work cleaning them inside and out, before they were returned to their point of despatch.

As they both approached their 18th birthday, Mr Cloverleaf put them on his permanent staff, thereby keeping them from being called up. Any work done in connection with the war was referred to as a 'reserved occupation'.

The blitz on London gave way to more terror in the shape of a pilotless aircraft which could travel at 400 miles per hour, carrying high explosives. It was called the V-1, but commonly known to the masses as the 'buzz bomb', or the 'doodle-bug'. People in their homes or in the street would stop at the whining sound that penetrated their ears, and wait for the sound to stop, which meant it had run out of fuel, and then in approximately 15 seconds, it could target them as it exploded. The silence of that waiting was terrifying. Charlie and Thomas would come out and watch when they heard the whining sound. The flame that issued from the rear of the plane would go out, and if that happened overhead or anywhere near, they would all run for cover, and pray that it would miss them.

In the house, near to the stairs where Mr Cloverleaf had built 'The Shelter', the boys had made a map of Europe on which they would stick pins as the Allied forces pushed their way slowly through to victory. The last pins were triumphantly stuck in as Berlin fell, and Italy surrendered to the Allies, and as a final gesture, a red-headed pin with a tiny union jack was placed in the centre of Germany, as peace came to a destroyed Europe.

It was all over. Katherine, Martha, Mr Cloverleaf, Flo, and all the boys danced around the garden in Acacia Avenue. Later they would join Katy Louise who had been on duty until the early hours, and had walked through the streets amongst the milling, singing crowd at 6 o'clock in the morning. Janet and Michael Fortesque, had met her in the grounds of the hospital, and had offered their congratulations on her success in becoming a state registered nurse. She was now 22 years old, and hopefully she could repay their trust and confidence in her in the coming years.

It all took quite a while for the realisation that the war was over to grow in the minds of the people. Mr Cloverleaf, while serving his country in a small way during the time when fire engines and ambulances hurtled around the capital, had made many acquaintances, and a few friends. One such friend was a young fireman who had on a particularly bad night taken a short rest in the canteen where Mr Cloverleaf often popped in for a cup of tea. They had started a conversation on interests and hobbies. Mr Cloverleaf boasted of his immaculate collection of stamps, and the young man confessed to an undying love and interest in the life of birds. He had, he said, just started reading a fascinating book written by a simply marvellous author called Adolphus Peregrine Fry. He didn't expect that Mr Cloverleaf would recognise the name, as you would have to have a very keen interest in his subject to have the slightest notion of his incredible insight into the life of these beautiful feathered creatures that travelled across continents and islands powered only by their own strength. Mr Cloverleaf recognised the words he used as being those of Adolphus. It wasn't fair not to tell him, and so by the time the young fireman left Mr Cloverleaf's company, he was flying himself, as he had an invitation to visit the house where the indomitable Mr Fry had lived until his death.

Apologising to Katherine for his most forward manner in inviting a stranger to her house, Mr Cloverleaf asked if it was possible for him to come on the next Sunday for a couple of hours, so that he could perhaps show him around Katherine's gallery, and maybe let him handle a couple of Adolphus's note books. 'The boy is besotted,' whispered Mr Cloverleaf to a tolerant Katherine.

'You had better speak to your wife and ask her if she can supply enough cakes and sandwiches to invite this young man for tea,' she answered.

The boy, according to Mr Cloverleaf, was besotted by birds, but Katy Louise, according to Katherine, was besotted by the boy. That meeting of Mr Cloverleaf, and Stephen Brown, heralded the beginning of a romance, and as the months went by Katy Louise and Stephen were inseparable. His visits became more frequent, and the more that Katherine got to know about him, the more she liked him. He was a young man with the most caring attitude to life, and to people, that Katherine had ever met, possibly with the exception of Adolphus. He sat with her, and asked her questions about the man who was obviously his idol, and Oh! How much he would have loved to have known him.

Katherine found talking to him incredibly easy, and on the day that he asked her if she would consider him as a future husband for Katy Louise, she was overjoyed. The young couple forged their love with the exchange of a friendship ring, each one to wear it until they became officially engaged and set the date for their marriage. Stephen would work hard for promotion, so as to not to have to go out fire fighting. He would aim to get to management status in the Fire Service, which would pay him well, and Katy Louise had some more exams that she wanted to pass before settling down to married life, and possibly raising a family.

Katherine decided that she would let them see what they could attain, before she offered them the other half of the house to live in. Their love was new, and the war had brought stress to all of them. She felt that they needed to enjoy one another's company, and live a little first. She remembered her days with Joseph and she wanted them to have such days. Children she hoped would come after marriage. The following years passed happily, and for Katherine they were a joy beyond compare. Katy Louise blossomed into a very beautiful woman, both in looks and in nature. Stephen was her life, and constant companion.

Thomas was forever in love with Katherine, but as yet she hadn't fulfilled her promise to tell him everything. As the years went by it didn't seem so important to him. He knew that she loved him, and that was enough. He had a good life, and enjoyed his work in the garage with Charlie. Katherine shared her life with him as if they were man and wife. No man at his age could ask for more than that he thought.

The war had been over for four years, and Katy had achieved success in her exams. Stephen was about to move from the fire fighting team to management, and so they thought that it was time to set the date, and get officially engaged.

It was 1949, and sadness hit Katherine once again. Her beautiful, wonderful Martha became seriously ill, and lost her fight for life in five short months. Katherine was devastated, as was Mr Cloverleaf who found living without her impossible and succumbed to pneumonia, after suffering a chest infection. He followed his beloved wife to heaven less than a month later. They were both 83 years old.

Katy Louise and Stephen were engaged at the end of the year, and planned to marry the following year. It was with Katherine's blessing, and with all the love in the world that she offered them the other half of the house to live in. Stephen was overwhelmed but refused to accept it without him paying any rent. He was a proud man, and Katherine was not in the least surprised, and so it was agreed that a rent be paid. She didn't tell them that she had opened a trust fund for any children that they may have, and that they would receive it, each of them, on their 20th birthday. Excitedly, they planned for their wedding, and made changes to the house that would now become 25 Acacia Avenue, while the one that Katherine lived in would be 25A. Stephen eventually got used to Katy Louise calling Katherine 'Kat'. It went back into history, Katy told him. She wasn't sure quite how far it went back, but Kat it was who had cared for her, and loved her all her life, and Kat it would stay. Stephen had no quarrel with that. He loved her, and nothing that she wanted would ever be denied her.

Katherine insisted on buying the wedding dress. She had been here before, and remembered all the trips to the dressmaker. At least now she was in London, and didn't have to travel all the way from Liverpool. One evening, as she discussed with Katy Louise her dress, and who she would have for bridesmaids, she passed her the box that had waited for so long for a moment like this. Katy Louise opened it and gasped. 'Oh Kat, that is so beautiful.' She lifted the tiara from the top of the veil, and held it up to the light, to watch it sparkle.

'It was your mother's,' Katherine said quietly, and I wondered if you would like to wear it. Katy Louise gently pulled the white tulle from the box, and put the tiara against it.

'I would love to wear it, but will you tell me of my mother, Kat?'

'Your mother died, darling, when you were five. She died in an accident, that wasn't her fault, and she loved you very much and hated leaving you. She would be so proud to know that you will wear her veil and tiara.'

Katy Louise did wear her mother's veil and tiara, and Katherine bought her the most beautiful lace dress that clung to her young figure perfectly, the train stretching behind her in layers of lace frills that bounced as she walked. Stephen's sister had the most lovely little daughter who made a delightful flower girl, dressed also in white, and carrying a mixture of pink and yellow roses. That was all that Katy Louise wanted. They were married at the little church that Adolphus attended, and came home to where Katherine had arranged a garden party. Lights and ribbons adorned all the trees, and tables had been set up by the caterers with chairs adorned with ribbons. Rose petals were strewn down the paths, and a little trio of musicians played in the background. It was a perfect day, and there were many more to come, said Thomas, as he made the speech that her father would have made. The lives of Stephen, Katy Louise, and Thomas were now the reason for Katherine living.

Thomas and Charlie had been left the business of the garage in the will of Mr Cloverleaf, and Charlie's boys were being trained to take over when Thomas and Charlie decided it was time to retire. Katherine was left with a feeling of contentment that at last in her life, something was normal. The marriage of Katy Louise to Stephen had for Katherine been the ultimate joy. She knew that she could leave them to live their lives, make their own decisions, but at the same time she could be near them to witness their happiness. Katy Louise, for her part, adored her husband, and took to the role of wife as if she had been born to it. The doors between the houses had been left unlocked, and Katherine was told in no uncertain manner that she had only to cross the gallery at any time she wanted, and likewise Katy Louise would do the same. Her Kat would always be her Kat, she said, as she walked with her into her kitchen, where the kettle was whistling and two cups sat in waiting.

The years passed by, five in all before Katy Louise produced a daughter, and then two years on, another little girl appeared at Katherine's door, held in her mother's arms, wrapped in a white shawl. Placing the baby in her arms, Katy Louise said, 'This one's for you, she has been yelling since I had her, so I told her to wait until I got her home, and Kat would sort her out. Kat did. Two minutes in her arms, and peace reigned. They all laughed, and Katherine hugged her newest challenge to her. The children grew quickly, and adored one another. They shared toys, and rabbit still lived on the shelf, as he had done since he arrived for Dorcas Louise more than fifty years ago. Katherine spent every breakfast time with the children, as she had done with their mother, and grandmother. Sometimes Jasper the cat would steal onto her lap, while she was knitting. She always had to have something to do, and she loved to make pretty things for the girls.

During the summer days, she would sit with Thomas in the garden that was now tended to by a gardener. He had been employed by Katherine soon after Mr Cloverleaf had died. Thomas had completely retired now, along with Charlie. The boys had taken over, and were doing exceedingly well, with Thomas and Charlie always at hand with advice. Katherine, feeling that age had caught up with her, complained to Thomas who said, 'Nothing will catch up with you, my love, you just have to slow down a bit, and give it a chance.'

Adolphus's cane was always in Katherine's hand. Thomas would watch her sometimes, and note that her fingers curled around it as if it gave her strength, and every now and then she would take her handkerchief and polish the silver top until it gleamed. She missed Martha with a pain that she couldn't explain. In the early morning when she awoke and came downstairs while Thomas slept, she was convinced that she could feel her presence, and late at night, long after Thomas had retired, she would go to the library, put on the green desk light, and she would write. Martha seemed to be at her side, willing her to finish the story that Adolphus had encouraged her to start.

It was the night before Joseph would have celebrated his birthday when she finally finished the story of her life. She touched the watch that was on the inkstand, and felt the locket around her neck. She tucked the book in the box that had replaced the little case that had travelled across the world. The contents of the case had been carefully placed there also, and she removed the locket, added it to the rest, and re-stuck the tape that held on the lid.

As she stood up, she raised her hands and said to herself, 'I am free now. No one can be hurt by my past. My secrets can now be told, and I will tell everyone in the morning.'

Putting out the light, she climbed the stairs, and with a smile as she crept into bed beside Thomas, she fell asleep.

Katherine Anne Carrera
passed away peacefully while asleep,
in the 77th year of her life,
on that night the 7th July 1963.